100
TINY
TALES
OF
TERROR

100
TINY
TALES
OF
TERROR

Edited by
Robert Weinberg,
Stefan Dziemianowicz,
& Martin H. Greenberg

BARNES
&NOBLE
BOOKS
NEW YORK

1996 Barnes & Noble Books

Text design by Stephen Morse

ISBN 0-76070-140-7

Printed and bound in the United States of America

96 97 98 99 00 M 9 8 7 6 5 4 3 2 1

BVG

Contents

Introduction

I s it horror—or, is it *terror?*

This question has engaged specialists of macabre fiction for nearly two centuries. Critics have developed classifications for horror and terror stories based on the degree and quality of emotions they evoke in the reader. Scholars have differentiated between the two on the basis of minute differences in the handling of story elements.

When asked in the 1930s to contrast the fiction contained in his magazines *Horror Stories* and *Terror Tales,* pulp magazine editor Rogers Terrill offered his own pithy definitions of horror and terror. "Horror," he wrote, "is what a girl would feel if, from a safe distance, she watched the ghoul practice diabolical rights upon a victim. Terror is what the girl would feel if, on a dark night, she heard the steps of the ghoul coming toward her and knew she was marked for the next victim."

From this example, you could generalize that horror is based in the physical experience, and terror is based in the imagination.

Then again, maybe Terrill was saying that any difference between the two labels is all in the mind. Indeed, no well-told scary story asks to be weighed on a scale that tips in favor of either horror or terror. Likewise, no reader engrossed in a tale of the macabre stops to ponder whether what he or she is experiencing is horror or terror. Even if the horror story and terror tale are as distinct from one another as their analysts would have us believe, they nevertheless share the common objective of stimulating the reader to a level of emotion where these distinctions have no meaning.

The stories collected in *100 Tiny Tales of Terror* are outstanding examples of fiction that frustrates any attempt to arrive at a clearer understanding of what distinguishes terror from horror. They span more than a century, but defy any efforts to explain terror in terms of historical perspective. Their settings range from Victorian England to the contemporary American Southwest, yet they provide no geographical road map to their underlying fears. And although their themes vary from traditional manifestations of the supernatural, as in E. F. Benson's "The Bus-Conductor" and Harriet Beecher Stowe's "Tom Toothacre's Ghost Story," to metaphysical quandaries that undermine our criteria for the natural and the supernatural, as in Joel Lane's "Wave Scars" and William R. Stotler's "Letter from Will Stotler, Dated October 32nd, As Received by D. E. LeRoss," the shocks they generate all resonate with the same disturbing power.

Such results derive in part from the shortness of the stories. Edgar Allan Poe explained this phenomenon best in his 1846 essay "The Philosophy of Composition," in which he wrote that "brevity must be in direct relation to the intensity of the intended effect." These stories are so focused on delivering terrors with a wallop that readers may find it impossible to dissect the tightly integrated elements into components for study under a critical microscope.

Our apologies, then, to readers who have picked up this volume in the hope of learning more about the unresolved debate over terror versus horror. You are forewarned that the artistry of the stories selected for this anthology does not lend itself easily to classroom discussion or clinical analysis.

Readers who have picked up this volume to directly experience the delights of terror might wait until some time after they have put the book down (assuming, of course, they *can* put it down), after their pulse has slowed, and after they have caught their breath, to ask themselves whether what they've read is horror, or *terror*.

And whether a scare by any other name wouldn't be just as frightening.

—*Stefan Dziemianowicz*
New York, 1996

Ashes of Circumstance

J. U. Giesy

"Come!" said the chief of police in response to a rap on his door.

An orderly entered.

"Chief, there's a man outside says he has information about that Arnaut business last night. He won't give it to anybody but you."

The chief puffed at the cigar he was smoking and nodded in decision.

"Show him in," he directed.

The orderly withdrew.

Presently the door opened again, to admit a dark-complexioned man with skin as sallow as yellow wax under the morning light. Dark eyes lurked at the back of shadowed sockets. He paused beside the end of the chief's desk.

"If I am correct," he began, speaking without any preliminary greeting, "your men were this morning summoned to the residence of a man known as Jean Arnaut. They found the dead bodies of a man and a woman in the drawing room of the house. The man was lying on the floor. The woman was decently placed upon a couch. She was Arnaut's wife."

The chief nodded again.

"You're correct enough," he said slowly. "Absolutely correct. They said you knew something about it. It appears they were right. Well?"

"Permit me to sit down."

His visitor sank into a chair.

"I would ask that you allow me to tell what I know in my own way. You see—I've taken all night to make up my mind as to my course in this affair. I've known Arnaut rather well for years.

"The double murder—for it was murder, chief, occurred last night. It was the climax of months of mental agony for Arnaut. But I am sure he never dreamed what real agony was until the last twelve hours. Do you know much about him, chief?"

1

The chief shook his head.

"At least you probably know that he is a man of large interests which frequently require his absence from the city for days at a time. He is rich. His home was such as gives one an instant appreciation of the owner's standing, if you know what I mean. At the time of his marriage, Jean spared no expense in preparing it for the reception of his bride. He wanted it to be, if anything, more beautiful and charming than the one she left—"

"Wait," the chief interrupted. "Why are you telling me all this!"

"Why?"

The man before him met his regard in what seemed a vague surprize.

"Why—because of what happened last night. Arnaut's wife was a beautiful woman—a woman in a thousand—the only one who ever stirred Arnaut's pulses. When he met her, he went mad. She became the main reason for his existence from that instant. And because she was the one woman, Arnaut, I think, became insanely jealous of her. Not that there was any reason for it, really, but that he fancied all other men must look upon her with his eyes. It was not that he did not trust her. She was a good woman, chief. It was just that he felt as the wearer of a priceless jewel may feel, when he knows that others envy him its possession. It was a sort of possessive fear that Arnaut felt. That, of course, was—at first.

"Arnaut, chief, is a peculiar man. Despite all his mad passion for his wife he gave little sign of what he felt. He is one of those men whose inner emotions do not easily disturb his surface. So while his love burned at a white heat within him, he was not given to outward manifestations of affection. He sought rather to act than to talk his love, to show what he felt by giving her everything she wanted, gratifying her every desire. His greatest delight was to find something he knew she wished and bring it to her. His love was a shrine at which he worshiped, and his wife was the madonna in that shrine. That, chief, is how Arnaut loved."

"You must have known him very well, to know so much," the chief suggested.

"I did. I was closer to him than any other, chief."

"But—what are you leading up to?"

The chief's cigar had gone out. He laid it aside.

"To what happened last night, and—the cause."

The chief leaned back in his chair.

"All right. Go on."

"Arnaut had a friend, chief. His name was Paul Leiss. They had been boys together. They had gone to school together, and in later years they remained bosom friends. Leiss was a single man. But after his marriage Arnaut took him to his house and presented him to his wife. What foul fiend of evil laughed at

2

the step, only the powers which laugh at us mortals can know. Yet for a long time, everything remained as it had been. Paul was frequently at the house, and often when Jean was out of town, he escorted Mrs. Arnaut to places of amusement or to social functions. He and she became very good friends.

"It was then that Jean's jealousy began to manifest itself, chief. He watched the growing intimacy between them with a smiling face that nonetheless masked the first stirrings of suspicion. Remember that he was a man of the world, and knew of other instances of a friend's forgetting his honor. One may say that his love and primal faith in his wife should have sustained him, but we—you and I—of the world, chief, also—know that jealousy is an insidious thing which feeds on little. Jean Arnaut became suspicious of his friend first, and then of his wife. In such a man, if the fire of love is hot, the fire of jealous doubt is as the flame of hell itself.

"Yet so far as I know, no one suspected. There was no reason why anyone should. It was there that the man's ability of repression showed itself. He still met Paul as always. He still treated his wife as he had treated her from the first. But he was watching—watching. Never an instant, when he was with them, but that his eyes were seeking a covert meaning in a glance, his ears listening for a veiled suggestion in a phrase. With the stealth of a prowling animal he kept his gnawing secret concealed, by a smile, and—watched. He even found a terrible pleasure in watching; in thinking that all the time they fancied him blind, he was looking on from what amounted to a screen. I am not saying that he was not warped in his judgment. He was. His jealousy of the beautiful woman he had married perverted his sense of proportion until every act, every word, took on a double meaning to his morbid fancy. But he thought then, sincerely, that he was justified in his suspicions. So—the result is as you see."

"You knew of this insane jealousy?" the chief inquired.

"Oh yes!" His visitor inclined his head.

"And let it go on—made no effort to stop it?"

"On the contrary, chief. I have labored with Jean for hours. He could see nothing save his suspicions—would consider nothing else."

"Go on," the chief prompted.

"One day Arnaut came home from a trip. That evening his wife related to him her life in the interval he had been absent. She spoke of Leiss again and again. Suddenly Arnaut turned upon her. He was drunk with rage.

" 'You care more for him than for me!' he cried.

"She laughed. He pressed for an answer. After a time she resented his attitude. She told him that his question was an insult, which she would answer by refusing to discuss the matter further. You see she had pride.

"The episode, however, was but the pouring of oil on the fire of Arnaut's suspicion. From that instant he began planning a trap for the two, that he might face them in the perfidy he was now convinced was theirs. And yet—so wonder-

3

ful was his craft, which amounted to insane guile—he was still outwardly much the same, gave no definite sign of the terrible thing in his soul. Only when alone did he pace the floor, grimacing, mouthing, swearing terrible oaths, till a froth gathered on his lips, and his eyes were bloodshot, and his tongue hot with fearful words.

"He laid his trap. It was nothing new. Merely he announced a journey— and on the night when he was supposed to be leaving the city he dined with Mrs. Arnaut. Never had she appeared more desirable, more alluring, more a thing to be adored. But he hardened his heart to his purpose and after dinner he went with her to her boudoir and sat in a chair by a little table, while he smoked a cigar.

" 'Paul coming tonight?' he asked, watching her through a half veil of smoke.

" 'Not that I know of,' she told him. She was in a soft negligee—plainly dressed for an evening at home.

"It should have meant nothing to Jean. Paul often came in unexpectedly, as he knew. But this time he had kept all mention of his projected trip from his friend, because he wanted to feel sure of the woman's guilt—that she called her lover to him, after he himself had gone. Hence into her words he read evasion. He nodded, got up and bade her good-bye. He left the house, saying he was going to his office for some papers and then to his train.

"In reality he never went beyond the end of the block. There he stopped. Crouched in the shadow of a railing, he watched his house.

"After a time a figure came down the street, and a man ran up the steps. Arnaut recognized the figure and carriage of his friend, Paul.

"For what seemed a long time after that, he still crouched where he was, nursing the terrible thing in his brain. Yet he kept sufficient control to adhere to the plan he had made. He meant to give them time to feel sure of his absence. At length he stepped out of the shadow and walked to the house, went up the steps and entered with his night key.

"His wife and Paul were sitting in the drawing room as he came in. Even then he noticed how beautiful she was. The next instant, however, his contempt for her treachery came back in a burning flood to his soul. He strode into the room and paused.

" 'Jean!' his wife cried out.

"Perhaps she was merely surprised. Perhaps for the first time some of Arnaut's control relaxed, and she saw something of his inner state peering at her from his burning eyes. Jean doesn't know, and he never will learn—now.

"Leiss rose. 'Hullo,' he said. 'We thought you'd left town, old man.'

"By an effort Arnaut steadied his voice. He explained that he had missed his train."

4

"Hold on!"

The chief leaned suddenly forward.

"See here—if you know that, you must have seen Arnaut since the murder."

"I have."

His informant's tone was matter of fact.

"Then—you know where he is now?"

"Yes. That is what caused me to spend a sleepless night—at least in part. I was trying to decide what to do about Arnaut."

"There is only one thing you can do."

The chief's finger crept toward a button on his desk.

"Tell me where he is at once."

"He will not escape." His visitor raised a hand. "Wait but a minute longer, chief, till my story's done. Arnaut left his wife with Leiss. He made an excuse of going to his room. But instead of doing so he went hastily to his wife's boudoir and began a search for any sign which might indicate his friend's prior presence in the room. He found it! On a little table which held his wife's basket of fancy work— she had a pretty taste, was always making pretty things—he found a white pile of tobacco ashes, staring up at him from the darkly polished wood—proof that a man had been admitted not so long before.

"His lips writhed for a moment, baring his teeth like the fangs of a wolf. He fairly ran to his own apartments, dragged out a drawer and procured a weapon. With it he returned to the drawing room. His mind was made up. He was going to kill Leiss. But first he meant to tell them both how he had watched, watched, watched, for months.

"Leiss was on his feet when he entered the room for the second time. He spoke as Arnaut appeared.

" 'I was just leaving, Jean. I only ran in for a moment on my way to the Greenville reception. I must be getting on.'

" 'Wait. I want a word with you.'

"Arnaut held up his hand. And then, like a man slipping the leash of a savage dog, he relaxed all the restraint which had held him. All his foul suspicions, all his fancied proof, all his agony of soul, all his love for his wife and his friend turned to hatred, he poured out upon them in a wild flood of rage and despair.

"In the midst of it, Leiss sought with a face of horror to stay him.

" 'Jean! Jean—you are mad to talk like this,' he cried. 'Stop! I will not permit even you to insult the woman who is your wife, in such fashion. If you were anyone save my old friend, I would strike you down for a great deal less. You—'

"Arnaut turned upon him with a frightful imprecation. He cursed him and he cursed his wife. And suddenly drawing his weapon, he shot Leiss through

5

the chest, so that he staggered and fell upon the floor. And at that he laughed, and turned on his wife, who had screamed and was cowering back beyond the body.

" 'There!' he shrieked at her, pointing to it. 'There is the thing you loved! Look at it and see how lovable it is—now!'

" 'Oh—my God!' said his wife. 'You believe that—really believe?'

"And she stretched out her hands like one groping in darkness and swayed on her feet.

"Arnaut answered her with a string of accusing oaths. But she was brave—brave. Arnaut admits that. Suddenly she drew herself up. She was very pale, and her eyes were wide. But her words lashed back at him in scorching scorn.

" 'Then—why don't you complete your work?'

"Arnaut says she stretched out her arms. He says her eyes, her face, will haunt him to the grave. But then he was mad—utterly mad. He lifted his smoking weapon and pointed it at her, and with what seemed to him then as absolute deliberation he fired.

"She swayed before him for a moment, and a spot of red grew on the filmy fabric of her gown. Then, then she bent forward slightly and coughed. Red blood spattered from her lips. 'Jean!' she choked, and fell on her knees, on her face.

"Arnaut nodded. He was quite satisfied. He had made all his plans. Yet even as he put his weapon away, something made him stoop and lift her up in his arms, and lay her on the couch. Having done that he straightened her limbs and composed her hands. She was still warm, seemed scarcely more than asleep. Then he walked out of the room without a single backward glance, and turned off the lights at the switch.

"All his rage had left him. He decided to leave the city at once. Going to his room, he took up the bags he had packed earlier in the day and started to leave the house. As he passed the door of his wife's boudoir, he noticed that the lights were burning. He set down his bags and stepped inside to turn them off. Then for the first time he saw what before had escaped his attention. It was a half-smoked cigar lying on the floor in the shadow of the table on the top of which he had seen the ashes. He crossed to it and picked it up. The band about it showed it to be one of the brand he habitually smoked.

"Suddenly, chief, as he stood there holding it in his hand, he began to tremble, because of a terrible thought. His supply of cigars was kept in his own room, in a cabinet to which he held the key, and which he always kept locked. He put down a finger slowly and touched the pile of ashes. They were cold—quite cold—but not more so than his own flesh had become. You see, chief, he had remembered—when it was too late. Now that it was all past—now that the terrible, irrevocable deed had been done, and two innocent souls sent to an unmerited fate—suddenly into his reeling brain came the recollection of the cigar he had smoked in that room before the pretended start on his journey. In that terrible moment which seared all the madness of suspicion from the soul of Jean Arnaut forever, I realized, chief, that the cigar and ashes were mine."

"Yours!"

The chief came to his feet in a bound.

"Mine," the man with the sunken eyes reaffirmed. "I—God help me!—am Jean Arnaut."

At the Bend of the Trail

Manly Wade Wellman

They stood at the bend of the trail, young Bruce Armstrong and white-haired Hubert Whaley, conversing while their black bearers raised their tent and built a cooking-fire. The sun was low on the African horizon and they whiled away the minutes before supper by conversation.

"As I was saying," Whaley told his young friend, "the natives invest every unusual object—rock, hill or what-not—with a supernatural personality and give it a wide berth. Look at this sharp curve in the trail. For years they've been dodging out to one side, just to avoid that root."

He pointed to a strange growth in the lush grass. It was long and crooked, lying in the shape of a letter S. If straight it might have been ten feet long, and it tapered from the size of a man's ankle at the point where it sprouted from the ground to a whiplash tip. It might have been the root of a tree, but there was no stem within yards to which it might attach.

"Rum thing. Looks as if a tree must be growing upside down," commented Armstrong. "Branches in the ground, root in the air, what? A chap could write books and books about uncatalogued plants in these parts. And you say the boys won't touch it?"

"Not one of them," replied Whaley. "Can't say that I blame them. It looks uncanny enough."

"What utter rot!" cried the younger man. "Come now, Whaley, do you mean to say you give a minute's serious thought to their superstitions?"

"I mean to say that Africa's full of strange beings and doings," was Whaley's sober response. "When you've been here as long as I have————"

"I'm turning missionary this moment," cut in Armstrong. "I don't be-grudge the blacks their ideas, but when a good friend and Englishman gets a touch of their religion I have to do something about it.—Hi, you Johnnies!" he cried to the bearers on the other side of the curved trail. "Tumble over here. Tell 'em, Whaley, I don't speak their lingo yet."

At Whaley's call a score of plum-colored men gathered, eyeing the whites with respectful interest.

"Look here, you chaps," said Armstrong. "What's all this about roots and spirits and such like? It's a lot of foolishness, you know.—Pass that on to 'em, Whaley, will you?"

When Whaley had translated, the headman replied that their tribal beliefs had been taught them by wise old men, who must have known the truth.

"Rot!" cried Armstrong when Whaley had rendered this into English. "Rot, I say, and I'll prove it. You're afraid to touch this root, are you?" He stepped close and set his boot-heel on the growth. "Well, then, suppose I show you that it's perfectly harmless."

A cry of alarm went up from the bearers—a cry echoed by Whaley.

"Look out, Armstrong! Look out, man, it's moving!"

The free tip of the root was swaying to and fro, like the head of a blind-worm. Even as Armstrong stared in chilled amazement it writhed up from the ground and curled back toward his foot. With a startled exclamation he jumped away. The root-tip sank quickly down and lay motionless again.

Whaley and Armstrong looked at each other, at the root, and at the retreating bearers.

"I call it odd," said Armstrong after a moment, in a voice that quivered ever so slightly. "Something to tell about back home, what?"

"Best leave it alone, old man," counseled Whaley. "Suppose we see what's for supper."

They ate in the gathering gloom, ate silently. In silence they smoked their pipes. The usual singing and laughing of the bearers were subdued also. Whaley noticed Armstrong's nervous fidgeting, wondered what to say, and said nothing. A dry rustle in the grass attracted their attention.

"What's that?" demanded Armstrong sharply. "A snake?"

"Let's have a look-see," suggested Whaley, taking the lantern from the tent-pole. "Dashed unpleasant things, snakes. Bring along the gun—it might be a big one."

But they found no snake, and the bearers, called to help look, said that there were few snakes in this part of the country. Finally the two whites returned to the fire to resume their smoking. Armstrong muttered, twitched and finally broke the silence.

"It's all nonsense, and I say it once for all."

"What's all nonsense? What do you mean?" asked Whaley, though he knew well enough.

8

"This beastly root business. It gets on my nerves. I can't forget it. When it writhed under my foot—ugh! My flesh crept."

"Don't try to worry it out," Whaley said. "You'll only go batty trying to explain it."

At that Armstrong jumped up, reached into the tool-box just inside the tent and grabbed a hand-ax. With this he strode away toward the trail.

"Don't be a silly ass, man," called Whaley, following him. "What are you going to do?"

"Going to cut that root out," flung back Armstrong. "I've bothered about it quite enough. I shan't sleep tonight, not while the thing's there."

"It's just on your nerves, Armstrong," said Whaley. "I tell you, it's nothing. Just a funny-looking plant that rustled when you kicked it.—Hm! What's this?"

They had come into the bend of the trail. The last rays of light showed them that there was no root there, no growing thing larger than a blade of grass, not even a hole to show where it might have been. The ax drooped in Armstrong's hand. The two stared at each other as the night rode down.

"Wood's scarce hereabouts," said Whaley in a low voice. "Perhaps the boys cut it up and used it for a fire."

Armstrong shook his head. "No, Whaley. You said yourself, and so did they, that it was a thing not to be touched."

They walked back to their camp. The brightness of the lantern shed a little comfort on them as they again sat in silence. "Bed?" suggested Whaley at last, and they entered the tent. "Now, forget———"

"You're a topping fellow, Whaley, but I don't need babying," said Armstrong, sitting on his cot to pull off his boots.

"Of course not. Go to sleep now, there's a good chap, and don't dream of roots."

"Dash it all, who's going to dream about 'em?" said Armstrong as they put out the light and lay down.

Silence yet again, and after a minute or two Whaley could hear Armstrong's deep, regular breathing. The young man was asleep, probably had dismissed the queer adventure of the evening as a trifle. But Whaley, as he himself had said, had lived too long in Africa to banish all strange things so lightly from his mind. He pondered long before he, too, dozed off.

He woke suddenly with a wild shriek splitting his ears, the shriek of a man in mortal terror. He sprang out of bed, shaking the sleep from his eyes. Moonbeams came through the half-opened flaps, showing Armstrong struggling on the ground between the cots. He was fighting somebody or something— Whaley could not see his antagonist. The older man dropped to his knees, reaching out to help. His hands fell on a quivering band that circled Armstrong's chest. He recoiled from it with a cry. He had touched wood, wood that moved and lived like flesh!

"Whaley—the thing—it's choking me!" gasped Armstrong in a rattling voice. "It has a spirit—it's after revenge————"

He writhed along the ground and half out of the tent, then collapsed. In the light from the moon Whaley saw a sight that stirred his white hair. A writhing, cable-like thing was grappling with Armstrong. It had wound twice around his body and arms, and the two loose ends were lashing to and fro like flails.

Whaley flung himself forward again. One of the flailing ends fell on his head, knocking him back into the tent. He went sprawling, half stunned and almost out of the fight. His hand fell into the open tool-box. A single grab found the handle of the ax that Armstrong had picked up earlier in the evening. The feel of the weapon seemed to restore Whaley's strength. Once more he charged into the battle.

Armstrong barely quivered now. Only the nameless attacker moved. Whaley put out his hand and clutched the larger coil that crushed his friend's chest. Sinking his nails into the coarse, splintery skin that coated it, he dragged it a little free of its hold and struck with the ax. The blade sank deeply into the tough tissue. He wrenched the ax free, and the moonlight fell upon the gash, as white as fresh-cut pine.

The floundering coils churned with new, hostile energy, loosening their hold on the fallen Armstrong. Whaley dragged at them, and they leaped and twisted in his hand like a flooded firehose. The smaller end glided across the ground and whipped around Whaley's ankle, climbing it in a spiral. Another loop snapped on his wrist like a half-hitch, almost breaking it. He grunted at the crushing agony, but with a supreme effort, drew a length almost taut between arm and leg. With all the strength of his right arm he drove the ax. He felt the steel edge bite deep. The grip on wrist and ankle relaxed and he freed himself with a sudden struggle. The two sundered halves of the thing flopped and twisted on the ground, like the pieces of a gigantic severed worm.

Whaley's mind whirled and he yearned to let himself drop and swoon, but he lifted the ax and struck again and yet again. His chest panted, his brow streamed sweat, but he chopped and chopped until only pulsating fragments lay around him. He dashed them all into the half-dead fire, which blazed quickly over this new food.

Then for the first time he realized that the native bearers were gathered, watching in frozen horror. He looked at them, then at the silent form of his partner. He knelt and passed his hands over the still body.

"Broken arm—three cracked ribs," he said aloud. "Not bad for an evil spirit." He called to the headman. "Build up the fire, heat water. Bring a bottle of brandy. You other boys, carry him into the tent, Lord, what a country!"

August Heat

William Fryer Harvey

Penistone Road, Clapham,
20th August, 190–.

I have had what I believe to be the most remarkable day in my life, and while the events are still fresh in my mind, I wish to put them down on paper as clearly as possible.

Let me say at the outset that my name is James Clarence Withencroft.

I am forty years old, in perfect health, never having known a day's illness.

By profession I am an artist, not a very successful one, but I earn enough money by my black-and-white work to satisfy my necessary wants.

My only near relative, a sister, died five years ago, so that I am independent.

I breakfasted this morning at nine, and after glancing through the morning paper I lighted my pipe and proceeded to let my mind wander in the hope that I might chance upon some subject for my pencil.

The room, though door and windows were open, was oppressively hot, and I had just made up my mind that the coolest and most comfortable place in the neighbourhood would be the deep end of the public swimming-bath, when the idea came.

I began to draw. So intent was I on my work that I left my lunch untouched, only stopping work when the clock of St. Jude's struck four.

The final result, for a hurried sketch, was, I felt sure, the best thing I had done.

It showed a criminal in the dock immediately after the judge had pronounced sentence. The man was fat—enormously fat. The flesh hung in rolls about his chin; it creased his huge, stumpy neck. He was clean-shaven (perhaps I should say a few days before he must have been clean-shaven) and almost bald. He stood in the dock, his short, clumsy fingers clasping the rail, looking straight in front of him. The feeling that his expression conveyed was not so much one of horror as of utter, absolute collapse.

There seemed nothing in the man strong enough to sustain that mountain of flesh.

11

I rolled up the sketch, and without quite knowing why, placed it in my pocket. Then with the rare sense of happiness which the knowledge of a good thing well done gives, I left the house.

I believe that I set out with the idea of calling upon Trenton, for I remember walking along Lytton Street and turning to the right along Gilchrist Road at the bottom of the hill where the men were at work on the new tram lines.

From there onwards I have only the vaguest recollection of where I went. The one thing of which I was fully conscious was the awful heat, that came up from the dusty asphalt pavement as an almost palpable wave. I longed for the thunder promised by the great banks of copper-coloured cloud that hung low over the western sky.

I must have walked five or six miles, when a small boy roused me from my reverie by asking the time.

It was twenty minutes to seven.

When he left me I began to take stock of my bearings. I found myself standing before a gate that led into a yard bordered by a strip of thirsty earth, where there were flowers, purple stock and scarlet geranium. Above the entrance was a board with the inscription:

CHS. ATKINSON.   MONUMENTAL MASON.
WORKER IN ENGLISH AND ITALIAN MARBLES.

From the yard itself came a cheery whistle, the noise of hammer blows, and the cold sound of steel meeting stone.

A sudden impulse made me enter.

A man was sitting with his back towards me, busy at work on a slab of curiously veined marble. He turned round as he heard my steps and I stopped short.

It was the man I had been drawing, whose portrait lay in my pocket.

He sat there, huge and elephantine, the sweat pouring from his scalp, which he wiped with a red silk handkerchief. But though the face was the same, the expression was absolutely different.

He greeted me smiling, as if we were old friends, and shook my hand.

I apologized for my intrusion.

'Everything is hot and glary outside,' I said. 'This seems an oasis in the wilderness.'

'I don't know about the oasis,' he replied, 'but it certainly is hot, as hot as hell. Take a seat, sir!'

He pointed to the end of the gravestone on which he was at work, and I sat down.

'That's a beautiful piece of stone you've got hold of,' I said.

He shook his head. 'In a way it is,' he answered; 'the surface here is as fine as anything you could wish, but there's a big flaw at the back, though I don't expect you'd ever notice it. I could never make really a good job of a bit of marble like that. It would be all right in a summer like this; it wouldn't mind the blasted heat. But wait till the winter comes. There's nothing quite like frost to find out the weak points in stone.'

'Then what's it for?' I asked.

The man burst out laughing.

'You'd hardly believe me if I was to tell you it's for an exhibition, but it's the truth. Artists have exhibitions: so do grocers and butchers; we have them too. All the latest little things in headstones, you know.'

He went on to talk of marbles, which sort best withstood wind and rain, and which were easiest to work; then of his garden and a new sort of carnation he had bought. At the end of every other minute he would drop his tools, wipe his shining head, and curse the heat.

I said little, for I felt uneasy. There was something unnatural, uncanny, in meeting this man.

I tried at first to persuade myself that I had seen him before, that his face, unknown to me, had found a place in some out-of-the-way corner of my memory, but I knew that I was practising little more than a plausible piece of self-deception.

Mr. Atkinson finished his work, spat on the ground, and got up with a sigh of relief.

'There! what do you think of that?' he said, with an air of evident pride.

The inscription which I read for the first time was this:

SACRED TO THE MEMORY

OF

JAMES CLARENCE WITHENCROFT.

BORN JAN. 18TH, 1860.

HE PASSED AWAY VERY SUDDENLY

ON AUGUST 20TH, 190—

'In the midst of life we are in death'

For some time I sat in silence. Then a cold shudder ran down my spine. I asked him where he had seen the name.

'Oh, I didn't see it anywhere,' replied Mr. Atkinson. 'I wanted some name, and I put down the first that came into my head. Why do you want to know?'

'It's a strange coincidence, but it happens to be mine.'

He gave a long, low whistle.

'And the dates?'

'I can only answer for one of them, and that's correct.'

'It's a rum go!' he said.

But he knew less than I did. I told him of my morning's work. I took the sketch from my pocket and showed it to him. As he looked, the expression of his face altered until it became more and more like that of the man I had drawn.

'And it was only the day before yesterday,' he said, 'that I told Maria there were no such things as ghosts!'

Neither of us had seen a ghost, but I knew what he meant.

'You probably heard my name,' I said.

'And you must have seen me somewhere and have forgotten it! Were you at Clacton-on-Sea last July?'

I had never been to Clacton in my life. We were silent for some time. We were both looking at the same thing, the two dates on the gravestone, and one was right.

'Come inside and have some supper,' said Mr. Atkinson.

His wife is a cheerful little woman, with the flaky red cheeks of the country-bred. Her husband introduced me as a friend of his who was an artist. The result was unfortunate, for after the sardines and watercress had been removed, she brought out a Doré Bible, and I had to sit and express my admiration for nearly half an hour.

I went outside, and found Atkinson sitting on the gravestone smoking.

We resumed the conversation at the point we had left off.

'You must excuse my asking,' I said, 'but do you know of anything you've done for which you could be put on trial?'

He shook his head.

'I'm not a bankrupt, the business is prosperous enough. Three years ago I gave turkeys to some of the guardians at Christmas, but that's all I can think of. And they were small ones, too,' he added as an afterthought.

He got up, fetched a can from the porch, and began to water the flowers. 'Twice a day regular in the hot weather,' he said, 'and then the heat sometimes gets the better of the delicate ones. And ferns, good Lord! they could never stand it. Where do you live?'

I told him my address. It would take an hour's quick walk to get back home.

'It's like this,' he said. 'We'll look at the matter straight. If you go back home to-night, you take your chance of accidents. A cart may run over you, and there's always banana skins and orange peel, to say nothing of falling ladders.'

He spoke of the improbable with an intense seriousness that would have been laughable six hours before. But I did not laugh.

'The best thing we can do,' he continued, 'is for you to stay here till twelve o'clock. We'll go upstairs and smoke; it may be cooler inside.'

To my surprise I agreed.

14

We are sitting now in a long, low room beneath the eaves. Atkinson has sent his wife to bed. He himself is busy sharpening some tools at a little oilstone, smoking one of my cigars the while.

The air seems charged with thunder. I am writing this at a shaky table before the open window. The leg is cracked, and Atkinson, who seems a handy man with his tools, is going to mend it as soon as he has finished putting an edge on his chisel.

It is after eleven now. I shall be gone in less than an hour.

But the heat is stifling.

It is enough to send a man mad.

Beside the Seaside

Ramsey Campbell

Milne left the garage and began to descend the hill to the town at the edge of the sea. Above the water the sun sank like an orange wind-blown seed, furred by a faint mist. He'd stopped to read *Playboy* in a layby, but when he'd closed the magazine the car had coughed weakly and had barely staggered to the lip of the hill down to the sea. It would be repaired in the morning, they'd told him, and he could stay in the town. He strode past white Victorian houses wedged into the hill, balancing his case full of samples of the new perfume; below, along the beach which was a leg stretched in a *Playboy* posture, a few figures hurried through April, and a lone green car vanished up the coast road.

The town's few streets were drawn to the promenade, and in the first hotel—one of a line whose intricate verandas had been chafed into sameness by sand—he found a room. "Oh, are you a salesman, Mr. Milne?" But it wasn't an echo of the inevitable joke, for she ushered him into his room with a smile, not a grin.

Well, the room would be gone in the morning, and he might find a club for the night. But his mind shouted: good God, what a holiday! Who could leap up eager for the day between these walls like slabs of yellow sand? Who could meet his face reflected between those patterns of wood tangled as brown seaweed? Who could live beneath the pencilled misspelt sign "No drinking in bedrooms" strung between two corners of the room like "Thou God Seest Me"? Beyond the balcony the thin line of the sea was russet, but the sun was sinking fast. Yet as Milne hurried from the room he glanced speculatively at the double bed.

15

At the end of the hall a net curtain unfurled across the window like a wing drifting forth from a cocoon. Milne locked his door and glanced up. A woman crouched on the ray of light along the floor, where the curtain's shadow bunched and spread. No, he hadn't seen her; he'd remembered seeing her, or remembered an insomniac notion, for the shadow whipped away and the floor was bare. A strange idea, given even his previous sleepless night in a disembowelled bed: it wasn't as if she had been crouching, more as if she had been a sketch glimpsed as she folded in half. He passed through the ray of light, his shoes crunching on sand.

In the dining-room, among the marine prints and the teapots in their knitted coats, sat groups Milne might have predicted: a family holidaying and laughing out of season, two pensioners and a stained wheelchair, a typist who couldn't afford Majorca. The last, a timid eager teenager who smiled with the family, sat alone. "I'll put you two together," the landlady said, taking Milne across to her. "You look right as rain now," she told the girl.

"Have you been ill?" Milne asked as he waited for his chop.

"A bit. I'm all right now, though. My friend went on a coach trip and she won't be back till late. I didn't want to spoil her week."

"How do you intend to pass the time?" Milne felt that was unequivocally conversational. Her nose was shiny, and fifteen years ago—at her age, in fact—he'd rejected women with shiny noses.

"There's not much to do down here," she said. "You can always walk along the prom, I suppose."

"No doubt you could."

"There always seem to be a lot of people on the beach at night. And other people watching."

"You've more or less sold me on an early night," Milne said, intending no ambiguity.

"Did you have to have a double bed? We got one even though we didn't want it."

"Oh, I'm surprised," Milne said.

But the room couldn't sustain an early night. Perhaps clubs were beyond her experience, Milne thought as he emerged to search, strolling along a quarter-mile of promenade to the first turn, past flurries of sand and shifting embryonic humps of the beach. In the inky light half the freaks of breeze and sand might have been embracing.

He made his way up the first hill. Already crumpled newspapers and trodden chips gathered outside the fish-and-chip shops; further on, buckets and spades clanked against a tube of fitful pink light in a shop doorway, and in an amusement arcade glowing plastic men leapt up and howled as they were shot. An alcoholic twitched away from a cracked Woolworth's window as Milne approached, snarling, "Now gerraway, boy! Gerraway, won't you?" and poking forth fingers coated with wet sand which Milne saw had smeared lines on the window.

Milne cut through an alley, past a lone string of garish cardboard fat women, and found himself in what might have been the same street. No, there was a cinema; the posters peeled like wallpaper in an abandoned house to advertise *Bullitt* or perhaps a tattered *Sound of Music*. Bored by the colorless night, Milne quickened his pace. Beyond the grey shop windows, the glowing gibbet of a neon sign, "The Submarine Club!" But when he came closer he saw the groups of shaved heads jostling down the steps, boys whose hair was minute tips like grains of sand, and the pursued groups of factory girls, vanguards of a new and equally disturbing race of close-cropped blondes. As he turned away, however, a Jaguar drew up and its driver coaxed forth a girl. Milne watched engrossed, as he might have pored over a *Playboy* centerfold. Even beneath the goosenecked sodium lamps she glittered, turning a cold facet to dazzle the defensive skinheads, whose laughter shattered. She was intricately perfect as a brooch, and Milne wavered in the shadows. Then she moulded back into the car and was gone.

Milne walked down toward the sea. Above a shop in whose doorway lay a broken plastic windmill, a room flickered around a television. He thought about the girl: during the night he knew her surfaces would melt from her, dangerous as ice over quicksand. He didn't envy the driver of the Jaguar. Neither, he realized with an insight he could usually avoid, did he envy himself.

He reached the promenade. A half-mile to his left it merged with the coast road which he would take tomorrow for the next large town, Liverpool. He turned in the opposite direction, toward the hotel. A chill breeze crept across the beach, which glimmered beneath a moon that bulged out briefly like white flesh from between strips of cloud. The sea was seeping darkly over the horizon. Yes, of course the old jokes were accurate; he had his transient women as he drove around the country, but hurriedly before he sped on to outdistance ennui or worse, reflection. It frightened him how fluid housewives were beneath their sleepy "Good morning," how their lives could slacken with their muscles. Sometimes he envied them their chameleon natures, although he suspected what that revealed of him. Sometimes he saw himself as a lone traveller—but he was no cowboy, for what did he leave except often a sample of perfume, and what did he take with him except some shreds of memory sticking to him like burrs, all anonymously smelling like his suitcase of the latest perfume?

"What do you want?" he demanded as he leaned on the railing and peered out at the sea. On the drowned sand, patches of mud glistened like dead bruised jellyfish. Perhaps ideally he needed a woman whose aspects he could fit together at leisure, like a jigsaw, fascinated then triumphant—not the eager typist, not the determinedly brittle girl in the Jaguar, for they would draw him down into themselves. "Go on then, where is she?" he demanded and pressed his lips together, for he was talking to the sea, whose refusal to be defined and violent ecstasy he detested. Not that this was violent; rather was it an oily sea which slumped sluggishly across the beach. That must be why so many couples lay down there, darkly huddled along the mile of beach. My God, they must be damp and daft, he thought. The grains of sand which settled on his own feet were clammy enough. Or perhaps they weren't couples. In the feeble bursts of moonlight it was difficult to see. Certainly one embrace on a glistening stain of mud was of coils of rope and limbs of sand.

He moved back from the railing and halted, disturbed. Along the railing, as far as he could see up the promenade, figures were leaning, peering out across the beach. He couldn't count them. The nearest man must have felt Milne's gaze, for he jerked out of his inertia and hurried away, almost running. The others still gazed down. What could they see? Milne wondered. Momentarily, before he erased it in fury, he had an autoerotic image of sand: once, gazing at a handful of sand slipping between his cupped palms, he'd thought how like a vagina it looked. Balls, he told himself, that's not the explanation. From what he'd seen of the town he could imagine that watchers had nothing else to do; why, even the sand which surged up the slope of stone below the promenade and trickled about his feet was more alive than they. He shook his toes free of the amoeba of sand, but already it glittered on his legs. His trousers were covered with the drifting grains; he might as well take the chance to slip beneath the railings and stride toward the sea. But he turned instead and strode toward the hotel, past the sign of a deserted taxi-rank through waves of sand which washed across the pavement.

It was close to midnight. The hotel was silent and paler than the moon. Over the table full of women's magazines and *Reader's Digests,* Milne stared blankly back at himself through the lounge door; his hair had yellowed. He hurried past the scatter of redirected letters on the hall table, past the vase of plastic ferns, and upstairs.

Before the entangled mirror in his room he combed sand from his hair; grains sprinkled whispering on the glass top of the dressing-table. The hotel was still quiet; the jovial family had taken a tour, the old couple and the typist were doubtless asleep. He lifted the window a little. A roll of moon squeezed out between two tight clouds, and Milne glimpsed the line of figures propped intent at the railing, above the beach where sand lifted palely whirling in the breeze. Slashed by a blade of the wind which pierced between window and frame, Milne undressed hurriedly and burrowed into bed.

A shout awoke him. Perhaps it echoed down a dream; perhaps it was the last laugh of the jovial family. Disorientated by sleep, Milne felt without believing that he was walled into a sand-pit. The sheets weighed on him heavily as sand and rustled like grains. He shifted restlessly, his eyes closing. Then he

18

blinked. Half-awake or not, he was sure he'd caught sight of something which had reared up on the balcony like a semi-opaque wave and vanished.

But the white sky streamed past and nothing else moved. He hung alert for a few minutes, then sank into sleep again.

Ants massed on his face, crawling. They pressed into his mouth, gritting between his teeth. He threw off the sheets and awoke—at least, he was sure that was the order of his actions. His face prickled and chafed against the pillow; his tongue grated against his teeth. He jerked upright and clutched the light-cord. As he pulled it and light blazed his fingers recoiled. They were excruciatingly gritty with sand.

He swung to sit on the edge of the bed, and grains rained on the carpet. The sand must have crept through the window on the breeze. He heaved the window shut, half-noticing that the air no longer moved but was an invisible block of ice. As he peered out at the faint dilution of night on the horizon, a shadow swept across the room behind him.

He stared at the light-bulb. Had the shadow been cast by an insect on the bulb? Somehow he associated the shadow with insects, a whole swarm of them crawling across the wall. He didn't intend to return to bed until he'd found the intruder.

Dressed, he began to search. In one corner of the room he killed a torpid earwig; in another he found a tiny blackened cog from a child's toy. Beneath the bed he found what seemed to be a plastic mouse's tail, and either a cat or the child had scraped the bed's legs to the bone. He peered beneath the dressing-table. The bottom drawer had sprinkled splinters on the carpet, but otherwise there was nothing. His face lifted in the mirror, and behind him the "No drinking" sign moved.

It couldn't have been an insect. One side of the string had risen and fallen back. It couldn't have been a swarm—yet unless his eyes were failing, one corner of the room had slipped out of focus because its entire surface was alive with minute specks. He caught up a shoe and rushed at the wall.

Nothing. But the corner of his eye caught movement, a swirl of shadow across the window. He stood in front of the bed, instinctively protective. A diagonal of movement streamed back to the first wall. In a second the wall scintillated like an anthill. Milne snarled incoherently and threw the shoe, then struggled to remove its twin. As he did so he saw in the mirror the reflected shoe strike the reflected wall, beneath a swarming yellow oval which might have been the unstable impression of a girl's face.

The wall screamed.

It might have been only the image of a scream that tore his mind. It was an echo, or a memory, before he could tell. Already it had disintegrated into a hiss like rain and pattered on the carpet. He was on his feet before he could think and clutching for the door. But his feet skidded on shifting sand and his nerves tore, for the doorknob was acrawl with grains unbearable as powdered glass.

He stared at his fingers, shocked not to see blood, and lunged for the window. The floor rolled apart beneath his feet. He fell. The floor and the walls were whispering voicelessly. He scrabbled to his feet, his fingers scraping together like rusty iron, and thrust at the window.

On the pane, against the dawn, stood the bed; and the sheets moved.

Milne turned as though in treacle and saw the girl's face on the pillow. No, it was too shapeless for a tanned girl's face; it must be a stain. But it moved, although it had fallen in half. The lower half of the face, from the upper lip downwards, swarmed into shape and crept up the pillow to meet the cheek-bones. And the sheets rose convulsively, furiously, as if limbs were drawing themselves up only to disintegrate and collapse again. As Milne watched mutely, the crawling particles of the face massed into a new pattern, and the mouth smiled.

He was across the room in one leap. The doorknob was clean. He fumbled and wrenched the door open. Behind him, a weight struck the floor with a spread flat thud which at once became a pursuing hiss. He stumbled limping down the stairs, his shoeless foot flayed by sand, and fell out into the dawn.

He peered about weakly. A quarter of a mile away one taxi slept at the taxi-rank. If Milne could reach the garage he could drive back later to collect his suitcase. He began to hobble along the promenade, shivering in a breeze which scooped up the sand from the pavement into his face. A few minutes and the dawn would splay forth. But now he could see little in the flecked crawling light; only the indistinct vista of the promenade dropping one edge to the beach, and at some distance still the taxi, guarded by a dim figure. Milne limped forward, brushing at his face, somehow unable to bring himself to call out or wave. There was so much sand in his eyes, like desiccated tears. Heedless of his chafed foot, he began to run.

Best of Luck

David Drake

A Russian-designed .51 caliber machine gun fires bullets the size of a woman's thumb. When a man catches a pair of those in his chest and throat the way Capt Warden's radioman did, his luck has run out. A gout of blood sprayed back over Curtis, next man in the column. He glimpsed open air through the RTO's middle: the hole plowed through the flailing body would have held his fist.

But there was no time to worry about the dead, no time to do anything but dive out of the line of fire. Capt Warden's feral leap had carried him in the opposite direction, out of Curtis' sight into the gloom of the rubber. Muzzle flashes flickered over the silver tree-trunks as the bunkered machine guns tore up Dog Company.

Curtis' lucky piece bit him through the shirt fabric as he slammed into the smooth earth. The only cover in the ordered plantation came from the trees themselves, and their precise arrangement left three aisles open to any hiding place. The heavy guns ripped through the darkness in short bursts from several locations; there was no way to be safe, nor even to tell from where death would strike.

Curtis had jerked back the cocking piece of his M16, but he had no target. Blind firing would only call down the attentions of the Communist gunners. He felt as naked as the lead in a Juarez floor show, terribly aware of what the big bullets would do if they hit him. He had picked up the lucky Maria Theresa dollar in Taiwan, half as a joke, half in unstated remembrance of men who had been saved when a coin or a Bible turned an enemy slug. But no coin was going to deflect a .51 cal from the straight line it would blast through him.

Red-orange light bloomed a hundred yards to Curtis' left as a gun opened up, stuttering a sheaf of lead through the trees. Curtis marked the spot. Stomach tight with fear, he swung his clumsy rifle toward the target and squeezed off a burst.

The return fire was instantaneous and from a gun to the right, unnoticed until that moment. The tree Curtis crouched beside exploded into splinters across the base, stunning impacts that the soldier felt rather than heard. He dug his fingers into the dirt, trying to drag himself still lower and screaming mentally at the pressure of the coin which kept him that much closer to the crashing bullets. The rubber tree was sagging, its twelve-inch bole sawn through by the fire, but nothing mattered to Curtis except the raving death a bullet's width above his head.

The firing stopped. Curtis clenched his fists, raised his head a fraction from the ground. A single, spiteful round banged from the first bunker. The bullet ticked the rim of Curtis' helmet, missing his flesh but snapping his head back with the force of a thrown anvil. He was out cold when the tree toppled slowly across his boots.

There were whispers in the darkness, but all he could see were blue and amber streaks on the inside of his mind. He tried to move, then gasped in agony as the pinioning mass shifted against his twisted ankles.

There were whispers in the darkness, and Curtis could guess what they were. Dog Company had pulled back. Now the VC were slipping through the trees, stripping the dead of their weapons and cutting the throats of the wounded. Wherever Curtis' rifle had been flung, it was beyond reach of his desperate fingers.

Something slurped richly near Curtis on his right. He turned his face toward the sound, but its origin lurked in the palpable blackness. There was a slushy, ripping noise from the same direction, settling immediately into a rhythmic gulping. Curtis squinted uselessly. The moon was full, but the clouds were as solid as steel curtains.

Two Vietnamese were approaching from his left side. The scuff of their tire-soled sandals paused momentarily in a liquid trill of speech, then resumed. A flashlight played over the ground, its narrow beam passing just short of Curtis' left hand. The gulping noise stopped.

"Ong vo?" whispered one of the VC, and the light flashed again. There was a snarl and a scream and the instant red burst of an AK-47 blazing like a flare. The radioman's body had been torn open. Gobbets of lung and entrails, dropped by the feasting thing, were scattered about the corpse. But Curtis' real terror was at what the muzzle flash caught in mid-leap—teeth glinting white against bloody crimson, the mask of a yellow-eyed beast more savage than a nightmare and utterly undeterred by the bullets punching across it. And the torso beneath the face was dressed in American jungle fatigues.

"Glad to have you back, Curtis," Capt Warden said. "We're way understrength, and replacements haven't been coming in fast enough. Better get your gear together now, because at 1900 hours the company's heading out on a night patrol and I want every man along."

Curtis shifted uneasily, transfixed by the saffron sclera of the captain's eyes. The driver who had picked him up at the chopper pad had filled Curtis in on what had gone on during his eight weeks in the hospital. Seventeen men had died in the first ambush. The condition of the radioman's body was blamed on the VC, of course; but that itself had contributed to rotted morale, men screaming in their sleep or squirting nervous shots off into the shadows. A month later, Warden had led another sweep. The lithe, athletic captain should have been a popular officer for his obvious willingness to share the dangers of his command; but when his second major operation ended in another disaster of bunkers and spider holes, the only emotion Dog Company could find for him was hatred. Everybody knew this area of operations was thick with VC and that it was Dog Company's business to find them. But however successful the operations were from the division commander's standpoint—the follow-ups had netted tons of equipment and abandoned munitions—Warden's men knew that they had taken it on the chin twice in a row.

It hadn't helped that the body of Lt Schaden, killed at the captain's side

22

in the first exchange of fire, had been recovered the next day in eerily mutilated condition. It looked, the driver whispered, as though it had been gnawed on by something.

They moved out in the brief dusk, nervous squads shrunk to the size of fire teams under the poundings they had taken. The remainder of the battalion watched Dog's departure in murmuring cliques. Curtis knew they were making bets on how many of the patrol wouldn't walk back this time. Well, a lot of people in Dog itself were wondering the same.

The company squirmed away from the base, avoiding known trails. Capt Warden had a destination, though; Curtis, again marching just behind the command group, could see the captain using a penlight to check compass and map at each of their frequent halts. The light was scarcely necessary. The mid-afternoon downpour had washed clean the sky for the full moon to blaze in. It made for easier movement through the tangles of trees and vines, but it would light up the GI's like ducks in a shooting gallery if they blundered into another VC bunker complex.

The trade dollar in Curtis' pocket flopped painfully against him. The bruise it had given him during the ambush still throbbed. It was starting to hurt more than his ankles did, but nothing would have convinced him to leave it in his locker now. He'd gotten back the last time, hadn't he? Despite the murderous crossfire, the tree, and the . . . other. Curtis gripped his sweaty M16 tighter. Maybe it hadn't been Maria Theresa's chop-scarred face that got him through, but he wasn't missing any bets.

Because every step he took into the jungle deepened his gut-wrenching certainty that Dog Company was about to catch it again.

The captain grunted a brief order into the phone flexed to his RTO. The jungle whispered "halt" from each of the platoon leaders. Warden's face was in a patch of moonlight. His left hand cradled the compass, but he paid it no attention. Instead his lean, dominant nose lifted and visibly snuffled the still air. With a nod and a secret smile that Curtis shivered to see, the captain spoke again into the radio to move the company out.

Three minutes later, the first blast of shots raked through them.

The bullet hit the breech of Curtis' rifle instead of simply disemboweling him. The dented barrel cracked down across both of his thighs with sledge-hammer force. His left thumb was dislocated, though his right hand, out of the path in which the .51 cal had snatched the rifle, only tingled. Curtis lay on his back amazed, listening to the thump-crack of gunfire and bullets passing over-head. He was not even screaming: the pain was yet to come.

An American machine gun ripped a long red streak to within six inches of Curtis' head, no less potentially deadly for not being aimed at him. The wounded soldier fumbled open his breast pocket and clutched at the lucky piece. It was the only action to which he could force his punished body. The moon glared grimly down.

Something moved near Curtis. Capt Warden, bare headed, was snaking across the jungle floor toward him. Warden grinned. His face slumped suddenly like lead in a mold, shaping itself into a ghastly new form that Curtis had seen once before. The Warden-thing's fangs shone as it poised, then leaped—straight into a stream of Communist fire.

A two-ounce bullet meat-axed through the thing's chest back to front, slapping it against a tree. Curtis giggled in relief before he realized that the creature was rising to its knees. Fluid shock had blasted a great crater in the flesh over its breastbone, and the lower half of its face was coated with blood gulped out of its own lungs. The eyes were bright yellow and horribly alive, and as Curtis stared in fascination, the gaping wound began to close. The thing took a step toward the helpless soldier, a triumphant grimace sweeping over its distorted features.

Without conscious direction, Curtis' thumb spun the silver dollar toward the advancing creature. The half-healed wound-lips in the thing's chest seemed to suck the coin in. The scream that followed was that of an animal spindled on white-hot wire, but it ended quickly in a gurgle as dissolution set in.

The stretcher team brought Curtis out in the morning. His right hand had been dipped into the pool of foulness soaking the ground near him, and the doctors could not unclench the fist from the object it was frozen on until after the morphine had taken hold.

The Boarded Window

Ambrose Bierce

In 1830, only a few miles away from what is now the great city of Cincinnati, lay an immense and almost unbroken forest. The whole region was sparsely settled by people of the frontier—restless souls who no sooner had hewn fairly habitable homes out of the wilderness and attained to that degree of prosperity which to-day we should call indigence than impelled by some mysterious impulse of their nature they abandoned all and pushed farther westward, to encounter new perils and privations in the effort to regain the meagre comforts which they had voluntarily renounced. Many of them had already forsaken that region for the remoter settlements, but among those remaining was one who had been of those first arriving. He lived alone in a house of logs surrounded on all sides by the great forest, of whose gloom and silence he seemed a part, for no one had ever known him to smile nor speak a needless word. His simple wants were supplied by the sale or barter of skins of wild animals in the river town, for not a thing did he grow upon the land which, if needful, he might have claimed by right of undisturbed possession. There were evidences of "improvement"—a few acres of ground immediately about the house had once been cleared of its trees, the decayed stumps of which were half concealed by the new growth that had been suffered to repair the ravage wrought by the ax. Apparently the man's zeal for agriculture had burned with a failing flame, expiring in penitential ashes.

The little log house, with its chimney of sticks, its roof of warping clapboards weighted with traversing poles and its "chinking" of clay, had a single door and, directly opposite, a window. The latter, however, was boarded up—nobody could remember a time when it was not. And none knew why it was so closed; certainly not because of the occupant's dislike of light and air, for on those rare occasions when a hunter had passed that lonely spot the recluse had commonly been seen sunning himself on his doorstep if heaven had provided sunshine for his need. I fancy there are few persons living to-day who ever knew the secret of that window, but I am one, as you shall see.

The man's name was said to be Murlock. He was apparently seventy years old, actually about fifty. Something besides years had had a hand in his aging. His hair and long, full beard were white, his gray, lustreless eyes sunken, his face singularly seamed with wrinkles which appeared to belong to two intersecting systems. In figure he was tall and spare, with a stoop of the shoulders—a burden bearer. I never saw him; these particulars I learned from my grandfather, from whom also I got the man's story when I was a lad. He had known him when living near by in that early day.

One day Murlock was found in his cabin, dead. It was not a time and place for coroners and newspapers, and I suppose it was agreed that he had died from natural causes or I should have been told, and should remember. I know only that with what was probably a sense of the fitness of things the body was buried near the cabin, alongside the grave of his wife, who had preceded him by so many years that local tradition had retained hardly a hint of her existence. That closes the final chapter of this true story—excepting, indeed, the circumstance that many years afterward, in company with an equally intrepid spirit, I penetrated to the place and ventured near enough to the ruined cabin to throw a stone against it, and ran away to avoid the ghost which every well-informed boy thereabout knew haunted the spot. But there is an earlier chapter—that supplied by my grandfather.

When Murlock built his cabin and began laying sturdily about with his ax to hew out a farm—the rifle, meanwhile, his means of support—he was young, strong and full of hope. In that eastern country whence he came he had married, as was the fashion, a young woman in all ways worthy of his honest devotion, who shared the dangers and privations of his lot with a willing spirit and light heart. There is no known record of her name; of her charms of mind and person tradition is silent and the doubter is at liberty to entertain his doubt; but God forbid that I should share it! Of their affection and happiness there is abundant assurance in every added day of the man's widowed life; for what but the magnetism of a blessed memory could have chained that venturesome spirit to a lot like that?

One day Murlock returned from gunning in a distant part of the forest to find his wife prostrate with fever, and delirious. There was no physician within miles, no neighbor; nor was she in a condition to be left, to summon help. So he set about the task of nursing her back to health, but at the end of the third day she fell into unconsciousness and so passed away, apparently, with never a gleam of returning reason.

From what we know of a nature like his we may venture to sketch in some of the details of the outline picture drawn by my grandfather. When convinced that she was dead, Murlock had sense enough to remember that the dead must be prepared for burial. In performance of this sacred duty he blundered now and again, did certain things incorrectly, and others which he did correctly were done over and over. His occasional failures to accomplish some simple and ordinary act filled him with astonishment, like that of a drunken man who wonders at the suspension of familiar natural laws. He was surprised, too, that he did not weep—surprised and a little ashamed; surely it is unkind not to weep for the dead. "Tomorrow," he said aloud, "I shall have to make the coffin and dig the grave; and then I shall miss her, when she is no longer in sight; but now—she is dead, of course, but it is all right—it *must* be all right, somehow. Things cannot be so bad as they seem."

He stood over the body in the fading light, adjusting the hair and putting the finishing touches to the simple toilet, doing all mechanically, with soulless care. And still through his consciousness ran an undersense of conviction that all was right—that he should have her again as before, and everything explained. He had had no experience in grief; his capacity had not been enlarged by use. His heart could not contain it all, nor his imagination rightly conceive it. He did not know he was so hard struck; *that* knowledge would come later, and never go. Grief is an artist of powers as various as the instruments upon which he plays his dirges for the dead, evoking from some the sharpest, shrillest notes, from others the low, grave chords that throb recurrent like the slow beating of a distant drum. Some natures it startles; some it stupefies. To one it comes like the stroke of an arrow, stinging all the sensibilities to a keener life; to another as the blow of a bludgeon, which in crushing benumbs. We may conceive Murlock to have been that way affected, for (and here we are upon

26

surer ground than that of conjecture) no sooner had he finished his pious work than, sinking into a chair by the side of the table upon which the body lay, and noting how white the profile showed in the deepening gloom, he laid his arms upon the table's edge, and dropped his face into them, tearless yet and unutterably weary. At that moment came in through the open window a long, wailing sound like the cry of a lost child in the far deeps of the darkening wood! But the man did not move. Again, and nearer than before, sounded that unearthly cry upon his failing sense. Perhaps it was a wild beast; perhaps it was a dream. For Murlock was asleep.

Some hours later, as it afterward appeared, this unfaithful watcher awoke and lifting his head from his arms intently listened—he knew not why. There in the black darkness by the side of the dead, recalling all without a shock, he strained his eyes to see—he knew not what. His senses were all alert, his breath was suspended, his blood had stilled its tides as if to assist the silence. Who—what had waked him, and where was it?

Suddenly the table shook beneath his arms, and at the same moment he heard, or fancied that he heard, a light, soft step—another—sounds as of bare feet upon the floor!

He was terrified beyond the power to cry out or move. Perforce he waited—waited there in the darkness through seeming centuries of such dread as one may know, yet live to tell. He tried vainly to speak the dead woman's name, vainly to stretch forth his hand across the table to learn if she were there. His throat was powerless, his arms and hands were like lead. Then occurred something most frightful. Some heavy body seemed hurled against the table with an impetus that pushed it against his breast so sharply as nearly to overthrow him, and at the same instant he heard and felt the fall of something upon the floor with so violent a thump that the whole house was shaken by the impact. A scuffling ensued, and a confusion of sounds impossible to describe. Murlock had risen to his feet. Fear had by excess forfeited control of his faculties. He flung his hands upon the table. Nothing was there!

There is a point at which terror may turn to madness; and madness incites to action. With no definite intent, from no motive but the wayward impulse of a madman, Murlock sprang to the wall, with a little groping seized his loaded rifle, and without aim discharged it. By the flash which lit up the room with a vivid illumination, he saw an enormous panther dragging the dead woman toward the window, its teeth fixed in her throat! Then there were darkness blacker than before, and silence; and when he returned to consciousness the sun was high and the wood vocal with songs of birds.

The body lay near the window, where the beast had left it when frightened away by the flash and report of the rifle. The clothing was deranged, the long hair in disorder, the limbs lay anyhow. From the throat, dreadfully lacerated, had issued a pool of blood not yet entirely coagulated. The ribbon with which he had bound the wrists was broken; the hands were tightly clenched. Between the teeth was a fragment of the animal's ear.

Boo, Yourself

Joe R. Lansdale

(For Jerry Williamson)

When Bob Randisi retired from bricklaying, he never expected to get married, and certainly not to a young looker like Bessie Williams. He was hardly marriage fodder. He was sixty-eight, about as exciting as a creosote post, and due to a cluster of warts that lived on his nose, and his odd silver eyes, very unattractive.

Had the idea been suggested to Bessie, she would have hooted you out of Tillie's Bar, the place she was most likely to be found. Marriage was not her style, especially to an old geezer like Bob. She was the freewheeling sort. Or as the bartender at Tillie's put it, "Near ever' man in town knows for a fact that Bessie ain't no natural blonde."

So neither party was contemplating matrimony. Bob wanted to open up his upholstery shop full-time, as his part-time work had already earned him a reputation as a wizard for turning cheap coverings into works of art. And Bessie, well, she just wanted to keep right on being Bessie. Least until she heard about the inheritance, then the idea of being Mrs. Randisi became kind of appealing.

Bob kept a schedule better than a clock. Monday through Friday he worked in his shop eight to five, except for an hour for lunch. After five was dinner and a bit of television before bed. Saturdays he read his week's worth of papers, and, at exactly seven o'clock, he walked into Tillie's and had his weekly beer. Sundays he rested.

It was on a faithful Saturday evening at Tillie's that Bessie noticed him. She made some crack about the warts on Bob's nose to the guy she was with, and the guy laughs and says, "Yeah, ain't it a shame a guy like that has all that money, and him probably gonna croak soon?"

"Money?" Bessie asked. And that is how she heard the story about the inheritance. Never mind that it was a sketchy story, she got the part about the hundred-thousand dollars down all right. And being a practical girl who knew fifty-six and fourteen a week crimping chairs down at the aluminum factory was not going to see her into a comfortable middle age, she set her sights on Bob.

Ditching the fellow she was with, she took a stool next to Bob. He took one look at that long, blonde hair, peaches and cream complexion, and those baby blues, and turned into hot shortening, ready to melt right off that bar stool. Fifteen minutes of well-planned chatter later, and Bessie had worked her way into Bob's heart secure as a blood vessel.

It would not have done any good to tell Bob what everyone else in town knew, that Bessie was a gold digger. He was too much in love. A whirlwind courtship followed, and a month later they married. Bob was so happy you could see stars in his silver eyes a block away.

Six months later Bessie had not gotten her hands on any money and Bob seemed healthy enough to live another sixty-eight years. And those silver eyes were starting to give Bessie the creeps. Furthermore, she was bored.

Enter Josh Stark, new man in town, self-styled stud.

Handsome in an oily way, with curly black hair and a blue and red sailing ship tattooed on his chest—visible most of the time due to his habit of unbuttoning his shirts to the navel—he was Bessie's sort of man. Cheap and fun-loving. After a chance meeting in the Food Mart, they took to each other like dogs to bones.

The whole town knew before Bob what was going on in his own house while he was out back in the shop. But he eventually figured it out. He was trusting, not stupid.

One morning at nine-thirty, Bob left his shop, stole into the house and found them in bed. "You sonofabitch," Bob screamed at Josh, "I'll skin you alive!"

Josh leaped out of bed, grabbed Bob by the collar—and got the surprise of his life. Years of bricklaying had made the little man as wiry as a steel cable. Bob's hairy, muscular hands closed on Josh's throat like tongs, and he tossed him out of the house on his naked butt. He then proceeded to kick Josh across the yard and down the street. Half the block got a look at Josh's tattoo as well as his other endowments.

As for Bessie, she found Bob was not as timid as she expected. He lashed her with a belt until she looked like a barber's pole. The way his silver eyes flashed while he was in the act convinced her solidly that, if properly provoked, here was a man capable of blind, passionate murder.

Afterwards, Bob did not throw her out, and Bessie was too scared to try and leave. Though the stars had gone out of Bob's eyes, she realized that he still wanted her. She was like an art treasure to him, something he could admire even if it did not admire him back. And there was that thing he had said while beating her, "If I can't have your loving face, no one will."

Josh was scared too and stayed away, but he could not get Bessie out of his mind. For the first time in his life, he was in love, or what passed for it. He gave the paperboy a dollar to sneak Bessie a note that said they should run off

Saturday while Bob was having his beer. He would come get her. The note then went on to describe her considerable charms.

Excited by the idea, Bessie wrote that she accepted, gave the paperboy a dollar and had him take her note to Josh. Things were set.

Josh's note was such a thrill to Bessie (her first true love note), that she could not part with it. She decided to hide it and take it with her Saturday. The only place she could think to stash it was in the hollow of the brass bedpost, the knob screwing off with surprising ease. She stuffed the note inside.

The reason the knob screwed off so easily was that Bob really did have some inheritance money, and he kept it hidden there. Bessie, in her haste, had not noticed the rolled greenbacks pushed slightly lower than her note.

Bob, however, noticed the note. He had promised Mrs. Gulley a rush order on her living room chair, only to discover he was running low on supplies. He went to the bedpost to get money for materials and found Josh's message. He read it, forgot about the money, calmly replaced the paper and looked toward the kitchen where he could hear Bessie singing "Ramblin' Rose."

Saturday night Josh crept alongside the hedges and peeked into Bob's yard. Bessie was sitting on the front porch swing looking out at the road. She was wearing a long dress and sandals. Her gold hair shimmered in the moonlight. In front of her was a little suitcase.

Josh checked his watch. Seven-fifteen. Bob would be at Tillie's now, having his beer. Smiling, Josh was about to step into the yard when a plan came to him. Why not give Bessie a playful, little scare?

Creeping from behind the shrubbery, he eased himself up on the porch, onto his hands and knees and began to crawl toward the unsuspecting Bessie. She was using her foot to swing herself a bit now, but her eyes had not moved one inch from the road.

Josh was almost snickering. It was all he could do to contain himself. God, this was fun! He crawled to the swing, jumped up suddenly and yelled, "Boo!"

Bessie bounced to her feet and grabbed Josh viciously by the throat. Josh looked her straight in the face. It was Bessie all right; blonde hair, soft skin, that pert little nose. But the moonlight in her eyes made them look . . . *silver*. And alongside her scalp and jaw line he could see *very delicate stitchings*.

Just as Josh was about to scream, Bessie's other hand came up holding a curved upholstery knife.

"Boo, yourself, you sonofabitch!" Bessie growled, and that was the last thing Josh ever heard.

A few hours later Bessie walked calmly into the sheriff's office. Or what first looked like Bessie. When the deputies realized what they were really seeing, they lost their chili dinner.

They had to cut Bob out of Bessie's well-skinned face and scalp, he had stitched himself into it so tightly. Afterwards, in his cell, still wearing Bessie's dress and sandals, he sat on his bunk and repeated over and over with a smile, "Boo, yourself, you sonofabitch."

When the sheriff and one of his deputies got over to Bob's place, they found what was left of Bessie on the bed. The deputy lost the rest of his chili, this time on the sheriff's boots.

Out in the shop they found Josh's remains. Fortunately for the deputy, and the sheriff's boots, the deputy was out of chili. Next to the body was Mrs. Gulley's living room chair. All finished. It was a beautiful upholstery job, marred only slightly by a rather cheap-looking backrest design. A blue and red sailing ship.

The Broken Thread

Kirk Mashburn

John Clayton was the best friend I ever had, and tomorrow I hang for his murder. I shot him; and that is all the state's attorney, or the exasperated young barrister appointed by the court to defend me when I neglected to employ my own counsel, ever got out of me at the trial.

The prosecution labeled me a cold-blooded murderer, which I am not. Shoot John Clayton I did, but not in cold blood, nor was it murder. Under like circumstances (which, thank God, cannot be) I would do it again.

I saw no reason to tell in court what I am about to write down now. They would have condemned me to the hangman with almost the same certainty, although there is a slight chance that I might have escaped the gallows for the madhouse. To me, that would have been no escape; and besides, *I believe Clayton needs me where he is!*

It all goes back to a woman, and too much leisure on our part; which is that much more evidence of the danger of both. We had proved up an oil concession in Venezuela, and sold it for more money than we knew there was in the world, and we did not know what to do with ourselves thereafter. It was the first time in ten years of knocking around together that we had ever had more than enough for a grubstake, or for a little fling between spells of chasing rainbows.

Out of sheer boredom, John blundered in on a spiritualistic séance, as he said, "to have his fortune told." I never knew exactly how he happened to meet

Madame Zara, as she called herself, but I do know that she fascinated him from the very start.

We've both had our palms read by some clever *Gitanos*—gipsies—in Spain, and seen Hindoo fakirs do some things that made us wonder a lot even while we scoffed; so I don't think Clayton took much more actual stock in Zara's clairvoyance than I did. He raved at length and in detail over her charms, which I had to admit were as genuine as I thought her spiritualistic pretensions spurious. Privately, I thought her more interested in a slice—a big slice—of the proceeds of our flyer in Venezuelan oil than in John. I disliked her for that, if for no other reason.

She had a medium's sensitiveness, all right, and she felt and returned my own antagonism. We both covered it up as well as we could; I, for my part, realizing that a whole lot of my feeling might be attributable to jealousy at her sharing John with me, perhaps supplanting me. I can't blame her for what happened. She had powers about which I knew nothing, and at which I sneered quite openly. God knows I have paid for that!

Clayton felt that something was wrong between Zara and me, and shrewdly guessed part of the cause. At least, I suppose that was why he insisted upon my accompanying him to innumerable of her private séances, to show me that I was still included in everything affecting him, as I had always been.

We heard and saw the usual clap-trap of knockings and writings, in a darkened room; or, sometimes, Zara gazed into a lighted crystal ball and said irrelevant nothings while seemingly in a trance. I had seen it all a dozen times before I ever heard of Zara, but John would drag me to it despite my protests, becoming angry if I persisted in refusing. It got on my nerves, and my irritation, as was inevitable, finally led me to openly expressed skepticism of such mummery. Zara caught me up like a flash.

"So! Eet ees fake, yes?" My trial brought out the fact that she was of Basque origin, and her accent was noticeable in proportion to the intensity of her feeling. "Well, suppose I show you sometheeng w'eech cannot be fake, eh? You weel belief our Juan, not so?"

I didn't see where she was leading, and said so.

"Suppose I put Juan een a trance—send hees *alma*—w'at you call soul—away from hees body, an' then let heem tell us w'at he see, eh?"

"Oh, rot!" I am afraid that I was deliberately rude, but I was sick of hocus-pocus, and this was a bit too much. "What difference does it make what I think, anyway? It isn't going to affect your paying clientele."

John, however, was eager for the experiment. It offered a possible chance to vindicate Zara in my eyes, and he insisted upon the attempt. It was only then that I realized what a grip she had on him.

Zara seemed considerably more hesitant, now that she had cooled from the flash of temper that had caused her to make the proposition. She knew better than we did, what she was trifling with. She half shook her head, something of uneasiness in her eyes, and it was at that precise moment that the Devil himself must have inspired me to smile, a little crookedly. Zara saw it, and stiffened instantly. It was enough. Even if she fully realized what she was about to do, her hot Basque temperament could not count costs in the face of ridicule. Whatever John might have been to her, he was not enough.

"Seet here!" she commanded him, motioning to the black velvet-covered table upon which rested the indispensable crystal. John sat as she bade. *"You"*—she fairly spat the word—"seet there, and *keep quiet!"*

I took the chair she indicated, about ten feet away from the table, opposite where John sat. Zara felt under the table, and all the lights in the sable-draped room switched off, leaving it in absolute darkness. Then a light flashed on, deep in the heart of the crystal, lighting it so that it seemed to retain all its refulgence within itself, though it disclosed John's tense, expectant face above it.

"Now," Zara's voice came through the darkness, "look into the creestal, my Juan, an' weel yourself to sleep. I weel help you."

John's face bent closer over the globe, his eyes focusing intently upon its shimmering depths. Zara began to speak in a low, monotonous voice. What language she spoke in, I do not know; nor, after the first few minutes, did it matter. The steady, unvarying monotone went on until it lost the seeming of voice and words and became but a lethean droning, with its burden the command: Sleep—*sleep!*

Even without the hypnotic influence of the lighted crystal into which Clayton gazed, I was powerfully affected by the changeless somnific quality of Zara's tones. Dimly I saw that John's head was sinking lower, his stare into the crystal becoming more fixed. Suddenly I was aware of a ghostly white hand thrusting out of the darkness, reaching stealthily toward him. My drowsiness vanished in a creeping sensation that prickled the hairs upon the back of my neck; and then I saw the hand cup softly under John's chin, and realized that Zara had quit her droning, and was gently forcing her subject backward to a more reclining position in his chair.

Although he was thereby moved away from the crystal, Clayton's face remained the only visible object in the room; the result, I suppose, of ingenious focusing of the lights in the globe.

Zara withdrew her hand, and her voice once more broke the silence.

"You are asleep." It was statement, rather than question.

"I am asleep," John's flat voice confirmed.

"Yet you are awake—onlee your body ees asleep, and the mind w'eech see through your earth-eyes." Zara paused, and when she resumed speaking, her words came slowly, as if she dreaded to utter them.

"You are abo't to leef your body, remaining connect' weeth eet onlee by a leetle thread w'eech ees my weel; you are leefeeng, ees not?"

For a perceptible space there was no answer; the lips framed in John's set, blank face remained motionless and silent. Then, heavily, as with an effort: "Yes, I—am—leaving——"

"Slow!" Zara's voice was tense. "Slow! An' keep connect' weeth me."

Again there was silence. Finally, after what seemed so long a time I was becoming restless, Zara spoke again.

"Are you free?"

"Yes." John's voice was fainter, but the answer came readily and distinctly enough.

"Tell me w'at you do, w'at you see?"

"I am——" The voice expressed puzzlement, paused. "I am still in the room with you, yet not with you. I see the city, but I am not in the city: I am in a void, a great blackness—a *blankness* . . . yet I see. . . ."

"W'at do you see?"

"Nothing. . . . Yes! Shapes—swirling shapes, all around me, everywhere."

"Ah! W'at are they like, Juan?"

The answer came hesitantly. "I don't know. . . . Some of them are like me; some are plainer than others. They have me surrounded, hemmed in."

"Are they—friendlee?" Zara was anxious.

"Most of them act curious: they just stare. I can see their eyes. . . . Some of them are sort of horrible-looking. . . . I don't like them. One is coming closer—good God! What a fearsome thing it is! I think it's inimical; I don't like it! I want to come back. It——"

Clayton's voice trailed off in a gasp. I was considerably impatient by this time. I held that Zara wasn't proving anything, as I had questioned her spiritualism, not her ability as a hypnotist. I took it for granted that John, in his present state, would say anything she willed him to say. Still, I had to admit there was an eery sense of realism to it that impressed me in spite of myself, which probably irritated me more than anything else.

"Cut it out, Zara! I've had enough of——"

"Quiet!" she cried. "In God's name, be quiet!"

Before I could say more, there was a cry from Clayton's lips that froze in my mouth whatever words I could have uttered.

"Zara!" It was pure anguish, if ever I heard it. "Zara! *It's breaking the thread!*"

Zara screamed: *"Ayudame, Dios! Maria Santissima!"* Then, with a mighty effort that wrung instinctive tribute from me even then, she forced her voice to a command, steady, but vibrant in its intensity. "You must not let eet break, Juan! Come back: I am help you! *Come back!*"

I heard a click, and the room was flooded with light at Zara's touch upon the switch. The sudden change from utter blackness blinded me for a moment. When my eyes adjusted themselves, I saw that Clayton's face was drained of color, and there was something shocking about the way it remained blank and staring and yet, at the same time, seemed to express a desperation that was reflected in Zara's own countenance.

She was speaking with a vital burden to her words that impresses me even now; but what she said, what words she used, I do not know. I sat staring, rigid in my chair.

There was a groan from out those colorless lips; and I thought I saw a swift spasm cross the pallid brow. What follows is something that, although I know that I am sane, as well and surely as I know that tomorrow I hang, I hesitate to set down.

First, there was a laugh from Clayton's lips—*but it was not Clayton who laughed!* The sound was more nearly a low, brief chuckle, obscene, utterly evil, and—*triumphant!* Without seeing her, I felt Zara sag, as if beneath a blow she could not withstand. Then—

(Am I mad? Or did I see this thing? Yes, I saw; tomorrow they hang me for the seeing!)

—then, before my torturing eyes, John Clayton's face changed: changed form, line and color. I *saw* it bloat and swell, and turn a mottled greenish hue; I saw the neck shorten and thicken, the hair give way to bony, sloping plates. The eyes opened, slyly, and I looked into the Pit. Zara sobbed, and It moved, swelled.

With an effort into which she threw all her heart and soul and will, Zara made her last attempt to recall Clayton, to send the Thing back to the place whence it came. Once more, I felt her without seeing, as she stiffened, hurled all the force and power in her to renewed attack.

It was not enough; but it sufficed in so much that the seeming of the monster faded, and John's poor face looked through for an instant. Once more, one last time, his voice broke feebly through what had been his lips. One word.

And the word was "Kill!"

Then what had been John Clayton was nearly all a Thing.

I carried a gun beneath my armpit, a habit formed in far places where it is advisable, if one would live long. Before I could use it, Zara had sprung at— It—with her bare hands. The Thing heaved up. In less time than it takes to write it, before I could even move, It had crushed her close, bent her backward. She screamed once, and then I sickened as I heard her spine snap.

At that, I shot It.

I stood over where It had fallen on the floor, and watched what had been

John Clayton and then a Thing, become John Clayton once again. Only, this time there was a bullet-hole in his forehead.

They say I put the bullet in Clayton's head, but that is truth which is yet a lie: I shot a Thing and not a friend. And they point to my great size and nod their heads, and say how easy it was for one of my strength to break so small a body as Zara's. But that is wholly a lie, for the Thing did it. I changed my estimate of Zara during those minutes I watched her battle with all her being to undo a folly that I, unwitting, drove her to. I would not have harmed her, at any rate.

Twice she has come to me in the night, through the steel walls of this condemned cell. Both times she has told me that she and Clayton need me—that the menace of the baffled Thing exists for them as yet.

Tomorrow—today, it may be, now—I go to help them.

The Bus-Conductor

E. F. Benson

My friend, Hugh Grainger, and I had just returned from a two days' visit in the country, where we had been staying in a house of sinister repute which was supposed to be haunted by ghosts of a peculiarly fearsome and truculent sort. The house itself was all that such a house should be, Jacobean and oak-panelled, with long dark passages and high vaulted rooms. It stood, also, very remote, and was encompassed by a wood of sombre pines that muttered and whispered in the dark, and all the time that we were there a southwesterly gale with torrents of scolding rain had prevailed, so that by day and night weird voices moaned and fluted in the chimneys, a company of uneasy spirits held colloquy among the trees, and sudden tattoos and tappings beckoned from the window-panes. But in spite of these surroundings, which were sufficient in themselves, one would almost say, to spontaneously generate occult phenomena, nothing of any description had occurred. I am bound to add, also, that my own state of mind was peculiarly well adapted to receive or even to invent the sights and sounds we had gone to seek, for I was, I confess, during the whole time that we were there, in a state of abject apprehension, and lay awake both nights through hours of terrified unrest, afraid of the dark, yet more afraid of what a lighted candle might show me.

Hugh Grainger, on the evening after our return to town, had dined with me, and after dinner our conversation, as was natural, soon came back to these entrancing topics.

"But why you go ghost-seeking I cannot imagine," he said, "because your teeth were chattering and your eyes starting out of your head all the time you were there, from sheer fright. Or do you like being frightened?"

Hugh, though generally intelligent, is dense in certain ways; this is one of them.

"Why, of course, I like being frightened," I said. "I want to be made to creep and creep and creep. Fear is the most absorbing and luxurious of emotions. One forgets all else if one is afraid."

"Well, the fact that neither of us saw anything," he said, "confirms what I have always believed."

"And what have you always believed?"

"That these phenomena are purely objective, not subjective, and that one's state of mind has nothing to do with the perception that perceives them, nor have circumstances or surroundings anything to do with them either. Look at Osburton. It has had the reputation of being a haunted house for years, and it certainly has all the accessories of one. Look at yourself, too, with all your nerves on edge, afraid to look round or light a candle for fear of seeing something! Surely there was the right man in the right place then, if ghosts are subjective."

He got up and lit a cigarette, and looking at him—Hugh is about six feet high, and as broad as he is long—I felt a retort on my lips, for I could not help my mind going back to a certain period in his life, when, from some cause which, as far as I knew, he had never told anybody, he had become a mere quivering mass of disordered nerves. Oddly enough, at the same moment and for the first time, he began to speak of it himself.

"You may reply that it was not worth my while to go either," he said, "because I was so clearly the wrong man in the wrong place. But I wasn't. You for all your apprehensions and expectancy have never seen a ghost. But I have, though I am the last person in the world you would have thought likely to do so, and, though my nerves are steady enough again now, it knocked me all to bits."

He sat down again in his chair.

"No doubt you remember my going to bits," he said, "and since I believe that I am sound again now, I should rather like to tell you about it. But before I couldn't; I couldn't speak of it at all to anybody. Yet there ought to have been nothing frightening about it; what I saw was certainly a most useful and friendly ghost. But it came from the shaded side of things; it looked suddenly out of the night and the mystery with which life is surrounded."

"I want first to tell you quite shortly my theory about ghost-seeing," he continued, "and I can explain it best by a simile, an image. Imagine then that you and I and everybody in the world are like people whose eye is directly opposite a little tiny hole in a sheet of cardboard which is continually shifting and revolving and moving about. Back to back with that sheet of cardboard is another, which also, by laws of its own, is in perpetual but independent motion. In it too there is another hole, and when, fortuitously it would seem, these two holes, the one through which we are always looking, and the other in the spiritual plane, come opposite one another, we see through, and then only do the sights and sounds of the spiritual world become visible or audible to us. With most people these holes never come opposite each other during their life. But at the hour of death they do, and then they remain stationary. That, I fancy, is how we 'pass over.'

"Now, in some natures, these holes are comparatively large, and are constantly coming into opposition. Clairvoyants, mediums are like that. But, as far as I knew, I had no clairvoyant or mediumistic powers at all. I therefore am the sort of person who long ago made up his mind that he never would see a ghost. It was, so to speak, an incalculable chance that my minute spy-hole should come into opposition with the other. But it did: and it knocked me out of time."

I had heard some such theory before, and though Hugh put it rather picturesquely, there was nothing in the least convincing or practical about it. It might be so, or again it might not.

"I hope your ghost was more original than your theory," said I, in order to bring him to the point.

"Yes, I think it was. You shall judge."

I put on more coal and poked up the fire. Hugh has got, so I have always considered, a great talent for telling stories, and that sense of drama which is so necessary for the narrator. Indeed, before now, I have suggested to him that he should take this up as a profession, sit by the fountain in Piccadilly Circus, when times are, as usual, bad, and tell stories to the passers-by in the street, Arabian fashion, for reward. The most part of mankind, I am aware, do not like long stories, but to the few, among whom I number myself, who really like to listen to lengthy accounts of experiences, Hugh is an ideal narrator. I do not care for his theories, or for his similes, but when it comes to facts, to things that happened, I like him to be lengthy.

"Go on, please, and slowly," I said. "Brevity may be the soul of wit, but it is the ruin of story-telling. I want to hear when and where and how it all was, and what you had for lunch and where you had dined and what—

Hugh began:

"It was the 24th of June, just eighteen months ago," he said. "I had let my flat, you may remember, and came up from the country to stay with you for a week. We had dined alone here—"

I could not help interrupting.

"Did you see the ghost here?" I asked. "In this square little box of a house in a modern street?"

"I was in the house when I saw it."

I hugged myself in silence.

"We had dined alone here in Graeme Street," he said, "and after dinner I went out to some party, and you stopped at home. At dinner your man did not wait, and when I asked where he was, you told me he was ill, and, I thought, changed the subject rather abruptly. You gave me your latch-key when I went out, and on coming back, I found you had gone to bed. There were, however, several letters for me, which required answers. I wrote them there and then, and posted them at the pillar-box opposite. So I suppose it was rather late when I went upstairs.

"You had put me in the front room, on the third floor, overlooking the street, a room which I thought you generally occupied yourself. It was a very hot night, and though there had been a moon when I started to my party, on my return the whole sky was cloud-covered, and it both looked and felt as if we might have a thunderstorm before morning. I was feeling very sleepy and heavy, and it was not till after I had got into bed that I noticed by the shadows of the window-frames on the blind that only one of the windows was open. But it did not seem worth while to get out of bed in order to open it, though I felt rather airless and uncomfortable, and I went to sleep.

"What time it was when I awoke I do not know, but it was certainly not yet dawn, and I never remember being conscious of such an extraordinary stillness as prevailed. There was no sound either of foot-passengers or wheeled traffic; the music of life appeared to be absolutely mute. But now, instead of being sleepy and heavy, I felt, though I must have slept an hour or two at most, since it was not yet dawn, perfectly fresh and wide-awake, and the effort which had seemed not worth making before, that of getting out of bed and opening the other window, was quite easy now and I pulled up the blind, threw it wide open, and leaned out, for somehow I parched and pined for air. Even outside the oppression was very noticeable, and though, as you know, I am not easily given to feel the mental effects of climate, I was aware of an awful creepiness coming over me. I tried to analyse it away, but without success; the past day had been pleasant, I looked forward to another pleasant day to-morrow, and yet I was full of some nameless apprehension. I felt, too, dreadfully lonely in this stillness before the dawn.

"Then I heard suddenly and not very far away the sound of some approaching vehicle; I could distinguish the tread of two horses walking at a slow foot's pace. They were, though not yet visible, coming up the street, and yet this indication of life did not abate that dreadful sense of loneliness which I have spoken of. Also in some dim unformulated way that which was coming seemed to me to have something to do with the cause of my oppression.

"Then the vehicle came into sight. At first I could not distinguish what it was. Then I saw that the horses were black and had long tails, and that what they dragged was made of glass, but had a black frame. It was a hearse. Empty.

"It was moving up this side of the street. It stopped at your door.

"Then the obvious solution struck me. You had said at dinner that your man was ill, and you were, I thought, unwilling to speak more about his illness. No doubt, so I imagined now, he was dead, and for some reason, perhaps because you did not want me to know anything about it, you were having the body removed at night. This, I must tell you, passed through my mind quite instantaneously, and it did not occur to me how unlikely it really was, before the next thing happened.

"I was still leaning out of the window, and I remember also wondering, yet only momentarily, how odd it was that I saw things—or rather the one thing I was looking at—so very distinctly. Of course, there was a moon behind the clouds, but it was curious how every detail of the hearse and the horses was visible. There was only one man, the driver, with it, and the street was otherwise absolutely empty. It was at him I was looking now. I could see every detail of his clothes, but from where I was, so high above him, I could not see his face. He had on grey trousers, brown boots, a black coat buttoned all the way up, and a straw hat. Over his shoulder there was a strap, which seemed to support some sort of little bag. He looked exactly like—well, from my description what did he look exactly like?"

"Why—a bus-conductor," I said instantly.

"So I thought, and even while I was thinking this, he looked up at me. He had a rather long thin face, and on his left cheek there was a mole with a growth of dark hair on it. All this was as distinct as if it had been noonday, and as if I was within a yard of him. But—so instantaneous was all that takes so long in the telling—I had not time to think it strange that the driver of a hearse should be so unfunereally dressed.

"Then he touched his hat to me, and jerked his thumb over his shoulder.

" 'Just room for one inside, sir,' he said.

"There was something so odious, so coarse, so unfeeling about this that I instantly drew my head in, pulled the blind down again, and then, for what reason I do not know, turned on the electric light in order to see what time it was. The hands of my watch pointed to half-past eleven.

"It was then for the first time, I think, that a doubt crossed my mind as to the nature of what I had just seen. But I put out the light again, got into bed, and began to think. We had dined; I had gone to a party, I had come back and written letters, had gone to bed and had slept. So how could it be half-past eleven? . . . Or—*what* half-past eleven was it?

"Then another easy solution struck me; my watch must have stopped. But it had not; I could hear it ticking.

"There was stillness and silence again. I expected every moment to hear muffled footsteps on the stairs, footsteps moving slowly and smally under the weight of a heavy burden, but from inside the house there was no sound whatever. Outside, too, there was the same dead silence, while the hearse waited at the door. And the minutes ticked on and ticked on, and at length I began to see a difference in the light in the room, and knew that the dawn was beginning to break outside. But how had it happened, then, that if the corpse was to be removed at night it had not gone, and that the hearse still waited, when morning was already coming?

"Presently I got out of bed again, and with the sense of strong physical shrinking I went to the window and pulled back the blind. The dawn was coming fast; the whole street was lit by that silver hueless light of morning. But there was no hearse there.

"Once again I looked at my watch. It was just a quarter-past four. But I would swear that not half an hour had passed since it had told me that it was half-past eleven.

"Then a curious double sense, as if I was living in the present and at the same moment had been living in some other time, came over me. It was dawn on June 25th, and the street, as natural, was empty. But a little while ago the driver of a hearse had spoken to me, and it was half-past eleven. What was that driver, to what plane did he belong? And again *what* half-past eleven was it that I had seen recorded on the dial of my watch?

"And then I told myself that the whole thing had been a dream. But if you ask me whether I believed what I told myself, I must confess that I did not.

"Your man did not appear at breakfast next morning, nor did I see him again before I left that afternoon. I think if I had, I should have told you about all this, but it was still possible, you see, that what I had seen was a real hearse, driven by a real driver, for all the ghastly gaiety of the face that had looked up to mine, and the levity of his pointing hand. I might possibly have fallen asleep soon after seeing him, and slumbered through the removal of the body and the departure of the hearse. So I did not speak of it to you."

There was something wonderfully straight-forward and prosaic in all this; here were no Jacobean houses oak-panelled and surrounded by weeping pine-trees, and somehow the very absence of suitable surroundings made the story more impressive. But for a moment a doubt assailed me.

"Don't tell me it was all a dream," I said.

"I don't know whether it was or not. I can only say that I believe myself to have been wide awake. In any case the rest of the story is—odd.

"I went out of town again that afternoon," he continued, "and I may say that I don't think that even for a moment did I get the haunting sense of what I had seen or dreamed that night out of my mind. It was present to me always as some vision unfulfilled. It was as if some clock had struck the four quarters, and I was still waiting to hear what the hour would be.

"Exactly a month afterwards I was in London again, but only for the day. I arrived at Victoria about eleven, and took the underground to Sloane Square in order to see if you were in town and would give me lunch. It was a baking hot morning, and I intended to take a bus from the King's Road as far as Graeme Street. There was one standing at the corner just as I came out of the station, but I saw that the top was full, and the inside appeared to be full also. Just as I came up to it the conductor, who, I suppose, had been inside, collecting fares or what not, came out on to the step within a few feet of me. He wore grey trousers, brown boots, a black coat buttoned, a straw hat, and over his shoulder was a strap on which hung his little machine for punching tickets. I saw his face, too; it was the face of the driver of the hearse, with a mole on the left cheek. Then he spoke to me, jerking his thumb over his shoulder.

" 'Just room for one inside, sir,' he said.

"At that a sort of panic-terror took possession of me, and I knew I gesticulated wildly with my arms, and cried, 'No, no!' But at that moment I was living not in the hour that was then passing, but in that hour which had passed a month ago, when I leaned from the window of your bedroom here just before the dawn broke. At this moment too I knew that my spy-hole had been opposite the spy-hole into the spiritual world. What I had seen there had some significance, now being fulfilled, beyond the significance of the trivial happenings of to-day and to-morrow. The Powers of which we know so little were visibly working before me. And I stood there on the pavement shaking and trembling.

"I was opposite the post-office at the corner, and just as the bus started my eye fell on the clock in the window there. I need not tell you what the time was.

"Perhaps I need not tell you the rest, for you probably conjecture it, since you will not have forgotten what happened at the corner of Sloane Square at the end of July, the summer before last. The bus pulled out from the pavement into the street in order to get round a van that was standing in front of it. At the moment there came down the King's Road a big motor going at a hideously dangerous pace. It crashed full into the bus, burrowing into it as a gimlet burrows into a board."

He paused.

"And that's my story," he said.

The Chill

Dennis Etchison

The thing that shocked him was that he wasn't shocked.

Morgan came out of the health food store, cut over the grass at the corner and was about to dig into his jeans for the keys when he clipped it with his foot. It was soft and rubbery.

Then he was stumbling into some kind of pothole, flailing one arm for balance—only there was no hole. At least there was not supposed to be.

It was then that he saw the people gathered around.

He laughed at himself and shook his head. But he wondered why they, all fifteen or twenty of them, continued to watch. He touched his fly, glanced down.

And saw that he was standing in a small hole in the sidewalk. The cement was cracked down in a concave circle, like a shallow crater.

"Now wait a minute," he muttered. He shifted his armload of groceries uneasily.

It was screwy. *I walked this way twenty minutes ago,* he thought. *Same side of the street, too. And there was no hole—there wasn't.*

"Move along, son."

"What?"

A cop supported Morgan's elbow, helping him out of the chuckhole.

"Keep the area clear," said the cop, to the others as well. He was big and flat-chested; Morgan got a close-up glimpse of his gun, the polished rosewood grip. As he led Morgan he kept his head down, as if afraid he might step on something.

Morgan looked down with him. And did a double-take.

The cop was high-stepping over a pair of white tennis shoes, set out on the pavement at a nice, neat angle. The laces were still tied.

"Wait a minute," he said again.

He stopped. The cop kept walking. His fingers left Morgan's elbow.

"What's going on?"

Some of the people turned away. A man in a shiny suit escorted a woman through the glass doors of a building. She glanced nervously back at Morgan. At Morgan's *feet.*

Morgan looked down again, and to the side and behind him, and saw finally what he had nearly stepped on the first time.

A hand. A man's hand, gray like the cement. The hand was attached to an arm that led under a mound of dull army-green canvas. The bulk of the tarpaulin lay in the street, between the wheels of a parked car.

Morgan stumbled backwards, staring at the formless shape. He stumbled again at the curb, regained his balance and crossed the street quickly to the parking lot.

He sloughed the groceries into the car and stood there by the open door. He started to step in onto the floorboard, then paused, balancing from foot to foot on the blacktop, watching over the roof of the car.

He thought about the body under the tarp. It must have hit at terrific speed—and, unbelievably, bounced, judging by the dented sedan at the curb.

Well, the building was tall enough, he guessed. He craned his neck. Ten, twelve . . . twenty-six stories. Offices or apartments, he couldn't tell which. Gray and black and hazy silver, layered between floors with a thin, dirty metallic icing: mid-twentieth century Crackerbox Imposing. It reminded Morgan of a stack of folded aluminum deck chairs. The filtered glare of the sun, down now behind the crow's feet TV antennae atop the laundromat, glazed the rows of smokey windows, the reflected light wavy on the glass panes that were lidded by unmoving metal awnings. At the very top, on the roof between a pair of block-like structures, stood two figures, their trouser legs blowing like flags.

Morgan considered. The vitamins would keep, certainly, but the half-gallon of raw milk, the natural cheddar, the pound of frozen DES-free ground beef . . .

He couldn't take long.

He locked the car and, dragging his feet, went back to the street.

He stood at a decent distance, his hands in his back pockets.

"That was the car, was it?" A man in walking shorts and black socks sidled up to him. The man inclined his head conspiratorially. "You saw him get hit, did you?"

Morgan made a noncommittal gesture. He needed answers himself. But he knew the police would not bother with his questions now; they were preoccupied with notebooks, with squad car radios, with each other, talking their own kind of reassuring shop in low voices that seemed not to move their lips. An un-uniformed man with crewcut handled a walkie-talkie officiously, aiming it like a pointer at the figures on the roof.

A woman in a sleeveless blouse came up and took possession of the man in walking shorts. Morgan heard a clucking begin in her throat.

"Excuse me," he said, and crossed the street.

At the curb one of his feet caught, nearly causing him to fall.

* * *

He felt a chill coming on as he hurried to the building.

At the doors a security guard waved him back.

"I live here," he tried. The guard hesitated. Morgan ducked inside, not looking back, and slipped through the milling crowd in the lobby.

The desk phones were all in use, hunched over by nervous, quick-eyed men who cupped their hands around the mouthpieces as they spoke. At the elevator he finally looked back at the glass doors. He saw a station wagon stenciled with the call letters of a local TV channel parking across the street. He punched the button and waited.

He waited while the other elevator opened and closed once, twice, three times; each time a full load of passengers squeezed out, followed by two officers who blocked the door with their shoulders as a third man checked names off a list; then the officers reboarded and took the elevator up again. He watched the light on the wall move up and down and up without a stop.

The light over his elevator never wavered from the top floor. After a few minutes it went off, and the words NOT IN SERVICE blinked on.

He pivoted slowly, casually—only to find himself reaching out for balance again. He groped, found an ashtray, steadied himself, hoping no one would notice.

He scanned the busy faces. No one had.

What happened?

His foot, no, his whole lower leg was asleep.

From standing, waiting so long? That was it.

He pretended to adjust the ashtray, a sand-filled canister into which countless cigarettes had plunged and extinguished. *Shake a leg*, he thought, *shake a leg*.

He made his way down the hall.

Morgan found a service elevator at the first turn, at the end of a row of offices, flanked by a maintenance closet and a restroom for EMP. ONLY.

He thumbed the button and tried to focus through the safety glass, waiting for the compartment to lower into view.

The double doors parted; it was already there.

He leaned his head back into the padded interior. He shut his eyes.

He squinted down through slitted lids at his legs. The right leg still felt cold. The foot, through some oddity of perspective, appeared very far away. He tried to thrum his toes but felt nothing, though the round, scuffed rubber end of the sneaker flexed like a mound of earth beneath which some unseen creature moved.

In fact the sensation, or lack of it, had now crept up to his knee; he rocked forward, took a step, but felt nothing. No blood coursing, no pins-and-needles. Only a coldness.

The floor locked into place, and the doors slid back.

Well, he could still walk.

He hobbled into the hall.

2642 . . . 2644 . . . twenty-sixth floor.

The elevator thumped closed behind him.

He had come up here for something. *What? So I'm just as morbid as the rest of them,* he thought. *Maybe worse.* No, he decided, not worse; they'd all be up here now, too, if they could, just to see where it happened, to savor the thought of it, turning it over and over before their minds' eyes like the secret behind the door at the end of the hall in the middle of the night in a house they thought they'd forgotten.

But he was already as high as the machinery would take him. He'd have to take the stairs the rest of the way, to the roof.

All but dragging one leg, Morgan tried to make it to the end of the long hall.

He passed door after door, yet he had the impression that they were moving past him while he remained in place, as if struggling on a treadmill. Each door was closed tight, sealed. Only if the doors were suddenly to swing wide could the lives they hid impinge upon him, or he upon them. And what then? Would their eyes recoil at the unexpected contact, would they slam soundproofed doors at his passing? Or would they stand frozen, fascinated?

Probably neither, he decided. They would most likely pretend that he was not there, that he did not exist.

He wondered in passing how many of the guests, insulated within these structures in which their lives played out—how many of them knew what was down there in the street right now? Would they *want* to know? What *about* the one who had chosen to leave his hermetic safety, to climb out under an alien sky, to scream down, straining to burn like a shooting star in the steely dusk?

He stopped, breathing heavily.

He leaned against a wall, and felt something cold touch his skin.

He turned: a fire extinguisher.

In the glass, behind the words BREAK IN CASE OF EMERGENCY, the reflection of his face.

The dim image reminded him: twenty-five, thirty extra pounds, so that the lines of his features were now soft, the face puffed, the skull beneath almost hidden by granola, wheat germ, yogurt, honey, unpasteurized milk, acidophilus culture, desiccated liver, torula yeast, turbinado sugar, dried fruits and cashew butter and whole wheat spaghetti and Brockmeyer's ice cream and date nut bread and carrot cake, and brown rice . . . it was *good* food. But now he looked at himself, unable for the moment to walk, and the fear returned, the fear that sapped and took the place of his will, and he forced himself to see and be reassured. But he could not look back, not for long. *That's right,* nodding sadly, turning away, *you can serve it up, can't you? But when it's on the plate, you can't see it. Can you?*

"Shit," he said aloud. The first thing he had thought when he saw him in the street was, *I'm glad it wasn't me!*

The left side of his body was cold, and growing colder.

But still he wanted to be there, to be up there, to be where *he* had been, to know what it was like.

He had to swing one leg around, using the other as the axis, and reach down with his good right hand and hold the knee from folding. In that way he managed to go on. To the fire door.

The stairs were a problem.

From here Morgan could see the Pacific Ocean beyond the shadow palm trees at the end of Wilshire Boulevard. The shoreline was broken by the ragged teeth of silhouetted buildings and, above it all, the clouds seemed to be bleeding dull colors that were illuminated from behind, masked by drifts of suspended particles.

He approached the edge of the roof.

He felt currents of air rising to meet him. He stopped between the two blocklike structures, which he now recognized as ventilation outlets. Droplets of moisture fell on his face and neck. They were like warm pinpricks.

The left side of his body, from toes to fingertips, was icy cold, numb.

He moved closer to the edge.

When he looked down, there was no sense of dizziness. At this distance the body on the street would be just another dark spot on the sidewalk.

He could not see it.

There were only a few raptorial stragglers left around the entrance, a single police car, the sedan with the dent and the TV station wagon. The man under the tarp had been cleared away. It had all started when he touched the hand, the empty hand curled heavenward; the cold hand. He wondered about the body. He pictured a collapsed sac, crushed bones, the pools of blood inside.

He heard a door slam. The door to the roof. But he had closed it. The wind? He stretched his neck but could not see around the air outlets.

Then he heard voices.

Police, probably. Or in-house security, checking, rehandling the details like beads until they satisfied themselves that it was a simple suicide.

And what would they think, finding him here?

But they could not see him. They would not, as long as they stayed away from the edge.

He turned back, swaying slightly.

Now several new dots angled on the sidewalk, and others moved jerkily across the street to gather at the front of the building. With a peculiar calmness, he realized that they were clustering together to watch him.

How long had he been standing here? Long enough for the police to notice, to send someone up? Did they think—

He waited, taking more and more of his weight onto his right side as the left side of his body grew heavy, a dead weight, unresponsive; and still he waited. He no longer had voluntary control over the stiffening joints, the leaden shoe. He watched with detachment as it began to move in the rising wind. The foot lost contact with the graveled roof, rose an inch, two inches into the air and swung, slowly at first, then in an increasing arc, nearer and nearer the edge. Now in space, now over the roof, now in space, now over the roof.

He waited, watching with growing concentration and concern, and presently he began to wonder which way it would fall.

Heads cocked and eyes fixed, his own and many others.

The Cleaning Machine

F. Paul Wilson

D r. Edward Parker reached across his desk and flipped the power switch on his tape recorder to the "on" position. "I want you to listen to this, Burke," he said. "She has classic paranoic symptoms; I wouldn't put much faith in anything she says."

Detective Ronald Burke, an old acquaintance on the city police force, sat across from the doctor. "She's all we've got," he replied with ill-concealed exasperation. "Over a hundred people disappear from an apartment house and the only person who might be able to tell us anything is a nut!"

Parker glanced at the recorder and noticed the glowing warm-up light. He pressed the button that started the tape. "Listen."

". . . and I guess I'm the one who's responsible for it but it was really the people who lived there in my apartment building who drove me to it—they were jealous of me.

"The children were the worst. Every day as I'd walk to the store they'd spit at me behind my back and call me names. They even got other little brats from all over town and would wait for me on corners and doorsteps. They called me terrible names and said that I carried awful diseases. Their parents put them up to it, I know it. All the people in my apartment building laughed at me. They thought they could hide it but I heard it. They hated me because they were jealous of my poetry. They knew I was famous and they couldn't stand it.

"Why just the other night I caught three of them rummaging through my desk. They thought I was asleep and so they sneaked in and tried to steal some of my latest works, figuring they could palm them off as their own. But I was awake. I could hear them laughing at me as they searched. I grabbed the butcher knife that I always keep under my pillow and ran out into the study. I must have made some noise when I got out of bed because they ran out into the hall and closed the door just before I got there. I heard one of them on the other side say, 'Boy, you sure can't fool that old lady!'

"They were fiends, all of them! But the very worst was that John Hendricks fellow next door who was trying to kill me with an ultra-frequency sonicator. He used to turn it on me and try to boil my brains while I was writing. But I was too smart for him! I kept an ice-pack on my head at all hours of the day. But even that didn't keep me from getting those awful headaches that plague me constantly. He was to blame.

"But the thing I want to tell you about is the machine in the cellar. I found it when I went down to the boiler room to see who was calling me filthy names through the ventilator system. I met the janitor on my way downstairs and told him about it. He just laughed and said that there hadn't been anyone down in the boiler room for two years, not since we started getting our heat piped in from the building next door. But I *knew* someone was down there—hadn't I heard those voices through the vent? I simply turned and went my way.

"Everything in the cellar was covered with at least half an inch of dust—everything, that is, except the machine. I didn't know it was a machine at that time because it hadn't done anything yet. It didn't have any lights or dials and it didn't make any noise. It just sat there being clean. I also noticed that the floor around it was immaculately clean for about five foot in all directions. Everywhere else was filth. It looked so strange, being clean. I ran and got George, the janitor.

"He was angry at having to go downstairs but I kept pestering him until he did. He was mighty surprised. 'What *is* that thing?' he said, walking towards the machine. Then he was gone! One moment he had been there, and then he was gone. There was no blinding flash or puff of smoke . . . just gone! And it happened just as he crossed into that circle of clean floor around the machine.

"I immediately knew who was responsible: John Hendricks! So I went right upstairs and brought him down. I didn't bother to tell him what that machine had done to George since I was sure he knew all about it. But he surprised me by walking right into the circle and disappearing, just like George.

"Well, at least I wouldn't be bothered by that ultra-frequency sonicator of his anymore. It was a good thing I had been too careful to go anywhere near that thing.

"I began to get an idea about that machine—*it was a cleaning machine!*

That's why the floor around it was so clean. Any dust or *anything* that came within the circle was either stored away somewhere or destroyed!

"A thought struck me: why not 'clean out' all of my jealous neighbors this way? It was a wonderful idea! I decided to start with the children . . .

"I went outside and, as usual, they started in with their name-calling (they always made sure to do it very softly but I could read their lips). There were about twenty of them playing in the street. I called them together and told them I was forming a club in the cellar. They all followed me down in a group. I pointed to the machine and told them that there was a gallon of chocolate ice cream behind it and that the first one to reach it could have it all. Their greedy little faces lighted up and they scrambled away in a mob.

"Three seconds later I was alone in the cellar.

"I then went around to all the other apartments in the building and told all those hateful people that their sweet little darlings were playing in the old boiler room and that I thought it was dangerous. I waited for one to go downstairs before I went to the next door. Then I met the husbands as they came home from work and told them the same thing. And if anybody came looking for someone, I sent him down to the cellar. It was all so simple: in searching the cellar they had to cross into the circle sooner or later.

"That night I was alone in the building. It was wonderful—no laughing, no name-calling and no one sneaking into my study. Wonderful!

"A policeman came the next day. He knocked on my door and looked very surprised when I opened it. He said he was investigating a number of missing persons reports. I told him that everyone was down in the cellar. He gave me a strange look but went to check. I followed him.

"The machine was gone! Nothing was left but the circle of clean floor. I told the officer all about it, about what horrible people they were and how they deserved to disappear. He just smiled and brought me down to the station where I had to tell my story again and they sent me here to see you.

"They're still looking for my neighbors, aren't they? Won't listen when I tell them that they'll never find them. They don't believe there ever *was* a machine! But they can't find my neighbors, can they? Well, it serves them right! I told them I'm the one responsible for 'cleaning out' my apartment building but they don't believe me. Serves them *all* right!"

"See what I mean?" said Dr. Parker with the slightest trace of a smile as he turned the recorder off. "She's no help at all."

"Yeah, I know she's as looney as they come," said Burke. "But how can you explain that circle of clean floor in the boiler room with all those footprints around it?"

"Well, I can't be sure, but the 'infernal machine' is not uncommon in the paranoid's delusional system. You found no trace of an 'ultra-frequency sonicator' in the Hendricks' apartment I trust?"

Burke shook his head. "No. From what we can gather, Hendricks knew nothing about electronics. He was a short-order cook in a greasy spoon downtown."

"I figured as much. She probably found everybody gone and went looking for them. She went down to the boiler room as a last resort and, finding *it* deserted, concluded that everybody has been 'cleaned out' of the building. She was glad but wanted to give herself the credit. She saw the circle of clean floor—probably left there by a round table top that had been recently moved—and started fabricating. By now she no doubt believes every word of her fantastic story. We'll never know what really happened until we find those missing tenants."

"I guess not," Burke said as he rose to go, "but I'd still like to know why we can find over a hundred sets of footprints approaching the circle but none leaving it."

Dr. Parker didn't have an answer for that one.

The Coffin Merchant

Richard Middleton

London on a November Sunday inspired Eustace Reynolds with a melancholy too insistent to be ignored and too causeless to be enjoyed. The grey sky overhead between the house-tops, the cold wind round every street-corner, the sad faces of the men and women on the pavements, combined to create an atmosphere of ineloquent misery. Eustace was sensitive to impressions, and in spite of a half-conscious effort to remain a dispassionate spectator of the world's melancholy, he felt the chill of the aimless day creeping over his spirit. Why was there no sun, no warmth, no laughter on the earth? What had become of all the children who keep laughter like a mask on the faces of disillusioned men? The wind blew down Southampton Street, and chilled Eustace to a shiver that passed away in a shudder of disgust at the sombre colour of life. A windy Sunday in London before the lamps are lit, tempts a man to believe in the nobility of work.

At the corner of Charing Cross Telegraph Office a man thrust a handbill under his eyes, but he shook his head impatiently. The blueness of the fingers that offered him the paper was alone sufficient to make him disinclined to remove his hands from his pockets even for an instant. But the man would not be dismissed so lightly.

"Excuse me, sir," he said, following him, "you have not looked to see what my bills are."

"Whatever they are I do not want them."

"That's where you are wrong, sir," the man said earnestly. "You will never find life interesting if you do not lie in wait for the unexpected. As a matter of fact, I believe that my bill contains exactly what you do want."

Eustace looked at the man with quick curiosity. His clothes were ragged, and the visible parts of his flesh were blue with cold, but his eyes were bright with intelligence and his speech was that of an educated man. It seemed to Eustace that he was being regarded with a keen expectancy, as though his decision on the trivial point was of real importance.

"I don't know what you are driving at," he said, "but if it will give you any pleasure I will take one of your bills; though if you argue with all your clients as you have with me, it must take you a long time to get rid of them."

"I only offer them to suitable persons," the man said, folding up one of the handbills while he spoke, "and I'm sure you will not regret taking it," and he slipped the paper into Eustace's hand and walked rapidly away.

Eustace looked after him curiously for a moment, and then opened the paper in his hand. When his eyes comprehended its significance, he gave a low whistle of astonishment. "You will soon be wanting a coffin!" it read. "At 606, Gray's Inn Road, your order will be attended to with civility and despatch. Call and see us!!"

Eustace swung round quickly to look for the man, but he was out of sight. The wind was growing colder, and the lamps were beginning to shine out in the greying streets. Eustace crumpled the paper into his overcoat pocket, and turned homewards.

"How silly!" he said to himself, in conscious amusement. The sound of his footsteps on the pavement rang like an echo to his laugh.

II

Eustace was impressionable but not temperamentally morbid, and he was troubled a little by the fact that the gruesomely bizarre handbill continued to recur to his mind. The thing was so manifestly absurd, he told himself with conviction, that it was not worth a second thought, but this did not prevent him from thinking of it again and again. What manner of undertaker could hope to obtain business by giving away foolish handbills in the street? Really, the whole thing had the air of a brainless practical joke, yet his intellectual fairness forced him to admit that as far as the man who had given him the bill was concerned, brainlessness was out of the question, and joking improbable. There had been depths in those little bright eyes which his glance had not been able to sound, and the man's manner in making him accept the handbill had given the whole transaction a kind of ludicrous significance.

"You will soon be wanting a coffin—!"

Eustace found himself turning the words over and over in his mind. If he had had any near relations he might have construed the thing as an elaborate threat, but he was practically alone in the world, and it seemed to him that he was not likely to want a coffin for anyone but himself.

"Oh damn the thing!" he said impatiently, as he opened the door of his flat, "it isn't worth worrying about. I mustn't let the whim of some mad tradesman get on my nerves. I've got no one to bury, anyhow."

Nevertheless, the thing lingered with him all the evening, and when his neighbour the doctor came in for a chat at ten o'clock, Eustace was glad to show him the strange handbill. The doctor, who had experienced the queer magics that are practised to this day on the West Coast of Africa, and who, therefore, had no nerves, was delighted with so striking an example of British commercial enterprise.

"Though, mind you," he added gravely, smoothing the crumpled paper on his knee, "this sort of thing might do a lot of harm if it fell into the hands of a nervous subject. I should be inclined to punch the head of the ass who perpetrated it. Have you turned that address up in the Post Office Directory?"

Eustace shook his head, and rose and fetched the fat red book which makes London an English city. Together they found the Gray's Inn Road, and ran their eyes down to No. 606.

" 'Harding, G. J., Coffin Merchant and Undertaker.' Not much information there," muttered the doctor.

"Coffin merchant's a bit unusual, isn't it?" queried Eustace.

"I suppose he manufactures coffins wholesale for the trade. Still, I didn't know they called themselves that. Anyhow, it seems as though that handbill is a genuine piece of downright foolishness. The idiot ought to be stopped advertising in that way."

"I'll go and see him myself to-morrow," said Eustace bluntly.

"Well, he's given you an invitation," said the doctor, "so it's only polite of you to go. I'll drop in here in the evening to hear what he's like. I expect that you'll find him as mad as a hatter."

"Something like that," said Eustace, "or he wouldn't give handbills to people like me. I have no one to bury except myself."

"No," said the doctor in the hall, "I suppose you haven't. Don't let him measure you for a coffin, Reynolds!"

Eustace laughed.

"We never know," he said sententiously.

III

Next day was one of those gorgeous blue days of which November gives but few, and Eustace was glad to run out to Wimbledon for a game of golf, or rather for two. It was therefore dusk before he made his way to the Gray's Inn Road in search of the unexpected. His attitude towards his errand despite the doctor's laughter and the prosaic entry in the directory, was a little confused. He could not help reflecting that after all the doctor had not seen the man with the little wise eyes, nor could he forget that Mr. G. J. Harding's description of himself as a coffin merchant, to say the least of it, approached the unusual. Yet he felt that it would be intolerable to chop the whole business without finding out what it all meant. On the whole he would have preferred not to have discovered the riddle at all; but having found it, he could not rest without an answer.

No. 606, Gray's Inn Road, was not like an ordinary undertaker's shop. The window was heavily draped with black cloth, but was otherwise unadorned. There were no letters from grateful mourners, no little model coffins, no photographs of marble memorials. Even more surprising was the absence of any name over the shop-door, so that the uninformed stranger could not possibly tell what trade was carried on within, or who was responsible for the management of the business. This uncommercial modesty did not tend to remove Eustace's doubts as to the sanity of Mr. G. J. Harding; but he opened the shop-door which started a large bell swinging noisily, and stepped over the threshold. The shop was hardly more expressive inside than out. A broad counter ran across it, cutting it in two, and in the partial gloom overhead a naked gas-burner whistled a noisy song. Beyond this the shop contained no furniture whatever, and no stock-in-trade except a few planks leaning against the wall in one corner. There was a large ink-stand on the counter. Eustace waited patiently for a minute or two, and then as no one came he began stamping on the floor with his foot. This proved efficacious, for soon he heard the sound of footsteps ascending wooden stairs, the door behind the counter opened and a man came into the shop.

He was dressed quite neatly now, and his hands were no longer blue with cold, but Eustace knew at once that it was the man who had given him the handbill. Nevertheless he looked at Eustace without a sign of recognition.

"What can I do for you, sir?" he asked pleasantly.

Eustace laid the handbill down on the counter.

"I want to know about this," he said. "It strikes me as being in pretty bad taste, and if a nervous person got hold of it, it might be dangerous."

"You think so, sir? Yet our representative," he lingered affectionately on the words, "our representative told you, I believe, that the handbill was only distributed to suitable cases."

"That's where you are wrong," said Eustace sharply, "for I have no one to bury."

"Except yourself," said the coffin merchant suavely.

Eustace looked at him keenly. "I don't see—" he began. But the coffin merchant interrupted him.

"You must know, sir," he said, "that this is no ordinary undertaker's business. We possess information that enables us to defy competition in our special class of trade."

"Information!"

"Well, if you prefer it, you may say intuitions. If our representative handed you that advertisement, it was because he knew you would need it."

"Excuse me," said Eustace, "you appear to be sane, but your words do not convey to me any reasonable significance. You gave me that foolish advertisement yourself, and now you say that you did so because you knew I would need it. I ask you why?"

The coffin merchant shrugged his shoulders. "Ours is a sentimental trade," he said. "I do not know why dead men want coffins, but they do. For my part I would wish to be cremated."

"Dead men?"

"Ah, I was coming to that. You see Mr.——?"

"Reynolds."

"Thank you, my name is Harding—G. J. Harding. You see, Mr. Reynolds, our intuitions are of a very special character, and if we say that you will need a coffin, it is—probable that you will need one."

"You mean to say that I—"

"Precisely. In twenty-four hours or less, Mr. Reynolds, you will need our services."

The revelation of the coffin merchant's insanity came to Eustace with a certain relief. For the first time in the interview he had a sense of the dark empty shop and the whistling gas-jet over his head.

"Why, it sounds like a threat, Mr. Harding!" he said gaily.

The coffin merchant looked at him oddly, and produced a printed form from his pocket. "If you would fill this up," he said.

Eustace picked it up off the counter and laughed aloud. It was an order for a hundred-guinea funeral.

"I don't know what your game is," he said, "but this has gone on long enough."

"Perhaps it has, Mr. Reynolds," said the coffin merchant, and he leant across the counter and looked Eustace straight in the face.

For a moment Eustace was amused; then he was suddenly afraid. "I think it's time I—" he began slowly, and then he was silent, his whole will intent on fighting the eyes of the coffin merchant. The song of the gas-jet waned to a point in his ears, and then rose steadily till it was like the beating of the world's heart. The eyes of the coffin merchant grew larger and larger, till they blended in one great circle of fire. Then Eustace picked a pen off the counter and filled in the form.

"Thank you very much, Mr. Reynolds," said the coffin merchant, shaking hands with him politely. "I can promise you every civility and despatch. Good-day, sir."

Outside on the pavement Eustace stood for a while trying to recall exactly what had happened. There was a slight scratch on his hand, and when he automatically touched it with his lips, it made them burn. The lit lamps in the Gray's Inn Road seemed to him a little unsteady, and the passers-by showed a disposition to blunder into him.

"Queer business," he said to himself dimly; "I'd better have a cab."

He reached home in a dream.

It was nearly ten o'clock before the doctor remembered his promise, and went upstairs to Eustace's flat. The outer door was half-open so that he thought he was expected, and he switched on the light in the little hall, and shut the door behind him with the simplicity of habit. But when he swung round from the door he gave a cry of astonishment. Eustace was lying asleep in a chair before him with his face flushed and drooping on his shoulder, and his breath hissing noisily through his parted lips. The doctor looked at him quizzically. "If I did not know you, my young friend," he remarked, "I should say that you were as drunk as a lord."

And he went up to Eustace and shook him by the shoulder; but Eustace did not wake.

"Queer!" the doctor muttered, sniffing at Eustace's lips; "he hasn't been drinking."

The Dancing Partner

Jerome K. Jerome

This story,' commenced MacShaugnassy, 'comes from Furtwangen, a small town in the Black Forest. There lived there a very wonderful old fellow named Nicholaus Geibel. His business was the making of mechanical toys, at which work he had acquired an almost European reputation. He made rabbits that would emerge from the heart of a cabbage, flop their ears, smooth their whiskers, and disappear again; cats that would wash their faces, and mew so naturally that dogs would mistake them for real cats, and fly at them; dolls, with phonographs concealed within them, that would raise their hats and say, "Good morning; how do you do?" and some that would even sing a song.

'But he was something more than a mere mechanic; he was an artist. His work was with him a hobby, almost a passion. His shop was filled with all manner of strange things that never would, or could, be sold—things he had made for the pure love of making them. He had contrived a mechanical donkey that would trot for two hours by means of stored electricity, and trot, too, much faster than the live article, and with less need for exertion on the part of the driver, a bird that would shoot up into the air, fly round and round in a circle, and drop to earth at the exact spot from where it started; a skeleton that, supported by an upright iron bar, would dance a hornpipe; a life-size lady doll that could play the fiddle; and a gentleman with a hollow inside who could smoke a pipe and drink more lager beer that any three average German students put together, which is saying much.

'Indeed, it was the belief of the town that old Geibel could make a man capable of doing everything that a respectable man need want to do. One day he made a man who did too much, and it came about this way:

'Young Doctor Follen had a baby, and the baby had a birthday. Its first birthday put Doctor Follen's household into somewhat of a flurry, but on the occasion of its second birthday, Mrs Doctor Follen gave a ball in honour of the event. Old Geibel and his daughter Olga were among the guests.

'During the afternoon of the next day some three or four of Olga's bosom friends, who had also been present at the ball, dropped in to have a chat about it. They naturally fell to discussing the men, and to criticizing their dancing. Old Geibel was in the room, but he appeared to be absorbed in his newspaper, and the girls took no notice of him.

' "There seem to be fewer men who can dance at every ball you go to," said one of the girls.

' "Yes, and don't the ones who can give themselves airs," said another; "they make quite a favour of asking you."

' "And how stupidly they talk," added a third. "They always say exactly the same things: 'How charming you are looking tonight.' 'Do you often go to Vienna? Oh, you should, it's delightful.' 'What a charming dress you have on.' 'What a warm day it has been.' 'Do you like Wagner?' I do wish they'd think of something new."

' "Oh, I never mind how they talk," said a fourth. "If a man dances well he may be a fool for all I care."

' "He generally is," slipped in a thin girl, rather spitefully.

' "I go to a ball to dance," continued the previous speaker, not noticing the interruption. "All I ask of a partner is that he shall hold me firmly, take me round steadily, and not get tired before I do."

' "A clockwork figure would be the thing for you," said the girl who had interrupted.

' "Bravo!" cried one of the others, clapping her hands, "what a capital idea!"

' "What's a capital idea?" they asked.

' "Why, a clockwork dancer, or, better still, one that would go by electricity and never run down."

'The girls took up the idea with enthusiasm.

' "Oh, what a lovely partner he would make," said one; "he would never kick you, or tread on your toes."

' "Or tear your dress," said another.

' "Or get out of step."

' "Or get giddy and lean on you."

' "And he would never want to mop his face with his handkerchief. I do hate to see a man do that after every dance."

' "And wouldn't want to spend the whole evening in the supper room."

' "Why, with a phonograph inside him to grind out all the stock remarks, you would not be able to tell him from a real man," said the girl who had suggested the idea.

' "Oh, yes, you would," said the thin girl, "he would be so much nicer."

'Old Geibel had laid down his paper, and was listening with both his ears. On one of the girls glancing in his direction, however, he hurriedly hid himself again behind it.

'After the girls were gone, he went to his workshop, where Olga heard him walking up and down, and every now and then chuckling to himself, and that night he talked to her a good deal about dancing men—asked what they usually said and did—what dances were most popular—what steps were gone through, with many other questions bearing on the subject.

'Then for a couple of weeks he kept much to his factory, and was very thoughtful and busy, though prone at unexpected moments to break into a quiet low laugh, as if enjoying a joke that nobody else knew of.

'A month later another ball took place in Furtwangen. On this occasion it was given by old Wenzel, the wealthy timber merchant, to celebrate his niece's betrothal, and Geibel and his daughter were again among the invited.

'When the hour arrived to set out, Olga sought her father. Not finding him in the house, she tapped at the door of his workshop. He appeared in his shirtsleeves, looking hot but radiant.

' "Don't wait for me," he said, "you go on, I'll follow you. I've got something to finish."

'As she turned to obey he called after her, "Tell them I'm going to bring a young man with me—such a nice young man, and an excellent dancer. All the girls will like him." Then he laughed and closed the door.

'Her father generally kept his doings secret from everybody, but she had a pretty shrewd suspicion of what he had been planning, and so, to a certain extent, was able to prepare the guests for what was coming. Anticipation ran high, and the arrival of the famous mechanist was eagerly awaited.

'At length the sound of wheels was heard outside, followed by a great commotion in the passage, and old Wenzel himself burst into the room and announced in stentorian tones:

' "Herr Geibel and a friend."

'Herr Geibel and his "friend" entered, greeted with shouts of laughter and applause, and advanced to the centre of the room.

' "Allow me, ladies and gentlemen," said Herr Geibel, "to introduce you to my friend, Lieutenant Fritz. Fritz, my dear fellow, bow to the ladies and gentlemen."

'Geibel placed his hand encouragingly on Fritz's shoulder, and the lieutenant bowed low, accompanying the action with a harsh clicking noise in his throat, unpleasantly suggestive of a death rattle. But that was only a detail.

' "He walks a little stiffly" (old Geibel took his arm and walked him forward a few steps. He certainly did walk stiffly), "but then, walking is not his forte. He is essentially a dancing man. I have only been able to teach him the waltz as yet, but at that he is faultless. Come, which of you ladies may I introduce him to as a partner? He keeps perfect time; he never gets tired; he won't kick you or tread on your dress; he will hold you as firmly as you like, and go as quickly or as slowly as you please; he never gets giddy; and he is full of conversation. Come, speak up for yourself, my boy."

'The old gentleman twisted one of the buttons at the back of his coat, and immediately Fritz opened his mouth, and in thin tones that appeared to proceed from the back of his head, remarked suddenly, "May I have the pleasure?" and then shut his mouth again with a snap.

'That Lieutenant Fritz made a strong impression on the company was undoubted, yet none of the girls seemed inclined to dance with him. They looked askance at his waxen face, with its staring eyes and fixed smile, and shuddered. At last old Geibel came to Annette, the girl who had conceived the idea.

' "It is your own suggestion, carried out to the letter," said Geibel, "an electric dancer. You owe it to the gentleman to give him a trial."

'She was a bright, saucy little girl, fond of a frolic. Her host added his entreaties, and she consented.

'Herr Geibel fixed the figure to her. Its right arm was screwed round her waist, and held her firmly: its delicately jointed left hand was made to fasten itself upon her right. The old toymaker showed her how to regulate its speed, and how to stop it, and release herself.

' "It will take you round in a complete circle," he explained; "be careful that no one knocks against you, and alters its course."

'The music struck up. Old Geibel put the current in motion, and Annette and her strange partner began to dance.

'For a while everyone stood watching them. The figure performed its purpose admirably. Keeping perfect time and step, and holding its little partner tight clasped in an unyielding embrace, it revolved steadily, pouring forth at the same time a constant flow of squeaky conversation, broken by brief intervals of grinding silence.

' "How charming you are looking tonight," it remarked in its thin, far-away voice. "What a lovely day it has been. Do you like dancing? How well our steps agree. You will give me another, won't you? Oh, don't be so cruel. What a charming gown you have on. Isn't waltzing delightful? I could go on dancing for ever—with you. Have you had supper?"

'As she grew more familiar with the uncanny creature, the girl's nervousness wore off, and she entered into the fun of the thing.

' "Oh, he's just lovely," she cried, laughing, "I could go on dancing with him all my life."

'Couple after couple now joined them, and soon all the dancers in the room were whirling round behind them. Nicholaus Geibel stood looking on, beaming with childish delight at his success.

'Old Wenzel approached him, and whispered something in his ear. Geibel laughed and nodded, and the two worked their way quietly towards the door.

' "This is the young people's house tonight," said Wenzel, as soon as they were outside; "you and I will have a quiet pipe and a glass of hock, over in the counting house."

'Meanwhile the dancing grew more fast and furious. Little Annette loosened the screw regulating her partner's rate of progress, and the figure flew round with her swifter and swifter. Couple after couple dropped out exhausted, but they only went the faster, till at length they remained dancing alone.

'Madder and madder became the waltz. The music lagged behind: the musicians, unable to keep the pace, ceased and sat staring. The younger guests applauded, but the older faces began to grow anxious.

' "Hadn't you better stop, dear," said one of the women; "you'll make yourself so tired."

'But Annette did not answer.

' "I believe she's fainted," cried out a girl who had caught sight of her face as it was swept by.

'One of the men sprang forward and clutched at the figure, but its impetus threw him down on to the floor, where its steel-cased feet laid bare his cheek. The thing evidently did not intend to part with its prize easily.

60

'Had anyone retained a cool head, the figure, one cannot help thinking, might easily have been stopped. Two or three men acting in concert might have lifted it bodily off the floor, or have jammed it into a corner. But few human heads are capable of remaining cool under excitement. Those who are not present think how stupid must have been those who were; those who are reflect afterwards how simple it would have been to do this, that, or the other, if only they had thought of it at the time.

'The women grew hysterical. The men shouted contradictory directions to one another. Two of them made a bungling rush at the figure, which had the result of forcing it out of its orbit in the centre of the room, and sending it crashing against the walls and furniture. A stream of blood showed itself down the girl's white frock, and followed her along the floor. The affair was becoming horrible. The women rushed screaming from the room. The men followed them.

'One sensible suggestion was made: "Find Geibel—fetch Geibel."

'No one had noticed him leave the room, no one knew where he was. A party went in search of him. The others, too unnerved to go back into the ballroom, crowded outside the door and listened. They could hear the steady whir of the wheels upon the polished floor as the thing spun round and round; the dull thud as every now and again it dashed itself and its burden against some opposing object and ricocheted off in a new direction.

'And everlastingly it talked in that thin ghostly voice, repeating over and over the same formula: "How charming you are looking tonight. What a lovely day it has been. Oh, don't be so cruel. I could go on dancing for ever—with you. Have you had supper?"

'Of course they sought for Geibel everywhere but where he was. They looked in every room in the house, then they rushed off in a body to his own place, and spent precious minutes in waking up his deaf old housekeeper. At last it occurred to one of the party that Wenzel was missing also, and then the idea of the counting-house across the yard presented itself to them, and there they found him.

'He rose up, very pale, and followed them; and he and old Wenzel forced their way through the crowd of guests gathered outside, and entered the room, and locked the door behind them.

'From within there came the muffled sound of low voices and quick steps, followed by a confused scuffling noise, then silence, then the low voices again.

'After a time the door opened, and those near it pressed forward to enter, but old Wenzel's broad shoulders barred the way.

' "I want you—and you, Bekler," he said addressing a couple of the elder men. His voice was calm, but his face was deadly white. "The rest of you, please go—get the women away as quickly as you can."

'From that day old Nicholaus Geibel confined himself to the making of mechanical rabbits, and cats that mewed and washed their faces.'

The Desert Lich

Frank Belknap Long

He has killed his wife, master! He is below, and he has killed his wife! All night he walked back and forth, beating upon the gate. With his bare hands, master! With his bare hands! All night upon the gate with his hands! Pound! pound! pound! It was like the desert drums, master. You have heard them? All night—and in the cold!"

Yes, I had expected him. I put my head out of the window and looked down upon him. Poor fellow! He was standing there in the cold, shivering and cursing. And whose fault was it? I had sold him a good wife, an excellent wife. He demanded too much of women; it was not in them to wear veils forever. I had warned him; I had said to him, "See here! You buy of me a woman! And she will betray you; it is to be expected. Why do you not shrug, why do you not philosophize, as do the English? Are not wives cheap; is it well to have them faithful too long? Would not anybody tire of an overfaithful woman? Faugh! I will get you another one!"

But no, he must kill his wife. It was to be expected. I descended the stairs, and let him in.

"Why is it," I demanded, "that you come here in the cold and disturb me? It is early, and I have had no coffee. The fumes of coffee go to our heads; when we have coffee we are happy, we smile, we furnish you with wives. That is the custom. But if you come here so early, what can you expect?"

He was bitter; he stormed. His shirt was open and I could see the long red hairs bristling on his chest.

"You must come with me! I shall show you what I have done, and then you will be happy. Come, it is not long. My camel is waiting."

What could I do? The wrath was in him and I had given him an unfaithful wife, and was in a measure to blame.

I gave directions and followed him. It was a pity. The camels had suffered too, and nuzzled my hand. I dissolved in sympathy; these fine beasts had suffered because a fool had murdered his wife. The sands whistled between our legs. There were drums all over the desert. I was so cold that my beard froze. But I was determined. I had made a bargain, and I would keep it.

"You do not mind?"

He was riding with his face turned toward Mecca. Poor fool! He was sentimental, and believed in devils! A bleak, freezing moment! We crossed dunes, the wind whistled through our beards. The silence of the morning drew in upon us. My teeth began to chatter, but I bit my tongue and urged my camel forward. Even then repentance might have come. I am not a fool and I have a conscience. It is not a pleasant thing to sell a man an unfaithful wife. Men have been buried in the sand for less! Once I saw a man's ears cut off for less! But what would you have? Assume that I decided to confess the fault mine. He would turn on me; I should have a knife in my side. It is not pleasant to anger a man who has red hairs on his chest. So I replied nothing, and we went on. The wind rose and lifted our saddles. It takes a tremendous wind to lift saddles. My lips began to freeze together. Would we never dismount?

What a cave! How can men live in such places? Eerily above the sands it rose, white, like a sepulcher. What madness drives men to bury themselves in such places? It rose high on each side, and slanted down in the middle. A camel's back rising out of the sand! And as white as clean-picked bones! There were bones in front, long rows of smooth, white bones. Human? Ah, yes, they were human. But no one wonders at it in the desert. For one thing, there are many lepers, and they die anywhere; like leaves they fall, and who is there to pick them up?

"For six years I have lived here!"

Poor fellow! I pitied him. To awake at night with your teeth on edge; to feel the cold in your bones; to know that you live in a tomb! And he had taken a wife to help him bear it! But is it any wonder that she rebelled?

We slid down from our poor, tired camels. We sidled across the sands. The wind licked furiously about the sepulcher! We stumbled over the bones; I groaned as a sharp point pricked through my sandals.

"Will you not enter first?"

He was bowing to me. I climbed up over the smooth, white stone. The opening was but three feet in diameter, a tiny hole in the top of a white sepulcher. I felt around inside with my foot for a ladder. But there was nothing.

"Drop!"

Was it a trap? Should I let myself go and drop down perhaps ten, perhaps twenty, perhaps a hundred feet? Desert sepulchers run deep. He was grinning like a malicious satyr. But if I hesitated there was the knife. And after all, what is a drop of fifty feet? A broken leg, perhaps, but when one has sold a man an unfaithful wife, is it too great a payment? Did I not owe him that much? And it might give him pleasure! I felt my hands slipping on the smooth stone. I closed my eyes, and let them slip.

I fell like a freighted pomegranate. For a moment I felt the darkness closing in about me, passing through my beard and over my head. I felt the darkness, and then I became light about the heart. I was falling a great distance. I thought of many things. Why had I not sounded the baggage in advance? I should have asked her, "Do you like this chap? Is it reasonable that I should ask you to live in a sepulcher?" But then, I did not know that the fool dwelt in a tomb!

When did I think of these things? Even as I fell. In less time than it takes a camel to sneeze, and then—a great weight on my shoulders!

I had landed upon my back. Ah, you may laugh, but it was horrible! My shoulders seemed on fire! Fierce contractions under my shoulders and arms! I cried out with the pain. I was a fool, of course. Who could have heard me! It was dark, and I had fallen a great distance. All of one hundred feet! Far above me I saw a miniature speck of light which wavered. Now it was here, now there. A tiny pin-prick of light, and a voice that laughed: "Fool! fool! fool!" Was it the light that spoke?

I passed my hand over my chest: I was dripping wet. The cold had disappeared. I was lying on a smooth, warm floor. Waves of intense heat passed over me. Somewhere near by there was fire—a furnace perhaps. It flickered occasionally across the darkness, lighting the vault. I tried to sit up. But a weight was on my shoulders; I lay panting.

Then deep thoughts began to run in my brain. It was a holiday season. Men would come for wives. With crates of pomegranates, with curds, with ewe's milk, bartering, scheming, seeking wives. They were fierce, determined men. What if my boy should say, "You must depart. There are no wives here! The master has gone away and there are no wives." Would they not storm; would they not scale the wall and carry away my women? And they would never pay me; I know them too well. But perhaps one will have a kinder heart; perhaps one will say, "Surely this man is not one to lose trade. If he is gone, there is mischief afoot. Some scoundrelly freelance may have murdered him! Hi, there, boy, in whose company did your master depart?" Ah, if they but think to ask that! But they will never ask it; I know them too well.

For hours, ages I lay there. Above me the spark of light vanished. In the night I lay, and groaned. But I saw things; objects made themselves visible to me. And there was the red-green illumination from beyond that flashed across the chamber. A small chamber! Twenty by twenty perhaps. And in the corner an object. It lay upon a round dais, and it repelled me. It possessed a blasphemous imperfection that I dared not openly acknowledge. It lacked the permanent quality of other objects. It had once boasted attributes—certain attributes— certain attributes! And now it was changing, becoming more unbearable before my eyes. I closed my eyes; I endeavored to shut out the object. But the outline of it forced itself beneath my eyelids; I could not blot out that long thin form from my tired brain. I saw very clearly that I had been a fool to sell a man an unfaithful wife.

And yet what a method of revenge! And had the idiot no sense of decorum? To drop a man one hundred feet into the sarcophagus of his wife!

The next day I could move. It was difficult, but I got to my feet. The furnace had gone out, and a chill had taken me. My eyes were glued together, and the knuckles of my hands were beginning to turn black. A misery in my bones! I felt them crack as I moved across the floor. My eyes could now distinguish objects without the aid of the light from the furnace. Plague on the idiot's stupidity! He might have left me the darkness! It is these little things that hurt, a lack of common decency between enemies.

It was not pleasant to look at her. The heat of the furnace had altered her monstrously. Now the cold might help, but things had gone atrociously far. I bit my knuckles and swore in my beard.

There was a disdain in her face. A horrible, bitter grimace. And I quailed before the justice of it. And yet it was not meant for me. Coward! He dared not face the contempt in his wife's face. He had sought me out, and he had forced the disdain upon me.

The cold increased; something loathsome slid across the floor. A snake or a rat? What did it matter? The agony was all within me. My anger warmed me against the cold without. But I did not like the thought of unknown things gliding between my legs, I was tempted to climb upon the bier. What if I put his wife upon the floor? The rats would be pleased. It was well to propitiate the vermin: they were insatiable in their greed. What if I should—and yet I had not descended so far! It was foolish to imagine such extremities! A man does not so abandon a woman for fear of rats! I could still hope.

I slid solemnly along the wall, feeling with my hands for a crevice, a crack, something definite to go upon. But nothing but damp mildew could I find—nothing but mildew one hundred feet below the desert. It came off in my hands, peeled layers of noisome greenish mildew. It was that, and the rats, which sent me back to the center of the room. I stood still, in the center, trying to rub my eyes open: they were gummy and stuck together. I could see, but only vaguely, as one perceives things in a prism. The blood pounded in my head; but I could not keep the cold out of my legs and arms. Fool! fool! fool! Something above reiterated it. It beat in through my frozen ears, it ran through my blood, and that shouted out from the tips of my fingers. Fool! fool! fool!

I might have known! To sell a man a piece of baggage for a wife! After all, the rats deserved her. Then the hunger came upon me! A longing for food, for plums, for raisins, pomegranates.

To feel both hunger and cold! To stand in the dark with rats running between your legs, and to long for pomegranates! I saw my women pressing the sweet fruit between their hands; in the darkness I could discern long rows of goblets filled with pomegranate juice! The figure on the bier appeared to mock me. Fool! fool! fool!

He was looking down upon me from above. I saw the tiny pin-prick of light, and tore at my beard. The long hairs came out in my hand. Already the skin on my face was beginning to freeze. I felt my ears: they were stiff and brittle. Low currents of air ran along the floor. I could feel the chill breeze whistling about my legs. But these things were soon forgotten—and then came back the dreams of pomegranates. Row on row of goblets filled with pomegranate juice. I stretched forth my hand to seize one, to drain it, and I slyly anticipated the ecstasy of the warm sweet liquid. Fool! The goblets vanished into thin air; and in my open mouth I tasted the necrophilic damp of a desert sepulcher.

During the next night I was very quiet. I lay upon my back, dumbly delirious. But I knew better than to dream of pomegranates. I filled the darkness with elaborate boards, overflowing with butter cakes, bowls of rice, dates, camel's meat, spices, rich red wine! Was I not shrewd? Even in the darkness did I drain goblet after goblet of Abyssinian wine.

In the morning I called upon Allah—for the first time! Then I repented, and blasphemed. Wallah! Wallah! Wallah! Even in the morning, in the gray cold, with slithery things crawling between my legs! I instinctively began to pity the woman on the bier. I crossed over and looked at her. Ah, she had changed.

There is a fascination in ugliness. We long to cover it up, but it attracts us. How I longed to put a cloth over that face! And yet how morbidly fascinating that monstrous grimace that seemed to dissolve and change as I watched it! Never in life had her face possessed such an attraction.

But how satisfy a longing for pomegranates by studying a face? What a longing for food obsessed me! I began to dream of snaring the rats. If they would walk into a trap! What if I should lie down and remain very quiet? Perhaps the rats would venture out and run over me. During the night I had several times felt tiny nostrils nuzzling my hand. And once something cold and loathsome had dashed across my face.

I lay down on the floor. It was a madness, for the chill was already in my bones. Already the gangrene had infected my armpits. I knew it too well, the dreadful, sickening pain. I knew also that my ears had turned black, that I should lose my ears. But a hunger fever was about me; I thought only of that. I was alone with my hunger.

I did not move; I did not breathe. Only above me I watched the light, the tiny white light that wavered and mocked. Fool! fool! fool! And there was the darkness and the stifling odors; horrible warm currents of air brushed across my face, and then something wet and slimy. My hand shot out and grasped it. It was soft and plump to the touch—a gigantic rat, a rare prize! What a fool a man is to barter an unfaithful wife! Yes, it was soft and I pressed it fiercely. I squeezed it as I would a pomegranate. I could feel it scratching, and struggling. The vermin!

I held it very close, sought to squeeze the air out of its detestable body. Then it bit me. The wet blood trickled over my palm. I let the rat go and sat up.

Was it only in imagination that I carried my hand to my lips and sucked greedily upon it? I had no clear evidence that I had so acted. Only, why had I gladly released the rat; what thrill had seized upon me at the thought of the warm blood trickling over my hand? Fool! fool! fool! Above me the ceaseless iteration; it had become a part of my every thought.

During the day I devoured my headdress. It was not pleasant, of course, but I got it down somehow. It had a sweet starchy taste. It weaned me from my pomegranates—for a time. But there were other insatiate longings. I dreamed of camels. I saw long processions of camels; I stood in a desert place, a land of dead seasons that wander, and watched them come solemnly up over the rim of the desert and disappear in the burning sands. I stood with a huge knife in my hand, and as each camel passed by I made a desperate lunge at his side with the knife. Great cuts would appear in the sides of the frightened animals, and I would put my lips to the lacerations and drink up gallon after gallon of fresh warm blood.

During the next night my longing reached its culmination. I might have known! From the very first his design had been that I should do what I was about to do. Have you the heart to blame me? My legs and arms were freezing. I could scarcely wriggle my fingers. Under my arms the pain was excruciating. My entire being cried out that I should do a vile thing to satisfy my craving for relief—for food, for pomegranates!

I approached the body. I drew back the cloth which covered it. I shrieked inwardly, but I was determined. There was no alternative. The damp and agony of the sarcophagus were in my blood; my soul was green and sick with noisome mildew. My soul was like the walls of the sepulcher—niter-encrusted and necrophilic.

But even as I bent there came a burst of merriment from above. The vault echoed with triumphant laughter, and the pin-point of light grew. Shafts of soft sunlight filtered through the darkness. In the center of the vault hung a rope! A rope!

"You did not mind? In my heart of hearts, I pitied you. But it was necessary to affirm, to act. Your offence was great, but under the stars, I pitied you! Is it not written: 'Thou shalt deal alone in women of sound heart?' But let enmity cease between us. Bind the rope about your waist. My wife you may leave: had you nibbled, I should have regretted—"

Quickly did I fasten the rope about me. And then up, up, up to sunlight—and pomegranates! My dear friend, never violate the Qoran.

Dickon the Devil

J. Sheridan Le Fanu

About thirty years ago I was selected by two rich old maids to visit a property in that part of Lancashire which lies near the famous forest of Pendle, with which Mr. Ainsworth's "Lancashire Witches" has made us so pleasantly familiar. My business was to make partition of a small property, including a house and demesne, to which they had a long time before succeeded as co-heiresses.

The last forty miles of my journey I was obliged to post, chiefly by cross-roads, little known, and less frequented, and presenting scenery often extremely interesting and pretty. The picturesqueness of the landscape was enhanced by the season, the beginning of September, at which I was travelling.

I had never been in this part of the world before; I am told it is now a great deal less wild, and, consequently, less beautiful.

At the inn where I had stopped for a relay of horses and some dinner—for it was then past five o'clock—I found the host, a hale old fellow of five-and-sixty, as he told me, a man of easy and garrulous benevolence, willing to accommodate his guests with any amount of talk, which the slightest tap sufficed to set flowing, on any subject you pleased.

I was curious to learn something about Barwyke, which was the name of the demesne and house I was going to. As there was no inn within some miles of it, I had written to the steward to put me up there, the best way he could, for a night.

The host of the "Three Nuns," which was the sign under which he entertained wayfarers, had not a great deal to tell. It was twenty years, or more, since old Squire Bowes died, and no one had lived in the Hall ever since, except the gardener and his wife.

"Tom Wyndsour will be as old a man as myself; but he's a bit taller, and not so much in flesh, quite," said the fat innkeeper.

"But there were stories about the house," I repeated, "that they said, prevented tenants from coming into it?"

"Old wives' tales; many years ago, that will be, sir; I forget 'em; I forget 'em all. Oh yes, there always will be, when a house is left so; foolish folk will always be talkin'; but I hadn't heard a word about it this twenty year."

It was vain trying to pump him; the old landlord of the "Three Nuns," for some reason, did not choose to tell tales of Barwyke Hall, if he really did, as I suspected, remember them.

I paid my reckoning, and resumed my journey, well pleased with the good cheer of that old-world inn, but a little disappointed.

We had been driving for more than an hour, when we began to cross a wild common; and I knew that, this passed, a quarter of an hour would bring me to the door of Barwyke Hall.

The peat and furze were pretty soon left behind; we were again in the wooded scenery that I enjoyed so much, so entirely natural and pretty, and so little disturbed by traffic of any kind. I was looking from the chaise-window, and soon detected the object of which, for some time, my eye had been in search. Barwyke Hall was a large, quaint house, of that cage-work fashion known as "black-and-white," in which the bars and angles of an oak framework contrast, black as ebony, with the white plaster that overspreads the masonry built into its interstices. This steep-roofed Elizabethan house stood in the midst of park-like grounds of no great extent, but rendered imposing by the noble stature of the old trees that now cast their lengthening shadows eastward over the sward, from the declining sun.

The park-wall was grey with age, and in many places laden with ivy. In deep grey shadow, that contrasted with the dim fires of evening reflected on the foliage above it, in a gentle hollow, stretched a lake that looked cold and black, and seemed, as it were, to skulk from observation with a guilty knowledge.

I had forgot that there was a lake at Barwyke; but the moment this caught my eye, like the cold polish of a snake in the shadow, my instinct seemed to recognize something dangerous, and I knew that the lake was connected, I could not remember how, with the story I had heard of this place in my boyhood.

I drove up a grass-grown avenue, under the boughs of these noble trees, whose foliage, dyed in autumnal red and yellow, returned the beams of the western sun gorgeously.

We drew up at the door. I got out, and had a good look at the front of the house; it was a large and melancholy mansion, with signs of long neglect upon it; great wooden shutters, in the old fashion, were barred, outside, across the windows; grass, and even nettles, were growing thick on the courtyard, and a thin moss streaked the timber beams; the plaster was discoloured by time and weather, and bore great russet and yellow stains. The gloom was increased by several grand old trees that crowded close about the house.

I mounted the steps, and looked round; the dark lake lay near me now, a little to the left. It was not large; it may have covered some ten or twelve acres; but it added to the melancholy of the scene. Near the centre of it was a small island, with two old ash trees, leaning toward each other, their pensive images reflected in the stirless water. The only cheery influence in this scene of antiquity, solitude, and neglect was that the house and landscape were warmed with the ruddy western beams. I knocked, and my summons resounded hollow and ungenial in my ear; and the bell, from far away, returned a deep-mouthed and surly ring, as if it resented being roused from a score years' slumber.

A light-limbed, jolly-looking old fellow, in a barracan jacket and gaiters, with a smile of welcome, and a very sharp, red nose, that seemed to promise good cheer, opened the door with a promptitude that indicated a hospitable expectation of my arrival.

There was but little light in the hall, and that little lost itself in darkness in the background. It was very spacious and lofty, with a gallery running round it, which, when the door was open, was visible at two or three points. Almost in the dark my new acquaintance led me across this wide hall into the room destined for my reception. It was spacious, and wainscoted up to the ceiling. The furniture of this capacious chamber was old-fashioned and clumsy. There were curtains still to the windows, and a piece of Turkey carpet lay upon the floor; those windows were two in number, looking out, through the trunks of the trees close to the house, upon the lake. It needed all the fire, and all the pleasant associations of my entertainer's red nose, to light up this melancholy chamber. A door at its farther end admitted to the room that was prepared for my sleeping apartment. It was wainscoted, like the other. It had a four-post bed, with heavy tapestry curtains, and in other respects was furnished in the same old-world and ponderous style as the other room. Its window, like those of that apartment, looked out upon the lake.

Sombre and sad as these rooms were, they were yet scrupulously clean. I had nothing to complain of; but the effect was rather dispiriting. Having given some directions about supper—a pleasant incident to look forward to—and made a rapid toilet, I called on my friend with the gaiters and red nose (Tom Wyndsour) whose occupation was that of a "bailiff," or under-steward, of the property, to accompany me, as we had still an hour or so of sun and twilight, in a walk over the grounds.

It was a sweet autumn evening, and my guide, a hardy old fellow, strode at a pace that tasked me to keep up with.

Among clumps of trees at the northern boundary of the demesne we lighted upon the little antique parish church. I was looking down upon it, from an eminence, and the park-wall interposed; but a little way down was a stile affording access to the road, and by this we approached the iron gate of the churchyard. I saw the church door open; the sexton was replacing his pick, shovel, and spade, with which he had just been digging a grave in the church-yard, in their little repository under the stone stair of the tower. He was a polite, shrewd little hunchback, who was very happy to show me over the church. Among the monuments was one that interested me; it was erected to commemo-rate the very Squire Bowes from whom my two old maids had inherited the house and estate of Barwyke. It spoke of him in terms of grandiloquent eulogy, and informed the Christian reader that he had died, in the bosom of the Church of England, at the age of seventy-one.

I read this inscription by the parting beams of the setting sun, which disappeared behind the horizon just as we passed out from under the porch.

"Twenty years since the Squire died," said I, reflecting as I loitered still in the churchyard.

"Ay, sir; 'twill be twenty year the ninth o' last month."

"And a very good old gentleman?"

"Good-natured enough, and an easy gentleman he was, sir; I don't think while he lived he ever hurt a fly," acquiesced Tom Wyndsour. "It ain't always easy sayin' what's in 'em though, and what they may take or turn to afterwards; and some o' them sort, I think, goes mad."

"You don't think he was out of his mind?" I asked.

"He? La! no; not he, sir; a bit lazy, mayhap, like other old fellows; but a knew devilish well what he was about."

Tom Wyndsour's account was a little enigmatical; but, like old Squire Bowes, I was "a bit lazy" that evening, and asked no more questions about him.

We got over the stile upon the narrow road that skirts the churchyard. It is overhung by elms more than a hundred years old, and in the twilight, which now prevailed, was growing very dark. As side-by-side we walked along this road, hemmed in by two loose stone-like walls, something running towards us in a zig-zag line passed us at a wild pace, with a sound like a frightened laugh or a shudder, and I saw, as it passed, that it was a human figure. I may confess now, that I was a little startled. The dress of this figure was, in part, white: I know I mistook it at first for a white horse coming down the road at a gallop. Tom Wyndsour turned about and looked after the retreating figure.

"He'll be on his travels to-night," he said, in a low tone. "Easy served with a bed, *that* lad be; six foot o' dry peat or heath, or a nook in a dry ditch. That lad hasn't slept once in a house this twenty year, and never will while grass grows."

"Is he mad?" I asked.

"Something that way, sir; he's an idiot, an awpy; we call him 'Dickon the devil,' because the devil's almost the only word that's ever in his mouth."

It struck me that this idiot was in some way connected with the story of old Squire Bowes.

"Queer things are told of him, I dare say?" I suggested.

"More or less, sir; more or less. Queer stories, some."

"Twenty years since he slept in a house? That's about the time the Squire died," I continued.

"So it will be, sir; and not very long after."

"You must tell me all about that, Tom, to-night, when I can hear it comfortably, after supper."

Tom did not seem to like my invitation; and looking straight before him as we trudged on, he said,

"You see, sir, the house has been quiet, and nout's been troubling folk inside the walls or out, all round the woods of Barwyke, this ten year, or more; and my old woman, down there, is clear against talking about such matters, and thinks it best—and so do I—to let sleepin' dogs be."

He dropped his voice towards the close of the sentence, and nodded significantly.

We soon reached a point where he unlocked a wicket in the park wall, by which we entered the grounds of Barwyke once more.

The twilight deepening over the landscape, the huge and solemn trees, and the distant outline of the haunted house, exercised a sombre influence on me, which, together with the fatigue of a day of travel, and the brisk walk we had had, disinclined me to interrupt the silence in which my companion now indulged.

A certain air of comparative comfort, on our arrival, in great measure dissipated the gloom that was stealing over me. Although it was by no means a cold night, I was very glad to see some wood blazing in the grate; and a pair of candles aiding the light of the fire, made the room look cheerful. A small table, with a very white cloth, and preparations for supper, was also a very agreeable object.

I should have liked very well, under these influences, to have listened to Tom Wyndsour's story; but after supper I grew too sleepy to attempt to lead him to the subject; and after yawning for a time, I found there was no use in contending against my drowsiness, so I betook myself to my bedroom, and by ten o'clock was fast asleep.

What interruption I experienced that night I shall tell you presently. It was not much, but it was very odd.

By next night I had completed my work at Barwyke. From early morning till then I was so incessantly occupied and hard-worked, that I had not time to think over the singular occurrence to which I have just referred. Behold me, however, at length once more seated at my little supper-table, having ended a comfortable meal. It had been a sultry day, and I had thrown one of the large windows up as high as it would go. I was sitting near it, with my brandy and water at my elbow, looking out into the dark. There was no moon, and the trees that are grouped about the house make the darkness round it supernaturally profound on such nights.

"Tom," said I, so soon as the jug of hot punch I had supplied him with began to exercise its genial and communicative influence; "you must tell me who beside your wife and you and myself slept in the house last night."

72

Tom, sitting near the door, set down his tumbler, and looked at me askance, while you might count seven, without speaking a word.

"Who else slept in the house?" he repeated, very deliberately. "Not a living soul, sir"; and he looked hard at me, still evidently expecting something more.

"That *is* very odd," I said returning his stare, and feeling really a little odd. "You are sure *you* were not in my room last night?"

"Not till I came to call you, sir, this morning; *I* can make oath of that."

"Well," said I, "there was some one there, *I* can make oath of that. I was so tired I could not make up my mind to get up; but I was waked by a sound that I thought was some one flinging down the two tin boxes in which my papers were locked up violently on the floor. I heard a slow step on the ground, and there was light in the room, although I remembered having put out my candle. I thought it must have been you, who had come in for my clothes, and upset the boxes by accident. Whoever it was, he went out and the light with him. I was about to settle again, when, the curtain being a little open at the foot of the bed, I saw a light on the wall opposite; such as a candle from outside would cast if the door were very cautiously opening. I started up in the bed, drew the side curtain, and saw that the door *was* opening, and admitting light from outside. It is close, you know, to the head of the bed. A hand was holding on the edge of the door and pushing it open; not a bit like yours; a very singular hand. Let me look at yours."

He extended it for my inspection.

"Oh no; there's nothing wrong with your hand. This was differently shaped; fatter; and the middle finger was stunted, and shorter than the rest, looking as if it had once been broken, and the nail was crooked like a claw. I called out 'Who's there?' and the light and the hand were withdrawn, and I saw and heard no more of my visitor."

"So sure as you're a living man, that was him!" exclaimed Tom Wyndsour, his very nose growing pale, and his eyes almost starting out of his head.

"Who?" I asked.

"Old Squire Bowes; 'twas *his* hand you saw; the Lord a' mercy on us!" answered Tom. "The broken finger, and the nail bent like a hoop. Well for you, sir, he didn't come back when you called, that time. You came here about them Miss Dymock's business, and he never meant they should have a foot o' ground in Barwyke; and he was making a will to give it away quite different, when death took him short. He never was uncivil to no one; but he couldn't abide them ladies. My mind misgave me when I heard 'twas about their business you were coming; and now you see how it is; he'll be at his old tricks again!"

With some pressure and a little more punch, I induced Tom Wyndsour to explain his mysterious allusions by recounting the occurrences which followed the old Squire's death.

"Squire Bowes of Barwyke died without making a will, as you know," said Tom. "And all the folk round were sorry; that is to say, sir, as sorry as folk will be for an old man that has seen a long tale of years, and has no right to grumble that death has knocked an hour too soon at his door. The Squire was well liked; he was never in a passion, or said a hard word; and he would not hurt a fly; and that made what happened after his decease the more surprising.

"The first thing these ladies did, when they got the property, was to buy stock for the park.

"It was not wise, in any case, to graze the land on their own account. But they little knew all they had to contend with.

"Before long something went wrong with the cattle; first one, and then another, took sick and died, and so on, till the loss began to grow heavy. Then, queer stories, little by little, began to be told. It was said, first by one, then by another, that Squire Bowes was seen, about evening time, walking, just as he used to do when he was alive, among the old trees, leaning on his stick; and, sometimes when he came up with the cattle, he would stop and lay his hand kindly like on the back of one of them; and that one was sure to fall sick next day, and die soon after.

"No one ever met him in the park, or in the woods, or ever saw him, except a good distance off. But they knew his gait and his figure well, and the clothes he used to wear; and they could tell the beast he laid his hand on by its colour—white, dun, or black; and that beast was sure to sicken and die. The neighbours grew shy of taking the path over the park; and no one liked to walk in the woods, or come inside the bounds of Barwyke: and the cattle went on sickening and dying as before.

"At that time there was one Thomas Pyke; he had been a groom to the old Squire; and he was in care of the place, and was the only one that used to sleep in the house.

"Tom was vexed, hearing these stories; which he did not believe the half on 'em; and more especial as he could not get man or boy to herd the cattle; all being afeared. So he wrote to Matlock in Derbyshire, for his brother, Richard Pyke, a clever lad, and one that knew nout o' the story of the old Squire walking.

"Dick came; and the cattle was better; folk said they could still see the old Squire, sometimes, walking, as before, in openings of the wood, with his stick in his hand; but he was shy of coming nigh the cattle, whatever his reason might be, since Dickon Pyke came; and he used to stand a long bit off, looking at them, with no more stir in him than a trunk o' one of the old trees, for an hour at a time, till the shape melted away, little by little, like the smoke of a fire that burns out.

"Tom Pyke and his brother Dickon, being the only living souls in the house, lay in the big bed in the servants' room, the house being fast barred and locked, one night in November.

"Tom was lying next the wall, and he told me, as wide awake as ever he was at noonday. His brother Dickon lay outside, and was sound asleep.

"Well, as Tom lay thinking, with his eyes turned toward the door, it opens slowly, and who should come in but old Squire Bowes, his face lookin' as dead as he was in his coffin.

"Tom's very breath left his body; he could not take his eyes off him; and he felt the hair rising up on his head.

"The Squire came to the side of the bed, and put his arms under Dickon, and lifted the boy—in a dead sleep all the time—and carried him out so, at the door.

"Such was the appearance, to Tom Pyke's eyes, and he was ready to swear to it, anywhere.

"When this happened, the light, wherever it came from, all on a sudden went out, and Tom could not see his own hand before him.

"More dead than alive, he lay till daylight.

"Sure enough his brother Dickon was gone. No sign of him could he discover about the house; and with some trouble he got a couple of the neigh bours to help him to search the woods and grounds. Not a sign of him anywhere.

"At last one of them thought of the island in the lake; the little boat was moored to the old post at the water's edge. In they got, though with small hope of finding him there. Find him, nevertheless, they did, sitting under the big ash tree, quite out of his wits; and to all their questions he answered nothing but one cry—'Bowes, the devil! See him; see him; Bowes, the devil!' An idiot they found him; and so he will be till God sets all things right. No one could ever get him to sleep under roof-tree more. He wanders from house to house while daylight lasts; and no one cares to lock the harmless creature in the workhouse. And folk would rather not meet him after nightfall, for they think where he is there may be worse things near."

A silence followed Tom's story. He and I were alone in that large room; I was sitting near the open window, looking into the dark night air. I fancied I saw something white move across it; and I heard a sound like low talking that swelled into a discordant shriek—"Hoo-oo-oo! Bowes, the devil! Over your shoulder. Hoo-oo-oo! ha! ha! ha!" I started up, and saw, by the light of the candle with which Tom strode to the window, the wild eyes and blighted face of the idiot, as, with a sudden change of mood, he drew off, whispering and tittering to himself, and holding up his long fingers, and looking at the tips like a "hand of glory."

Tom pulled down the window. The story and its epilogue were over. I confess I was rather glad when I heard the sound of the horses' hoofs on the court-yard, a few minutes later; and still gladder when, having bidden Tom a kind farewell, I had left the neglected house of Barwyke a mile behind me.

The Doll's Ghost

F. Marion Crawford

It was a terrible accident, and for one moment the splendid machinery of Cranston House got out of gear and stood still. The butler emerged from the retirement in which he spent his elegant leisure, two grooms of the chambers appeared simultaneously from opposite directions, there were actually housemaids on the grand staircase, and those who remember the facts most exactly assert that Mrs. Pringle herself positively stood upon the landing. Mrs. Pringle was the housekeeper. As for the head nurse, the under nurse, and the nursery-maid, their feelings cannot be described. The head nurse laid one hand upon the polished marble balustrade and stared stupidly before her, the under nurse stood rigid and pale, leaning against the polished marble wall, and the nursery-maid collapsed and sat down upon the polished marble step, just beyond the limits of the velvet carpet, and frankly burst into tears.

The Lady Gwendolen Lancaster-Douglas-Scroop, youngest daughter of the ninth Duke of Cranston, and aged six years and three months, picked herself up quite alone, and sat down on the third step from the foot of the grand staircase in Cranston House.

"Oh!" ejaculated the butler, and he disappeared again.

"Ah!" responded the grooms of the chambers, as they also went away.

"It's only that doll," Mrs. Pringle was distinctly heard to say, in a tone of contempt.

The under nurse heard her say it. Then the three nurses gathered round Lady Gwendolen and patted her, and gave her unhealthy things out of their pockets, and hurried her out of Cranston House as fast as they could, lest it should be found out upstairs that they had allowed the Lady Gwendolen Lancaster-Douglas-Scroop to tumble down the grand staircase with her doll in her arms. And as the doll was badly broken, the nursery-maid carried it, with the pieces, wrapped up in Lady Gwendolen's little cloak. It was not far to Hyde Park, and when they had reached a quiet place they took means to find out that Lady Gwendolen had no bruises. For the carpet was very thick and soft, and there was thick stuff under it to make it softer.

Lady Gwendolen Douglas-Scroop sometimes yelled, but she never cried.

It was because she had yelled that the nurse had allowed her to go downstairs alone with Nina, the doll, under one arm, while she steadied herself with her other hand on the balustrade, and trod upon the polished marble steps beyond the edge of the carpet. So she had fallen, and Nina had come to grief.

When the nurses were quite sure that she was not hurt, they unwrapped the doll and looked at her in her turn. She had been a very beautiful doll, very large, and fair, and healthy, with real yellow hair, and eyelids that would open and shut over very grown-up dark eyes. Moreover, when you moved her right arm up and down she said "Pa-pa," and when you moved the left she said "Ma-ma," very distinctly.

"I heard her say 'Pa' when she fell," said the under nurse, who heard everything. "But she ought to have said 'Pa-pa.' "

"That's because her arm went up when she hit the step," said the head nurse. "She'll say the other 'Pa' when I put it down again."

"Pa," said Nina, as her right arm was pushed down, and speaking through her broken face. It was cracked right across, from the upper corner of the forehead, with a hideous gash, through the nose and down to the little frilled collar of the pale green silk Mother Hubbard frock, and two little three-cornered pieces of porcelain had fallen out.

"I'm sure it's a wonder she can speak at all, being all smashed," said the under nurse.

"You'll have to take her to Mr. Puckler," said her superior. "It's not far, and you'd better go at once."

Lady Gwendolen was occupied in digging a hole in the ground with a little spade, and paid no attention to the nurses.

"What are you doing?" enquired the nursery-maid, looking on.

"Nina's dead, and I'm diggin' her a grave," replied her ladyship thoughtfully.

"Oh, she'll come to life again all right," said the nursery-maid.

The under nurse wrapped Nina up again and departed. Fortunately a kind soldier, with very long legs and a very small cap, happened to be there; and as he had nothing to do, he offered to see the under nurse safely to Mr. Puckler's and back.

Mr. Bernard Puckler and his little daughter lived in a little house in a little alley, which led out off a quiet little street not very far from Belgrave Square. He was the great doll doctor, and his extensive practice lay in the most aristocratic quarter. He mended dolls of all sizes and ages, boy dolls and girl dolls, baby dolls in long clothes, and grown-up dolls in fashionable gowns, talking dolls and dumb dolls, those that shut their eyes when they lay down, and those whose eyes had to be shut for them by means of a mysterious wire. His daughter Else was only just over twelve years old, but she was already very clever at mending dolls' clothes, and at doing their hair, which is harder than you might think, though the dolls sit quite still while it is being done.

Mr. Puckler had originally been a German, but he had dissolved his nationality in the ocean of London many years ago, like a great many foreigners. He still had one or two German friends, however, who came on Saturday evenings, and smoked with him and played picquet or "skat" with him for farthing points, and called him "Herr Doctor," which seemed to please Mr. Puckler very much.

He looked older than he was, for his beard was rather long and ragged, his hair was grizzled and thin, and he wore horn-rimmed spectacles. As for Else, she was a thin, pale child, very quiet and neat, with dark eyes and brown hair that was plaited down her back and tied with a bit of black ribbon. She mended the dolls' clothes and took the dolls back to their homes when they were quite strong again.

The house was a little one, but too big for the two people who lived in it. There was a small sitting-room on the street, and the workshop was at the back, and there were three rooms upstairs. But the father and daughter lived most of their time in the workshop, because they were generally at work, even in the evenings.

Mr. Puckler laid Nina on the table and looked at her a long time, till the tears began to fill his eyes behind the horn-rimmed spectacles. He was a very susceptible man, and he often fell in love with the dolls he mended, and found it hard to part with them when they had smiled at him for a few days. They were real little people to him, with characters and thoughts and feelings of their own, and he was very tender with them all. But some attracted him especially from the first, and when they were brought to him maimed and injured, their state seemed so pitiful to him that the tears came easily. You must remember that he had lived among dolls during a great part of his life, and understood them.

"How do you know that they feel nothing?" he went on to say to Else. "You must be gentle with them. It costs nothing to be kind to the little beings, and perhaps it makes a difference to them."

And Else understood him, because she was a child, and she knew that she was more to him than all the dolls.

He fell in love with Nina at first sight, perhaps because her beautiful brown glass eyes were something like Else's own, and he loved Else first and best, with all his heart. And, besides, it was a very sorrowful case. Nina had evidently not been long in the world, for her complexion was perfect, her hair was smooth where it should be smooth, and curly where it should be curly, and her silk clothes were perfectly new. But across her face was that frightful gash, like a sabre-cut, deep and shadowy within, but clean and sharp at the edges. When he tenderly pressed her head to close the gaping wound, the edges made a fine grating sound, that was painful to hear, and the lids of the dark eyes quivered and trembled as though Nina were suffering dreadfully.

"Poor Nina!" he exclaimed sorrowfully. "But I shall not hurt you much, though you will take a long time to get strong."

He always asked the names of the broken dolls when they were brought to him, and sometimes the people knew what the children called them, and told him. He liked "Nina" for a name. Altogether and in every way she pleased him more than any doll he had seen for many years, and he felt drawn to her, and made up his mind to make her perfectly strong and sound, no matter how much labour it might cost him.

Mr. Puckler worked patiently a little at a time, and Else watched him. She could do nothing for poor Nina, whose clothes needed no mending. The longer the doll doctor worked, the more fond he became of the yellow hair and the beautiful brown glass eyes. He sometimes forgot all the other dolls that were waiting to be mended, lying side by side on a shelf, and sat for an hour gazing at Nina's face, while he racked his ingenuity for some new invention by which to hide even the smallest trace of the terrible accident.

She was wonderfully mended. Even he was obliged to admit that; but the scar was still visible to his keen eyes, a very fine line right across the face, downwards from right to left. Yet all the conditions had been most favourable for a cure, since the cement had set quite hard at the first attempt and the weather had been fine and dry, which makes a great difference in a dolls' hospital.

At last he knew that he could do no more, and the under nurse had already come twice to see whether the job was finished, as she coarsely expressed it.

"Nina is not quite strong yet," Mr. Puckler had answered each time, for he could not make up his mind to face the parting.

And now he sat before the square deal table at which he worked, and Nina lay before him for the last time with a big brown paper box beside her. It stood there like her coffin, waiting for her, he thought. He must put her into it, and lay tissue paper over her dear face, and then put on the lid, and at the thought of tying the string his sight was dim with tears again. He was never to look into the glassy depths of the beautiful brown eyes any more, nor to hear the little wooden voice say "Pa-pa" and "Ma-ma." It was a very painful moment.

In the vain hope of gaining time before the separation, he took up the little sticky bottles of cement and glue and gum and colour, looking at each one in turn, and then at Nina's face. And all his small tools lay there, neatly arranged in a row, but he knew that he could not use them again for Nina. She was quite strong at last, and in a country where there should be no cruel children to hurt her she might live a hundred years, with only that almost imperceptible line across her face to tell of the fearful thing that had befallen her on the marble steps of Cranston House.

Suddenly Mr. Puckler's heart was quite full, and he rose abruptly from his seat and turned away.

"Else," he said unsteadily, "you must do it for me. I cannot bear to see her go into the box."

So he went and stood at the window with his back turned, while Else did what he had not the heart to do.

"Is it done?" he asked, not turning round. "Then take her away, my dear. Put on your hat, and take her to Cranston House quickly, and when you are gone I will turn round."

Else was used to her father's queer ways with the dolls, and though she had never seen him so much moved by a parting, she was not much surprised.

"Come back quickly," he said, when he heard her hand on the latch. "It is growing late, and I should not send you at this hour. But I cannot bear to look forward to it any more."

When Else was gone, he left the window and sat down in his place before the table again, to wait for the child to come back. He touched the place where Nina had lain, very gently, and he recalled the softly tinted pink face, and the glass eyes, and the ringlets of yellow hair, till he could almost see them.

The evenings were long, for it was late in the spring. But it began to grow dark soon, and Mr. Puckler wondered why Else did not come back. She had been gone an hour and a half, and that was much longer than he had expected, for it was barely half a mile from Belgrave Square to Cranston House. He reflected that the child might have been kept waiting, but as the twilight deepened he grew anxious, and walked up and down in the dim workshop, no longer thinking of Nina, but of Else, his own living child, whom he loved.

An undefinable, disquieting sensation came upon him by fine degrees, a chilliness and a faint stirring of his thin hair, joined with a wish to be in any company rather than to be alone much longer. It was the beginning of fear.

He told himself in strong German-English that he was a foolish old man, and he began to feel about for the matches in the dusk. He knew just where they should be, for he always kept them in the same place, close to the little tin box that held bits of sealing-wax of various colours, for some kinds of mending. But somehow he could not find the matches in the gloom.

Something had happened to Else, he was sure, and as his fear increased, he felt as though it might be allayed if he could get a light and see what time it was. Then he called himself a foolish old man again, and the sound of his own voice startled him in the dark. He could not find the matches.

The window was grey still; he might see what time it was if he went close to it, and he could go and get matches out of the cupboard afterwards. He stood back from the table, to get out of the way of the chair, and began to cross the board floor.

Something was following him in the dark. There was a small pattering, as of tiny feet upon the boards. He stopped and listened, and the roots of his hair tingled. It was nothing, and he was a foolish old man. He made two steps more, and he was sure that he heard the little pattering again. He turned his back to the window, leaning against the sash so that the panes began to crack, and he faced the dark. Everything was quite still, and it smelt of paste and cement and wood-filings as usual.

"Is that you, Else?" he asked, and he was surprised by the fear in his voice.

There was no answer in the room, and he held up his watch and tried to make out what time it was by the grey dusk that was just not darkness. So far as he could see, it was within two or three minutes of ten o'clock. He had been a long time alone. He was shocked, and frightened for Else, out in London, so late, and he almost ran across the room to the door. As he fumbled for the latch, he distinctly heard the running of the little feet after him.

"Mice!" he exclaimed feebly, just as he got the door open.

He shut it quickly behind him, and felt as though some cold thing had settled on his back and were writhing upon him. The passage was quite dark, but he found his hat and was out in the alley in a moment, breathing more freely, and surprised to find how much light there still was in the open air. He could see the pavement clearly under his feet, and far off in the street to which the alley led he could hear the laughter and calls of children, playing some game out of doors. He wondered how he could have been so nervous, and for an instant he thought of going back into the house to wait quietly for Else. But instantly he felt that nervous fright of something stealing over him again. In any case it was better to walk up to Cranston House and ask the servants about the child. One of the women had perhaps taken a fancy to her, and was even now giving her tea and cake.

He walked quickly to Belgrave Square, and then up the broad streets, listening as he went, whenever there was no other sound, for the tiny footsteps. But he heard nothing, and was laughing at himself when he rang the servants' bell at the big house. Of course, the child must be there.

The person who opened the door was quite an inferior person, for it was a back door, but affected the manners of the front, and stared at Mr. Puckler superciliously under the strong light.

No little girl had been seen, and he knew "nothing about no dolls."

"She is my little girl," said Mr. Puckler tremulously, for all his anxiety was returning tenfold, "and I am afraid something has happened."

The inferior person said rudely that "nothing could have happened to her in that house, because she had not been there, which was a jolly good reason why"; and Mr. Puckler was obliged to admit that the man ought to know, as it was his business to keep the door and let people in. He wished to be allowed to speak to the under nurse, who knew him; but the man was ruder than ever, and finally shut the door in his face.

When the doll doctor was alone in the street, he steadied himself by the railing, for he felt as though he were breaking in two, just as some dolls break, in the middle of the backbone.

Presently he knew that he must be doing something to find Else, and that gave him strength. He began to walk as quickly as he could through the streets, following every highway and byway which his little girl might have taken on her errand. He also asked several policemen in vain if they had seen her, and most of them answered him kindly, for they saw that he was a sober man and in his right senses, and some of them had little girls of their own.

It was one o'clock in the morning when he went up to his own door again, worn out and hopeless and broken-hearted. As he turned the key in the lock, his heart stood still, for he knew that he was awake and not dreaming, and that he really heard those tiny footsteps pattering to meet him inside the house along the passage.

But he was too unhappy to be much frightened any more, and his heart went on again with a dull regular pain, that found its way all through him with every pulse. So he went in, and hung up his hat in the dark, and found the matches in the cupboard and the candlestick in its place in the corner.

Mr. Puckler was so much overcome and so completely worn out that he sat down in his chair before the work-table and almost fainted, as his face dropped forward upon his folded hands. Beside him the solitary candle burned steadily with a low flame in the still warm air.

"Else! Else!" he moaned against his yellow knuckles. And that was all he could say, and it was no relief to him. On the contrary, the very sound of the name was a new and sharp pain that pierced his ears and his head and his very soul. For every time he repeated the name it meant that little Else was dead, somewhere out in the streets of London in the dark.

He was so terribly hurt that he did not even feel something pulling gently at the skirt of his old coat, so gently that it was like the nibbling of a tiny mouse. He might have thought that it was really a mouse if he had noticed it.

"Else! Else!" he groaned right against his hands.

Then a cool breath stirred his thin hair, and the low flame of the one candle dropped down almost to a mere spark, not flickering as though a draught were going to blow it out, but just dropping down as if it were tired out. Mr. Puckler felt his hands stiffening with fright under his face; and there was a faint rustling sound, like some small silk thing blown in a gentle breeze. He sat up straight, stark and scared, and a small wooden voice spoke in the stillness.

"Pa-pa," it said, with a break between the syllables.

Mr. Puckler stood up in a single jump, and his chair fell over backwards with a smashing noise upon the wooden floor. The candle had almost gone out.

It was Nina's doll voice that had spoken, and he should have known it among the voices of a hundred other dolls. And yet there was something more in it, a little human ring, with a pitiful cry and a call for help, and the wail of a hurt child. Mr. Puckler stood up, stark and stiff, and tried to look round, but at first he could not, for he seemed to be frozen from head to foot.

Then he made a great effort, and he raised one hand to each of his temples, and pressed his own head round as he would have turned a doll's. The candle was burning so low that it might as well have been out altogether, for any light it gave, and the room seemed quite dark at first. Then he saw something. He would not have believed that he could be more frightened than he had been just before that. But he was, and his knees shook, for he saw the doll standing in the middle of the floor, shining with a faint and ghostly radiance, her beautiful glassy brown eyes fixed on his. And across her face the very thin line of the break he had mended shone as though it were drawn in light with a fine point of white flame.

Yet there was something more in the eyes, too; there was something human, like Else's own, but as if only the doll saw him through them, and not Else. And there was enough of Else to bring back all his pain and to make him forget his fear.

"Else! my little Else!" he cried aloud.

The small ghost moved, and its doll-arm slowly rose and fell with a stiff, mechanical motion.

"Pa-pa," it said.

It seemed this time that there was even more of Else's tone echoing somewhere between the wooden notes that reached his ears so distinctly, and yet so far away. Else was calling him, he was sure.

His face was perfectly white in the gloom, but his knees did not shake any more, and he felt that he was less frightened.

"Yes, child! But where? Where?" he asked. "Where are you, Else?"

"Pa-pa!"

The syllables died away in the quiet room. There was a low rustling of silk, the glassy brown eyes turned slowly away, and Mr. Puckler heard the pitter-patter of the small feet in the bronze kid slippers as the figure ran straight to the door. Then the candle burned high again, the room was full of light, and he was alone.

Mr. Puckler passed his hand over his eyes and looked about him. He could see everything quite clearly, and he felt that he must have been dreaming, though he was standing instead of sitting down, as he should have been if he had just waked up. The candle burned brightly now. There were the dolls to be mended, lying in a row with their toes up. The third one had lost her right shoe, and Else was making one. He knew that, and he was certainly not dreaming now. He had not been dreaming when he had come in from his fruitless search and had heard the doll's footsteps running to the door. He had not fallen asleep in his chair. How could he possibly have fallen asleep when his heart was breaking? He had been awake all the time.

He steadied himself, set the fallen chair upon its legs, and said to himself again very emphatically that he was a foolish old man. He ought to be out in the streets looking for his child, asking questions, and enquiring at the police stations, where all accidents were reported as soon as they were known, or at the hospitals.

"Pa-pa!"

The longing, wailing, pitiful little wooden cry rang from the passage, outside the door, and Mr. Puckler stood for an instant with white face, transfixed and rooted to the spot. A moment later his hand was on the latch. Then he was in the passage, with the light streaming from the open door behind him.

Quite at the other end he saw the little phantom shining clearly in the shadow, and the right hand seemed to beckon to him as the arm rose and fell once more. He knew all at once that it had not come to frighten him but to lead him, and when it disappeared, and he walked boldly towards the door, he knew that it was in the street outside, waiting for him. He forgot that he was tired and had eaten no supper, and had walked many miles, for a sudden hope ran through and through him, like a golden stream of life.

And sure enough, at the corner of the alley, and at the corner of the street, and out in Belgrave Square, he saw the small ghost flitting before him. Sometimes it was only a shadow, where there was other light, but then the glare of the lamps made a pale green sheen on its little Mother Hubbard frock of silk; and sometimes, where the streets were dark and silent, the whole figure shone out brightly, with its yellow curls and rosy neck. It seemed to trot along like a tiny child, and Mr. Puckler could almost hear the pattering of the bronze kid slippers on the pavement as it ran. But it went very fast, and he could only just keep up with it, tearing along with his hat on the back of his head and his thin hair blown by the night breeze, and his horn-rimmed spectacles firmly set upon his broad nose.

On and on he went, and he had no idea where he was. He did not even care, for he knew certainly that he was going the right way.

Then at last, in a wide, quiet street, he was standing before a big, sober-looking door that had two lamps on each side of it, and a polished brass bell-handle, which he pulled.

And just inside, when the door was opened, in the bright light, there was the little shadow, and the pale green sheen of the little silk dress, and once more the small cry came to his ears, less pitiful, more longing.

"Pa-pa!"

The shadow turned suddenly bright, and out of the brightness the beauti-

84

ful brown glass eyes were turned up happily to his, while the rosy mouth smiled so divinely that the phantom doll looked almost like a little angel just then.

"A little girl was brought in soon after ten o'clock," said the quiet voice of the hospital doorkeeper. "I think they thought she was only stunned. She was holding a big brown-paper box against her, and they could not get it out of her arms. She had a long plait of brown hair that hung down as they carried her."

"She is my little girl," said Mr. Puckler, but he hardly heard his own voice.

He leaned over Else's face in the gentle light of the children's ward, and when he had stood there a minute the beautiful brown eyes opened and looked up to his.

"Pa-pa!" cried Else, softly, "I knew you would come!"

Then Mr. Puckler did not know what he did or said for a moment, and what he felt was worth all the fear and terror and despair that had almost killed him that night. But by and by Else was telling her story, and the nurse let her speak, for there were only two other children in the room, who were getting well and were sound asleep.

"They were big boys with bad faces," said Else, "and they tried to get Nina away from me, but I held on and fought as well as I could till one of them hit me with something, and I don't remember any more, for I tumbled down, and I suppose the boys ran away, and somebody found me there. But I'm afraid Nina is all smashed."

"Here is the box," said the nurse. "We could not take it out of her arms till she came to herself. Should you like to see if the doll is broken?"

And she undid the string cleverly, but Nina was all smashed to pieces. Only the gentle light of the children's ward made a pale green sheen in the folds of the little Mother Hubbard frock.

The Dreamclown

Nancy A. Collins

The wind slammed against the bedroom window, pressing its hand on the thin glass pane. This sudden movement on nature's behalf startled Jere into wakefulness. The wind was gusting, shaking the bare-limbed trees about in a macabre October danse that transformed them into windowshade skeletons. Jere was reminded of the first time he had seen the Dreamclown. Niles had still been alive then . . .

The house William and Doreen Campbell raised their two young sons in was old. Not dilapidated or seedy, mind you. Not old in that sense of the word. It was a faithful Saint Bernard of a building that had settled down for a long, well-served nap. And the arthritic groaning of settling timbers and the asthmatic wheezing of the steam pipes added to the illusion that they were living inside a benign giant.

It was there Jere and Niles discovered all the things every generation of young boys learn anew. How to whistle through your teeth without using your fingers. How to rub a long-haired cat the wrong way until sparks flew. How to make fart noises with your cupped hands. How to make a kazoo with a cheap plastic comb and a piece of waxed paper. All the things that drive mothers up the wall.

Jere was the junior member of the partnership, forever following in the footsteps of his elder brother, Niles.

Niles was the Boy Wonder of the two, his eight-year-old's face hiding the future lines of a handsome man in the folds of his childhood. The brothers were as different as night and day. Niles was dark-haired and dusky-skinned. Jere was fair-skinned, true to his father's Scottish genes. His hair was an exuberant golden-red. The only sign of their brotherhood was in their eyes; eyes so dark they swallowed the pupils.

Niles was three years the senior; and those three years had made a sizable impact in their relationship. Niles was boss; he had the muscle, experience and the knowledge to exert himself as the dominant brother. He was brave, daring, inquisitive, and fearless. Or so it seemed to his five-year-old brother.

Niles was the trail-blazer for all the adventures (and mischief) they got into. He would discover a dead cat in the bushes near Mrs. Pickett's, then relate the news of his find to Jere—who was, naturally, interested. Death always fascinates children, since, like sex, discussion of it is taboo in their presence. So the chance to see a dead cat (likewise a picture of a nekkid lady) was never to be missed. But Jere was a little kid, so squeamishness was expected of him. While Niles poked and prodded the dead cat with a stick (in case anything jumped out), Jere would nervously observe from a safe distance. Thus the chemistry of their relationship was defined: Niles was the intrepid Doer, while Jere served as Appreciative Audience. From a safe distance, of course.

Jere awoke that night, his bladder swollen to the size of a football. He got up, blearily locating his brother's bed. Since their shared bedroom was on the second floor and the john was on the ground floor, mother had instigated the rule that Niles must escort his little brother to the toilet, in case Jere might accidentally stumble and take a header down the stairs. Niles had never been too thrilled with his enforced duty, since Jere was (in his words) "a garden sprinkler." But he had doggedly accepted his fate with all the disdain and put-upon martyrdom of a big brother.

So, still sleep-fuzzed, Jere stood next to his big brother's bed and discovered Niles was missing. For a moment he was terrified. He was terrified of having to go downstairs by himself, where it was dark and the monsters dwelt. Then he saw Niles standing at the window, staring beyond as if mesmerized. Jere had heard of people sleep-walking. He had even seen Bugs Bunny do it on the Saturday morning cartoons.

"Niles?" he whispered, struggling to keep his voice from squeaking. "I gotta pee, Niles."

His brother's head swiveled toward him and Jere could see that Niles was not asleep at all. He placed one finger to his full child's lips. "Sssh, you stupe! You wanna scare him off?" He gestured for Jere to join him at the windowsill.

As he looked down into the autumn streets of Cornelius, Missouri, far below them, performing in the midnight darkness, was The Dreamclown.

He wasn't an American circus clown with the baggy pants, flipper feet, seltzer bottle and fright wig. Nothing so grotesque or so gaudy. The Dreamclown was far more sublime. In the years to come Jere would be able to identify the particular breed of clown as the French mime-acrobat called *Pierrot.* But at the age of five, he only knew that the white-faced creature was a clown. And a wondrous clown he was, too.

The Dreamclown was a phantom of black and white, the only break in his color scheme being his brightly painted lips. His white face seemed sweetly androgynous, with its delicately painted eyebrows and grease-paint tear.

If the Dreamclown had hair, Jere couldn't see it. His head was topped by a tight-fitting black velvet skullcap. The voluminous white silk costume he wore whipped and fluttered in the wind, hinting at a willowy acrobat's frame beneath. Jere had never seen anyone so beautiful in his life.

The Dreamclown paused in mid-pirouette, drifting back into place like a leaf. He smiled at the boys, his painted eyes reaching out and snaring them. And he bowed, acknowledging their presence. And he began to dance anew, leaping and twisting to the sounds of an orchestra only he could hear. Fascinated, the two boys stared as a performance unlike any other Cornelius, Missouri, had ever witnessed unfolded before them.

Neither boy noticed how long they had watched the weirdling dancer. Minutes? Hours? The time seemed unimportant. Until the Dreamclown made a grand flourish of a bow that shouted finality. Slowly, like a mechanical doll on its last gears, the Dreamclown righted himself and Jere was aware of being watched. Intently. He began to fidget. He had never liked the feeling of being watched, even at such an early age.

"Niles?"

Niles didn't move to hush him. He was staring at the Dreamclown as if he had never had a pissant little brother. There was a look of what—love? longing? on Niles' face. And that was when Jere suddenly became scared.

Then the Dreamclown made a hand gesture. Nothing obscene. But it *was* seductive. It was unspoken yet spoke with the richness of mime. It said, "Come with me."

There was a low groan as Niles pushed against the windowsill, his face blanched in the moonlight and his dark eyes full of something Jere knew he'd never be part of. And he knew that Niles would keep pushing until he joined the Dreamclown on the street, wrapped in a cold shower of shattered glass and splintered wood.

"Niles!" His whisper was nearly a sob of panic. But it brought his brother back to him.

"Jere?" Niles blinked as if awakened from a daydream. The Dreamclown mocked a heartbroken frown and with a *c'est la vie* shrug of his shoulders, executed a stunning backward somersault.

And was swallowed by the night.

The two boys stared at the spot where the mysterious Dreamclown had been, then at each other.

"This never happened!" hissed Niles. "You don't tell no one. Not Mom, not Dad, not no one! You do an' I won't have a two-timing little sneak for my brother, understand?"

"Yeah, sure. Sure, Niles. I unnerstand."

"Good. Now, get to bed. You've got kinnergarden in the morning."

"Niles?"

"What is it?"

"I still have to go pee-pee."

That was the first time they saw the Dreamclown. But it was not the last. Over the next few months the visits became the centerpiece of their young lives. But Jere was more than a little guilty and frightened by their "secret." It was the secrecy that Niles had sworn him to that ate at Jere's young mind. The concept of keeping something from his parents was a completely new and alien one to the pre-schooler. But as much as he feared parental disapproval and rage, he feared being locked away from Niles' company far worse. So he kept silent.

Niles, on the other hand, lived for the midnight shows, which were infrequent at first, then became as regular as clockwork. He had his own theories as to the origin of the Dreamclown, and he often repeated them to Jere, his eyes bright and his voice edged with the euphoria of the obsessed.

"I figure he's kind of like an angel, a fairy, kinda. He leads all the kids into this really neat world full of magic and fun. Maybe that's why he's here—to take us to a world like that, kinda like Disneyland."

Jere wasn't too sure about that last one. It *sounded* good; as good as kids could expect the world to get. But he remembered the movie his parents had taken him to see not so long ago. It was *Pinocchio*. In it, Pinocchio and his best friend thought they were being taken to a wonderful world where they could do

88

as they pleased, but ended up being turned into donkeys. The part where the bad little boys pulled on their donkey ears, their screams turning into hee-haws, had upset him so much his mother had to take him to the lobby to get a drink of water.

He had been asleep, dreaming fitfully. Niles usually woke him up around midnight so he could watch the Dreamclown's performances. But for some reason Niles had let him sleep and it was a nightmare that woke Jere. He forgot what horrors had chased him from his sleep as soon as he opened his eyes.

He sat up, strangling on an unvoiced whimper. He didn't want Niles to think he was a baby, not with his sixth birthday coming up. Then he saw Niles standing frozen in front of the window, so much like the very first night. But something was different. He had never seen his brother stand so rigidly before.

"Niles?"

No sound, no movement, not even a hint that Niles had heard him.

"Niles?"

What happened next made his spine tighten, and if he had seen himself in a mirror he was certain his hair would have been standing on end, like Buck Wheat in the old Our Gang comedies. His bladder felt like it was full of ground glass. As he sat in his bed and watched his brother, Niles moved, heading back to bed. But he also stayed at the window. There were *two* Niles.

The Niles at the window looked funny. And then Jere realized that he could see through his brother. The ghost-Niles flickered and glowed like a feeble candle in the window. And as Jere watched, he seeped through the frame.

Sobbing, Jere stumbled from his bed and went to the window. Somehow, he knew what he would see. He sensed it with the uncanny foresight of the very young, although he prayed he wouldn't see his brother down on the street. That by some miracle the ghost-Niles wouldn't be there.

Unfortunately, he was.

There was the Dreamclown, standing in a mellow pool of lamplight. He was smiling, his arms stretched outward as if in welcome. It took Jere a second to locate the ghost-Niles, a pale half-shadow in the night. The ghost-Niles was smiling as well, moving closer to the Dreamclown.

Jere pressed his hands against the chill of the windows, his fascination and terror running in contradicting patterns. Part of him wanted to scream, to yell at Niles and tell him it was a trick and to come back and be safe. Yet, another part of him wanted to see what was going to happen.

The ghost-Niles extended a hand, and it seemed to Jere that his brother began to burn. No, burn wasn't an accurate word. It was like Niles was being filled with a strong, unwarming light. It streamed from his hair, his fingertips, his eyes, weaving an aura of silvery light around his ghostly body. It made him look like the illustration of the Boy Jesus in the Children's Bible in Sunday School.

"Niles! No! Noooo!"

Jere was surprised to hear his own voice. He had come out of his shock with the realization that Niles was leaving him. Leaving him behind to go with the black-and-white stranger with the bleeding lips.

The Dreamclown looked up and caught Jere in his placid, painted gaze. The pleas dried up in his throat and his heart constricted with a wretched surge of fear.

Jere watched helplessly as the Dreamclown led Niles into the darkness beyond the lights. One minute they were there, and the next they were gone. They had walked into the Twilight Zone, but no chain-smoking Rod Serling was going to walk into view and announce the moral of the teleplay.

Jere staggered back from the window, his youngster's face leeched of all color and his eyes the feverish wet-color of black marbles. He bruised his hip against something and looked down at his brother's bed. Niles lay there, twisted amongst the bedclothes. Jere touched his brother's exposed hand and felt the flesh rapidly cooling beneath his fingers. It was then his child's brain gripped the full extent of the horror he had witnessed.

He had been left behind.

Jere screamed. It was far more than a simple, shrill child-scream. It was the sum of his muscles and blood and bones. It was a long, strong sustained shriek that threatened to rupture his throat with its magnitude.

He was vaguely aware of his parents thundering up the stairs, then he collapsed at the foot of his brother's bed, the face of the Dreamclown smiling darkly in his head, the screams of donkeys ringing in his ears.

Ember

Fred Chappell

When I came out of Paradise they were shooting at me. Shotguns and pistols mostly, whatever they could grab hold of. I jumped into my old green pickup truck in the parking lot and drove off. I couldn't shoot back because I'd already pitched my .44 pistol away. I wouldn't have shot back anyway, so I stepped on the gas. Probably it was rocks thrown up against the undercarriage, but it might have been bullets hitting the truck, so I ducked my head down.

Scared, Hell yes, I was scared. Couldn't breathe except in gulps and my hands were shaking and two drops of dead cold sweat inched from my armpit down my left side. It wasn't so much getting shot at—though I hear tell you never get used to that—but the faces of the people, faces of them that used to be my friends and neighbors turned red and murderous. I couldn't stand up to that.

Ten minutes later I felt a little easier and stopped trembling so much, not seeing the headlights after me in my mirror. But I knew they'd be coming and I knew they'd already called the sheriff and the highway patrol. I was a wanted man now, the only time in my life. I didn't know what to think.

I had already made one big mistake. If I had turned right coming out of the parking lot there at West End Tavern Dance I'd be traveling toward the broad highways, the ones that connected with Georgia and all the other states and all the nations of the world. But I'd turned left instead and there was nothing in front of me but the brushy mountains of western North Carolina, briar thickets and tear-britches rocks over the steep slopes. And especially there was Ember Mountain where nobody went in the dark, nobody that would anyhow talk about it in the daylight.

But I started thinking maybe some things wouldn't be so bad. I had fished the streams around here and knew my way some, and the more the men that were trailing me didn't know Ember, the better. So I made a turn-off onto a little clay road that goes up Burning Creek and crosses it three times. At the third ford the trail's no wider than a cowpath and I pulled the truck over into a stand of laurel and cut the motor and the lights and opened the door.

Then it was like stepping into another world because the silence came down so sudden and the darkness. The world of Paradise Township where I'd shot with my .44 my untrue sweetheart Phoebe Redd was sure enough a world away, I was thinking, and then the silence let up a little and I could hear the hood of the truck ticking as the motor cooled and the feathery swishing of the wind in the treetops and the low mutter of Burning Creek off to my left. Those noises brought me back to myself and how I had to keep running.

I scrambled down to the edge of the creek and got down on all fours and drank like a dog, tasting the mountain in the water, the mossy rocks above me in the dark and the humus and the secret springs of Ember. When I stood up again I could hear the other night sounds of late August, the crickets and cicadas and somewhere a long way off to my right the longdrawn empty call of a hoot owl.

But there was nowhere to go but up the mountain. The farther I got in the nighttime, the farther away I'd be come sunup. Let them try to find me in six hours, or eight. Carolina wouldn't hold me nor Georgia either, once I got past Ember Mountain.

I dreaded to have to do it, though. It wasn't only what they say about the ridges and hollers of Ember, and I'd heard plenty of that and put stock in some of it. But just any old mountain in the dark of the night is a reckless time, and if there hadn't been so many certain dangers behind me, I wouldn't have been traveling on to meet new ones.

So I started up, my pants wet and my feet soaked in my shoes. My breath began to pound in my chest and my knees felt weak, but I climbed any way I could, tripping over tree roots and crawling on all fours and sliding down on the loose shale; it was a wonder I didn't just tumble to the bottom and lie at the end of the valley like a rag doll a little girl has lost on her picnic.

But I kept on going and the rocks and roots and bushes kept tearing at me. The left side of my face got laid open by a bramble or a twig and I could feel the blood oozing down my neck into my shirt. I had to stop and rest a lot of times but I didn't like to and it got worse the higher I climbed because the silence got deeper and I began to remember more and more what folks said about Ember.

Oh Phoebe, I thought, *oh Phoebe Redd. See what your faithless ways have brought on me.*

I went on. I kept going till I thought I couldn't stand it any more and then I came to the backbone of a stony ridge and struck south along with it, still climbing and climbing till I came to a weedy clearing. Then I saw a point of orange light up the mountain to my left. The more I tried to make it out, the more I couldn't see it clear. That's the way it is in the dark silence with trees everywhere.

But when I climbed some more, not breathing as hard now, I saw it again, clear and shining but shadowed over by something every now and again so that it flickered. I figured it to be a hunter's campfire, even though I had not heard his dogs running. Not everybody was scared of the tales and there was a plenty of game varmints up here, I could tell that just by listening.

I started toward the light. Not a wise decision, maybe, but it wasn't like I decided. A picture in my mind drew me: I could see how there'd be a fellow there by his campfire and how he'd have coffee or a sip of whiskey and maybe both. I was hot and cold and sick of the rocks and the bruising. I'd make up some lie to tell him about what I was doing up there, any lie that would stick.

But the ridge led down before it led up, and going downhill in the dark without a trail is a fool's job. Rocks and sawbriars all the way down and then a slick mud gulley at the bottom, then laurel thicket when I was climbing again, as puzzledy as a roll of barb wire. But I could just smell that coffee and taste it in my mouth, so I kept on and on. Might be a hunting man would appreciate some company up here in the lonesome midnight. Or it might be he wouldn't. It was a chancy notion.

But then when I came to the edge of the clearing I found it was no campfire. Here was a neat mountain cabin with a hearth fire inside and the clearing about me was for a garden. I could make out the shape of the cabin

92

pretty well. It was a clean place, the shingle roof mossed over, the little porch propped up on flat rocks. From the chinked rock chimney rose the ghost-colored smoke of the fire I'd spied so far away.

I waited at the edge, watching and listening. There were no dogs. I took it strange there were no dogs. A man at midnight walking up to a house in the solitary woods—he expects to hear the hounds begin to racket and come out to meet him.

Who was it lived here anyhow? Nobody I'd ever heard about.

I tried to walk quiet, but they'd have to be stone deaf in there not to hear me rustling and crackling through the goldenrod and the cornstalks. But I came right to the side of the house without anybody raising a holler and saw that it was just a cabin like many another I know. Weathered oak boards and mud-chink rock foundations and on the porch flowers growing in lard buckets and a cane-bottom rocking chair empty but for starlight and shadow. There was silence all around.

On this side there was a little square window curtained with dotted swiss, just above the eye level. I stretched up on tiptoe to see inside.

The room was neat and cheery in the firelight. There was a hooked rug on the floor and another bigger one hanging on the wall and two little tables with dried flowers in vases and a couple of straight chairs. There was a tall dark rocking chair beside the fire and in it sat a little old granny woman with iron-colored hair. She was wearing a washed-pale blue gingham dress and a blue-gray apron. She wasn't rocking in her chair, just sitting there as still as a tombstone, but she was not asleep. I could see the firelight glinting yellow in her eyes like they were cat's eyes.

I let down flat on my feet to ease my legs. It was nothing strange to see, an old woman remembering in front of her fire, but I had to wonder. How could it be only her up here and no menfolk about to help her do? It all looked all right, but when I thought, there was nothing right about it.

I decided to take another look and this time it wasn't an old woman in her rocking chair but another kind of thing hard to tell about. All gnarled and rooty like the bottom of a rotted oak stump turned up. Or all wattly, the way toad-stools will grow on fallen timber. Maybe more like it looks at the bottom of a candle burnt halfway down, where the wax has gathered in smooth pulpy lumps.

I can't say exactly because it was nothing exact to see. Something alive that nobody would ever think could live, something that knew about me out here by the window without seeing me, something that was an old woman in a chair and was no old woman any way in the world.

All right, Bill Puckett, I thought. *This is what comes of your jealous murdering. You have landed in the hardest place a man can land.*

I figured that maybe my third glimpse might be the true one and when I peeped again it was the same old woman as before, sitting just the way she was at first, with her eyes still shining yellow and not rocking in her rocking chair.

So maybe I'd imagined the rooty thing there, tired and scared as I was, and I was determined to get the good of her hearth fire, no matter. Ember Mountain with its ditches and brambles was too much for me this night; I was willing to take my chances with the old woman.

I went around to the front and up the five worn porch steps, trying to fix on a lie to tell her and whoever was with her here. I rapped three times and thought I heard a "Come-in," but the door planks were mighty thick. Anyhow, I shot back the smooth-handled latch and entered.

When she craned her head to look it came to my mind what a sorry marvel I must appear. I was all wet and muddy and my clothes were ripped and one side of my face and neck was probably still bleeding from a gash. Not a handsome sight to look on.

But she didn't show the least surprise. "Come in," she said. "Come to the fire where it's warm."

I was grateful. I crossed over to the clean rock hearth and held my hands palm up to the fire, the way you can't help doing. I warmed one side of myself and turned to warm the other.

She was looking me up and down. "You appear to been a good while in the woods," she said.

"Yes mam, I have been."

"Even on a summer night you can get cold and tore up on this mountain."

"Yes mam."

She was just a nice old granny woman. Even with her sitting down, I could tell she was real short. Short and thick, I thought, before I observed she was a humpback woman. I couldn't place her age, the skin of her face being so smooth and ruddy. Apple cheeks, folks call that, but she was old. Her hands were wrinkled and looked powdery and her voice was shrewd and trembly with her years.

"You got to be careful," she said. "There's many a good man been lost on Ember in the night."

"Yes mam."

She turned her head sideways and the firelight caught in her eyes till they shone like pieces of gold. "Why are you up here, then, so late into the night?"

I hadn't made up my lie yet and now when I tried to I couldn't do it. It stuck in the middle of my throat and I coughed and choked. I couldn't make sense in my head except just the truth and finally that was what I told her. "The law is after me," I said, "and some other people too. They're wanting to hang me on a big hickory tree, I reckon."

"What for?"

"I shot a woman," I said.

"Did you kill her?"

"*I* don't know. But it was an awful big pistol I pulled the trigger on."

"Who was she?"

"She was just a woman that treated me wrong. There ain't no use to say her name."

"Sit down," she said. "Pull up a chair to the fire and sit you down. It's good you told me the straight of it and not some infernal lie."

I felt better leaning forward in the chair and soaking up the heat. My pants legs were steaming as the denim dried. "I didn't take no pleasure in it," I said. "It just came over me too powerful. She swore time after time she was my woman and no other man's. But when I went to the West End Tavern Dance I saw them both and I shot and threw down my pistol and fled away."

"Wasn't it Phoebe Redd, this woman?"

"How did you know that? How could you ever hear about it up on this mountain?"

Her voice dropped to a mumble and it was hard to hear her. I thought she said: "Because it's not the first time, never ever the first time."

"What did you say?" I asked.

She looked at me then with a look as straight as a broomstick. "How old a man would you be?"

"My name is Bill Puckett," I told her. "I'm twenty-seven years old."

"Ain't you surely old enough to know better about women?"

"It came over me. I was in a fever where I couldn't think."

She nodded and got up and limped to the fire, showing she had a bad leg. She took up a big wrought iron poker and shifted the three logs. Red and orange sparks went up fantail and the wood snapped and sizzled. Her bunched-up shadow divided into three on the walls. "Well, what's done is done," she said. "What you'll be doing next, that's the question."

"I don't know anything to do but to just keep running," I said. "Because all they're going to do is just keep coming after me."

"You could give up and hand yourself over."

"I don't know," I said. "They're riled pretty hot. No telling what they might do to me."

"Sit you back," she said, "and take your ease. I've got some herb tea already made that I can warm up for you. It'll take some of the ache out of your bones."

I didn't say no but began to rub my ankles and the calves of my legs. My skin was itching where my pants legs dried by the hearth fire.

With her heavy poker she swung the iron crane out from the fireplace wall over the blaze and lifted down a black kettle from the adze-scarred mantelpiece beam. She hung the kettle on the crane hook. "Take off your shoes and your stockings," she said, and when I did she drew them to the hearth with the poker and arranged them to dry. "Won't take a minute for the tea to warm," she said. "A good strong herb tea. Here now, move over into my rocking chair and rest a little easier."

I did that too and began to unloosen a little in my muscles. I leaned back and looked into the fire and then when I looked at her again she blurred in front of me because of the firelight. I put it down to the firelight. "You'll need you a cup and saucer," she said. "I'll go and get them from the kitchen."

I tried to get up.

"You just stay here. You'll be needing all the rest you can get."

I listened to her shuffling about and I wondered again about her being lame and how she managed up here on the mountainside all alone by herself. I wondered too a great deal about how she heard of Phoebe, only I expected she had a radio back there in the kitchen that she would listen to a-nights, though I hadn't seen any power lines when I found the house. But the fact that she knew the name of Phoebe Redd just showed how soon they'd be catching up with me.

I must have dozed a little because next I remember her face close to mine, her apple cheeks smooth and reddish, and her eyes away from the firelight not yellow now but black-dark as two soot spots. And something I hadn't seen before: there were dents in her skin here and there, two in her forehead and one in her left cheek just below the eye and three dents in her throat, little pushed-in places like the thumbprints you'd leave in biscuit dough. The skin was smooth in the dents, smooth as isinglass. Wounds that have healed over, I thought, old wounds. Except for one in her throat just under her chin: that one was healed but looked fresh too, as red and rare as a scarlet flower.

She'd had a bad time too, I thought and right then that was all I thought.

"Here now," she said. "Drink this all down." She offered me a china saucer with little blue painted flowers and a gilt edge and on it a blue enamel cup almost brimful of steaming tea. I remember the look of that cup and saucer as clear as the bluest sky. "It'll be good and strong for you," she said.

I knew I'd spill it if I tried to hold the saucer, my hands unsteady as they were. I set the saucer on the floor and held the cup in my thumb and first finger by its fragile little handle. When I sipped at it, the taste of its heat went right to my breastbone. It was strong and rank and bitter and it tasted of something that reminded me of *far away.* That is the best I know how to tell: it tasted of *far away,* every bit as strong as she had said. Just the steam lifting out of the cup clambered in my head.

"There now," she said. "Can you feel anything from that?"

"It's mighty good," I said.

She was standing close over me again, her face almost touching mine and looking deep into my eyes. "Go on. Drink it down."

I didn't want to look into her eyes so it was her throat I saw, the red new-healed smooth place beneath her chin. Right then I recognized that wound for the first time as the place on her body where my .44 bullet had struck my deceitful Phoebe back in Paradise. It was the exact same spot.

I wanted to understand that, I wanted to try to make some sense, but it was too late. The old woman's tea was too strong in me and the little china cup slipped out of my unnerved fingers onto the hearthstones. It didn't break into a hundred splinters; it stuck solid and quivering on the rock like an arrow shot into a tree trunk. I stared at it there unharmed.

I kept staring at the cup because I didn't want to look at the granny woman. It shivered my body to know if I looked at her I'd see her again all ugly roots and lumps and with her firelit yellow eyes deformed.

But that's what I knew and not what I saw. All I saw was a heavy black roaring before my eyes and a sick shaking and I dropped then into a deep swoon, the deepest I reckon that a man can endure.

And when I came back to myself I was not sitting in the rocking chair and there was no hearth before me and not even a cabin around me. I was lying flat on my back under the stars in the middle of a fair-sized grassy bald, a circle with edges so sharp against the trees and bushes it looked like it was cut here with a knife.

It took a long time for me to get steady and sit up and when at last I do I find you-all here, all twelve of you men sitting crosslegged on the edge of the circle, all watching me with your wild eyes.

And when one of you, the tall dark-complected man there in his ancient buckskins, asked me to tell my whole story I didn't hold back the least little crumb of it. Awful as it is, it's the truth and I know you know that.

Because you don't need to explain anything to me. I can see in your bitter faces and in the bitter shadows of your eyes how it is and how it is going to be, that we are the men who ever killed Phoebe Redd; over the years and generations and centuries it was us that left the marks of our pistol balls on her again and again. Mine was the freshest one just beneath her chin, as red as a scarlet rose. I know how her revenge on us is everlasting and how we are to be scattered howling to and fro on the mountain; and how there is no rest for us and no surcease, but only being driven miserable on the rocks and thorns until Ember Mountain perishes and time itself passes all away.

The Empty House

Maurice Level

When he had picked the lock, the man went in, shut the door carefully and stood listening intently.

Although he knew the house was empty, the complete silence and inky darkness made an extraordinary impression on him. Never before had he experienced at one and the same time such a longing for and fear of solitude. He stretched out his hand, felt about the wall and fastened the bolt of the door. A little reassured, he took from his pocket a small electric lamp and looked round. The white patches of light that broke the darkness moved up and down with the beating of his heart. To give himself courage he murmured:

"It's like being in my own house."

Forcing a smile, he stepped cautiously into the dining-room.

Everything was in the most scrupulous order. Four chairs were pushed in round the table; the reflections of the legs of another were mirrored in the shining parquet floor. Vague odors of tobacco and fruit floated in the air. He opened the drawers of a sideboard where table-silver stood in orderly piles: "That's better than nothing," he thought as he put it in his pocket. But at every movement the spoons and forks jingled, and though he knew that the house was empty and he could not disturb any one, the noise agitated him and he turned away on tiptoe, leaving untouched a case of silver and enamel fruit knives and forks.

"That is not what I have come to get," was what he said to himself to excuse his hesitation.

But the same want of resolution kept him standing by the table fingering the silver that weighed heavily in his pocket as he looked at the door of the little salon where the closely-drawn, heavy curtains made the darkness still more dense. He made a supreme effort to dominate this unusual cowardice; and finally he walked calmly into the room with the easy step of a man who is returning to his own home after an evening with friends. He had suddenly lost the sensation of fear, and seeing a candelabra on an old chest he struck a match, lit the candles, and carried the light round to examine the pictures on the walls, the gold photograph frames, the ornaments, the piano, the mantel-piece from beneath which there came the smell of cinders and soot. He glanced at some papers that he raised with a finger, weighed a silver statuette in his hand and put it down again, then with a last look round the room, placed the candelabra on the table, blew out the candles and opened the door of the bedroom.

There was no longer any shadow of hesitation. Under pretext of looking over the house, which was to let, he had some days before been able to find out where every piece of furniture stood, and its nature. At one glance his practised eye had noted the bureau where the old man was sure to keep his valuable documents, the chest where his money ought to be, the bed in the alcove, and the big wardrobe with glass doors and many drawers, the contents of which he would probably find it well worth while to examine. He put out his lamp, stretched out his arm, and without knocking against even a chair, walked towards the bureau. He felt the top, drew his hand along the front, placed one finger of the left hand on the lock and felt in his pocket for his keys.

He had lost a little of his calm. It was not that he had any return of the curious fear of the darkness and silence of the house he had broken into; he now felt the feverish haste of the gambler who fingers his card before turning it up. What would he find? . . . Title-deeds? . . . Bank-notes? . . . And how much? What fortune lay waiting for him here behind this plank of wood? . . .

But he could not get at his keys. He had forgotten to take them out of his pocket before putting in the silver, and they had become entangled in it. As he fumbled, the spoons got into the rings of the keys, the prongs of the forks bent and pierced the lining of his coat, scratching his flesh. His impatience increased his clumsiness; he stamped his foot, swore, clenched his teeth and pulled so violently that the stuff gave way, and the keys and silver flew out and scattered over the floor with a sound like that of old iron . . . He was losing his nerve again . . . he had so nearly attained his object, and time was flying! . . . He did not know the exact hour, and it seemed as if he had been there a very long time. For the first time he became aware of the tic-tac of a clock, and the minutes seemed to be galloping along . . .

He knelt down, took a key and tried it, his ear close to the lock; no use. He took another, then a third, still another, trying them with careful movements . . . No good. No use at all! . . . His anger blazed up again, and he laughed harshly:

"Enough of that . . . Why should I spare the furniture?"

And seizing his jimmy, with one skillful movement he had the lock off. Then he opened the drawer and turned on his lamp.

A sigh of joy burst from him as his eyes fell on a collection of notes pinned together in packets. Slowly, methodically, he took them up, counted them, held them up to the light, then smoothed them with the back of his hand. He drew up a chair, sat down and continued to search at ease. Under a bag of gold there was a thick packet of share-certificates made out in the name of the holder, shares that amounted to twenty thousand francs—a fortune! . . .

"What a pity to leave them," he thought. "But they're no use to me . . ."

He replaced them. Sure now of his booty, he took his time; weighing the gold coins in his hand, comparing the surfaces and inscriptions on the forty- and fifty-franc pieces before putting them in his breast pocket. There was no longer any haste or agitation; success had ousted every feeling but those of relief and exultation. A heavy cart passed along the street, rattling the windows, shaking the furniture, making the silver on the floor vibrate. The familiar sound brought him back to a sense of where he was, and he took out his watch. Four o'clock—it was growing late! Gathering up the money without counting it, he looked quickly through the other drawers. There was nothing of any value to him. Some loose money had strayed among the papers and letters, and this he put in his vest pocket, murmuring:

"For out-of-pocket expenses."

A beautiful bronze paper-weight lay on the table. He had been wise enough to leave the share-certificates and some jewelry, but this—might he not take this as a charming little souvenir? . . . He was stretching out his hand when a noise startled him; the clock was striking, four sharp little strokes. He stood still, his hand out, his fingers open . . . the silence, broken for a moment by the decisive sounds, seemed suddenly to become oppressive, solemn. There was not a vibration within the four walls, not even the imperceptible murmur of hangings when the folds stir, not a crack from the dry boards that seem to sleep by day and wake into a sort of attempt at life during the night . . . Nothing but the beating of his own pulses, the sound of the quickened tide of the blood that throbbed in his temples . . . Fear gripped him again, a stupid, unusual fear—surely there was something abnormal about the nature of this silence? Why did he feel that he dare not disturb it by even a gesture? . . . He had ceased pressing the button of his lamp and stood there in the darkness, his shoulders bent, his neck stretched forwards, his nostrils dilated, his ears straining as he bent towards the mantelshelf where the little clock had ticked so quickly . . . The ticking had ceased! Well, the clock had stopped, that was all. Was there anything terrifying about that? . . . Nevertheless, a shiver ran down his back; some immediate and terrible danger seemed to be threatening him, and he seized his knife, turned on the lamp and wheeled quickly round.

In the alcove, half hidden in the shadow, he saw the face of an old man. The mouth was half open, and two terrible eyes were looking fixedly at him. There was no expression of fear; the eyes looked unflinchingly into his own, the hand that was stretched out over the sheet did not tremble, the leg that hung down below the covering was steady. Some one was going to take him by the throat; in a moment he would feel on his face the breath of this pale and silent adversary.

Without daring to move his head, he turned his eyes to look for the door.

The bank-notes had fallen to the floor, forgotten; he had but one idea—to flee! But from the menace in the eyes he saw that he would never manage to reach the door, that the old man was opening his mouth to cry for help, and that once the cry had sounded, it would be too late to escape; and without a second's hesitation, like a beast defending itself, he rushed to the bed, raised the knife and with a gasp of rage thrust it twice in the body up to the hilt. There was no moan, not a sound; a pillow fell softly to the ground and the head slipped sideways on the bolster, the lips half open, the chin on the chest.

Still trembling with fear and passion, he drew back and looked at his victim. The light of the lamp was too small to allow him to distinguish either the rent made by the knife in the disordered shirt or any trace of blood. Apparently the stroke had gone straight to the heart, for the expression of the face had not changed. The first thrust, well-aimed and lightning-swift, had stopped life as if it had been a shot from a revolver. Proud of his skill, he muttered menacingly:

"So you were at home watching me! Well, you have seen, haven't you?"

But as he bent over the quiet face and noted that the expression was the same, it flashed into his mind that the knife might only have pierced the coverings, that perhaps the old man was still alive, still watching him with the same supreme irony.

He raised the knife again and drove it in, drew it out and brought it down with savage frenzy, and intoxicated by the dull sound it made as it entered the chest, he continued to strike, exciting himself by oaths and exclamations that he forgot to stifle. The shirt was now in rags, the flesh one large wound. But untouched by the knife, the face still kept its impassive calm, its terrifying stare. He lost his head, and flinging his lamp away, seized the old man by the throat to give a last certain stroke.

But his right hand remained up in the air and the cry of rage did not pass his lips, for under the other hand he felt, not the damp and throbbing flesh from which life was escaping in a flow of blood, but flesh that had no last quiver of life in it, which was cold with the awful iciness that is like nothing else in the world—dead flesh, dead for long hours! . . . His arm fell.

He had never been afraid of crime. His knife had often been red: his face had been wet with the warm stream that leaped from severed arteries: he knew the smell of blood, the death-rattle that comes when life is flowing from the body . . . Death caused by his own hands was nothing . . . But this! . . . And instinctive respect for the Dead suddenly rose from some obscure depth in his murderer's soul, and a superstitious fear of the Great Mystery froze him . . . He had believed the house was empty, and he had shut himself in with a corpse! . . . A corpse . . . this, then, accounted for the unearthly silence and the pall-like mystery of the darkness! . . .

Somewhere in the far distance a clock struck five, and without daring to turn his head towards the abandoned spoils, with his hat in his hand and vague memories of prayers rising in his terrified mind, he stumbled over the furniture and fled from the house . . .

The Epiphany of Death

Clark Ashton Smith

(Dedicated to the memory of H. P. Lovecraft)

I find it peculiarly difficult to express the exact nature of the sentiment which Tomeron had always evoked in me. However, I am sure that the feeling never partook, at any time, of what is ordinarily known as friendship. It was a compound of unusual esthetic and intellectual elements, and was somehow closely allied in my thoughts with the same fascination that has drawn me ever since childhood toward all things that are remote in space and time, or which have about them the irresolvable twilight of antiquity. Somehow, Tomeron seemed never to belong to the present; but one could readily have imagined him as living in some bygone age. About him, there was nothing whatever of the lineaments of our own period; and he even went so far as to affect in his costume an approximation to the garments worn several centuries ago. His complexion was extremely pale and cadaverous, and he stooped heavily from poring over ancient tomes and no less ancient maps. He moved always with the slow, meditative pace of one who dwells among far-off memories and reveries; and he spoke often of people and events and ideas that have long since been forgotten. For the most part, he was apparently unheedful of present things, and I felt that for him the huge city of Ptolemides, in which we both dwelt, with all its manifold clamor and tumult, was little more than a labyrinth of painted vapors. There was a like vagueness in the attitude of others toward Tomeron; and though he had always been accepted without question as a representative of the noble and otherwise extinct family from whom he claimed descent, nothing appeared to be known about his actual birth and antecedents. With two servants, who were both deaf-mutes, who were very old and who likewise wore the raiment of a former age, he lived in the semi-ruinous mansion of his ancestors, where it was said, none of the family had dwelt for many generations. There he pursued the occult and recondite studies that were so congenial to his mind; and there, at certain intervals, I was wont to visit him.

I cannot recall the precise date and circumstances of the beginning of my acquaintance with Tomeron. Though I come of a hardy line that is noted for the sanity of its constitution, my faculties had been woefully shaken by the horror of the happening with which that acquaintance ended. My memory is not what it was, and there are certain lacunae for which my readers must contrive to forgive me. The only wonder is, that my powers of recollection have survived at all, beneath the hideous burden they have had to bear; for, in a more than metaphoric sense, I have been as one condemned to carry with him, at all times and in all places, the loathsome incubi of things long dead and corrupt.

I can readily recall, however, the studies to which Tomeron had devoted himself, the lost demonian volumes from Hyperborea and Mu and Atlantis with which his library shelves were heaped to the ceiling, and the queer charts, not of any land that lies above the surface of the earth, on which he pored by perpetual candle-light. I shall not speak of these studies, for they would seem too fantastic and too macabre for credibility; and that which I have to relate is incredible enough in itself. I shall speak, however, of certain strange ideas with which Tomeron was much preoccupied, and concerning which he so often discoursed to me in that deep, guttural and monotonous voice of his, that had the reverberation of unsounded caverns in its tones and cadences. He maintained that life and death were not the fixed conditions that people commonly believed them to be; that the two realms were often intermingled in ways not readily discerned, and had penumbral border-lands; that the dead were not always the dead, nor the living the living, as such terms are habitually understood. But the manner in which he spoke of these ideas was extremely vague and general; and I could never induce him to specify his meaning or to proffer some concrete illustration that would render it more intelligible to a mentality such as mine, that was unused to dealing in the cobwebs of abstraction. Behind his words, there hovered, or seemed to hover, a legion of dark, amorphous images that I could never formulate or depict to myself in any way, until the final denouement of our descent into the catacombs of Ptolemides.

I have already said that my feeling for Tomeron was never anything that could be classified as friendship. But even from the first, I was well aware that Tomeron had a curious fondness for me—a fondness whose nature I could not comprehend, and with which I could hardly even sympathize. Though he fascinated me at all times, there were occasions when my interest was not unalloyed with an actual sense of repulsion. At whiles, his pallor was *too* cadaverous, too suggestive of fungi that have grown in the dark, or of leprous bones by moonlight; and the stoop of his shoulders conveyed to my brain the idea that they bore a burden of centuries through which no man could conceivably have lived. He aroused always a certain awe in me; and the awe was sometimes mingled with an indeterminate fear.

I do not remember how long our acquaintance had continued; but I do remember that he spoke with increasing frequency, toward the end, of those bizarre ideas at which I have hinted. Always I felt that he was troubled about something, for he often looked at me with a mournful gleam in his hollow eyes;

and sometimes he would speak, with peculiar stress, of the great regard that he had for me.

And one night he said, 'Theolus, the time is coming when you must know the truth—must know me as I am, and not as I have been permitted to seem. There is a term to all things, and all things are obedient to inexorable laws. I would that it were otherwise, but neither I nor any man, among the living or among the dead, can lengthen at will the term of any state or condition of being, or alter the laws that decree such conditions.'

Perhaps it was well that I did not understand him, and that I was unable to attach much importance to his words or to the singular intentness of his bearing as he uttered them. For a few more days, I was spared the knowledge which I now carry.

Then, one evening, Tomeron spoke thus: 'I am now compelled to ask an odd favor of you, which I hope you will grant me, in consideration of our long friendship. The favor is, that you accompany me this very night to those vaults of my family which lie in the catacombs of Ptolemides.'

Though much surprised by the request, and not altogether pleased, I was nevertheless unable to deny him. I could not imagine the purpose of such a visit as the one proposed; but, as was my wont, I forbore to interrogate Tomeron, and merely told him that I would accompany him to the vaults if such were his desire.

'I thank you, Theolus, for this proof of friendship,' he replied earnestly. 'Believe me, I am loath to ask it; but there has been a certain deception, an odd misunderstanding which cannot go on any longer. Tonight, you will learn the truth.'

Carrying torches, we left the mansion of Tomeron and sought the ancient catacombs of Ptolemides, which lie beyond the walls and have long been disused, for there is now a fine necropolis in the very heart of the city. The moon had gone down beyond the desert that encroaches toward the catacombs; and we were forced to light our torches long before we came to the subterranean adits; for the rays of Mars and Jupiter in a sodden and funereal sky were not enough to illumine the perilous path we followed among mounds and fallen obelisks and broken graves. At length we discovered the dark and weed-choked entrance of the charnels; and here Tomeron led the way with a swiftness and surety of footing that bespoke long familiarity with the place.

Entering, we found ourselves in a crumbling passage where the bones of dilapidated skeletons were scattered amid the rubble that had fallen from the sides and roof. A choking stench of stagnant air and age-old corruption made me pause for an instant; but Tomeron scarcely appeared to perceive it, for he strode onward, lifting his torch and beckoning me to follow. We traversed many vaults in which mouldy bones and verdigris-eaten sarcophagi were piled about the walls or strewn where desecrating thieves had left them in bygone years.

104

The air was increasingly dank, chill and miasmal; and mephitic shadows crouched or swayed before our torches in every niche and corner. Also, as we went onward, the walls became more ruinous and the bones we saw on every hand were greener with the mould of time.

At length we rounded a sudden angle of the low cavern we were following. Here we came to vaults that evidently belonged to some noble family, for they were quite spacious and there was but one sarcophagus in each vault.

'My ancestors and my family lie here,' announced Tomeron.

We reached the cavern's end and were confronted by a blank wall. At one side was the final vault, in which an empty sarcophagus stood open. The sarcophagus was wrought of the finest bronze and was richly carven.

Tomeron paused before the vault and turned to me. By the flickering, uncertain light I thought that I saw a look of strange and unaccountable distress on his features.

'I must beg you to withdraw for a moment,' he said, in a low and sorrowful voice. 'Afterward, you can return.'

Surprised and puzzled, I obeyed his request and went slowly back along the passage for some distance. Then I returned to the place where I had left him. My surprise was heightened when I found that he had extinguished his torch and had dropped it on the threshold of the final vault. And Tomeron himself was not visible anywhere.

Entering the vault, since there was seemingly no other place where he could have hidden himself, I looked about for him, but the room was empty. At least, I thought it empty till I looked again at the richly carven sarcophagus and saw that it was now tenanted, for a cadaver lay within, shrouded in a winding-sheet of a sort that has not been used for centuries in Ptolemides.

I drew near to the sarcophagus, and peering into the face of the cadaver, I saw that it bore a fearful and strange resemblance to the face of Tomeron, though it was bloated and puffed with the adipocere of death and was purple with the shadows of decay. And looking again, I saw that it was indeed Tomeron.

I would have screamed aloud with the horror that came upon me; but my lips were benumbed and frozen, and I could only whisper Tomeron's name. But as I whispered it, the lips of the cadaver seemed to part, and the tip of its tongue protruded between them. And I thought that the tip trembled, as if Tomeron were about to speak and answer me. But gazing more closely, I saw that the trembling was merely the movement of worms as they twisted up and down and to and fro and sought to crowd each other from Tomeron's tongue.

The Everlasting Club

Ingulphus

There is a chamber in Jesus College the existence of which is probably known to few who are now resident, and fewer still have penetrated into it or even seen its interior. It is on the right hand of the landing on the top floor of the precipitous staircase in the angle of the cloister next the Hall—a staircase which for some forgotten story connected with it is traditionally called "Cow Lane." The padlock which secures its massive oaken door is very rarely unfastened, for the room is bare and unfurnished. Once it served as a place of deposit for superfluous kitchen ware, but even that ignominious use has passed from it, and it is now left to undisturbed solitude and darkness. For I should say that it is entirely cut off from the light of the outer day by the walling up, some time in the eighteenth century, of its single window, and such light as ever reaches it comes from the door, when rare occasion causes it to be opened.

Yet at no extraordinarily remote day this chamber has evidently been tenanted, and, before it was given up to darkness, was comfortably fitted, according to the standard of comfort which was known in college in the days of George II. There is still a roomy fireplace before which legs have been stretched and wine and gossip have circulated in the days of wigs and brocade. For the room is spacious and, when it was lighted by the window looking eastward over the fields and common, it must have been a cheerful place for a sociable don.

Let me state in brief, prosaic outline the circumstances which account for the gloom and solitude in which this room has remained now for nearly a century and a half.

In the second quarter of the eighteenth century the University possessed a great variety of clubs of a social kind. There were clubs in college parlours and clubs in private rooms, or in inns and coffee-houses: clubs flavoured with politics, clubs clerical, clubs purporting to be learned and literary. Whatever their professed particularity, the aim of each was convivial. Some of them, which included undergraduates as well as seniors, were dissipated enough, and in their limited provincial way aped the profligacy of such clubs as the Hell Fire Club of London notoriety.

Among these last was one which was at once more select and of more evil fame than any of its fellows. By a singular accident, presently to be explained, the Minute Book of this Club, including the years from 1738 to 1766, came into the hands of a Master of Jesus College, and though, so far as I am aware, it is no longer extant, I have before me a transcript of it which, though it is in a recent handwriting, presents in a bald shape such a singular array of facts that I must ask you to accept them as veracious. The original book is described as a stout duodecimo volume bound in red leather and fastened with red silken strings. The writing in it occupied some forty pages, and ended with the date November 2, 1766.

The Club in question was called the Everlasting Club—a name sufficiently explained by its rules, set forth in the pocket-book. Its number was limited to seven, and it would seem that its members were all young men, between twenty-two and thirty. One of them was a Fellow-Commoner of Trinity: three of them were Fellows of Colleges, among whom I should specially mention a Fellow of Jesus, named Charles Bellasis: another was a landed proprietor in the county, and the sixth was a young Cambridge physician. The Founder and President of the Club was the Honourable Alan Dermot, who, as the son of an Irish peer, had obtained a nobleman's degree in the University, and lived in idleness in the town. Very little is known of his life and character, but that little is highly in his disfavour. He was killed in a duel at Paris in the year 1743, under circumstances which I need not particularise, but which point to an exceptional degree of cruelty and wickedness in the slain man.

I will quote from the first pages of the Minute Book some of the laws of the Club, which will explain its constitution:—

"1. This Society consisteth of seven Everlastings, who may be Corporeal or Incorporeal, as Destiny shall determine.

2. The rules of the Society, as herein written, are immutable and Everlasting.

3. None shall hereafter be chosen into the Society and none shall cease to be members.

4. The Honourable Alan Dermot is the Everlasting President of the Society.

5. The Senior Corporeal Everlasting, not being the President, shall be the Secretary of the Society, and in this Book of Minutes shall record its transactions, the date at which any Everlasting shall cease to be Corporeal, and all fines due to the Society. And when such Senior Everlasting shall cease to be Corporeal he shall, either in person or by some sure hand, deliver this Book of Minutes to him who shall be next Senior and at the time Corporeal, and he shall in like manner record the transactions therein and transmit it to the next Senior. The neglect of these provisions shall be visited by the President with fine or punishment according to his discretion.

6. On the second day of November in every year, being the Feast of All Souls, at ten o'clock *post meridiem*, the Everlastings shall meet at supper in the place of residence of that Corporeal member of the Society to whom it shall fall

in order of rotation to entertain them, and they shall all subscribe in this Book of Minutes their names and present place of abode.

7. It shall be the obligation of every Everlasting to be present at the yearly entertainment of the Society, and none shall allege for excuse that he has not been invited thereto. If any Everlasting shall fail to attend the yearly meeting, or in his turn shall fail to provide entertainment for the Society, he shall be mulcted at the discretion of the President.

8. Nevertheless, if in any year, in the month of October and not less than seven days before the Feast of All Souls, the major part of the Society, that is to say, four at the least, shall meet and record in writing in these Minutes that it is their desire that no entertainment be given in that year, then, notwithstanding the two rules last rehearsed, there shall be no entertainment in that year, and no Everlasting shall be mulcted on the ground of his absence."

The rest of the rules are either too profane or too puerile to be quoted here. They indicate the extraordinary levity with which the members entered on their preposterous obligations. In particular, to the omission of any regulation as to the transmission of the Minute Book after the last Everlasting ceased to be "Corporeal," we owe the accident that it fell into the hands of one who was not a member of the society, and the consequent preservation of its contents to the present day.

Low as was the standard of morals in all classes of the University in the first half of the eighteenth century, the flagrant defiance of public decorum by the members of the Everlasting Society brought upon it the stern censure of the authorities, and after a few years it was practically dissolved and its members banished from the University. Charles Bellasis, for instance, was obliged to leave the college, and, though he retained his fellowship, he remained absent from it for nearly twenty years. But the minutes of the society reveal a more terrible reason for its virtual extinction.

Between the years 1738 and 1743 the minutes record many meetings of the Club, for it met on other occasions besides that of All Souls Day. Apart from a great deal of impious jocularity on the part of the writers, they are limited to the formal record of the attendance of the members, fines inflicted, and so forth. The meeting on November 2nd in the latter year is the first about which there is any departure from the stereotyped forms. The supper was given in the house of the physician. One member, Henry Davenport, the former Fellow-Commoner of Trinity, was absent from the entertainment, as he was then serving in Germany, in the Dettingen campaign. The minutes contain an entry, "Mulctatus propter absentiam per Presidentem, Hen. Davenport." An entry on the next page of the book runs, "Henry Davenport by a Cannonshot became an Incorporeal Member, November 3, 1743."

The minutes give in their own handwriting, under the date November 2, the names and addresses of the six other members. First in the list, in a large bold hand, is the autograph of "Alan Dermot, President, at the Court of His Royal Highness." Now in October Dermot had certainly been in attendance on the Young Pretender at Paris, and doubtless the address which he gave was understood at the time by the other Everlastings to refer to the fact. But on October 28, five days *before* the meeting of the Club, he was killed, as I have already mentioned, in a duel. The news of his death cannot have reached Cambridge on November 2, for the Secretary's record of it is placed below that of Davenport, and with the date November 10: "this day was reported that the President was become an Incorporeal by the hands of a french chevalier." And in a sudden ebullition, which is in glaring contrast with his previous profanities, he has dashed down "The Good God shield us from ill."

The tidings of the President's death scattered the Everlastings like a thunderbolt. They left Cambridge and buried themselves in widely parted regions. But the Club did not cease to exist. The Secretary was still bound to his hateful records: the five survivors did not dare to neglect their fatal obligations. Horror of the presence of the President made the November gathering once and for ever impossible: but horror, too, forbade them to neglect the precaution of meeting in October of every year to put in writing their objection to the celebration. For five years five names are appended to that entry in the minutes, and that is all the business of the Club. Then another member died, who was not the Secretary.

For eighteen more years four miserable men met once each year to deliver the same formal protest. During those years we gather from the signatures that Charles Bellasis returned to Cambridge, now, to appearance, chastened and decorous. He occupied the rooms which I have described on the staircase in the corner of the cloister.

Then in 1766 comes a new handwriting and an altered minute: "Jan. 27, on this day Francis Witherington, Secretary, became an Incorporeal Member. The same day this Book was delivered to me, James Harvey." Harvey lived only a month, and a similar entry on March 7 states that the book has descended, with the same mysterious celerity, to William Catherston. Then, on May 18, Charles Bellasis writes that on that day, being the date of Catherston's decease, the Minute Book has come to him as the last surviving Corporeal of the Club.

As it is my purpose to record fact only I shall not attempt to describe the feelings of the unhappy Secretary when he penned that fatal record. When Witherington died it must have come home to the three survivors that after twenty-three years' intermission the ghastly entertainment must be annually renewed, with the addition of fresh incorporeal guests, or that they must undergo the pitiless censure of the President. I think it likely that the terror of the alternative, coupled with the mysterious delivery of the Minute Book, was answerable for the speedy decease of the two first successors to the Secretaryship. Now that the alternative was offered to Bellasis alone, he was firmly resolved to bear the consequences, whatever they might be, of an infringement of the Club rules.

The graceless days of George II. had passed away from the University. They were succeeded by times of outward respectability, when religion and morals were no longer publicly challenged. With Bellasis, too, the petulance of youth had passed: he was discreet, perhaps exemplary. The scandal of his early conduct was unknown to most of the new generation, condoned by the few survivors who had witnessed it.

On the night of November 2nd, 1766, a terrible event revived in the older inhabitants of the College the memory of those evil days. From ten o'clock to midnight a hideous uproar went on in the chamber of Bellasis. Who were his companions none knew. Blasphemous outcries and ribald songs, such as had not been heard for twenty years past, aroused from sleep or study the occupants of the court; but among the voices was not that of Bellasis. At twelve a sudden silence fell upon the cloisters. But the Master lay awake all night, troubled at the relapse of a respected colleague and the horrible example of libertinism set to his pupils.

In the morning all remained quiet about Bellasis' chamber. When his door was opened, soon after daybreak, the early light creeping through the drawn curtains revealed a strange scene. About the table were drawn seven chairs, but some of them had been overthrown, and the furniture was in chaotic disorder, as after some wild orgy. In the chair at the foot of the table sat the lifeless figure of the Secretary, his head bent over his folded arms, as though he would shield his eyes from some horrible sight. Before him on the table lay pen, ink and the red Minute Book. On the last inscribed page, under the date of November 2nd, were written, for the first time since 1742, the autographs of the seven members of the Everlasting Club, but without address. In the same strong hand in which the President's name was written there was appended below the signatures the note, "Mulctatus per Presidentem propter neglectum obsonii, Car. Bellasis."

The Minute Book was secured by the Master of the College, and I believe that he alone was acquainted with the nature of its contents. The scandal reflected on the College by the circumstances revealed in it caused him to keep the knowledge rigidly to himself. But some suspicion of the nature of the occurrences must have percolated to students and servants, for there was a long-abiding belief in the College that annually on the night of November 2 sounds of unholy revelry were heard to issue from the chamber of Bellasis. I cannot learn that the occupants of the adjoining rooms have ever been disturbed by them. Indeed, it is plain from the minutes that owing to their improvident drafting no provision was made for the perpetuation of the All Souls entertainment after the last Everlasting ceased to be Corporeal. Such superstitious belief must be treated with contemptuous incredulity. But whether for that cause or another the rooms were shut up, and have remained tenantless from that day to this.

Fair Trade

William F. Nolan

He tole me to speak all this down into the machine, the Sheriff did, what all I know an' seen about Lon Pritchard an' his brother Lafe an' what they done, one to the other. I already tole it all to the Sheriff but he says for sure that none'a what I tole him happened the way I said it did but to talk it all into the machine anyhow. He figgers to have it all done up on paper from this talkin' machine so's folks kin read it an' laugh at me I reckon. If you don' believe it why should I talk it all down I wanted to know but he says it's for legal when they stan' me afore Judge Henry for Lon Pritchard's killin' which I sure never done. I witnessed it done, with the blood an' all, but I never done it personal.

Well, anyways, here goes . . .

First, my name is Jace Ridling. I guess that's Jason but none as ever called me the name formal. I was born right here in this part'a Virginia where I been all my life but I'm not rightly sure about my years due to my bein' alone an' all with no kinfolk alive to testify my age. I don't recall I ever had no blood kinfolk—'cept my Ma and my Pappy an' I never knew 'em proper. Not enough to hang a recollection on 'em. They both took off when I was a tad an' left me at the county home an' I run away an' jus growed as best I could, livin' off the woods an' what you find there. Guess I've et everthin' that grows there in my time—grub worms an' wiggly bugs under dead logs an' squinch owls an' frogs an' crickets an' skittery squirrils an' what all else I can't rightly recall. Don't matter none to this story, 'cept that's why I saw what I did. Livin' out in deep woods like I do I see what goes on when town folk are abed of a night. Lotsa funny things go on in deep woods if yer a mind ta look for 'em.

Like I tole Sheriff Meade this here story begun a week back, at the tail end'a that real mean rain spell we had. Hard black rain, the worst anybody kin recollect, worst ever in this county, slicin' inta that yella clay out there on Cemetery Ridge, makin' the ground all soft an' slidey. It was the rain, jes comin' down an' comin' down what done it—what caused the box they had Lafe Pritchard nailed inside to bust open at the bottom'a Calder's Hill. Rain loosed it—an' that wet clay run like yella blood down the hill, carryin' the box hard onto the rocks. Knocked the top clean off, lettin' the rain in onto Lafe an soakin' his nice black fifty-dollar store-bought suit, the one they buried him in.

Now comes the part Sheriff Meade says is looney talk—but as the Lord A'mighty is my witness it happened jes like I tole him it did. 'Bout Lafe Pritchard I mean, 'bout how the rain—God's Tears some call it—come peltin' down into that cold split-open wood box an' woke ole Lafe till he rose up to sit straight as a soldier there in his fine black suit . . .

I was no more'n ten feet away—huggin' the side'a the hill the way I was to shelter me some agin' the storm—with my shiny rain slicker curled 'round me like a tent there in the blowin' dark—watchin' that dead man blinker his dead eye an' move his dead mouth like he was testin' 'em to see if they still worked proper.

I was down wind'a him—an' even past the smell'a the rain I caught his scent, strong as sin on Sunday. I could nose him plain, all sour an' gone to rot, the kinda smell a crushed rat gives off inside a barn after the wagon wheel has run him over an' him bein' there on the barn floor awhile.

For sure, I was scart. Never seen me no livin' dead men afore, but I'd heard tell of 'em a'plenty an' knew it could happen, that the dead could raise up if they had a mind to do so. An' a *reason*. They's a reason behind everythin' men do, livin' an' dead. An' Lafe, he sure had hisself a reason. The rain was the thing that woke him from his uneasy rest, gave him the chance to do what he *had* to do. It jes happened I was there to see it . . .

I tole myself Jace, you calm on down now, boy, 'cuz Lafe was yer friend an' it don't figger he means to harm ya none. Jes speak up to him kindly.

Lafe, I say . . . standin' close to him an' lookin' down at him sittin' there in that cold wet box with his rain-slicked hair all plastered along the dead white of his face. His one eye rolls up to look me over. There's jes a hole where the other was. Worms got it likely. His face is half gone. Parts of him have fell off, parts'a his nose is missin' an' his upper lip is been most et away till the teeth shine out at me like he's smilin' even when he's not.

He's a plain fright, Lafe Pritchard is—but I say to him, Lafe, oh sweet Jesus, Lafe, you're the first livin' dead I ever come across. What brung ya back?

He don't answer right off. First, he stands up slow, looks around with that one eye at the dark on Calder's Hill an' up at the other graves on Cemetery Ridge an' at the wind-shook trees an' he stretches like a long-asleep cat, his arms up above his head, stretchin' those dead muscles an' I stand there a'side him wonderin' if there's still any blood in him. For sure not. But *somethin'* keeps him there, tall in the dark. Somethin' fires his dead flesh an' moves those long arms a'his.

Lon. He says that name to me, soft an' raspy, deep as a well. It's Lon I want to see. Where's Lon?

112

To home, most likely, on a night like this I say back to him.

Lon. I must see my brother Lon, he says. Can't sleep proper till I do.

That voice a'his was somethin' to remember. Like no voice I ever heard a'fore or since or ever will agin' I'd guarantee.

Can the dead walk? Can they move through hollers an' gullies an' through deep woods? Oh *yes* they can!

Lafe did, that night, walkin' his dead legs along steady as you please past drippin' oak and evergreen, through tangle-weeds an' waist-high grass, his shoes suckin' at yella clay or lost in leaf loam an' me with him an' the black rain peltin' down like buckshot on us both an' neither of us sayin' nary a word as it final gave way to a smoky-burnt sun which come up slow over the trees.

Sure enough, the storm was over. Over an' spent. Jes like it had stayed long enough to wake ole Lafe an' havin' done that job took off for other woods. A bird, kingfisher most likely, sang high an' sweet for us, an' frogs moved morning-soft in the marsh.

We're almost into town I say to Lafe.

He nods an' I step back a mite from the scent of him. The sun makes him smell worse as it heats him up. Already our wet clothes is steamin' like smoke.

I ask him do you aim to walk right down the main street? Somehow it don't seem proper to me.

I aim to, he tells me in that raspy voice that sounds like it comes from inside a holla log.

What'll folks say, seein' as how you look an' all? Seein' as how they know you belong dead an' buried on Cemetery Ridge?

They'll be none up to say, he tells me. They'll most be abed.

You intendin' to go straight through town to Lon's?

Straight through. That's my proper intent.

Now he stops at the edge of the wood, lookin' toward the town with that one spit-shiny eye, with his teeth gapin' an' his dead white skin all flaked half away to raw bone.

I coulda cut an' run, right then. I didn't hafta go in an' see what I saw, witness what I witnessed, an' sure as God's grace I'd be safe off this minute in the deep woods if I'd done jes that 'stead'a bein' here inside this jailhouse talkin' at this machine an' not bein' believed by nobody.

But I never run.

I went in with Lafe.

The town was dawn-silent 'cept for a big splotchy dog that came snuffin' an' barkin' outa Red's Cafe toward us, till he got a whiff'a Lafe an' down-tailed it quick back inside. Lafe paid him no mind.

We walked the length'a that street to Lon's house at the far side where the road turns back to deep wood. Lon he's lived there alone since Lafe died. Nice, with climbin' vines along one side an' big sunny windas.

I had no fear in me then, jes a burnin' curiosity to see what Lafe would do when he found Lon, an' what Lon would do when he laid sight'a him—seein' his own dead brother standin' there fresh from the grave.

Jace boy, I tole myself, keep yer eyes wide open 'cuz it ain't never 'afore happened that a dead man walks bold as brass beside you toward a brother he hated more than Satan himself 'afore he died.

Because see, it was *hate* that brung Lafe here—hate fer Lon that druv him up from that coffin to walk the woods here to face the brother that deviled his woman an' ruint his life an' drove him to fire that bullet into his own heart.

Hate was the blood that filled Lafe Pritchard's body that mornin'—hate was the coal that fed the furnace of him.

What you gonna do when you find Lon to home I asked?

You'll see, Lafe says to me an' knocks on that door as calm as you please, a dead man knockin' to be let in an' Lon comin' up from sleep in his gray long-johns to open the door an' seein' his horror of a brother standin' there—an' screamin' like a stuck pig as Lafe reaches out to take him by the throat.

It all happened fast . . .

Lon claws at those bone-white fingers an' staggers back inside, eyes bugged, an' Lafe, all swole up an' stinkin' from the sun havin' been at him, drags Lon down the hall by the neck, me follerin' to the kitchen. Not a word betwixt 'em. Just the horror of it, the stench of it, in that dark mornin' room with the shades down an' the light still outside.

Now comes the part that got me sick, so I don't rightly want to dwell on it.

Sheriff Meade says he's certain convinced that what I'm really doin' here is confessin' up to killin' Lon Pritchard an' that this is my way'a tryin' to slip past the law's penalty by blamin' a dead man for what *I* done.

He's wrong. Lafe done in Lon, right there in front'a me that mornin' in that kitchen an' it was Lafe that cut the hole in him with the carvin' knife. I didn't do it. I jes watched it gettin' done, gaggin' the while, sick with the raw sight of it all, yet with my gaze plain fixed to it.

After it was done Lafe steps back an' says to me, we're even now, me an' Lon. I got what I come fer. I can sleep proper now. It's a fair trade. He owed me an' I collected.

So that's all there is to it. If you don't believe me you go out an' see fer yourself. Out to Cemetery Ridge where he's sleepin' now inside that box agin with the lid nailed shut an' a fresh hole dug an' him at the bottom where he asked me to put him.

I done it fer a friend. I buried him proper so's he could finally rest easy.

I don't judge him fer what he done. Lon Pritchard was bad clean through, we all knew that. Stealin' other folks wommin, an' cheatin' at his store business an' gettin' sod-drunk on God's Sunday. Deserved what he got, if truth be tole. It's the Lord's own justice what Lafe done to him.

114

An' the trade's been made. You'll find it in there, in the box with him. He's a'holdin' it fast in those bony fingers, claspin' it to his bosom like a lost pup. I didn't take it. Not me. Nosir. It's down there with him—the thing that was missin' when Sheriff Meade found the deceased.

Lon Pritchard's heart.

The Family Underwater

Lucy Taylor

I t was soon after my fifteenth birthday that I came home from school one day to find that our frame house on the corner of Monument Avenue and Malvern Street had filled up with water all the way to the second-floor ceiling. I don't mean it was *under* water—it was *full* of water, like a toy house that you'd put in the bottom of an aquarium for the guppies to swim through and the bottomsuckers to clean. Inside, my mother and my ten-year-old sister Babette floated from room to room like big soft ballerinas doing a *pas de deux* in soggy slow motion. I stared through the living room window, afraid to open the front door for fear a torrent of water would rush out, depositing a waterlogged Mom and Babette and all our tacky furniture and used clothing from Second Hand Rose in a big sopping heap on the lawn.

So I hung around outside until Dad staggered home, listing side to side like a ship with an unbalanced cargo, sweat stains the size of volleyballs under his arms and that mean glint in his eyes that suggested his reception that evening at The Tramp Lounge had not been worthy of his stature in Tampa's dominant social class, the Fraternal Order of Drunkards, Bullies, and Buttholes.

But I digress, as Ms. Flannahan in English 202 used to say.

In his own sodden state, Dad didn't even notice the condition of the interior of our house, but opened the door and plunged right into a stationary wall of water, while I gaped through the window. The water didn't seem to distract Dad at all from his mission, which, as usual, was to dump shit onto his nearest and dearest. In that respect, we all functioned at one time or another as toilets. Tonight, Dad's face was red as a clown's carnation, and his mouth hung open like a piranha with a bad overbite. He was flailing his arms about, but it was all taking place in slow motion, and—best of all—there was almost no sound. Oh, I could hear little gurgles that might have been "goddamn bitch" and "lousy fag bartender" but mostly it was just soft, sucky sounds, like a baby's farts, not scary, but instead almost comical.

115

Mom scowled and said something that came out of her mouth in a long string of silvery bubbles. It looked like she was puking up pearls or the egg cases of some exotic sea creature.

Then I saw Dad raise his hand and strike Mom alongside the head, but underwater like that, it took about ten seconds for his hand to connect with her jaw, and a good fifteen more for Mom to go down—in slow, graceful silence, her dress floating up high in the water so I could see her blue underpants billowing, her shoulder striking the edge of the coffee table with a muffled, wet *thrump*.

Something tiny and gold, about the size of a corn kernel, floated past the window. It took me a minute to realize it was one of Mom's teeth. I took a deep breath, planning to hold it just long enough to drag Mom and Babette out of the house, and I plunged into the submerged living room.

As soon as I entered the water, Dad came at me, his rubbery lips twisted like a riled moray eel, his mouth working but no sound coming out except the glug-glug of bubbles that sounded like the toilet tank when it backs up. He grabbed for me, but before he could hit me, Babette floated by, breaststroking like crazy, her red hair fanning out around her head like a halo of flame. She made a shooshing gesture with one finger, then clasped my hand in a motion so graceful and serene, you'd never have guessed the desperation behind it, and floated up the stairs ahead of me like a drowned angel. It wasn't until we swam into our room and hid in the closet, hovering up level with the coat hangers that I realized I'd been breathing all along. The water was thick and cold and cloying, like breathing snot, and it took some getting used to, but after a while I didn't notice anymore. I was just grateful for the bizarre fact that I was able to breathe at all.

Those first few weeks adjusting to life underwater were difficult. I slept a lot and had strange, murky dreams in which I drowned and revived and drowned again, but I also began to feel a new and welcome calm, a safe-feeling numbness as if a dentist doing a root canal had missed my gum and shot the novocaine directly into my brain. Cotton candy La-La Land, safe and soft and cushiony, where even the most violent fights erupted in silence and serenity, and blood spilling from my lip or Mom's nose unfurled like gorgeous underwater snakes that slowly dissipated into the pale layers of cornflower blue water. Dad's yelling didn't frighten me, and physical pain, what I felt of it at all, seemed to take place in someone else's body, the sensations distant, like the echo of a train disappearing far down a tunnel.

I began to regret all those years I'd spent living in the air.

At night, Babette and I would lie together in our submerged bed and whisper back and forth, her bubbles breaking on my nose and mouth like kisses.

"How do you suppose it happened?" I said. "I mean, this isn't possible.

For one thing, our house never even kept out a good hard rain—how can it hold in all this water without any of it leaking out?"

"What are you talking about?" said Babette. "Our house has always been full of water. Ever since I was three years old. Don't you remember? It filled up with water the day of GrandMa's funeral. Dad got drunk and fell against the coffin, and Mom started screaming at him, and Dad smacked her in the face. When we got home, the house was full of water. I wondered why you never said anything about it."

"Is that why I've never seen you cry? You've been underwater all these years?"

Babette nodded. "I'm sorry. I should have told you. I really thought you were just pretending not to know."

"But that still doesn't explain how it happened. How a house can just fill up with water all by itself."

"Because we need it to be full of water," Babette said. "So we can live here without going crazy."

If there was a downside to living in a house full of water, it was that, after a while I got used to it. To the silence, the slowness, to swimming or floating from room to room instead of walking. Then, *bam,* it was time to go to school or to church or to the grocery store, and the outside world, full of noise and hard edges and sharp, prickly people would hit me like a brick in the teeth, and all I wanted was to dive back underwater.

What was weird, too, was when someone from outside came over to our house, and there I was, safe under the water, but the visitor wasn't, so we'd be moving in two different worlds, a creature of the land and a creature of the sea, hopelessly miscommunicating. After a while I realized that, except for Mom and Babette, it was easier just to be alone.

I remember one disaster that happened right around my first underwater Thanksgiving. I let this boy I liked, Luke Marshak, come over to watch a video. I knew it was a mistake, but Mom had been nagging me to have my friends over, so I did it to appease her. So right in the middle of *Terminator* Dad burst in, floated right into the antique hatrack and knocked it flat, then did a kind of underwater imitation of an airplane with only one engine trying to take off. He was swinging his arms around, careening into lamps and picture frames. Objects were sinking slowly toward the floor, a glass lamp shattering in silence, stained glass shards floating up toward the ceiling, gorgeous as a splintered rainbow, and a tiny fleck of rainbow nicked Luke right above the eye. Big shiny drops of crimson floated out of his forehead and stained the water as Dad went down with a big muffled *flump* onto the floor.

I was so used to this by now, I hardly noticed, but Luke turned the color of skim milk and ran outside like a skinny monkey hopped up on speed. All I could think was what a nerd he was to jump around like that when all he had to do was lie back and float.

I thought I had adapted pretty well to my underwater world until the day Dad ate Babette. Mom was upstairs floating around in the attic, doing the spring cleaning. Dad was downstairs watching WWF wrestling on TV, well on his way to replacing all the blood in his body with beer. I was making like Mike Nelson on the old *Sea Hunt* reruns, finning languid as a porpoise, doing slow-motion somersaults in my room.

Suddenly Babette gave a screech that was sharp and terrifying even underwater. I swam downstairs in time to see Dad on the floor with Babette pinned underneath him. The water around the bottom of her shorts was turning red. She squirmed away, but Dad caught onto her ankles. Babette began to swim, swimming and screaming, when suddenly Dad's body stiffened and darkened and elongated. Fins sprouted from his spine and belly, and he became a shark, a great white shark with hideous metallic-colored jaws and eyes that looked like they'd been plucked from a deep-frozen corpse. He opened his mouth and sucked Babette in. He gulped her feet and legs down his throat, then her waist, then her just-budding breasts. The water in the living room churned scarlet. Morsels of what looked like albacore tuna but that had to be flesh floated past my face. I couldn't think, couldn't fight, couldn't swim, and Babette's skull was being crushed in like an empty beer can—I saw her eyes, glassy and huge, full of terror as her face slid down into his maw, and then our Father the Great White Shark looked toward me and focused on me his unspeakable hunger, that gluttonous urge to devour and destroy. Without hesitating a moment, I opened a second floor window, took a deep breath, swam outside into the air and—

—fell into the zinia border and the bright, loud outside world of sharp edges and air where I couldn't swim anymore, so I got to my feet and I ran, I ran for my life.

A funny thing about how you change when you've lived underwater. The world of light and air never feels right, never quite works. It's like being E.T. for the rest of your life, always searching for a home you can't quite remember and aren't sure you even liked, but the only place that ever felt "normal."

I spent quite a few years in the air world. Moved into a shelter for runaway kids in Phoenix, finished high school, got a job selling ads for a radio station. With a little effort, I learned not to blow bubbles or try to breaststroke across a room, because people would look at me funny. After a while, you'd never have thought I grew up in any place but the air.

Then one evening, coming home after work, I saw a blond boy with a cigarette and a smirk leaning up against the laundromat on the corner. Hard raptor eyes, a ripe, biteable mouth with just a faint trace of cruelty at the corners, a lump in his Levi's that made my heart melt down all slick and hot and wet into my underpants.

I went home with him.

I wasn't disappointed.

His name was Darius. His apartment was a walk-up on the third floor over a liquor store. The apartment was underwater. He opened the door and swam inside. I swam in behind him. We fucked like fish, in silence and cold-blooded splendor, while the water protected us, kept us separate, a buffer through which hate and fear and violence barely registered. Where blood was beautiful and pain an interesting diversion.

I knew I had come home.

Fear

Guy de Maupassant

We went up on deck after dinner. Before us the Mediterranean lay without a ripple and shimmering in the moonlight. The great ship glided on, casting upward to the star-studded sky a long serpent of black smoke. Behind us the dazzling white water, stirred by the rapid progress of the heavy bark and beaten by the propeller, foamed, seemed to writhe, gave off so much brilliancy that one could have called it boiling moonlight.

There were six or eight of us silent with admiration and gazing toward faraway Africa whither we were going. The commandant, who was smoking a cigar with us, brusquely resumed the conversation begun at dinner.

"Yes, I was afraid then. My ship remained for six hours on that rock, beaten by the wind and with a great hole in the side. Luckily we were picked up toward evening by an English coaler which sighted us."

Then a tall man of sunburned face and grave demeanor, one of those men who have evidently traveled unknown and far-away lands, whose calm eye seems to preserve in its depths something of the foreign scenes it has observed, a man that you are sure is impregnated with courage, spoke for the first time.

"You say, commandant, that you were afraid. I beg to disagree with you. You are in error as to the meaning of the word and the nature of the sensation that you experienced. An energetic man is never afraid in the presence of urgent danger. He is excited, aroused, full of anxiety, but fear is something quite different."

The commandant laughed and answered: "Bah! I assure you that I was afraid."

Then the man of the tanned countenance addressed us deliberately as follows:

"Permit me to explain. Fear—and the boldest men may feel fear—is something horrible, an atrocious sensation, a sort of decomposition of the soul, a terrible spasm of brain and heart, the very memory of which brings a shudder of anguish, but when one is brave he feels it neither under fire nor in the presence of sure death nor in the face of any well-known danger. It springs up under certain abnormal conditions, under certain mysterious influences in the presence of vague peril. Real fear is a sort of reminiscence of fantastic terror of the past. A man who believes in ghosts and imagines he sees a specter in the darkness must feel fear in all its horror.

"As for me I was overwhelmed with fear in broad daylight about ten years ago and again one December night last winter.

"Nevertheless, I have gone through many dangers, many adventures which seemed to promise death. I have often been in battle. I have been left for dead by thieves. In America I was condemned as an insurgent to be hanged, and off the coast of China have been thrown into the sea from the deck of a ship. Each time I thought I was lost I at once decided upon my course of action without regret or weakness.

"That is not fear.

"I have felt it in Africa, and yet it is a child of the north. The sunlight banishes it like the mist. Consider this fact, gentlemen. Among the Orientals life has no value; resignation is natural. The nights are clear and empty of the somber spirit of unrest which haunts the brain in cooler lands. In the Orient panic is known, but not fear.

"Well, then! Here is the incident that befell me in Africa.

"I was crossing the great sands to the south of Onargla. It is one of the most curious districts in the world. You have seen the solid continuous sand of the endless ocean strands. Well, imagine the ocean itself turned to sand in the midst of a storm. Imagine a silent tempest with motionless billows of yellow dust. They are high as mountains, these uneven, varied surges, rising exactly like unchained billows, but still larger, and stratified like watered silk. On this wild, silent, and motionless sea, the consuming rays of the tropical sun are poured pitilessly and directly. You have to climb these streaks of red-hot ash, descend again on the other side, climb again, climb, climb without halt, without repose, without shade. The horses cough, sink to their knees and slide down the sides of these remarkable hills.

"We were a couple of friends followed by eight spahis and four camels with their drivers. We were no longer talking, overcome by heat, fatigue, and a thirst such as had produced this burning desert. Suddenly one of our men uttered a cry. We all halted, surprised by an unsolved phenomenon known only to travelers in these trackless wastes.

120

"Somewhere, near us, in an indeterminable direction, a drum was rolling, the mysterious drum of the sands. It was beating distinctly, now with greater resonance and again feebler, ceasing, then resuming its uncanny roll.

"The Arabs, terrified, stared at one another, and one said in his language: 'Death is upon us.' As he spoke, my companion, my friend, almost a brother, dropped from his horse, falling face downward on the sand, overcome by a sunstroke.

"And for two hours, while I tried in vain to save him, this weird drum filled my ears with its monotonous, intermittent and incomprehensible tone, and I felt lay hold of my bones fear, real fear, hideous fear, in the presence of this beloved corpse, in this hole scorched by the sun, surrounded by four mountains of sand, and two hundred leagues from any French settlement, while echo assailed our ears with this furious drum beat.

"On that day I realized what fear was, but since then I have had another, and still more vivid experience——"

The commandant interrupted the speaker:

"I beg your pardon, but what was the drum?"

The traveler replied:

"I cannot say. No one knows. Our officers are often surprised by this singular noise and attribute it generally to the echo produced by a hail of grains of sand blown by the wind against the dry and brittle leaves of weeds, for it has always been noticed that the phenomenon occurs in proximity to little plants burned by the sun and hard as parchment. This sound seems to have been magnified, multiplied, and swelled beyond measure in its progress through the valleys of sand, and the drum therefore might be considered a sort of sound mirage. Nothing more. But I did not know that until later.

"I shall proceed to my second instance.

"It was last winter, in a forest of the Northeast of France. The sky was so overcast that night came two hours earlier than usual. My guide was a peasant who walked beside me along the narrow road, under the vault of fir trees, through which the wind in its fury howled. Between the treetops, I saw the fleeting clouds, which seemed to hasten as if to escape some object of terror. Sometimes in a fierce gust of wind the whole forest bowed in the same direction with a groan of pain, and a chill laid hold of me, despite my rapid pace and heavy clothing.

"We were to sup and sleep at an old gamekeeper's house not much farther on. I had come out for hunting.

"My guide sometimes raised his eyes and murmured: 'Ugly weather!' Then he told me about the people among whom we were to spend the night. The father had killed a poacher, two years before, and since then had been gloomy and behaved as though haunted by a memory. His two sons were married and lived with him.

"The darkness was profound. I could see nothing before me nor around me and the mass of overhanging interlacing trees rubbed together, filling the night with an incessant whispering. Finally I saw a light and soon my companion was knocking upon a door. Sharp women's voices answered us, then a man's voice, a choking voice, asked, 'Who goes there?' My guide gave his name. We entered and beheld a memorable picture.

"An old man with white hair, wild eyes, and a loaded gun in his hands, stood waiting for us in the middle of the kitchen, while two stalwart youths, armed with axes, guarded the door. In the somber corners I distinguished two women kneeling with faces to the wall.

"Matters were explained, and the old man stood his gun against the wall, at the same time ordering that a room be prepared for me. Then, as the women did not stir: 'Look you, monsieur,' said he, 'two years ago this night I killed a man, and last year he came back to haunt me. I expect him again to-night.'

"Then he added in a tone that made me smile:

"'And so we are somewhat excited.'

"I reassured him as best I could, happy to have arrived on that particular evening and to witness this superstitious terror. I told stories and almost succeeded in calming the whole household.

"Near the fireplace slept an old dog, mustached and almost blind, with his head between his paws, such a dog as reminds you of people you have known.

"Outside, the raging storm was beating against the little house, and suddenly through a small pane of glass, a sort of peep-window placed near the door, I saw in a brilliant flash of lightning a whole mass of trees thrashed by the wind.

"In spite of my efforts, I realized that terror was laying hold of these people, and each time that I ceased to speak, all ears listened for distant sounds. Annoyed at these foolish fears, I was about to retire to my bed, when the old gamekeeper suddenly leaped from his chair, seized his gun and stammered wildly: 'There he is, there he is! I hear him!' The two women again sank upon their knees in the corner and hid their faces, while the sons took up the axes. I was going to try to pacify them once more, when the sleeping dog awakened suddenly and, raising his head and stretching his neck, looked at the fire with his dim eyes and uttered one of those mournful howls which make travelers shudder in the darkness and solitude of the country. All eyes were focused upon him now as he rose on his front feet, as though haunted by a vision, and began to howl at something invisible, unknown, and doubtless horrible, for he was bristling all over. The gamekeeper with livid face cried: 'He scents him! He scents him! He was there when I killed him.' The two women, terrified, began to wail in concert with the dog.

"In spite of myself, cold chills ran down my spine. This vision of the animal at such a time and place, in the midst of these startled people, was something frightful to witness.

"Then for an hour the dog howled without stirring; he howled as though in the anguish of a nightmare; and fear, horrible fear came over me. Fear of what? How can I say? It was fear, and that is all I know.

"We remained motionless and pale, expecting something awful to happen. Our ears were strained and our hearts beat loudly while the slightest noise startled us. Then the beast began to walk around the room, sniffing at the walls and growling constantly. His maneuvers were driving us mad! Then the countryman, who had brought me thither, in a paroxysm of rage, seized the dog, and carrying him to a door, which opened into a small court, thrust him forth.

"The noise was suppressed and we were left plunged in a silence still more terrible. Then suddenly we all started. Someone was gliding along the outside wall toward the forest; then he seemed to be feeling of the door with a trembling hand; then for two minutes nothing was heard and we almost lost our minds. Then he returned, still feeling along the wall, and scratched lightly upon the door as a child might do with his fingernails. Suddenly a face appeared behind the glass of the peep-window, a white face with eyes shining like those of the cat tribe. A sound was heard, an indistinct plaintive murmur.

"Then there was a formidable burst of noise in the kitchen. The old gamekeeper had fired and the two sons at once rushed forward and barricaded the window with the great table, reinforcing it with the buffet.

"I swear to you that at the shock of the gun's discharge, which I did not expect, such an anguish laid hold of my heart, my soul, and my very body that I felt myself about to fall, about to die from fear.

"We remained there until dawn, unable to move, in short, seized by an indescribable numbness of the brain.

"No one dared to remove the barricade until a thin ray of sunlight appeared through a crack in the back room.

"At the base of the wall and under the window, we found the old dog lying dead, his skull shattered by a ball.

"He had escaped from the little court by digging a hole under a fence."

The dark-visaged man became silent, then he added:

"And yet on that night I incurred no danger, but I should rather again pass through all the hours in which I have confronted the most terrible perils than the one minute when that gun was discharged at the bearded head in the window."

Fluffy

Theodore Sturgeon

Ransome lay in the dark and smiled to himself, thinking about his hostess. Ransome was always in demand as a house-guest, purely because of his phenomenal abilities as a raconteur. Said abilities were entirely due to his being so often a house-guest, for it was the terse beauty of his word-pictures of people and their opinions of people that made him the figure he was. And all those clipped ironies had to do with the people he had met last weekend. Staying awhile at the Joneses, he could quietly insinuate the most scandalously hilarious things about the Joneses when he week-ended with the Browns the following fortnight. You think Mr. and Mrs. Jones resented that? Ah, no. You should hear the dirt on the Browns! And so it went, a two-dimensional spiral on the social plane.

This wasn't the Joneses or the Browns, though. This was Mrs. Benedetto's ménage; and to Ransome's somewhat jaded sense of humor, the widow Benedetto was a godsend. She lived in a world of her own, which was apparently set about with quasi-important ancestors and relatives exactly as her living-room was cluttered up with perfectly unmentionable examples of Victorian rococo.

Mrs. Benedetto did not live alone. Far from it. Her very life, to paraphrase the lady herself, was wound about, was caught up in, was owned by and dedicated to her baby. Her baby was her beloved, her little beauty, her too darling my dear, and—so help me—her bobbly wutsi-wutsikins. In himself he was quite a character. He answered to the name of Bubbles, which was inaccurate and offended his dignity. He had been christened Fluffy, but you know how it is with nicknames. He was large and he was sleek, that paragon among animals, a chastened alley-rabbit.

Wonderful things, cats. A cat is the only animal which can live like a parasite and maintain to the utmost its ability to take care of itself. You've heard of little lost dogs, but you never heard of a lost cat. Cats don't get lost, because cats don't belong anywhere. You wouldn't get Mrs. Benedetto to believe that. Mrs. Benedetto never thought of putting Fluffy's devotion to the test by declaring a ten-day moratorium on the canned salmon. If she had, she would have uncovered a sense of honor comparable with that of a bedbug.

Knowing this—Ransome pardoned himself the pun—categorically, Ransome found himself vastly amused. Mrs. Benedetto's ministrations to the phleg-

124

matic Fluffy were positively orgiastic. As he thought of it in detail, he began to feel that perhaps, after all, Fluffy was something of a feline phenomenon. A cat's ears are sensitive organisms; any living being that could abide Mrs. Benedetto's constant flow of conversation from dawn till dark, and then hear it subside in sleep only to be replaced by a nightshift of resounding snores; well, that *was* phenomenal. And Fluffy had stood it for four years. Cats are not renowned for their patience. They have, however, a very fine sense of values. Fluffy was getting something out of it—worth considerably more to him than the discomforts he endured, too, for no cat likes to break even.

He lay still, marvelling at the carrying power of the widow's snores. He knew little of the late Mr. Benedetto, but he gathered now that he had been either a man of saintly patience, a masochist or a deaf-mute. A noise like that from just one stringy throat must be an impossibility, and yet, there it was. Ransome liked to imagine that the woman had calluses on her palate and tonsils, grown there from her conversation, and it was these rasping together that produced the curious dry-leather quality of her snores. He tucked the idea away for future reference. He might use it next week-end. The snores were hardly the gentlest of lullabies, but any sound is soothing if it is repeated often enough.

There is an old story about a lighthouse tender whose lighthouse was equipped with an automatic cannon which fired every fifteen minutes, day and night. One night, when the old man was fast asleep, the gun failed to go off. Three seconds after its stated time, the old fellow was out of his bed and flailing around the room, shouting, "What was that?" And so it was with Ransome.

He couldn't tell whether it was an hour after he had fallen asleep, or whether he had not fallen asleep at all. But he found himself sitting on the edge of the bed, wide awake, straining every nerve for the source of the—what was it?—sound?—that had awakened him. The old house was as quiet as a city morgue after closing time, and he could see nothing in the tall, dark guest-room but the moon-silvered windows and the thick blacknesses that were drapes. Any old damn thing might be hiding behind those drapes, he thought comfortingly. He edged himself back on the bed and quickly snatched his feet off the floor. Not that anything was under the bed, but still—

A white object puffed along the floor, through the moonbeams, toward him. He made no sound, but tensed himself, ready to attack or defend, dodge or retreat. Ransome was by no means an admirable character, but he owed his reputation and therefore his existence to this particular trait, the ability to poise himself, invulnerable to surprise. Try arguing with a man like that sometime.

The white object paused to stare at him out of its yellow-green eyes. It was only Fluffy—Fluffy looking casual and easy-going and not at all in a mood to frighten people. In fact he looked up at Ransome's gradually relaxing bulk and raised a long-haired, quizzical eyebrow, as if he rather enjoyed the man's discomfiture.

Ransome withstood the cat's gaze with suavity, and stretched himself out on the bed with every bit of Fluffy's own easy grace. "Well," he said amusedly, "you gave me a jolt! Weren't you taught to knock before you entered a gentleman's boudoir?"

Fluffy raised a velvet paw and touched it pinkly with his tongue. "Do you take me for a barbarian?" he asked.

Ransome's lids seemed to get heavy, the only sign he ever gave of being taken aback. He didn't believe for a moment that the cat had really spoken, but there was something about the voice he had heard that was more than a little familiar. This was, of course, someone's idea of a joke.

Good God—it had to be a joke!

Well, he had to hear that voice again before he could place it. "You didn't say anything, of course," he told the cat, "but if you did, what was it?"

"You heard me the first time," said the cat, and jumped up on the foot of his bed. Ransome inched back from the animal. "Yes," he said, "I—thought I did." Where on earth had he heard that voice before? "You know," he said, with an attempt at jocularity, "you should, under these circumstances, have written me a note before you knocked."

"I refuse to be burdened with the so-called social amenities," said Fluffy. His coat was spotlessly clean, and he looked like an advertising photograph for eiderdown, but he began to wash carefully. "I don't like you, Ransome."

"Thanks," chuckled Ransome, surprised. "I don't like you either."

"Why?" asked Fluffy.

Ransome told himself silently that he was damned. He had recognized the cat's voice, and it was a credit to his powers of observation that he had. It was his own voice. He held tight to a mind that would begin to reel on slight provocation, and, as usual when bemused, he flung out a smoke-screen of his own variety of glib chatter.

"Reasons for not liking you," he said, "are legion. They are all included in the one phrase—'You are a cat.' "

"I have heard you say that at least twice before," said Fluffy, "except that you have now substituted 'cat' for 'woman.' "

"Your attitude is offensive. Is any given truth any the less true for having been uttered more than once?"

"No," said the cat with equanimity. "But it is just that more clichéd."

Ransome laughed. "Quite aside from the fact that you can talk, I find you most refreshing. No one has ever criticized my particular variety of repartee before."

"No one was ever wise to you before," said the cat. "Why don't you like cats?"

A question like that was, to Ransome, the pressing of a button which released ordered phrases. "Cats," he said oratorically, "are without doubt the most self-centered, ungrateful, hypocritical creatures on this or any other earth. Spawned from a mésalliance between Lilith and Satan—"

Fluffy's eyes widened. "Ah! An antiquarian!" he whispered.

"—they have the worst traits of both. Their best qualities are their beauty of form and of motion, and even these breathe evil. Women are the ficklest of bipeds, but few women are as fickle as, by nature, any cat is. Cats are not true. They are impossibilities, as perfection is impossible. No other living creature moves with utterly perfect grace. Only the dead can so perfectly relax. And nothing—simply nothing at all—transcends a cat's incomparable insincerity."

Fluffy purred.

"Pussy! Sit-by-the-fire-and-sing!" spat Ransome. "Smiling up all toadying and yellow-eyed at the bearers of liver and salmon and catnip! Soft little puffball, bundle of joy, playing with a ball on a string; making children clap their soft hands to see you, while your mean little brain is viciously alight with the pictures your play calls up for you. Bite it to make it bleed; hold it till it all but throttles; lay it down and step about it daintily; prod it with a gentle silken paw until it moves again, and then pounce. Clasp it in your talons then, lift it, roll over with it, sink your cruel teeth into it while you pump out its guts with your hind feet. Ball on a string! Play-actor!"

Fluffy fawned. "To quote you, that is the prettiest piece of emotional clap-trap that these old ears have ever heard. A triumph in studied spontaneity. A symphony in cynicism. A poem in perception. The unqualified—"

Ransome grunted.

He deeply resented this flamboyant theft of all his pet phrases, but his lip twitched nevertheless. The cat was indeed an observant animal.

"—epitome of understatement," Fluffy finished smoothly. "To listen to you, one would think that you would like to slaughter earth's felinity."

"I would," gritted Ransome.

"It would be a favor to us," said the cat. "We would keep ourselves vastly amused, eluding you and laughing at the effort it cost you. Humans lack imagination."

"Superior creature," said Ransome ironically. "Why don't you do away with the human race, if you find us a bore?"

"You think we couldn't?" responded Fluffy. "We can outthink, outrun and outbreed your kind. But why should we? As long as you act as you have for these last few thousand years, feeding us, sheltering us and asking nothing from us but our presence for purposes of admiration—why then, you may remain here."

Ransome guffawed. "Nice of you! But listen—stop your bland discussion of the abstract and tell me some things I want to know. How can you talk, and why did you pick me to talk to?"

Fluffy settled himself. "I shall answer the question Socratically. Socrates was a Greek, and so I shall begin with your last question. What do you do for a living?"

"Why I—I have some investments and a small capital, and the interest—" Ransome stopped, for the first time fumbling for words. Fluffy was nodding knowingly.

"All right, all right. Come clean. You can speak freely."

Ransome grinned. "Well, if you must know—and you seem to—I am a practically permanent house-guest. I have a considerable fund of stories and a flair for telling them; I look presentable and act as if I were a gentleman. I negotiate, at times, small loans—"

"A loan," said Fluffy authoritatively, "is something one intends to repay."

"We'll call them loans," said Ransome airily. "Also, at one time and another, I exact a reasonable fee for certain services rendered—"

"Blackmail," said the cat.

"Don't be crude. All in all, I find life a comfortable and engrossing thing."

"Q. E. D.," said Fluffy triumphantly. "You make your living being scintillant, beautiful to look at. So do I. You help nobody but yourself; you help yourself to anything you want. So do I. No one likes you except those you bleed; everyone admires and envys you. So with me. Get the point?"

"I think so. Cat, you draw a mean parallel. In other words, you consider my behavior catlike."

"Precisely," said Fluffy through his whiskers. "And that is both why and how I can talk with you. You're so close to the feline in everything you do and think; your whole basic philosophy is that of a cat. You have a feline aura about you so intense that it contacts mine; hence we find each other intelligible."

"I don't understand that," said Ransome.

"Neither do I," returned Fluffy. "But there it is. Do you like Mrs. Benedetto?"

"No!" said Ransome immediately and with considerable emphasis. "She is absolutely insufferable. She bores me. She irritates me. She is the only woman in the world who can do both those things to me at the same time. She talks too much. She reads too little. She thinks not at all. Her mind is hysterically hidebound. She has a face like the cover of a book that no one has ever wanted to read. She is built like a pinch-type whiskey bottle that never had any whiskey in it. Her voice is monotonous and unmusical. Her education was insufficient. Her family background is mediocre, she can't cook, and she doesn't brush her teeth often enough."

"My my," said the cat, raising both paws in surprise. "I detect a ring of sincerity in all that. It pleases me. That is exactly the way I have felt for some years. I have never found fault with her cooking, though; she buys special food for me. I am tired of it. I am tired of her. I am tired of her to an almost unbelievable extent. Almost as much as I hate you."

"Me?"

"Of course. You're an imitation. You're a phony. Your birth is against you, Ransome. No animal that sweats and shaves, that opens doors for women, that dresses itself in equally phony imitations of the skins of animals, can achieve the status of a cat. You are presumptuous."

"You're not?"

"I am different. I am a cat, and have a right to do as I please. I disliked you so intensely when I saw you this evening that I made up my mind to kill you."

"Why didn't you? Why—don't you?"

"I couldn't," said the cat coolly. "Not when you sleep like a cat . . . no, I thought of something far more amusing."

"Oh?"

"Oh yes." Fluffy stretched out a foreleg, extended his claws. Ransome noticed subconsciously how long and strong they seemed. The moon had gone its way, and the room was filling with slate-gray light.

"What woke you," said the cat, leaping to the window-sill, "just before I came in?"

"I don't know," said Ransome. "Some little noise, I imagine."

"No indeed," said Fluffy, curling his tail and grinning through his whiskers. "It was the stopping of a noise. Notice how quiet it is?"

It was indeed. There wasn't a sound in the house—oh yes, now he could hear the plodding footsteps of the maid on her way from the kitchen to Mrs. Benedetto's bedroom, and the soft clink of a teacup. But otherwise—suddenly he had it. "The old horse stopped snoring!"

"She did," said the cat. The door across the hall opened, there was the murmur of the maid's voice, a loud crash, the most horrible scream Ransome had ever heard, pounding footsteps rushing down the hall, a more distant scream, silence. Ransome bounced out of bed. "What the hell—"

"Just the maid," said Fluffy, washing between his toes, but keeping the corners of his eyes on Ransome. "She just found Mrs. Benedetto."

"Found—"

"Yes. I tore her throat out."

"Good—God! Why?"

Fluffy poised himself on the window-sill. "So you'd be blamed for it," he said, and laughing nastily, he leaped out and disappeared in the gray morning.

Footprints in the Water

Poppy Z. Brite

Dru sat at his desk for hours, hunching his bony shoulders, never bothering to push the childishly fair hair out of his face, staring until he still saw the roundabout in front of his eyes when he blinked. When he closed his eyes, a bright phantom roundabout swam in the pinpricked phosphorescent darkness behind his eyelids. When he opened them, the roundabout was tauntingly solid and still, a needle stuck in a cork, a folded triangle of paper balanced on the tip of a needle. He squinted at it, stared without blinking, visualized the piece of paper beginning to turn as the author of the book on psychic power had said to do. He willed it to turn. He blew on it to see what it looked like turning, then tried to keep it turning by the force of his mind. He vowed he would not close his eyes again until the paper began to turn. He touched it with the tip of his finger and made it turn, pushed it with his mind, forced his will upon it. It sat still, a pale brown creased slip of paper balanced on the tip of a rusty needle. It would turn. It would turn. It had to turn. He knew he could harness every scrap of power that nestled in every corner of his brain if only he could make that roundabout turn. He pushed at it with his mind. He would not close his eyes. His eyelids were stretched open. His eyeballs were dry, burning. If he blinked now, the lids would scrape against his eyes. The roundabout swam and began to dissolve, fading into a field of light that crept in from the edges of his vision. The slip of paper was absolutely still, stirred by no breath, no current. It would never turn.

In disgust, Dru squeezed his eyes shut and turned his head away. The needle shot up out of the cork and skimmed past his face, just missing his eye, scratching his cheek deeply enough to make him need three stitches. Bright and vital drops of blood spattered the roundabout, soaked into the tipped-over cork.

Dru was fifteen then. After that, he knew, the earth was his.

Nineveh. Pacing through the crop of stones, the only pale thing in a black night. Nineveh always dresses in white now, white silk jacket, white shoes with soft white soles, hair of the palest silver-blond falling like wings of light along his pale, pale cheeks and forehead. He moves through the yard. A brittle slice of moon gives off a cold light, fluorescently harsh, in which Nineveh nearly disappears. He cannot live in harsh light. Harsh light is for the electric white ceilings of morgues. The stones glitter and he moves among them, paler than they are and less sharp-edged. The moonlight paints the stones, runs off them and soaks the ground; at the base of each stone is its black reflection. The mirror image of a gravestone. But there can be no more mirror images. All is lost. Your mirror image only dazzles and sinks as you stare into his eyes, his eyes obscured by black water. The moon is not Nineveh's twin.

He stops and stands over a stone, his eyes hidden under a wing of silvery hair, but perhaps glittering, painted by the moon. His feet are hidden in the black pool at the base of the stone. The shadow melts over his ankles. He stands there until the moon, no longer hard-edged, fades into a delicate yellow-pink sky that becomes whitely hot by midday. The sun bleaches the grass and the stones. It cannot burn Nineveh's pale, pale skin: his cheeks never show a tinge of rose; his lips are translucent. The sunlight, hot as white metal, burns a sheet of fire into the gravestone of his twin brother.

The house of Frixtons, Dru's mother and father, began to be plagued. Records, books, random desirable things appeared on Dru's bed, things he had seen in shops but hadn't been able to stretch his pocket money to buy. His parents made him return them to the shops, but they kept coming back. Water and a slightly thicker, clear substance drooled from the ceiling, but the plaster was always found to be dry to the touch. Often the walls shook with invisible raps, and objects—antique chairs, marble eggs, small Chinese statues—flew about like heavy wingless birds. When Dru told the disturbances to stop, they ceased, but would begin again within a few hours.

Dru still sat hunched at his desk over the roundabout, his hair hanging in his eyes, a long, slender tail of a braid snaking halfway down his back. Sometimes he pulled the braid up over his shoulder and sucked absently at it, staring at the roundabout, staring, willing. He still could not make it turn. He could slam doors without looking at them; he could make an empty glass fill up with water; he could make a small truck roll up a hill and stop, but that tiny, creased piece of paper stayed still. Now and then a breath of air stirred it, and his heart leaped. He turned sixteen, seventeen. His fair hair darkened two shades.

Dru was interviewed, tested in laboratories. He bent spoons, emerged from empty locked rooms. They put a paper-and-cork roundabout in front of him, but he could not make it go around. He produced living snakes out of the air; they were albino, and their eyes were always red. Two books were published, a scholarly journal study, and a glossy paperback with a mystic eye on the front. Both featured the name Dru Frixton prominently on their covers. When Dru was eighteen, he caused a mouse's neck to be broken by an invisible blow. After the mouse had been examined and pronounced dead, Dru restored it to life.

Headlines glared off the newspapers. Nineveh's pale hand rested on the glossy cover of the paperback. His finger sought the address of the publisher, whereby this boy might be found, and hovered indecisively: he could not write the letter.

Nineveh's twin brother Dylan had been dead three years.

Dylan is laughing. The inside of his mouth is dark pink and his eyes are wet and happy. He was never as pale as Nineveh, never as colorless; now he seems a warm and joyous blaze of color, with his bright hair, with his pink laughing mouth. He shakes his head and his mouth opens wider, and he beats his hands on his knees helplessly as he used to do when he couldn't stop laughing, back when he and Nineveh were children. Now he is laughing at himself for laughing so much, and his laughter is breathy and jagged. He must ache from so much laughing. His hand is in the air, messing Nineveh's hair, entwined there. He teases Nineveh for being so neat, so pale, and a smile touches Nineveh's lips. Nineveh's only smiles are for Dylan. They are floating together in water, water as warm and thick as the sea they must have shared before they were born. Dylan's mouth is closed now; open, closed on Nineveh's, wet. And the water is black. Black under an electric white sky. Dylan is being sucked into a glittering black vortex of water. His mouth is open, gulping for air, and Nineveh wants to shout not to do that, not to swallow the water, that the black water is bitter, bilious, poisonous. Nineveh cannot hang on to his brother's hand. Dylan is pulling away, screaming for Nineveh to let go, not to get sucked in with him. He is screaming for Nineveh to save himself. His voice is choked, gulping. Dylan is strangling on the black water. It is seeping into his lungs, covering his head. And with the last semiconscious effort he can make, he pushes Nineveh away from the vortex, wills him with smooth, strong strokes toward the white shore far in the distance. When Nineveh has made it halfway there, Dylan's face floats up in the water beside him, still under the water, under the glossy black film, and Dylan's eyes are open and full of water and his mouth is open, gaping, letting the water fill him—

Nineveh surfaces from the dream screaming, floundering in the white sea of his bed. The sheets twine over his mouth and he spits them out; they are dry. He reaches for Dylan's hand, tries to touch Dylan's face before he remembers that the dream is real. Drowned. Drowned on holiday, far out in the water where no one could see them, not parents, not even God. Nineveh's idea to swim out there with Dylan. Drowned. All Nineveh's smiles, drowned. His love gone into the black water.

Nineveh's trailing hand touches the cover of the glossy paperback on the floor, next to the bed. His fingers pause over it for a moment; then he strokes it gently and takes it into bed with him, flipping through the pages again.

Dru has taken to wearing black eyeliner when he and Nineveh meet. They sit in the coffeeshop, ignoring the afternoon outside. Dru's fingers pull the braid over his shoulder and twist it, play with it. Several times he brings it to his lips and takes it away again. He is dressed in black. Nineveh, luminescently pale in the coffeeshop gloom, stirs sugar into his tea.

Three years, says Dru.

Nineveh is quiet.

Transfer of energy into matter, says Dru. Infusion of the life force into inanimate matter. Transport of an entity from place to place through another dimension. Restoration.

Nineveh will not meet his eyes.

Dru becomes ashamed of his cheap mediumistic babble. He makes Nineveh's teacup slide away, dance on its rim around the edges of the table, and return to rest primly between Nineveh's outstretched hands on the tabletop. Not a drop of tea is spilled.

Nineveh smiles. His lips are very pale. Glory, he says.

It is a night of drooling rain and sluggish, dim flashes of lightning. Dru is in Nineveh's house, in the bed where Dylan once slept. The sheets are white and cold. On the couch, Nineveh pretends to sleep.

Dru is concentrating, willing, pushing his mind. The tip of his braid is in his mouth; he sucks fiercely without being aware of it. Behind Dru's eyelids, the field of stones spreads. The stones glisten with moonlight filtered through clouds and the wetness of the viscous rain. A stirring. A rupturing. Dru gasps; his black-rimmed eyes fly open. Glory wasn't worth the price.

Minutes later, the mud outside the front door sucks with footsteps. Nineveh darts to answer a knock at the door.

Dru huddles under the cold sheet, trying to disappear into the sea of white. The smell is not what he had expected. No corruption, no gray-green fluid rot. A dark, wet smell, this, a smell of earthworms, of soggy leaves disintegrating and falling away under the ground.

I could have loved bones, says Nineveh's voice.

Independent of his brain, Dru's fingers twist the sheet away from his face. Two shapes are in the doorway. No shadows-and-bars framework of bones. A mass far softer and darker. A black smiling mouth with black gums. Somehow he had expected the eyes to be red, like those of the snakes he materialized. But they are dark, softly, deeply dark, far darker than they could be if there were anything in the sockets. The shape shifts in the doorway. Nineveh is holding its hand.

You are glorious, says Nineveh to Dru.

So you are, says another voice, a wet, gulping parody of Nineveh's. The shapes move toward the bed.

How can you harm me? asks Dru. His voice quavers. The tip of his braid slips out of his mouth and streaks his cheek with spit.

Harm you? says the gulping voice. I love you. You gave me back my life.

And mine, says Nineveh.

Two figures slip into the bed, one so pale it seems to fade into the sheets, one dark and seeping. Their hands are touching Dru. His skin is streaked with darkness. On his lips is the taste of rot, soft and dark and sweet. He realizes that he is being kissed.

Dylan's mouth is open now. Open, wet.

The Frenzied Farmhouse

Stefan Grabinski
Translated by Miroslaw Lipinski

I stand in the shimmering light of the sun and bathe in its blood-red streams while the deeply melancholic wind wails so loudly above my head.

I look at the vast, empty steppe, disfigured by weeds, while the mournful crows weep so profusely above me.

I stand alone in the rubble, a homeless, childless father, and despair lives and breathes in the ruins.

Clouds are gathering on the horizon, converging along the slopes. A layer of smoke stings my eyes, soot gets stuck in my throat, cutting into it like a knife. . . .

Yesterday I returned from the institution: I am no longer dangerous. Let it be so. But I swear that anyone, under similar circumstances, would have eventually done the same thing.

I am not sick, nor was I ever sick—even then, yes, even then. What I did was not an aberration but was as necessary as the forces of nature, as necessary as life and death. Without a doubt, what happened occurred as a result of my surroundings. I am not, nor was I ever, a psychopath.

Instead, I was a complete skeptic. I did not adhere to any principle or doctrine; my temperament was not a suggestible one. In this respect, my friend K., whom I had always considered to be extremely superstitious, stood at the opposite extreme. His strange, at times crazy views and theories constantly raised strong opposition on my part, and we quarrelled continually, which resulted in us frequently severing contact with each other for long periods of time. And yet, it appears, he was not mistaken in everything. At least one of his views fulfilled itself with fatal consequence in regard to me—maybe precisely because I came out most fiercely against it, as if sensing that I would serve as an example of its veracity.

K. maintained that in certain places certain events had to occur. In other words, that places exist whose character, nature and spirit await the fulfillment of events connected with them. He called this a "stylistic consequence," though I sensed in all this a pantheistic element. Whatever else he might have understood by this, I did not hold a similar view, and I steered clear of even a hint of any mystery that life could possibly offer.

Yet this concept gave me no peace, and a desire to prove its groundlessness tempted me even after my final parting with K. I would soon satisfy my curiosity, and when that happened, it left me, in my thirtieth year, with the white hair of an old man and broken forever. My flesh crawls at the thought of that unforgettable moment of horror that has crushed me so completely.

I don't know why I still live and for what, and how I can live after all that has happened. Yet I don't believe in punishment; besides, I don't feel guilty. . . .

Even though the setting sun is bleeding and its crimson light gushes over my head, I don't feel at fault.

Yet my agony has been too long and my torment too intense.

Though my blood curdles at the memory of what I've done and my mind is drenched in pools of blood, my forehead is clean and my hands are deathly pale.

Yet my end is overly delayed, and I understand everything too clearly, too keenly. My thoughts have become unusually focused. I am cold like steel, and like steel I cut into my arteries. . . .

The sun flickers and covers me with crimson.

I am dripping with blood, genuine blood. . . .

I was the father of two children, our poor children. Agnes loved them madly, perhaps even more than I. She left them prematurely, dying a couple of years after the birth of our girl.

My Agnes! My sweet Agnes! . . .

Her death upset me greatly. Unable to be pacified by a structured life, I began to travel with my children, who were my only comfort during those times. In order to tear my thoughts away from painful memories, I read a lot, jumping from subject to subject, from books full of licentiousness and brutality to those replete with mysticism and symbolism. And on top of that, I never forgot about K. and his theories.

One day we stopped for a longer time at * with the intention of spending the autumn there. What charmed me most about this bustling, cultural city were its beautiful outlying districts.

My children and I started out for such a district one sunny August Sunday. As we left the city limits, our carriage passed between two rows of poplars, cut across railroad tracks and hurried along fields. We were already a few miles beyond the city, when I noticed, on the right side of the road, in a barren area a small distance away, a rather strange, seemingly uninhabited solitary structure in the midst of a neglected orchard. I stopped the carriage and went to inspect the building.

While I was examining its details, a shrivelled old woman suddenly came out from behind a pile of rubble in front of the building, and, with fear in her eyes, whispered to me:

"Leave this house while there is still time, leave it if you love God and if your life and the lives of your children are dear to you!"

Afterward, she dashed to the side, disappearing in the bent grass.

This incident merely strengthened my curiosity and stimulated a desire to solve the problem—if, in general, one could speak of something like this here. After my return to the city, I already had a plan: I decided to move into the abandoned farmhouse immediately. It seemed to have been created to test the theories of my eccentric friend. If these theories had any validity, then they could be proven here. I was struck, namely, by the aforementioned scene at the ruin, as well as by certain details of the place that corresponded to what K. had once told me.

As to my scepticism, it did not lessen at all. I continually maintained the cold reserve of an objective investigator. Eventually I would shift from this role to that of an actor; but this occurred later and without my awareness.

Meanwhile, the temptation was too great, and the following day, taking everything with me, I moved to the secluded farmstead with my children.

What surprised me was that not even the smallest difficulty arose when I wanted to come to an understanding with the community concerning the lease, and I was allowed to occupy the place at a dirt-cheap price. I had complete freedom and didn't have to concern myself with snooping villagers, as people kept away from my house, and often I saw them superstitiously making a sign of the cross as they passed it in the distance. Thus, weeks would go by and I would not see a human face, unless someone came along the road, a rare occurrence as traffic here had already died down for several years, moving a couple of kilometers to the west.

Therefore, I began my observations.

What intrigued one, above all, was the farmhouse itself. The structure did not at first glance differentiate itself from the typical farmsteads that one came across in the suburbs or on country roads, and yet. . . .

As a result of a certain proportional arrangement, it appeared more nar-

136

row toward the bottom, so that the base, in comparison to the highest point, was amazingly small and thin; the roof, with its upper section, simply weighed down the foundation. The entire building was comparable to a human freak who bends under the weight of an abnormally large head. This construction gave the building a brutal character, like that of the strong bullying the weak. I never understood how this structure could have arisen and how it could ever stand.

The minuscule windows made a similar impression in comparison to the walls. Squeezed into the thick walls, they were almost lost in their grip. At least that's the way they looked from the outside; though, as I found out eventually, the windows were not really so narrow, and they let in as much light as, under normal circumstances, windows much larger.

Added to this, was the predatory look of a ruin tainted with a multitude of holes and gouges. Exposed bricks dotted the outside walls like splattered pustules of congealed gore.

The interior presented a no less sorry state. Consisting of three rooms, it was full of cracks and holes, through which the wind freely slipped in, rolling into the half-collapsed hearth, swirling the ashes there and pounding the smoke hole.

The corner room, however, where I frequently spent my time, proved to be the most bizarre. Lichens, formed on one of the walls where the plaster had fallen off, had created a puzzling image.

From the beginning I wasn't able to get a proper fix on it. I copied it down roughly on a piece of paper and got a fairly strange picture, or rather, a fragment of a picture.

At the bottom of the wall, right above the floor, were the contours of a child's legs. One leg, bent at the knee, had the foot resting against the other leg, which was stiffened tensely toward the ground. The backwardly inclining body was depicted as far as the chest—the rest was missing.

Small, frail arms were raised in a helpless gesture of self-defense.

The entire form, which could have represented the body of a several-year-old boy, had a corpse-like inertia to it.

Somewhat higher, in the direction of the non-existing head, two hands were clenched about something . . . unknown. The space between the fingers was empty. These hands, however, belonged to someone else: they were considerably bigger and veined. To whom they belonged, the picture didn't tell. The arms stopped short above the elbow, disappearing somewhere on the white background of the wall.

This image, as well as the entire room, had a special illumination during sunny days. The sun's rays that fell through the windows refracted in such a way that the light split into blood-red whorls, bathing one of the rafters; then, it seemed, thick drops of blood dripped from it into a pool below.

I explained this unpleasant phenomenon on an optical illusion and the particular chemical composition of the glass, which was otherwise clean and completely transparent.

After exploring this abode, I passed to the orchard, or garden, which formed with it a single, inseparable and stylistic whole.

It was very old and neglected. Luxuriant thickets had enclosed it for many years from the outside, jealously guarding its mysterious interior. Slender, prematurely decayed young trees rotted away amidst sickly rampant grass and thorn apples. They had not been overthrown by winds, which didn't have access here, but by the slow, malignant sucking of their sap by older trees. And so they had dried up like skeletons, their leaves a dry eczema. Those younger trees that had not yet been reached by the sucking branches of the old colossuses were withering in shadows created by a brutal overgrowth.

In one place a young alder leaned out from the spans of a neighboring oak, and with a yearning for liberation, was wallowing in the sun; a muscular branch had overtaken it, however, burying itself into the still-soft core and breaking through to the other side. The young alder's roots hung in tatters, its fibers and grains were twisted in forceful contractions. The young tree was dying. . . .

Elsewhere, lipped polypores covered shoots with poisonous kisses, taking them in with the milk of forgetfulness. Some type of hideous, blood-swelled parasites ensnared juvenile stems and then, swallowing, strangled them. Elongated sycamore boughs rested their weight on barely robust seedlings, pressing them to the ground. Under this excessive pressure, the seedlings either bent sorrowfully to the subsoil or gave birth to monstrous, odd scrubs. . . .

The orchard was never quiet. There was always some twittering and disruptive howling. With an unpleasant uproar, birds wailed strange things about the shrubs; they wandered from branch to branch, they nestled in the hollows of trees. Sometimes hellish chases began about the entire garden, and a dangerous battle of life and death ensued. Parents went after their young. In futile endeavors, the poor chicks, unaccustomed to flight, smashed themselves against trees, broke their wings, tore their feathers, until fatigued and bleeding, they sank to the ground; then their persecutors struck from above with their beaks until no sign remained of the mutilated bodies.

This strange orchard possessed my children with instinctive fear, and they avoided it, confining their play to the front of the cottage. I, on the contrary, almost never left it. I studied its degenerate manifestations and penetrated ever deeper into its secrets. Somehow, imperceptibly, I allowed myself to be drawn into its enchanted circle and become tangled up in the swarm of crime and madness. I wasn't able to follow the progression of the spiritual process I went through—everything developed almost unconsciously. Only today are its more subtle phases opening up before me.

In the beginning, the atmosphere of the farmhouse and its surroundings was so repugnant to me that had it not been for my desire to uncover the truth, I would have gladly left. With time, I got used to the environment; it even became indispensable to me: I became familiar with it. The place began to transform me to its tone, and I succumbed to a law I would call "psychic mimicry"—I conformed to the background. I allowed myself to become brutalized.

This transformation found its clearest expression in the sympathy I started to feel for the elements of force and compulsion as I surveyed the character of the farmhouse and what was occurring around it. I became wicked and vicious. With villainous pleasure, I helped birds persecute their young, the trees torture shoots. Human intelligence was terribly blunted at that time and turned into a desire for mindless destruction.

Months passed in this manner, while my madness increased and assumed greater dissolute forms. Along with me, the entire environment accelerated in frenzy, as if expecting a resolution soon. Even I had to have sensed this, for I remember how I would, near the end, stare for hours at the chimerical fragment on the wall, anticipating in its completion an answer to the problem of the farmhouse. Finally, I knew only this: I had to unravel something and make something clear—but what was happening to me, I was unaware of.

Concurrent with these symptoms, my relationship with my children changed dramatically. I would not say that I stopped loving them—on the contrary; but my love transformed itself into something horrible, into a joy at maltreating the objects of my feelings: I began to beat my children.

Terrified, astonished at the severity of a once gentle father, they ran away from me, hiding in corners. I remember those pathetic, bright little eyes flooded with tears, a silent grievance deep inside. I was roused only once. It happened when my poor son groaned out in the midst of being beaten:

"Daddy, why are you hitting me?"

I choked up with tears, but the next day repeated my beatings. . . .

One day I woke up in a considerably more peaceful frame of mind and feeling reborn, as if after a long, feverish sleep. I clearly understood the situation: to remain longer in this secluded spot would be dangerous. That's why I decided to leave the next day, giving up further research. This was the last impulse of the will.

That evening, on the eve of our departure, I was sitting with my children in the house; all of us were gazing wistfully at the setting sun that trailed over the wheat fields.

The sun was bloody and sad. Cold coppery streaks of autumn light, wrapped in the chill of evening, lay on the fields in plaintive agony. . . .

In the orchard it suddenly grew quiet; soporific ash-trees murmured, crickets chirped. The world waited with bated breath. A pregnant moment. . . .

I slowly turned my glance to the puzzle on the wall.

"This has to be completed; yes, it has to be completed. . . ."

I am swept away by affection. I am warm, and my eyes are full of tears.

"Jerzy! Come here, child!"

He sits on my knees, trustful, grateful. He must have sensed the sincerity in my voice. My hands stroke my son's blond head . . . and slowly encircle his neck. . . .

"Daddy! Don't squeeze so strongly! Da-a-ad—"

He wheezes.

My second child, terrified, runs quickly to the door.

"I'll get away from you!"

I cast aside Jerzy's dead body, catch up to my daughter and smash her head against a beam. . . .

Blood mingles with the sun's crimson light.

I stare at the bottom of the wall, where lies my son. He is pressed against the picture, completing it exactly. His body does not go beyond its contours even one inch.

I stare and recognize the hands that no longer encircle an empty space, but are strangling his neck. They are my own. . . .

The clanging caravan of insane thoughts has ridden over and crunched the dead to vanish in the storm. . . .

The problem of the farmhouse was solved.

Gobble, Gobble!

William F. Nolan

Right now I'm a young, healthy female human being. I haven't always been human (didn't start that way) and I probably won't stay human for too much longer, but I'm having fun these days so I'll stick with it for a while. Not that I'm from outer space or anything, but in human terms I'm an alien organism.

What I am is a feeder.

I don't feed very often—maybe once every six months or so—but when I do get hungry it takes a lot to satisfy me. But that's cool. I can always find things to eat.

And each time I feed, I change. But I'll get to that. Guess my changing can seem kind of icky, kind of a grossout, but it's really cool. Hey, I *know* I use the word cool too much, okay? But so do all of my friends.

If I sound like a dippy high school chick writing in her school notebook or something, well, that's what I am right now. That's the latest me. Sixteen and pretty. I mean, not an absolute knockout, not like some cheerleaders I know with super boobs and real cute butts, but pretty enough to make the guys go for me. Sharp looking. And I dress sharp. Plenty of boys ask me out. To dances and parties and stuff. (And to a lot of dumb movies!)

Of course, I don't eat what my friends do: gooky burgers with fries (heavy on the ketchup), jelly doughnuts and candy and junk like that. Most of my girlfriends scarf down Big Macs and pizza like mad, and a lot of them drink beer. That's sicko stuff as far as I'm concerned. Sure, I can *fake* eating junk like that (and I have to) but there's no real food value in any of it. I go for basics. I seem to get extra hungry around the holidays, especially Thanksgiving (gobble, gobble!).

My pattern as a feeder has been pretty consistent. I select a town, and a species, move in, live with them for six months or so, do my feeding (yum, yum) and then move on to another place. (I really dig France. Had me some good eating in Paris, you bet!)

I've been a bird and an insect (beetle) and a dog and an ant (African) and once I was a male housecat named Ari. Since I was "fixed" (you know, like no balls!) I didn't go around chasing females. I was real skinny, with all the little knobs on my backbone sticking out. Vet said I was hyper-thyroid and I had to swallow pills with my catfood. Real drag.

You're mixed up, right? About my feeding. Look, I didn't say I never ate "normal" food when I go between feedings; it's just that I don't *like* it and have to fake liking it.

After a few months I start to get bored, no matter what change I've made. But by the time the boredom really sets in I'm usually like *starved*. So I feed, change, and move on. (Usually eat more than once, when I begin a feeding, but I'll get to that later.)

I guess you figure I'm a creep, huh? Just because I'm different. I'm with my girlfriends at a movie and this guy in a ski mask chops off a nice lady's head with an axe and we go, ugh, that's *gross*. So I guess, to you, I'm in the same bag. A gross old feeder.

Old. That's an interesting word. How old am I? Jeez, who the freak knows? I've been around a long time, that's for sure. Feeders just keep going. We don't age like you do because we keep adapting and we're never the same long enough to get old. So I don't really have any idea of how old I am. Or care, for that matter.

Right now (existential time), as Judy Ann Singer, I'm sixteen. And I live in Lawton City, Illinois. In a green, quiet little town of three thousand. And I go to Lawton High where I'm president of the Drama Club (I'm good at acting roles, been doing it all my life).

Being female again is a blast (as my pals say). Last three times I fed I was a male and I like being female better. Everything is *softer*, somehow. It's a silky feeling, being female. Males have hard edges; they live in a rougher world. But I'd freak out, having to stay one or the other. We feeders have a choice.

Well, I guess I've done enough rambling. Since this is what I call an alien record then I'd better start recording, eh? Instead of just blah, blah, blah on paper. Get down to the important stuff. The nitty-gritty.

Okay, then. I'll start by telling you about Rick. He's my latest boyfriend. Been going steady with him for just over three months. Do we *do* it? Sure. He's cool. Safe sex, right? Anyhow . . .

Rick's on the football team. Not captain yet, but he could be next year. And he also plays basketball and baseball. All-round jock. I go to a *lot* of games, take my word!

Football is cool, with all the guys bashing away at each other. Blood sport. Basketball's okay, too, but baseball's a drag. The pits. Bore-ing.

One of our fun things to do is go to the drive-in on Fridays in Rick's yellow Mustang convertible. We put the top up (for privacy) and just make out like crazy for most of the dumb movie. Unless it's a Clint Eastwood. When he's Dirty Harry. I always have Rick cool down when big Clint's doing his thing. And he doesn't mind, really. He digs Clint. That's when we actually *watch* the movie.

So it's Friday night and Rick asks me to go to the drive-in with him to a horror flick called *The Bloodsuckers* about a bunch of vampires on Fifth Avenue in New York who suck blood out of rich people who live in million-dollar townhouses or condos or whatever.

I dig horror flicks because I can do a lot of screaming and Rick thinks it's neat, my screaming and grabbing at him. Actually, vampires don't scare me. First of all, they don't exist and if they did they'd be real easy to fight off with garlic and crosses (two crossed tablespoons will do) and holy water and all like that. But I *do* like to watch the stakes get hammered into their chests (spurt, spurt!). That's neat.

So off we go to the Big Clock Drive-In to see this new bloodsucker movie, and right away Rick gets real attentive. You know, he's hot to trot. We haven't made it in about two weeks and he's all steamed up about the idea of being with me in my tight black-leather outfit. Boots and the whole bit. Rick's a freak for black leather. Wears it himself when he rides his Honda. (Yeah, he's a biker, too. Macho man!)

They know us at the Big Clock. We go there a lot (no other drive-ins in Lawton) and the ticket guys know us and when they see me in some of my sexy outfits they kind of drool, you know. ("Way to go, Ricko! Way to go.")

Rick keeps the Mustang real cherry. Wax job every other Sunday. It's a classic, and he treats it like one. Like he treats me. (Thinks he knows me. Oh, wow, does he ever *not* know me!)

It's dark now and we've got the top up and the black metal speaker's inside so we can hear the soundtrack, and we're eating popcorn. (Well, *he* is; I'm faking.)

Then Rick goes, "Today my parents told me they want me to go to UCLA in California for college. Wha'dya think?"

And I go, "It's a neat school. And I hear that L.A. is neat, too."

"My ole man went to UCLA so he wants me to go there." Rick leans in close. "Will you go with me?"

"In a year? You kidding? I never plan ahead that far."

"Hey, I don't want to go unless you do."

"I'll think about it. Yeah. Maybe I'll go to California. Who knows?" I giggle. "Quit being so serious. We're here to see some vampires, right?"

And he goes, "Right," and gives me a squeeze as the screen noise starts and the previews come on.

It's really dark now, the kind of deep dark you get in an Illinois summer, and pretty soon the chief bloodsucker is sinking his fangs into the throat of some blonde rich bitch who owns a lot of Texas oil and wears a ton of diamonds around the house.

That's when I realize I haven't fed in over six months, when this ham actor is scarfing away at the blonde's neck.

Hungry. It always hits me sudden like this. I never plan a feeding, it just happens. Like pow! One second I'm doing my act, as a human or whatever, and the next I'm like into my feeding mode.

When the time comes to feed, look out world! The hunger just *consumes* me, like a wave washing over a shore. And right then, watching the rich blonde getting fanged by this chief vampire . . . I . . . am . . . suddenly . . . *starved!*

Rick goes, "You look funny, Jude."

And I go, "Yeah? Funny how?"

"Your eyes. The way you're staring at me. Kind of super intense. What's with you?"

"It's time to eat is all. I'm hungry. Gobble, gobble!"

"Eat? We ate before we came here, remember? At the break I'll get some chili dogs an' Cokes, like always. How come all of a sudden you're hungry?"

"It's been almost six and a half months," I tell him.

He goes, "Huh?" Real surprised at what I just said.

Which is when I went for him. Like that shark went for the swimmer at the beginning of *Jaws*.

I've got a lot of interior strength. All feeders do. We can summon it up when we need it. Like now. And my teeth are sharp.

But this is for the record, so I don't want to mix you up about what happened to Rick.

I'm Rick now. I mean, after we left the drive-in I was behind the wheel of the Mustang and Judy Ann Singer was inside me, all part of the change, okay?

Let me try and explain. I don't feed like you'd think I would. I don't just go around gobbling up people and things the way girls at the school do Big Macs. That's not how a feeder operates.

We absorb.

We go inside and eat out the whole center of our victims (if you want to call them that), kind of leaving them hollow but still looking and acting ordinary on the outside.

And we usually go for two or three at once. At least I do. You know, I told you how it takes a lot to satisfy me once I really settle down to feed after maybe half a year. I'm starved, for sure.

So Rick wasn't enough. He was like the first course of the meal. I was still real hungry.

His parents were home, watching TV, when I parked the Mustang outside their house and used Rick's key to get in.

They're in the living room, watching a Late Night movie about some lady doctor who was saving babies in Calcutta.

I go, "Hi!" giving them a smile.

They make me wait for the next commercial before they'll talk to me.

"You're home early, son," goes Rick's father.

And his mother goes, "Yes, where's Judy?"

I shrug. "She's dead."

They go all pale.

"My God!" says Rick's old man, standing up from the couch. "Did you have an accident?"

"Nope." I walk over and switch off the TV. "No accident. She just isn't around anymore."

"You're not making sense," says Rick's mother.

I smile at her. I walk toward her. I'm strong and I'm fast and I'm *still* very hungry.

"Gobble, gobble!" I say.

Graven Images

William Browning Spencer

Well, what have we got today?" the man said, seating himself in the chair, his back to the window so that he was silhouetted against the twilight.

"Back already?" Benny said. One of the things Benny hated about the man was his heartiness, the slick, salesman's boom of his voice. "I thought I had seen the last of you for a while."

"I can leave if you'd like," the man said. He had the blackmailer's upper hand, and he knew it.

"Okay, okay," Benny said, reaching over to the nightstand and opening the drawer. He took the photographs out and spread them on the bed.

The man leaned forward. "We could use some more light," he said.

Benny walked to the door and flipped a switch. The room brightened, and he walked back as the man lifted one of the photographs and held it up.

"Tell me about this one," the man said.

Benny took the photo and sat on the edge of the bed. His shoulders sagged. "Well, that's my daughter Lucy. She was nine years old or thereabouts. And in the wagon is our dog, Zenith. She would haul that dog all over town, dress him up, go rolling down a hill with him clutched to her chest. Zenith doted on Lucy and so he let her do most anything. I guess men and dogs are alike in that respect. They'll tolerate some rough handling from the women they love."

"The house in the background," the man said. "Yours?"

"Well, we lived there. That's on Cedar Avenue. We rented it for three years in the early fifties. Our landlord lived next door, an old Italian man who didn't speak much English and always wore a suit. They sold the house shortly after he hanged himself, so we had to move. I remember it was his brother who came to our door and told us the news. I didn't know who he was. There was this small, tearful man in suspenders standing at my door. He was wearing a white shirt with the sleeves rolled up, and he looked real frail, and the first words he spoke were: 'My brother he is suicided with the chair.' And I didn't know what he was talking about or who he was, but Eileen came up behind me—she always saw straight to a person's heart—and walked quick past me and took him in her arms and he went to sobbing on her shoulder while she held him."

Benny sighed. "She was good with people, Eileen."

"I'll take it," the man said, standing up.

Benny blinked. "What?"

"The photo. This one will do," the man said.

That was in the summer—at Brodin Memorial Hospital. In November, Benny woke in his own home in the middle of the night to relieve his bladder, and he heard a sound in the kitchen.

It was the man again, seated at the kitchen table. He had poured himself a glass of milk.

"Just make yourself at home," Benny said.

The man smiled broadly. "Oh, I'm comfortable most anywhere," the man said.

"I bet," Benny said. He knew why the man had come. Without saying a word, he left the kitchen and returned with the photographs. He tossed them on the kitchen table.

The man finished his glass of milk, and tapped one of the photos.

"That's Lucy graduating from high school," Benny said. "What's to say? The day was hot, I remember that. She's wearing a bathing suit under that black gown. So were a lot of the kids. They went . . . look, you want it, you got it." Benny handed the photo to the man.

"They went to the beach," the man said.

"Yeah." Benny stood up. "You got your photo. It's two in the morning, and I'm going back to bed. You know the way out."

The man shook his head. "No. I'm not interested in that one. This one, perhaps. That's your wife, isn't it? And the young man, who's he?"

"That's Danny Miller. He played clarinet in a band. And that's Eileen, all right. She wasn't my wife then. Hey, maybe you want this picture. It's yours."

"I'll take it," the man said.

"You son of a bitch."

"Well, I'm not a fool. She looks quite luminous in this picture, breathless, and the lights in her hair . . . you kissed her for the first time that night, or I can't read a photo."

"Take it and get out," Benny said.

As the man walked toward the door, Benny shouted at his back: "I don't need a photograph to call up that night. There ain't so goddam many perfect moments in a man's life that they get clouded with time. Ask me what perfume she wore. Ask me what the band played or how the champagne tasted or what the night air felt like or how the back of her neck surprised my hand that first time I kissed her."

The man didn't turn around. He walked down the hall and out the door without a word.

*   *   *

A year later, the week before Christmas, Benny was watching the rain fall, a grim, flat attack on the hospital's parking lot. The man came up behind him.

"You gave me a start," Benny said.

The man apologized. He seemed to have put on weight since Benny had last seen him. He seemed, in fact, tired, disheartened.

"Well," Benny said. "Here's what I've got."

This time the man sat on the bed next to Benny, and Benny showed him the photographs.

"This is Aunt Kate," Benny said. "She made the best fudge brownies. And she loved to sing. She would sing 'Amazing Grace' while washing the dishes."

"No," the man said. He was shaking his head. He stood up and thumbed through the photos in his hands. "You insult me. These are not the goods. These are not . . . these are not your photographs."

Benny chuckled. "You are sharp. I got to give you that, you are sharp."

The man threw the photos on the floor. "In all our dealings, we have been above board. I am disappointed in you."

"Those are Lou Himmel's photographs. Perhaps you recognized them. That really is Aunt Kate. Lou's Aunt Kate, not mine, Lou being dead, I figured he wouldn't mind."

"I wish to see your photographs."

Benny shrugged. "I burned them."

"You know what this means."

Now Benny stood up. "Yeah, it means I don't give a goddam. Now get out of here."

The man sighed and looked around the room as though seeking a reasonable audience. "I'll complete the paperwork, then."

"Whatever lights your fire," Benny said. "Whatever honks your horn."

The storm raged outside. Benny was watching the six o'clock news when Nurse Cable—everyone on the ward called her Julie—entered. She was a pretty young woman with black hair, cut rather severely, and a lush Georgia accent. She took Benny's blood pressure. "How are you doing?" she asked.

"Poorly," Benny said. "I'm an old man, and anyone my age who says he is feeling great has simply forgotten what it means to feel great. I'm going to die, you know."

"Oh, I don't think so. These tests are perfectly routine. We all die someday, but I don't think you'll die today, Mr. Levin."

"Oh, I don't mind," Benny said. "I'm sick of the game, frankly. What sort of a game is it when your opponent can look at the cards when he deals the hands? I'm beginning to think that Lucy had the best of it."

147

"Lucy?"

"My daughter."

"I didn't know you had a daughter."

"I did. She drowned."

"I'm sorry."

"Well, that's the point, isn't it? We are all sorry for what's inevitable. Piece by piece it is taken away from us. We appear to bargain, but it all comes to the same thing in the end. Death and condolences."

Julie fluffed the old man's pillow. "You are in a morbid frame of mind tonight, Mr. Levin, I'll say that. I'm not sure I can absorb so much philosophy this evening. There are three very sick people on the ward, and some less sick ones that need a bit of coddling."

Benny chuckled. "That's the spirit. Youth has no business mucking with philosophy and despair."

"Not during work hours anyway," Julie said. She left.

It was nearly ten when she returned. Benny was sitting up in bed looking at a photograph.

"He missed this one," Benny said. "He held it right in his hand, but he thought it was one of Lou's."

"I'm afraid I don't understand," Julie said. She had to go. There were meds to disperse, I.V.'s to regulate.

He handed the photo to her. "It doesn't look like much, I suppose."

It didn't. The photo was black and white, and showed a motel looking like a grey shoe box on its side. There were some vague mountains in the background hoarding rain clouds, and you could almost hear the hiss of tires on a wet highway. A sign said: Parkway Motel. The camera, a cheap box-camera judging by the quality of the image, had been jarred during the exposure, tilting and blurring everything.

"Eileen hugged me just as I snapped it," Benny said. Benny laughed and took the photo back. "Oh, I don't expect you to admire the beauty of the photo. Its charms are all internal. That was our honeymoon. We stayed there the first day on our way down to Key West."

Julie said she had been to Key West a year ago with her parents, and the conversation turned to the despicable nature of land developers and the apathy of the powerful. Then Julie had to get back to work.

Benny watched the eleven o'clock news that evening and then turned the TV off and went into the bathroom. He turned the shower on, brushed his teeth.

When Benny turned back to the shower, the man was standing under the fall of water, his dark suit soaked, his hair plastered against his forehead, his small eyes grim and veiled by the twin waterfalls pouring over the bony ridge of his brow.

148

"Son of a bitch!" Benny said, stepping backward as though bitten. He slipped then, reached out for a handhold, and caught only a draped towel that came away from its rung, falling with him. The back of his head slammed against the tiled floor.

"Are you all right?" Eileen asked. Her face was inches from his. The shower was still on, the pouring water making a mist behind her head.

"I slipped," Benny said. "Wow." Eileen helped him up, an arm around his waist. She was still fully dressed, a dark dress with white dots, and she was soaked. Benny was suddenly aware of his nakedness. He had never been naked with Eileen, and he felt awkward and ungainly. The throb at the back of his head was insignificant.

Eileen dried him and hustled him under the covers. "Are you okay?" she asked, leaning over him.

"I'm fine," he said, reaching to touch her cheek. "But you are soaked."

"That's easily remedied," his new bride said, and she shucked her dress in one effortless motion, the wet garment rising over her head, her slip following. She walked toward him, glowing, her crooked smile enriched by the fullness of her hips.

"I wish I had a photograph of you right now," Benny said.

"Not on your life, fellow," she said, crawling under the covers. "You'll have to settle for a snapshot of this motel."

And the shock of her body, its full length falling upon him, clicked the shutter of his heart.

The Greater Festival of Masks

Thomas Ligotti

There are only a few houses in the district where Noss begins his excursions. Nonetheless, they are spaced in such a way that suggests some provision has been made to accommodate a greater number of them, like a garden from which certain growths have been removed or have yet to appear. It even seems to Noss that these hypothetical houses, the ones now absent, may at some point change places with those which can be seen, in order to enrich the lapses in the landscape and give the visible a rest within nullity. And of these houses now stretching high or spreading low there will remain nothing to be said, for they will have entered the empty spaces, which are merely blank faces waiting to gain features. Such are the declining days of the festival, when the old and the new, the real and the imaginary, truth and deception, all join in the masquerade.

But even at this stage of the festival some have yet to take a large enough interest in tradition to visit one of the shops of costumes and masks. Until recently Noss was among this group, for reasons neither he nor anyone else could clearly explain. Now, however, he is on his way to a shop whose every shelf is crammed and flowing over, even at this late stage of the festival, with costumes and masks. In the course of his little journey, Noss keeps watching as buildings become more numerous, enough to make a street, many narrow streets, a town. He also observes numerous indications of the festival season. These signs are sometimes subtle, sometimes blatant in nature. For instance, not a few doors have been kept ajar, even throughout the night, and dim lights are left burning in empty rooms. On the other hand, someone has ostentatiously scattered a bunch of filthy rags in a certain street, shredded rags that are easily disturbed by the wind and twist gaily about. But there are many other gestures of festive abandonment: a hat, all style mangled out of it, has been jammed into the space where a board is missing in a high fence; a poster stuck to a crumbling wall has been diagonally torn in half, leaving a scrap of face fluttering at its edges; and into strange pathways of caprice revelers will go, but to have *shorn* themselves in doorways, to have littered the shadows with such wiry clippings and tumbling fluff. Reliquiae of the hatless, the faceless, the tediously groomed. And Noss passes it all by with no more, if no less, than a glance.

His attention appears more sharply awakened as he approaches the center of the town, where the houses, the shops, the fences, the walls are more, much more . . . close. There seems barely enough space for a few stars to squeeze their bristling light between the roofs and towers above, and the outsized moon—not a familiar face in this neighborhood—must suffer to be seen only as a fuzzy anonymous glow mirrored in silvery windows. The streets are more tightly strung here, and a single one may have several names compressed into it from end to end. Some of the names may be credited less to deliberate planning, or even the quirks of local history, than to an apparent need for the superfluous, as if a street sloughed off its name every so often like an old skin, the extra ones insuring that it would not go completely nameless. Perhaps a similar need could explain why the buildings in this district exhibit so many pointless embellishments: doors which are elaborately decorated yet will not budge in their frames; massive shutters covering blank walls behind them; enticing balconies, well-railed and promising in their views, but without any means of entrance; stairways that enter dark niches . . . and a dead end. These structural adornments are mysterious indulgences in an area so pressed for room that even shadows must be shared. And so must other things. Backyards, for example, where a few fires still burn, the last of the festival pyres. For in this part of town the season is still at its peak, or at least the signs of its termination have yet to appear. Perhaps revelers hereabouts are still nudging each other in corners, hinting at preposterous things, coughing in the middle of jokes. Here the festival is not dead. For the delirium of this rare celebration does not radiate out from the center of things, but seeps inward from remote margins. Thus, the festival may have begun in an isolated hovel at the edge of town, if not in some lonely residence in the woods beyond. In any case, its agitations have now reached the heart of this dim region, and Noss has finally resolved to visit one of the many shops of costumes and masks.

A steep stairway leads him to a shrunken platform of a porch, and a little slot of a door puts him inside the shop. And indeed its shelves *are* crammed and flowing over with costumes and masks. The shelves are also very dark and mouth-like, stuffed into silence by the wardrobes and faces of dreams. Noss pulls at a mask that is over-hanging the edge of one shelf—a dozen fall down upon him. Backing away from the avalanche of false faces, he looks at the sardonically grinning one in his hand.

"Excellent choice," says the shopkeeper, who steps out from behind a long counter in the rearguard of shadows. "Put it on and let's see. Yes, my gracious, this is excellent. You see how your entire face is well-covered, from the hairline to just beneath the chin and no farther. And at the sides it clings snugly. It doesn't pinch, am I right?" The mask nods in agreement. "Good, that's how it should be. Your ears are unobstructed—you have very nice ones, by the way—while the mask holds on to the sides of the head. It is comfortable, yet secure enough to stay put and not fall off in the heat of activity. You'll see, after a while you won't even know you're wearing it! The holes for the eyes, nostrils, and mouth are perfectly placed for your features; no natural function is inhibited, that is a must. And it looks so good on you, especially up close, though I'm sure also at a distance. Go stand over there in the moonlight. Yes, it was made for you, what do you say? I'm sorry, what?"

Noss walks back toward the shopkeeper and removes the mask.

"I said alright, I suppose I'll take this one."

"Fine, there's no question about it. Now let me show you some of the other ones, just a few steps this way."

The shopkeeper pulls something down from a high shelf and places it in his customer's hands. What Noss now holds is another mask, but one that somehow seems to be . . . impractical. While the other mask possessed every virtue of conformity with its wearer's face, this mask is neglectful of such advantages. Its surface forms a strange mass of bulges and depressions which appear unaccommodating at best, possibly pain-inflicting. And it is so much heavier than the first one.

"No," says Noss, handing back the mask, "I believe the other will do."

The shopkeeper looks as if he is at a loss for words. He stares at Noss for many moments before saying: "May I ask a personal question? Have you lived, how shall I say this, *here* all your life?"

The shopkeeper is now gesturing beyond the thick glass of the shop's windows.

Noss shakes his head in reply.

"Well, then there's no rush. Don't make any hasty decisions. Stay around the shop and think it over, there's still time. In fact, it would be a favor to me. I have to go out for a while, you see, and if you could keep an eye on things I would greatly appreciate it. You'll do it, then? Good. And don't worry," he says, taking a large hat from a peg that poked out of the wall, "I'll be back in no time, no time at all. If someone pays us a visit, just do what you can for them," he shouts before closing the front door behind him.

Now alone, Noss takes a closer look at those outlandish masks the shop-keeper had just shown him. While differing in design, as any good assortment of masks must, they all share the same impracticalities of weight and shape, as well as having some very oddly placed apertures for ventilation, and too many of them. Outlandish indeed! Noss gives these new masks back to the shelves from which they came, and he holds on tightly to the one that the shopkeeper had said was so perfect for him, so practical in every way. After a vaguely explor-atory shuffle about the shop, Noss finds a stool behind the long counter and there falls asleep.

It seems only a few moments later that he is awakened by some sound or other. Collecting his wits, he gazes around the dark shop, as if searching for the source of hidden voices which are calling to him. Then the sound returns, a soft thudding sound behind him and far off into the shadowy rooms at the rear of the shop. Hopping down from the stool, Noss passes through a narrow doorway, descends a brief flight of stairs, passes through another doorway, ascends an-other brief flight of stairs, walks down a short and very low hallway, and at last arrives at the back door. It rumbles again once or twice.

"Just do what you can for them," Noss remembers. But he looks uneasy. On the other side of that door there is only a tiny plot of ground surrounded by a high fence.

"Why don't you come around the front?" he shouts through the door. But there is no reply, only a request.

"Please bring five of those masks to the other side of the fence. That's where we are now. There's a fire, you'll see us. Well, can you do this or not?"

Noss leans his head into the shadows by the wall: one side of his face is now in darkness while the other is indistinct, blurred by a strange glare which is only an impostor of true light. "Give me a moment, I'll meet you there," he finally replies. "Did you hear me?"

There is no response from the other side. Noss turns the door handle, which is unexpectedly warm, and through a thread-like crack peers out into the backyard. There is nothing to be seen except a square of blackness surrounded by the tall wooden slabs of the fence, and a few thin branches twisting against a pale sky. But whatever signs of pranksterism Noss perceives or is able to fabricate to himself, there is no defying the traditions of the festival, even if one can claim to have merely adopted this town and its seasonal practices, however *rare* they may be. For innocence and excuses are not harmonious with the spirit of this fabulously infrequent occasion. Therefore, Noss retrieves the masks and brings them to the rear door of the shop. Cautiously, he steps out.

When he reaches the far end of the yard—a much greater distance from the shop than it had seemed—he sees a faint glow of fire through the cracks in the fence. There is a small door with clumsy black hinges and only a hole for a handle. Setting the five masks aside for a moment, Noss squats down and peers through the hole. On the other side of the fence is a dark yard exactly like the one on his side, save for the fire burning upon the ground. Gathered around the blaze are several figures—five, perhaps four—with hunched shoulders and spines curving toward the light of the flames. They are all wearing masks which at first seem securely fitted to their faces. But, one by one, these masks appear to loosen and slip down, as if each is losing hold upon its wearer. Finally, one of the figures pulls his off completely and tosses it into the fire, where it curls and shrinks into a wad of bubbling blackness. The others follow this action when their time comes. Relieved of their masks, the figures resume their shrugging stance. But the light of the fire now shines on four, yes four, smooth and faceless faces.

"These are the wrong ones, you little idiot," says someone who is standing in the shadows by the fence. And Noss can only stare dumbly as a hand snatches up the masks and draws them into the darkness. "We have no more use for *these!*" the voice shouts.

Noss runs in retreat toward the shop, the five masks striking his narrow back and falling face-up on the ground. For he has gained a glimpse of the speaker in the shadows and now understands why *those* masks are no good to them now.

Once inside the shop, Noss leans upon the long counter to catch his breath. Then he looks up and sees that the shopkeeper has returned.

"There were some masks I brought out to the fence. They were the wrong ones," he says to the shopkeeper.

"No trouble at all," the other replies. "I'll see that the right ones are delivered. Don't worry, there's still time. And how about you, then?"

"Me?"

"And the masks, I mean."

"Oh, I'm sorry to have bothered you in the first place. It's not at all what I thought. . . . That is, maybe I should just—"

"Nonsense! You can't leave now, you see. Let me take care of everything.

153

Listen to me, I want you to go to a place where they know how to handle cases like this, at times like this. You're not the only one who is a little frightened tonight. It's right around the corner, this—no, *that* way, and across the street. It's a tall gray building, but it hasn't been there very long so watch you don't miss it. And you have to go down some stairs around the side. Now will you please follow my advice?"

Noss nods obediently.

"Good, you won't be sorry. Now go straight there. Don't stop for anyone or anything. And here, don't forget these," the shopkeeper reminds Noss, handing him an unmatching pair of masks. "Good luck!"

Though there doesn't seem to be anyone or anything to stop for, Noss does stop once or twice and dead in his tracks, as if someone behind him has just called his name. Then he thoughtfully caresses his chin and his smooth cheeks; he also touches other parts of his face, frantically, before proceeding toward the tall gray building. By the time he reaches the stairway at the side of the building, he cannot keep his hands off himself. Finally Noss puts on one of the masks—the sardonically grinning one. But somehow it no longer fits him the way it once did. It keeps slipping, little by little, as he descends the stairs, which look worn down by countless footsteps, bowed in the middle by the invisible tonnage of time. Yet Noss remembers the shopkeeper saying that this place hadn't been here very long.

The room at the bottom, which Noss now enters, also looks very old and is very . . . quiet. At this late stage of the festival the room is crowded with occupants who do nothing but sit silently in the shadows, with a face here and there reflecting the dull light. These faces are horribly simple; they have no expression at all, or very slight expressions and ones that are strange. But they are finding their way back, little by little, to a familiar land of faces. And the process, if the ear listens closely, is not an entirely silent one. Perhaps this is how a garden would sound if it could be heard growing in the dead of night. It is that soft creaking of new faces breaking through old flesh. And they are growing very nicely. At length, with a torpid solemnity, Noss removes the old mask and tosses it away. It falls to the floor and lies there grinning in the dim glow of that room, fixed in an expression that, in days to come, many will find strange and wonder at.

For the old festival of masks has ended, so that a greater festival may begin. And of the old time nothing will be said, because nothing will be known. But the old masks, false souls, will find something to remember, and perhaps they will speak of those days when they are alone behind doors that do not open, or in the darkness at the summit of stairways leading nowhere.

The Green Scarab

Willis Knapp Jones

S o that's the kind of fellow you are, Gil, killing me with curiosity when I let you smear paint all over my room. When are you going to let me see your picture?" Manchester nodded toward the easel that faced the window.

"This morning—no, not yet!" the artist shouted, but he was too late. Manchester had already thrown off the cloth covering the painting.

"Oh, pretty nice! Who is she, Gil?" he exclaimed.

"I don't know." Burgess was slipping off his street coat.

"Don't know?"

"No."

"I mean, who was the model?"

The artist was silent for a minute. "Maybe I can make you understand. After our four years of college together, you ought to know me fairly well. I haven't any model. You see, Dick, for about a year I have been seeing this girl in a hazy sort of way. Awhile ago—a month ago yesterday, to be exact—she suddenly became so vivid that I felt I must paint her."

"Sort of a dream girl, eh? But what's this? The King Tut craze has struck your lady, apparently. It's clever. The little spot of green exactly balances the mass of shadow above."

"What do you mean?" Burgess was putting on his sketching jacket without paying much attention to the picture.

"Why, this necklace and the pendant."

"She hasn't any necklace." He came across the room, the coat dangling from one arm. As he saw the painting, he stopped in astonishment, then rubbed his eyes. "Well, I'll be darned!" he gasped. "Where did that thing come from?"

"How should I know?" It was Manchester's turn to be surprized.

"But what is it? Looks like one of those bugs you brought back from Egypt last year."

"Certainly. It's a scarab. But I didn't know you were interested in Egyptology."

"I'm not, particularly. The only time I go through your museum is when you are around to explain things."

"Then where did you get the details for the scarab? You're wasting your

155

talents in this line. You ought to be a miniature painter, for I can even read the inscription: 'REDET-N-PTAH,' eldest royal daughter. Where did you get it?"

"I don't know," replied Burgess in a daze. "I never saw the thing before. Last night I was having the devil's own time with the neck of that girl. It was either too flat or it looked as if she had a swelling. Finally I gave up and went home intending to finish it before you saw it. Now look at it. I'm sure I don't know who did it."

"Probably the scrubwoman painted it while she was resting," observed Manchester dryly.

The canvas was filled by a life-size portrait of a young girl, a brunette whose eyes had something magnetic about them. In fact, the whole picture gave the impression that the painted girl was about to step, Galatea-like, into life. To one looking more attentively, the face seemed to be that of a sleeper suddenly and rudely awakened.

But it was not the face which held their attention. They were occupied with a chain which the picture girl wore about her neck, a golden chain from which dangled a green oval pendant.

Burgess stared at the chain as if he doubted his own eyes. He stretched out his finger and touched the dry color. "Well, I'll be darned!" he ejaculated.

"Are you trying to tell me you don't know who painted that scarab?" his friend demanded.

"I never saw it before you told me about it."

"Of course I believe you, implicitly! Any other stories you want to unload? My credulity is unlimited."

"But is it really there?" The artist was struggling into his coat now.

"Are you crazy, Gil?"

"It's been here again, then."

"What's been here?"

"The *thing.*"

"The what?"

"I don't know what it is. Once I was having difficulties with one of the eyes, trying to make it match the other. It wouldn't come out right. In the morning I found that someone had corrected it. I searched the studio then. Only through your room or through the museum can anyone get in here. I know you are not an artist. This isn't the kind of thing a person would do as a joke. It gave me the shivers. Sometimes as I work, I feel a presence behind me. Once, when I was doing this drapery, I know someone had hold of my hand, guiding the brush. I couldn't go on. I ran from the room, and when I came back—look at that fold! Nobody but a great artist could have done it."

"Which of the *Arabian Nights* stories have you been reading lately, Gil?" Manchester gazed with real alarm at his chum.

"I know it sounds like a fairy tale. I wish I could think it was. Do you remember the night I slept here? You wanted me to come in with you. Well, that night I arranged an alarm to go off at the slightest movement of the cloth covering the picture. Then I slept in the corner. About 2 it went off. I lit the light. The cloth was just as I had left it, but the air had a touch of the most curious perfume. Tell me that I'm crazy, that I'm dreaming, or explain it somehow. I'm just about frantic."

"Did you ever consider the idea that you yourself painted those parts that you mention?"

"I? I wasn't here. Don't you think I'd know if I did them?"

"I'm not sure. By the way, do those noises from the unpacking room of the museum next door annoy you while you are working?"

"No, I never hear them after I begin."

"That proves my point." Manchester gestured with his finger. "When you start painting, you forget everything. Why, I don't believe you even know you are painting. I came in here yesterday afternoon and you were sitting there scowling and talking to yourself. You didn't answer me when I spoke to you. You artist chaps are so temperamental that you almost go into trances when you are working."

"Of course I saw you. I was worrying about this neck, and you said some silly thing that didn't deserve to be answered. Besides, even if I agreed about the trance, can the sage explain how I could paint an Egyptian scarab, a thing I know nothing about, and do it so accurately that you can read the inscription?"

"That's just the point that sticks me. But your painting is done and ready for the exposition. You need a rest. Why don't you learn something of Egyptology? That stuff that we've had in the storeroom for a couple of weeks is to be unpacked after supper. Dr. Sheridan, the man who directed the excavations, will be in charge. And if you want wild stories, I'll stir up the Egyptian excavators."

"Thanks, I'll be there."

"All right, Gil, and if you can think up any additional details to make your story more convincing, I'll be glad to hear them." And with this Parthian shot, Manchester went out.

For a long time, Burgess stared at the door through which his friend had disappeared. Then he turned to his canvas and picked up his palette. After one glance at it, he rushed to call Manchester back. He had the final proof of the truth of his story, and he was all agog with eagerness to impart the information to his friend. Of all the colors on his palette, there was not the slightest trace of that peculiar blue-green of the scarab.

That evening when Gilbert Burgess entered the receiving room of the museum he was faced by pile upon pile of boxes and crates. Three of the foremost Egyptian scholars of their day were unpacking the treasures. Manchester introduced him to them as an artist, and whispered that they were going to unwrap one of the mummies a little later. Burgess made himself as unobtrusive as possible and listened to their talk, most of which he did not in the least understand.

When they had uncrated six mummy cases, Dr. Sheridan turned to the visitor. "We want to show the public just how a mummy is preserved. Would you like to choose the one? It makes no difference to us. Here is one of about the Sixth Dynasty, perhaps 4000 B.C. This one is of the Eighteenth, two thousand years later. Here is a recent one, 1000 B.C. He is a king and might be most interesting."

Burgess pointed to one. "Who is that?" he asked.

"I don't know, exactly; somebody in the royal family, perhaps a queen or her daughter. But it was before the Middle Kingdom, and they had not learned the most perfect embalming."

"Yet, I'd like to see that one, if you don't mind." He could not tell what strange impulse made him go against the suggestions of the authority.

"Just as you like. We'll open the Sleeping Beauty, then," and the men started on the seals of the heavy case. The priest who had prepared her for burial had evidently meant to preserve the body forever. It was some time before the mummy proper could be lifted out.

"Your choice was evidently a beauty," laughed Dr. Sheridan, holding up a small cube of stone. "Here is her vanity case. It was in this mortar that she ground up the green malachite which she put under her eyes. And look at the scarabs!" He caught up several. "Indeed your choice was good. Usually the outside wrapping is poor, but this is fine stuff." Indeed it was, unusually soft, and creamy yellow from age. The bandages were about eight inches wide.

The other men, who had seen too many mummies unwrapped to be interested, worked on other packages. Only Dr. Sheridan and his assistant and Burgess witnessed the removal of the burial garb of this princess nearly five thousand years dead. They worked in silence, unwinding the linen.

Finally Dr. Sheridan pointed to the head. "One more turn around will uncover the face. That was a superstition the Egyptians had. Sometimes in their elaborate ceremonies, the feet would be wrapped a month before the head. Only when they were ready to put the body into the case would they cover the mouth. Ah! There's her Highness!" Her face was entirely visible.

Where had Burgess seen that face before? It was like none of his acquaintances. Then with startling suddenness it came over him. The girl, except that she had an olive complexion, was identical with his painting!

"Take off some more," he commanded. "I must see the scarab around her neck."

"Oh, there'll be no more scarabs, Mr. Burgess. Nothing now but the

158

opening on the left side, made by the embalmers. This is too early in Egyptian history for the pectoral scarab. That did not come until—What?"

His exclamation came with the appearance, after the removal of more bandage, of just the scarab of which Burgess had spoken.

"This is very unusual," Dr. Sheridan was muttering to himself. But Burgess had forgotten him. "Dick!" he shouted; "come quick!"

Urged to haste by his tone, Manchester hurried over.

"Well?" Burgess waited.

"It is! It's the image of your painting, Gil!" burst from the astounded man. "But this makes it worse than ever!"

The others clamored to hear the details. When Burgess had finished, they were as puzzled as Manchester had been. "If you had not proved part of your story," observed Dr. Sheridan, "I should be inclined to call you a second Munchausen. Where is the picture?"

"The other side of that wall, in the studio. I'd like to bring it over tomorrow when the light's good, simply to see how nearly alike they are."

Manchester, who had been examining the pectoral scarab, looked up. "You remember, Gil, I translated your scarab this morning. If this is not the identical inscription, I don't known Egyptian. When you bring it over tomorrow you'll see."

Dr. Sheridan was the only one in the museum the next morning when Burgess brought in the canvas. The receiving room did not seem so mysterious now with light creeping into every corner. Burgess looked for the mummy.

"It's moved to the Egyptian Room," explained the scientist, interpreting his questioning glance. "Bring your picture there."

The Egyptian Room was fitted like a huge tomb. Draperies and vessels adorned the walls. In the corner stood several mummy cases. One of them Burgess remembered seeing the night before. "All this is new," Dr. Sheridan explained. "They've been here only a couple of weeks."

"Can you tell me how long, exactly?" the artist asked, struck by a sudden idea.

"No, but I can find out. I just got back myself. But there's your princess."

In the center of the room a standard held the body of the partially unwrapped princess, upon her forehead the gold uræus of nobility.

There was something weird about the atmosphere. Burgess sniffed. "What's the odor?" he asked. "It's like the perfume in my studio the night I almost discovered the painter of my picture."

"It is the spice the Egyptians used for embalming. The body remained in it for seventy days. It is natron, mostly. But let's see the picture."

Except for the costume and the difference of complexion, point for point they were identical. There was even a similarity in the arrangement of the hair. It was a puzzle that the Egyptian authority could not solve.

While they were talking, one of the assistants came in to ask about the disposition of some of the material, and Dr. Sheridan excused himself. "I'll be back in a moment," he said.

Once alone, Burgess made a more careful comparison of the painting and the princess, even taking measurements. The more he contrasted, the more he was sure that they were the same. "Well, it's got me!" he ejaculated, sitting on a mummy case to await the return of his friend.

The air seemed very heavy. He rubbed his eyes. He felt drowzy. He looked at the canvas leaning against the side of the tomb, and then at the dead princess.

Suddenly he started up. Was she breathing? There was surely a slight movement of her breast.

Finally, like a sleeper awaking, she stirred. An instant later she opened her eyes. Her face had the suddenly-awakened look of the girl in the painting. Her listless gaze wandered around the room, settling with a start upon the portrait. She sat up and stared at the canvas. Then she shook her head as if angry. The presence of the artist seemed to puzzle her for a moment, but she waved her hand with an imperious gesture. Her meaning was very evident, though Burgess could not understand why the one who was responsible for it should want the picture destroyed. He laid it to a woman's whim, and shook his head, smiling as he refused.

The princess suddenly arose and, taking no notice of him, glided to one of the mummy cases. The linen windings had somehow disappeared, and she was dressed in a long flame-colored robe. Remembering the difficulty the men had had in opening a case, Burgess was astonished at the ease with which she turned back the cover. A few blocks of color fell to the floor as a young man stepped out, carrying in his hand several artists' brushes.

Burgess gave a gasp of surprize. If the princess resembled the portrait, the young man was a perfect duplicate of himself, several shades darker.

The young Egyptian seemed momentarily astonished at seeing Burgess, but before he could do anything, the princess touched her companion's arm, and they talked earnestly together. Several times they looked at the canvas. Finally the Egyptian nodded assent, holding out his brushes. He then took a step toward the portrait. Burgess, however, had other ideas about the destruction of his exposition picture, and rushed to intercept him.

The lady stretched her hand toward him. To Burgess, it seemed as if a claw of ice had clutched his heart. He stood still. His breath came in gasps. The room was making dizzying circles. His head pained. Then all grew blank before him.

160

Suddenly the princess struck him and shouted in his ear, "Wake up! You must have been asleep for half an hour." Or was it Manchester?

Burgess opened his eyes. The first thing he saw was the princess lying on the standard as she had been placed. "I know who painted that picture!" the artist shouted. "Look in that case."

"That reminds me," Manchester remarked as they were breaking the seals. "Sheridan asked me to tell you that these mummies came a month ago, day before yesterday. He's sorry he couldn't come back, but some of the men are in trouble about a vase that came broken, and he has to help them."

"But a month ago," mused Burgess; "the very day I began my picture. Do you see any connection?"

They opened the stone lid.

"Why, he was an artist, Gil," Manchester exclaimed as several color pots rolled out. "And of the same period as the princess. You and he, if you really believe he helped you, did a good job. I'm interested in seeing how the portrait compares with the original."

He looked around. The canvas was lying face down on the floor. Manchester lifted the picture. His face grew white and he dropped it again.

Burgess sprang to catch the painting. Then he, too, uttered a cry as he set up the huge frame. It was absolutely blank, except that in the canvas, a third of the way from the top, was a small, accurate reproduction of a little green scarab.

The Grim Passenger

Donald Edward Keyhoe

Because of the ridicule generally attaching itself to anyone admitting the possibility of the supernatural, I have until now refrained from setting forth the details of certain events which apparently led to a widely known and regretted disaster in mid-Atlantic several years ago. But the opening of the tomb of King Tut-Ankh-Amen and the attending publicity brought the matter back to my mind, and I shall offer it to the public to believe or not as it chooses. Even now I do not admit that there was anything supernatural about it; that there was something strange and terrible about it no one will deny.

For obvious reasons, certain names have been omitted or changed, but with these exceptions I have related everything exactly as it occurred. In my position as secretary to the president of the B——— Museum of London, I have charge of the sending out of expeditions in search of valuable specimens, ancient and otherwise. For some time during the year of 19— we had been on the trail of a mummy-case supposed to contain the dead body of a certain king whose name is to be found in history of centuries long past. Creditable information having at last been obtained as to the location of the tomb containing the mummy, I sent for a man whose name may be remembered even now as that of a famous museum supplier, a man who was well versed in such work and who was thoroughly dependable because of his matter-of-fact and common-sense nature. I shall call him Thomas D. Stevenson. Acquainting him with all the facts at my disposal, I gave him an order for such equipment as he would need and sufficient funds to cover all expenses of the trip. Two days later he left London for a spot not very far from that at which the present activities are taking place. Less publicity was given the matter, however, than at the present time because of reasons which concerned a slight difficulty in regard to the law.

After reaching his destination, Stevenson encountered obstacles in obtaining guides and other natives to help in the excavation. They were finally obtained, however, and after considerable effort the Englishman and his party located the long-lost tomb; within a few days the main entrance to the great vault was partially uncovered and preparations were made for opening it, when the natives suddenly drew off to one side, muttering and casting awestruck looks at the door, which bore in ancient language an inscription that had been cut into the metal that formed the outer part. When Stevenson peremptorily ordered them back to their work, the head native approached him, tremblingly, and pointed out a little, dried-up old man who seemed to hold a position of importance among the others.

"Master," he said, "he has told us the meaning of the words and we are afraid."

"You fools!" Stevenson stormed. "What is there on that door to frighten men living hundreds of years after it was erected?"

"It says," answered the cowed native, "that he who sleeps there has left his spirit to guard his body and that any who touch it shall die."

"Damned nonsense!" roared the other, and went on trying to drive the men back to their work.

But neither threats, cajolery nor offers of higher pay would move them. The little old man had frightened them with his translation of the words on the door, and the inbred superstitions of generations did the rest.

Seeking a full solution of the problem, Stevenson asked the old native for a translation of the warning, and this is what he heard: "Turn ye away lest ye become as I. On them who heed not my warning shall my curse fall, and it shall so be until my body rests again undisturbed."

At the bottom of these words was a seal bearing the profile of a crowned head. Even Stevenson felt a vague uneasiness and misgiving at this, but he

162

shook off his doubts with a laugh at his momentary weakness, and again attempted to force the men to the work. Finding them determinedly against it, he dismissed them and set about getting other aid, which was no small matter in that out-of-the-way place.

Finally a nondescript outfit of drifters and ne'er-do-wells was assembled and the vault was opened. To the relief of Stevenson and the disappointment of the men, there was very little treasure found, although this is now believed to have been in a second vault near by. The much desired mummy-case, however, lay in state on a terraced stonework, covered with symbols and signs which later proved to be an almost complete history of the life of the dead king. On closer examination Stevenson was startled to find reproduced in the center of the case the identical warning that had been seen on the door. For a moment the Englishman had an almost overpowering impulse to drop the whole thing and return to England and the museum empty-handed; he quickly stifled this and curtly gave the order that started the body of the dead monarch on its journey far from his wished-for resting place to the bustling, unmindful city of London.

Then began the journey to the nearest seaport. Singularly restless and impatient for one of his stolid nature, Stevenson rushed his men, already tired from work, until fever set in and delayed him while he attended to the sick. Instead of yielding to rest and recognized remedies, the fever took a more malignant form, and before the party reached their port five men had succumbed. The others, a curious fear having descended upon them, cursed the mummy, Stevenson and the expedition heartily and impartially, nor did they lose any time in severing their connection with the outfit, once the mummy-case was on board ship and their pay was in their pockets.

Stevenson, his mind wearied and in a turmoil from the trying happenings of the preceding weeks, turned in at his hotel hoping to enjoy a good rest, but instead tossed and turned throughout most of the night. Arising early, preparatory to embarking on his ship, he was astonished to find a local police official awaiting him.

"What is it?" demanded the Englishman bruskly, short-tempered from worry and lack of sleep.

"Sir, it is that we wish you to identify some bodies," answered the smiling, suave official, as if he were suggesting a stroll in the cool of the morning.

"Bodies?" gasped the other. "Whose—what bodies?"

"Sir, they are five men who are said to have come with you from Z——— yesterday. Last night they became very drunk in one of the places down on the old docks, and started a brawl in which several were hurt and three of your party were killed; the other two attempted escape when our men arrived, and were fatally wounded before they submitted to arrest. One died at once and the other but a few minutes ago."

It was with an effort that Stevenson shook off the depression that this news brought to him, and complied with the police regulations in identifying the dead men and giving his rather slight knowledge of each one. This done, he hurried back to his hotel and at once proceeded to his ship, endeavoring all the time to shake off a foreboding that had begun to be a very part of his mind. Insistently the thought hammered itself into his every waking moment and brought him sinister dreams, that of all the men who had entered the forbidden tomb and had defied the warning that had protected the dead king for centuries, he alone still lived. Again and again he told himself that the deaths were accidental and in the course of natural events. Fever was a common thing, and scores of men were killed in just such quarrels as had occurred on the preceding night. Then before him would come a vision of the mummy-case with its silent warning, and his bolstered-up confidence and courage would fall like a house of cards. He had been guiltier than the men who helped him in violating that warning. How long would *he* escape the vengeance of the power that had taken the lives of the rest?

Already unwell from his efforts in the desert, Stevenson rapidly became worse, until by the time his ship had reached England he was a mental and physical wreck. Then it was that we of the museum heard of his plight and went to his aid, removing him to a hospital and the mummy-case to the basement of the museum.

At the bedside of the sick man several of the lesser officials of the institution listened to his story, but when he related the details of the horrors that had attended every moment since the removal of the dead king from the tomb, they raised their eyebrows and nodded to each other in expression of their belief that the heat and the solitude had been a little too much for him. Little attention was paid then, when at the close of his narrative Stevenson raised himself up on one shoulder and, his eyes gleaming in a fierce, unnatural way, cried out, "Don't let them keep the mummy! Have him taken back! Take him back before it is too late!" An attendant rushed up quickly, and soothingly pushed the sick man back into his bed, while the others withdrew, hardly giving a second thought to the words of the man they had just left, feeling only a natural sorrow at the affliction which his long stay in the tropics had brought him.

Two days later Stevenson died, raving about the mummy and uttering warnings to the effect that it should be taken back to the tomb. His words were ascribed to delirium, and no attention was paid to them at the time.

Then the mummy-case was brought to the central exhibition room and placed within a case especially prepared for it. While someone was studying the symbols on the case the inscription was noted and its meaning found by referring to our records of ancient languages. But the thing was taken more as a joke by everyone in the museum than as anything of serious meaning.

And then, without farther warning, tragedy invaded the museum itself. For the very next morning the night watchman was found dead directly in front of the mummy-case, his eyes wide open, with a look of mortal terror in them, while his face was rigid and drawn with fear, as if the man had died while looking on something so dreadful that his mind had instantly become crazed even as his overtaxed heart burst from horror.

No reason could be assigned, and after a searching investigation a verdict was reached by the coroner's jury that death was due "to failure of the heart, the unnatural pose in which the dead man was found to be due to his fear at dying, being added to by the darkness and silence in which he was when the attack seized him." This was most unsatisfactory, but no other explanation was forthcoming.

Hardly had we recovered from this shock when, early one afternoon, I was startled to hear the sound of a fall, and rushing into the president's room, I found him lying on the floor, breathing his last.

As I raised his head up from the floor, the dying man gasped out, "Send back the mummy—send him back to—"

Before he could finish the words, he sank back limply. A quickly summoned doctor pronounced his death due to a nervous disorder that had affected the heart.

That ended the stay of the mummy in the museum. Before another day we had it carried to the basement, although it was with difficulty that we could prevail on anyone to go near the now greatly feared body. Arrangements were under way for sending it back to its former resting place when we received a call from Basil G. Stoddard, the representative of an American museum of no small fame. Mr. Stoddard wished to see the cause of the mysterious events, which had by that time been well discussed in the newspapers. He was insistent, and I finally gave in to the extent of allowing him to enter the room where we had locked up the mummy-case. The upshot of it all was that he decided to buy it from us, although we told him every known happening that had been attributed to its baleful influence.

"I do not believe any of the deaths were caused by this dried-up old body," he said. "As for the warning, it was only a natural desire to keep robbers from prying into his tomb that caused him to take such a course. Knowing the superstitious nature of the people, he saw that such a caution would be his best protection. The value to me and to the institution I represent is in the mummy itself and the case, which has certain unusual figures worked into it."

"Well, I shall be glad to be rid of it," I returned. "I do not like to believe that there is anything connecting the deaths and the mummy itself which cannot be explained by psychology of fear, but at any rate we shall all breathe more easily when the thing is no longer under our care."

165

Just one week later Stoddard sailed for New York. With flags flying bravely, bands playing inspiring music, and hundreds of passengers waving good-bye to their friends on shore, the then largest ship of her class slowly dropped down stream and commenced her maiden voyage. With not a thought of anything but a wonderful journey before them on that floating palace, the passengers began their customary plans for shortening the time and making it most agreeable.

There was but one exception to this. One passenger lay deep in the hold, unmoving, apparently an inanimate, though rather gruesome, bit of cargo. But who knows but that there radiated from that dead body a terrible malevolence which was destined to bring death and disaster to the gay crowds that thronged the decks above? Who knows but that this malevolent influence—all-powerful because of centuries through which it had existed and grown—perhaps penetrated to the minds of those who guided the destinies of the great ship? That it did not give to the captain of the vessel an all-consuming desire to break the highest records for speed to the American port? And that this desire would render him careless of danger, of reports of drifting icebergs, causing him to drive his ship farther and farther into peril?

Who knows but that this influence (if such there was), vicious, unpitying and ruthless in its desire for vengeance at its violated warning, perhaps swerved each mind to its purpose, even reaching up to the lookout in the crow's nest and making him slow in seeing that vast floating danger which loomed up in the path of the ship carrying those precious souls, until the colossal mass of ice crashed into the oncoming ship, crushing it like a shell and dooming many of those on board to death or separation from loved ones and the others to terrible memories that will live with them forever?

And perhaps as that once proud ship settled below the waves to its final resting place the dead king exulted in fiendish triumph as he went down to rule over the world of dead about him in that greatest of tombs, the steamship *Titanic*.

Have You Seen Me?

Nancy Holder

Have you seen me?

"C'mon, Dane," Chris urged as she hurried toward the post office doors. Air-conditioning frosted the glass panes with condensation—or maybe it was steam; man, it was blistering out today. Her skin seemed to lift off her bones and ripple dry and itchy; there was no sweat on Dane's grubby little fingers, wrapped inside her grip. California desert heat, no moisture, no quarter.

"C'mon, hon," she said.

"C'mon, hon," he parroted, and she glanced back at him in mild surprise. He repeated everything these days. You had to watch yourself. Two years old, and he knew how to say "fuck it." But not when to.

"You're a silly-billy." She gave his hand a playful shake. He grinned up at her. Looked so like his dad, with his white-blond hair, his three-corner, deep blue eyes, the dimples. So cute, though he was in his terrible two's—which, to be honest, weren't really so terrible. Chris had a sense of humor, and she supposed that gave her an edge over the young mothers she hung out with. Debi, Kathy, Silvia—they were all going wacko, like they'd caught it from each other or something. Just couldn't hack it, they claimed; there was lots of grabbing the nippers and going out roaming, getting out of their small, baking houses and into the malls and the four-plex, where it was cool and things were more interesting.

Chris did that kind of thing, too—got out—but she didn't mind staying home with Dane. They had an air-conditioner in the front room, and at night she and Dane and Tommy—when he was home; Tommy was a trucker—they'd lie on the roll-out couch with a light sheet on top and sleep in each other's arms, all three of them. How could life be so perfect? Contrary to everyone's expectations, she and Tommy were doing great: getting married right out of high school had worked after all. Believe it, dude.

And also contrary, the airhead cheerleader (she knew that's what they all thought) was the world's best mother. The best. Even her own mother was amazed.

"Oh, thank you," Chris said, as a man in a pair of faded jeans and a T-shirt held the glass door open for her. She scooted Dane in, and came in after. Her son looked at the man and said, "Oh, thank you," and the two adults laughed.

Then she saw the long line and murmured, "Shit," and Dane said, "Shit," and the man laughed once more as he left the frigid haven.

It was a very long line, and she didn't have anything to occupy Dane with; he would certainly get bored before it was their turn to buy stamps and mailing tape. Maybe she should hunt for the envelope the mailman had left in the box and buy stamps through him; and she could get some tape at the grocery store, where she was going next.

She debated, shuffling forward as the line moved ahead and one of the postal clerks shouted, "Next!" It was nice and cool inside, and last time they hadn't had the right kind of tape at the store; and she'd be hanged if she knew where that envelope was.

"Next!"

And the line was moving pretty fast. She put her hands on Dane's shoulders and he idly bounced himself against her knee caps. Both of them had shorts on; now, in the post office, she was getting goosebumps.

"You okay, little guy?" she asked him.

"Next!"

"Next," Dane said. With a lopsided smile, Chris tousled his hair. He was such a knucklehead. He certainly was becoming his own person.

"Next!" And they all shuffled forward. Chris rested her arm on the waist-high table to her right. All kinds of forms for Express Mail stood in blue boxes, and pens attached to the table with chains, and brochures advertising stamp collecting sets. And in the middle of the table, encased in plastic, was an 8½ by 11-inch flyer. It was labeled "Have You Seen Me?" and it consisted of photographs of children, perhaps six to a row, perhaps six rows. Beneath each one was typed:

Name:
Birthdate:
Last Seen:
Description:

Chris glanced away, took a deep breath, and made herself look at it. Thirty-six missing children. Thirty-six tragedies. She didn't know what she would do if Dane were abducted, or got lost somewhere. Just thinking about it gave her a twist in the gut. But for the sake of those other children, the unlucky ones, and their parents, she scanned the flyers whenever she saw them. You never knew when you might see one of these kids. Someone had spotted one from *America's Most Wanted*, and the child had been missing for three whole years. Imagine how his parents had suffered. Imagine his terror. But imagine how much worse it would have been if no one had paid attention to the TV program or the flyers. "Have You Seen Me?" they read; but you could be standing right next to a missing kid and never know it, if you didn't pay attention.

Thirty-six missing lives. Thirty-six headaches. How did they go missing? She thought of car doors opening and old men offering candy. She thought of desperate women who would do anything to feel a child in their arms. Angry divorced parents. Or kids who wandered off, plain and simple, just didn't pay attention to how far they had drifted away from the loving watch of Mommy and Daddy. They wandered crying in the woods, or fell down ravines, or starved.

Bad karma. The very worst.

This was all too awful. She forced herself to imagine instead the recent rescue of the little boy. A neighbor of the child's, the tube on, maybe some nachos and a beer on a small oak table. Turning to his wife and saying, "Wow, that looks like little Kevin."

The wife nodding, startled.

And wondering for a while, and hesitating, and probably losing sleep over it. It would take a lot of courage to make a call to the police. What if you were wrong? The whole neighborhood would probably shun you for the rest of your life. The whole town, actually. But how could you not speak up if you had a suspicion; how could you respect yourself if some child suffered because you were too chicken shit to—

Chris's mouth dropped open.

Second on the left, second row. The little boy in the small, grainy picture could've been Dane's twin. Blue eyes, blond hair, dimples. Missing for six months. Age now: two.

Dane was two.

She peered at the photograph. The child looked exactly like Dane. Exactly.

"Next!" the clerk called. Chris tapped Dane's head and he pranced forward like a horse. It looked like him down to his flyaway bangs, the shape of his nose.

Suddenly she was aware of eyes upon her. She turned her head slightly.

The man behind her was dressed in a suit, and his gaze ticked from her face to the flyer and back again. Down to Dane, to the flyer and back again.

She opened her mouth to say, "Isn't the resemblance amazing?" Then she realized he was thinking—he was suspecting—

Floored, she turned back around. Her face went hot. How embarrassing. She didn't blame him, not really. They did look like the same boy. But how could he even consider, for even a second, that she would, that Dane—

169

"Next!"

She shrugged her shoulders. This was something to tell Tommy when he got home tomorrow night. Have a good laugh. After all, she had a great sense of humor.

But God, what if her kid had been missing for six months? That was nothing to laugh at. There was absolutely nothing funny about it. She shivered.

Have you seen me? The chant of lost children. That poor mother, wherever she was. Whoever she was. Chris looked at the photograph. Steven Magnuson. Poor Mrs. Magnuson. Poor Steven. He could be dead. Or living through hell, begging someone in his mind, *Please, notice me. Please, make me visible. Save me.*

She winced at her own thought and gave Dane a squeeze. "Ow!" he wailed, and a few heads swiveled in her direction.

She felt the man's scrutinizing stare.

"Next!" bellowed another clerk, this one a woman.

The man cleared his throat. Her cheeks went hot again.

"Hurry up, hon," she said to Dane, pushing him forward. But there was nowhere for him to go, and he stumbled into the elderly woman in front of him, who made a point of glaring at Chris.

"Sorry," she murmured.

The man was very close behind her.

The line shuffled forward, shuffled forward. Dane sang an off-key version of "Bingo" to himself, said, "Oh, thank you! Next!"

The man's body heat seeped through the cold air. Chris started to sweat. If he was going to say something, he should just say it, damn it. Who did he think he was, someone from the FBI?

Oh, my God, maybe he was. Maybe they staked out the post offices and other public places, looking for those missing kids. Maybe he would haul her in for questioning, as they said on TV. Separate her and Dane for hours, as she got more and more frantic, and they tried to find Tommy and—

Shit, she had to stop watching so much TV.

"Uh," the man said.

"Next!" It was Chris's turn. She scooted Dane to the window. Asked for her stamps, forgot the tape, almost forgot her change, and hurried out of the post office.

The heat slapped her as she went through the doorway. It brought her up short, until she heard the footfalls behind her. The man was coming. She said, "Dane-o, let's book"—an old *Hawaii Five-O* joke—and dragged her son by the arm.

"Mommy! Too hard!" Dane squalled.

"Excuse me," the man said. Finally said something. Chris broke into a light, innocent trot and got to her car. Unlocked it easily, slid Dane into the car seat, hopped in—how had she moved so fast?

The man watched her go as he slid into his own car, a run-down station wagon with out-of-state plates. The father of the missing boy, she thought. An uncle. One of those rumpled policemen, like Columbo.

"Too much TV," she said aloud.

"Next!" Dane chirruped. "TV!"

"Yeah, we'll go home and watch TV," she said, but as she drove out of the post office parking lot and slid into the traffic, she thought about how foolishly she had acted. Or reacted. Tommy said she over-dramatized things. Said it was cuz she was bored; it wasn't easy living in a small town saddled with a little one, while he was out on the road so much. That's what he said, anyway, though she was inclined to disagree. She had everything she wanted in life—a great husband, a great kid—and if she could change anything, it would only be that Tommy was home more.

"The hell with it," she muttered. She was being really dumb. The man had probably wanted to ask if she knew how to get to the interstate, or if she could recommend a good restaurant—not that she could, they didn't eat out much, and mostly at Mickey D.'s or Burger King—something like that. That kid hadn't really looked like Dane.

Oh, yes he had. He was the spitting image of her boy.

Well, so what? She hadn't abducted Dane. She had given birth to him. He was her son. There was no reason to act guilty, even less to feel guilty. It had just been . . . insulting. Yes. That he should even think that Dane was a missing child. She was a good mother.

So were all those other moms bad ones? Shame, Chris, she told herself. It was just bad luck.

She swung down the road and turned left on Avocado, and pulled into the grocery store parking lot.

"C'mon, hon!" Dane sang, kicking his legs.

"You goofy-goo." Chris bent over him and unstrapped his car seat, gave him a kiss. "Love you, baby."

"Mommy," he said adoringly.

They went into the store.

She pulled out a cart and they sailed up and down the aisles. Chris remembered the envelope full of coupons in her purse and began sorting through them in the frozen foods section, where it was coolest. The sun through the storefront windows was a blazing ball of mustard yellow. It was going to be a hot night. Too hot for cooking much of anything. She didn't make a big fuss over meals when Tommy was on the road; she could microwave something. Had been meaning to get back on Weight Watchers anyway. And they had a special on—

Dane said, "Hiya," in a cheerful voice, and Chris glanced at him. He was looking at something very intently. She followed his line of vision.

The man from the post office stood at the end of the aisle, his hands in his pockets. Slowly he moved his gaze from Dane to her, held it levelly.

Have you seen me?

She drew in her hands as if she'd been caught stealing. Gripped the handle of the cart and whirled in the opposite direction.

Coincidence. Of course. He had to eat, too, didn't he?

No. He had followed her. He was trailing her. And Tommy wasn't home.

Should she go to the police station? And tell them what? That she believed a man was following her around because her son looked like someone else's missing child? In a small town, you didn't bother the police unnecessarily. Otherwise, they might not come when you really needed them.

She headed down the dairy section, looking backward as she hurried along. Not there. She stopped. Her mind was racing. Milk. They needed low fat for them, and regular for Dane.

She put her hand out, let it drop. She was too shaken to do the marketing. She was going to go home.

But this was crazy. He hadn't threatened her or anything. There was no reason to be so upset.

In this day and age, there was. With all the psychos and druggies and all the crime, even in small towns like hers, there sure enough was. You couldn't be too careful, or your kid would end up on—

Jesus, on a milk carton. She swallowed. She had never noticed before that the pictures in the post office matched the ones on the milk carton. But there he was, the post office boy, the Magnuson-Dane clone, his picture duplicated a hundred times, a thousand, on the sweating wax cartons.

And there *he* was. The man, less than twenty feet away. He was dark-skinned—

—that shouldn't make a difference, Chris told herself firmly—

—and tall, and his suit didn't look right on him, somehow.

Her heart pounded. She was being prejudiced. Just because a man was dark and not too well tailored didn't mean he was dangerous. Just because he happened to be in two places where she was. Just because—

"Bullshit," she said, and Dane caroled proudly, "bullshit, bullshit, bullshit," as she hurried the cart toward the exit.

"Bullshit, bullshit," Dane warbled. Tight-lipped, Chris said nothing.

"Bullshit, bullshit, bullshitttt!"

"C'mon, hon, out of the cart," she pleaded with him, wrapping her arms around his waist and hefting him up. Dane locked his feet under the seat, as he sometimes did, and giggled.

172

"Candy."

"Dane, Mommy wants to go home."

He kicked the underside of the seat.

The man strode toward them. Fast. Faster.

"Hey," he called.

"Candy! Candy!" Dane bellowed.

"Christ, Dane!" she shouted, and Dane started, let her pick him up and spirit him past the magazines and dog food and out of the store.

"Hey!" The man was running after them.

Chris threw Dane in the back seat, not his car seat, and said, "No standing! Do you hear? No standing!"

"Mommy!" Dane cried, confused.

She started the car and peeled out of the parking lot. She saw him in the rearview mirror, hands on his hips, looking maybe a little confused.

On the way home, she calmed down. Okay, okay, it's over, she told herself. It was strange, but it's over. She checked the mirror again and again. He wasn't following her; there was no one at all behind her, in fact. He had probably given up, or realized that Dane wasn't the missing child. Who knew what had gone through his mind? He was gone, and that was the end of that. And if she'd flown off the handle, so what? Mothers had instincts, and hers had gone on alert. She believed in woman's intuition, trusted it. Too much caution was better than not enough.

All the way home, she watched the road behind her. Never saw his station wagon. Hell, maybe he'd just been making a pass at her. It happened.

But not this time. Of that she was positive.

Dane sang "Bingo" and made "rrr-rrr" motor noises. Totally unaffected. Kids. You never knew how they'd react to things.

"Okay," she said, as she pulled into the driveway. "Home free."

"Home! Home!" Dane sounded like E.T.

"Well, at least we got the stamps." She put the brake on and got out. The sun was still blazing. The house would be an oven for a while, until she got the air-conditioner going.

She opened the door and Dane half-crawled, half-tumbled out. One of his toys, a small, metal sixteen-wheeler, was clutched in his hand. He seemed all right. Never again, no matter what, she promised herself, would she not put him in his car seat. If something ever happened to him, she would never forgive herself. Never, never, never.

And then, for the first time, it occurred to her that the man himself might have been trying to abduct Dane. He might have seen the picture and somehow been inspired to take him, some kind of copy-cat thing. She started to shake, forced herself to stop. It didn't matter. They were home.

But what about that other boy, the one who looked so much like Dane? What of him?

"God, Dane, what a day," she said, as she unlocked the door. "What a strange, hot day." Dane giggled.

They went into the house. She put her house keys back in her purse and laid it on the table in the foyer. Dropped the stamps; they tumbled to the floor beside Dane's left foot.

"Shit," she muttered, and dropped onto her heels to pick them up.

Dane let go of his truck and it smacked the back of her hand. "Ow, Dane!" she cried. She wobbled back, forth, lost her balance, and tumbled sideways onto her elbow.

"Shit!" Dane clapped his hands.

A jab of pain shot through her forearm as she sat up. "Dane, you're not supposed to—"

Something slammed into the house with the shock of a bomb. The windows rattled; plaster cascaded from the ceiling.

"Jesus!" Chris jumped.

Something crashed against the door—*wham, crash, smash.* The entire door bowed inward, as if it were made of putty. The joints screeched.

With a cry, Chris scrabbled forward and threw her arms around Dane. Her knee came down on the truck but she was barely aware of it, only that it made it hard to get to her feet.

"What is it? What is it?" she shrieked at Dane, as if he would know. The door was being battered. The noise was deafening. She started to drag him away, God, into the kitchen, or down the hall or—

A long piece of the door splintered, shattered, fell into the foyer. Chris screamed again as the hot sun poured through; and the silhouette of a . . . an

not an axe, not an arm.

And someone shouted through the door, started to climb through the wreckage, a foot, a leg—

—the man, she knew it was him, she knew it was the dark man, calling—

"Are you in there, my darling? My silly-billy?"

She grabbed Dane's wrist and started to run; unable to remember the layout of her house in her panic, she took the corner to the kitchen too hard and ran into the wall.

Before she regained her footing, Dane batted her hand, saying, "Too hard, Mommy! Too hard." He pulled free. She flailed for him.

"Dane!"

He ran back toward the door.

"C'mon, hon!" he said eagerly. "Next! Next! Next!"

And he hurtled himself against the door as it burst completely apart, and something dark threw itself inside and slammed down on top of him; and Chris

174

screamed and screamed and screamed as the shadow moved back through the door and her son was gone

his giggle trailing after.

Have you seen me?
   No, you knucklehead.
   Not you.
   Not yet.
   The chant of the lost.
   The despair of the found.
   Have you seen me?
   No, but I'm looking for you, my sugar-spice girl, my silly-billy-boy.
   And I will find you.
   Poster or milk carton or summer-camp sleepover,
   I will find you.
   And *you* will see *me*.

Heroes

Richard T. Chizmar

1

I've always watched him. Secretly. From the time I was a child. Watched the way his eyebrows danced when he laughed. The way he lit his pipe or handled a tool, like a magician wielding a magic wand. The way he walked the family dog; bending to talk with it or ruffle its fur, but only when he was sure no one was watching. The way he read the newspaper or one of his tattered old paperbacks, peering over the worn pages every few minutes to keep me in check. The way his eyes twinkled when he called me "son." I've always watched him.

2

The detective's name was Crawford and when he disappeared into the crowd, I wondered for what had to be the tenth time tonight if I was truly insane for trusting him.

It was Thursday, December 21, and Baltimore-Washington International

Airport was suffering under the strain of thousands of holiday travelers. A river of lonely businessmen and women, sweatshirt-clad college students, and entire families flowed by North Gate 23, blocking my view of the exit tunnel. I remained sitting on one of the orange-padded seats in the waiting area while Crawford tried to get close enough to look out the airport windows. Our man was due on an 8:30 P.M. flight from Paris—a private charter—so the computer screens all around me offered no news of its arrival.

I stared at the clock on the far wall. It was almost time. Months of research and planning were about to come to an end. My stomach felt like it was bubbling over and I was tempted to duck into the bathroom. Instead, afraid to leave my seat, I popped another Tums and waited for it to dissolve under my tongue.

Crawford reappeared, trailing behind an overweight couple who were moving with the grace and speed of a pair of hermit crabs. I could see by the expression on his face that the news was not good. I'd hired Ben Crawford, a Philadelphia-based private detective, two months earlier. He'd been the only one of the half-dozen detectives who'd been recommended to me who was willing to take my case. A fifty-thousand-dollar certified check—half payment in advance—had sealed the deal.

We made an odd pair. I stood over six feet tall but tipped the scales at only one-sixty. Crawford, on the other hand, could best be described as a human stump; only five-four, he weighed in with one hundred and seventy pounds of compressed muscle. His arms and legs strained against his clothing, and like many other muscular men of his size, he more waddled than walked. Despite my edginess, I smiled and almost laughed aloud at the sight before me: the waddling detective and Mr. and Mrs. Hermit Crab.

"What's so damn funny?" he asked, moving his coat from the chair next to me and sitting down.

"What . . . oh, nothing. Nervous tension, I guess."

He checked his watch. "The plane just landed. It'll be another ten minutes or so."

I nodded, my throat suddenly dry, my stomach tightening another notch.

Now it was Crawford's turn to smirk. "Hey, take it easy, you're white as a sheet. Don't worry, he'll be on that plane." He glanced at his watch again. "Another couple of hours and it'll all be over. Trust me."

I nodded again. I trusted him all right. I had no other choice.

3

Twenty years ago, when I was seventeen and still in high school, each student in our senior English class was assigned to write a paper about the person he or she most admired. The class was a large one and the list of heroes was long and impressive: Martin Luther King, Abraham Lincoln, John F. Kennedy, Joe Namath, Willie Mays, John Glenn, and dozens of other famous figures. I was the only student who chose to write about his father. A nine-page tribute. My father cried at the kitchen table when he read it. Stood up and hugged me real close. I'll never forget that day. Never.

4

Our man was the only passenger in the tunnel. A shadow. Moving slow. Carrying no luggage.

Even in the dim light, I could see that he was a striking man. Tall. Elegant. Draped in a fine black overcoat, dark slacks, and shiny, zippered boots. His face contrasted sharply with his slicked, black hair and his dark apparel. Deathly pale flesh appeared almost luminous in the airport lights, and sharp, high cheekbones seemed to hide his eyes under his forehead. Eyes as dark as midnight.

"Jesus," I whispered.

"Yeah, I know," Crawford said, leaning close enough that I could feel his breath. "He's something, ain't he?"

Before I could answer, the detective stepped past me and met our visitor at the side of the walkway, away from the swelling crowd. I stumbled blindly after him, not wanting to be separated.

"It's a pleasure to see you again, sir," Crawford said.

Neither man offered forth a hand, and I noticed that our visitor's hands were covered by black leather gloves. He nodded and smiled. A quick flash of teeth. Like a shark. A chill swept across my spine.

"As promised, I am here." His voice was mesmerizing, his words soft and melodic like music. I wanted to hear more.

"Yes, you certainly are," Crawford said, sounding infinitely more civilized than I had ever heard him. "I trust your trip was satisfactory."

"Indeed, it was quite comfortable. But, my friend, I long for the journey home, so may we continue on quickly?"

"Yes, yes, of course." Crawford eased me forward, his fingers digging into my arm. "This is—"

"Mr. Francis Wallace," he interrupted, smiling again. I felt a wave of nausea rush forward and began to sway. The detective's fingers tightened on my arm again. "I have crossed an entire ocean to make his acquaintance."

"I . . . I really must thank you for coming here," I said. I looked helplessly at Crawford. "I'm not sure I believed him until I saw you walking up the tunnel. I was so terribly afraid that I had been wrong all this time."

"It is not necessary to thank me, Mr. Wallace. I have thought about this moment many times since your friend's visit to my home. I admit, initially, I was wary, hesitant to come. But yours is such a strange story, such a strange reason for my journey. My decision to come here was much easier than your decision to seek me, I trust."

A pack of giggling children skittered past us, brushing the man's coat. He cringed and turned to Crawford. "I am ready to proceed now."

The detective led us through the busy airport, outside into the bitter December air, to his rental car in the upper-level parking lot. The traffic on the interstate was moderate. We drove north in silence.

5

It was my father who stood at my side on my wedding day, and I by his, eight months later, when Mother passed away. Barely a year later, and it was my father again, his arms around me, who broke the news to me that my precious Jennifer had been killed in an accident. It was the worst of times, but still we had each other.

6

The house I grew up in was dark, the street deserted. The rental car was parked in the driveway, its ticking engine the only sound in the night. I sat on the front porch, Crawford on my left side, smoking a cigarette. Snow flurries danced around us, drifting to the ground and melting. I played with the zipper on my coat for a long time before I looked up.

He was staring at me.

"You okay?" he asked, his breath visible in the chill air.

"I don't know." I took a deep breath and looked over my shoulder at the front door, which our visitor had disappeared into just minutes earlier. "I planned this for so long . . . thought about it for so long, but I don't know. I'm still not sure it's right."

He shook his head. "Listen to me, I gotta admit that I thought you were a genuine nutcase when you hired me. Offered me a hundred thousand to go find this guy and convince him of your little plan. Hell, I only signed on because I was short on cash and long on bills."

He stood up and inhaled on his cigarette. Began pacing the walkway. "I mean, I thought he was a fantasy, something made up for the movies and books. But the more you showed me about this guy—the papers, the files, the photos; all dated over hundreds of years—and the more time I spent around this house, getting to know you and your old man . . . the more I understood. You've gone to an awful lot of trouble, Wallace, an awful lot. Now, you don't know me very well; not well at all, in fact. But if you're asking for my opinion, my view of all this, I think you did good. I think you did damn good."

A soft thud sounded from the house and I jerked around.

Crawford kneeled at my side, pointed a finger at me. "You did good, Wallace. Trust me."

"Oh, God, I hope so."

7

I don't watch my father anymore. It hurts too much.

Ten months ago, on a Friday night, he forgot my name. I had just returned from the grocery store with the week's supplies—he was no longer able to drive himself—when he called me into the den. The television was on the wrong channel and he couldn't figure out how to work the remote control. He looked me straight in the eyes and said, "Charlie, could you please turn on HBO?" I laughed, thinking he was acting the smart-ass, one of his favorite pastimes.

But later at dinner, he asked, "Charlie, pass me the salt and pepper."

I looked at him; there was no humor in his voice, no mischief in his eyes. "Dad," I said, scared, "who is Charlie?"

A confused expression creased his face. "What the hell kind of question is that?"

"Just tell me who Charlie is, Dad."

He laughed. "Hell, you are. Don't you even remember your own name? We served in the war together, Charlie. You were my wing man, for Christsakes."

It came to me then. Charlie Banks—my father's best friend, dead over fifteen years now.

It was a long night, but the next morning, everything was back to normal. I was his son again, Charlie Banks completely forgotten.

But I could see the signs then. No longer able to drive, arthritis, failing eyesight and hearing, advancing stages of senility . . . the list continued to grow as every month passed.

As did my own depression and anxiety. I remember someone once said that there is nothing sadder, nothing more heartbreaking, than watching your hero die.

They were right.

It was during that time I decided I couldn't let that happen.

8

The snow was falling harder now. The narrow streets were covered, neighborhood yards of dead grass just beginning to glisten a beautiful white.

I was standing by the rental car, nervously running my bare hand over the cold metal. The two of them stood huddled together on the porch, Crawford's cigarette aglow. The man had emerged from the house several minutes ago, but the detective had insisted on talking to him first. Alone. I'd trusted him this far, so I'd agreed.

Five minutes later, twenty minutes before midnight, they finished talking and walked to the driveway.

Crawford pulled me aside and said, "Your dad was sleeping like a baby. Just as we planned. There was no pain, no surprise."

I closed my eyes, nodded my head. "Thank you," I whispered. "Thank you so much."

"It's been my pleasure," the detective said, reaching for my hand. "And I mean that. Now, don't worry about anything. I'm going to get our friend back to the airport and back on that plane. You get inside." He waved at me from the car. "I'll be in touch."

Before he joined Crawford, the man laid a hand on each of my shoulders, touched a single gloved finger to my face. "Immortality is a rare and wonderful thing, Mr. Wallace. But it is not without its failings. It will not always be easy. Cherish this gift, protect it, as I know you will, and you and your father will be truly rewarded."

Tears streamed down my cheeks. I opened my mouth to thank him, but the words did not come.

He held a finger to his lips. "Say nothing. I must go."

I watched the car back out of the driveway, pull away into the night, its brake lights fading to tiny red sparks in the falling snow. I looked at the second-floor window—my father's bedroom—then at the front door. A snowflake drifted to my lips, and I opened my mouth, tasted it like I had done so many times before as a child. I looked skyward and caught another on my tongue. Then, I started across the lawn, his words still in my head.

Immortality is a rare and wonderful thing.

God, I hoped so.

The Hollow

David B. Silva

That day, that mystical day when the warm winds of fantasy first whispered secrets in Michael Carpenter's ears, had been long overdue. It was a summer day, parched and windless and climbing toward the low one hundreds. The kind of day a rabid dog might feel just right about. The kind of day twelve-year-old Michael had spent a lifetime waiting for.

Using a stick of driftwood he had snatched up from the dry, rocky bed of Moss Creek, Michael macheted his way through a field of knee-high grass, looking to kick-up a pheasant or a coyote pup or some such thing. Anything to change the dull routine that shadowed the town of Appleton every January 1st like a dark thundercloud and stayed uninvited all year round, reminding, always reminding the townspeople that their lives were insipid little lives. He marched helter-skelter through the grass with no particular destination in mind, stopping on occasion and looking back at the serpentine path he had left in his wake, a path that led back home, back to where Cheryl-the-babysitter sat entranced by *All My Children* or *General Hospital* or whatever other strip of celluloid nonsense occupied the airwaves at the moment, then he would swallow his loneliness down and turn away again. Off to the wonders of the world, even though in all his summer days of searching he had yet to stumble across anything he could possibly call a wonder.

But this was a different summer day, a new summer day.

In his wandering, his searching for marvels, he came upon a lonely oak which guarded a field of grass as a scarecrow might guard acres of corn. As tall as old Mister Potter's barn, the oak reached skyward on the strength of four arms. The frayed end of a thick cord rope dangled from one arm and Michael knew a swing had once swayed from the mighty branch, swayed with the laughter of summer children and autumn winds. Through the mesh of tiny leaves, the sun slithered and seeped until it fell across his face in a web of spider lines. And he decided the little bit of shade wasn't that bad an idea about then.

He slid down the lumpy trunk of the great oak until his butt rested comfortably in the soft, dusty dirt.

If cousin Brian were there, they would tell jokes about school and Buddy Markham and maybe even Cheryl-the-babysitter. And they would laugh out loud before their eyes would meet suddenly, like two dogs face-to-face in a

181

stand-off, then they would grow perfectly still until one of them couldn't hold it any longer and he would snicker and instantly a wrestling match would break out. Clouds of dirt would fly then, drifting back to earth, back to their squeals of laughter. And it wouldn't seem so hot.

And it wouldn't seem so lonely.

If Brian were there.

Michael sighed.

Then, as he watched a black ant scurrying madly about, herky-jerky here and there, something long and thin and alive soft-slithered out of the hollow of the great oak, floated over the loose dirt and in a blink, sucked the frantic ant from the face of the earth.

Michael Carpenter's eyes nearly exploded from their sockets.

The long, slender *something*—it was surely alive—slithered back into the hidden safety of the old oak hollow.

And Michael listened as the world suddenly held its breath, hushed by the wonder of what it had seen, waiting expectantly for what would happen next.

"God, did you see that?" he shouted. "Did you see that?"

He was on his feet, staring at the dark hollow of the tree, keeping a safe distance in case the adventurous tentacle—*it was a tentacle, wasn't it? like the wiggly arm of an octopus?*—might dare to snake out into the sunlight again.

"Did you see that?"

It was something incredible, something so wondrous that the town of Appleton would just have to come alive again. Appleton would just have to stir awake from its Rip Van Winkle slumber now. And all because Michael Carpenter was in the right place at the right time and had witnessed the weedy arm gobbling up a no-good black ant.

He held tight to the stick of driftwood as he stepped within an arm's length of the hollow. It was dark inside, and quiet.

"I know you're in there," he said, giving the trunk a whack with his stick. "I saw you gobble that ant."

Yes, I'm here.

He heard the words in his head. The *something* was talking to him, talking right inside his head like his very own thoughts did. Like it was right there inside his head with him, filling up the weird furrowed canals of his brain.

"Come out," he said. "I want to see what you look like."

But his head was quiet.

"I won't tell anyone, I promise." As if it made a difference, as if a promise made to a *something* would otherwise have to be kept, he crossed his fingers behind his back. "Please?"

The raw tip of a tentacle appeared cautiously out of the darkness. Pink and moist and looking as if a finger-touch would sink deep into its flesh, the tentacle arched skyward, allowing a line of squirming feelers to sniff the air.

Michael moved back a step.

"Come on," he said. "I won't hurt you."

Then another tentacle ventured forth.

And another.

And another.

Until there were six in all, six long slender arms that reached and probed from a strangely-formed body with two dark eyes and a mouth lined with rows of teeth, like the shark-mouth he had seen on television once.

"Wow!" he shouted, feeling his heart pounding against his chest. And he took another retreating step.

The *thing*—now that he had seen all of it, it wasn't any longer a *some-thing*, it was a *thing*—seemed bothered by the sunlight. Translucent inner lids, like crocodile eyes, opened and closed with a slow, purposeful motion. And it stared with a wonder of its own at the young boy before finally extending a single tentacle in Michael's direction.

The pink flesh wrapped itself harmlessly around his finger, feeling like the soft belly of a snake.

"That tickles," he said with a smile.

Then, as if hurt by the comment, the probing tentacle unwound itself from his tiny index finger, and raised a cloud of dust as it fell back to the ground and slithered away.

"I'm sorry."

Huge eyes blinked as if they didn't understand.

"I didn't mean to scare you."

It's hot, the *thing* said in his head. And it waddled back into the shade of the hollow, back so far in the darkness that nothing was left to be seen. As if there had never been a *thing* at all.

"Go on, take a look," Michael told her. "It's there, honest it is."

Cheryl-the-babysitter was kneeling before the great oak. She had fussed about coming all the way out to the great tree, complaining that she would miss the end of *General Hospital*. But he had insisted. Even after she had accused him of being a liar, of having an overactive imagination, he had insisted that she come, and he had taken her by the hand and dragged her away from the RCA. After all, she was the babysitter. She was being paid to look after him, wasn't she?

"I don't see anything," she insisted, whisking a fallen strand of hair back behind her ear. "If you're lying to me, Michael Carpenter, I'll lock you in your bedroom for a week. I swear I will."

"It's there." This wasn't one of his made-up stories. Not like the tale about a man with a mask and long knife that he had seen slipping through the back bedroom window. No, this wasn't anything like that. This was real. "It had six arms with little feelers on the bottom that wiggled and squirmed like white baby worms."

"That's sick," she said, and she started to rise. But before she could, a soft, pink tentacle slithered out from the dark hollow and wrapped itself around her ankle.

"I told you," Michael shouted. "I told you!"

Then a second tentacle wrapped itself around her other ankle. And while Michael was feeling so happy about the sudden appearance, so happy that he wouldn't be thought a liar, the other tentacles were suddenly all there, wrapping around Cheryl-the-babysitter, choking off gurgling screams before they even had a chance to leave her throat.

"No!" Michael screamed. "You're not supposed to do that!"

He tried.

He tried to keep the *thing* from pulling Cheryl-the-babysitter into the hollow, into the dark of the hollow where no one would ever hear from her again. But the *thing* was stronger than him. And it had six arms instead of only two. And . . . and it was hungry.

That's what it told him. *Hungry*, it said in his head.

Michael fell to his knees and watched in silence until the dust had settled again. *Hungry* kept sounding in his head. *Just hungry*. His eyes followed the tiny drops of moisture leading a path back to the hollow, a thin crust of dirt floating innocently atop the moist redness.

"NO!" he screamed, but the scream was trapped somewhere inside his head, trapped with his understanding of what had happened. "You weren't supposed to do that."

Then everything was suddenly too quiet.

Michael wiped away the tears that had stained his face. He looked over his shoulder, back at the path that led home, wondering if he should follow it, wondering if Cheryl-the-babysitter would still be there watching the last of *General Hospital*, wondering if there was the slightest chance it had all been a nightmare.

But he knew better.

Appleton was still asleep back there, minus Cheryl-the-babysitter, but still yawning at its own apathy just the same, as if nothing had ever happened. Nothing at all.

But something had happened.

Things had changed.

Everything had changed.

And Michael had to tell someone. He couldn't simply keep it a secret. Even though he had discovered the *thing*, even though he had practically fed Cheryl-the-babysitter to it, he couldn't keep what had happened a secret. No, that wouldn't do at all.

Not at all.

He had to tell someone.

Oh God, he had to tell someone.

"In there," he said, pointing an uncertain finger. "Back where it's dark like the bottom of Spinner's Pond. Back inside where your eyes can't see nothing."

"You sure?" Brian asked. He knelt in the dirt, trying to see into the darkness without venturing too near the hollow. He wanted to believe, Michael could see that he wanted to believe. Even though he was a year older than Michael, he was hoping that there really was a *thing* hiding in the old oak, still munching on Cheryl-the-babysitter. "Don't look like there's enough room in there for a whole body. You really sure?"

"Room enough," Michael said.

Then, in a soft whisper, a slender pink arm of the *thing* was there, wrapping itself around cousin Brian like they were long-lost friends, and dragging him screaming back into the hollow.

Michael's muscles locked when he tried to move. He wanted to cup his hands over his ears, wanted to shut out the high-pitched screams that were calling his name, screaming for him to do something about the hungry *thing*. But what could he do? It had so many arms, was so much stronger than his twelve-year-old body.

And then he remembered the stick of driftwood he had snatched from the bed of Moss Creek.

And the stick was suddenly in his hand.

And with all his strength, he let the stick fall against the soft pink flesh of the *thing* . . .

. . . again

. . . and again

. . . and again

until the *thing* had disappeared into the darkness of the hollow, disappeared with cousin Brian under arm, back into the world of the old oak where no one would ever know what it had done.

No one but Michael.

Then the stick slipped from his fingers, falling lifeless to the ground, lifeless like cousin Brian must be, lifeless like Cheryl-the-babysitter must be.

All because the *thing* was hungry.

And he cried.

He studied the trail left by the dragging, and the bright red moisture which spotted the ground, and the redness which coated the end of the stick. And he cried because they were both dead now, because what had begun as such a special day had ended so terribly wrong.

It wasn't supposed to be hungry.

It was supposed to be friendly, just friendly.

That's all.

She stood behind him, his mother did, holding him by the shoulders as he stared through seemingly lifeless eyes at the flashing blue and red lights. It was dusk now, the sun was sinking beyond the line of distant oak trees which lined Spinner's Pond. The evening air was quickly cooling the town of Appleton.

Cousin Brian and Cheryl-the-babysitter had been taken away in black, zippered bags. Michael's mother had held her hands over his eyes when the bodies had spilled out from the hollow, but he'd already known what they would look like.

"Just playing," he had answered when someone asked how he had found the bodies. He didn't tell them about the *thing*. They wouldn't have believed him anyway. It was the sort of thing adults wouldn't believe if it came from the mouth of a young boy. And he was twelve, old enough now that he shouldn't be making up stories. Even when they showed him the murder weapon, a big old stick of driftwood all wrapped in plastic, he didn't tell them about the *thing*. Though he thought the stick looked familiar, thought he could almost feel it in his hands as it came crashing down against the soft pink flesh of . . .

(cousin Brian's skull?)

(Cheryl-the-babysitter's chubby face?)

. . . the *thing*.

But there was nothing to say, nothing he could add. Enough rumors were already spreading through the town about the drifter that had been seen sleeping under the great oak the night before, the drifter that maybe stopped just long enough to stuff cousin Brian and Cheryl-the-babysitter into the hollow before moving along again.

There was nothing he could add to that.

Nothing he wanted to add.

There was only one thing that really mattered now. Something wondrous had finally happened to the sleepy-eyed town of Appleton. Something the townsfolk would be talking about for years to come. And if Michael Carpenter could only tell the truth, it might keep the good folks of Appleton talking forever more. But it was their secret, just between the two of them—Michael and the *thing*. Because they had both known that morning that Appleton needed a little excitement if it was ever to shake loose from its Rip Van Winkle slumber.

And now sleepy-eyed Appleton was as wide awake as ever.

The House of Shadows

Mary Elizabeth Counselman

The train pulled up with a noisy jerk and wheeze, and I peered out into the semi-gloom of dusk at the little depot. What was the place?—"Oak Grove." I could read dimly the sign on the station's roof. I sighed wearily. Three days on the train! Lord, I was tired of the lurching roll, the cinders, the scenery flying past my window! I came to a sudden decision and hurried down the aisle to where the conductor was helping an old lady off.

"How long do we stop here?" I asked him quickly.

"About ten minutes, ma'am," he said, and I stepped from the train to the smooth sand in front of the station. So pleasant to walk on firm ground again! I breathed deeply of the spicy winter air, and strolled to the far side of the station. A brisk little wind was whipping my skirts about my legs and blowing wisps of hair into my eyes. I looked idly about at what I could see of Oak Grove. It was a typical small town—a little sleepier than some, a little prettier than most. I wandered a block or two toward the business district, glancing nervously at my watch from time to time. My ten minutes threatened to be up, when I came upon two dogs trying to tear a small kitten to pieces.

I dived into the fray and rescued the kitten, not without a few bites and scratches in the way of service wounds, and put the little animal inside a store doorway. At that moment a long-drawn, it seemed to me derisive, whistle from my train rent the quiet, and as I tore back toward the station I heard it chugging away. I reached the tracks just in time to see the caboose rattling away into the night.

What should I do? Oh, why had I jumped off at this accursed little station? My luggage, everything I possessed except my purse, was on that vanished train, and here I was, marooned in a village I had never heard of before!

Or had I? "Oak Grove" . . . the name had a familiar ring. Oak Grove . . . ah! I had it! My roommate at college two years before had lived in a town called Oak Grove. I darted into the depot.

"Does a Miss Mary Allison live here?" I inquired of the station-master. "Mary Deane Allison?"

I wondered at the peculiar unfathomable look the old man gave me, and

187

at his long silence before he answered my question. "Yes'm," he said slowly, with an odd hesitancy that was very noticeable. "You her kin?"

"No," I smiled. "I went to college with her. I . . . I thought perhaps she might put me up for the night. I've . . . well, I was idiot enough to let my train go off and leave me. Do you . . . is she fixed to put up an unexpected guest, do you know?"

"Well"—again that odd hesitancy—"we've a fair to middlin' hotel here," he evaded. "Maybe you'd rather stay there."

I frowned. Perhaps my old friend had incurred the disapproval of Oak Grove by indiscreet behavior—it seems a very easy thing to do in rural towns. I looked at him coldly.

"Perhaps you can direct me to her house," I said stiffly.

He did so, still with that strange reluctance.

I made my way to the big white house at the far end of town, where I was told Mary Allison lived. Vague memories flitted through my mind of my chum as I had seen her last, a vivacious cheerful girl whose home and family life meant more to her than college. I recalled hazy pictures she had given me of her house, of her parents and a brother whose picture had been on our dresser at school. I found myself hurrying forward with eagerness to see her again and meet that doting family of hers.

I found my way at last to the place, a beautiful old Colonial mansion with tall pillars. The grounds were overgrown with shrubbery and weeds, and the enormous white oaks completely screened the great house from the street, giving it an appearance of hiding from the world. The place was sadly in need of repairs and a gardener's care, but it must have been magnificent at one time.

I mounted the steps and rapped with the heavy brass knocker. At my third knock the massive door swung open a little way, and my college friend stood in the aperture, staring at me without a word. I held out my hand, smiling delightedly, and she took it in a slow incredulous grasp. She was unchanged, I noticed—except, perhaps, that her dancing bright-blue eyes had taken on a vague dreamy look. There was an unnatural quiet about her manner, too, which was not noticeable until she spoke. She stood in the doorway, staring at me with those misty blue eyes for a long moment without speech; then she said slowly, with more amazement than I thought natural, "Liz! Liz!" Her fingers tightened about my hand as though she were afraid I might suddenly vanish. "It's . . . it's good to see you! Gosh! How . . . why did you come here?" with a queer embarrassment.

"Well, to tell the truth, my train ran off and left me when I got off for a breath of air," I confessed sheepishly. "But I'm glad now that it did . . . remembered you lived here, so here I am!" She merely stared at me strangely, still clutching my hand. "There's no train to Atlanta till ten in the morning." I hesitated, then laughed, "Well, aren't you going to ask me in?"

"Why . . . why, of course," Mary said oddly, as if the idea were strange and had not occurred to her. "Come in!"

I stepped into the great hall, wondering at her queer manner. She had been one of my best friends at college, so why this odd constraint? Not quite as if she did not want me around—more as if it were queer that I should wish to enter her house, as if I were a total stranger, a creature from another planet! I tried to attribute it to the unexpectedness of my visit; yet inwardly I felt this explanation was not sufficient.

"What a beautiful old place!" I exclaimed, with an effort to put her at ease again. Then, as the complete silence of the place struck me, unthinkingly I added, "You don't live here alone, do you?"

She gave me the oddest look, one I could not fathom, and replied so softly that I could hardly catch the words, "Oh, no."

I laughed. "Of course! I'm crazy . . . but where is everybody?"

I took off my hat, looking about me at the Colonial furniture and the large candelabra on the walls with the clusters of lighted candles which gave the only light in the place—for there were no modern lighting fixtures of any kind, I noted. The dim candle light threw deep shadows about the hall—shadows that flickered and moved, that seemed alive. It should have given me a sense of nervous fear; yet somehow there was peace, contentment, warmth about the old mansion. Yet, too, there was an incongruous air of mystery, of unseen things in the shadowy corners, of being watched by unseen eyes.

"Where is everybody? Gone to bed?" I repeated, as she seemed not to have heard my question.

"Here they are," Mary answered in that strange hushed voice I had noticed, as if some one were asleep whom she might waken.

I looked in the direction she indicated, and started slightly. I had not seen that little group when I entered! They were standing scarcely ten feet from me just beyond the aura of light from the candles, and they stared at me silently, huddled together and motionless.

I smiled and glanced at Mary, who said in a soft voice like the murmur of a light wind, "My mother . . ."

I stepped forward and held out my hand to the tall kind-faced woman who advanced a few steps from the half-seen group in the shadows. She seemed, without offense, not to see my hand, but merely gave me a beautiful smile and said, in that same hushed voice Mary used, "If you are my daughter's friend, you are welcome!"

I happened to glance at Mary from the corner of my eye as she spoke, and I saw my friend's unnatural constraint vanish, give place to a look, I thought wonderingly, that was unmistakably one of relief.

"My father," Mary's voice had a peculiar tone of happiness. A tall distinguished-looking man of about forty stepped toward me, smiling gently. He too seemed not to see my outthrust hand, but said in a quiet friendly voice, "I am glad to know you, my dear. Mary has spoken of you often."

I made some friendly answer to the old couple; then Mary said, "This is Lonny . . . remember his picture?"

The handsome young man whose photograph I remembered stepped forward, grinning engagingly.

"So this is Liz!" he said. "Always wanted to meet one girl who isn't afraid of a mouse . . . remember? Mary told us about the time you put one in the prof's desk." He too spoke in that near-whisper that went oddly with his cheery words, and I found myself unconsciously lowering my voice to match theirs. They were unusually quiet for such a merry friendly group, and I was especially puzzled at Mary's hushed voice and manner—she had always been a boisterous tomboy sort of person.

"This is Betty," Mary spoke again, a strange glow lighting her face.

A small girl about twelve stepped solemnly from the shadows and gave me a grave old-fashioned curtsey.

"And Bill," said Mary, as a chubby child peeped out at me from behind his sister's dress and broke into a soft gurgling laugh.

"What darling kids!" I burst out.

The baby toddled out from behind Betty and stood looking at me with big blue eyes, head on one side. I stepped forward to pat the curly head, but as I put out a hand to touch him, he seemed to draw away easily just out of reach. I could not feel rebuffed, however, with his bright eyes telling me plainly that I was liked. It was just a baby's natural shyness with strangers, I told myself, and made no other attempt to catch him.

After a moment's conversation, during which my liking for this charming family grew, Mary asked if I should like to go to my room and freshen up a bit before dinner. As I followed her up the stairs, it struck me forcibly—as it had before only vaguely—that this family, with the exception of Mary, were in very bad health. From father to baby, they were most pasty-white of complexion—not sallow, I mused, but a sort of translucent white like the glazed-glass doors of private offices. I attributed it to the uncertain light of the candles that they looked rather smoky, like figures in a movie when the film has become old and faded.

"Dinner at six," Mary told me, smiling, and left me to remove the travel-stains.

I came downstairs a little before the dinner hour, to find the hall deserted—and, woman-like, I stopped to parade before a large cheval-glass in the wall. It was a huge mirror, reflecting the whole hall behind me, mellowly illumined in the glow of the candles. Turning about for a back-view of myself, I saw the little baby, Bill, standing just beside me, big eyes twinkling merrily.

"Hello there, old fellow," I smiled at him. "Do I look all right?" I glanced back at the mirror . . . and what it reflected gave me a shock.

I could see myself clearly in the big glass, and most of the hall far behind me, stretching back into the shadows. But the baby was not reflected in the glass at all! I moved, with a little chill, just behind him . . . and I could see my own reflection clearly, but it was as if he were simply not there.

At that moment Mary called us to dinner, and I promptly forgot the disturbing optical illusion with the parting resolve to have my eyes examined. I held out my hand to lead little Bill into the dining-room, but he dodged by me with a mischievous gurgle of laughter, and toddled into the room ahead of me.

That was the pleasantest meal I can remember. The food was excellent and the conversation cheery and light, though I had to strain to catch words spoken at the far end of the table, as they still spoke in that queer hushed tone. My voice, breaking into the murmur of theirs, sounded loud and discordant, though I have a real Southern voice.

Mary served the dinner, hopping up and running back into the kitchen from time to time to fetch things. By this I gathered that they were in rather straitened circumstances and could not afford a servant. I chattered gayly to Lonny and Mary, while the baby and Betty listened with obvious delight and Mary's parents put in a word occasionally when they could break into our chatter.

It was a merry informal dinner, not unusual except that the conversation was carried on in that near-whisper. I noticed vaguely that Mary and I were the only ones who ate anything at all. The others merely toyed with their food, cutting it up ready for eating but not tasting a bite, though several times they would raise a fork to their lips and put it down again, as though pretending to eat. Even the baby only splashed with his little fork in his rice and kept his eyes fixed on me, now and then breaking into that merry gurgling laugh.

We wandered into the library after the meal, where Mary and I chatted of old times. Mr. Allison and his wife read or gave ear to our prattling from time to time, smiling and winking at each other. Lonny, with the baby in his lap and Betty perched on the arm of his chair, laughed with us at some foolish tale of our freshman days.

At about eleven Mary caught me yawning covertly, and hustled me off to bed. I obediently retired, thankful for a bed that did not roll me from side to side all night, and crawled in bed in borrowed pajamas with a book, to read myself to sleep by the flickering candle on my bedside table.

* * *

I must have dropped off to sleep suddenly, for I awoke to find my candle still burning. I was about to blow it out and go back to sleep when a slight sound startled the last trace of drowsiness from me.

It was the gentle rattle of my doorknob being turned very quietly.

An impulse made me feign sleep, though my eyes were not quite closed and I watched the door through my eyelashes. It swung open slowly, and Mrs. Allison came into the room. She walked with absolute noiselessness up to my bed, and stood looking down at me intently. I shut my eyes tightly so my eyelids would not flutter, and when I opened them slightly in a moment, she was moving toward the door, apparently satisfied that I was fast asleep. I thought she was going out again, but she paused at the door and beckoned to some one outside in the hall.

Slowly and with incredible lack of sound, there tiptoed into my room Mr. Allison, Lonny, Betty, and the baby. They stood beside the bed looking down at me with such tender expressions that I was touched.

I conquered an impulse to open my eyes and ask them what they meant by this late visit, deciding to wait and watch. It did not occur to me to be frightened at this midnight intrusion. There swept over me instead a sense of unutterable peace and safety, a feeling of being watched over and guarded by some benevolent angel.

They stood for a long moment without speaking, and then the little girl, bending close to me, gently caressed my hand, which was lying on the coverlet. I controlled a start with great effort.

Her little hand was icy cold—not with the coldness of hands, but with a peculiar *windy* coldness. It was as if some one had merely blown a breath of icy air on me, for though her hand rested a moment on mine, it had no weight!

Then, still without speaking but with gentle affectionate smiles on all their faces, they tiptoed out in single file. Wondering at their actions, I dropped off at last into a serene sleep.

Mary brought my breakfast to my bed next morning, and sat chattering with me while I ate. I dressed leisurely and made ready to catch my ten o'clock train. When the time drew near, I asked Mary where her family was—they were nowhere in the house and I had seen none of them since the night before. I reiterated how charming they were, and how happy my visit had been. That little glow of happiness lighted my friend's face again, but at my next words it vanished into one that was certainly frightened pleading. I had merely asked to tell them good-bye.

That odd unfathomable expression flitted across her face once more. "They . . . they're gone," she said in a strained whisper. And as I stared at her perplexedly, she added in confusion, "I . . . I mean, they're away. They won't be back until . . . nightfall," the last word was so low it was almost unintelligible.

So I told her to give them my thanks and farewells. She did not seem to want to accompany me to the train, so I went alone. My train was late, and I wandered to the ticket window and chatted with the station-master.

"Miss Allison has a charming family, hasn't she?" I began conversationally. "They seem so devoted to each other."

Then I saw the station-master was staring at me as if I had suddenly gone mad. His wrinkled face had gone very pale.

"You stayed there last night?" His voice was almost a croak.

"Why, yes!" I replied, wondering at his behavior. "I did. Why not?"

"And . . . you saw . . . them?" His voice sank to a whisper.

"You mean Mary's family?" I asked, becoming a little annoyed at his foolish perturbation. "Certainly I saw them! What's so strange about that? What's wrong with them?"

My approaching train wailed in the distance, but I lingered to hear his reply. It came with that same reluctance, that same hesitancy, after a long moment.

"They died last year," he whispered, leaning forward toward me and fixing me with wide intent eyes. "Wiped out—every one of 'em exceptin' Mary—by smallpox."

In Kropfsberg Keep

Ralph Adams Cram

To the traveller from Innsbrück to Munich, up the lovely valley of the silver Inn, many castles appear, one after another, each on its beetling cliff or gentle hill,—appear and disappear, melting into the dark fir trees that grow so thickly on every side,—Laneck, Lichtwer, Ratholtz, Tratzberg, Matzen, Kropfsberg, gathering close around the entrance to the dark and wonderful Zillerthal.

But to us—Tom Rendel and myself—there are two castles only: not the gorgeous and princely Ambras, nor the noble old Tratzberg, with its crowded treasures of solemn and splendid mediævalism; but little Matzen, where eager hospitality forms the new life of a never-dead chivalry, and Kropfsberg, ruined, tottering, blasted by fire and smitten with grievous years,—a dead thing, and haunted,—full of strange legends, and eloquent of mystery and tragedy.

We were visiting the von C——s at Matzen, and gaining our first wonderful knowledge of the courtly, cordial castle like in the Tyrol,—of the gentle and delicate hospitality of noble Austrians. Brixleg had ceased to be but a mark on a map, and had become a place of rest and delight, a home for homeless wanderers on the face of Europe, while Schloss Matzen was a synonym for all that was gracious and kindly and beautiful in life. The days moved on in a golden round of riding and driving and shooting: down to Landl and Thiersee for chamois, across the river to the magic Achensee, up the Zillerthal, across the Schmerner Joch, even to the railway station at Steinach. And in the evenings after the late dinners in the upper hall where the sleepy hounds leaned against our chairs looking at us with suppliant eyes, in the evenings when the fire was dying away in the hooded fireplace in the library, stories. Stories, and legends, and fairy tales, while the stiff old portraits changed countenance constantly under the flickering firelight, and the sound of the drifting Inn came softly across the meadows far below.

If ever I tell the Story of Schloss Matzen, then will be the time to paint the too inadequate picture of this fair oasis in the desert of travel and tourists and hotels; but just now it is Kropfsberg the Silent that is of greater importance, for it was only in Matzen that the story was told by Fräulein E——, the gold-haired niece of Frau von C——, one hot evening in July, when we were sitting in the great west window of the drawing-room after a long ride up the Stallenthal. All the windows were open to catch the faint wind, and we had sat for a long time watching the Otzethaler Alps turn rose-color over distant Innsbrück, then deepen to violet as the sun went down and the white mists rose slowly until Lichtwer and Laneck and Kropfsberg rose like craggy islands in a silver sea.

And this is the story as Fräulein E—— told it to us,—the Story of Kropfsberg Keep.

A great many years ago, soon after my grandfather died, and Matzen came to us, when I was a little girl, and so young that I remember nothing of the affair except as something dreadful that frightened me very much, two young men who had studied painting with my grandfather came down to Brixleg from Munich, partly to paint, and partly to amuse themselves,—"ghost-hunting" as they said, for they were very sensible young men and prided themselves on it, laughing at all kinds of "superstition," and particularly at that form which believed in ghosts and feared them. They had never seen a real ghost, you know, and they belonged to a certain set of people who believed nothing they had not seen themselves,—which always seemed to me *very* conceited. Well, they knew that we had lots of beautiful castles here in the "lower valley," and they assumed, and rightly, that every castle has at least *one* ghost story connected with it, so they chose this as their hunting ground, only the game they sought was ghosts, not chamois. Their plan was to visit every place that was supposed to be haunted, and to meet every reputed ghost, and prove that it really was no ghost at all.

There was a little inn down in the village then, kept by an old man named Peter Rosskopf, and the two young men made this their headquarters. The very first night they began to draw from the old innkeeper all that he knew of legends and ghost stories connected with Brixleg and its castles, and as he was a most garrulous old gentlemen he filled them with the wildest delight by his stories of the ghosts of the castles about the mouth of the Zillerthal. Of course the old man believed every word he said, and you can imagine his horror and amazement when, after telling his guests the particularly blood-curdling story of Kropfsberg and its haunted keep, the elder of the two boys, whose surname I have forgotten, but whose Christian name was Rupert, calmly said, "Your story is most satisfactory: we will sleep in Kropfsberg Keep to-morrow night, and you must provide us with all that we may need to make ourselves comfortable."

The old man nearly fell into the fire. "What for a blockhead are you?" he cried, with big eyes. "The keep is haunted by Count Albert's ghost, I tell you!"

"That is why we are going there to-morrow night; we wish to make the acquaintance of Count Albert."

"But there was a man stayed there once, and in the morning he was dead."

"Very silly of him; there are two of us, and we carry revolvers."

"But it's a *ghost*, I tell you," almost screamed the innkeeper; "are ghosts afraid of firearms?"

"Whether they are or not, we are *not* afraid of *them.*"

Here the younger boy broke in,—he was named Otto von Kleist. I remember the name, for I had a music teacher once by that name. He abused the poor old man shamefully; told him that they were going to spend the night in Kropfsberg in spite of Count Albert and Peter Rosskopf, and that he might as well make the most of it and earn his money with cheerfulness.

In a word, they finally bullied the old fellow into submission, and when the morning came he set about preparing for the suicide, as he considered it, with sighs and mutterings and ominous shakings of the head.

You know the condition of the castle now,—nothing but scorched walls and crumbling piles of fallen masonry. Well, at the time I tell you of, the keep was still partially preserved. It was finally burned out only a few years ago by some wicked boys who came over from Jenbach to have a good time. But when the ghost hunters came, though the two lower floors had fallen into the crypt, the third floor remained. The peasants said it *could* not fall, but that it would stay until the Day of Judgment, because it was in the room above that the wicked Count Albert sat watching the flames destroy the great castle and his imprisoned guests, and where he finally hung himself in a suit of armor that had belonged to his mediæval ancestor, the first Count Kropfsberg.

No one dared touch him, and so he hung there for twelve years, and all the time venturesome boys and daring men used to creep up the turret steps and stare awfully through the chinks in the door at that ghostly mass of steel that held within itself the body of a murderer and suicide, slowly returning to the dust from which it was made. Finally it disappeared, none knew whither, and for another dozen years the room stood empty but for the old furniture and the rotting hangings.

So, when the two men climbed the stairway to the haunted room, they found a very different state of things from what exists now. The room was absolutely as it was left the night Count Albert burned the castle, except that all trace of the suspended suit of armor and its ghastly contents had vanished.

No one had dared to cross the threshold, and I suppose that for forty years no living thing had entered that dreadful room.

On one side stood a vast canopied bed of black wood, the damask hangings of which were covered with mould and mildew. All the clothing of the bed was in perfect order, and on it lay a book, open, and face downward. The only other furniture in the room consisted of several old chairs, a carved oak chest, and a big inlaid table covered with books and papers, and on one corner two or three bottles with dark solid sediment at the bottom, and a glass, also dark with the dregs of wine that had been poured out almost half a century before. The tapestry on the walls was green with mould, but hardly torn or otherwise defaced, for although the heavy dust of forty years lay on everything, the room had been preserved from further harm. No spiderweb was to be seen, no trace of nibbling mice, not even a dead moth or fly on the sills of the diamond-paned windows; life seemed to have shunned the room utterly and finally.

The men looked at the room curiously, and, I am sure, not without some feelings of awe and unacknowledged fear; but, whatever they may have felt of instinctive shrinking, they said nothing, and quickly set to work to make the room passably inhabitable. They decided to touch nothing that had not absolutely to be changed, and therefore they made for themselves a bed in one corner with the mattress and linen from the inn. In the great fireplace they piled a lot of wood on the caked ashes of a fire dead for forty years, turned the old chest into a table, and laid out on it all their arrangements for the evening's amusement: food, two or three bottles of wine, pipes and tobacco, and the chess-board that was their inseparable travelling companion.

All this they did themselves: the innkeeper would not even come within the walls of the outer court; he insisted that he had washed his hands of the whole affair, the silly dunderheads might go to their death their own way. *He* would not aid and abet them. One of the stable boys brought the basket of food and the wood and the bed up the winding stone stairs, to be sure, but neither money nor prayers nor threats would bring him within the walls of the accursed place, and he stared fearfully at the hare-brained boys as they worked around the dead old room preparing for the night that was coming so fast.

At length everything was in readiness, and after a final visit to the inn for dinner Rupert and Otto started at sunset for the Keep. Half the village went with them, for Peter Rosskopf had babbled the whole story to an open-mouthed crowd of wondering men and women, and as to an execution the awe-struck crowd followed the two boys dumbly, curious to see if they surely would put their plan into execution. But none went farther than the outer doorway of the stairs, for it was already growing twilight. In absolute silence they watched the two foolhardy youths with their lives in their hands enter the terrible Keep, standing like a tower in the midst of the piles of stones that had once formed walls joining it with the mass of the castle beyond. When a moment later a light showed itself in the high windows above, they sighed resignedly and went their ways, to wait stolidly until morning should come and prove the truth of their fears and warnings.

In the meantime the ghost hunters built a huge fire, lighted their many candles, and sat down to await developments. Rupert afterwards told my uncle that they really felt no fear whatever, only a contemptuous curiosity, and they ate their suppers with good appetite and an unusual relish. It was a long evening. They played many games of chess, waiting for midnight. Hour passed after hour, and nothing occurred to interrupt the monotony of the evening. Ten, eleven, came and went,—it was almost midnight. They piled more wood in the fireplace, lighted new candles, looked to their pistols—and waited. The clocks in the village struck twelve, the sound coming muffled through the high, deep-embrasured windows. Nothing happened, nothing to break the heavy silence; and with a feeling of disappointed relief they looked at each other and acknowledged that they had met another rebuff.

Finally they decided that there was no use in sitting up and boring themselves any longer, they had much better rest; so Otto threw himself down on the mattress, falling almost immediately asleep. Rupert sat a little longer, smoking, and watching the stars creep along behind the shattered glass and the bent leads of the lofty windows; watching the fire fall together, and the strange shadows move mysteriously on the mouldering walls. The iron hook in the oak beam, that crossed the ceiling midway, fascinated him, not with fear, but morbidly. So it was from that hook that for twelve years, twelve long years of changing summer and winter, the body of Count Albert, murderer and suicide, hung in its strange casing of mediæval steel; moving a little at first, and turning gently while the fire died out on the hearth, while the ruins of the castle grew cold, and horrified peasants sought for the bodies of the score of gay, reckless, wicked guests whom Count Albert had gathered in Kropfsberg for a last debauch, gathered to their terrible and untimely death. What a strange and fiendish idea it was, the young, handsome noble who had ruined himself and his family in the society of the splendid debauchees, gathering them all together, men and women who had known only love and pleasure, for a glorious and awful riot of luxury, and then, when they were all dancing in the great ballroom, locking the doors and burning the whole castle about them, the while he sat in the great keep listening to their screams of agonized fear, watching the fire sweep from wing to wing until the whole mighty mass was one enormous and awful pyre, and then, clothing himself in his great-great-grandfather's armor, hanging himself in the midst of the ruins of what had been a proud and noble castle. So ended a great family, a great house.

But that was forty years ago.

He was growing drowsy; the light flickered and flared in the fireplace; one by one the candles went out; the shadows grew thick in the room. Why did that great iron hook stand out so plainly? why did that dark shadow dance and quiver so mockingly behind it?—why—But he ceased to wonder at anything. He was asleep.

It seemed to him that he woke almost immediately; the fire still burned, though low and fitfully on the hearth. Otto was sleeping, breathing quietly and regularly; the shadows had gathered close around him, thick and murky; with every passing moment the light died in the fireplace; he felt stiff with cold. In the utter silence he heard the clock in the village strike two. He shivered with a sudden and irresistible feeling of fear, and abruptly turned and looked towards the hook in the ceiling.

Yes, It was there. He knew that It would be. It seemed quite natural, he would have been disappointed had he seen nothing; but now he knew that the story was true, knew that he was wrong, and that the dead *do* sometimes return to earth, for there, in the fast-deepening shadow, hung the black mass of wrought steel, turning a little now and then, with the light flickering on the tarnished and rusty metal. He watched it quietly; he hardly felt afraid; it was rather a sentiment of sadness and fatality that filled him, of gloomy forebodings of something unknown, unimaginable. He sat and watched the thing disappear in the gathering dark, his hand on his pistol as it lay by him on the great chest. There was no sound but the regular breathing of the sleeping boy on the mattress.

It had grown absolutely dark; a bat fluttered against the broken glass of the window. He wondered if he was growing mad, for—he hesitated to acknowledge it to himself—he heard music; far, curious music, a strange and luxurious dance, very faint, very vague, but unmistakable.

Like a flash of lightning came a jagged line of fire down the blank wall opposite him, a line that remained, that grew wider, that let a pale cold light into the room, showing him now all its details,—the empty fireplace, where a thin smoke rose in a spiral from a bit of charred wood, the mass of the great bed, and, in the very middle, black against the curious brightness, the armored man,

198

or ghost, or devil, standing, not suspended, beneath the rusty hook. And with the rending of the wall the music grew more distinct, though sounding very still, very far away.

Count Albert raised his mailed hand and beckoned to him; then turned, and stood in the riven wall.

Without a word, Rupert rose and followed him, his pistol in hand. Count Albert passed through the mighty wall and disappeared in the unearthly light. Rupert followed mechanically. He felt the crushing of the mortar beneath his feet, the roughness of the jagged wall where he rested his hand to steady himself.

The keep rose absolutely isolated among the ruins, yet on passing through the wall Rupert found himself in a long, uneven corridor, the floor of which was warped and sagging, while the walls were covered on one side with big faded portraits of an inferior quality, like those in the corridor that connects the Pitti and Uffizzi in Florence. Before him moved the figure of Count Albert,—a black silhouette in the ever-increasing light. And always the music grew stronger and stranger, a mad, evil, seductive dance that bewitched even while it disgusted.

In a final blaze of vivid, intolerable light, in a burst of hellish music that might have come from Bedlam, Rupert stepped from the corridor into a vast and curious room where at first he saw nothing, distinguished nothing but a mad, seething whirl of sweeping figures, white, in a white room, under white light, Count Albert standing before him, the only dark object to be seen. As his eyes grew accustomed to the fearful brightness, he knew that he was looking on a dance such as the damned might see in hell, but such as no living man had ever seen before.

Around the long, narrow hall, under the fearful light that came from nowhere, but was omnipresent, swept a rushing stream of unspeakable horrors, dancing insanely, laughing, gibbering hideously; the dead of forty years. White, polished skeletons, bare of flesh and vesture, skeletons clothed in the dreadful rags of dried and rattling sinews, the tags of tattering grave-clothes flaunting behind them. These were the dead of many years ago. Then the dead of more recent times, with yellow bones showing only here and there, the long and insecure hair of their hideous heads writhing in the beating air. Then green and gray horrors, bloated and shapeless, stained with earth or dripping with spattering water; and here and there white, beautiful things, like chiselled ivory, the dead of yesterday, locked it may be, in the mummy arms of rattling skeletons.

Round and round the cursed room, a swaying, swirling maelstrom of death, while the air grew thick with miasma, the floor foul with shreds of shrouds, and yellow parchment, clattering bones, and wisps of tangled hair.

And in the very midst of this ring of death, a sight not for words nor for thought, a sight to blast forever the mind of the man who looked upon it: a leaping, writhing dance of Count Albert's victims, the score of beautiful women

199

and reckless men who danced to their awful death while the castle burned around them, charred and shapeless now, a living charnelhouse of nameless horror.

Count Albert, who had stood silent and gloomy, watching the dance of the damned, turned to Rupert, and for the first time spoke.

"We are ready for you now; dance!"

A prancing horror, dead some dozen years, perhaps, flaunted from the rushing river of the dead, and leered at Rupert with eyeless skull.

"Dance!"

Rupert stood frozen, motionless.

"Dance!"

His hard lips moved. "Not if the devil came from hell to make me."

Count Albert swept his vast two-handed sword into the fœtid air while the tide of corruption paused in its swirling, and swept down on Rupert with gibbering grins.

The room, and the howling dead, and the black portent before him circled dizzily around, as with a last effort of departing consciousness he drew his pistol and fired full in the face of Count Albert.

Perfect silence, perfect darkness; not a breath, not a sound: the dead stillness of a long-sealed tomb. Rupert lay on his back, stunned, helpless, his pistol clenched in his frozen hand, a smell of powder in the black air. Where was he? Dead? In hell? He reached his hand out cautiously; it fell on dusty boards. Outside, far away, a clock struck three. Had he dreamed? Of course; but how ghastly a dream! With chattering teeth he called softly,—

"Otto!"

There was no reply; and none when he called again and again. He staggered weakly to his feet, groping for matches and candles. A panic of abject terror came on him; the matches were gone! He turned towards the fireplace: a single coal glowed in the white ashes. He swept a mass of papers and dusty books from the table, and with trembling hands cowered over the embers, until he succeeded in lighting the dry tinder. Then he piled the old books on the blaze, and looked fearfully around.

No: It was gone,—thank God for that; the hook was empty.

But why did Otto sleep so soundly; why did he not awake?

He stepped unsteadily across the room in the flaring light of the burning books, and knelt by the mattress.

So they found him in the morning, when no one came to the inn from Kropfsberg Keep, and the quaking Peter Rosskopf arranged a relief party;—found him kneeling beside the mattress where Otto lay, shot in the throat and quite dead.

In the Triangle

Howard Wandrei

He listened.

In the familiar woods surrounding the house was some exotic beast, making its presence known in a most puzzling manner. Arnold closed the book he had been reading and walked over to the open window. The August afternoon was at its pitch, and the heavy, moist, hazy air had suffocated all other living things into silence. The man looked through the woods in the direction of the sound, and then cocked his head, listening intently, trying to identify the sound. It was a broken succession of growlings, a gobbling curiously interrupted so as to sound like a mechanical and humorless chuckling.

He was disturbed. There could be no beast on earth that could make a sound like that. Its utterly mechanical nature seemed all exact repetition. He thought of a phonograph, whose arm soullessly and maddeningly played the same groove of a record over and over and over again. His house was remotely situated, and no one from town would be here on such a stifling afternoon. The empty lightness of children was not in the noise, and it could hardly be made with implements. It was a throaty evidence of life, and now it cut regularly through the air like a vocal saw.

Arnold knew the woods very well, having lived there many years; the origin of the disturbance was not difficult to locate. Having listened intently at the window for some minutes, he dropped his book on the window-seat and crossed the room to the door. Here he stopped for a moment, but decided not to lock it. The small animals of the woods might take a bright object or two, so he returned to close the window. Then he closed the door, and after looking up at the dead blue sky and around at his greening acres, made off through the trees. No human being was likely to visit, especially on a day like this. Only one white-haired old man had come by in the last two weeks. Curious old fellow. He had eyed Arnold as though he were taking pictures of his ways, his body, and his brain; and he had taken his own time in leaving.

No air stirred. The birds were silent, and the trees stood so still they seemed waiting for life. Arnold walked rapidly and softly, peering through the trees ahead and to either side. The ground was not entirely free of brush, nor was it level. But the loose collocations of elms, oaks, and cottonwoods which were commonest in this country admitted a fairly unobstructed view for some

201

distance ahead. As he walked he looked familiarly on his property, identifying a stump, touching a tree where he had carved his initials a year or two ago. Now he was ascending a broad, low knoll, the first site he had chosen for his house, and decided against because of the magnificent trees growing here. From the continued noise of the beast he knew that discovery was close at hand. The sound was even more puzzling than before, and it would be difficult to say whether it was caused by throat or machine. There would be enlightenment on the other side of the knoll.

As he walked, the exotic growling had assumed the character of a struggle, and now, as he advanced more carefully, a thin, plaintive human voice, oddly familiar, augmented the sound of eccentric senseless chuckling. So it was a struggle, and one of the contenders was a man calling weakly for help.

Arnold quickly crested the knoll, shouting, "Hold on! I'm with you in a moment!"

The struggle, instead of ceasing at his now noisy approach, increased, and the chuckle became magnified to a broken, staccato barking. Arnold shouted again encouragingly, and, breaking through a clinging screen of creepers and clutching brush, stopped dead as he sighted the struggling figures before him.

In this spot three venerable cottonwoods formed an almost perfect triangle, within which the ground was almost free of all growth. In this triangle was lying prone an old man with long white hair. It was the old fellow who had dropped in two weeks ago. He was plainly and neatly dressed in coarse gray cloth, and he was striving fearfully to protect his throat and abdomen from the teeth and disemboweling claws of a strange beast.

The beast was of human size, and seemed to have something of the characteristics each of ape, pig, and dog. Its fangs were of extraordinary length, however, and it made such a violent caricature of life that Arnold looked on it with disgust and horror. Coarse black hair covered the body and a short tail jerked convulsively as the beast made its barking noises and its arching fangs worried the old man's throat. A hybrid? Odd animals have appeared most unaccountably at the strangest times in the most unexpected places. There was the dog-boar monstrosity that was found in France. This might not be the worst nor the least of nature's baroque experiments.

Completely revolted by the appearance of the queer animal, Arnold hastily looked for a convenient weapon, answering the piteous appeal in the old man's eyes. If he had taken fuller account of the situation, he might have hesitated, and thought the struggle even stranger than at first glance.

In the first place, aside from the affair in the triangle, the woods were uncommonly still, so still that the air seemed charged with waiting and expectancy. There was so marked a contrast between the apparent violence in the triangle and the deadly summer stillness of the air and brush and trees that the whole affair was denied both purpose and reality. The background of silence, suggesting a toleration that approached human understanding, gave the struggle the character of highest artificiality.

Arnold missed the significance in the attacking fangs of the beast. The teeth were terribly sharp, and, though repeatedly closing on the old man's throat, never dented the skin. The disemboweling claws, full of raking death, exerted convulsive pressure and nothing more. The claws themselves scarcely caught in the old man's neat gray cloth. Arnold had heard the ugly, ghoulish barking aright, but didn't see its meaning. The barks were unfinished growlings, animal sounds continually started and never completed. The old man exhibited no evidences of physical harm; his plain garments were unsullied, and were disposed in careful folds. The waiting woods and the struggling forms insidiously represented a composite threat and nothing more.

But Arnold, unable to find either stick or stone in the enclosed triangle, and daring to take no time looking through the brush encroaching on this particular spot, flung himself bodily on the assaulting beast. The impact of his body liberated the old man, who took to his feet at once, and circled the two on the ground gingerly.

"Kill him! Kill him!" he squeaked querulously.

"Get a stick!" said Arnold, furiously struggling. But the old man stood by, watching the two interestedly.

The beast emitted magnified, full-throated barkings now, and a long violence of growlings. Its rank, intolerable animal odor was suffocating and charnel in the stagnant air, and Arnold fought to finish the thing as soon as possible. Oddly enough, he thought at this moment of his pleasant room and the book he had been reading. The time-spread initials he had carved in the tree seemed stamped on the beast's rugose, leonine forehead. The hateful feeling of the moist, swine-like skin was a difficulty in itself, but more important was the fact that the animal's body afforded no firm grasp. He was holding the creature desperately by its wrists, and his superior position prevented it from using its deadly legs. Neither of them was free to use his hands.

"For God's sake, hit it! Kick its head!" he said, and looked up at the old man, his eyes full of violent entreaty. But the old man only skipped about tensely, eyeing the beast and looking at Arnold nervously. Arnold cursed his luck in hearing the beast from his untroubled house. Better the old man had died. Or would he have died anyhow? The animal might have been the old devil's pet, to all appearances. At any rate the old fellow didn't seem to have a scratch on his body from the curious encounter.

As Arnold looked into the beast's flaming eyes his brain flushed with desperation, purpose, and horror. The creature's wide, fixed stare seemed an attempt to take possession of his will, and he felt himself drowning in the engulfing shadows of the beast's mindlessness. He shook his head dizzily, freeing himself from the hypnotizing stare, and, as his one resort, sickly forced his jaws to the beast's throat. He found his face wet and warm, and the taste of blood on his lips. The reek of the thing's skin checked his breath. Convinced now that the situation demanded the beast's life or his own, he worked with distasteful hurry: there was the sanctuary afterward of his room and his books, nor would he ever bury this vileness on his loved property. The old man would hear a word or two, moreover. He had offered no help in the least, only dancing about like a gray-headed, delighted monkey.

During this time the creature had made no effort to use its own powerful jaws, only barking and growling savagely. And at Arnold's sudden determination to take its life, it closed its jaws for his convenience and merely continued the sound through its nose and throat. Its body lurched about with all the appearances of deadly intent, but it made no effort at definite harm. Arnold missed this singularity, and his revolted jaws clipped the beast's jugular.

The mingled incidents of the situation resolved themselves into coincidences. Arnold found himself lying prone, looking dimly at the sky. His throat hurt terribly, and he raised his arm to find his neck mangled, the large veins severed, and his life ebbing away in warm spurts. The arm was bare and swarthy, like pigskin, as was his whole unfamiliar body. The leathery tongue with which he tried to lick his straining lips encountered strange, curving fangs. Above him stood the beast, and his dying brain burned with shame as he recognized his own garments, his own watchful attitude, and himself, looking down eagerly with his own now weirdly glittering eyes.

Now the quiet summer afternoon afforded the scene of a hairy beast lying on the ground in the center of triangulated cottonwoods, clawing horribly at its breast. A young man and an old man with long white hair were walking off through the woods to Arnold's house, and, as the strange beast's head rolled sidewise, the eyes filming in death glimpsed finally the brisk figure of the old man looking back gleefully.

In the Vault

H. P. Lovecraft

There is nothing more absurd, as I view it, than that conventional association of the homely and the wholesome which seems to pervade the psychology of the multitude. Mention a bucolic Yankee setting, a bungling and thick-fibered village undertaker, and a careless mishap in a tomb, and no average reader can be brought to expect more than a hearty albeit grotesque phase of comedy. God knows, though, that the prosy tale which George Birch's death permits me to tell has in it aspects beside which some of our darkest tragedies are light.

Birch acquired a limitation and changed his business in 1881, yet never discussed the case when he could avoid it. Neither did his old physician, Doctor Davis, who died years ago. It was generally stated that the affliction and shock were results of an unlucky slip whereby Birch had locked himself for nine hours in the receiving-tomb of Peck Valley Cemetery, escaping only by crude and disastrous mechanical means; but while this much was undoubtedly true, there were other and blacker things which the man used to whisper to me in his drunken delirium toward the last. He confided in me because I was his doctor, and because he probably felt the need of confiding in some one else after Davis died. He was a bachelor, wholly without relatives.

Birch, before 1881, had been the village undertaker of Peck Valley, and was a very calloused and primitive specimen even as such specimens go. The practises I heard attributed to him would be unbelievable today, at least in a city; and even Peck Valley would have shuddered a bit had it known the easy ethics of its mortuary artist in such matters as the ownership of costly "laying-out" apparel invisible beneath the casket's lid, and the degrees of dignity to be maintained in posing and adapting the unseen members of lifeless tenants to containers not always calculated with sublimest accuracy. Most distinctly Birch was lax, insensitive, and professionally undesirable; yet I still think he was not an evil man. He was merely crass of fiber and function—thoughtless, careless, and liquorish, as his easily avoidable accident proves, and without that modicum of imagination which holds the average citizen within certain limits fixed by taste.

Just where to begin Birch's story I can hardly decide, since I am no practised teller of tales. I suppose one should start in the cold December of 1880, when the ground froze and the cemetery delvers found they could dig no more graves till spring. Fortunately the village was small and the death rate low, so that it was possible to give all of Birch's inanimate charges a temporary haven in the single antiquated receiving-tomb. The undertaker grew doubly lethargic in the bitter weather, and seemed to outdo even himself in carelessness. Never did he knock together flimsier and ungainlier caskets, nor disregard more flagrantly the needs of the rusty lock on the tomb door which he slammed open and shut with such nonchalant abandon.

At last the spring thaw came, and graves were laboriously prepared for the nine silent harvests of the grim reaper which waited in the tomb. Birch, though dreading the bother of removal and interment, began his task of transference one disagreeable April morning, but ceased before noon because of a heavy rain that seemed to irritate his horse, after having laid but one body to its permanent rest. That was Darius Peck, the nonagenarian, whose grave was not

205

far from the tomb. Birch decided that he would begin the next day with little old Matthew Fennet, whose grave was also near by; but actually postponed the matter for three days, not getting to work until Good Friday, the fifteenth. Being without superstition, he did not heed the day at all; though ever afterward he refused to do anything of importance on that fateful sixth day of the week. Certainly, the events of that evening greatly changed George Birch.

On the afternoon of Friday, April fifteenth, then, Birch set out for the tomb with horse and wagon to transfer the body of Matthew Fenner. That he was not perfectly sober, he subsequently admitted; though he had not then taken to the wholesale drinking by which he later tried to forget certain things. He was just dizzy and careless enough to annoy his sensitive horse, which as he drew it viciously up at the tomb neighed and pawed and tossed its head, much as on that former occasion when the rain had seemingly vexed it. The day was clear, but a high wind had sprung up; and Birch was glad to get to shelter, as he unlocked the iron door and entered the side-hill vault. Another might not have relished the damp, odorous chamber with the eight carelessly placed coffins; but Birch in those days was insensitive, and was concerned only in getting the right coffin for the right grave. He had not forgotten the criticism aroused when Hannah Bixby's relatives, wishing to transport her body to the cemetery in the city whither they had moved, found the casket of Judge Capwell beneath her headstone.

The light was dim, but Birch's sight was good, and he did not get Asaph Sawyer's coffin by mistake, although it was very similar. He had, indeed, made that coffin for Matthew Fenner; but had cast it aside at last as too awkward and flimsy, in a fit of curious sentimentality aroused by recalling how kindly and generous the little old man had been to him during his bankruptcy five years before. He gave old Matt the very best his skill could produce, but was thrifty enough to save the rejected specimen, and to use it when Asaph Sawyer died of a malignant fever. Sawyer was not a lovable man, and many stories were told of his almost inhuman vindictiveness and tenacious memory for wrongs real or fancied. To him Birch had felt no compunction in assigning the carelessly made coffin which he now pushed out of the way in his quest for the Fenner casket.

It was just as he had recognized old Matt's coffin that the door slammed to in the wind, leaving him in a dusk even deeper than before. The narrow transom admitted only the feeblest rays, and the overhead ventilation funnel virtually none at all; so that he was reduced to a profane fumbling as he made his halting way among the long boxes toward the latch. In this funereal twilight he rattled the rusty handles, pushed at the iron panels, and wondered why the massive portal had grown so suddenly recalcitrant. In this twilight, too, he began to realize the truth and to shout loudly as if his horse outside could do more than neigh an unsympathetic reply. For the long-neglected latch was obviously broken, leaving the careless undertaker trapped in the vault, a victim of his own oversight.

The thing must have happened at about three-thirty in the afternoon. Birch, being by temperament phlegmatic and practical, did not shout long; but proceeded to grope about for some tools which he recalled seeing in a corner of the tomb. It is doubtful whether he was touched at all by the horror and exquisite weirdness of his position, but the bald fact of imprisonment so far from the daily paths of men was enough to exasperate him thoroughly. His day's work was sadly interrupted, and unless chance presently brought some rambler hither, he might have to remain all night or longer. The pile of tools soon reached, and a hammer and chisel selected, Birch returned over the coffins to the door. The air had begun to be exceedingly unwholesome, but to this detail he paid no attention as he toiled, half by feeling, at the heavy and corroded metal of the latch. He would have given much for a lantern or bit of candle; but, lacking these, bungled semi-sightlessly as best he might.

When he perceived that the latch was hopelessly unyielding, at least to such meager tools and under such tenebrous conditions as these, Birch glanced about for other possible points of escape. The vault had been dug from a side-hill, so that the narrow ventilation funnel in the top ran through several feet of earth, making this direction utterly useless to consider. Over the door, however, the high, slit-like transom in the brick façade gave promise of possible enlargement to a diligent worker; hence upon this his eyes long rested as he racked his brains for means to reach it. There was nothing like a ladder in the tomb, and the coffin niches on the sides and rear, which Birch seldom took the trouble to use, afforded no ascent to the space above the door. Only the coffins themselves remained as potential stepping-stones, and as he considered these he speculated on the best mode of arranging them. Three coffin-heights, he reckoned, would permit him to reach the transom; but he could do better with four. The boxes were fairly even, and could be piled up like blocks; so he began to compute how he might most stably use the eight to rear a scalable platform four deep. As he planned, he could not but wish that the units of his contemplated staircase had been more securely made. Whether he had imagination enough to wish they were empty is strongly to be doubted.

Finally he decided to lay a base of three parallel with the wall, to place upon this two layers of two each, and upon these a single box to serve as the platform. This arrangement could be ascended with a minimum of awkwardness, and would furnish the desired height. Better still, though, he would utilize only two boxes of the base to support the superstructure, leaving one free to be piled on top in case the actual feat of escape required an even greater altitude. And so the prisoner toiled in the twilight, heaving the unresponsive remnants of mortality with little ceremony as his miniature Tower of Babel rose course by

207

course. Several of the coffins began to split under the stress of handling, and he planned to save the stoutly built casket of little Matthew Fenner for the top, in order that his feet might have as certain a surface as possible. In the semi-gloom he trusted mostly to touch to select the right one, and indeed came upon it almost by accident, since it tumbled into his hands as if through some odd volition after he had unwittingly placed it beside another on the third layer.

The tower at length finished, and his aching arms rested by a pause during which he sat on the bottom step of his grim device, Birch cautiously ascended with his tools and stood abreast of the narrow transom. The borders of the space were entirely of brick, and there seemed little doubt but that he could shortly chisel away enough to allow his body to pass. As his hammer blows began to fall, the horse outside whinnied in a tone which may have been encouraging and may have been mocking. In either case, it would have been appropriate, for the unexpected tenacity of the easy-looking brickwork was surely a sardonic commentary on the vanity of mortal hopes, and the source of a task whose performance deserved every possible stimulus.

Dusk fell and found Birch still toiling. He worked largely by feeling now, since newly-gathered clouds hid the moon; and though progress was still slow, he felt heartened at the extent of his encroachments on the top and bottom of the aperture. He could, he was sure, get out by midnight; though it is character-istic of him that this thought was untinged with eery implications. Undisturbed by oppressive reflections on the time, the place, and the company beneath his feet, he philosophically chipped away the stony brickwork, cursing when a fragment hit him in the face, and laughing when one struck the increasingly excited horse that pawed near the cypress tree. In time the hole grew so large that he ventured to try his body in it now and then, shifting about so that the coffins beneath him rocked and creaked. He would not, he found, have to pile another on his platform to make the proper height, for the hole was on exactly the right level to use as soon as its size would permit.

It must have been midnight at least when Birch decided he could get through the transom. Tired and perspiring despite many rests, he descended to the floor and sat awhile on the bottom box to gather strength for the final wriggle and leap to the ground outside. The hungry horse was neighing repeatedly and almost uncannily, and he vaguely wished it would stop. He was curiously unelated over his impending escape, and almost dreaded the exertion, for his form had the indolent stoutness of early middle age.

As he remounted the splitting coffins he felt his weight very poignantly; especially when, upon reaching the topmost one, he heard that aggravated crackle which bespeaks the wholesale rending of wood. He had, it seems, planned in vain when choosing the stoutest coffin for the platform; for no sooner was his full bulk again upon it than the rotting lid gave way, jouncing him two feet down on a surface which even he did not care to imagine. Maddened by the sound, or by the stench which billowed forth even to the open air, the waiting horse gave a scream that was too frantic for a neigh, and plunged madly off through the night, the wagon rattling crazily behind it.

Birch, in his ghastly situation, was now too low for an easy scramble out of the enlarged transom, but gathered his energies for a determined try. Clutching the edges of the aperture, he sought to pull himself up, when he noticed a queer retardation in the form of an apparent drag on both his ankles. In another moment he knew fear for the first time that night; for struggle as he would, he could not shake clear of the unknown grasp which held his feet in relentless captivity. Horrible pains, as of savage wounds, shot through his calves; and in his mind was a vortex of fright mixed with an unquenchable materialism that suggested splinters, loose nails, or some other attribute of a breaking wooden box. Perhaps he screamed. At any rate, he kicked and squirmed frantically and automatically whilst his consciousness was almost eclipsed in a half-swoon.

Instinct guided him in his wriggle through the transom, and in the crawl which followed his jarring thud on the damp ground. He could not walk, it appeared, and the emerging moon must have witnessed a horrible sight as he dragged his bleeding ankles toward the cemetery lodge, his fingers clawing the black mold in brainless haste, and his body responding with that maddening slowness from which one suffers when chased by the phantoms of nightmare. There was evidently, however, no pursuer; for he was alone and alive when Armington, the lodge-keeper, responded to his feeble clawing at the door.

Armington helped Birch to the outside of a spare bed and sent his little son Edwin for Doctor Davis. The afflicted man was fully conscious, but would say nothing of any consequence, merely muttering such things as "Oh, my ankles!", "Let go!", or ". . . shut in the tomb." Then the doctor came with his medicine-case and asked crisp questions, and removed the patient's outer clothing, shoes and socks. The wounds—for both ankles were frightfully lacerated about the Achilles tendons—seemed to puzzle the old physician greatly, and finally almost to frighten him. His questioning grew more than medically tense, and his hands shook as he dressed the mangled members, binding them as if he wished to get the wounds out of sight as quickly as possible.

For an impersonal doctor, Davis's ominous and awestruck cross-examination became very strange indeed as he sought to drain from the weakened undertaker every last detail of his horrible experience. He was oddly anxious to know if Birch were sure—absolutely sure—of the identity of that top coffin of the pile, how he had chosen it, how he had been certain of it as the Fenner coffin in the dark, and how he had distinguished it from the inferior duplicate coffin of vicious Asaph Sawyer. Would the firm Fenner casket have caved in so readily? Davis, an old-time village practitioner, had of course seen both at the respective funerals, as indeed he had attended both Fenner and

Sawyer in their last illnesses. He had even wondered, at Sawyer's funeral, how the vindictive farmer had managed to lie straight in a box so closely akin to that of the diminutive Fenner.

After a full two hours Doctor Davis left, urging Birch to insist at all times that his wounds were due entirely to loose nails and splintering wood. What else, he added, could ever in any case be proved or believed? But it would be well to say as little as could be said, and to let no other doctor treat the wounds. Birch heeded this advice all the rest of his life until he told me his story, and when I saw the scars—ancient and whitened as they then were—I agreed that he was wise in so doing. He always remained lame, for the great tendons had been severed; but I think the greatest lameness was in his soul. His thinking processes, once so phlegmatic and logical, had become ineffaceably scarred, and it was pitiful to note his reaction to certain chance allusions such as "Friday," "tomb," "coffin," and words of less obvious concatenation. His frightened horse had gone home, but his frightened wits never quite did that. He changed his business, but something always preyed upon him. It may have been just fear, and it may have been fear mixed with a queer belated sort of remorse for bygone crudities. His drinking, of course, only aggravated what he sought to alleviate.

When Doctor Davis left Birch that night, he had taken a lantern and gone to the old receiving-tomb. The moon was shining on the scattered brick fragments and marred façade, and the latch of the great door yielded readily to a touch from the outside. Steeled by old ordeals in dissecting-rooms, the doctor entered and looked about, stifling the nausea of mind and body that everything in sight and smell induced. He cried aloud once, and a little later gave a gasp that was more terrible than a cry. Then he fled back to the lodge and broke all the rules of his calling by rousing and shaking his patient, and hurling at him a succession of shuddering whispers that seared into the bewildered ears like the hissing of vitriol.

"It was Asaph's coffin, Birch, just as I thought! I knew his teeth, with the front ones missing on the upper jaw—never, for God's sake, show those wounds! The body was pretty badly gone, but if ever I saw vindictiveness on any face—or former face! . . . You know what a fiend he was for revenge—how he ruined old Raymond thirty years after their boundary suit, and how he stepped on the puppy that snapped at him a year ago last August. . . . He was the devil incarnate, Birch, and I believe his eye-for-an-eye fury could beat time and death! God, his rage—I'd hate to have it aimed at me!

"Why did you do it, Birch? He was a scoundrel, and I don't blame you for giving him a cast-aside coffin, but you always did go too damned far! Well enough to skimp on the thing in some way, but you knew what a little man old Fenner was.

"I'll never get the picture out of my head as long as I live. You kicked hard, for Asaph's coffin was on the floor. His head was broken in, and everything was tumbled about. I've seen sights before, but there was one thing too much here. An eye for an eye! Great heavens, Birch, but you got what you deserved! The skull turned my stomach, but the other was worse—*those ankles cut neatly off to fit Matt Fenner's cast-aside coffin!*"

Itself

Seabury Quinn

"No," Dr. Applegate said reflectingly, "I'm not at all sure we can refer everything to science for an explanation, at least, not to science as we know it."

Renouard, the demonstrator of anatomy, gave his diminutive beard a quick, nervous tug and smiled like an amiable Mephistopheles. "Ah, yes," he mocked, " 'In earth and sky and sea, strange things there be,' eh? Can you give us any sign, doctor?"

Applegate drew thoughtfully at his cigar. "I wouldn't be too anxious for a sign, if I were you, Renouard," he warned. "Patrick O'Loughlin wanted a sign, and got one.

"It was last spring that O'Loughlin came down with a touch of influenza. Nothing serious; just a case for careful diet and bed-rest treatment; but the family wanted a nurse, so I got them Miss Sandler. Wonderful girl, Sarah Sandler. None better. If she were on night duty and the devil himself came into the sick room, she'd tell him to make as little noise as possible when he put his pitchfork behind the door, and step softly, lest he wake her patient.

"I dropped in to see O'Loughlin toward the end of the week and found him lying on his back, trying to stare a spot of sunlight off the ceiling.

" 'How are you, Pat?' I asked when he took no more notice of me than if I'd not come in. 'Let's see the chart. Ah, fine; you'll be up and attending to business by this time next week.'

" 'No, I won't, doctor,' he answered in a hollow voice. 'I'll never get out of this bed till Mike Costello comes to dress me for my funeral.'

" 'Rats!' I answered. 'You're healthy as a herd of elephants, O'Loughlin. A little touch of flu won't have any more effect on you than a drink of liquor. Why, your chart shows a steady decline in temperature. You're as good as recovered this minute, man.'

" 'No, doctor,' he replied with the stubbornness only an Irishman can show. 'I'm a doomed man; I've had the sign.'

" 'Sign?' I repeated testily. 'What d'ye mean?'

" 'The comb sign, sir,' he replied. 'Mary Ann had it before she went, and go she did, spite of all you could do to keep her.'

" 'Your daughter had an aggravated case of interstitial nephritis,—it's particularly deadly in the young,' I told him. 'We caught the disease too late, and no power on earth could have saved her. You're a husky man, sound as a trivet, except for a touch of flu—'

" 'She had the sign, and she went, doctor,' he interrupted doggedly, 'and I've had it, and *I'll* go, too. It's no use your trying to save me; I'm going.'

" 'What do you mean?' I asked, seating myself on the bedside. When a patient gets in such a frame of mind the doctor has to think fast, if he doesn't want to lose another case.

" 'It came to us three months before Mary Ann died,' he answered. 'There was a crowd of young people at the house, and 'long toward midnight someone suggested they try some table-tipping. I didn't want to interfere with their fun; but I didn't like it. Table-tipping and such like things aren't good for the soul, sir, as any man from the old country can tell you.

" 'Well, sir, they all sat down to the little table in the hall, and put their hands on it, little fingers touching, so as to make a complete circle, and one of the young men called out, "Are there any spirits here tonight? If there are, let them answer our questions. One rap on the table means *a*, two, *b*, and so on through the alphabet. Now, then, are there any spirits here tonight?"

" 'Dr. Applegate, you can believe it or not; but that table—a brand-new piece of furniture it was—began to quiver like a mettlesome horse when something startles him, and all 'round its edge there started a series of rappings as though someone was marching about it beating a tattoo with a pair of drumsticks.

" 'Then I lost my temper, for I don't hold with that sort o' thing, and I said, "Whoever's knocking on that table, quit it. I won't have it in my house."

" 'The young folks jumped up from their chairs, doctor, but the drumming kept up, and Mary Ann suddenly cried out, "Why, father, they're calling for *you!* Hear the rappings? 'Patrick O'Loughlin; Patrick O'Loughlin,' is what they're spelling."

" 'And so they were. "Who calls?" I wanted to know, and the rappings stopped like a drum corps' music when the drum major brings down his baton.

" ' "Who calls?" I asked again, and the thing spelled out the answer: "Itself."

" 'You're not Irish, doctor, and you most likely don't know what that word meant to an Irishman. Over in the old country we have fairy folk and such like, and those we call the little good people, though the holy saints know they're not good at all. But we call 'em good lest they hear our real opinion of 'em and steal away our children or burn our homes over our heads. But bad and troublesome

212

as the little good people are, they're holy angels compared to some o' the things that hover 'round in the air. And these terrible things, the very sight or sound of which means death, we don't name at all, though we know their names well enough. We refer to 'em by the use of a pronoun, and the worst of 'em all we call simply "themselves."

" ' "And what does Itself want with Patrick O'Loughlin?" I asked, though my breath was coming so fast in my throat it near choked the speech from my lips.

" 'And it answered me and said, "Patrick O'Loughlin, you have called to me and here I am. Never, while there's a man or woman of your blood in this new land will I desert you. You shall know when Death and I are near by the movements of the comb."

"I could have laughed in the man's face. Who but an Irishman could have dreamed such a fantastic story? Table-tipping, a message from an old-world fairy, delivered by rappings on a piece of Grand Rapids furniture!

" 'You're crazy, Pat,' I told him.

" 'Am I, indeed, doctor?' he answered seriously. 'Then listen to this: Never a word more could we get from the table after that one message had been delivered, and what the night-thing meant by "the movements of the comb" was more than any of us could imagine.

" 'But you recall well enough when Mary Ann was taken sick. You remember how she seemed so much better just the day before she died? Well, sir, the very night the poor lamb went away I went a-tiptoe into her room to kiss her good-night, and she was lying in bed, staring at me with her big blue eyes like a little child lost in the woods. "Did you put my comb on the bed, daddy?" she asked as I came into the room.

" ' "Comb, child? What comb?" I asked, curious to know what she meant.

" ' "My big comb, there," she says, and points to the foot of the bed where, lying on the folded comfort, was the big Spanish tortoise-shell comb her Uncle Timothy, who was a sea captain in the Lamport and Holt service, had brought her from Barcelona for a gift on her fifteenth birthday. She always kept the trinket in a blue velvet case on her dressing table, and most of the time the case was locked, for you never can tell when a servant will pick up a piece of bric-a-brac like that and make off with it.

" ' "It was in the case this morning, I'm sure," she told me, "for Miss Jarvis, the nurse, was admiring it then; but just now I chanced to look at the foot of the bed, and there it was, shining in the electric light more beautifully than I'd ever seen it glisten before."

" ' "It must have got put there by mistake, child," I told her as I picked the thing up and restored it to its case; but there was a feeling of dread running through me as I spoke, for I recalled the message I'd had.

" 'That very morning the angel came for her, doctor. You yourself remember how we called you from your bed past midnight, and how her little white soul had gone to heaven before you could get here?'

" 'Yes; I remember, Pat,' I answered soothingly, 'but what has all this to do with your getting well?'

" 'Just this, doctor,' he replied earnestly. 'Mary Ann's room has been left untouched, save for the necessary cleaning, since the day we took her from it, and the comb has always lain in its velvet case on her dressing table, exactly as I put it the night she died. Last night, sir, as I was lying here, trying to sleep, and not able to for the way my thoughts kept turning on Mary Ann, I felt a soft thump on the foot of my bed, as though a cat had leaped up there. Dr. Applegate, sir, it was my daughter's comb lying there, though the Holy Mother herself only knows how it came down a flight of stairs and through two closed doors to get there.

" 'I've had the sign, doctor. You mean well, and your medicine's as good as any; but there's nothing you can do. 'Tis a priest I need to doctor my sinful soul, not a medical man to patch my body up, sir.'

" 'H'm, where is this comb?' I asked.

" 'Upstairs, in Mary Ann's room,' he answered.

" 'Well, then, Patrick,' I told him, 'here's where we play a Yankee trick on this old-country goblin of yours. I'm going to take that comb home with me, and lock it in my office safe, and if "Itself" comes snooping around my place I'll give him a dose of medicine that'll send him back to Ireland by the non-stop route.'

"He grinned wanly at my suggestion as he answered, 'All right, doctor, do as you please; but it's no use. I've had the sign and nothing earthly can help me now.'

"Half an hour later I left the O'Loughlin house, the blue velvet case containing the carved tortoise-shell comb under my arm. I locked the thing securely in my wall safe, attended to my office calls, ate dinner and went to the club for a rubber of bridge.

"It must have been just past midnight when I got back to the house, for the policeman on our beat was putting in his call at the patrol box across the street as I unlocked my front door.

"The shrilling of my telephone bell greeted me as I stepped from the vestibule. 'Hello?' I called.

" 'This is Miss Sandler, Dr. Applegate,' a voice came over the wire. 'Mr. O'Loughlin has died. Shall I—'

" 'I'll be right over,' I said.

" 'He died while I was out of the room, doctor,' the nurse told me. 'I made sure Mr. O'Loughlin was sleeping easily before I slipped downstairs at midnight to

214

pour myself a cup of coffee—I was gone less than five minutes by my wrist watch. When I came back he seemed still sleeping, but a second look told me he'd never wake again in this world.'

"She busied herself with the bottles on the bedside table a minute, then looked up at me, almost diffidently. 'Did Mr. O'Loughlin say anything to you about a comb this afternoon?'

" 'Yes, he said something about a sign, and as it was preying on his mind, I took the thing home with me.'

" 'You *did?*' she replied incredulously.

" 'Yes; why?'

" 'Why—why,' she seemed at a loss for words—'you're sure you took that comb home with you, doctor?'

" 'Of course I'm sure,' I answered.

" 'Well, sir, when I came back from drinking my coffee—just after I noticed Mr. O'Loughlin had gone—I happened to look down on the foot of the bed, and—and I saw this there.' She lifted a cushion from the couch and produced the exact duplicate of the comb I'd taken from O'Loughlin's house that afternoon.

" 'I've been nursing for nearly ten years, doctor,' she went on,—'two years in the army during the war—and I didn't think anything could unstring my nerves; but—well, Mr. O'Loughlin told me about this comb tonight, and I thought it was funny—then. Now I don't know what to think. It gives me the creeps.'

" 'You're not the only one who has the creeps,' I told her as I took the comb. 'Call Costello's undertaking establishment and tell them I'll have the death certificate ready when they get here.'

"When we'd completed the clerical details I drove Miss Sandler to her apartment, then hustled back to my office. 'Now we'll see what's what,' I promised myself as I took from my pocket the comb the nurse had found on O'Loughlin's death bed and began to turn the knob of my safe.

"My fingers seemed all thumbs and my hand shook in spite of myself. I laid the comb on the corner of my desk, grasped the safe knob in both hands, and spun the combination.

"There was the blue velvet case, exactly as I had placed it in the safe ten hours earlier. I fairly snatched it open in my eagerness. In its setting of white satin, the tortoise-shell comb lay glistening in the light.

" 'That settles that,' I murmured: 'now for the other one.' I turned to the desk, then blinked in stupefaction. The comb I'd laid there two minutes before was gone.

"High and low, over every inch of my office, I searched for that bit of feminine frippery like the woman in the parable hunting her lost piece of silver. Daylight was coming through the office windows before I gave up.

"Explain it any way you will, or don't explain it at all. I can swear I locked up one physical, tangible comb in my safe that afternoon; Miss Sandler found exactly the same comb on the bed beside O'Loughlin's body, and I will take oath that I carried that very comb home with me. But from the moment I turned my back on it to open my safe, I never saw that second comb again."

Jason, Come Home

Darrell Schweitzer

> Why this is Hell, nor am I out of it.
> —*Marlowe*

Jason lived in a closed little world, in the upstairs bedroom he had occupied since earliest childhood, surrounded by all the accumulating strata of boyhood and adolescence and early manhood. Model airplanes dangled from the ceiling. Plastic battleships, which had once lined the shelves, were now crowded awkwardly by heaps of books and records. The walls were covered with posters: Frazetta, psychedelics, reproductions of classic paintings, and even a huge map of James Branch Cabell's imaginary land of Poictesme. This room was home to him. He went out from it, into the larger world when he had to, always to return, though, to its cluttered comfort.

His father had vanished from his life early, when he was nine, one summer night after concluding a particularly spectacular quarrel with his mother. There had been a knock at the door, and his father came in and merely said, "Goodbye son." Then he went out of the house, "to get a Goddamned newspaper," as he'd shouted when Mother demanded an explanation, and he never came back. After that, Jason lived alone, his mother reduced to a noise in the background, a figure seen on the stairs, but seldom a true presence. His father had been the parent who mattered.

He remained in his room after college, puttering away at his drawing table, selling an occasional cartoon to the syndicates, but otherwise just sliding from one day into the next, with nothing more demanded or hoped for or even wanted.

The end came when he was thirty, when his mother died and he was forced out, into a kind of exile. His uncle got him a job with an advertising agency in New York. So he left the Philadelphia suburb; and his new, closed-in world was a dingy apartment in the Bronx, where the elevated trains roared by his window at all hours, and between them the traffic on the Cross Bronx Expressway was a steady whisper, like a bitter wind.

He returned to his apartment one sweltering June evening, panting after walking up five flights of stairs because the elevator wasn't working. He let himself in, then carefully locked the three locks, one after another, and wedged the iron bar of the police lock diagonally between the door and the floor. It was as he stepped into the kitchen and had one hand on the refrigerator door, with a no more complicated thought in his mind than a glass of lemonade, that he heard the distinct sound of someone rummaging through his bedroom.

He froze, unable to feel anything but a kind of resignation, as one might in that last second in front of an oncoming train, when even terror is useless. But he was able to step silently into the hall. His hands knew what they were doing. He got out his keys and unlocked one lock, then another.

Suddenly a huge, sweating black man, a complete stranger, stepped out of the bedroom with Jason's videocasette recorder in his arms.

"Hey, man . . ."

The burglar set the VCR down on a chair. A switchblade flicked open in his hand.

Jason grabbed the bar of the police lock, but the black man only grinned. A second burglar materialized out of nowhere and yanked the bar from his hands, then tossed it to the first. It was only as he stood dumbly staring at his empty hands that Jason realized that the partner must have been standing in the doorway to the bathroom, opposite the kitchen, just out of sight behind a bookcase, no more than three feet away all the time he'd been working at the locks.

The second burglar caught him by the collar and lifted him against the door. He too had a switchblade, weaving the point back and forth in front of Jason's eyes.

"You make one little sound, motherfucker . . ."

"Shit, just kill him and get the fuck outa here," the other burglar said.

The one holding Jason laughed. "He can't do nothing. You know how us folks all look *alike* . . ." To Jason he said, *"Ain't that right?"*

Jason's only response was a gasp as a fist slammed into his solar plexus and a knee caught him in the groin. After that he lay still on the floor, doubled up, just wishing the pain would go away, that everything would go away. It might have been hours before he realized he was alone in the apartment.

He staggered into the bedroom, standing in the doorway with his eyes closed, not daring to look. But he couldn't stand there forever, and eventually he opened his eyes and saw what he had been expecting. All the drawers had

217

been dumped out. The books had been swept from the shelves and trampled, the posters ripped from the walls. A solitary plastic biplane dangled from the ceiling, minus its upper wing.

He sank down in the doorway and covered his face with his hands, sobbing gently. He felt like he had been raped, his innermost *self* violated. The outer world had burst in brutally, through the window overlooking the elevated tracks. As if to mock him, a particularly noisy train went by just then, rattling the apartment. The last plastic battleship slid off a shelf and broke.

He knew he was completely alone, with no one to turn to and nowhere to go. It occurred to him, in an abstract way—he couldn't apply the thought to himself, no, not really—that if he had somehow directed his life differently, years ago, he might not be here now, like this. But he had lived himself into a corner, and here he was.

He thought, too, of calling the police, but never did. He was sure they had enough statistics already.

Instead, with that same feeling of utter resignation he'd had before, he waded through the debris and reverently set up his drawing table. He re-attached the clamp-on lamp and plugged it in. Fortunately the bulb was not broken.

Then he found a pencil and righted a chair, and began to draw.

Hours passed, and he lost himself in the act of drawing. The pain of the outer world receded a little.

Then somewhere, far away, a phone was ringing.

The night seemed to go on forever, and still he worked, with faint, light touches of the pencil, his hand guided almost unconsciously, without any plan or design. It was only after a long while that he realized what he was doing: remembering and reconstructing the only place in the world he had ever been safe or happy, his old room at home. His hand called back every object in perfect detail, reproducing precisely the order of the books on the shelves, the angle of the fake polar-bear throw-rug in relation to the bed, the formation of the model planes on the ceiling.

The dark, noisy New York world retreated beyond his window once more, and he was comforted.

But the phone was still ringing. It had been doing so for an hour. Slowly he came to realize that the sound was from *his* phone, at his feet among the wreckage. He picked it up.

"Jason, come home," a voice said softly.

He put his pencil down carefully.

"Who is this?"

"It's Dad. Come home, son."

He was even more afraid now than he had been when the burglar seemed about to slit his throat. He knew that voice. He had long treasured it in his memory.

"Stop it! Whoever you are, stop it!"

"Jase—"

"My father went away when I was nine. We never heard from him. He's dead."

"You sure, Jase?"

No one had ever called him *Jase* except his father. He'd once fought with a boy at school for doing it, because *Jase* was the secret name his father had given him, and no one else was allowed to use it.

"Look," he said weakly. "I can't. The house was sold to developers. It's offices now. I don't live there. Neither do you."

"Don't bother to pack, Jase. Everything is here for you. Just come home."

His journey was like a dream. The burglars hadn't taken his wallet. No, in this dream, which he secretly and deeply knew *wasn't* anything as simple as a dream, as night finally paled into dawn, he had money and he bought a ticket and boarded an Amtrak train. Penn Station rolled away, and at ill defined intervals the loudspeaker called out Newark, Princeton Junction, Trenton, and finally Thirtieth Street, Philadelphia. As long as he didn't think about it, as long as he let himself drift with the current of his dream or whatever it was, everything was easy. He felt as if a great burden were lifted from him.

A local took him past familiar sights. The station names were like a litany: Wynnewood, Ardmore, Bryn Mawr, Rosemont. At last he stood on a familiar platform. Slowly, trembling with expectation, he descended the wooden steps into the parking lot, while the early morning traffic of school children and cleaning ladies melted away around him. He was alone, gazing up the hill he had so often climbed, where a Tudor house stood among oak and mimosa trees.

He climbed the hill, still unable to bring himself to question what he was doing, or even wonder why there was no sign in front of the house proclaiming its conversion into the offices of assorted doctors, lawyers, and real estate brokers. Nor did he hesitate when he found that he still had the key to the front door on his key chain.

The lock had not been changed.

He went inside, and he knew at once that he belonged here. It was something he could feel, almost as if only here he could truly breathe. He stood in the little hall at the bottom of the front stairs for a while, looking at the familiar things all around him: the grandfather clock gleaming darkly in the living room to his left, the framed tintypes of his great-grandparents on the wall to his right, the antique lantern on the mail table. There was mail there, a few letters, and a copy of *Treasure Chest* magazine. That startled him. He had subscribed to *Treasure Chest* as a child, but was sure it had long since ceased publication.

Then, at last, because he inevitably had to, he went reverently up the carpeted stairs, past the familiar old prints his mother had carefully restored and framed, to his own room, where the books and airplanes and the plants in the windowsill were all exactly as they had always been.

He lay down on the bed and realized that he was home now, truly and for good, and he slept peacefully, his whole New York exile no more than a rapidly fading, unpleasant dream.

Downstairs, in the kitchen, plates clacked. Silverware clinked on a glass. A teapot whistled.

He sat up suddenly, disoriented for a few seconds, remembering. He rubbed his face and shook his head.

It was still morning. He wondered if he had slept through the whole day and night, into the following morning. It felt like a long time.

He gazed slowly around the room, running his hand along the bookcase by the bed, noting the familiar titles and arrangement.

This isn't possible, he thought, but there was too much pain in thoughts like that. So he took the path of least resistance and merely rose and prepared himself for breakfast. In the bathroom, he paused to stare at himself in the mirror. The face looking back at him was not a thirty-year-old man's, but much younger, eighteen or nineteen at most. It seemed right that way.

Afterward, he put on blue jeans and a college t-shirt and went downstairs barefoot.

He hesitated before the kitchen door, his heart racing, his thoughts a muddle.

"Mom?"

There was no answer. He gently pushed the door open. The kitchen was empty, but a place had been set, and pancakes steamed. He walked around the kitchen and peered out into the yard. Everything was as it always had been, the woodpile, the shed, the few boards nailed up from an abandoned attempt to build a tree house.

Nothing moved out there. He listened. Nothing moved inside the house either. The grandfather clock in the living room ticked patiently. He sat down and ate, then washed his dishes and put them away, and went back to his room.

For a while he lay back on the bed daydreaming, and then he reached over for a random book. It was *The Count of Monte Cristo*, which had been his favorite once. He opened it near the beginning and reread the prison sequence, caught up in the hero's desperation and the joy of his escape.

Once more he heard someone moving about the house. He put the book down and listened, but did not get up from the bed. The kitchen door opened and closed. Footsteps came up the carpeted stairway.

He sat up, tense, waiting for the door to his room to open. It had to open, any second now.

But it didn't.

"Mom?" he called out, and when no answer came, he called again, his voice breaking into an awkward squeak. *"Dad?"*

He got up and opened the door himself. No one was there, but a tray had been placed on the post at the top of the stairs, with a sandwich and a glass of milk on it.

That afternoon he put on sneakers, got the lawn mower out of the shed in the back yard, and mowed the lawn. It was so easy, falling into the familiar pattern, doing what he always did, what was always expected of him.

But when he finished, and had put the lawn mower away, a disquieting thought came to him. He almost remembered being someone else, somewhere else. That other person wasn't able to accept what was happening to him. That other person said again and again, *No, this isn't possible.*

He hardly knew what he was doing. Something gave him the impulse, and he walked slowly to the end of the driveway. There he stopped, looking up and down the street at the familiar houses, at the names on the mailboxes which he knew from his paper route. When he was a small child, he had ranged through all the back yards, discovering the secrets of the tangle of bushes behind the houses that all the neighborhood kids called The Jungle.

The houses were silent, the street empty.

And the vaguely remembered person said again, *No, this isn't possible.*

But Jason knew that it merely *was*, possible or not, that he was *here*, and he turned and went back into the house, up to his room.

He must have napped. It was dusk when he awoke. His legs didn't quite reach the floor. He slid off the bed, then hurried down to the living room, turned on the TV set, and plopped down on the floor, holding his face up between his fists. He watched *The Lone Ranger* first, then *Ramar of the Jungle.*

Someone was moving about in the kitchen. He heard kitchen sounds, and after a while he could smell roast chicken.

"Jase, it's time to eat," a voice said.

He got up, switched off the set, and went in to his dinner. Again he ate alone, but this time two places were set.

A door swung shut upstairs. Floorboards creaked overhead.

He stopped eating then. He sat still and remembered so many secret things, and wished, and remembered some more. He was almost crying when he finally ran to the stairs and up them.

His father was waiting at the top of the stairs. He hadn't changed at all since that night he'd gone out for the newspaper.

"Daddy?"

His father smiled and beckoned him up the stairs with a gentle flicking motion of his fingers.

"Welcome home, son. Welcome, welcome home."

He began to climb the stairs slowly, his heart pounding, his eyes wide. Halfway up he stopped, and merely stared.

"Come on, Jase. Come on."

He backed down one step, then two, then three.

"Daddy, I . . . can't."

"What's the matter, Jase?"

"I don't know, Daddy. It's like I . . . don't belong here."

"This is your home, son. Of course you belong here. Now come upstairs."

"No." He turned and ran the rest of the way down the stairs and bounded against the front door, his fingers working furiously at the chain and the lock. He said, aloud, in a voice that wasn't that of a child, *"No, this isn't possible."*

Then he was outside and running in the darkness, along the familiar street, and something seemed to fall away from his mind, and he could think more clearly, and remember, and he began to become someone else, and the memory and the actuality changed places.

It was suddenly morning, and he wasn't running, merely walking swiftly, looking at his watch and afraid he would miss his train. He was dressed in a suit and carrying his art portfolio. Businessmen with briefcases hurried up the wooden stairs, onto the train platform.

As he waited among the commuters, and as the conductor called out the familiar stops, he seemed to be surfacing out of some depth, like a swimmer rising toward the sunlight from the bottom of a deep pool. He changed trains at 30th Street, Philadelphia, and soon the flat New Jersey landscape slid by the window. Then he saw New York again, and that view, too, was familiar, the gray-blue towers of Manhattan rising beyond a house-covered hill shortly before the train went underground.

He went to work that day, but he accomplished little. His mind was a muddle of shifting impressions and memories that weren't memories, all summed up by the question *Did any of it really happen?* For a while that was a comfort, the thought that none of it, including the burglary, had ever happened, that it was a bad dream, a mere vapor of the mind. But at the same time he felt a strange *newness* about everything, the agency, the other employees, the restaurant where he went for lunch. It was as if he didn't belong here, and had somehow been inserted into someone else's life.

Did any of it really happen?

He knew, of course, that in the end he would have to find out. He delayed

222

as long as possible that evening, wandering the streets after dark even though he was often afraid to wander the streets, trying to put off that final moment of discovery and confirmation.

But in the end, he returned to his apartment, and he saw the remains of everything he had managed to cling to from his home, from his room, the trampled books and clothing, the ripped posters, the broken airplanes.

He could not weep now. He was beyond all that. The weeping had been done by someone else, it seemed, long ago. Now all he could do was sit down at the drawing table, clamp a fresh piece of paper in place, and begin to draw.

The thought came to him that he would draw the burglars and turn the result over to the police. He had seen them both clearly enough.

But that was someone else's thought, an intrusion, and he put it out of his mind.

The elevated train rumbled past the window.

He drew his room again, his room back home, once more calling back every detail. He worked with a desperate urgency, as if time were running out, his last chance slipping away.

He sat, barefoot and in blue jeans and a college t-shirt, in the middle of a ravaged apartment in a strange and frightening place remembering, remembering, while someone died inside him, someone who was no more than a vaguely familiar stranger, someone who shouted for the last time, *No, this isn't possible.*

The phone rang.

Johnny on the Spot

Frank Belknap Long

I was Johnny on the spot. I had left a guy lying in a dark alley with a copper jacketed bullet in him, and the cops were naming me. They were also naming a torpedo named Jack Anders. Anders had ducked out of the alley, the back way, without stopping to see if I was tagging after. The bullet had come out of Anders' gun, but I was as much to blame as he was for what had happened.

Wait—I've got to be honest about this, I was more to blame. He was the trigger man, but I had put the finger on the guy in the first place. I wanted to get away from the bright lights, because when I stared at my hands in the glare of the street lamps they seemed to change color. I couldn't stand the sight of myself in the light. My red hands—

In the dark I could forget about my hands. I wanted to dance in darkness to the strains of soft music. It was a screwy sort of urge—considering. All over town the teletype was naming me. By going into that taxi dance hall I was exposing myself to more publicity on the same night.

I should have stayed with the crowds in the street. But I'm a restless sort of guy. When I get a yen I have to satisfy it, even if it means extra legwork for the cops.

A dozen heavily rouged dolls in romper suits were standing around under dim lights when I entered the hall. I walked past the ticket window and mingled with the sappy-looking patrons. The Johnnies who patronize taxi dance halls are all of one type—dumb, awkward-looking clucks who have to shell out dough to get favors from dames.

With me it's different. All I have to do is snap my little finger. I don't mean I could have got by in there without buying a ticket. Not for long. But there's a rule which says you can look the dames over and walk out again if you're not suited. All I did at first was mingle with the patrons and size up the dames. And that's how I came to overhear the conversation.

The two dames who were whispering together were standing off in one corner, away from the ropes. One was a blonde with cold eyes and an "I've been around" look.

The other girl was young and sweet. I could tell just by looking at her that she hadn't been around at all.

The blonde's eyes were boring like a dental drill into the younger girl's face. I stood close beside her, listening to what she was saying. She wasn't giving that poor kid a ghost of a break.

"You're pretty smart, aren't you?" she taunted. "You think you've got something."

The dark-haired girl shook her head. "No, Dixie, no, I didn't say that. I don't know why he likes me. I swear I don't."

"Quit stalling, hon. You know how to use what you've got. You're smart, all right, but not as smart as I am. I'm taking him away from you, see?"

Sudden terror flared in the younger girl's eyes. She grasped her companion's wrist and twisted her about.

"You can't do that! I love him. I love him, do you hear!"

The blonde wrenched her wrist free. "You'll get over it hon," she sneered, her lips twisting maliciously. "They all do. I can't help it if I like the guy."

"You like him because he's rich. Not for what he is. You got lots of men crazy about you."

"Sure, I have. But Jimmy's different. Maybe I do love his dough. So what? Don't you love his dough?"

"I swear I don't, Dixie. I'd love him if he didn't have a cent."

"He's all you've got, eh? Well, ain't that too bad?"

"You won't take him away, Dixie. Promise me you won't."

224

Dixie laughed. "I'm taking him tonight, hon. I've had plenty of experience with guys like Jimmy."

I knew then that Dixie was the girl for me. I stepped up to her and held out my arms.

"Dance, honey?" I said.

She was plenty startled. She stared at me for an instant in a funny sort of way. Like she knew I was standing there, but couldn't see me.

Then her arms went out and around my shoulders. We started to dance, moving out into the hall.

We were in the middle of the floor when something seemed to whisper deep inside of me: "Now, now, while the lights are low and the music is like a whisper from the tomb."

I stopped dancing suddenly and clasped her in my arms. "You'll never take Jimmy away from her," I whispered.

She was a smart one, that girl. She recognized me an instant before I kissed her. She whimpered in terror and struggled like a pinioned bird in my clasp.

"Spare me," she moaned. "Come back in a year, a month. I'll be waiting for you. I won't run out on you, I swear it."

"You played me for a sap," I said. "You were warned about your ticker, but you went right on dancing."

"I'll stop tonight," she promised wildly. "Give me a few days—a week."

I shook my head. "Sorry, girlie. This is the payoff."

It's funny how near I can get to people without frightening them. When she sagged to the floor the couples about us went right on dancing. The lights were so dim they didn't notice her lying still and cold at my feet.

For three or four seconds no one noticed her. Then one of the girls saw her and screamed. All over the floor men and women stopped dancing and crowded about her. I knew that in a moment they would be naming me again. So I slipped silently from the place.

I do not like to be named. In that dance hall I was just a lonely guy looking for a dance to waltz with. I am only Death when I strike, and between times I am like the people about me.

Maybe you'll meet me sometime in a crowd. But you won't recognize me because I take color from my surroundings. I am always fleeing from what I have to do. I am a Johnny on the spot. But in the end—in the end I meet up with practically everyone.

Justice

Brian Stableford

In the days when Swabia was one of the five grand duchies and the *Schlegerbund* were a great power in the land there came to the town of Ravensburg a man named Nikolaus Makri, who had fled from Lombardy upon a tide of dark rumours which alleged that he was overactive in the cause of change and progress.

Swabia's nobles considered theirs a more advanced realm than decadent Lombardy, and so Makri was made welcome there—all the more because he claimed to be a wise and artful physician, and also to be expert in the amputation of limbs. In Swabia the work of surgery had long been the prerogative of barbers rather than physicians, but the march of progress had reduced the barber's guild to a mean and powerless thing. The status of barbers was so reduced that they had little enough success in persuading certain stubborn souls that it was evil for a man to cut his own hair, so their protestations failed to inhibit the ardent Nikolaus from plying his saws and razors as he wished. He became a well-respected man in Ravensburg, and became enthusiastic for the improvement of his adopted town.

There was in Swabia at this time a very violent highway robber who had also come to the duchy from Lombardy. His name was Zorillo, and the depredations which he practised around the shores of Lake Konstanz had become the stuff of legend. The *Schlegerbund* finally condescended to send a company of mercenaries to pursue him, and he was eventually seized by them while hiding in a cheesemaker's shop on the outskirts of Ravensburg. He was quickly brought to trial before the three magistrates of the district.

Knowing that he was doomed, Zorillo confessed all his crimes and pleaded guilty. This was a wise move, for Swabia was at that time the most civilized region of the Empire, and the law of the land was meek enough to licence torture only in cases where the guilty would not admit their crimes.

The presiding magistrates laboured long and hard to find a way in which they could increase the robber's punishment, for he was guilty of many heinous crimes against the property of noblemen as well as the murder of a few lesser folk, but the law was quite clear. They could pass no harsher sentence on a robber who confessed his guilt than to order that he be hanged by the neck and choked by slow degrees. No doubt they considered the possibility of an accusation of heresy, which—if substantiated—would permit Zorillo to be burned, but however reluctant the robber had been to abide by the laws of the Church, he had never openly questioned their propriety, nor had he ever been so vile as to play the cutpurse with men of the cloth.

Thus it was that Zorillo was sentenced to go to the merciful gallows with his limbs unextended by the rack and his joints uncrushed by the boot. The voices of his victims, whose gold had never been recovered, were loud in proclaiming that such gentle treatment could not be an effective deterrent to other Lombard thieves, who would surely flock across the border in ever-greater numbers. The fact that Zorillo had become something of a hero to the poor folk who were not worth robbing only amplified these fears.

When Zorillo's trial was over, however, Nikolaus Makri visited the frustrated magistrates, and told them that he knew of a way by which the bandit's suffering might be prolonged within the letter of the law. He said that he had been encouraged to speak in the interests of serving justice, and in the interests of encouraging the thieves of decadent and hateful Lombardy to stay at home.

Makri proposed that the magistrates should allow him to make a small incision in the lower part of Zorillo's throat before the robber was sent to the scaffold. This, he explained, would allow a trickle of air into the felon's lungs even when the rope was drawn exceedingly tight, and might prolong the hanged man's agony for an hour or more.

The magistrates were sceptical at first, objecting that a slit throat was the easiest way of all to die, but when Nikolaus Makri had demonstrated his technique on a stray dog they were convinced, and gave him a licence to proceed, so that the vengeful ends of justice might be seen to be properly served in spite of the gentleness of the law.

When the time came for him to meet his destiny Zorillo objected most strenuously to the making of the incision, declaring that it amounted to unlawful torture, but the magistrates gleefully replied that Master Nikolaus was a certified physician, whose vocation was to discover how life might be prolonged. They pointed out to the miserable villain that wise men everywhere were quite agreed that the actions of physicians—no matter how painful and nauseating they might sometimes seem to the ignorant—could not possibly qualify as torture.

The robber could not be persuaded to agree with this judgement, and he appealed to the Bishop of Ravensburg, asking that the Church should intercede on his behalf. Alas for Zorillo, the Bishop—whose own wealth had been somewhat reduced by Zorillo's zeal for theft—agreed with the magistrates that the ends of justice would best be served by letting Makri proceed with his experiment.

When he heard this, the condemned man fell to cursing everyone on sight—but he dared not call upon the devil's name lest he provide grounds for his own burning. The magistrates, being good and pious Christians, had not the least fear of his feeble invocations. Indeed, they were convinced that God would wholeheartedly approve of the lesson which they were about to offer to all those who might contemplate interference with the divine ordering of men's estates— which clearly insisted that the best of men were destined to be rich and the worst of them poor.

When the appointed hour came, the incision in Zorillo's neck was duly made by the ingenious Makri, before the hangman's rope was made secure. Then the robber was hauled most carefully upwards, and made secure to the gibbet, so that the weight of his body might cause the noose to tighten by patient degrees. The whole town had heard of the physician's bold scheme, and everyone was there to see how long it took for the condemned man to die, and what wrigglings and writhings he might contrive to make in the meantime. How many there were who wished to see the experiment fail—in addition to Ravensburg's three barbers, who had an understandable prejudice in the matter—it is impossible to judge.

There was much discussion regarding the longest time that it had ever taken anybody to die upon a Swabian scaffold, and veterans of a hundred public executions were earnestly consulted as authorities upon the matter. Some said fifteen minutes, others twenty, and one ancient crone swore by her rotting teeth that she had seen the infamous murderer Homstein kick his legs for half an hour before the inevitable stink gave evidence of his dying spasm. Wagers began to be laid as to how long Zorillo would last, and there was such excitement generated by these speculations that marked candles were brought from a nearby Benedictine monastery in order to measure the result—for all of this occurred in the days before the invention of mechanical clocks.

The most popular predictions were clustered between forty minutes and an hour, and within five minutes of Zorillo's suspension more gold had been wagered upon the length of his life than he had ever stolen. Whatever redistribution of Swabia's wealth he might have contrived by the manner of his life paled into insignificance by comparison with the redistribution which would be accomplished by the manner of his death.

When the first of the twenty-minute marks upon the candle-timer was passed, a great cheer went up from the crowd. Zorillo was still writhing and kicking his feet in a thoroughly vigorous fashion, and though his eyes were bulging from their sockets he was still capable of looking wildly about. He was still trying to speak, though the cord about his neck would not permit it, and a sorrowful priest was heard to remark that this enforced silence would at least keep his soul safe, by preventing any weakening of his resolve to refrain from calling upon the devil for aid.

As the second twenty-minute mark was passed in its turn there was a greater cheer, and loud applause for clever Nikolaus Makri—especially from those who had wagered on a longer interval. Zorillo was quieter now, and his bulbous gaze had ceased to roam the crowd, but his fists continually clenched and unclenched in a strained and calculated manner which was clearly not the work of some posthumous agitation, and his bowels had not yet let go of their burden to signal the moment of expiry. The gamblers were counting seconds now, calling them in scrupulous unison, held taut by the knowledge that fortunes might be won or lost on the passing of each moment.

By the time that the hour mark was passed the chanting of the seconds had begun to waver, because the greater proportion of the wagers laid had by then been settled or given up for lost. Only the boldest of the speculators had put pledges on times in excess of the hour, and though another cheer went up at the melting of the mark it was somewhat muted by comparison with the last. The crowd were no less inclined to marvel at what Makri had accomplished, but there was now less praise and more anxiety in the exclamations, for Zorillo had again commenced to struggle fiercely against the rope which held him, as though he sought by furious effort to hurry on the moment of his release.

If the robber's efforts were indeed directed to that end, they failed him. He continued to dance, and his dance now seemed as uncanny as it was desperate. Though his eyes were blank and fixed, his blackened tongue still moved like a slug within his gaping mouth, and in the quieter moments there were those in the crowd who believed that the hanged man was somehow contriving to make audible sounds. More than one was later to claim that they heard words, but German is the kind of language which, when whispered, can easily sound like the gaggings, gaspings and gurglings of a strangled throat.

When another hour had elapsed, and Zorillo still moved on the end of his rope, the wonderment of the crowd was beginning to turn to horror. None had dared to bet on such an interval as this, and the minds of the watchers began to turn—as the minds of men inevitably do when they are faced with the unprecedented—to the fear that some awful magic might have been involved in procuring Zorillo's amazing longevity. Nikolaus Makri was still standing by the magistrates, proud as a peacock to see what he had achieved, but he was now the target of uneasy glances from many of the humble folk—who were ever inclined, in their ignorance, to suspect physicians of secret sorcery.

When a further twenty minutes had elapsed without Zorillo being reduced to stillness or incontinence, the magistrates conferred, and then sought a second opinion from the Bishop, who was also in attendance. They decided, though not without a certain reluctance, that enough was enough, and that justice had now been seen to be done. The public executioner was commanded to go forward and grip Zorillo's body firmly round the waist while lifting his own feet off the ground, so that his extra weight would further tighten the noose and hasten the robber's demise.

The executioner obeyed, but he quickly let go, saying that he could not bear to feel the hanged man struggling so fervently to throw him off. While he was making this excuse he suffered the consequence of standing too close to the gibbet, for Zorillo caught him with a well-directed kick which knocked him sprawling on the ground. Some of those in the crowd cheered, but the greater number were too anxious to be amused. The suspicion was abroad that the devil's hand was in the business now, and there were many who were willing to suppose that Zorillo might have secretly turned heretic after all.

"You have done your work well enough," said one of the magistrates to Nikolaus Makri. "Now will you tell us, if you please, how much longer it will take this wicked man to die?"

But Nikolaus Makri did not know, and he could only shake his head. An anxious frown had appeared upon his face.

All of a sudden, the hanged man began to shake and quiver in a new way, as though he had been seized by a bout of wild laughter which, because it could not escape from his sealed throat, was forced to eddy and echo inside him.

"Well," said the bruised and bitter executioner, picking himself up from where he had fallen, "there is one sure way to put an end to the farce." So saying, he took a dagger from his belt, and thrust it hard into the hanged man's breast, intending to puncture the heart which was still beating within.

But the wound inflicted by the executioner refused to bleed, and the hanged man skilfully kicked his persecutor in the head again, sending him sprawling in the dirt for a second time.

"It is not Zorillo!" cried a voice from the crowd. "It is a demon sent by the Lord of Hell to possess his body, and there will be a dire time in Swabia while it hangs undying there!"

When this was said the priests and friars who were present became angry, for they alone had a licence to detect the hand of the devil in earthly affairs, but they made no shift to offer an alternative explanation. Even the bishop seemed fearful, and he was evidently beginning to regret that he had given his approval to an action which, however virtuous it seemed, had no obvious precedent in the scriptures.

The crowd began to melt away, as the common people began to run to their homes, anxious for the consequences of what their masters had wrought.

Now it proved quite impossible to approach the hanging body, for if anyone stepped towards it, its booted feet would lash out very fiercely—and Zorillo did not seem to be in any way aware of the fact that the hilt of a dagger stood out prominently from his breast, set firmly in a deep but unbleeding wound.

The face of the hanged man was very dark and bloated now, but the protuding eyes did not seem sightless—instead they seemed possessed of a stare more wrathful than could ever be worn by a man who had not a strangling noose around his neck. While the sun stood high in the sky the baleful glare was difficult enough to bear, but when sunset stained the western sky blood-red Zorillo's eyes became so fierce and fiery that there was not a man in Ravensburg who dared meet that stare. In the end, even the priests and magistrates went away, and the watchmen whom they set to guard the gibbet stood with their backs to the unsleeping man who still danced beneath it.

When night had completely fallen, the hangman was instructed to creep up on the gibbet under cover of darkness, with the object of cutting Zorillo down so that his body might be dealt with another way. He agreed to try it, for he was a man of courage and he had not forgotten or forgiven the indignities to which he had been subjected. But when he approached the scaffold, as stealthily as he was able, he was kicked yet again, more savagely than before. He instantly resigned from his position.

All through the next day, and the next after that, Zorillo hung unquietly where he was, with his bulging eyes staring horribly at everyone who passed him by. Although his face began to show signs of corruption, with white maggots creeping upon his darkened flesh, still his body squirmed and still his legs lashed out if anyone approached. No one any longer doubted that the adversary who took delight in all the sufferings of men had been moved by Nikolaus Makri's cunning ploy to take too keen an interest in the duchy of Swabia—and if any proof were needed that Satan was abroad in the land, fevers broke out in the town, and animals in the fields began to sicken.

When a week had passed, and the rotting body on the gibbet still gave every indication that there was unnatural life in it, Nikolaus Makri was seized by the constable and taken to the prison, where he was swiftly tried for sorcery, and convicted in spite of his denials.

He complained very loudly that he was a physician and a devout follower of Christ—and this refusal to make a proper confession of his foul sins entitled his judges to torment him until he acknowledged the justice of their action. His limbs were stretched until the joints popped, his skin was vigorously raked with iron combs, and his eyes—when their stare began to remind his uncomfortable questioners of the staring eyes of the undead Zorillo—were melted and sealed by boiling tar.

When this business was concluded, Makri should by law have been taken to the place where Zorillo's scaffold stood, and properly burned in order to make certain that his soul could not be darkened by any failure of his hard-won repentance, but this was not possible while the demon-inhabited corpse still hung there. So Ravensburg's churchmen and lawyers were forced to continue their lately-established tradition of innovation, and in view of the fact that the position of public executioner remained unfilled, they ruled that the guild of barbers must supply a razorman to cut the physician's throat.

The guild of barbers was only too happy to oblige, and the three candidates drew lots to see which one would be afforded the honour of carrying out the execution.

When the act had been done—more neatly than any mere physician could ever have managed it, the perpetrator proudly claimed—the bloodstained body of Nikolaus Makri was taken to the gibbet, and laid down nearby. All the free citizens of the district were called to public prayer, and the Bishop piously led them in imploring Jesus the merciful to undo what his direr enemy Satan had contrived, allowing Zorillo to go to that eternal rest—or perhaps eternal torment—from which the people of the town had tried so foolishly to keep him for a while.

But in the morning, it proved that the hanged man was still staring, and still squirming, and that the plague had still to run its horrid course throughout the region; and so the people of Ravensburg learned that once the common order of things has been deliberately upset, it is not so readily restored.

Doubtless this single example of the dangers of tampering with tradition was of little significance in the greater scheme of things, but it contributed in its own small way to that great tide of misfortunate events which eventually caused Swabia to turn its back on the dubious causes of justice and progress, and which ultimately swept the entire duchy on to the rubbish-heap of history.

The Law of the Hills

Grace M. Campbell

I have grown old and credulous. Such a thing simply could not happen. Not in this country, and not in this day. But—believe me or not, as you please—I tell you I saw it.

Ever since Ken Graham first walked into my classroom, I have wished that I might have had such a son. And as the years went by, my fondness for him grew, and I began to dream that some day he should take my place, and complete the collection of minerals which has brought me and this old school fame.

Why not? After graduating with honors, the boy had two years of study in the best schools abroad, and then a year of practical work in the field. What else did he need? Only that I should pull the strings my own departmental Punch dances to, and have him designated assistant professor of mineralogy.

So I pulled the strings, and the appointment was made. But he answered with a strange, incoherent letter begging delay.

I could not understand it. Perhaps that chit of a girl he had married in Norway preferred a director of mines with five thousand a year to an assistant professor with half that salary. Idiot! Couldn't she see that I meant to make him head of the department?

I took out of my desk the picture they had sent from Norway, and all my suspicions vanished.

Surely there was no stupid selfishness of that sort in the mate Ken Graham had chosen. A sweet, unspoiled young face, with a fine delicacy of feature. And yet such a strange suggestion of wildness! That fluffy aureole of whitish hair! Those keen, deep-set eyes! Those sharply outlined features! She looked like a beautiful wild thing.

Hush! A jealous old man's imaginings.

In the end I decided that I would go to them. I would seek them out, and bring them back. This old stone house was big enough for all of us to be happy in, if happiness was possible. Old men are arrogant sometimes—and I had set my mind on spending the rest of my days near the boy I had learned to love as a son.

When I got off the train, they told me where I should find him. It was late, but he would still be in his office, the expressman said.

"A bear for work, that Graham. He's never stopped since his wife died. Too bad about his wife. The wolves got her and Louis Barjon one night, just a few weeks ago. A great pity—a great pity."

Oh, my boy! My poor, poor boy!

I could see him, as I came up the walk, his head bent over his hands before the uncurtained window.

I tapped on the door, and walked in.

"You, Professor? You? What brought you here?"

"Rocks, my boy," I lied. "Rocks. Specimens. Clarke at Ten Mile has unearthed a curious fossil—some sort of pig, he says. He claims it's Jurassic Permian. He's set it far too early, of course, but I came along to look at it. But there's time for that tomorrow. I wanted to have a chat with you."

"And no one could be more welcome," he returned. "Come inside. It's late, and you have had a long, hard trip in."

Of course I had—a damned hard trip in. I'm getting old, and thirty hours on a little, one-horse railroad is no joke to me. But I did not intend to be bundled off to bed until I had got to the bottom of this thing that was making my boy look like a man who had been through the Valley of Death.

233

"I'm sleeping here now," he explained, as he took me into a little room off his office. "I had this place built some weeks ago, after——"

He did not finish, but stooped, and set a match to the fire. The great pine knots flamed and roared in the open fireplace. He boiled water, and made tea, talking all the time of mines, and mine-management, and minerals.

We smoked in silence a long while after he had put the cups away. Then I leaned over and put my hand on his knee.

"Ken, my boy. Could you tell the old man?"

He started, and looked at me searchingly.

"You wouldn't believe me, Professor."

"I am not a scoffer, son," I answered.

He rose, and threw another knot of pine on the fire. I watched the flames curl up and around it. The young man's face was lost in shadow.

"Do you believe in lycanthropy?"

"Of course not. There is no such thing."

"Of course not. There never was such a thing. And yet, I tell you, I have seen it happen."

Was the boy insane? Why, that was old English superstition. It belonged to the days of witchcraft and burnings. Never since the Sixteenth Century had intelligent men of any country in the world, save Russia, talked of such things seriously. Absurd!

"My wife," he went on, without looking up, "never knew much about her father. He was killed, it was said, in a hunting accident the second winter after his marriage. His wife died of shock the day the news reached her, and left a little daughter two hours old. That is all Hilde ever knew of her parents.

"She was brought up on the old estate, under the personal direction of her grandfather. He was passionately fond of her, but he watched with an eagle eye over all her study and her play. The old man was a constant contradiction to Hilde. He would never allow her living pets of any kind, for one thing. He took her to England, France, and Egypt, but never permitted her to holiday in the mountains of her own beloved Norway. Even when she went to Torghatten, her course of study was laid down by that inconsistent old man. He seemed to show his affection for her by suppressing all the instincts that were strongest.

"It was at Torghatten that I met her—and we loved each other.

"The old gentleman received me with great kindness, when I visited him. He had many questions to ask me about my parentage, and my work. I answered them all as I could, and did not wonder much at the seriousness with which he asked them, though I had the impression continually that there was something he wanted to say to me, something that preyed upon his mind. At times, he seemed happy in our happiness, and planned with us the details of our mar-

234

riage. Then, in the very midst of the planning, he would start up with fear in his face, and speak as if it all must stop.

"Once he started to say something about his son, Hilde's father, but stopped short before he had well begun.

"To the very day we sailed from Norway, he was a constant puzzle to us.

"When this offer came from Meakins & Company, I hesitated to bring my bride into a rough camp like this. But Hilde insisted she would love it. All her life she wanted to live in the solitary places, to climb hills, and be free. She begged me to accept at once.

"We came north a few days later, as you know. I built her a little bungalow on the hill yonder, just across the river. Before I had the foundation laid, she had flowers growing all about the place, native flowers which she had never seen before, but which she transplanted and tended with passionate care.

"She turned our little cabin into a very bower of beauty, and there was not in the world anyone more exultantly happy than she.

"Often she took long walks alone, while I was at the mill. I have come home many times to find a note on the table to say that we would have tea on the Baldman. She would be waiting there with a picnic supper. And all through the long summer days we were happier by far than I had ever dreamed of being.

"Then came winter.

"All of a sudden it came. The cold set in overnight. A driving storm that lasted for three days buried the countryside in drifts. It was the northern winter at its worst.

"One night"—here the boy paused to breathe heavily, and his face was set—"one night we were sitting cozily by the fire reading, when suddenly a wolf howled quite near.

"Hilde went deathly white, and clutched my hand.

"I took her in my arms, and laughed at her, and told her there was no cause for alarm, and that his majesty would be bold indeed, and very hungry, before he would dare attack any human.

"But nothing that I could say really comforted her, and from that time on, she was in terror of being left alone, especially at night.

"A month or so later, I was kept late at the mill, and it was nearly eleven before I started home. Going up the hill, I heard the wolves again. There is no mistaking the cry of the timber wolf, and I ran up the steps hoping that Hilde had not heard.

"There was no light in the house, and I tiptoed into her room, trying not to wake her till the sound had died away.

"The moon shone in the window, and there was my girl, crouched down on the floor, peering out into the night. She seemed in the grip of an agony of emotion dreadful to see, and did not know that I was there at all.

"I touched her on the shoulder. She turned like a flash, and looked at me for a moment with only fear in her face. Then she crumpled up in my arms, and sobbed hysterically until she fell asleep."

Ken drew a gusty sigh and paused, his pipe forgotten in his hand.

"I could not understand it at all," he went on. "She was not a coward. There's a little lake up in the hills where we used to swim, and I have seen her dive into the water from twenty feet up the cliff. So it was more than fear that troubled her. It was some deeper dread of which she could not speak.

"She was never her old self after that night when she cried herself to sleep. At times she would lavish passionate, tearful love on me. At other times, she was absent-minded and lost in somber reflections of her own.

"One night, when I came home early, she was not there. I was searching frantically for her when she came quietly up the path, bareheaded and alone. There was such a look in her eyes as I have seen in the eyes of the dead, and I followed her in silence into the house, fear clutching at my heart.

"The wolves were frequently to be heard in those days. The heavy snow had made them very bold. Once they came so close to the house that I reached for my rifle determined to teach at least one of them a lesson in restraint. But Hilde caught my arm, and stopped me.

"I knew her tenderness for wild things, and put my .22 away in the shed.

"When I came back into the room, she was not there. Vaguely uneasy, I searched for her in the bedroom. She was not there. But the window was open, and I saw among the trees a lithe, gray-white form that flashed across the shadows and was gone.

"I won't go into the details of that night. All sorts of horrors came to me—old folk-tales of Norway that the people of the hills believed in, stories of the taint that ran in certain families and of the dread deeds done at night 'by the will of the Foul Fiend.' I kept wondering, too, about the death of Hilde's father, and asking over and over again whether I had gone out of my mind.

"Suddenly the door opened and there stood Hilde, her fair hair white with loose fluffs of snow. She looked tired and worn, and with only a furtive glance at me she hurried to her room and slept heavily till noon.

"She was frequently absent after that, and I never knew, when I came home at night, whether she would be there or not."

Again the boy paused, staring at the fire. And again he went on.

"One day, there was an explosion at the northern mine, and I went up to try and get things moving again. No train came out that night, so I decided to tramp the eleven miles back rather than leave Hilde alone.

"Just a few miles from home, I realized that I was being followed by wolves. I was not armed, and there was nothing for it but to climb a tree. A broken-off oak stump stood near the track. It offered no protection from the

236

wind, but I knew that from it I should be able to hail the log train in the morning if necessary. So I scrambled up in some haste.

"Within two minutes there were fourteen timber wolves squatting in a circle about that stump. You know their method—a short wait to see if you're going to run for it, then a half turn to the left, and a steady circling march around their victim.

"I don't know what the end of that death-march would have been, for just as I was bending all my will-power to fight the hypnotism of it, there dashed down the railway track a slender white wolf. Like a mad thing she darted here and there about that circle, then flashed away among the trees, with the whole pack behind her.

"I waited till their cry had died away in the distance, then climbed stiffly down, and hurried home. Hilde was waiting for me at the door. There was a curious brightness in her eyes, and she listened with some tension, I thought, to the explanation of my lateness. But I said nothing at all of my adventure with the wolves.

"A few nights later, Louis Barjon dropped in after supper. For once Hilde was almost herself. She was reading by the fire, while Louis and I smoked.

" 'Never saw the wolves so bold as this year,' said Louis. 'Have you seen the white one? White as a snow-drift, she is, and swift as the wind. She seems to come out of nowhere to join the pack, and they're devils when she's with them. She's the most beautiful animal I've ever seen, but I bet she's as keen on the kill as any of the dirty crew.'

"Hilde dropped her book. 'The white wolf never kills,' she said.

"Louis turned and looked at her in astonishment. Was it merely girlish sentiment for a lovely wild thing? Evidently Louis thought so, for he laughed tolerantly and went on, 'Well, maybe. But folks is laying for her. It's hardly safe to go out at night, so keep your rifle handy, boy.'

"I remembered the one night when I did take my rifle down. I glanced at Hilde. Her eyes were wide, and her nostrils dilated. What was the emotion that swayed her? My heart contracted.

" 'Did you ever see her?' demanded Louis again. I thought of the gray-white form I had seen flitting among the trees, and of the beautiful white beast that had saved me from the pack only a few nights before. But I shook my head in denial.

" 'I've seen her twice,' he went on. 'The other night I took a flying shot at her, and I caught her on the right front paw. But it was just a scratch, I guess, for there was only a bit of blood on the snow.'

"In spite of myself, I glanced at Hilde's right forearm. She had it tightly bandaged. I looked up at her face. Her eyes were fixed on the back of Louis' head as he picked a coal out of the fire for his pipe.

"Was it only fancy, or did her lips draw back from her white teeth?

"My heart seemed to stop beating. That picture is engraved on my mind forever. Old Louis, bluff and weatherbeaten, leaning down over the fire; Hilde watching him with a sort of sinister ferocity; and I dumb with terror.

"In silence I let him rise, and wind his long scarf about his neck, and go out into the night.

"I shut the door behind him, and turned hastily to Hilde. I was too late. She was gone. I went to her bedroom. She was not there, nor in any other room in the house.

"A sense of black tragedy engulfed me. I clung with all my might to my love for her, and I prayed to know the secret the old man in Norway would have told me before we came away.

"My whole soul revolted at the conclusions that were forcing themselves on me, and I waited in horror for what the morning would bring. I don't think I thought much after a while. My mind seemed numbed. I just sat and waited, with a curious sense of waiting for more than her coming home.

"Toward morning it started to snow heavily. I built up the fire, and put the kettle on to boil.

"Then I heard a sound outside, a whining and a heavy scratching sound. I flung open the door.

"Call me mad, if you will—but there in the snow was the white wolf. She was staggering and covered with blood, and scarcely able to drag her hindquarters into the room. The beautiful animal crawled weakly to my feet, and rubbed her head against my knee like a dog.

"I took her head between my hands, and she looked up with those pleading eyes I knew, licked my hand once or twice, and sank on the floor—dead.

"I knew my girl would never come home again.

"I knew—God! that such things should be!—that the old law of the hills had held, that ancient, dreadful law that said there was no return for the werewolf that once had spilled the blood of humankind.

"I knew, too, what they would tell me that day—that old Louis was dead, that he had accounted for half the pack before they had got him, but that they had got him in the end.

"And then I told them that my wife had gone with Louis, that she had gone to spend a day with his wife, to help her with the quilting. They were deeply distressed, and searched everywhere. But they found no trace or sign of her at all.

"I buried the white wolf that night, under the pine trees. And the wolves howled about the place till dawn.

"Since then I have waited, hoping against hope that some day I will wake and find that I have only been insane.

"I have not the courage to sleep at the cottage now, but I go there every day to see if perhaps she has come home. But I know, as there is a God in heaven, that all that is mortal of my girl lies buried there under the pine trees, where her garden was last year."

For an hour he sat there, his head bowed in suffering, till from sheer weariness he slept in his chair.

I threw a coat around him, and built up the fire, and sat there thinking, thinking, thinking in amazement and dread.

The thing could not be, of course. Yet, I had lived near enough to Mother Earth to know that there are more things under heaven than science has ever dreamed of.

But the proof of it? I had to have some proof.

I sat there till daylight. Then I made strong coffee for the lad, and we had breakfast when he woke. I told him all that was going on around the old halls, confessed that I had lied to him about Clarke's fossilized pig, and saw a hint of the old twinkle return to his eyes.

Then I slipped away.

Now I should test this thing. Within the hour I should know whether the lad had dreamed an ugly dream or had been the victim of devil's work.

The cottage door was unlocked, waiting Hilde's return. Things were just as she had left them, no doubt—her work bag in the corner, the book she had been reading open on the table. But I did not pause there. I went on through to the garden.

The grave was clearly marked by a blazed cross on the giant pine. Frantically I began to dig, and as I turned out the loose sand I prayed that I might prove that the boy had only dreamed.

I made my gruesome find. With my hands I scraped away the earth that covered the bare skull and the bony paws. With my fingers I pried the long rows of teeth apart, and looked.

God! Was I too gone mad?

In the sharp canines were little pits of yellow, and one large molar had a solid cap of gold.

Letter from Will Stotler, Dated October 32nd As Received by D. E. LeRoss

I submit to you the following letter which I received on October fifteenth.

Dillon,

I'd ask about the kids I know you don't have, ask about the weather, pretend to care, but I have a big big bad problem and I wasn't sure what to do. The children have stopped their screaming, the weather is fine here. I wanted to call you but your number's unlisted. The FBI came yesterday, I'm a mess, that's what I wanted to call you about. (Cold eyes opening.) It's Jemain, Dillon, he went south.

Jemain's notes stacked, lines and bridges, a complex schemata for soul-searching, for reading the world, all felt-tip and ball-point and full of truth. When I first read his notes, Jemain had been gone for about a week. (Cold eyes glaring.) That was in August. He was on his way even before he left, going south. I've said that five times, haven't I? (Shrill screams of terror, of children, of vocal response.) No, I've only said it twice, I checked. God!

June 26th, 1994

Will! A quick story. There is this really Fat Guy with a bushy beard that goes into a video store named Video Implosion and rents the *Cannibal Bride–Emerald Jungle* type gore-flick trash. He comes back and rents another arm-load. (We've got them all at the Implosion, Steve buys 'em cheap.) I just smile. After the guy rents all of the splatter-ick he doesn't come back. Two weeks later I'm in HardCore. See the Fat Guy in the ever-shrinking horror section—replaced by erotic thrillers, sex and knives and plot holes covered with lotsa skin. I don't see what he rents but I can guess. (At least he isn't renting holocaust documentaries.) The quick story ends. Last week's headline on the Weekly World News: CANNIBAL FILM-

240

MAKERS IN MEXICO CITY. Thought about that article from Paranoia magazine (GHOULS TRAFFIC STREET KIDS' BODIES FOR RICH TRANSPLANT PATIENTS). Some people wanna live forever, eh? Went to the library and found it's common for street-children to disappear. They lose a thousand kids a year in Rio alone. The Natives don't mind; the kids are a pain in the butt. The World Health Organization believes the missing kids go sick from disease and run from the cities. Harvest organs, play it off as poverty taking a toll, make stomach-pumping Teevee commercials . . . Bet you can buy pickled five-year-old spleen in Hong Kong. Well, I rented (um, borrowed) Lenzi's *Emerald Jungle* from the Implosion. I have two big questions. One. How did Lenzi get all the carnage to look so real? Two. Who would want to watch cannibals in action? Well, in the quick story, the Fat Guy likes them. (That's the *who*. The why please.) And I'm sick of bumping into him. So big you just can't miss. You know he works for the phone company? Watched him pole-climb. There was a sight! 400 lbs. up a pole. What if he dropped into traffic? Talk about terror. Check my new diagram. Page 17. Red line shows progression, retrogression. I am the black line across the page.

More lines and notes and lines and notes. (Children are shrieking.) I've sent you copies of some of Jemain's better diagrams. (I've kept the originals—even the FBI didn't get them.) Maybe the pages will make sense to you and you can tell me what you think. Does friendship happen this way, a transaction? (Cold eyes flickering.) Here's the other letter out of the packet Jemain left for me before he went to Delaware.

July 4th, 1994

Great great. Another 4th and here I still am. Gotta get outta here. Writing about the Lenzi thing. New lines added to page 17. Found more at the library on a tip. Book titled *The Gnostics* by Lacarriere, page 62. "For knowledge itself, in a world of illusions, can only be illusory?" Questions questions. Let me tell you a strange little story. Starts like: The Fat Guy doesn't come back to the Implosion but my phone dies. I go to Benny's and call Pac Bell. They send the Fat Guy and he fiddles with the technicolor wires in the apartment's phone box. He recognizes me, has runny snot on his beard. I get to talk film as he splices wires. Doesn't mention Lenzi's stuff until I bring it up. He finds Lenzi's stuff "distasteful. Very bad." I don't bother to ask why he rented them if he knew from the box that they'd be so very bad. He then recommends *The Gnostics* and says

Lenzi's films document seven steps to sloffing off this "too heavy body." He says Lenzi is a very gnostic man. Phone repaired, exit Fat Guy, end strange little story. Heavy bodies? Lenzi cannibal training films for the gnostic? Check out page 17. Retrogression. The aquamarine line crosses the orange line, port-ten-cious . . .

(A bit of blood smeared on a blue wall.) You just read the last letter that Jemain wrote before he went to Delaware. It was in a packet he gave me that also had notes and legal pads full of words and sheets covered with lines. (A cold eye, a finger, a twisted braid of hair.) The scribbles and lines and screams and words are all mixed up, metered out, metaphorical depth-rope streaming from the chapped hands of a metaphorical riverboat steward. Jemain went across the country then down the coast to Delaware, to the beach, and got another job at a video store. (Mucus and tears.) I got this next letter in the beginning of September. By then I'd carefully read his notes and made a little sense out of them. I wish the screaming would just stop. (Cold eye opens, pupil wide.)

August 24th, 1994

Hey! My new address is at the top of this sheet. Found more about Lenzi. He ends up in Mexico! Why stop in Mexico? Everybody stops. In Mexico it seems. Well, I watched all of Lenzi's films. I can see why the Fat Guy thought they were instructional. Graphic scenes of eating parts. Hearts beating and all that. Cults with papier-mâché phalluses. Immortality. Jim Jones wannabes without the old-Elvis look. Followers lunching. Kerouac and Burroughs and Leary and McKenna went to Mexico, right? What drew them there? History and something else. Everybody goes there. Wanna live forever, eh? Touch the Other. The Aztecs (Mayans? Oltecs?) were in Mexico before the Spanish came. Early doctors. Food (um, human) fed to the Gods. Missing street kids. Early Aztec (Mayan, Oltec?) doctors. Hmmmm . . . In other news. I don't have a phone here, don't need one. The guy I work for at The Store is named Steve. Different last name. My apartment number is still 7. (I have housemates, though.) The Different but Same. See the lines of influence in my new diagram. Watch that orange line, it's going to eventually merge with my black one. (In October, if I'm right.)

The legal pads piling up next to Jemain's sleeping bag. I looked up Lacarriere's *The Gnostics* about the time I got his first letter from Delaware. I was not startled to find page 64 dog-eared. A lot of pages in libraries get folded, how many chains of thought marked by those creased pages?

Let me sum up the gnostics. (I know you may know but bear with me, I think this is important.)

There were two main groups; those that were true ascetics, didn't marry, didn't procreate, didn't hardly eat or drink. Truly ascetic to the point of extinction. They died out. Then there were the false ascetics, or, better, reverse-ascetics. These men (and women) believed that in order to purge the flesh you had to indulge in everything, break every taboo, eat children and each other, procreate madly, overload the world with flesh and all the human element they could muster.

Both gnostic groups were closed to outsiders, obviously knowing something worth sealing away. The Christians persecuted them, didn't they? (Brows sinking over open eyes.) Both groups believed there were connections everywhere, this-event-to-that-result, everything a veil. When and if you pull back that veil there's another veil. And another. What did they know? What were they protecting? That was my question. I just wanted something, some learning, that would help Jemain break his chain of unlogic. I sent Jemain a letter about the time I got the one you just read, explaining that I mostly understood and suggesting he get somebody to help him. He'd gone weird before but pulled out of it on his own. (Screaming loud and long and eternal. Brows sigh.)

September 17th, 1994

Yeah. The guy at the county referred me to Brockman, a *shrink* on 7th street. Figures, huh? I saw her yesterday and she was helpful. I explained almost everything. She probably diagnosed me with something not too severe but ugly-sounding. I don't buy it. *You* and *she* don't understand. You especially. The gnostics didn't die out— they advanced. Moved forward and out from the massacre at Montsegur. Spread to quiet places near the equator. You know about Moses, right? Stood and looked out over the Jordan and *saw* and died. (They don't know where his body is.) Lenzi hasn't made a film in ten years, since he's been in Mexico. To Hell With It. I'll *show* you what I mean, where I'm going. Just a hint. Go look up *hexad* and *Pentateuch* in the Oxford English dictionary. Yeah. The BIG dictionary. It'll make sense later. Yeah it will. Look at the new diagram I sent you, follow the orange line. (That's YOU.) That'll come clear later, too. Can you hear the screaming? Oh. Say hi to Debbie for me.

Really concerned, and curious, I made a trip to the library and examined the Oxford English dictionary. The print was tiny.

A *hexad* is a group of six, usually related to the first six days of creation.

"The Pythagoreans held the number six to be perfect . . . The names of the *hexad* are these."

"The *pentateuch:* 'of five books' (five + 'implement vessel')." The definition: "1. Name for the first five books of the New Testament . . . taken together as a connected group, traditionally ascribed to Moses." The five books of Moses? What is the implement vessel? (Cold eyes burning. Children smiling without lips. Pattern of brown lines on a blue wall.)

Jemain's last letter came three days ago, beating the FBI and his telegram. There was another diagram with it. This one in red and simple, thirty-two dots all connected in a circle, a black dot in the center, the whole page marked with slashes, the slashed area filled with the word LENZI.

September 32

That's right. It's the thirty-second. So I can't see my shrink or anybody today. Only the Earth as God intended is really here. Not much left. Nothing's too solid. Hope you'll join me in Mexico. Doubt it. But hope. I'm tracking Lenzi. Wanna know what he knows. Paid my dues for entry. There was an article in an issue of *Film Threat,* September '92, that said he was living near Mexico City. Moses disappeared after seeing the promised land. That's why I'm leaving. On the thirty-second day. Not the first of October. That's tomorrow. This day should last until I reach Mexico. At least until Texas. I can't hitch. Everything has stopped. Everyone is gone. No roads. My room is here only because I woke up in it. I'll be surprised if the mailman can read the address on this envelope. If my housemates find it. I don't know if anything can leave the thirty-second day. Maybe even I can't. We'll see. Your address may not be readable. I'm in between the lines. My script might be too. These days happen every seventh day. When God is resting. *Any* day is the seventh or the thirty-second. Did the children smile at you? If you look, you can find them too. Lenzi did, along with his crew. Enclosed: Two photographs of Lenzi. One current. One old. Lenzi's face hasn't aged a day. In fifteen years. The picture of me in this letter is for your reference. If you look you can find. It only takes stamina. And a willingness to move through thought and action. No matter how bloody. Action then thought then push.

I got a telegram from Telcomex two days ago. The Mexican related the message from Jemain, coughed, had trouble with the words. It simply said: LOOK UP MIRMIR. ODINS EYE. I AM BLIND. FOUND LENZI. JEMAIN.

Four days ago, on the sixth, my phone went dead again trying to connect with UC Davis. Pacific Bell sent somebody I haven't seen before, for some reason I expected the Fat Guy. After all, my new license plate number is M32IR6.

I called UC Davis after he re-connected my phone and looked for MIRMIR and got a simple tale, as recounted from *Ancient Egyptian Myths and Legends* by Lewis Spence: "Thus Odin pledged his eye to Mirmir for a draught from the well of wisdom, and we find that sacred wells famous for the cure of blindness are often connected with legends of saints who sacrificed their own eyesight. The allusion in those legends is probably to the circumstance that the sun as reflected in water has the appearance of an eye."

Lenzi is quoted in September's *Film Threat* as replying: "Oh yes. Mexico City was built on a lake that has been closed like an eye . . . the city built atop landfills over the waters and wells. Wells of people tainted with blood and flesh."

A plainclothes FBI woman came to my door on the tenth. She had rings under her eyes and too much makeup. She'd flown in with her partner from Delaware. They were asking around. They found children's bodies, Dillon, in a deep grave outside of Dover. They found papers in the grave and for each paper a piece of each child was missing. Somehow they connected the whole thing to Jemain and went to his apartment. In his room there were thirty-two diagrams, arranged in a neat circle, the word LENZI written on each sheet, on the floor, on the walls, even on the ceiling and back of the door. Blood was written all over each LENZI. Jemain was gone. Well, I told her what I knew, gave her everything but Jemain's letters and the best diagrams. My phone worked when she called her partner at Video Implosion. She gave me her business card with the blue Bureau seal, told me to call ASAP if I remembered anything.

The Somebody that came to connect my phone on the sixth (before I called and looked up MIRMIR) told me, when I asked: "Really fat guy with a long beard? You mean Joseph. Yeah. Split to Mexico."

The FBI woman told me similar homicides had happened near *here*, a telephone employee, did I know anything about it? The name on her business card was Debora Clarez. Debbie. I didn't say hi. I almost screamed. I offered her coffee.

I called Steve and he told me the Implosion's Lenzi videos had been erased. HardCore's copies of the films had all been erased, the clerk told me I was the fifth person today to ask about them. Four more! Who were the four others?

Dillon. I was proofing this letter and noticed something. Something bad. There are FIVE letters from Jemain and SIX MAIN PARTS from me. He's made his own *pentateuch*. I've made a *hexad*. And the diagrams aren't so cryptic anymore. The orange line is always me and I'm in the first diagram and his last. My line follows his to a single point, like all the other lines, and all the lines become one line. (Eyes are open, open. Children scream.) One line, Dillon. Call me. CALL ME. Why do you need an unlisted number? (Cold eye shifts, pupil the eye.) Why did you never call? (Cold eye is. Is.) Please call me as soon as you get this. I really need to talk to somebody who understands. I do. Please call. Please. (Is.)

Will

When I read Will's letter I immediately called the number he left on its back. The telephone lines were down but I kept trying. I gave up and called the next day. I verified the number was his with the operator, but his phone had been disconnected.

I did examine the diagrams he'd sent and they were familiar. The lines in Jemain's work compare to blood paths shown in *Gray's Anatomy*, roughly, matching veins in eyes, hands, and lips. Some of the other diagrams matched the placement of stars, but none of the intersections lined-up with constellations, instead they made their own constellations. Those same lines also outlined a rough map, a map that leads to Mexico City *from my home* in Kempton.

To add to this, Telcomex called to give me a message from Will, which has been passed on to a specialist at the FBI. (That same specialist securing permission for me to publish these letters. The case is stone cold at their end.) Will's telegram read: FOUND JEMAIN. I AM BLIND.

Two young men passing notes back and forth, one goes south, the other follows. I guess I should book my reservations to sunny Mexico City and complete this cycle, I had a map, after all. Sorry, Will, wherever you may be, I don't know which line on these damned diagrams is mine and I'm not asking.

D. E. LeRoss
Kempton, Pennsylvania

Lightning Rod

Melanie Tem

Her body spasmed. The newspaper flew in pieces from her hands, and the lamp swayed. She was flung hard against the wall; amid all the other, surging pain, the impact barely registered.

Heat sizzled from her fingertips, then shot back through the pathways of her nervous system. Her eyes teared and her nose stung from the familiar, bitter odor of her own singeing flesh and hair.

'Mom?'

246

Kevin was standing by the bed. Instinctively, Emma reached for him. Then, appalled by her own carelessness and selfish need to heal, she snatched her hands back. Just in time: she saw electricity spark between them, but it didn't quite reach Kevin.

'I'm all right,' Emma managed to say.

'But what's wrong?'

As the shock subsided, Emma found herself tingling with resentment. Self-absorbed teenager or not, how could Kevin ask such a question? Reminding herself that maternal sacrifices often go unnoticed—that, in fact, in order to work they must go unnoticed—she said only, 'I was missing your father,' which, she'd come to understand, was not precisely true.

'Oh. Still?'

Emma pulled herself up to a shaky sitting position against the hot pillows and pressed her knuckles against the buzzing in her temples. Sometimes it seemed to her that, if she could create a complete circuit, the current travelled more smoothly through her, with less painful arcing. She knew it was dangerous to try to make things easier for herself, but for the moment Kevin seemed safe enough.

'You have another headache, huh?'

Emma nodded. 'Not a really bad one, though.' It had, in fact, been much worse, and would be again before Kevin was grown.

Kevin hesitated, then reached toward her. 'Want me to rub your neck?'

'No!' Emma cried in alarm, then added more gently, 'It's already getting better.' To keep her son from guessing that the headache still raged, she forced her hands open and to her lap.

Kevin settled himself companionably among the rumpled bedclothes but didn't try to touch her again. From this distance, Emma studied him: downy thighs, cheeks and chest with no hint of hair, Adam's apple as yet apparent only to the touch, iridescent grey eyes so much like Mitchell's before the cancer had flooded them. So far, Emma concluded again, it seemed she was doing her job with this one; at thirteen, Kevin had suffered no real pain in his life.

The thought of Mitchell missing his little boy growing up brought Emma a burning sadness, and she thought about it with deliberate regularity, the only thing left that she could do for her husband. The sorrow of Kevin's fatherlessness was actually heart-stopping. Holly had already been grown and living across town with her grandfather when Mitchell had died, but Emma still had a duty to protect her son from ever understanding how much he'd lost.

'I was thinking about him, too,' Kevin said now, dry-eyed, even smiling a little. 'But just when I was starting to get really sad, I heard you yelling and I had to come in here and make sure you were okay.'

Emma closed her eyes in relief. Disaster averted one more time. This, at least, she could do.

'I don't think about him like you do, though. I never did.'

Kevin was regarding her warily. Ears still ringing, vision still blurred, breath still coming short, Emma managed to nod approval.

'Most of the time I'm pretty happy, you know? Even right after he died, a few days or so, I was okay.'

Those first few thunderous days, before Emma had been able to get her bearings, she hadn't been able to stop Kevin from crying and vomiting and calling for his father. 'That's good, honey,' she told him now. 'That's what I want for you.'

'Or I'm worried about other stuff. Normal stuff, like grades or something.'

'But not *too* worried,' Emma protested. 'You don't worry *too* much, do you?'

'Or girls.' He blushed. Emma caught her breath at how beautiful he was, how perfect and innocent and utterly vulnerable without a mother's protection.

'You're too young to worry about girls.'

'Is it okay to still be happy even if your father died?'

'That's exactly the way it's supposed to be.'

'But my life didn't really change. Don't you think that's weird? It's like he never died. Or never lived.'

A slight contraction marred his face; Kevin was sad. Emma's throat prickled, but she was able to say, 'You're going on with your life. That's what you're supposed to do.'

'But what about you? What about your life?'

'This *is* my life.' Emma judged it an acceptable risk now to hug her son. He buried his face childishly against her, rubbing the new wounds on her chest, but she didn't wince.

'I don't miss him! I don't know how, and I want to!' Kevin burst into tears. Confused, Emma held him until the sobbing had stopped, which didn't take long. Almost immediately, he grew restless, sat up, wiped his nose with the back of his hand, and asked, 'Are Holly and Grandpa coming over for dinner tonight?'

'Of course.'

'Gee, they're here every day. Good thing they live close.'

'Holly's only twenty-one. She can't be expected to do everything for him. It's enough that she lives there.'

'When I grow up, I'm not gonna take care of anybody.'

Emma smiled fondly at her son and said nothing.

'What time are they supposed to get here?'

'About six o'clock.' Emma felt the brief surge of panic that always accompanied the realisation that she was not ready for her father. 'What time is it?'

Kevin shrugged.

'Oh, Kevin, what happened to the brand new watch I just bought you?'

'Lost it, I guess. How come you don't wear a watch?'

'I can't. They stop.'

'You used to wear watches. You had that real pretty one with the diamonds that Dad gave you for your anniversary that year.' Without warning, the smooth little face registered a slight tremor, and the grey eyes glistened with tears. 'Oh, I wish Daddy—'

Emma clenched her teeth. The hair on her arms stood up, and she was hot, then cold. It didn't last long and, when she relaxed from it, all trace of Kevin's own sadness had been overridden by concern for her. 'We'd better get dinner started,' she told him.

'Spaghetti, right? I'll get the pans out.'

He clattered off down the stairs. Emma called after him, 'Don't turn the stove on till I get there!' though she knew he wouldn't; he was afraid of the burners, as she intended him to be.

Gingerly, Emma swung her legs over the edge of the bed. For as long as she could remember her body had ached, and the aching had worsened since Mitchell had died, joints stiffening and muscles tearing little by little. She made her way across the room, carefully rolling up her shirt so that, by the time she was standing in front of the full-length mirror on the door, the entire front of her torso was exposed to her own view.

Three new scars twisted among the hardened and raised edges of older ones, bright pink amid darker red and brown and white. One descended along her breastbone for an inch or two; one disappeared into her thinning pubic hair; the largest branched out into the vulnerable pale underside of her left arm. The absorbent flesh around her heart was so thickly patterned that she could neither see nor find by tracing with her fingertips where the new marks began.

Below all the other scars, most of which nested together on her chest like those terrible photos of the backs of slaves after the Civil War, was the birthmark that coiled like a red-brown tail out of her navel. Emma touched it. It didn't hurt. She seemed to remember that it had once, but that couldn't be right; she knew birthmarks didn't hurt. It had always embarrassed her until she'd met Mitchell, who used to kiss it with tender awe.

For just an instant, Emma missed Mitchell. But she pushed it away; there was no room for her own sadness amid the sadness of everyone else.

She hadn't saved Mitchell from the cancer. She thought now that she should have seen it coming, should have known he was in danger before he did, before the doctors had given the danger a name. If she'd been braver or more skilful, she could have taken the disease into her own body.

It gave her some comfort to know that she had been able to absorb much of his pain and his fear of dying. Because of her, he'd been peaceful at the end, while Emma's terror of his leaving her had spread and hardened like scar tissue.

She had stayed in bed with him those last long days and nights. Kevin had brought them his homework and the morning paper. Holly had brought them soup. 'Why don't you take a break, Mama? I'll stay with him.' But Emma knew better than to leave. If she left him, Mitchell would hurt, and he would be afraid. She could feel the wounding and scarring across her internal organs and in the cavities of her mind and body. Finally the circuit had made itself continuous, a self-perpetuating loop, and she'd felt closer to Mitchell than ever before.

Just before he died, Mitchell had whispered, 'Something's wrong. I feel like it's somebody else who's dying.' Emma had accepted that as measure of how well she'd done her job.

Emma's father had come to the funeral. He'd never paid much attention to Mitchell, and he didn't seem to be paying much attention now. He was safe this time. He hadn't lost anyone he'd loved.

Emma's father had no name.

She knew he had a given name, of course, and a surname that related him to generations of people besides her, but she never thought of herself as that named man's child. She did her best not to call him anything, to keep him where she could watch him, in direct relationship to her—'my father', and nothing else. On the few occasions that had required some form of address, 'Dad' and 'Daddy' and 'Pa' had frightened her, and always a bad shock and deep scarring had followed. For a long time, Emma hadn't known what the pain was that threatened her father at those times, but she could always feel it gathering.

'We can't let your father be hurt any more.' Mama had told her that from as early as she could remember, in lullabies and fairy tales and happy birthday songs. Emma didn't remember what Mama looked like or anything they'd done together, just the two of them, but she remembered the sound of her voice saying that, and the scarring on the older woman's chest and stomach like a blooming thorn tree. Mama had never been shy about letting Emma see her body, and every time it seemed there was a new branch on the scar tree, a new pink flower. 'That's what you do when you love somebody like him. You protect him. He can't take any more pain.'

Her father's father had died when Emma was six. She'd never met him, and Mama said she never had, either; he lived hundreds of miles away and had been estranged from his son for years. In the car all the way to the funeral, Emma and her mother had cried, and Emma, in the back seat, had watched the occasional twitching of Mama's head, the tensing of her shoulders. Her father hadn't said anything, except that they'd have to stop for gas and wasn't that the juncture of Route 36 where they were supposed to turn? He'd looked at his father's body in the coffin without expression, while Mama had wailed. Without comment and without taking a thing, he'd cleaned out the house he'd grown up in; Mama had by this time been so upset that she couldn't help, and Emma's chest had hurt for days.

'He's been hurt enough.'

Emma knew the story, although not from her father. She would have been afraid to hear it from him. Before she'd even existed, before there'd been any need for her, he'd had another family, a wife named Mary-Ellen and two little boys named Joseph and John. They'd all died when their house burned down while he was away at work. Just thinking their names made Emma catch her breath painfully; she tried to remember to think their names every day, and she'd made sure to teach them to Holly.

'Our job is to bring him joy and to keep pain away from him.' Mama had still been saying that the day she left; Emma was thirteen, no longer a child.

She'd been awakened in the night by her father's cry, followed almost at once by a flash of lightning that lit her room purple, a fierce thunderclap, the acrid smell of ozone, and a jolt of electricity that pinned her for long moments to her bed. She'd felt the progress of the burn, travelling from the base of her throat to her lower abdomen in split-seconds; she'd cried out, but weakly, and her father hadn't heard. The burn had scarred badly, her first scar, and had formed the trunk and roots for all the other scars to come.

Grief threatened her father constantly that first year, and Emma was terrified that she wasn't good enough, that some of it would get through to him and he'd explode. But she learned. 'I'm learning, Mama.' Before long, she could sense when he was in danger of being sad even if she was away from him. The school nurse thought she was having seizures; the doctor concurred and gave her medicine, which she pretended to take, afraid that even the pretence of self-protection would make them stop.

Once, not looking, she'd crossed the street too close in front of a speeding car. She'd heard its frantic honking and her father's shouting her name at the same moment, and by the time he'd reached her on the other side of the street Emma had been trembling violently, holding onto a signpost, and panting, 'I'm sorry! Oh, I'm so sorry!' But her father had been utterly calm; later, she'd wondered if he'd even realised that she'd been in danger.

The fall of her senior year in high school, her father had been transferred to California. Emma had barely started to think about all she was leaving behind when she'd come upon her father standing desolately in the back yard. 'I built this house,' he'd told her. She hadn't known that. 'I've lived here twenty-three years. Your mother—' Emma had collapsed on the grass. Her father had helped her to her feet. When her head had cleared, they'd finished packing their belongings, and both of them had left the emptied house without a backward glance. Now Emma could not remember how one room had opened into another in that house, or how sunlight had come into the back yard.

Her father reminded her of a sock puppet with no face, a thumb-smoothed lump of modelling clay. Approaching eighty now, he was very nearly featureless. He had no hair left, no residue of moustache or beard. His sparse eyebrows were almost the same color as his flesh. He had no wrinkles. It had been years since Emma had seen him laugh or frown or even yawn and, since the night Mama'd left and she had understood her job, she had never seen him cry.

'We take his pain away. That's why he married me. That's why you were born.'

Abruptly Emma stepped closer to the mirror and peered at the birthmark that spun like thin red wire from her navel. She touched it. It didn't hurt, but it once had. This, she suddenly realised, was what connected her to her father. This was her first scar.

Emma lowered her shirt and tried to bring her reflection into focus. Since Mitchell's death she could hardly see herself, but she didn't think any of the scars showed.

The shirt, however, was badly wrinkled, and a faint brownish burn pattern spread like charred twigs across the front. Her father and Kevin wouldn't notice, but Holly would. Emma changed quickly into a clean shirt and ran a comb through her hair without really looking, trying to smooth the static with her palms. Her father would be here soon and, although Holly took care of him now, Emma would have to go downstairs.

Emma kept looking around the dinner table. Again and again she studied each of these people she loved, trying to gauge their shifting mental states. Her taut nerves keened like wires in a hot, mounting wind. She hardly ate; she wasn't hungry, and she dared not divert any attention away from her father, son, daughter, father, son. Again and again she focused on each of them; loving them, she was charged with keeping them safe from pain.

Mitchell should have been sitting at the end of the table. His place had been gutted, as if by fire. Emma should have been able to stop that from happening.

Across the table, Holly was watching, too, and Emma saw how little she ate. Now and then, the glances of mother and daughter crossed like antennae; once, for an instant, they locked, and Emma felt a tiny reverberation of loss, something drained away from her, before she looked away.

'Neat, huh, Grandpa?'

Emma snapped her attention back to her son, afraid she was already too late and he'd already been hurt by her father's blankness. Kevin was leaning sideways in his chair and ducking his head childishly to see up into his grandfather's averted face.

252

'Mmm,' said Emma's father, which was virtually all he seemed to say these days. When he took another forkful of salad, he bent his head even further, and Kevin nearly fell off his chair.

Pain was gathering around her son. Emma readied herself. At a very early age she'd stopped trying to interest her father, seeing how uncomfortable it made him; stopped saying she loved him because it put him in danger. Holly had done the same. But Kevin, oblivious or stubborn, wouldn't give up. 'I love you, Grandpa,' he still insisted, and his grandfather, if he said anything, said, 'Mmm.'

He hadn't yet stopped demanding of her, 'Does Grandpa love us?'

'Of course he does.'

'Why doesn't he say it? Or act like it?'

'He can't, sweetheart. At first he was too afraid, and now he's forgotten how.'

Kevin had just told a joke. Emma had missed most of it, but she smiled encouragingly at the punchline. Holly chuckled. Kevin was looking expectant and pleased with himself. Emma's father sipped impassively at his coffee.

'You know any good jokes, Grandpa?' The old man regarded him flatly and then, minimally, shook his head. His face caught the light like the surface of an egg.

'Wanna see my turtle?'

Kevin was taking too many chances. Emma intervened. 'Kevin. Let Grandpa finish his meal.'

'He's finished! He's just sitting there!'

'Kevin. Stop.'

Her son left the table scowling then, close to tears. But before he was out of the room, the soft spot just below Emma's breastbone tingled, and she saw Holly flinch. A moment later, Kevin went out the back door whistling.

'He's okay,' Emma found herself saying to Holly, and then for the first time saw the faint red line emerging from her daughter's open collar. A scratch, she told herself, or the edge of a sunburn. But she knew what it was.

Abruptly, Emma stood up and carried her dishes into the kitchen. Kevin was safely outside; she heard him playing with the dog, whooping like a much younger child. The others were out of her line of sight, but she could hear her daughter talking gently to her father, could hear his silences.

Emma leaned heavily against the counter and sobbed. She pressed her fingers over her mouth to still the noise, but it burst through like a frantic Morse code. *I miss Mitchell. I want my mother.* Quite unexpectedly, this was no one else's grief but her own.

The pain was enormous and exquisite. Emma embraced it, claimed it, fell with it to her knees.

Then it was gone. As if a switch had been thrown, a current diverted.

'No!' she whispered. 'It's mine!'

She raised her head and saw Holly in the doorway, collapsed against the jamb. Her sturdy young body jerked, and her hair stood out wild around her head. Emma thought she smelled burning, and her ears rang as if from a loud close noise. Long red burns were steadily making their way along the undersides of her daughter's outflung arms.

'Holly, don't!'

'Oh, Mama, let me. You always take care of everybody else. Let me take care of you. I know how.'

'Give it back to me.'

Holly shook her head fiercely, and her hair flew. 'I love you. I don't want you to be sad.'

'It's *mine!*' Emma cried. 'It belongs to *me!*'

She lunged at her daughter and tried to take her in her arms. But Holly was stronger. She forced Emma into her lap and cradled her like a baby. She stroked her, and Emma felt her facial muscles going limp as Holly's fingers twisted and splayed.

'I miss them,' she whimpered, but she no longer knew whom she meant. Holly had taken it all.

The Lions in the Desert

David Langford

". . . further information on the elusive topic of polymorphism is said by some sources to be held in the restricted library of the Jasper Trant Bequest (Oxford, England)."
                                   —*(Various references, from about 1875 onward.)*

How shall one catch the lions in the desert?" said young Keith Ramsey in his riddling voice, as he poured hot coffee into the unavoidable instant coffee.

After a week of nights on the job with him, I knew enough to smile guardedly. Serious proposals of expeditions, nets, traps, or bait were not required. Despite his round pink face and general air of being about sixteen, Keith was a mathematics D.Phil. (or nearly so) and had already decided to educate me in some of the running jokes of mathematicians. It could be interesting, in an obsessive way. The answers to the riddle were many and manifold.

254

"I thought of a topological method," he said. "See, a lion is topologically equivalent to a doughnut . . ."

"What?"

"Well, approximately. A solid with a hole through it—the digestive tract, you know. Now if we translate the desert into four-dimensional space, it becomes possible to *knot* the lion by a continuous topological deformation, which would leave it helpless to escape!"

I have no higher mathematics, but dire puns were allowed, "parallel lions" and the like. "Er, geometrically the desert is approximately a plane," I suggested. "With the lions on it. Simply hijack the plane, and . . ."

He groaned dutifully, and we both drank the awful coffee supplied by the Trant to its loyal security force. Keith had converted his to the usual syrup with four spoonfuls of sugar. After all my care in dosing the sugar bowl, I was pleased that he took the correct measure.

"Deformation," he said again, with what might have been a shiver. "You know, Bob, I wish they hadn't shown us that picture. For me it's night-watchman stuff or the dole, but every time I put on this wretched imitation policeman rig, I can feel things crawling all over my grave."

"I never feel things like that—I'm too sensible. The original Man Who Could Not Shudder. But I sort of know what you mean. It reminded me of that bit in *Jekyll and Hyde*, if you ever read it . . . ?"

He looked into the half-drunk coffee and sniffed; then snapped his skinny fingers. "Oh, ugh, yes. The awful Mr. Hyde walking right over the kid in the street. Crunch, crunch, flat against the cobbles. Ta *very* much for reminding me. Yes, I suppose it was like that."

"They say down at the Welsh Pony that the turnover of guards here is pretty high for a cushy job like this. I have the impression they last about six weeks, on average. Funny, really."

"Hilarious, mate. Look, what do *you* think happened to that bloke last year?"

"Maybe he opened one of the forbidden books," I offered. "A hell of a thing when even a trusty pair like us gets told to keep clear of Area C."

A gray man in a gray suit had hired me on behalf of the Trant Trustees. Amazingly little was said about career prospects, union representation or even—the part I was naturally curious about—the precise nature of what the two night guards actually guarded. Books were said to enter into it.

Instead: "I should warn you, Mr. Ames, that certain people are intensely interested in the Trant Bequest. Last year, just outside the . . . that is, outside Area C, one of your predecessors was found like this. His colleague was not found at all." He showed me a photograph without apparently caring to glance at it himself. The spread-eagled remains did not slot handily into anyone's definition of how a corpse should look. Someone had, as Keith would have put it, tried bloody hard to translate him into two-dimensioned space.

"How shall one catch the lions in the desert?" he repeated, now badly slurred. The sugar treatment had taken longer than I had expected. "The method of the Sieve of Eratosthenes is to make an exhaustive list of all the objects in the desert and to cross off all the ones which on examination prove . . . prove not to be . . . To cross off . . ." Abandoning thought experiment number umpty-tum, he slumped to the table, head on arms, dribbling slightly over the sleeve of his nice navy-blue uniform. I thought of hauling him across to his bunk, but didn't want to jog him back into wakefulness. With any luck he'd reach the morning with nothing worse than a touch of cramp. I rather liked young Keith: some day, maybe, he'd make a fine maths tutor with his games and jokes. If he could rouse interest in a dull pragmatist like me . . .

Certain people are intensely interested in the Jasper Trant Bequest. I am one of them. I slotted my special disk into the sensor-control PC and moved quietly out of the room.

Area A of the big house on Walton Street is mostly an impressive front hall, crusted with marble, chilled by a patterned quarry-tile floor too good (the Trustee said) to cover up with carpeting. Maggie, the black, shiny and very nearly spherical receptionist, reigns here from nine to five, Monday to Saturday—grumbling about the feeble electric fan-heater, nodding to the daily Trustee delegation, repelling any and all doomed enquiries for a reader's card. I had yet to research the turnover time of Maggie's job. The "guardroom" and a small, unreconstructed Victorian lavatory complete Area A.

Once upon a time, it was said, Jasper Trant saw something nasty in the woodshed. The people who strayed into the Bequest between nine and five had often gathered as much from odd sources—a footnote in Aleister Crowley, a sidelong reference in (of all places) H. P. Lovecraft. They came hoping for secret words of power, the poor fossils. Modern spells are written in bright new esoteric languages like C++ and 80486 extended assembler. This was the glamour I'd cast over the real-time monitoring system that logged all movement in Area B.

"It's like something out of fucking *Alien,*" Keith Ramsey had said the day before. "All those narrow twisty corridors . . . it's *designed* to make you expect something's going to jump out at you from round the next corner, or chase you through the bits where you can't run because you've got to go sideways."

Naturally I'd been thinking about it, too, and had replied: "My guess is, it was designed that way to make it hard to bring in heavy cutting equipment. Or a trolly big enough to truck out the library. Assuming there really is a library."

"Mmm . . . or maybe it was just fun to design. Everyone likes mazes, and why not old Trant? He was a maths don, wasn't he? You know there's a

256

general algorithm for solving any maze. No, not just 'follow the left-hand wall,' that only works without unconnected internal loops. To find the center as well as getting out again, what you do is . . ."

I was fascinated, but Area B isn't quite that complex. It fills almost all the building, winding up, down and around to pass every one of the (barred) windows, and completely enclosing the central volume in its web of stone and iron. You might get lost for a while, but there are no actual dead ends, or only one.

"You wouldn't get planning permission for *that* nowadays," Keith had said gloomily. "Bloody indoor folly."

I moved along the eighteen-inch passageways now. The dull yellow lamps, too feeble and too widely spaced, bred a writhing mass of shadows. (When the gas-brackets were in use, it must have been far worse.) Our desultory patrols were set to cover the whole labyrinth, with one exception: the short spur where the sensors clustered thickest. Daily at 10 AM the gray-headed Trustee and his two hulking minders went down this forbidden path to—consult? check? dust? pay homage to? *"Feed* the Bequest," came Keith's remembered voice, now artificially hollow. "His expensive leather briefcase, Bob, simply has to be packed with slabs of raw meat. Flesh which is . . . no longer of any human shape!"

Remembering the photograph of a certain ex-guard, it was possible to feel apprehension. I thought also of my reconnaissance down at the Welsh Pony pub off Gloucester Green, where it was almost a standing joke that people didn't wear a Trant guard's navy uniform for long. They did not all suffer freak accidents: that would be absurd. By and large, they merely tended to leave after that average six weeks. You could speculate, if you chose, that something had frightened them. The heavy, regulation torch was a comfort in my hand.

Somewhere the real-time watchdog system dreamed its dreams, fed a soothingly "normal" pattern of patrol movements by my rogue software, registering nothing at all in the dense minefield of IR and ultrasonic pickups that guarded the way to Area C.

Left, right, left, and there in torchlight was the door: big, grim, banded with iron, deep-set in its massive frame, with a lock the size of a VCR unit. I was half inclined to turn back at that point, because it was a joke. Modern burglars flip open those jumbo Victorian lever-and-ward efforts almost without breaking step. As part of my personal quest, I'd entered other restricted libraries (including sections of the BM and Bodleian known to very few) and had never seen such a lumbering apology for a lock. But after all, and hearteningly, there was the maze and the electronic network . . . something here was surely worth guarding.

"How shall one catch the lions in the desert?" I quoted to myself as I felt for the lock-spring, remembering one of Keith's sillier answers: the hunter builds a cage, locks himself securely in, and performs an inversion transformation so that he is considered to be outside while all the lions are inside, along with the desert, the Earth, the universe . . . Perhaps Jasper Trant had liked mathematical jokes. He was here at just about the right time to have known Lewis Carroll, another of Keith's heroes whom I must look up some day.

I was here because of a rumor that Trant's preoccupations, Trant's bequest, had a personal connection with—well—myself.

Click and *click* again. The door swung ponderously inward, and the first torchlit glimpse swept away half my uncertainties. Area C, where the movement sensors did not extend, was indeed a library—a forty-foot-square room with wooden bookcases scattered along its iron walls. Ceiling and floor were likewise made of, or lined with, dull iron. A vault.

All this profusion was a disappointment. I had flicked through libraries before. The literature of the occult is stupendously boring and repetitive . . . it may contain many small secrets, but I had very much hoped that dead Jasper Trant knew one big secret.

Must smells: old books, old iron, and a thin reek of what might have been oil. Keeping close to the wall, I moved cautiously clockwise to the first bookcase. An average turnover time of six weeks. Easing out a random volume with a cracked calf spine, I shone the torch on its title page to find what blasting, forbidden knowledge . . .

The Principles of Moral and Political Philofophy by William Paley, D.D.: The Twelfth Edition, corrected by The Author. Vol I. MDCCXCIX. Crammed with edifying stuff about Chriftianity.

Jesus Christ.

The next one was called *The Abominations of Modern Society.* These included swearing, "leprous newspapers" and "the dissipations of the ballroom," and the author didn't approve of them at all. Then another volume I of Paley . . . sermons . . . more sermons . . . numbing ranks of sermons . . . a *third* copy of the identical Paley tract.

I scanned shelf after shelf, finding more and more of the same dull bookdealers' leavings. Junk. All junk. The Bequest library was a fake. Not even a volume of dear old Ovid's *Metamorphoses.*

On the other hand, where does the wise man hide a pebble? On the beach. Where does the wise man hide a leaf . . . ?

Perhaps. In the center of the far wall, opposite the door, my flicking circle of torchlight found a cleared space and a long metal desk or table. On the steel surface, an old-fashioned blotting pad; on the pad, a book like a ledger that lay invitingly open. Cautiously, cautiously, now. There was something almost too tempting about . . .

What I felt was minute but inexplicable. I might have put it down to nerves, but I never suffer from nerves. A sinking feeling? I backed rapidly away, and my bootheel snagged on something, a slight step in the floor. The floor had been smooth and even. Now the torch beam showed bad news: a large rectangle of iron had sunk noiselessly, with the metal table and myself on it, just less than half an inch into the floor. I thought *hydraulics,* whipped around instantly and blurred toward the door faster than anyone I have ever met could have managed. Too late.

It was all very ingenious. Victorian technology, for God's sake. The 3-D maze construction of Area B must have concealed any amount of dead space for tanks, conduits, and machinery. Now, tall vertical panels within the deep door frame had hinged open on either side to show iron under the old wood, and oiled steel bars moved silkily out and across, barring the way. By the time I reached the door, the closing space was too narrow: I could have thrust myself a little way in, only to have neat cylinders punched out of me. The heavy rods from the left finished gliding into their revealed sockets at the right. And that was that.

The space between the bars was about four unaccommodating inches. I thought hard. I still knew one big thing, but was it needed? "Well, I was just curious," I imagined myself saying with a slight whine to Gray Suit in the morning. "It's a fair cop. I don't suppose, ha ha, there's any chance you could keep me on? No? Oh well, that's the luck of the game," and bye-bye to the Jasper Trant Bequest.

Everyone gets curious after a while. Practically anybody would grow overcome with curiosity in an average time of, say, six weeks. Thus the staff turnover. Thus . . .

No. I don't pretend to be an expert on human psychology, but surely sooner or later the Trant would end up hiring someone too loyal or too dull to take a peep, and they'd duly hold down the job for years on end.

For the sake of form I tested the bars—immovable—and went back to learn what I might from the disastrous ledger. It was all blank sheets except for where it had lain open. That page carried a few lines of faded blue-black ink, in the sort of clerkly hand you might expect from Bob Cratchit.

> *Jasper Trant said in his Last Will and Testament that once as a magistrate of the Oxford courts he saw a shape no man could believe, a thing that crawled from a cell window where no man might pass and left nought behind. All through his life he puzzled over this and sought a proof. Here is his bequest.*

Here was what bequest? Was this slender snatch of gossip the root of all those rumors about Trant's secret lore of shape-shifters and changelings? Something was missing. Or perhaps I had not thought it through. The path seemed clear: wait till morning, own up like a man, and walk out of the building forever. No problem.

It was then that I looked properly at the steel table which supported the book. It was dreadfully like a medical examination couch. Two huge minders always accompanied the Trustee on his morning visit to Area C. Suddenly I was sure that no errant security guard was allowed to say good-bye without being carefully prodded and probed. Which would not do at all.

The Trant Bequest had circulated its own damned rumors, and fed the fires by refusing any access to its worthless collection. Bait.

How shall one catch the lions in the desert? There was one answer that Keith repeated with a tiny sneer because it wasn't pure maths but mathematical physics. I know even less physics than maths, but swiftly picked up the jeering tone . . . protective coloration. The theoretical physicist's answer: Build a securely locked cage in the centre of the desert. Wave mechanics says there is always a tiny but non-zero probability that any particular wave / particle, including a lion, might be in the cage. Wait.

With the long patience of the dead, Jasper Trant had waited.

Shit, I thought, seeing another facet. After six weeks on average, if they hadn't given way to curiosity, each successive Trant guard would be sacked on some excuse or another, to make way for the testing of the next in line. No one who wanted to infiltrate the Bequest would have to wait for long.

I sighed. Four inches between the bars. This would take time and not be at all comfortable. I could not stay around for a possible medical examination: every instinct screamed against it, and I trust my instincts. The Trant Bequest had nothing more to tell me about myself.

So. Off with that smart uniform. The dull, painful trance of change, writhing to and fro on that death-cold iron floor, in the dark. Bones working as in a dream. Muscle-masses shifting, joints dislocating, rewriting the map of myself. The ribs are one thing; the pelvic and cranial sutures are very much harder work to part and rejoin. It went on and on, until at length I was a grotesque flat parody of the Bob Ames who had entered an eternity before. Even so, it would be a long hard wriggle. By now I must look like . . .

Well, specifically, like the dead and flattened guard in that photograph. Could *he* have been—? No, it wouldn't make sense, there was a real autopsy and everything. But I did examine the bars more closely, in fear of some hidden trap. Then I stood back and glimpsed the trap too obvious to be noticed.

Jasper Trant himself had seen something slip from an Oxford jailhouse cell. Through the bars, no doubt. Bars, no doubt, set just as far apart as those now blocking the Area C door. There was another subtlety here. If this was a snare for people like myself, set by his long-departed curiosity, why the loophole?

260

Almost I could hear Keith's voice, the eager voice of the mathematician: Didn't you read the mention of "proof" in the book? Wasn't I telling you last night about the austere kind of maths reasoning we call an existence proof? Trant wasn't collecting for a zoo . . . he was a mathematician and all his Trustees want is the existence proof. Which they'd certainly have, if after walking in there and triggering the hydraulics you got out through that impossible gap. Don't you *see?*

I saw, and was profoundly grateful to Keith for the patterns of reasoning he'd shown me. It was heady stuff, this reason, a shiny and unfamiliar tool. I couldn't stay and I couldn't go. Knowledge is power and human ignorance is my safeguard. After the long years' trek from that damned children's home in search of more of my kind, whatever kind that might be, I did not propose the betrayal of confirming to these . . . others . . . that my own kind existed. Which left me caught, like the lion in the desert who ("Ever heard the psychologist's method, Keith?") builds around him, deduction by deduction, the bars of his own intangible cage.

Yes, I owe a great deal to young Keith. Education is a wonderful thing; he taught me how to be a lion. And at the last I remembered one thing that he'd explained to me, sentences falling over each other in his enthusiasm . . . the technique of reducing a difficulty to a problem that has already been solved. All else then follows. Q.E.D.

It was solved, I think, last year.

Caught in this exact dilemma, what did my anonymous cousin do then? He could escape the cage, but at the cost of leaving the Trustees their proof. I salute him for his splendid piece of misdirection. Then as now, there was a second guard, no doubt asleep back in the control room. No live man could have slipped through those bars after springing the trap, but a dead man, topologically equivalent but stamped and trampled and flattened . . . In the morning, outside the barred doorway of Area C, there lay an object that might just have been—that to any rational mind must have been—hauled and crushed with brutal force through one narrow space. Hauled from outside the cage. A bizarre and suspicious circumstance, but not one which quite *proved* anything.

So logic points the way. I'm sorry to be doing this, Keith. I'm truly grateful for all our conversations, and will try to make quite sure that you feel no pain.

The Little Green Ones

Les Daniels

He never knew who it was that he followed into the cemetery, much less why. His mind was on something else entirely as he wandered down the leafy London street, and evidently he had fallen into step behind some stranger, for when he looked up he was just inside the gate. He felt as if he were teetering on the edge of a dream. Behind him was a modern street, and he knew that if he turned his head he would see a photocopy shop with a bright orange sign, but in front of him was a shady expanse of ancient trees and weathered stone.

'The Public Are Permitted to Walk in the Cemetery Daily,' proclaimed a sign, as if it were the most natural thing in the world for people to stroll through rows of corpses for their pleasure, and in fact he saw figures in the distance, moving slowly through the autumn haze. He couldn't see their faces. He wondered what his friends in Phoenix would say if they saw him go inside himself; it certainly wasn't like him to be morbid, but somehow this spot aroused his curiosity. He felt that this was the real London, that the cars and television sets outside were only a façade hiding something much less modern. Even the cemetery, apparently Victorian, was only a few layers deeper into the layers of disguise that covered something almost sinister in the city, something unutterably old.

He didn't like that, and he wanted to go home.

He had come on business, but there wasn't much business: he wouldn't have been walking around if someone hadn't cancelled an appointment. He didn't even have a room at the convention hotel: some mix-up had shunted him off to a dingy, dark place where the elevator creaked and his room was a box just barely big enough to hold a bed. He was beginning to think he didn't even care if franchises for Cowboy Bob's Bar-B-Q sprang up all over London or not. All that glass and plastic and concrete would be just another trick to fool the eye; the real London stretched out before him.

He stepped through the stone arch in the wall and went into the cemetery. It was quiet, and so big he couldn't see the end of it. Dead leaves littered the pathway, crunching unpleasantly under his feet, but there was still green in the trees overheard. He noticed a squirrel fleeing frantically from his intrusion, and scrambling up the side of a small mausoleum. The motion drew his eyes to the words 'Devoted and Gentle Son', and to the pale stone face of a youth beside them. He looked to be about twenty, but his countenance was blackened in spots by time, especially around the eyes. The sculpture was giving way to some sort of rot, like the decay that long ago had turned the face inside the tomb to putrid fruit.

He felt the first hint of a shudder, looked away, and saw the children. There were two of them, standing on the other side of the path, and they were green.

He realized almost at once that they were statues, but somehow he was not reassured. Both of them, the girl and the boy, were staring at him with that disconcerting directness which only small children can summon; they appeared to be about seven, and they had been made lifesize. Except for their colour, which really was quite odd, they looked like figures from an antiquated text-book, a typical pair of typical children from several generations ago. The girl wore a dress that hung straight down from her shoulders to her knees; her shoes had little straps and there was a big bow in her short hair. The boy wore a sailor suit, complete with cap and kerchief; he had short pants and long stockings. They had their heads thrust forward, as if to increase the intensity of their gaze, and they had their arms behind their backs. They stood straight, almost at attention, yet time had tilted each one slightly away from the other, as if they might at any moment fall rigid to the ground. Their faces were earnestly expressionless.

He was only a few paces from the gate, yet in the presence of these little ones he felt terribly alone; he decided on the spot that he would not venture any further into the realm they seemed to guard. After all, he had no business in a graveyard anyway. Still, he stepped across the path to take a closer look at them. He couldn't quite resist the pull of these odd little figures, which seemed so commonplace and yet so horrible. Evidently someone's kids had died, and been commemorated in a fashion that was perhaps not in the best of taste, especially since the statues had turned green. He never would have contemplated such a thing if anything had happened to his two boys, who of course were safe at home, and certain to outlive him in any case. There was no connection with his family anyway; these really quite atrocious little figures were from another time and place.

The girl and boy stood watch over a slab of granite, conventionally grey and shaped somewhat like a coffin. There was an inscription on either side of it, and he discovered to his astonishment that the people buried here were a married couple who had died in middle age. She had given up the ghost in 1927, and he had followed her less than a year later. These were not the graves of children after all.

Then what was the significance of these little green ones who gazed at him so balefully, their loathsome, almost iridescent colour a match for the few leaves clinging to a tumorous old tree behind them? Why were they looking at him, and why was he looking back?

What weird sentiment had inspired these nasty little statues? Who had commissioned them? Was it some whimsical relative, or perhaps the grieving husband, who realized that his time was near and chose to commemorate their early days as childhood sweethearts? Had he killed himself to join her? Had he been hanged for killing her? And why were they so damned green?

It was a sickly, milky green, like lichen or moss, although it might have been oxidation if the things were made of metal. He could have found out easily enough, but he was damned if he was going to touch them. It was too easy to imagine them crumbling beneath his touch, held together by nothing but the strange stuff that encrusted them. Worse yet, his hand might sink into a mass of fungus. People thought green was the colour of life, but this was a festering life that fed on death.

He hurried away from there, hardly taking time to notice another sign beside the gate: 'Persons in Charge of Children Are Required to Control Them.'

His nerves were shot, no doubt. The trip wasn't going well, and he hadn't been sleeping much: jet-lag. But it was this city, too, and the whole country, really. It was on the wrong side of the world. The gravity was wrong here, and so was the light. He longed to be back in God's country, where things stood new and clean against a desert sky, where nothing was old and nothing was green.

On his way back to the hotel, he had to wait for a hateful and ridiculous traffic signal. Instead of an honest and direct 'WALK' or 'DON'T WALK', the electric sign displayed a slumped red figure to keep pedestrians immobile, and a strutting, glowing green figure when it was time to march. He stared at something green taking its first step and felt his eyelids twitch.

He was bone weary, no doubt about that, and he would be expected to perform like a happy salesman at the reception that was only a few hours away. He stumbled into his hotel, made his way to his room, locked the door behind him and fell into his little bed. He told himself he was taking a nap. After all, your health is more important. The room grew dark around him while he lay like a man who had been poleaxed.

Half asleep in his overpriced coffin, he heard a quiet voice, something between a groan and a sigh. It was right there in the cramped confines of his room. He jerked upright like an old-fashioned mechanical toy and peered into the twilight. Was someone there? Or had he made that noise himself?

He got up, more drained than ever, and turned on the light. There was nothing to be seen, but the bathroom door was closed and he decided to leave it that way. He went out to the convention without bothering to shave or shower or change his clothes.

The party was noisier and stupider than he would have thought possible. He drank heavily and tried not to talk to anyone. A man got up on a table and took his pants down. The future of Cowboy Bob's Bar-B-Q was in his hands. Amazingly, nobody seemed to object. Even the English seemed crude and crass, oblivious to the verdant mysteries that slept beneath their soil. Christ, even Robin Hood had dressed in green. Was everybody blind?

He took a cab back to his hotel and wondered whether his wife was going to leave him. He was in London, but there wasn't even any goddam fog. He could see every landmark they passed, even Brompton Cemetery. The gates, thank God, were locked, and the little green ones safe inside—unless they'd been out for hours. Do you know where your children are tonight?

The cab dropped him off, and every building he could see around him was the work of men long dead. The sky was gigantic. Everyone was going to die, no matter what they did, and something small was going to come around the corner unless he got inside. Why was this happening to him? He hadn't done anything—he'd only looked.

He stood outside his room, so sure the little green ones were inside that he couldn't even bring himself to open the door. He thought about them for a long time, then said the hell with it and went inside, which was a reasonable plan since they didn't visit him until after he was asleep. It wasn't sleep, really, just the fitful snooze of the ageing and the afraid, but it was good enough until he saw the kids again, their arms locked behind their backs as if they were tied. They didn't reach out for him, and they didn't come toward him; instead they went into the bathroom and stood in the shower. They made no sound, but all at once the silence seemed shrill, as if someone had turned up the volume on an unplugged radio. The boy and the girl waited under the running water, their little faces bland and boring and reproachful, and the green that covered them dribbled away, filling the tub and overflowing on to the floor. It slopped toward him, while the children, washed free of it, gave forth a blistering white light that streamed into his eyes and woke him up.

It was sunlight, of course, and it was his last day in London. All he had to do was survive this; and he would be safe.

A phoney banquet at the big hotel. International food franchise folks, eat this. It couldn't have been worse. Everything was green.

He had walked past the cemetery on his way, and had peered in for long enough to see the kiddies still standing there, but he sensed that they were not through with him, and every course he ate confirmed it. Watercress soup. Avocado salad. Lamb with mint sauce, the green flecks swimming up through the innocuous oil. Green beans, potatoes sprinkled with parsley. Lime mousse for dessert, and mints wrapped in green foil. It was all fucking green, and he didn't eat much. Green Perrier bottles were all around him, but he was slugging back cheap Scotch.

He ran for the plane.

Whatever it was that there was dropped behind him as he soared into the sky, but not before he looked out of the window and saw the whole accursed island spread out below him. It was green, green from stem to stern, green for hundreds of miles in every direction, as far as the eye could see. An alien empire, drifting into insignificance. Christopher Robin's dead.

It was hard to shake them, of course. Their grave little features were engraved on each one of the peas in his plastic plate, and when the plane hit an air pocket he would see their small, sad faces.

They were gone, however, by the time he got to Phoenix, and Death was something that grew in the old world.

He told himself that, even when his wife showed up in a green rented car and asked him for a divorce. She had spent his money on green contact lenses, which transformed her eyes into something glassy, cold, and enigmatic. Maybe she was right, but how could fake and hate bring happiness? It was all non-sense, right up to the last moment, the land around him brown and clean and honest and American. The dead kids were a thousand, thousand miles away. There was nothing to remind him of them.

Dead was dead, and green was green, and that was the end of it.

Yet when his own children ran out to greet him at the door, he saw to his dismay that they were not alone.

Miracles

Barry Pain

I

Best and Bliss, at that time unknown to one another, enlisted at the beginning of the Great War, Best making a declaration as to his age which was untrue, but accepted, for Best was very hard stuff. At the time, Best was building up a small business as a greengrocer, and had recently and indiscreetly married. Bliss was the son of a poor parson. He had just taken his degree in honours at Cambridge, and was reading for the Bar, his expenses being meanwhile defrayed by a wealthy uncle.

The middle-aged greengrocer and the young student met somewhere in France, and became fast friends. Both of them had the gift of rapid observation and memory to a quite unusual and remarkable extent, and they had weird competitions to see which was the better in these respects. Best would collect twenty or more small, miscellaneous articles, and put them on a table. Bliss would be allowed to see them for five seconds, and no more. Without making any written note of what he had seen he was required to say, twenty-four hours later, what each of the articles was, and to describe any peculiarity that any of them possessed. Then Bliss would put Best through a similar test. There was a system of marking, and the winner took half a crown from the loser. They were very equal. Neither of them ever got ten shillings ahead of the other.

It was while he was lying in hospital that Bliss thought out the code for thought-reading which the two men afterwards used. It was a very good code, involving no speaking, but certain movements so slight as to be practically imperceptible. But it was not a code that everybody could use. It required very quick observation and a marvellous memory. Later, Best learned the code, and they practised together. Occasionally, they gave a friendly performance, calling it *Miracles*. One of the war correspondents saw it, and gave it rather an enthusiastic notice.

Best and Bliss both did well in France, but at home fortune was not kind to them. Best's friend, who had promised to keep an eye on the business for him, let him down, and the business was shut up. He also ran away with Best's wife, and as she had taken to drink and miscellaneousness, Best considered that about balanced the account. Best broke the man's nose without showing much interest in the performance.

"More a matter of etiquette than anything else," he said to Bliss.

Bliss's career at the Bar had to be abandoned. His wealthy uncle died, and left all that he possessed to the woman to whom he had long been secretly married. And Bliss said that he supposed that after the War he would have to be a blinking schoolmaster. Blinking was not the exact word used.

"What price *Miracles?*" asked Best.

"What do you mean?" said Bliss.

"We might do it on the halls. We might do it at shows in private houses. It's my belief there's a living in it, and nobody here has come within a million miles of finding out how the trick's done."

"Worth thinking over, anyhow," said Bliss.

And ultimately they did it. It was then that they took the assumed names, Best and Bliss, by which they are known in this story. They had the right to put certain letters, which both gain and deserve respect, after their real names, but these did not appear on their business card, which simply bore the words:

BEST AND BLISS

"MIRACLES"

Once more their fortunes turned. At the very first private engagement which they obtained through an entertainment agency, it chanced that Sir Charles Brotherton was present. He came late and left early as was his custom at such functions. He saw only the last part of the performance of Best and Bliss, but he recognized that this was something which he had never seen before, and for which he was unable to offer any explanation. He went up to Bliss and gave him his card. Bliss knew the name. Everybody did.

"If you and Mr Best can come to the office of the *Daily Triumph* for about ten minutes at three o'clock to-morrow afternoon I think it might do you some good."

Bliss looked at Best. Best nodded.

"Thank you very much, Sir Charles," said Bliss. "We shall be there without fail."

They were punctual at the office and were shown up immediately to Sir Charles's private room.

"I've not much time," said Sir Charles. "Show me the best you can do as quickly as you can."

"Very good," said Best. "Will you ring and have my friend taken to some room where he cannot see or hear what goes on here, and arrange to have him brought back when you ring again?"

"Certainly," said Sir Charles. And it was done.

"You will excuse me," said Best, "if I seem to give directions, but will you take some object from your pocket and hide it anywhere you like?"

Sir Charles drew a handful of silver from his pocket, selected a sixpence, and put it under one of the three ink-bottles on his plain roll-top desk.

"And will you also write a telegram which you will permit me to see?"

"I will," said Sir Charles. "As a matter of fact, it is a telegram which I shall be sending presently."

"I think that will do," said Best. "If you will leave the telegram on the desk and close the top over it, you can then ring for my friend and we will start."

Sir Charles pulled down the top of the desk, rang, and Bliss was brought in. Best was seated in an easy natural attitude in a chair and did not speak. It was the impression of Sir Charles that he did not subsequently move any part of his body until the trick was over. But this was not quite correct.

Bliss talked slowly, but he began at once.

"Inside that desk, Sir Charles, you have an inkstand of walnut wood with three bottles in it. They are marked on ivory labels fixed to the wood, Black, Red, and Copying. Underneath the bottle marked Copying is the sixpence which you took from your pocket. The date of it is 1918, and there is a noticeable scratch right across it on the other side. You have a good deal of silver in that pocket—twenty-three shillings in all. Eight of the coins are half-crowns, and there is also a florin and a shilling. There is a blotting-pad inside that desk, and the colour of the blotting-pad is green. On it lies a telegram addressed to Peterson, 23 Shell Street, Brixton. The message consists of the two words,

268

'Nothing doing.' There is no signature on the front of the telegram, nor by the way, is the name and address filled in at the back. You have no less than eleven penholders on your desk, and I notice that you write with a gilt J. But the telegram is not written in ink. That was written with a common indelible pencil, which you took from your lower right-hand waistcoat-pocket."

Sir Charles showed no signs of surprise. "I know something of conjuring," he said, "but I am not an expert. Are you prepared to give me a similar performance to-morrow afternoon at the same time here, when experts will be present who will suggest test conditions?"

"Certainly," said Best.

Sir Charles scribbled a few words on a slip of paper and handed it to Best.

"Good afternoon, gentlemen," said Sir Charles. "Give that slip of paper to the cashier downstairs. Anybody will tell you where to find him."

The slip instructed the cashier to pay Best and Bliss ten guineas, and to take their receipt.

At the next performance there were present two expert illusionists, a man of science who was also a spiritualist, a very good descriptive writer, and of course Sir Charles Brotherton. Best and Bliss gave a more extended and elaborate show, and left when it was over.

"How's it done?" Sir Charles asked the illusionists.

"Code, of course. Couldn't be done any other way."

"What code?"

"Well, we might have to see that show twenty times before we could state that completely."

"Good. Will you two do all that Best and Bliss do in three weeks' time for a fee of two-fifty?"

But they did not like to give a fixed guarantee, and besides they were very busy.

"I see," said Sir Charles, and turned to the man of science. "Would you mind telling me your views?"

"There is no code at all. The amount could not be transmitted in the time. The gift of Mr Bliss, I take it, is analogous to the gift of a good medium. He probably is himself a good medium, though, of course, he may not know it."

There was a shortage of news at the time, and Best and Bliss got two columns in the next day's *Daily Triumph*. A leading article dealt with them judicially. Either these two men had some supernormal gift or they were amazingly clever. In a short time the public would probably have an opportunity of seeing them on the stage and could then form their own judgment. The only thing that Best and Bliss disliked about it was the interview with Professor Moon, the scientific spiritualist, suggesting that they had the gift of mediums, and the floods of letters from those who believed or were trying to believe in spiritualism, which immediately followed. They had been in war. They had seen the real thing. The idea that a dishonest medium should take money from a bereaved mother for pretending to put her into communication with her lost son, moved them to disgust, expressed in very plain and improper terms. They sent the briefest of letters to the *Daily Triumph*, saying that they made no claim to any supernatural gift whatever, and would be extremely sorry to be classed as mediums.

II

They had been in London for a year. Best had thought there might be a living in it. It seemed to them now that there was something approaching a fortune in it. During that year they had worked very hard and taken no holidays. But they were able to do the provincial tour which the agent had mapped out for them quite comfortably in a four-figure motor-car.

They had played for a week in Manchester. On the fourth night they drove back to their hotel after the show and had a whisky-and-soda as their custom was.

Suddenly Best said to Bliss: "What about that woman in black?"

"Yes," said Bliss. "She's been there every night and also at the *matinée*. Third row of the stalls and the seat nearest the gangway on the right—stage right. Wonder what on earth she does it for?"

"She looks pretty awful," said Best. "Looks sort of as if some one was hurting her. Must have been a good-looking girl in her time too."

"She looks to me about half mad," said Bliss.

They thought no more about the subject until the following day, when a letter was handed to them at the theatre, signed Edna Durnavel.

She said that her only son, Arthur, had been killed in the War. Ever since then she had been trying to communicate with him, but she wished to be sure that the communication was genuine and authentic. And for that reason her first step was to make herself acquainted with the tricks practised by mediums. She had spent much money on mediums, and had found nothing—nothing that she could trust.

She had, however, recalled an article which appeared a long time ago in the *Daily Triumph*, in which Professor Moon expressed his opinion that Mr Bliss was certainly possessed of inexplicable and supernormal gifts, and was almost certainly, though perhaps unconsciously, a medium. Professor Moon had said much the same thing about Mr Best. She recalled also that they had written and disclaimed any such gift, but she thought there might have been a reason for that.

At any rate, she had now witnessed their performance several times, and all her study of the arts of illusion did not suggest to her any possible explana-

270

tion, except that they really did possess some such power as Professor Moon had described.

If they were able and willing to put her into communication with her son, Arthur, they would have her undying gratitude. She might add that she was a wealthy woman, and would be glad to pay any fee they asked.

"Nothing doing," said Best.

"We'll talk about it afterwards," said Bliss. "We've got to hurry. The orchestra's started."

"Look here," said Bliss, after the show. "You remember our Mr Arthur Durnavel, don't you?"

"Yes," said Best, "and wish I could forget him. Oh, chuck it. He's dead, anyhow. And there are things that don't stand talking about."

"I can't chuck it," said Bliss. "I've got that woman in my mind. Lucky for Durnavel the Huns got him when they did. It would have been far worse for him otherwise. But I suppose she thought a lot of him. Looks as if she hadn't thought of much else these last years. Suppose we put up something for her? Just to—well, sort of comfort her."

Best had been pacing up and down the room. He paused and said angrily, "I won't touch it. Do it on your own if you must. I won't take any of the money."

"Did you think I meant to take any myself?"

"No, not really. Sorry."

They talked the matter over further, and in consequence Mrs Durnavel received a letter next day saying that Messrs Best and Bliss would, on certain conditions, attempt automatic writing on her behalf if she would come round to their dressing-room after the evening performance.

At the interview Mrs Durnavel was pale and trembled visibly with excitement. Her voice was very low and she seemed to find a difficulty in speaking. She thanked them for seeing her and said she was willing to accept any conditions.

"You must hear what the conditions are first," said Best. "Firstly, you will offer us no money or present of any kind for what we are going to do. Secondly, you will never let anybody know that we have done it. And lastly, you will promise never to ask us to do anything of the kind again."

"I agree and promise," said Mrs Durnavel.

"One more point. If we get a message it will naturally have a great effect upon you. We think it will be better for you if you go the moment you have read it. We wish to avoid emotional scenes."

"Yes, yes. Anything you wish."

"We will begin, then. Are you ready, Bliss?"

Bliss sat down at a little table at which was a writing-pad and pencil. He took up the pencil.

"Quite ready."

Best crossed over to him and made a few passes in the air before Bliss's eyes. This had been arranged between them. Suddenly Bliss's eyes closed. And this had not been arranged.

Best stood behind Bliss to read what he wrote, but Bliss's hand remained motionless. Outside in the dark and dirty passage some girl laughed loudly and uncontrollably.

Then the laughter stopped abruptly. Nothing could be heard but the dim sounds of traffic, like a distant sea. And immediately the hand moved and the pencil began to write. It wrote a few lines very rapidly and then the pencil dropped from the fingers.

Best's round and rubicund face showed no vestige of surprise or wonder. Nothing could upset that man's stolidity. Yet the words that Bliss had written were not what had been arranged between them. And there was another point that puzzled Best. He took the sheet from the pad and handed it over to Mrs Durnavel.

"But it's his handwriting," she said, breathless. "My boy's own hand-writing!"

She read the message and pressed it close to her. She looked up, her eyes full of tears. But all the tension and twist had gone from the face, and it was only happiness that was overpowering her. Bliss still sat with his eyes closed, quite motionless, his right hand on the table, his left arm hanging limply.

Best opened the door.

"You can find your way out, Mrs Durnavel?"

"Yes, yes. My maid's waiting for me at the further end of the passage. Good-bye. I can never thank you enough. It's hopeless."

She came towards the door. As she passed the table where Bliss was sitting, with an uncontrollable impulse she bent down and kissed the hand that had written the message. Then she went out quietly.

Best walked quickly to Bliss and tapped him on the shoulder. "Wake up," he said.

Bliss stood up and rubbed his eyes.

"I think I've been dead," he said.

"Dead asleep. But everything went all right. She's quite satisfied. Here, get your hat and let's get back to the hotel. If ever we wanted a drink we want one to-night."

As they sat over their whisky-and-soda, Best said: "Did you know that our Mr Arthur Durnavel called his mother 'Dearest,' and signed his letters to her 'Chick'?"

"I didn't."

"You wrote it anyhow."

"And what else did I write?"

"Oh, the usual things. It was all right."

272

"I didn't write a word of it," said Bliss. "And I don't know who did."

Best remembered every word of that letter perfectly, especially this sentence: "Within one hour we shall be happy together."

He thought of it next morning when he read in the newspaper the account of Mrs Durnavel's death in an accident to her motor when she was returning from the theatre. Bliss was not given a chance to see the paper that morning.

Morella

Edgar Allan Poe

Αυτο χαθ' αυτο μεθ αυτου, μονοειδεξ αει ον.
Itself, by itself solely, one everlastingly, and single.

Plato—Sympos.

With a feeling of deep yet most singular affection I regarded my friend Morella. Thrown by accident into her society many years ago, my soul, from our first meeting, burned with fires it had never before known; but the fires were not of Eros, and bitter and tormenting to my spirit was the gradual conviction that I could in no manner define their unusual meaning, or regulate their vague intensity. Yet we met; and fate bound us together at the altar; and I never spoke of passion, nor thought of love. She, however, shunned society, and, attaching herself to me alone, rendered me happy. It is a happiness to wonder; it is a happiness to dream.

Morella's erudition was profound. As I hope to live, her talents were of no common order, her powers of mind were gigantic. I felt this, and, in many matters, became her pupil. I soon, however, found that, perhaps on account of her Presburg education, she placed before me a number of those mystical writings which are usually considered the mere dross of the early German literature. These, for what reason I could not imagine, were her favorite and constant study; and that, in process of time, they became my own should be attributed to the simple but effectual influence of habit and example.

In all this, if I err not, my reason had little to do. My convictions, or I forget myself, were in no manner acted upon by the ideal, nor was any tincture of the mysticism which I read, to be discovered, unless I am greatly mistaken, either in my deeds or in my thoughts. Persuaded of this, I abandoned myself implicitly to the guidance of my wife, and entered with an unflinching heart into the intricacies of her studies. And then—then, when poring over forbidden

273

pages, I felt a forbidden spirit enkindling within me, would Morella place her cold hand upon my own, and rake up from the ashes of a dead philosophy some low, singular words, whose strange meaning burned themselves in upon my memory. And then, hour after hour would I linger by her side, and dwell upon the music of her voice, until, at length, its melody was tainted with terror, and there fell a shadow upon my soul, and I grew pale and shuddered inwardly at those too unearthly tones. And thus joy suddenly faded into horror, and the most beautiful became the most hideous, as Hinnon became Gehenna.

It is unnecessary to state the exact character of those disquisitions which, growing out of the volumes I have mentioned, formed, for so long a time, almost the sole conversation of Morella and myself. By the learned in what might be termed theological morality they will be readily conceived, and by the unlearned they would, at all events, be little understood. The wild Pantheism of Fichte; the modified Παλιγγενεσια of Pythagoreans; and, above all, the doctrines of Identity as urged by Schelling, were generally the points of discussion presenting the most of beauty to the imaginative Morella. That identity which is termed personal, Mr. Locke, I think, truly defines to consist in the saneness of a rational being. And since by "person" we understand an intelligent essence having reason, and since there is a consciousness which always accompanies thinking, it is this which makes us all to be that which we call ourselves, thereby distinguishing us from other beings that think, and giving us our personal identity. But the *principium individuationis*—the notion of that identity which at death is or is not lost forever—was to me, at all times, a consideration of intense interest; not more from the perplexing and exciting nature of its consequences than from the marked and agitated manner in which Morella mentioned them.

But, indeed, the time had now arrived when the mystery of my wife's manner oppressed me as a spell. I could no longer bear the touch of her wan fingers, nor the low tone of her musical language, nor the lustre of her melancholy eyes. And she knew all this, but did not upbraid; she seemed conscious of my weakness or my folly, and, smiling, called it fate. She seemed also conscious of a cause, to me unknown, for the gradual alienation of my regard; but she gave me no hint or token of its nature. Yet was she woman, and pined away daily. In time, the crimson spot settled steadily upon the cheek, and the blue veins upon the pale forehead became prominent; and, one instant, my nature melted into pity, but, in the next, I met the glance of her meaning eyes, and then my soul sickened and became giddy with the giddiness of one who gazes downward into some dreary and unfathomable abyss.

Shall I then say that I longed with an earnest and consuming desire for the moment of Morella's decease? I did; but the fragile spirit clung to its tenement of clay for many days, for many weeks and irksome months, until my tortured nerves obtained the mastery over my mind and I grew furious through delay, and, with the heart of a fiend, cursed the days, and the hours, and the bitter moments, which seemed to lengthen and lengthen as her gentle life declined, like shadows in the dying of the day.

But one autumnal evening, when the winds lay still in heaven, Morella called me to her bedside. There was a dim mist over all the earth, and a warm glow upon the waters, and, amid the rich October leaves of the forest, a rainbow from the firmament had surely fallen.

"It is a day of days," she said, as I approached; "a day of all days either to live or die. It is a fair day for the sons of earth and life; ah, more fair for the daughters of heaven and death!"

I kissed her forehead and she continued:

"I am dying, yet shall I live."

"Morella!"

"The days have never been when thou couldst love me; but her whom in life thou didst abhor, in death thou shalt adore."

"Morella!"

"I repeat that I am dying. But within me is a pledge of that affection—ah, how little!—which thou didst feel for me, Morella. And when my spirit departs shall the child live, thy child and mine, Morella's. But thy days shall be days of sorrow—that sorrow which is the most lasting of impressions, as the cypress is the most enduring of trees. For the hours of thy happiness are over; and joy is not gathered twice in a life, as the roses of Pæstum twice in a year. Thou shalt no longer, then, play the Teian with time, but, being ignorant of the myrtle and the vine, thou shalt bear about with thee thy shroud on the earth, as do the Moslemin at Mecca."

"Morella!" I cried, "Morella! how knowest thou this?" But she turned away her face upon the pillow, and, a slight tremor coming over her limbs, she thus died, and I heard her voice no more.

Yet, as she had foretold, her child, to which in dying she had given birth, which breathed not until the mother breathed no more—her child, a daughter, lived. And she grew strangely in stature and intellect, and was the perfect resemblance of her who had departed, and I loved her with a love more fervent than I had believed it possible to feel for any denizen of earth.

But, ere long, the heaven of this pure affection became darkened, and gloom and horror and grief swept over it in clouds. I said the child grew strangely in stature and intelligence. Strange, indeed, was her rapid increase in bodily size, but terrible, oh! terrible were the tumultuous thoughts which crowded upon me while watching the development of her mental being! Could it be otherwise, when I daily discovered in the conceptions of the child the adult powers and faculties of the woman? when the lessons of experience fell from the lips of infancy? and when the wisdom or the passions of maturity I found hourly gleaming from its full and speculative eye? When, I say, all this became evident to my appalled senses, when I could no longer hide it from my soul, nor throw it off from those perceptions which trembled to receive it, is it to be wondered at that suspicions of a nature fearful and exciting crept in upon my spirit, or that my thoughts fell back aghast upon the wild tales and thrilling theories of the entombed Morella? I snatched from the scrutiny of the world a being whom destiny compelled me to adore, and in the rigorous seclusion of my home watched with an agonizing anxiety over all which concerned the beloved.

And, as years rolled away, and I gazed, day after day, upon her holy and mild and eloquent face, and pored over her maturing form, day after day did I discover new points of resemblance in the child to her mother, the melancholy and the dead. And hourly grew darker these shadows of similitude, and more full, and more definite, and more perplexing, and more hideously terrible in their aspect. For that her smile was like her mother's I could bear, but then I shuddered at its too perfect identity; that her eyes were like Morella's I could endure, but then they too often looked down into the depths of my soul with Morella's own intense and bewildering meaning. And in the contour of the high forehead, and in the ringlets of the silken hair, and in the wan fingers which buried themselves therein, and in the sad, musical tones of her speech, and above all, oh! above all, in the phrases and expressions of the dead on the lips of the loved and the living, I found food for consuming thought and horror, for a worm that would not die.

Thus passed away two lustra of her life, and, as yet, my daughter remained nameless upon the earth. "My child," and "my love" were the designations usually prompted by a father's affection, and the rigid seclusion of her days precluded all other intercourse. Morella's name died with her at her death. Of the mother I had never spoken to the daughter; it was impossible to speak. Indeed, during the brief period of her existence, the latter had received no impressions from the outer world, save such as might have been afforded by the narrow limits of her privacy. But at length the ceremony of baptism presented to my mind, in its unnerved and agitated condition, a present deliverance from the terrors of my destiny. And at the baptismal fount I hesitated for a name. And many titles of the wise and beautiful, of old and modern times, of my own and foreign lands, came thronging to my lips, with many, many fair titles of the gentle, and the happy, and the good. What prompted me, then, to disturb the memory of the buried dead? What demon urged me to breathe that sound, which, in its very recollection, was wont to make ebb the purple blood in torrents from the temples to the heart? What fiend spoke from the recesses of my soul, when, amid those dim aisles, and in the silence of the night, I whispered within the ears of the holy man the syllables Morella? What more than fiend convulsed the features of my child, and overspread them with hues of death, as, starting at that scarcely audible sound, she turned her glassy eyes

276

from the earth to heaven, and, falling prostrate on the black slabs of our ancestral vault, responded, "I am here!"

Distinct, coldly, calmly distinct, fell those few simple sounds within my ear, and thence, like molten lead, rolled hissingly into my brain. Years—years may pass away, but the memory of that epoch, never! Nor was I indeed ignorant of the flowers and the vine, but the hemlock and the cypress overshadowed me night and day. And I kept no reckoning of time or place, and the stars of my fate faded from heaven, and therefore the earth grew dark, and its figures passed by me, like flitting shadows, and among them all I beheld only Morella. The winds of the firmament breathed but one sound within my ears, and the ripples upon the sea murmured evermore—Morella. But she died; and with my own hands I bore her to the tomb; and I laughed with a long and bitter laugh as I found no traces of the first, in the charnel where I laid the second, Morella.

Moving Out

Nicholas Royle

I don't know what she told her friends about her reasons for moving out, but I wasn't convinced it was just because of the new job. It was based on the east coast, seventy miles away. She could hardly commute, could she? her look seemed to say.

But did she really have to shift *all* her stuff and *buy* a flat rather than rent somewhere?

I thought we'd got on OK in my flat; it seemed to work fine. There was no indication that she tired of my frequent games and traps, which were never anything more than elaborate jokes.

Sometimes, for fun, I used to try and frighten her; tense my muscles and affix an expression to my face, then move slowly toward her. She'd return the stare as long as she could, then fear crept suddenly into her eyes and I had to laugh to break the spell. "Did I really frighten you?" "Yes," she said, hurt. "I'm sorry." I showed concern and concealed my pleasure. It was only a game.

She took everything. Her collection of masks left a very empty wall in the bedroom, stubbled with nails. The bathroom shelf was suddenly made bare; forgotten tubs of moisturizing cream and rolled-up flattened tubes of toothpaste, even these things were taken. I saw her cast a mournful eye over my tailor's dummy.

"When I get my own place," she had once said, "will you give me this?" She often asked. I didn't know why it was so important to her; she could have picked one up in any junk shop. I saw her from the kitchen one day, when she hadn't heard me come in from outside. She was kneeling at the mannequin's castors and clinging to its waist. Crying her eyes out.

I still didn't understand its significance.

She moved on a Saturday. I went along to help. Her new job came with a car, an estate, which was good because she would never have squeezed everything into my Mini.

I was ignored when I offered to drive. I knew what she'd say if she bothered to answer: I wasn't insured because we weren't married.

She didn't even give me a chance to climb in next to her, before moving swiftly away from the curb, spinning her wheels through gutterfuls of litter.

I looked at the features of the Mini as I approached it. The radiator grille—the car's mouth—had been buckled for a couple of weeks, and one of the eyes had a smashed lens. I had to wrench the door open. The engine wheezed into life and I moved off. The front offside wheel scraped against the wheel arch, but a bald tire was a small sacrifice. I'd said I'd help her move, and help her I would, with or without her cooperation.

I had my work cut out keeping up with her. She darted and surged, switching lanes in her haste like there was no one else on the road. I had to rely on steady progress, the weight of the boxes in the back of her car and the re-tuning I'd had done two months earlier.

Her block of flats had a lift. If there hadn't been so many heavy boxes and bags to carry, she would have climbed the stairs, despite her flat being on the sixth floor. She had always hated lifts.

It wasn't just the discomfort of being crammed into what was basically a large tin, with a number of strangers; nor was it the embarrassment of awkward silences and accidentally crossed stares. Lifts terrified her.

Which offered me endless opportunities whenever we went anywhere and had to use a lift.

I only had to stand there, glaze my eyes over and turn slowly toward her, and she would panic.

"No, Nick! No!"

She once bolted out of a lift in a multi-story carpark and ran straight into an old Vauxhall. She might have got away with a few bruises, had the car been stationary.

Some months later, one afternoon when she had gone out for a walk to help build up her strength, I rigged up a dummy out of some of my clothes, which I found in the wardrobe, and had it hanging in a noose from the kitchen doorway by the time she got back.

The relapse set her back about three months.

I regretted doing it but as I explained, it was only a joke.

278

It always puzzled me why she liked masks when she was so easily frightened by faces.

"A mask is only a mask," she said. "It's not ambiguous. There's nothing behind it." But in order to frighten her, I always had to start off by masking my features.

"There's nothing but wall behind my masks," she'd explained.

"Why do you like them so much?" I demanded.

"People used to believe that traumatic events that had not yet taken place could send back echoes from the future," she explained. "These echoes would sometimes register in masks."

"Like a satellite dish?" I quipped.

She gave me a black look.

"Why don't they show up in faces?" I asked.

"Because we block them. A mask can't. That's why you scare me when you fix your face like a mask. Sometimes the echoes are like the real thing."

I stared at her now from the corner of the lift in her new home, but she looked no more distressed than she had when I'd snatched glances in her mirror during the drive up. Now it was her turn to wear a mask, the mask of tragedy. Yes, it would hurt, but she had to make the break. That kind of thing. Stony-faced resolve, with just the occasional glimpse of what looked like terror animating her glass eyes. She only had to say, if she didn't want me there.

But not a word was uttered. In fact, I couldn't recall the last time she had addressed me at all. I was blurring reality and imagination, not sure afterward if she had said something or if I had imagined it from the look on her face.

The flat was on two floors. Not bad for the price and with a sweeping view of the sea front and port. At night the lights on the promenade would be pretty.

The staircase leading to the upper rooms was situated in the middle of the flat between the kitchen and the living room. You could walk right around the enclosed staircase, through the kitchen, the hallway and the living room. Actually under the stairs there was a cupboard, at its tallest about as tall as me.

I was able to follow her around from room to room and remain unseen. I tailed her just close enough to let her know I was there. She stopped and looked round, eyes flashing with anger and fear, but I was always just out of sight.

Later, after a light meal, I tried to talk to her. As if *I'd* done anything to upset *her*. "What's wrong?" I asked her.

She didn't feel like talking.

She slumped in a chair in front of the French windows. The curtains were closed, which meant she couldn't see the view. I pulled them back for her. It was dark now. The lights *were* pretty.

But with a snort she'd jumped up and quit the room as soon as I opened the curtain.

Anyone can take a hint, but it's somehow nicer to sit down and talk things out.

She clung to the edge of the sink, her face white as enamel. "I'll make a drink," I suggested.

Thrusting out an arm she opened the fridge door and bent down to get the milk out. She started when she saw the car keys next to the butter. I'd put them there just after we'd arrived.

"What's the matter?" I pleaded.

I'd often hidden her things in the fridge at my flat, as a joke; her reaction never more than a laugh or a groan.

She slammed the fridge door, ignoring me, and ran upstairs where she shut herself in her bedroom.

I took the keys out of the fridge and put them quietly down on the table, then sat down and thought about what might happen next. The simplest would be for me just to go. Would that be seen as giving in or a dignified withdrawal? Two of her Malaysian leather masks gazed unresponsively down at me from the wall above the portable television.

I became aware of a murmur of conversation through the ceiling. I stood up and craned my neck. Although the actual words were indistinguishable, I could tell it was her voice, and unanswered.

I walked quietly down the hall to the telephone extension. Hoping she wouldn't hear the click, I lifted the receiver to my ear.

". . . Mini was his."

I frowned. What were they talking about?

". . . but the things that are happening here, I'm terrified. I feel like I'm going mad or something. I keep hearing this terrible squealing."

I dropped the phone and rubbed my forehead, which was prickling with perspiration.

I couldn't decide what was the best thing to do, given her state of mind. But since my presence was obviously not helping, I decided to call it a day.

Closing the front door quietly behind me, I stepped into early morning darkness and thick fog. The car was some minutes' walk away. The plastic-covered seat was cold and sweating, the windscreen obscured inside and out. I proceeded, hunched over the wheel, the choke full out, wiping the condensation away with tissues and the fog with protesting wipers. The headlamps pushed into the fog, illuminating nothing but clouds of billowing moisture. The full beam was less help.

More by chance than navigation I found the dual carriageway and caught up with a set of red lights, which, when I narrowed the gap to eighteen inches, I could see belonged to a large container lorry.

In order to continue to enjoy the false security of the lorry's slipstream, I was obliged to accelerate to sixty miles per hour. I could scarcely credit the drivers who from time to time overtook me in the outside lane. My own knees had liquified in the fear that I would fail to register the lorry's brake lights, should they come on.

Because of the unshrinking blanket of fog, I never saw the sign warning of roads merging and so remained ignorant of the danger until six lanes of traffic suddenly tried to squeeze into three.

Given the appalling visibility and the speed the influx of traffic was traveling at (coming from the west, where the fog would be thinner), there were bound to be some casualties.

A USAF jeep shunted me into the lorry I'd been sheltering behind, and an Audi overtaking on the outside caught my wing.

Then, dimly, I began to understand what she had meant about the echoes. Sometimes, she had said, the echoes are like the real thing.

I only stayed long enough to pick up the tailor's dummy.

It would function as a present and as a surprise. Hopefully, she would have calmed down overnight and was probably already indulging herself in contrition.

Driving back up with the dummy lying silently on the back seat, I saw its bulk whenever I checked the rear-view mirror. Was it not too silent and bland? It needed a mask.

Also in the mirror I saw the mask I would give it.

The car coughed and clanked, but somehow made it.

She was out, at work, as I'd anticipated.

I went to the cupboard under the stairs. Three boxes sat in a corner and a couple of coats hung on hooks. The dummy, with its mask, was the same height as me.

Patiently I awaited the end of the working day.

I heard the key in the front door, the shuffle of letters, the tap of an executive briefcase on kitchen linoleum.

Footsteps. A yawn. More steps.

She pulled open the door.

A tremor went through her body; she stepped back; her mouth fell open but any sound was choked in her throat.

All apologies, I slid forward toward her, castors squealing.

"No, Nick! No!" she managed to scream.

Mr. Lupescu

Anthony Boucher

The teacups rattled and flames flickered over the logs.

"Alan, I *do* wish you could do something about Bobby."

"Isn't that rather Robert's place?"

"Oh you know *Robert.* He's so busy doing good in nice abstract ways with committees in them."

"And headlines."

"He can't be bothered with things like Mr. Lupescu. After all, Bobby's only his *son.*"

"And yours, Marjorie."

"And mine. But things like this take a *man,* Alan."

The room was warm and peaceful; Alan stretched his long legs by the fire and felt domestic. Marjorie was soothing even when she fretted. The firelight did things to her hair and the curve of her blouse.

A small whirlwind entered at high velocity and stopped only when Marjorie said, "Bob-*by!* Say hello nicely to Uncle Alan."

Bobby said hello and stood tentatively on one foot.

"Alan. . . ." Marjorie prompted.

Alan sat up straight and tried to look paternal. "Well, Bobby," he said. "And where are you off to in such a hurry?"

"See Mr. Lupescu, 'f course. He usually comes afternoons."

"Your mother's been telling me about Mr. Lupescu. He must be quite a person."

"Oh, gee, I'll say he is, Uncle Alan. He's got a great big red nose and red gloves and red eyes—not like when you've been crying but really red like yours 're brown—and little red wings that twitch, only he can't fly with them 'cause they're rudder-mentary he says. And he talks like—oh, gee, I can't do it, but he's swell, he is."

"Lupescu's a funny name for a fairy godfather, isn't it, Bobby?"

"Why? Mr. Lupescu always says why do all the fairies have to be Irish because it takes all kinds, doesn't it?"

"*Alan!*" Marjorie said. "I don't see that you're doing a *bit* of good. You talk to him seriously like that and you simply make him think it *is* serious. And you *do* know better, don't you, Bobby? You're just joking with us."

"Joking? About *Mr. Lupescu?*"

"Marjorie, you don't—Listen, Bobby. Your mother didn't mean to insult you or Mr. Lupescu. She just doesn't believe in what she's never seen, and you can't blame her. Now supposing you took her and me out in the garden and we could all see Mr. Lupescu. Wouldn't that be fun?"

"Uh, uh." Bobby shook his head gravely. "Not for Mr. Lupescu. He doesn't like people. Only little boys. And he says if I ever bring people to see him then he'll let Gorgo get me. G'bye now." And the whirlwind departed.

Marjorie sighed. "At least thank heavens for Gorgo. I never can get a very clear picture out of Bobby, but he says Mr. Lupescu tells the most *terrible* things about him. And if there's any trouble about vegetables or brushing teeth all I have to say is *Gorgo* and hey presto!"

Alan rose. "I don't think you need worry, Marjorie. Mr. Lupescu seems to do more good than harm, and an active imagination is no curse to a child."

"You haven't *lived* with Mr. Lupescu."

"To live in a house like this, I'd chance it," Alan laughed. "But please forgive me now—back to the cottage and the typewriter. Seriously, why don't you ask Robert to talk with him?"

Marjorie spread her hands helplessly.

"I know. I'm always the one to assume responsibilities. And yet you married Robert."

Marjorie laughed. "I don't know. Somehow there's something *about* Robert. . . ." Her vague gesture happened to include the original Degas over the fireplace, the sterling tea service, and even the liveried footman who came in at that moment to clear away.

Mr. Lupescu was pretty wonderful that afternoon all right. He had a little kind of an itch like in his wings and they kept twitching all the time. Stardust, he said. It tickles. Got it up in the Milky Way. Friend of his has a wagon route up there.

Mr. Lupescu had lots of friends and they all did something you wouldn't ever think of not in a squillion years. That's why he didn't like people because people don't do things you can tell stories about. They just work or keep house or are mothers or something.

But one of Mr. Lupescu's friends now was captain of a ship only it went in time and Mr. Lupescu took trips with him and came back and told you all about what was happening this very minute five hundred years ago. And another of the friends was a radio engineer only he could tune in on all the kingdoms of faery and Mr. Lupescu would squidgle up his red nose and twist it like a dial and make noises like all the kingdoms of faery coming in on the set. And then there was Gorgo only he wasn't a friend, not exactly, not even to Mr. Lupescu.

They'd been playing for a couple of weeks only it must've been really hours 'cause Mamselle hadn't yelled about supper yet but Mr. Lupescu says Time is funny, when Mr. Lupescu screwed up his red eyes and said, "Bobby, let's go in the house."

"But there's people in the house and you don't—"

"I know I don't like people. That's why we're going in the house. Come on, Bobby, or I'll—"

So what could you do when you didn't even want to hear him say Gorgo's name?

He went into father's study through the French window and it was a strict rule that nobody ever went into father's study, but rules weren't for Mr. Lupescu.

Father was on the telephone telling somebody he'd try to be at a luncheon but there was a committee meeting that same morning but he'd see. While he was talking Mr. Lupescu went over to a table and opened a drawer and took something out.

When father hung up he saw Bobby first and started to be very mad. He said, "Young man, you've been trouble enough to your mother and me with all your stories about your red-winged Mr. Lupescu, and now if you're to start bursting in—"

You have to be polite and introduce people. "Father, this is Mr. Lupescu. And see he does, too, have red wings."

Mr. Lupescu held out the gun he'd taken from the drawer and shot father once right through the forehead. It made a little clean hole in front and a big messy hole in back. Father fell down and was dead.

"Now, Bobby," Mr. Lupescu said, "a lot of people are going to come here and ask you a lot of questions. And if you don't tell the truth about exactly what happened, I'll send Gorgo to fetch you."

Then Mr. Lupescu was gone through the French window onto the gravel path.

"It's a curious case, Lieutenant," the medical examiner said. "It's fortunate I've dabbled a bit in psychiatry; I can at least give you a lead until you get the experts in. The child's statement that his fairy godfather shot his father is obviously a simple flight-mechanism, susceptible of two interpretations. A, the father shot himself; the child was so horrified by the sight that he refused to accept it and invented this explanation. B, the child shot the father, let us say by accident, and shifted the blame to his imaginary scapegoat. B has of course its more sinister implications; if the child had resented his father and created an ideal substitute, he might make the substitute destroy the reality. . . . But there's the solution to your eyewitness testimony; which alternative is true, Lieutenant, I leave it up to your researches into motive and the evidence of ballistics and fingerprints. The angle of the wound jibes with either."

284

The man with the red nose and eyes and gloves and wings walked down the back lane to the cottage. As soon as he got inside he took off his coat and removed the wings and the mechanism of strings and rubbers that made them twitch. He laid them on top of the ready pile of kindling and lit the fire. When it was well started, he added the gloves. Then he took off the nose, kneaded the putty until the red of its outside vanished into the neutral brown of the mass, jammed it into a crack in the wall, and smoothed it over. Then he took the red-irised contact lenses out of his brown eyes and went into the kitchen, found a hammer, pounded them to powder, and washed the powder down the sink.

Alan started to pour himself a drink and found, to his pleased surprise, that he didn't especially need one. But he did feel tired. He could lie down and recapitulate it all, from the invention of Mr. Lupescu (and Gorgo and the man with the Milky Way route) to today's success and on into the future when Marjorie, pliant, trusting Marjorie would be more desirable than ever as Robert's widow and heir. And Bobby would need a *man* to look after him.

Alan went into the bedroom. Several years passed by in the few seconds it took him to recognize what was waiting on the bed, but then Time is funny.

Alan said nothing.

"Mr. Lupescu, I presume?" said Gorgo.

Mr. Templeton's Toyshop

Thomas Wiloch

The Porcelain Doll

Mr. Templeton's toyshop is quite unique. He has glass animals, lead soldiers, and wooden ships. There are paper kites, crystal rings, marbles of all shapes and sizes, and music boxes made of gleaming dark wood. And high on a shelf is the beautiful Alice, a porcelain doll so dainty and lifelike as to rival even the little girls in the village. The old woman buys Alice. "It will be a gift for my granddaughter," she explains. "I'm sure she will enjoy it," Mr. Templeton says politely. He carefully wraps the doll and takes the money she hands him. It is late and he is closing shop and she is the last to leave. They say goodnight and Mr. Templeton closes the door behind her. As she walks home in the darkness, the woman fancies a movement in the package she carries. There seems to be a wriggling. She is surprised when a tiny hand pokes out of the paper. She is even more surprised when the hand pushes a little knife into her throat. She can only gurgle incoherently as she falls. Later, we see Mr. Templeton in his toyshop window. His eyes are sparkling with expectation. Soon he spies his little Alice strutting down the moonlit street, a bloodstained pocketbook in one hand, and a gleaming knife in the other.

The Kaleidoscope

Mr. Templeton holds the kaleidoscope to the young boy's eye. "Look in here," he says. The boy peeks inside the cardboard tube while Mr. Templeton twists the other end. "See the colors?" Mr. Templeton says. "Oh, yes," says the boy. "What pretty patterns it makes!" Mr. Templeton smiles. Then he twists the kaleidoscope the other way. The boy's mouth opens wide, he inhales, then he screams. "There we are," says Mr. Templeton, pulling the kaleidoscope from the child's bloody socket. "Now let's get the other eye." Later, a woman comes to the toyshop to buy a stuffed bear for her nephew. "That one is perfect," she says, pointing out a particular bear. "It has the prettiest blue eyes, just like my little nephew Randy." Mr. Templeton raises his eyebrows, a trifle surprised. "I believe I've met your Randy," he tells her.

The Music Box

He buys a music box, carved of dark oak and with hinges of brass, at Mr. Templeton's toyshop. "It will play the Salzbach waltz," says Mr. Templeton, "when I set the mechanism." He is sure she will like it. "Please deliver it today," he says, and Mr. Templeton nods sagely. Later, she opens the package the deliveryman has brought. "A music box," she cries. It is so very beautiful. She reads the card he has enclosed and she smiles. How sweet of him. Wanting to hear the song the box plays, she lifts the lid. A melody begins. A soft and lilting melody. She finds herself dancing. It is a most compelling tune. That night he stops by to see how she likes his gift. He knocks on the door. He knocks again. He opens the door and enters the room. She is crumpled on the floor, gasping and holding her heart. Her feet kick back and forth, scraping the wooden floor in time with the tinkling melody. "My dear!" he cries, rushing forward. But he cannot reach her. He cannot bend down to help her. Instead, he finds himself dancing . . .

The Toy Boat

Mr. Templeton hands the toy boat to the boy at the counter. Its white sails glow in the darkness of the musty toyshop and its single red running light shines like a malignant eye. The boy gapes at this treasure which, after long weeks of saving, is finally his alone. "Enjoy your boat!" says Mr. Templeton as the boy leaves the shop. "I will!" the boy calls back. "Right away!" Mr. Templeton smiles. The boy gathers some friends together and, amid a flurry of excited voices, the children hurry to the river. There, the boy places his boat into the water and, majestically, it drifts away. The children jump and shout and run along the shore, following the craft. Suddenly, a change comes over the boat. The white sails swell, the wooden frame widens, and the masts sprout from twig size to poles. The boat is growing. Presently there is a sailing ship before their startled, delighted eyes. The ship comes to a halt. A gangplank is lowered. The children scramble aboard. They have never been on a ship before. Some of them climb the rigging, others examine the cannon, and still others spin the great wheel that steers the ship. Behind them the gangplank is quietly hoisted. Then, magically, the ship seems to vibrate. It grows less clear, its image blurred and smaller. In a moment it is gone. There is only empty space. Space, and a small boat bumping against the rocks of the shore. We see Mr. Templeton approach and pluck the boat from the water. Later, in the privacy of his dark study, Mr. Templeton sits at his desk. The toy boat has been placed before him while he holds one of the children in a pair of tweezers. With his free hand, he carefully pulls at the child's tiny fingers. The child raises quite a fuss as, one by one, Mr. Templeton removes the fingers and places them in a neat row upon a sheet of white paper. The noise is really more than Mr. Templeton can stand. Why must children be so loud? This was to be, he had hoped, a quiet evening of scientific study. He puts an end to the child's complaints with a well-placed pin.

The Figurines

The figurines on the glass shelf are delicately fashioned. "Even the eyelashes are perfect," the woman says. Mr. Templeton smiles proudly. "However do you carve them so?" she asks, examining a little man in a business suit. She unbuttons the man's coat and a tiny label displays the manufacturer's name. "Such detail," she marvels. "These figures are not carved," Mr. Templeton explains. "Come here, I'll show you." He leads her into the back of the store. Lifting a cloth, he reveals a metal bird cage. Inside the cage are a crowd of tiny people, each three inches tall. "A simple hypodermic injection," Mr. Templeton says. "I do a bit of experimenting as a hobby." He opens a trapdoor on the top of the cage and, reaching in with a pair of tongs, he lifts out a tiny woman. The woman kicks her legs and swings her arms and the sounds she makes are like squeaky shoes. "I will show you how it is done," Mr. Templeton says. He places the tiny woman in a glass jar and sprays a mist at her from a squeeze bottle. The woman coughs, twitches, and then is stiff. She stands impossibly still, staring. Mr. Templeton picks her up and hands her to his customer. "Here you are," he says. "Isn't it lovely?" The woman gasps and drops the figurine on the floor. It shatters like a teacup. "Oh my," says Mr. Templeton. "A most unfortunate accident. I'm afraid you will have to replace that for me." The nervous woman reaches into her purse. "Oh no," says Mr. Templeton, grabbing the woman's arm and poking her with a hypodermic, "that is not what I meant at all."

The Magnifying Glass

The shelf of magnifying glasses has attracted the man's attention. "I'm looking for a toy for my son. Something mentally stimulating," he says. "Try this one," says Mr. Templeton, handing him a large magnifying glass with a black handle. "Go stand by the window so you get the best light." The man walks to the window and peers through the magnifying glass, examining his hand. "This is a good lens," he tells Mr. Templeton. "That's an amazing lens," Mr. Templeton agrees. The man shifts the glass to investigate the pattern on his tie, but there is something abnormal. The hand he has just been looking at has changed. It has enlarged and grown warped, as if the distortion of the magnifying glass has taken hold and set. "Oh my god," says the man. His torso feels odd. He has been holding the lens to his tie and now his chest, too, has expanded strangely. As he frantically drops the magnifying glass it slides against his leg, distorting it so that the misshapen limb can no longer support him. He falls. "What's going on?" the man says to Mr. Templeton, who comes around the counter and carefully picks up the magnifying glass. "I have been doing some experiments with this glass," he explains. "It only does this in sunlight." He stoops over the frightened man and holds the lens to his panicked face. "Now," says Mr. Templeton, "let's see what this glass can really do."

The Slide Projector

Mr. Templeton shows the new slide projector his toyshop is selling. "It comes with this box of pretty slides," he explains. The man nods his head. "Is it reliable?" he asks. "I don't want it to break right away. My Gloria would be so brokenhearted." "No one," Mr. Templeton assures him, "has ever complained to me about it." That satisfies the man. Later, a little girl sits on the rug while her father sets up the projector. "We will show the pictures on this wall, Gloria," he says. The little girl claps her hands and laughs. "You shouldn't have spent so much," his wife reproaches him quietly. He waves a hand. "She'll like it," he says. "And it wasn't that much." His wife shuts off the lamp and the projector lights the wall. He clicks a switch and a slide moves into place. A picture of a lion. "Oh, look at that, dear," says the woman. Gloria giggles and points. The picture wobbles. "Must be something wrong with the slide," the man says, squinting inside the projector. The picture wobbles again. Then the lion blinks his eyes, paws at the ground, and roars. "Is this a moving picture?" his wife asks. He is about to say no when the lion leaps off the wall and quiets him forever with a swipe of his huge paw. The man's face gleams in bright red lines for a moment before he falls, knocking over the projector and plunging the room into chaotic darkness. Later that night we see Mr. Templeton walking through the dim light towards his shop, carrying a projector under his arm and leading a large animal on a rope. "And how was little Gloria?" he asks the animal as they stroll along.

The Tea Set

"Look what I bought you at Mr. Templeton's," he says. The little girl opens the box and then gives a squeal of delight. "A tea set!" she says. "Oh, thank you, daddy!" He smiles at her. "Now you go play with that, dear, but be careful you don't break anything." She hurries off to her room. Soon there is a little party going on. A teddy bear and doll sit solemnly at a table with plates and teacups set before them. "Drink up," she tells her guests, pouring out water from the teapot. "This is good tea." She holds a teacup to the teddy bear's lips and then to the doll's lips, too. "There, wasn't that good?" she says. Then she takes a sip of the water from her own teacup. Later, her father enters the room. The teddy bear and doll sit quietly, their arms and legs at stiff angles. "Having fun?" he asks. The girl does not reply. She sits staring at her two companions. "Dear?" he says, walking over to her. "What's wrong?" Her face is a smooth mask, shiny as the china teacup she holds in her hand. Her eyes are white and vacant, looking at the air. He reaches for her hand. It is stiff and glasslike. With a snap, it falls off. There is a tinkling sound as it hits the floor and shatters into a sprinkling of white fragments. Then there is the sound a man makes when he is trying to destroy the world with a single, wailing scream.

The Halloween Candy

Halloween is Mr. Templeton's favorite holiday. He stands in the doorway of his toyshop and gives candy to the neighborhood children who come begging. One little girl is dressed as a bear. "Is that what you really want to be?" asks Mr. Templeton. "Grrr!" the girl says through the hole in her plastic mask. Mr. Templeton chuckles and hands her a piece of candy. Other children come, display their gaudy costumes, and take the candy Mr. Templeton offers. "Is that what you really want to be?" he asks each child in turn. "Oh yes," say the werewolf, the snake and the gorilla. "Oh yes," say the dinosaur, the vampire and the crocodile. And to each of the children Mr. Templeton gives his candy. Late that night Mr. Templeton is awakened by screams. He opens his bedroom shutters and looks down into the narrow street below. Small, colorful figures are roaming in the dim light, some snarling, others hissing or howling. Two of the figures pull open the door of a house down the way and all of them clamber inside. A few moments later there are more screams. Screams cut short. And then the strange little creatures bustle out into the street again, licking dark liquid from their faces and hands. "Mr. Templeton!" a voice calls from down below. He leans out and sees a woman at his toyshop door. "Mr. Templeton, please let me in! Please!" From up the street the bothersome creatures are drawing closer. The woman pounds on the specially-reinforced metal doors which guard the toyshop. "I open in the morning," Mr. Templeton calls down to her. "Come back then." He secures the shutters, muffling the last of the woman's hysterical pleas. Soon there are more screams outside. Then the padding of many little feet on the cobblestones, drifting away, finally, into the night.

Mrs. Bentley's Daughter

August Derleth

Sac Prairie sweltered in the July sun. The warm, dusty air was lifeless, and in the heat of early afternoon the green of the trees was lost in the dull gray haze. The drooping flowers made curious splotches of color around Mrs. Vaile's porch; the light pink of late roses, the red of garden carnations, the orange and yellow of nasturtiums, and the deep blue of canterbury bells and clematis, that crept up along the porch floor and trailed along over the rail and the pillar.

The door of her house opened, and Mrs. Vaile herself came out upon the porch. She was dressed for the street, and as she came out she drew on her white gloves, holding her sunshade close to her body with the pressure of her elbow. She had trouble with the gloves and finally put the sunshade down to get at them better. One was already on, the other half-way on, when she drew them both off again and flung them to a chair on the porch.

"It's too hot to wear them, anyway," she said.

Then she raised her sunshade and stepped out into the sun. A car came down the road and swung around the corner in a perfect storm of dust.

"Land's sakes!" exclaimed Mrs. Vaile. "Never saw such dust." She reflected that unless they had rain soon, the house and the flowers would soon be a dusty brown. She turned and looked at the flowers, bent away from the sun.

Then she went on her way, marching sedately down the walk and out upon the street. From the shade of her parasol she looked over at the house that was her destination. She should really have called sooner, she reflected, it being her place as a new neighbor to do so. Oh, well. She crossed the dirt road with little, mincing steps and came up before the white-washed fence about the house. She opened the gate and began to walk up the path toward the house.

Then she saw the child. It was sitting on the stone curb of an old, evidently unused well, for the opening was neither covered over nor marked with the paraphernalia of usage. The child was playing about, quite dangerously, too, Mrs. Vaile thought. It was a little girl, Mrs. Vaile saw as she came closer. What if she should fall into the well? The thought sent Mrs. Vaile from her path over to the child.

"Hello, darling," said Mrs. Vaile in her kindest voice.

The child looked up at her. "H'lo!" she said.

"Does your mother know you're out here, sitting at the well?" asked Mrs. Vaile, leaning slightly forward.

"Mama doesn't care."

Mrs. Vaile puckered brow. She smiled a bewildered smile, and looked more closely at the child. The little girl smiled back at her.

"I don't think you ought to sit on the curb there, darling; you might fall into the well."

The child turned her head slightly and looked down into the well. She laughed gayly and tossed her curls. Then she shook her head.

"I can't fall down into the well," said the child simply.

Mrs. Vaile glanced nervously toward the house, half expecting the child's mother to come out to her. She thought it very odd that they should leave the well uncovered with a child about the house. Once more she entreated her.

"Do come with me to your mother, won't you? Come to the house with me."

"Oh, no, I couldn't. I must stay here." The child shook her head vehemently.

Mrs. Vaile sighed. "Oh! very well, then." She picked her way over the grass back to the walk and went on up toward the house. She mounted the porch steps and rang the bell; then she looked back at the child. Somewhat unruly, that girl; Mrs. Vaile felt it.

Then suddenly she saw her neighbor's smiling face framed in the doorway, and in a moment she was sitting in a rather old-fashioned parlor—there were so many of them in Sac Prairie, she had been told. The walls were papered with light tan paper, on which were great red splotches of flowers—almost gaudy, thought Mrs. Vaile—but she was smiling at her hostess who was saying something about her flowers. The horsehair furniture felt very odd, somehow. Across from her on the mantel she saw several old chromos. On one of these she saw three people—a woman, a man—her husband, no doubt—and a child. The woman was her hostess, and the child was the child on the well curb. A family group, thought Mrs. Vaile. She turned to her hostess now, and smiled as if she had heard and appreciated every word that had dimly come to her.

"I know I should have come sooner, but I was frightfully busy. Moving, you know. And if it hadn't been for your adorable little girl, whom I saw on the well curb as I came in—"

Mrs. Vaile stopped abruptly. There was a sudden odd pallor on the face of her hostess. She heard the woman saying, more to herself than to her:

"On the well curb again?"

"Yes," said Mrs. Vaile affably. "She was sitting there quite pertly, and answered me when I spoke to her."

"Ah!" the woman exclaimed, and leaned forward. "And what did she say?"

Mrs. Vaile hesitated. Would it do to tell this woman that she had reprimanded her child? "Not much, certainly not," said Mrs. Vaile. "I told her I thought she hadn't ought to sit on the well curb, but she said you didn't mind; so I came on in."

"Ah! yes. Dorothy was always like that. A bit unruly, perhaps, just a little bit. But such a dear, and such a comfort to me. She comes and she goes, but she seems to like the well curb best. It's a bit extraordinary, too, when you come to think of it."

Mrs. Vaile thought her hostess was becoming steadily more incoherent; she thought it best to change the subject. She led off on the last meeting of the Ladies' Aid, and her hostess entered into this topic with fervor.

It was after five when Mrs. Vaile emerged from the house. She saw as she came down the path that the child was no longer at the well. She was most probably playing in the dense bushes to the left, from which came the shrill screaming of a group of children at play. Behind her, the woman was leaning over the porch railing and staring at the well.

She closed the gate after her, and stepped briskly across the street. It was at her doorstep that she met Mrs. Walters, from the other end of the block. Mrs. Vaile did not like Mrs. Walters; she had been warned that Mrs. Walters was an accomplished gossip, and she detested gossips. But she was already coming to feel that gossiping was one of the few means of passing the time in Sac Prairie.

She greeted Mrs. Walters, and the woman responded with a sharp nod.

"Have you been visiting Mrs. Bentley?" she asked.

Mrs. Vaile nodded. "Yes. We have had a very pleasant chat about"—she could not tell this woman that they had been discussing the Ladies' Aid—"about Mrs. Bentley's daughter, Dorothy."

Mrs. Walters jerked her head about and stared at Mrs. Vaile in open-eyed astonishment.

"Do you tell me she talks about her?" she demanded.

"Why, yes," answered Mrs. Vaile. "After I saw the girl on the well curb—"

"Saw the girl on the well curb!" Mrs. Walters almost screamed the words; she seemed to be leaning away from Mrs. Vaile, and at the same time boring her eyes into her.

Mrs. Vaile was nonplussed. What had she said now? Dear me! she thought, what a queer person! But something Mrs. Walters was saying brought her up sharply.

"How you talk, Mrs. Vaile! Why, that girl fell into the well over a year ago. I can't believe that Mrs. Bentley would talk about it!"

Mrs. Vaile nodded. "It is rather queer, isn't it? If a daughter of mine fell into the well once, I'd be sure not to let her play around it again. But there she was, smart as you please, sitting right on top of the well curb!"

"What *are* you saying, Mrs. Vaile?" asked Mrs. Walters coldly. Then, in a voice that seemed to come from far away, "Surely you know that the child drowned when she fell into the well!"

Mrs. Edmonds' Pantry

Tina L. Jens

Burke . . . Burke!" The old lady screeched down the back stairs. As usual, she stood tottering on the top landing of the three-flat, one fist mashed against her hip and the other clutched tight to the railing. She glared down the crack between the banisters. She knew her son-in-law, on the ground floor, could hear her.

"Burke, I need food! And don't go bringin' me no more of them green beans and canned chicken!

"I got enough of that blamed canned chicken to stuff a horse," she muttered. Mrs. Edmonds hobbled back inside and slammed the door. She made her way through the kitchen and into the pantry adjoining it.

"Meanness. Blamed meanness. That's all it is." She scowled grimly at the pantry shelves. All three were stocked top to bottom. In fact the whole pantry was overflowing—with cans of green beans and canned chicken.

She'd had enough of Burke's beans and chicken. She grabbed the nearest can and made a feeble toss toward the garbage.

"Ever since Edgar died, that devil has treated me like this. He wouldn't have gotten away with it while Edgar was alive. No sir! And Susan . . ." she moaned. "Bless her soul. We should have kicked that fool Burke out when Susan died. But Edgar was too soft-hearted for that. Look where his kindness has gotten me!"

Mrs. Edmonds tugged the garbage pail closer to the shelves. "Burke!" she screeched again.

"When I ask for something different that devil brings me a different brand of green beans! But he'll pay for it. Someday he'll pay . . ." With that, she jabbed her arm across the shelf and swept it clean. The cans bounced off the counter and onto the floor. It was only sheer luck that none of the falling cans crushed Mrs. Edmonds' toes.

"Well? Lisa, Jonathan, what do you think? Is this not the greatest apartment you've ever seen?"

Lisa saw Jonathan grin, and rolled her eyes at him. The rental agent was a real trip. The spiky black hair and flowing robes aside, the woman had to be on the wrong side of fifty. And her vocabulary consisted of nothing but clichés.

Still, the agent was right about one thing. It *was* a great apartment, in an even better neighborhood. Jonathan was still in the living room drooling over the built-in bookcases and fireplace, but he joined her to check out the kitchen. They'd be willing to compromise on many things like closet space and yard access, but if the kitchen didn't meet their standards, they'd pass on the apartment.

Lisa surveyed it critically. The room was on the narrow side—they'd have to push their table against the wall to leave enough floor space for them both to work.

And the refrigerator sat in an awkward spot, pushed up against a closed door, so that it stuck out in the middle of the floor. But, unlike the newer apartments they'd seen, this one had a gas stove with a large oven.

"The dishwasher looks a little old," Jonathan said. "Do you think the landlord would replace it? We do too much fancy cooking to have to worry about scrubbing pots and pans."

"Gourmet cooks, are you?" the rental agent asked.

"We dabble," Jonathan conceded.

"What's back here?" Lisa asked, eyeing the door behind the refrigerator.

"I guess it was a pantry once," the agent said vaguely. "None of the tenants ever bother to use it."

Lisa arched an eyebrow.

"With a hundred restaurants in walking distance—who cooks?" the agent asked philosophically.

"We do," Jonathan said firmly.

A test shove revealed that the refrigerator was on wheels. Jonathan shouldered it out of the way while Lisa fiddled with the slide bolt on the door. It was stuck with rust and new paint drippings.

"Here, let me try," Jonathan said.

"Who ever heard of locking the pantry?" Lisa asked.

"And painting it closed," Jonathan added over the screech of the broken seal of paint.

She followed him into the small L-shaped space. A layer of dust covered the counter and shelves, not quite hiding the stains and ring marks made by a previous cook. The room obviously hadn't been treated to the same coat of paint that its outer door had received. Just as odd, was the gaping space obviously designed for a refrigerator.

Lisa called out to the rental agent, "Why on earth is the refrigerator parked in the middle of the kitchen? There's a perfect place for it in here."

"Oh, boys will be boys," the woman said from the doorway.

Lisa frowned suspiciously. The agent caught her look, and stuttered an excuse.

"I believe the room was closed off before the boys moved in. I guess they never opened it up because they just never needed the space.

"I mean, how much room do you need for paper plates, a couple frozen dinners, and a case of beer?" she said airily.

Jonathan gave her a rude look and she hurried on.

"The boys were only here for a few months before they broke the lease. They didn't really have time to unpack. That's why the owners are so excited about having a married couple in here—people who will really think of this as a 'home.' " The agent made quotation signs in the air around "home."

Lisa hated people who made quotation signs in the air—but that was no reason to reject an apartment. And the agent was only asking them to sign an eight-month lease, to fill out "the boys' " term. Like so many Chicago landlords, the owners liked to keep their leases on a May–October schedule. They'd take it.

"Halloo-oo!"

Jonathan looked up from unloading the van. A middle-aged woman in a house-frock was hurrying across the yard waving a dish towel at him.

"Honey, either we're about to get a weird visit from Welcome Wagon, or the next-door neighbor wants help with the dishes."

"Jonathan! Shhh!" Lisa scolded him. She smiled and clambered out from among the boxes to greet the woman.

"How do you do?" the woman chirped, in an accent Lisa couldn't quite place. "I'm Ava. Pete's my husband. We live next door. We have a little present for you—some shelves for your back porch. You'll be needing them for your groceries." Ava nodded knowingly.

"That's sweet of you. But I don't think we'll need them. Our apartment has a pantry."

"Oh, but that was Mrs. Edmonds' pantry," Ava said solemnly. "No one uses Mrs. Edmonds' pantry. It wouldn't be right."

Ava grabbed Lisa's arm, glanced around quickly, and whispered, "She choked to death on a chicken bone, you know. And out of canned chicken too." The lady clucked sadly. "That's why I always fix mine from scratch. Well, must hurry now, lots of work to do—for me and you!" She giggled and scampered off.

"Pete will bring over those shelves!" she called back over her shoulder.

Lisa turned to Jonathan. With one finger, he made a crazy circle near his temple, shrugged, and reached for the nearest box.

After a day of moving furniture and boxes, Jonathan had gone back to work. As a freelance graphic artist, Lisa could afford to take more time off. She wandered through the rooms trying to decide where to start. She decided to tackle the kitchen first. She couldn't eat lunch till she unpacked the dishes.

She devoted the morning to scrubbing cabinets, lining shelves, and unpacking the mountain of boxes labeled *Kitchen*. Then, for a change of scenery, she decided to visit the neighborhood co-op.

Things are starting to look presentable, Lisa thought, as she lugged the last bag of groceries up the stairs and into the kitchen. *At least there is a path through every room, now.* She pushed the other bags aside and thumped the last one down on the table.

She unloaded the refrigerator stuff first, then double-wrapped the fish. Jonathan would love the orange roughy, but not if it spoiled everything else in the fridge.

She set the little bags of whole spices aside to grind later and hauled the rest of the groceries into the pantry. Boxed goods went on the bottom shelf. Cans and jars on the middle, including the home-canned green beans and tomatoes and those wonderful fruit preserves from Maine. The co-op had been filled with wonderful stuff.

Lisa bent down to grab the last can out the sack on the floor. She heard a soft scratching sound above her. Straightening quickly, she found a jar of tomatoes had slid perilously close to the edge of the shelf.

"The bottom must have been wet," Lisa mumbled to herself.

She grunted as she hoisted the bags of whole grain flour and sugar to the top shelf. Then she hid the small cans of chicken behind the soups and vegetables. Jonathan would make fun of her if he saw them. But sometimes she liked a quick chicken salad sandwich. And making it from scratch was a lot of work.

She grabbed the nearest bag to fold it. She'd take them with her when she went back to the co-op.

"Burrrkkke!"

"Who's there?" Lisa whirled around. The pantry door had swung closed. She felt foolish.

A little oil would take care of that squeak. "But right now, I'm taking a break. When you start talking to squeaking doors it's time to quit."

She made herself a cup of tea and settled in on the couch, channel-surfing through the soaps. *Maybe I'll just close my eyes for a bit,* she thought, and snuggled deeper into the couch pillows.

Lisa jerked awake. The clock said she'd slept more than an hour. But she was more concerned with the sound that had awakened her. There it was again. A muffled "Thwock!" from the other room. She got up to investigate.

She flipped on the bedroom ceiling light. Nothing seemed amiss. The dining room was still so messy she couldn't be sure.

Lisa groped across the kitchen till she found the light switch on the far wall. It was a stupid place for a light switch, convenient only when you were coming in the back door.

She glanced at the sink. The dishes were stacked just as she had left them. There was nothing on the counters or floor. She pulled open the pantry door and went in. It swung closed behind her as she reached for the light.

"Ick!"

She was standing in something squishy. Lisa waved her arm in front of her searching for the dangling light cord. She wasn't taking another step without some light. She found the cord and tugged it.

Kernels of creamed corn were squishing up between her toes. Lisa bent down to pick up the can. She cut her finger on the jagged edge of the lid. "Damn it!"

She sucked on her bleeding finger and reached for another empty can lying in the corner. It looked like it had exploded. Something dropped in her hair.

"Now what?" She looked up. The entire room was splattered with creamed corn. Bits of sauce and kernels were dropping from the ceiling. She stood up and started to back out, still sucking her finger.

She heard a scraping sound on the shelves. She saw a can of corn slide from the back of the shelf. Gathering speed as it moved, it launched across the pantry and exploded against the far wall. Lisa whimpered. Corn dribbled down the newly-painted plaster.

"Jonathan, I'm telling you, those cans flew across the pantry and crashed into the far wall!" Lisa kicked off her slippers and sat down on the bed. "They slid across the shelf—like they were getting a running start or something. No strings, no jet propulsion, nothing. They did it by themselves." She glared at her husband.

"Lisa, come on! Flying creamed corn? What'd the potatoes do—jump through a hoop?"

"Jonathan, I watched those cans—"

"It was faulty metal in the cans. Or they got the pressurization too high at the factory. Something like that."

"So the would-be engineer is telling me that internal pressure can make a can slide across a shelf, fly through the air and—"

"Lisa, drop it!" Jonathan snapped at her. "You're just tired. You've been working too hard. Come to bed and forget it."

Jonathan switched out his light.

"Easy for you to say!" Lisa grumbled. "You didn't have to clean it up." She lay back and stared at the ceiling.

"It was the cheap stuff anyway," Jonathan said, his voice muffled by his pillow. "Go back to the co-op tomorrow and get some of that good home-canned stuff."

298

"Yeah, right," Lisa muttered. She didn't press the point. Obviously, Jonathan thought she was loony.

It wasn't Lisa's fault that Jonathan didn't get much sleep that night. Around 2 A.M. they were both awakened by a loud splintering *Crack!* that was quickly followed by a series of crashes.

Jonathan leaped out of bed and grabbed for the lamp. He missed and it crashed to the floor.

Lisa sat up in bed leisurely and called after her husband. "You might want to put some shoes on before you go in there—unless you're partial to walking in cold vegetables."

Lisa sat at the kitchen table sipping her coffee. Jonathan was putting the finishing coat of paint on the new pantry shelves. Lisa had helped him clear away the avalanche of broken glass, cans, boxes, and splintered wood.

The top and bottom shelves had cracked down the middle, and both sides had torn away from the wall, leaving four gaping holes in the plaster.

She had retreated to her present position after she saw the middle shelf. It remained securely fastened to the wall. It was empty—except for five jars of green beans and three cans of chicken. Jonathan snorted when he saw the canned chicken. Lisa had been right to hide them.

"You know, maybe we should take Pete and Ava up on their offer," Lisa said. "Those metal shelves aren't so bad. And there's room on the back porch."

Jonathan just snorted again.

She shrugged. Jonathan claimed the old shelves simply gave out from stress. He was adding reinforcements to each of them.

But she didn't buy it. A few cans of soup weren't enough to give a piece of wood an anxiety attack. And it didn't explain the middle shelf.

"Done!" Jonathan plopped down in a chair with a self-satisfied smile. "The paint should be dry by this afternoon. You can load them up again tonight. Why don't you pick up some dried cranberries and marjoram? I want to try a new sauce on the Cornish hens. I wasn't crazy about the raspberries last time, were you?"

The shelves had stayed up all week. And none of the cans had done any flying lately, much to Jonathan's smug amusement. Maybe he was right, Lisa thought as she finished setting the dining room table and went back in the kitchen.

But she didn't believe for a minute that the previous tenants had moved the refrigerator into the middle of the floor just for convenience sake. Floor space was too valuable in an apartment this size to shut off an entire room for no reason.

They had closed the pantry and *locked* it. And what about Ava's warning? *"You don't want to use that, that was Mrs. Edmonds' pantry."*

Lisa went to the sink to scrub the mushroom caps. Mrs. Edmonds, there was a strange story. Choked to death on a chicken bone. "Out of canned chicken—Good Lord." Lisa scrubbed faster.

She was making pork mornay with cubed vegetables. The veggies had to be pre-cooked and she was running out of time. She decided to cheat and used canned vegetables. She knew Jonathan would complain that it was a waste of quality meat to serve it with anything but fresh vegetables. But he could peel his own if he wanted them so bad.

Lisa pulled open the pantry door and made a mental note to have Jonathan take the door off. It was inconvenient when she had her hands full.

"A couple cans of mixed vegetables and some stewed tomatoes should do it."

Before she could reach them, the designated cans skidded across the shelf. They hurled into the air and slammed into her chest. Knocked off balance, she fell against the back wall.

Lisa's eyes grew the size of spring potatoes as the cans and jars began shifting into formation. Lining up for an attack. The assault began. Rapid fire—vegetables and tomato sauce alternated shots, battering her ribs and arms. Every fourth round, a can of stewed tomatoes zinged out, like tracer fire, to improve their aim.

A volley of canned fruits pounded her face and head. Preserves teetered at the edge of the shelf, then dropped straight down. Her toes a clear target.

In prize-fighter fashion she weaved and ducked the missiles. But it was impossible to protect her body and bare feet at the same time. Lisa's arms were bruised in a dozen places where she had warded off blows. A can of blueberries hit their secondary mark—breaking at least two of her toes.

Lisa couldn't dodge the next wave of attack. A pyramid of soup cans slammed into her stomach. It knocked the breath out of her. She bent double. Immediately she knew that was a mistake. Her arms gave little protection to her head. Boxes and cans continued to rain down.

Bruised and shell-shocked, Lisa didn't see the five-pound bags of flour and sugar wobbling on the top shelf. They landed with deadly aim on the back of her neck.

When Jonathan came home that night, the acrid air of burnt meat permeated the apartment.

"Lisa! What smells?" Jonathan ran into the kitchen and hit a wall of black smoke.

A few open windows reduced the black wall to a grey fog. It improved visibility enough to reveal the outline of one arm across the pantry doorway.

Jonathan found his wife buried under a gooey avalanche of fruit and vegetables, empty cans, and splintered wood.

The top and bottom pantry shelves had been ripped away. The middle shelf was intact but clear—except for a five-can pyramid of green beans and three neatly stacked tins of canned chicken.

The Music on the Hill

Saki

Sylvia Seltoun ate her breakfast in the morning-room at Yessney with a pleasant sense of ultimate victory, such as a fervent Ironside might have permitted himself on the morrow of Worcester fight. She was scarcely pugnacious by temperament, but belonged to that more successful class of fighters who are pugnacious by circumstance. Fate had willed that her life should be occupied with a series of small struggles, usually with the odds slightly against her, and usually she had just managed to come through winning. And now she felt that she had brought her hardest and certainly her most important struggle to a successful issue. To have married Mortimer Seltoun, "Dead Mortimer" as his more intimate enemies called him, in the teeth of the cold hostility of his family, and in spite of his unaffected indifference to women, was indeed an achievement that had needed some determination and adroitness to carry through; yesterday she had brought her victory to its concluding stage by wrenching her husband away from Town and its group of satellite watering-places and "settling him down," in the vocabulary of her kind, in this remote wood-girt manor farm which was his country house.

"You will never get Mortimer to go," his mother had said carpingly, "but if he once goes he'll stay; Yessney throws almost as much a spell over him as Town does. One can understand what holds him to Town, but Yessney—" and the dowager had shrugged her shoulders.

There was a sombre almost savage wildness about Yessney that was certainly not likely to appeal to town-bred tastes, and Sylvia, notwithstanding her name, was accustomed to nothing much more sylvan than "leafy Kensington." She looked on the country as something excellent and wholesome in its way, which was apt to become troublesome if you encouraged it overmuch. Distrust of town-life had been a new thing with her, born of her marriage with Mortimer, and she had watched with satisfaction the gradual fading of what she called "the Jermyn-Street-look" in his eyes as the woods and heather of Yessney had closed in on them yesternight. Her will-power and strategy had prevailed; Mortimer would stay.

Outside the morning-room windows was a triangular slope of turf, which the indulgent might call a lawn, and beyond its low hedge of neglected fuschia bushes a steeper slope of heather and bracken dropped down into cavernous combes overgrown with oak and yew. In its wild open savagery there seemed a stealthy linking of the joy of life with the terror of unseen things. Sylvia smiled complacently as she gazed with a School-of-Art appreciation at the landscape, and then of a sudden she almost shuddered.

"It is very wild," she said to Mortimer, who had joined her; "one could almost think that in such a place the worship of Pan had never quite died out."

"The worship of Pan never has died out," said Mortimer. "Other newer gods have drawn aside his votaries from time to time, but he is the Nature-God to whom all must come back at last. He has been called the Father of all the Gods, but most of his children have been stillborn."

Sylvia was religious in an honest, vaguely devotional kind of way, and did not like to hear her beliefs spoken of as mere aftergrowths, but it was at least something new and hopeful to hear Dead Mortimer speak with such energy and conviction on any subject.

"You don't really believe in Pan?" she asked incredulously.

"I've been a fool in most things," said Mortimer quietly, "but I'm not such a fool as not to believe in Pan when I'm down here. And if you're wise you won't disbelieve in him too boastfully while you're in his country."

It was not till a week later, when Sylvia had exhausted the attractions of the woodland walks round Yessney, that she ventured on a tour of inspection of the farm buildings. A farmyard suggested in her mind a scene of cheerful bustle, with churns and flails and smiling dairymaids, and teams of horses drinking knee-deep in duck-crowded ponds. As she wandered among the gaunt grey buildings of Yessney manor farm her first impression was one of crushing stillness and desolation, as though she had happened on some lone deserted homestead long given over to owls and cobwebs; then came a sense of furtive watchful hostility, the same shadow of unseen things that seemed to lurk in the wooded combes and coppices. From behind heavy doors and shuttered windows came the restless stamp of hoof or rasp of chain halter, and at times a muffled bellow from some stalled beast. From a distant corner a shaggy dog watched her with intent unfriendly eyes; as she drew near it slipped quietly into its kennel, and slipped out again as noiselessly when she had passed by. A few hens, questing for food under a rick, stole away under a gate at her approach. Sylvia felt that if she had come across any human beings in this wilderness of barn and byre they would have fled wraith-like from her gaze. At last, turning a corner quickly, she came upon a living thing that did not fly from her. Astretch in a pool of mud was an enormous sow, gigantic beyond the town-woman's wildest computation of swine-flesh, and speedily alert to resent and if necessary repel the unwonted intrusion. It was Sylvia's turn to make an unobtrusive retreat. As she threaded her way past rickyards and cowsheds and long blank walls, she started suddenly at a strange sound—the echo of a boy's laughter, golden and equivocal. Jan, the only boy employed on the farm, a tow-headed, wizen-faced yokel, was visibly at work on a potato clearing half-way up the nearest hill-side, and Mortimer, when questioned, knew of no other probable or possible begetter of the hidden mockery that had ambushed Sylvia's retreat. The memory of that untraceable echo was added to her other impressions of a furtive sinister "something" that hung around Yessney.

Of Mortimer she saw very little; farm and woods and trout-streams seemed to swallow him up from dawn till dusk. Once, following the direction she had seen him take in the morning, she came to an open space in a nut copse, further shut in by huge yew trees, in the centre of which stood a stone pedestal surmounted by a small bronze figure of a youthful Pan. It was a beautiful piece of workmanship, but her attention was chiefly held by the fact that a newly cut bunch of grapes had been placed as an offering at its feet. Grapes were none too plentiful at the manor house, and Sylvia snatched the bunch angrily from the pedestal. Contemptuous annoyance dominated her thoughts as she strolled slowly homeward, and then gave way to a sharp feeling of something that was very near fright; across a thick tangle of undergrowth a boy's face was scowling at her, brown and beautiful, with unutterably evil eyes. It was a lonely pathway, all pathways round Yessney were lonely for the matter of that, and she sped forward without waiting to give a closer scrutiny to this sudden apparition. It was not till she had reached the house that she discovered that she had dropped the bunch of grapes in her flight.

"I saw a youth in the wood today," she told Mortimer that evening, "brown-faced and rather handsome, but a scoundrel to look at. A gipsy lad, I suppose."

"A reasonable theory," said Mortimer, "only there aren't any gipsies in these parts at present."

"Then who was he?" asked Sylvia, and as Mortimer appeared to have no theory of his own, she passed on to recount her finding of the votive offering.

"I suppose it was your doing," she observed; "it's a harmless piece of lunacy, but people would think you dreadfully silly if they knew of it."

"Did you meddle with it in any way?" asked Mortimer.

"I—I threw the grapes away. It seemed so silly," said Sylvia, watching Mortimer's impassive face for a sign of annoyance.

"I don't think you were wise to do that," he said reflectively. "I've heard it said that the Wood Gods are rather horrible to those who molest them."

"Horrible perhaps to those that believe in them, but you see I don't," retorted Sylvia.

"All the same," said Mortimer in his even, dispassionate tone, "I should avoid the woods and orchards if I were you, and give a wide berth to the horned beasts on the farm."

It was all nonsense, of course, but in that lonely wood-girt spot nonsense seemed able to rear a bastard brood of uneasiness.

"Mortimer," said Sylvia suddenly, "I think we will go back to Town some time soon."

Her victory had not been so complete as she had supposed; it had carried her on to ground that she was already anxious to quit.

"I don't think you will ever go back to Town," said Mortimer. He seemed to be paraphrasing his mother's prediction as to himself.

Sylvia noted with dissatisfaction and some self-contempt that the course of her next afternoon's ramble took her instinctively clear of the network of woods. As to the horned cattle, Mortimer's warning was scarcely needed, for she had always regarded them as of doubtful neutrality at the best: her imagination unsexed the most matronly dairy cows and turned them into bulls liable to "see red" at any moment. The ram who fed in the narrow paddock below the orchards she had adjudged, after ample and cautious probation, to be of docile temper; today, however, she decided to leave his docility untested, for the usually tranquil beast was roaming with every sign of restlessness from corner to corner of his meadow. A low, fitful piping, as of some reedy flute, was coming from the depth of a neighbouring copse, and there seemed to be some subtle connection between the animal's restless pacing and the wild music from the wood. Sylvia turned her steps in an upward direction and climbed the heather-clad slopes that stretched in rolling shoulders high above Yessney. She had left the piping notes behind her, but across the wooded combes at her feet the wind brought her another kind of music, the straining bay of hounds in full chase. Yessney was just on the outskirts of the Devon-and-Somerset country, and the hunted deer sometimes came that way. Sylvia could presently see a dark body, breasting hill after hill, and sinking again and again out of sight as he crossed the combes, while behind him steadily swelled that relentless chorus, and she grew tense with the excited sympathy that one feels for any hunted thing in whose capture one is not directly interested. And at last he broke through the outermost line of oak scrub and fern and stood panting in the open, a fat September stag carrying a well-furnished head. His obvious course was to drop down to the brown pools of Undercombe, and thence make his way towards the red deer's favoured sanctuary, the sea. To Sylvia's surprise, however, he turned his head to the upland slope and came lumbering resolutely onward over the heather. "It will be dreadful," she thought, "the hounds will pull him down under my very eyes." But the music of the pack seemed to have died away for a moment, and in its place she heard again that wild piping, which rose now on this side, now on that, as though urging the failing stag to a final effort. Sylvia stood well aside from his path, half hidden in a thick growth of whortle bushes, and watched him swing stiffly upward, his flanks dark with sweat, the coarse hair on his neck showing light by contrast. The pipe music shrilled suddenly around her, seeming to come from the bushes at her very feet, and at the same moment the great beast slewed round and bore directly down upon her. In an instant her pity for the hunted animal was changed to wild terror at her own danger; the thick heather roots mocked her scrambling efforts at flight, and she looked frantically downward for a glimpse of oncoming hounds. The huge antler spikes were within a few yards of her, and in a flash of numbing fear she remembered Mortimer's warning, to beware of horned beasts on the farm. And then with a quick throb of joy she saw that she was not alone; a human figure stood a few paces aside, knee-deep in the whortle bushes.

"Drive it off!" she shrieked. But the figure made no answering movement.

The antlers drove straight at her breast, the acrid smell of the hunted animal was in her nostrils, but her eyes were filled with the horror of something she saw other than her oncoming death. And in her ears rang the echo of a boy's laughter, golden and equivocal.

The Mystery of the Semi-Detached

Edith Nesbit

He was waiting for her; he had been waiting an hour and a half in a dusty suburban lane, with a row of big elms on one side and some eligible building sites on the other—and far away to the south-west the twinkling yellow lights of the Crystal Palace. It was not quite like a country lane, for it had a pavement and lamp-posts, but it was not a bad place for a meeting all the same: and farther up, towards the cemetery, it was really quite rural, and almost pretty, especially in twilight. But twilight had long deepened into night, and still he waited. He loved her, and he was engaged to be married to her, with the complete disapproval of every reasonable person who had been consulted. And this half-clandestine meeting was tonight to take the place of the grudgingly sanctioned weekly interview—because a certain rich uncle was visiting at her house, and her mother was not the woman to acknowledge to a moneyed uncle, who might 'go off' any day, a match so deeply ineligible as hers with him.

So he waited for her, and the chill of an unusually severe May evening entered into his bones.

The policeman passed him with but a surly response to his 'Good night.' The bicyclists went by him like grey ghosts with fog-horns; and it was nearly ten o'clock, and she had not come.

He shrugged his shoulders and turned towards his lodgings. His road led him by her house—desirable, commodious, semi-detached—and he walked slowly as he neared it. She might, even now, be coming out. But she was not. There was no sign of movement about the house, no sign of life, no lights even in the windows. And her people were not early people.

He paused by the gate, wondering.

Then he noticed that the front door was open—wide open—and the street lamp shone a little way into the dark hall. There was something about all this that did not please him—that scared him a little, indeed. The house had a gloomy and deserted air. It was obviously impossible that it harboured a rich uncle. The old man must have left early. In which case—

He walked up the path of patent-glazed tiles, and listened. No sign of life. He passed into the hall. There was no light anywhere. Where was everybody, and why was the front door open? There was no one in the drawing-room, the dining-room and the study (nine feet by seven) were equally blank. Every one was out, evidently. But the unpleasant sense that he was, perhaps, not the first casual visitor to walk through that open door impelled him to look through the house before he went away and closed it after him. So he went upstairs, and at the door of the first bedroom he came to he struck a wax match, as he had done in the sitting-rooms. Even as he did so he felt that he was not alone. And he was prepared to see *something;* but for what he saw he was not prepared. For what he saw lay on the bed, in a white loose gown—and it was his sweetheart, and its throat was cut from ear to ear. He doesn't know what happened then, nor how he got downstairs and into the street; but he got out somehow, and the policeman found him in a fit, under the lamp-post at the corner of the street. He couldn't speak when they picked him up, and he passed the night in the police-cells, because the policeman had seen plenty of drunken men before, but never one in a fit.

The next morning he was better, though still very white and shaky. But the tale he told the magistrate was convincing, and they sent a couple of constables with him to her house.

There was no crowd about it as he had fancied there would be, and the blinds were not down.

As he stood, dazed, in front of the door, it opened, and she came out.

He held on to the door-post for support.

'*She*'s all right, you see,' said the constable, who had found him under the lamp. 'I told you you was drunk, but you *would* know best—'

When he was alone with her he told her—not all—for that would not bear telling—but how he had come into the commodious semi-detached, and how he had found the door open and the lights out, and that he had been into that long back room facing the stairs, and had seen something—in even trying to hint at which he turned sick and broke down and had to have brandy given him.

'But, my dearest,' she said, 'I dare say the house was dark, for we were all at the Crystal Palace with my uncle, and no doubt the door was open, for the maids *will* run out if they're left. But you could not have been in that room, because I locked it when I came away, and the key was in my pocket. I dressed in a hurry and I left all my odds and ends lying about.'

'I know,' he said; 'I saw a green scarf on a chair, and some long brown gloves, and a lot of hairpins and ribbons, and a prayerbook, and a lace handkerchief on the dressing-table. Why, I even noticed the almanack on the mantelpiece—October 21. At least it couldn't be that, because this is May. And yet it was. Your almanack is at October 21, isn't it?'

'No, of course it isn't,' she said, smiling rather anxiously; 'but all the other things were just as you say. You must have had a dream, or a vision, or something.'

He was a very ordinary, commonplace, City young man, and he didn't believe in visions, but he never rested day or night till he got his sweetheart and her mother away from that commodious semi-detached, and settled them in a quite distant suburb. In the course of the removal he incidentally married her, and the mother went on living with them.

His nerves must have been a good bit shaken, because he was very queer for a long time, and was always inquiring if any one had taken the desirable semi-detached; and when an old stockbroker with a family took it, he went the length of calling on the old gentleman and imploring him by all that he held dear, not to live in that fatal house.

'Why?' said the stockbroker, not unnaturally.

And then he got so vague and confused, between trying to tell why and trying not to tell why, that the stockbroker showed him out, and thanked his God he was not such a fool as to allow a lunatic to stand in the way of his taking that really remarkably cheap and desirable semi-detached residence.

Now the curious and quite inexplicable part of this story is that when she came down to breakfast on the morning of the 22nd of October she found him looking like death, with the morning paper in his hand. He caught hers—he couldn't speak, and pointed to the paper. And there she read that on the night of the 21st a young lady, the stockbroker's daughter, had been found, with her throat cut from ear to ear, on the bed in the long back bedroom facing the stairs of that desirable semi-detached.

The Ninth Skeleton

Clark Ashton Smith

It was beneath the immaculate blue of a morning in April that I set out to keep my appointment with Guenevere. We had agreed to meet on Boulder Ridge, at a spot well known to both of us, a small and circular field surrounded with pines and full of large stones, midway between her parents' home at Newcastle and my cabin on the north-eastern extremity of the Ridge, near Auburn.

Guenevere is my fiancée. It must be explained that at the time of which I write, there was a certain amount of opposition on the part of her parents to the engagement—an opposition since happily withdrawn. In fact, they had gone so far as to forbid me to call, and Guenevere and I could see each other only by stealth, and infrequently.

The Ridge is a long and rambling moraine, heavily strewn in places with boulders, as its name implies, and with many outcroppings of black volcanic stone. Fruit-ranches cling to some of its slopes, but scarcely any of the top is under cultivation, and much of the soil, indeed, is too thin and stony to be arable. With its twisted pines, often as fantastic in form as the cypresses of the California coast, and its gnarled and stunted oaks, the landscape has a wild and quaint beauty, with more than a hint of the Japanesque in places.

It is perhaps two miles from my cabin to the place where I was to meet Guenevere. Since I was born in the very shadow of Boulder Ridge, and have lived upon or near it for most of my thirty-odd years, I am familiar with every rod of its lovely and rugged extent, and, previous to that April morning, would scarcely have refrained from laughing if anyone had told me I could possibly lose my way. . . . Since then—well, I assure you, I should not feel inclined to laugh. . . .

Truly, it was a morning made for the trysts of lovers. Wild bees were humming busily in the patches of clover and in the ceanothus bushes with their great masses of white flowers, whose strange and heavy perfume intoxicated the air. Most of the spring blossoms were abroad: cyclamen, yellow violet, poppy, wild hyacinth, and woodland star; and the green of the fields was opalescent with their colours. Between the emerald of the buck-eyes, the grey-green of the pines, the golden and dark and bluish greens of the oaks, I caught glimpses of the snow-white Sierras to the east, and the faint blue of the Coast Range to the west, beyond the pale and lilac levels of the Sacramento valley. Following a vague trail, I went onwards across open fields where I had to thread my way among clustering boulders.

My thoughts were all of Guenevere, and I looked only with a casual and desultory eye at the picturesqueness and vernal beauty that environed my path. I was half-way between my cabin and the meeting-place, when I became suddenly aware that the sunlight had darkened, and glanced up, thinking, of course, that an April cloud, appearing unobserved from beyond the horizon, had passed across the sun. Imagine, then, my surprise when I saw that the azure of the entire sky had turned to a dun and sinister brown, in the midst of which the sun was clearly visible, burning like an enormous round red ember. Then, something strange and unfamiliar in the nature of my surroundings, which I was momentarily at a loss to define, forced itself upon my attention, and my surprise became a growing consternation. I stopped and looked about me, and realized, incredible as it seemed, that I had lost my way; for the pines on either hand were not those that I had expected to see. They were more gigantic, more gnarled, than the ones I remembered; and their roots writhed in wilder and more serpentine contortions from a soil that was strangely flowerless, and where even the grass grew only in scanty tufts. There were boulders large as druidic monoliths, and the forms of some of them were such as one might see in a nightmare. Thinking, of course, that it must all be a dream, but with a sense of utter bewilderment which seldom if ever attends the absurdities and monstrosities of nightmare, I sought in vain to orient myself and to find some familiar landmark in the bizarre scene that lay before me.

A path, broader than the one I had been following, but running in what I judged to be the same direction, wound on among the trees. It was covered with a grey dust, which, as I went forward, became deeper and displayed footprints of a singular form—footprints that were surely too attenuate, too fantastically slender, to be human, despite their five toe-marks. Something about them, I know not what, something in the nature of their very thinness and elongation, made me shiver. Afterwards, I wondered why I had not recognized them for what they were; but at the time, no suspicion entered my mind—only a vague sense of disquietude, an indefinable trepidation.

As I proceeded, the pines amid which I passed became momentarily more fantastic and more sinister in the contortions of their boughs and boles and roots. Some were like leering hags; others were obscenely crouching gargoyles; some appeared to writhe in an eternity of hellish torture; others were convulsed as with a satanic merriment. All the while, the sky continued to darken slowly, the dun and dismal brown that I had first perceived turning through almost imperceptible changes of tone to a dead funereal purple, wherein the sun smouldered like a moon that had risen from a bath of blood. The trees and the whole landscape were saturated with this macabre purple, were immersed and steeped in its unnatural gloom. Only the rocks, as I went on, grew strangely paler; and their forms were somehow suggestive of headstones, of tombs and monuments. Beside the trail, there was no longer the green of vernal grass—only an earth mottled by drying algae and tiny lichens the colour of verdigris. Also there were patches of evil-looking fungi with stems of a leprous pallor and blackish heads that drooped and nodded loathsomely.

The sky had now grown so dark that the whole scene took on a semi-nocturnal aspect, and made me think of a doomed world in the twilight of a dying sun. All was airless and silent; there were no birds, no insects, no sighing of the pines, no lisping of leaves: a baleful and preternatural silence, like the silence of the infinite void.

The trees became denser, then dwindled, and I came to a circular field. Here, there was no mistaking the nature of the monolithal boulders—they were headstones and funeral monuments, but so enormously ancient that the letterings or figures upon them were well-nigh effaced; and the few characters that I could distinguish were not of any known language. About them there was the hoariness and mystery and terror of incomputable Eld. It was hard to believe that life and death could be as old as they. The trees around them were inconceivably gnarled and bowed as with an almost equal burden of years. The sense of awful antiquity that these stones and pines all served to convey increased the oppression of my bewilderment, confirmed my disquietude. Nor was I reassured when I noticed on the soft earth about the headstones a number of those attenuate footprints of which I have already spoken. They were disposed in a fashion that was truly singular seeming to depart from and return to the vicinity of each stone.

Now, for the first time, I heard a sound other than the sound of my own footfalls in the silence of this macabre scene. Behind me, among the trees, there was a faint and evil rattling. I turned and listened; there was something in these sounds that served to complete the demoralization of my unstrung nerves; and monstrous fears, abominable fancies, trooped like the horde of a witches' sabbat through my brain.

The reality that I was now to confront was no less monstrous! There was a whitish glimmering in the shadow of the trees, and a human skeleton, bearing in its arms the skeleton of an infant, emerged and came towards me! Intent as on some ulterior cryptic purpose, some charnel errand not to be surmised by the living, it went by with a tranquil pace, an effortless and gliding tread, in which, despite my terror and stupefaction, I perceived a certain horrible and feminine grace. I followed the apparition with my eyes as it passed among the monuments without pausing and vanished in the darkness of the pines on the opposite side of the field. No sooner had it gone, than a second, also bearing in its arms an infant skeleton, appeared and passed before me in the same direction and with the same abominable and loathsome grace of movement.

310

A horror that was more than horror, a fear that was beyond fear, petrified all my faculties, and I felt as if I were weighted down by some ineluctable and insupportable burden of nightmare. Before me, skeleton after skeleton, each precisely like the last, with the same macabre lightness and ease of motion, each carrying its pitiful infant, emerged from the shadow of the ancient pines and followed where the first had disappeared, intent as on the same cryptic errand. One by one they came, till I had counted eight! Now I knew the origin of the bizarre footprints whose attenuation had disturbed and troubled me.

When the eighth skeleton had passed from sight, my eyes were drawn as by some irresistible impulsion to one of the nearer headstones, beside which I was amazed to perceive what I had not noticed before: a freshly opened grave, gaping darkly in the soft soil. Then, at my elbow, I heard a low rattling, and the fingers of a fleshless hand plucked lightly at my sleeve. A skeleton was beside me, differing only from the others through the fact that it bore no infant in its arms. With a lipless and ingratiating leer, it plucked again at my sleeve, as if to draw me towards the open grave, and its teeth clicked as if it were trying to speak. My senses and my brain, aswirl with vertiginous terror, could endure no more: I seemed to fall and fall through deeps of infinite eddying blackness with the clutching terror of those fingers upon my arm, till consciousness was left behind in my descent.

When I came to, Guenevere was holding me by the arm, concern and puzzlement upon her sweet oval face, and I was standing among the boulders of the field appointed for our rendezvous.

'What on earth is the matter with you, Herbert?' she queried anxiously. 'Are you ill? You were standing here in a daze when I came, and didn't seem to hear or see me when I spoke to you. And I really thought you were going to faint when I touched your arm.'

No Eye-Witnesses

Henry S. Whitehead

There were blood stains on Everard Simon's shoes. . . .

Simon's father had given up his country house in Rye when his wife died, and moved into an apartment in Flatbush among the rising apartment houses which were steadily replacing the original rural atmosphere of that residential section of swelling Brooklyn.

Blood stains—and forest mold—on his shoes!

The younger Simon—he was thirty-seven, his father getting on toward seventy—always spent his winters in the West Indies, returning in the spring, going back again in October. He was a popular writer of informative magazine articles. As soon as his various visits for week-ends and odd days were concluded, he would move his trunks into the Flatbush apartment and spend a week or two, sometimes longer, with his father. There was a room for him in the apartment, and this he would occupy until it was time for him to leave for his summer camp in the Adirondacks. Early in September he would repeat the process, always ending his autumn stay in the United States with his father until it was time to sail back to St. Thomas or Martinique or wherever he imagined he could write best for that particular winter.

There was only one drawback in this arrangement. This was the long ride in the subway necessitated by his dropping in to his New York club every day. The club was his real American headquarters. There he received his mail. There he usually lunched and often dined as well. It was at the club that he received his visitors and his telephone calls. The club was on Forty-fourth Street, and to get there from the apartment he walked to the Church Avenue subway station, changed at De Kalb Avenue, and then took a Times Square express train over the Manhattan Bridge. The time consumed between the door of the apartment and the door of the club was exactly three-quarters of an hour, barring delays. For the older man the arrangement was ideal. He could be in his office, he boasted, in twenty minutes.

To avoid the annoyances of rush hours in the subway, Mr. Simon senior commonly left home quite early in the morning, about seven o'clock. He was a methodical person, always leaving before seven in the morning, and getting his breakfast in a downtown restaurant near the office. Everard Simon rarely left the apartment until after nine, thus avoiding the morning rush-hour at its other end. During the five or six weeks every year that they lived together the two men really saw little of each other, although strong bonds of understanding, affection, and respect bound them together. Sometimes the older man would awaken his son early in the morning for a brief conversation. Occasionally the two would have a meal together, evenings, or on Sundays; now and then an evening would be spent in each other's company. They had little to converse about. During the day they would sometimes call each other up and speak together briefly on the telephone from club to office or office to club. On the day when Everard Simon sailed south, his father and he always took a farewell luncheon together somewhere downtown. On the day of his return seven months later, his father always made it a point to meet him at the dock. These arrangements had prevailed for eleven years. He must get that blood wiped off. Blood! How—?

During that period, the neighborhood of the apartment had changed out of all recognition. Open lots, community tennis-courts, and many of the older one-family houses had disappeared, to be replaced by the ubiquitous apartment houses. In 1928 the neighborhood which had been almost rural when the older

Simon had taken up his abode "twenty minutes from his Wall Street office" was solidly built up except for an occasional, and now incongruous, frame house standing lonely and dwarfed in its own grounds among the towering apartment houses, like a lost child in a preoccupied crowd of adults whose business caused them to look over the child's head.

One evening, not long before the end of his autumn sojourn in Flatbush, Everard Simon, having dined alone in his club, started for the Times Square subway station about a quarter before nine. Doubled together lengthwise, and pressing the pocket of his coat out of shape, was a magazine, out that day, which contained one of his articles. He stepped on board a waiting Sea Beach express train, in the rearmost car, sat down, and opened the magazine, looking down the table of contents to find his article. The train started after the ringing of the warning bell and the automatic closing of the side doors, while he was putting on his reading-spectacles. He began on the article.

He was dimly conscious of the slight bustle of incoming passengers at Broadway and Canal Street, and again when the train ran out on the Manhattan Bridge because of the change in the light, but his closing of the magazine with a page-corner turned down, and the replacing of the spectacles in his inside pocket when the train drew in to De Kalb Avenue, were almost entirely mechanical. He could make that change almost without thought. He had to cross the platform here at De Kalb Avenue, get into a Brighton Beach local train. The Brighton Beach expresses ran only in rush hours and he almost never travelled during those periods.

He got into his train, found a seat, and resumed his reading. He paid no attention to the stations—Atlantic and Seventh Avenues. The next stop after that, Prospect Park, would give him one of his mechanical signals, like coming out on the bridge. The train emerged from its tunnel at Prospect Park, only to re-enter it again at Parkside Avenue, the next following station. After that came Church Avenue, where he got out every evening.

As the train drew in to that station, he repeated the mechanics of turning down a page in the magazine, replacing his spectacles in their case, and putting the case in his inside pocket. His mind entirely on the article, he got up, left the train, walked back toward the Caton Avenue exit, started to mount the stairs.

A few moments later he was walking, his mind still entirely occupied with his article, in the long-familiar direction of his father's apartment.

The first matter which reminded him of his surroundings was the contrast in his breathing after the somewhat stuffy air of the subway train. Consciously he drew in a deep breath of the fresh, sweet outdoor air. There was a spicy odor of wet leaves about it somehow. It seemed, as he noticed his environment with the edge of his mind, darker than usual. The crossing of Church and Caton Avenues was a brightly lighted corner. Possibly something was temporarily

313

wrong with the lighting system. He looked up. Great trees nodded above his head. He could see the stars twinkling above their lofty tops. The sickle edge of a moon cut sharply against black branches moving gently in a fresh wind from the sea.

He walked on several steps before he paused, slackened his gait, then stopped dead, his mind responding in a note of quiet wonderment.

Great trees stood all about him. From some distance ahead a joyous song in a manly bass, slightly muffled by the wood of the thick trees, came to his ears. It was a song new to him. He found himself listening to it eagerly. The song was entirely strange to him, the words unfamiliar. He listened intently. The singer came nearer. He caught various words, English words. He distinguished "merry," and "heart," and "repine."

It seemed entirely natural to be here, and yet, as he glanced down at his brown clothes, his highly polished shoes, felt the magazine bulging his pocket, the edge of his mind caught a note of incongruity. He remembered with a smile that strange drawing of Aubrey Beardsley's, of a lady playing an upright cottage pianoforte in the midst of a field of daisies! He stood, he perceived, in a kind of rough path worn by long usage. The ground was damp underfoot. Already his polished shoes were soiled with mold.

The singer came nearer and nearer. Obviously, as the fresh voice indicated, it was a young man. Just as the voice presaged that before many seconds the singer must come out of the screening array of tree boles, Everard Simon was startled by a crashing, quite near by, at his right. The singer paused in the middle of a note, and for an instant there was a primeval silence undisturbed by the rustle of a single leaf.

Then a huge timber wolf burst through the underbrush to the right, paused, crouched, and sprang, in a direction diagonal to that in which Everard Simon was facing, toward the singer.

Startled into a frigid immobility, Simon stood as though petrified. He heard an exclamation, in the singer's voice, a quick "heh"; then the sound of a struggle. The great wolf, apparently, had failed to knock down his quarry. Then without warning, the two figures, man and wolf, came into plain sight; the singer, for so Simon thought of him, a tall, robust fellow, in fringed deerskin, slashing desperately with a hunting-knife, the beast crouching now, snapping with a tearing motion of a great punishing jaw. Short-breathed "heh's" came from the man, as he parried dexterously the lashing snaps of the wicked jaws.

The two, revolving about each other, came very close. Everard Simon watched the struggle, fascinated, motionless. Suddenly the animal shifted its tactics. It backed away stealthily, preparing for another spring. The young woodsman abruptly dropped his knife, reached for the great pistol which depended from his belt in a rough leather holster. There was a blinding flash, and the wolf slithered down, its legs giving under it. A great cloud of acrid smoke drifted about Everard Simon, cutting off his vision; choking smoke which made him cough.

But through it, he saw the look of horrified wonderment on the face of the young woodsman; saw the pistol drop on the damp ground as the knife had dropped; followed with his eyes, through the dimming medium of the hanging smoke, the fascinated, round-eyed stare of the man who had fired the pistol.

There, a few feet away from him, he saw an eldritch change passing over the beast, shivering now in its death-struggle. He saw the hair of the great paws dissolve, the jaws shorten and shrink, the lithe body buckle and heave strangely. He closed his eyes, and when he opened them, he saw the figure in deerskins standing mutely over the body of a man, lying prone across tree-roots, a pool of blood spreading, spreading, from the concealed face, mingling with the damp earth under the tree-roots.

Then the strange spell of quiescence which had held him in its weird thrall was dissolved, and, moved by a nameless terror, he ran, wildly, straight down the narrow path between the trees. . . .

It seemed to him that he had been running only a short distance when something, the moon above the trees, perhaps, began to increase in size, to give a more brilliant light. He slackened his pace. The ground now felt firm underfoot, no longer damp, slippery. Other lights joined that of the moon. Things became brighter all about him, and as this brilliance increased, the great trees all about him turned dim and pale. The ground was now quite hard underfoot. He looked up. A brick wall faced him. It was pierced with windows. He looked down. He stood on pavement. Overhead a streetlight swung lightly in the late September breeze. A faint smell of wet leaves was in the air, mingled now with the fresh wind from the sea. The magazine was clutched tightly in his left hand. He had, it appeared, drawn it from his pocket. He looked at it curiously, put it back into the pocket.

He stepped along over familiar pavement, past well-known façades. The entrance to his father's apartment loomed before him. Mechanically he thrust his left hand into his trousers pocket. He took out his key, opened the door, traversed the familiar hallway with its rugs and marble walls and bracket side-wall light-clusters. He mounted the stairs, one flight, turned the corner, reached the door of the apartment, let himself in with his key.

It was half-past nine and his father had already retired. They talked through the old man's bedroom door, monosyllabically. The conversation ended with the request from his father that he close the bedroom door. He did so, after wishing the old man good-night.

He sat down in an armchair in the living-room, passed a hand over his forehead, bemused. He sat for fifteen minutes. Then he reached into his pocket for a cigarette. They were all gone. Then he remembered that he had meant to buy a fresh supply on his way to the apartment. He had meant to get the cigarettes from the drug-store between the Church Avenue subway station and the apartment! He looked about the room for one. His father's supply, too, seemed depleted.

He rose, walked into the entry, put on his hat, stepped out again into the hallway, descended the one flight, went out into the street. He walked into an unwonted atmosphere of excitement. People were conversing as they passed, in excited tones; about the drug-store entrance a crowd was gathered. Slightly puzzled, he walked toward it, paused, blocked, on the outer edge.

"What's happened?" he inquired of a young man whom he found standing just beside him, a little to the fore.

"It's a shooting of some kind," the young man explained. "I only just got here myself. The fellow that got bumped off is inside the drug-store—what's left of him. Some gang-war stuff, I guess."

He walked away, skirting the rounded edge of the clustering crowd of curiosity-mongers, proceeded down the street, procured the cigarettes elsewhere. He passed the now enlarged crowd on the other side of the street on his way back, returned to the apartment, where he sat, smoking and thinking, until eleven, when he retired. Curious—a man shot; just at the time, or about the time, he had let that imagination of his get the better of him—those trees!

His father awakened him about five minutes before seven. The old man held a newspaper in his hand. He pointed to a scare-head on the front page.

"This must have happened about the time you came in," remarked Mr. Simon.

"Yes—the crowd was around the drugstore when I went out to get some cigarettes," replied Everard Simon, stretching and yawning.

When his father was gone and he had finished with his bath, he sat down, in a bathrobe, to glance over the newspaper account. A phrase arrested him:

". . . the body was identified as that of 'Jerry the Wolf,' a notorious gangster with a long prison record." Then, lower down, when he had resumed his reading:

". . . a large-caliber bullet which, entering the lower jaw, penetrated the base of the brain. . . . no eye-witnesses. . . ."

Everard Simon sat for a long time after he had finished the account, the newspaper on the floor by his chair. "No eye-witnesses!" He must, really, keep that imagination of his within bounds, within his control.

Slowly and reflectively, this good resolution uppermost, he went back to the bathroom and prepared for his morning shave.

Putting on his shoes, in his room, he observed something amiss. He picked up a shoe, examined it carefully. The soles of the shoes were caked with black mold, precisely like the mold from the woodpaths about his Adirondack camp. Little withered leaves and dried pine-needles clung to the mold. And on the side of the right shoe were brownish stains, exactly like freshly dried bloodstains. He shuddered as he carried the shoes into the bathroom, wiped them clean with a damp towel, then rinsed out the towel. He put them on, and shortly afterward, before he entered the subway to go over to the club for the day, he had them polished.

The bootblack spoke of the killing on that corner the night before. The bootblack noticed nothing amiss with the shoes, and when he had finished, there was no trace of any stains.

Simon did not change at De Kalb Avenue that morning. An idea had occurred to him between Church Avenue and De Kalb, and he stayed on the Brighton local, secured a seat after the emptying process which took place at De Kalb, and went on through the East River tunnel.

He sent in his name to Forrest, a college acquaintance, now in the district attorney's office, and Forrest received him after a brief delay.

"I wanted to ask a detail about this gangster who was killed in Flatbush last night," said Simon. "I suppose you have his record, haven't you?"

"Yes, we know pretty well all about him. What particular thing did you want to know?"

"About his name," replied Simon. "Why was he called 'Jerry the Wolf'—that is, why 'The Wolf' particularly?"

"That's a very queer thing, Simon. Such a name is not, really, uncommon. There was that fellow, Goddard, you remember. They called him 'The Wolf of Wall Street.' There was the fiction criminal known as 'The Lone Wolf.' There have been plenty of 'wolves' among criminal 'monikers.' But this fellow, Jerry Goraffsky, was a Hungarian, really. He was called 'The Wolf,' queerly enough, because there were those in his gang who believed he was one of those birds who could change himself into a wolf! It's a queer combination, isn't it?—for a New York gangster?"

"Yes," said Everard Simon, "it is, very queer, when you come to think of it. I'm much obliged to you for telling me. I was curious about it somehow."

"That isn't the only queer aspect of this case, however," resumed Forrest, a light frown suddenly showing on his keen face. "In fact that wolf-thing isn't a part of the case—doesn't concern us, of course, here in the district attorney's office. That's nothing but blah. Gangsters are as superstitious as sailors; more so, in fact!

"No. The real mystery in this affair is—the bullet, Simon. Want to see it?"

"Why—yes; of course—if you like, Forrest. What's wrong with the bullet?"

Forrest stepped out of the room, returned at once, laid a large, round ball on his desk. Both men bent over it curiously.

"Notice that diameter, Simon," said Forrest. "It's a hand-molded round ball—belongs in a collection of curios, not in any gangster's gat! Why, man, it's like the slugs they used to hunt the bison before the old Sharps rifle was invented. It's the kind of a ball Fenimore Cooper's people used—'Deerslayer!' It would take a young cannon to throw that thing. Smashed in the whole front of Jerry's ugly mug. The inside works of his head were spilled all over the side-walk! It's what the newspapers always call a 'clue.' Who do you suppose resur-rected the horse-pistol—or the ship's blunderbuss—to do that job on Jerry? Clever, in a way. Hooked it out of some dime museum, perhaps. There are still a few of those old 'pitches' still operating, you know, at the old stand—along East Fourteenth Street."

"A flintlock, single-shot horse-pistol, I'd imagine," said Everard Simon, laying the ounce lead ball back on the mahogany desk. He knew something of weapons, new and old. As a writer of informational articles that was part of his permanent equipment.

"Very likely," mused the assistant district attorney. "Glad you came in, old man."

And Everard Simon went on uptown to his club.

Old Clothes

Ramsey Campbell

C ome on, lad, let's be having you," Charlie shouted, and let the back of the van down with a clatter that sent pigeons flying from the cracked roadway. "Anyone'd think it were Fort Knox."

"Don't call me lad," Eric muttered, shoving all his weight against the door of the house. The July sunlight on his shoulders felt like a weight too, but the door didn't budge, not until Charlie stumped along the weedy path and threw his weight against the door. It cracked, then stuttered inward, crumpling bills and final reminders and circulars and advertising newspapers, which trailed along the grayish hall toward the ragged staircase. "Go on, lad," Charlie urged. "What are you waiting for?"

"Christmas. Christmas, and the fairy to come off the tree and give me a million pounds." Eric was waiting for his eyes to adjust, that was all. Specks of light, dust that had found sunlight, rose above the stairs, but the house seemed darker than it ought to be.

Charlie gave him a push. "Don't be going to sleep, lad. Time enough for a rest when we've cleared the house."

I'm forty years old, Eric snarled inside himself, and I don't like being pushed. "Try finding someone else who'll put up with you," he muttered as Charlie threw open the first door. "We'll start in here," Charlie said.

The room didn't look as if it had been cleaned for months. Plants with gray fur wilted in pots; cobwebs hung beneath the round table, draped the lopsided chairs. Nevertheless, someone had been in the house since the old lady had died, for the drawers of a bureau had been pulled out, spilling letters. Charlie stuffed the letters into the drawers. "Take the chairs," he said over his shoulder. "You can manage them."

Eric resented being made to feel he'd said he couldn't. By the time he'd finished shifting the chairs, he was wearing gray gloves and a wig. Charlie stared at him as if he'd made a stupid joke. "Give us a hand with the table," he growled.

They had to dance back and forth along the hall and up and down the stairs. As they manhandled the table into the sunlight, Eric thought he glimpsed a pattern round the edge, of pairs of hands or the prints of hands. "Get a move on, lad," Charlie panted, glancing at the darkening sky.

The old lady's relatives must have kicked the papers along the hall, Eric decided as he stooped to a wad of letters that had been wedged behind the bureau. They were thank-you letters, one from a woman who lived a few streets away from Eric: Thank you for putting me in touch with my father; thank you, said another, for my wife, for my son . . . "Never mind prying," Charlie said. "I don't care if she's dead, some things are private."

They were starting on the dining room—spiders fled when Charlie lifted the fat tablecloth—before Eric realized what the letters meant. "What was she, anyway? You never said."

"You never bloody asked, lad. What difference does it make? One of them spiritists, if it's any of your business."

Perhaps it offended him, or maybe he felt that it should, as Eric's father had after Eric's mother died. Eric remembered his father on his knees in church and at bedtime, praying for a sign. They were both dead now, but he'd never felt tempted to contact them, had never been interested in that kind of thing. All the same, he couldn't help peering into each room as he followed Charlie, couldn't help feeling like an intruder as they stripped the beds and unbolted the frames. Venturing into her bedroom, he almost expected to see her or her shape made of dust in the bed. He flinched when something moved, scraping, behind him. It was a raincoat hanging on the door.

The sky was darker when they carried out the bed. By the time they took out the wardrobe, the sky was black. The downpour began as they were about to clear the attic, and so they sat in the cab of the van and ate the sandwiches

Charlie's wife had made. She always made half for Eric since she'd taken pity on him, though Charlie gave him less than half. They drank coffee from Charlie's flask, too sweet for Eric's taste, and then Charlie said, "Can't wait all day. Back to work."

The gray road looked like a river of tar now, jumping with rain. Charlie shrugged into his plastic raincoat; too bad for Eric if he hadn't brought one. Swallowing the words he would have liked to say, Eric ran out of the cab and into the house. Hall and rooms were squirming with large vague shadows of rain; he thought of the ectoplasm mediums were supposed to ooze, but he grabbed the raincoat from the hook on the bedroom door.

A few shakes and the dust almost blinded him. At least the coat was wearable. He fumbled in the pockets to make sure they were empty. A hint of clamminess in the sleeves made him shiver, but it had gone by the time he'd buttoned the coat on the man's side. Charlie watched him from the bedroom doorway with a kind of dull contempt. "My God, what do you look like."

Eric didn't care, or so he told himself. They cleared the attic. Then he slammed the door of the house. For a moment he thought he heard movement inside; it must be the papers flapping. Charlie was already starting the van, and he had to run.

Charlie left him in the drizzle while he drove along the coast to sell the vanload of furniture and ornaments. Eric strolled around town, reading job advertisements that always asked for people younger or more qualified than he was; then he climbed the streets above the factories that nobody wanted to rent, to his flat.

He reached in the right-hand pocket of the raincoat without thinking. Of course his key wasn't in there, but neither was the pocket empty, though the object was only a flower, easy enough to overlook. Nevertheless, he'd never seen a flower like it, especially one looking so fresh when it must have been in the pocket for weeks. He found an old glass and stood the flower in water.

Later he bought chips in the next street and fried himself an egg; then he tried to watch a film about Hawaii through the snow on the television Charlie had given him from one of the houses. Exhausted by the day's work, he was in bed before it was dark. He saw handprints dancing around a table, heard his parents calling to each other, almost saw a shape with arms that could reach around the world. Once he thought he heard metal jingling further down the room he lived and ate and slept in.

The morning was colder. He waited for Charlie to ring the shaky bell and watched newspapers chasing along the back alleys, birds darting out of the steep slate roofs. He changed the water in the glass on the mantelpiece—the flower was already drooping—then he decided to wait downstairs in case the bell had stopped working. He opened the door of his flat, and metal jingled among the coats on the hook.

He'd hung the borrowed raincoat on top. In the left-hand pocket he found two tarnished coins of a kind he'd never seen before. On an impulse he put one in his mouth and bit timidly. The metal was soft to his teeth.

He was gazing at the bite-mark when Charlie rang the bell. He hid the coins under the glass on the mantelpiece and searched the pockets twice to make sure they were empty; then, abruptly, his mind a tangle of half-formed thoughts—Long John Silver, nothing up my sleeve—he buttoned himself into the raincoat. He didn't want to leave it when he could take it with him.

Charlie looked as if he mightn't even let him in the van. "Slept in it, did you?" he said in disgust. "I'm having my doubts about you."

"I thought it'd keep the dust off."

"No dust where we're going." Nor was there, neither in the house they were clearing nor the one to which the young couple were moving. The wife fussed around them all day, telling them to be careful and not to put that there, and Eric seldom had a chance to feel in the raincoat pockets. There was never anything. Soon he felt more like a stooge than ever, especially when he realized that somehow he'd managed to button the coat on the wrong side, though he remembered buttoning it properly. No wonder the husband avoided looking at him.

Eric half expected the flower and the coins to have vanished: he'd remembered his mother reading him a bedtime story about fairy gold. No, the coins were still there, and the wilting flower. He hung up the coat and tried not to watch it, then made himself go out to the Weights & Scales for a drink. An hour of listening to people decades younger than he complaining about unemployment and immigrants and governments and prophesying the football match up the hill next Saturday, and he went home. The pockets were empty, and so, when he slept, were his dreams.

As soon as he got up, he rummaged in the pockets. Still empty. Much more groping in the old material and he would be finding holes. He put the coat on, out of defiance to Charlie if nothing else, and plunged his hands into the pockets so as to look uncaring as he waited on the doorstep. The right-hand pocket contained a diamond as big as his thumbnail.

He ran upstairs and hid the diamond under his pillow. He ran down, then back up, and hid the coins next to the diamond. The van was just drawing up. Charlie gave him a look that made words superfluous, and took his time in handing over Eric's wages, which were supposed to include Eric's cut from the sale of the contents of the cleared house. The cut seemed smaller than it ought to be. Remembering the diamond, he didn't care. Charlie stared at him when he unbuttoned the raincoat to stow the money in his shirt, but he didn't want to put anything in those pockets in case it might be spirited away.

The diamond made him careless, and so did the old lady whose house they were clearing. "That's not mine," she kept crying as they lifted furniture.

"Someone's trying to play a trick on me. Don't bother taking it, I won't have it in my house." They carried on doggedly, hoping her son would arrive soon, and Eric almost dropped a tea chest full of crockery for reaching in his pocket when he thought he felt it move, and kept on reaching in there for something that would make the day worthwhile.

The son, a middle-aged man with pinched eyes and a woeful mouth, arrived as they started on the bedrooms, and calmed his mother down as best he could while they brought down a wardrobe. "Where have you been? I thought you were never coming," she cried as Eric hurried back to the house, missing a step when something rattled in his pocket. It was a pearl necklace. "That's mine. Look at him," the old lady screeched, "you've brought a thief into my house."

"I don't think that's one of yours, Mummy."

"It is, it is. You all want to rob me."

Before Eric could think what to say, Charlie snatched the necklace. "So that's what you've been up to with your bloody silly coat. I ought to give you your cards right now." He handed the necklace to the old lady. "Of course it's yours, ma'am. Please accept my apologies. I've never had anything like this happen before in thirty-eight years of removals."

"Go on then, give me my cards." Eric was sure there must be plenty more where the necklace had come from. "Don't you be making out I'm a thief. You're a thief."

"Watch your tongue, lad, or I'll knock you down." Charlie nodded fiercely at the son as if to tell him to be angry. "And he will, too."

"Don't call me lad. I'm not a lad, I'm forty, and I'm not a thief—you are. You steal my money you get from selling stuff I carried. And he steals my sandwiches," he told the old lady, thinking that should show her—she was a mother, after all.

"Who said anything about sandwiches? You'll get no sandwiches from me. I wouldn't make you a cup of tea," she screeched, "except to pour it over your head."

Eric had had enough. "See how much you can shift by yourself," he told Charlie. "And when you get tired, Muscles here can help you."

He strode home, feeling as if all he'd said was a burden he'd thrown off, leaving him lighter, almost capable of flying. He didn't need Charlie or his cards, he didn't need anyone. The coat would keep him, however it worked—he didn't need to know how. He restrained himself from searching the pockets until he arrived home, in case it mightn't work in the open. But when he'd closed himself in, he found they were empty.

He hung the coat on the door and went out to the Nosebag Cafe for a pie and chips. When he returned to find the coat empty, he put it on. For a while he watched television so as not to keep reaching in the pockets; then he switched off the set and kept counting one to a hundred with his arms folded. Eventually he dozed and almost saw the face of the shape with arms or hands that could reach around the world, that were reaching into his pockets or out of them. Once he awoke with his hands in his pockets, and snatched them out in a panic.

In the morning he found a stone the size of the palm of his hand, a smooth stone that glittered and looked precious. As soon as he was dressed, he bought the cheapest newspaper to wrap the coins and jewel and stone individually before placing them in a supermarket bag. That left one sheet of newspaper, which he folded around the dead flower.

He clutched the bag to him in both hands all the way to the museum: there were too many thieves about these days. He wouldn't let the girl behind the desk at the museum see what he had; the fewer people who knew, the better. He waited for the top man and occasionally felt in his pockets.

He refused to open the bag until he was in the curator's office. The first item that came to hand was the flower. He didn't expect it to be worth anything; he just wanted to know what it was, while he anticipated learning how wealthy he was. But the curator frowned at the flower, then at Eric. "Where did you get this?"

"An old lady gave it to me. She didn't know what it was."

"And where did she get it? You can't say? I thought not." The curator picked up the phone on his desk. "She ought to know it's a protected species."

Eric gripped the bag and prepared to flee if the curator was calling the police. Instead he called some doctor to find out if any flowers had been taken from a garden, flowers with a long name that included Himalayas. None had, nor apparently had any other garden been robbed, and he put down the receiver. "What else have you in there?"

"Nothing. I've brought the wrong things." Eric tried not to back away too conspicuously. "I'll have to come back," he lied, and managed not to run until he was out of the museum.

He wandered the thirsty streets. Football fans looking for pubs or mischief elbowed him out of the way. He wasn't sure if he wanted to hide the contents of the bag at home or dump them in the nearest bin. He couldn't take them to be valued until he knew where they'd come from, and how was he to find that out? He was beginning to hate the damned coat; it had made a fool of him, had nearly got him arrested. He'd begun to grow furious, trying to unbutton it and fumbling helplessly, when he remembered the address on the letter he'd seen in the medium's house. At once he made for the hill.

An old lady opened the door of the terraced house and rubbed her eyes as if she had been asleep or weeping. She glanced sharply at his raincoat, then shook her head at herself. "I don't want anything today," she mumbled, starting to close the door.

"I've lost my parents." He couldn't just ask as if she knew about the coat. "Someone said you could help me."

"I don't go in for that anymore." Nevertheless, she stood back for him. "You do look lost. Come in if you want to talk."

He didn't, not about his parents: even using them to trick his way in had made him feel guilty. As soon as he was seated in the parlor, which smelled of old furniture and lavender, he said, "Why did you give it up?"

She stared, then understood. "The lady who used to put me in touch died herself."

"Was she a good medium? Did they bring her things?"

He thought he'd been too direct, for she stiffened. "That's what killed her, I think."

His hands recoiled from the pockets, where they had been resting. "What, being brought things?"

"Apports, they're called. Them, aye, and growing old." She shivered. "One of her guides was evil, that's what she didn't know."

He gaped at her, out of his depth. "He brought her flowers and treasures until he got to be her favorite," she said. "Then he started bringing other things until she was afraid to hold séances at all, but that didn't stop him. He started putting them in her bed when she was asleep."

Eric was on his feet before he knew it, and struggling to unbutton the coat until he realized that he meant to leave it in her house. She didn't deserve that or the contents of the supermarket bag. "I've got to go now," he stammered, and collided with furniture and doors on his way out of the house.

Football fans came crowding up the hill toward the football ground, singing and shouting and throwing empty beer cans. He went with them, since he didn't know where best to go. He couldn't be sure that the old lady's story had anything to do with the coat, with whatever brought him presents. Nevertheless, when something in the right-hand pocket bumped against him, he found he couldn't swallow.

He wanted desperately to stand still, to prepare himself, if he could, to find out what was there, but the crowd crammed into the narrow streets shoved him onward, wouldn't let him out of its midst. He scarcely had room to reach down to the pocket; he wished he could use that as an excuse not to find out, but he couldn't bear not knowing what was scraping against him with every step. Nor could he simply reach in. His fingers ranged shakily and timidly over the outside of the pocket to trace the shape within.

It felt like a cross. It must be; he could trace the chain it would hang from. He slipped his hand into the pocket and grabbed the chain before he could flinch, managed to raise it to eye level. Yes, it was a cross, a silver cross, and he'd never felt so relieved in his life; the old lady's tale couldn't have anything to do with him. He dangled the cross into the supermarket bag and

324

lifted his hand to his mouth, for a splinter from somewhere had lodged in his finger. As he pulled out the splinter with his teeth, he noticed that his hand smelled of earth.

He had just realized that the cross was very like the one his father had always worn when he realized there was something in the left-hand pocket too.

He closed his eyes and plunged his hand in, to get it over with. His fingertips flinched from touching something cold, touched it again and discovered it was round, somewhat crusted or at least not smooth, a bulge on it smoother, less metallic. A stone in a ring, he thought, and took it out, sighing. It was the ring his mother had worn to her grave.

Something else was rolling about in the pocket—something which, he realized, choking, had slipped out of the ring. He snatched it out and flung it away blindly, crying out with horror and fury and grief. Those nearest him in the crowd glanced at him, warning him not to go berserk while he was next to them; otherwise the crowd took no notice of him as it drove him helplessly uphill.

He tore at the buttons and then at the coat. The material wouldn't tear; the buttons might have been sewn through buttonholes too small for them, they were so immovable. He felt as if he were going mad, as if the whole indifferent crowd were too—this nightmare of a crowd that wasn't slowing even now that it had come in sight of the football ground and the rest of itself. His hands were clenched on the supermarket bag at the level of his chest so as not to stray near his pockets, in which he thought he felt objects crawling. He was pleading, almost sobbing, first silently and then aloud, telling his parents he was sorry, he would never have stolen from them, he would pray for them if they wanted, even though he had never believed . . . Then he closed his eyes tight as the crowd struggled with itself, squeezed his eyes shut until they ached, for something was struggling in his pocket, feebly and softly. He couldn't bear it without screaming, and if he screamed in the midst of the crowd, he would know he was mad. He looked down.

It was a hand, a man's hand. A man had his hand in Eric's pocket, a scrawny youth who blinked at Eric as though to say the hand was nothing to do with him. He'd been trying to pick Eric's pocket, which had closed around his wrist just as the holes had closed around the buttons. "My God," Eric cried between screaming and laughter, "if you want it that badly, you can have it," and all at once the buttonholes were loose and the coat slipped off his arms, and he was fighting sideways out of the crowd.

He looked back once, then fought free of the crowd and stumbled uphill beyond the streets, toward the heath. Perhaps up there he would know whether to go to Charlie for his cards or his job. At last he realized he was still holding his mother's ring. He slipped it into his safest pocket and forced himself not to look back. Perhaps someone would notice how wild the pickpocket's eyes were growing; perhaps they might help him. In any case, perhaps it had only been the press of the crowd that had been giving him trouble as he struggled with the coat, one hand in the pocket, the other in the sleeve. Perhaps Eric hadn't really seen the sleeve worming, inching. He knew he'd seen the youth struggling to put on the coat, but he couldn't be sure that he'd seen it helping itself on.

One-Night Strand

Donald R. Burleson

It wasn't much of a motel. Eric had started forming that opinion while edging the Toyota off the highway and onto the bumpy drive in front of the office, where a neon sign proclaimed "VACANCY" in sputtering yellow hesitancies as if laboring under the ravages of some strange electrical disease. The opinion grew a little stronger while he was checking in, under the ministrations of a sallow desk clerk whose breath conjured up impressions of beer-vomit and unwashed dentures. And the opinion grew stronger still when Eric saw his room, number 18, where he suspected he was not to be the only guest, not if you counted tiny ones with more than two legs. But maybe it wasn't that bad, maybe he was just tired. A quick look around revealed dinginess but no obvious vermin, and the plumbing did seem to work, minimally.

At any rate, it was dark, and he had had to get off the road and get some sleep. This certainly wasn't one of those places with key-cards and free coffee and color TV, but it was going to have to do for tonight.

Room 18 at least had the virtue of being at the end of a row of rooms, with number 17 on the right but with nothing on the left but an open field stretching off into the night. Not that noisy neighbors would have been a problem anyway, he thought, surveying the place as he closed up the car and took his single bag to the door; there were only a few other cars here and there, down the way, and it was already pretty late. It appeared that nobody was in number 17, next door, and that was fine with him. He was going to be sleeping like a mummy as soon as his head hit the pillow.

But he didn't sleep. Lying on the spongy bed, he found himself wide-eyed in the dark. It was going to be one of those nights when he was paradoxically too tired to sleep. And it seemed a waste, when he had all this quiet around him, no noise from outside at all except a distant swish of passing highway traffic, and nobody in the room next door.

The thought was scarcely formed when a quick wash of headlights filtered through the drawn blinds, scattering a wild profusion of jittery shadows. Someone had pulled up in front of number 17 and shut off their engine. For a few seconds it was so quiet that he could hear the low tick-tick-tick of the engine cooling. Then the opening of a car door, then other sounds: laughter, footsteps, a car door closing, someone fumbling with a key at the door of number 17, muttering, more footsteps, laughter again, a man's voice, then apparently a female voice, a chittering sort of giggle that Eric found somehow disquieting.

He had to get up and have a look.

Prying the edge of the blinds back an inch or two, he peered out. A dim bulb somewhere nearby cast a faint illumination on the scene. There next to the Toyota was a rusty-looking blue Dodge Colt, its front doors both hanging open, making it look like some giant insect. A tall, cadaverously thin man in a wrinkled light gray suit was standing next to the car door on the passenger side and appeared to be struggling to lift something out of the front seat, something large and lumpy under a blanket. Whatever it was, when the man got clear of the car with it, it seemed to poke angularly up into the blanket in places, and made Eric think vaguely of several bottles of champagne sticking up out of a large tub, as if anyone would bother to conceal such a thing under a blanket, especially at this hour and in a dump like this. That odd, chittering laughter came again, from somewhere, and Eric surmised that the mystery woman must already be inside the room. He just hoped they didn't make noise all night, but maybe that was hoping for too much.

As he watched, the thin man disappeared into Room 17 with his odd burden. Through the adjoining wall there filtered more mumbling and more laughter, his in a muffled bass, hers in that high staccato chirp that he found so uncomfortable. Momentarily the thin man reappeared, returning to the car and fumbling in the back seat for something. He went around slamming car doors and came stumbling back toward the motel room carrying a second burden even stranger than the first. Eric, watching from the dark of his room, blinked and tried to see more clearly in the wan light.

Mr. Bones, as Eric had decided to call him, was clutching a double armload of women's high-heeled shoes, maybe half a dozen pairs. They were all white, gaudy with sequins, and seemed to have holes cut in the soles, leaving just the toe and the spiky heel on each shoe, and a rim or outline of what would have been the sole. Mr. Bones dropped a few of the shoes on the pavement and bent over, wheezing and mumbling, to gather them up. Was this going to be how he got his thrills, then? Watching his companion for the evening change shoes repeatedly? The world was becoming a peculiar place to live. Well—let them do whatever they wanted, as long as they were reasonably quiet about it.

But of course there was no chance of that. Lying back in bed, he listened in the dark, and his anger grew.

Through the thin intervening wall, sounds kept coming. He writhed in the bedsheets, trying to get comfortable, trying to ignore the sounds. Muffled talking, muttering, laughing, now his deep and hollow voice, now her insane piping and chirping, now the bedsprings groaning. Eric put a pillow over his head, but that was intolerable; he felt as if he couldn't breathe. It was hot now, and muggy, and he was more uncomfortable by the minute.

Through the wall, the sounds would swell from time to time into a medley of murmuring gruffness and chittering giggles. Suddenly there came a succession of sounds not just through but along the wall, a frenzied clack-clack-clack-clack-clack-clack-clack-clack that sounded, for God's sakes, like high-heeled shoes on the opposite side of the wall. Was *that* it, then? Did Mr. Bones get his jollies watching her put a pair of the shoes on her hands and clack them in a noisy path across the wall? Were people, even these days, really crazy enough and rude enough to do things like that in a motel where other people were trying to sleep? Thoughtless bastards!

A near-quiet had fallen, over there, broken only by a sort of dry rustling like bedsheets. Maybe they were tired, ready for some sleep themselves. But the sounds came crashing through again to shatter the silence—gruff bass mumblings, protestations of bedsprings, the high, mindless chittering laughter and, without warning, another round of shoe-clatterings across the wall, so many and so fast that Eric figured they must *both* be up doing it this time. He'd heard of some strange ways of getting aroused, but this was a new one, and one he wished he hadn't discovered, at least not at this juncture in his life.

Silence fell again, and Eric lay rigid in his rumpled sheets, waiting. Nothing, nothing for a long while. Then a low suggestion of whispering and quiet laughing, and unplaceable *other* sounds, strange arid sounds like the rustling and crackling of dry grass. A voice came through, gruff and low-timbred.

"Mm, that's good. Another strand. Oh, yeah. Tie me good and tight."

Eric sighed in the dark. Bondage, yet? Tying him to the goddamn bed. What else?

As if in reply, the sounds swelled out into a riot of shouting, thumping, giggling, with the clatter of shoes again in an invisible arc across the wall. "Oh, g'haaaa—oh! Uh!" It sounded like a man in pain, but then there was no surprise in that, considering the source, Eric reflected. "H-hh-uuuh! Uh!" A sound like gurgling in the throat, and more of that idiotic chirping laughter, more thumping, more shoes across the wall, this time in a wider arc that seemed to go off the adjoining wall and fade onto the other walls of number 17, as if the lunatic woman were "running" the shoes clear around the room, and all the while no letup on the muttering and gurgling and chirping.

Eric was up on his feet, furious. If these inconsiderate sons of bitches thought they were going to go at this all night, they were going to have to reconsider their plans, and that was a pure fact. Pulling his trousers on, he made for the door.

Outside, the sounds were of course even louder. Eric had his fist poised over number 17, ready to knock, but thought: hmm, who knows what kind of loony-bin types we're really talking about here? The kind, perhaps, that would pick up a gun and blow you away, right through the door? Maybe he'd better check things out. Surprisingly, the blinds in number 17 were open, and he bent to look in, cupping his hands around his eyes to block out the reflection of the light behind him.

There was a low lamp on in the room, in fact, across on the far wall, and it served to lend a little illumination to objects in there, but it still took him a minute to understand what he was looking at.

In the uncertain light the bed looked rather like a large spool of thread, with wrappings of some fibrous matter in sticky-looking strands around a moving lump in the middle, a lump with a protruding head that bobbed and brayed with laughter. The threads were wound loose, actually, because Eric could see patches of the thin, naked body of Mr. Bones, and indeed the groin area had been left clear.

She was there, all right, all of her, bigger than Mr. Bones, her head down between his legs, her own angular legs and arms splayed out to clutch the sides of the mattress. Only it wasn't really arms and legs—it was just legs. Eric must have made some involuntary sound at the window, because suddenly her body turned, without relinquishing her multiple hold on the bed. As it came around, the shiny, bulbous abdomen scattered a silky froth on the air above the bed, and the face jerked toward him. Its unthinkable arachnid contours were smeared with lurid splashes of lipstick and rouge—obscene red markings that folded and refolded as the nightmare mouth continued to work, sucking the air. Eric froze at the window, and the myriad clustered little eyes seemed to pierce him, seemed to pin him to the night like a bug on velvet.

But she was up off the bed now, moving, making her way across the lefthand wall again, toward the window, chirping and chittering as she came. Eric had overestimated the supply of gaudy white high-heeled shoes; there were exactly four pairs, and she was wearing them all. As she came clattering around, he caught a glimpse of the bed, where the head in the silky wrappings lifted a thin, bemused face that grinned as if in vague drunken approval.

It was the high heels reaching the window that broke Eric's trance. And broke the window as she came trundling through, fiddling her legs over the sill, dropping two or three sequin-spangled high-heeled shoes off onto the cement. One sinewy leg actually touched his face before he could move away. Recoiling, he scrambled blindly and collided with the front end of his car, frantic not to have her touch him again. She plopped heavily to the ground and came after him.

He had a frantic sensation of dodging a hideous flurry of movement that seemed to come at him from everywhere, a deranged sensation of running around the car to find that she had scuttered under it to meet him as he fumbled

329

the car door open. By the time his head began to clear a little, he could only infer that he had managed to get inside the car, and that his keys must have been in his pants pockets, because he was driving headlong into the night somewhere, not looking back at all, and trying not to think.

But some furtive corner of his mind kept remembering all the tiny bound bundles he'd ever seen suspended jittering in spiderwebs, tragic little scenarios in dusty corners of garages and toolsheds and attics, and he thought of Mr. Bones, and gave the Toyota some more gas.

One Size Eats All
A Campfire Tale For Children

T. E. D. Klein

The words had been emblazoned on the plastic wrapper of Andy's new sleeping bag, in letters that were fat and pink and somewhat crudely printed. Andy had read them aloud as he unwrapped the bag on Christmas morning.

" 'One size eats all.' What's that supposed to mean?"

Jack, his older brother, had laughed. "Maybe it's not really a sleeping bag. Maybe it's a *feed* bag!"

Andy's gaze had darted to the grotesquely large metal zipper that ran along the edge of the bag in rows of gleaming teeth. He'd felt a momentary touch of dread.

"It's obviously a mistake," Andy's father had said. "Or else a bad translation. They must have meant 'One size *fits* all.' "

He was sure that his father was right. Still, the words on the wrapper had left him perplexed and uneasy. He'd slept in plenty of sleeping bags before, but he knew he didn't want to sleep in this one.

And now, as he sat huddled in his tent halfway up Wendigo Mountain, about to slip his feet into the bag, he was even more uneasy. What if it *wasn't* a mistake?

He and Jack had been planning the trip for months; it was the reason they'd ordered the sleeping bags. Jack, who was bigger and more athletic and who'd already started to shave, had picked an expensive Arctic Explorer model from the catalogue. Nothing but the best for Jack. Andy, though, had hoped that if he chose an obscure brand manufactured overseas, and thereby saved his parents money, maybe they'd raise his allowance.

330

But they hadn't even noticed. The truth was, they'd always been somewhat inattentive where Andy was concerned. They barely seemed to notice how Jack bullied him.

Jack did bully him—in a brotherly way, of course. His bright red hair seemed to go with his fiery temper, and he wasn't slow to use his fists. He seemed to best the younger boy in just about everything, from basketball to campfire-building.

Which was why, just before they'd set out for Wendigo Mountain, Andy had invited his friend Willie along. Willie was small, pale, and even less athletic than Andy. His head seemed much too big for his body. On a strenuous overnight hike like this one, Andy thought, it was nice to have somebody slower and weaker than he was.

True to form, Willie lagged behind the two brothers as they trudged single-file up the trail, winding their way among the tall trees that covered the base of the mountain, keeping their eyes peeled for the occasional dark green trail-markers painted on the trunks. It was a sunny morning, and the air had begun to lose some of the previous night's chill.

By the time Willie caught up, winded and sweating beneath his down jacket, Andy and Jack had taken off their backpacks and stopped for a rest.

"It's *your* tough luck," Jack was telling him. "You've heard the old saying, 'You made your bed, now lie in it'?"

Andy nodded glumly.

"Well, it's the same thing," said Jack. "You *wanted* the damn bag, so tonight you're just gonna have to lie in it."

All morning, that's exactly what Andy had been worrying about. He eyed the pack at his feet, with the puffy brown shape strapped beneath it, and wished the night would never come. *You made your bed,* he told himself. *Now die in it.*

"Andy, for God's sake, stop obsessing about that bag!" said Willie. "You're letting your fears get the best of you. Honest, it's a perfectly ordinary piece of camping gear."

"Willie's right," said Jack. Hoisting his backpack onto his shoulders, he grinned and added cruelly, "And the people it eats are perfectly ordinary, too!"

As they continued up the trail, the trees grew smaller and began to thin; the air grew cooler. Andy could feel the weight of the thing on his back, heavier than a sleeping bag ought to be and pressing against him with, he sensed, a primitive desire—a creature impatient for its dinner.

Ahead of him, Jack turned. "Hey, Willie," he yelled. "Did Andy tell you where his bag is from?"

"No," said Willie, far behind them. "Where?"

Jack laughed delightedly. "Hungary!"

* * *

They made camp at a level clearing halfway up the mountain. Andy and Willie would be sharing a tent that night; Jack had one to himself. Late afternoon sunlight gleamed from patches of snow among the surrounding rocks.

The three unrolled their sleeping bags inside the tents. Andy paused before joining the others outside. In the dim light his bag lay brown and bloated, a living coffin waiting for an occupant. Andy reminded himself that it was, in fact, a fairly normal-looking bag—not very different, in truth, from Jack's new Arctic Explorer. Still, he wished he had a sleeping bag like Willie's, a comfortable old thing that had been in the family for years.

Willie lagged behind again as the brothers left camp and returned to the trail. They waited until he'd caught up. Both younger boys were tired and would have preferred to stay near the tents for the rest of the day, but Jack, impatient, wanted to press on toward the summit while it was still light.

The three took turns carrying a day pack with their compasses, flashlights, emergency food, and a map. The slope was steeper here, strewn with massive boulders, and the exertion made them warm again. Maybe, thought Andy, he wouldn't even need the bag tonight.

The terrain became increasingly difficult as they neared Wendigo's peak, where the trail was blanketed by snow. They were exhausted by the time they reached the top—too exhausted to appreciate the sweeping view, the stunted pines, and the small mounds of stones piled in odd patterns across the rock face.

They raised a feeble shout of triumph, rested briefly, then started down. Andy sensed that they would have to hurry; standing on the summit, he'd been unnerved at how low the sun lay in the sky.

The air was colder now, and shadows were lengthening across the snow. Before they'd gotten very far, the sun had sunk below the other side of the mountain.

They'd been traveling in shadow for what seemed nearly an hour, Jack leading the way, when the older boy paused and asked to see the map. Andy and Willie looked at one another and realized, with horror, that they had left the day pack at the top of the mountain, somewhere among the cairns and twisted trees.

"I thought you had it," said Andy, aghast at the smaller boy's carelessness.

"I thought *you* did," said Willie.

No matter; it was Andy that Jack swore at and smacked on the side of the head. Willie looked pained, as if he, too, had been hit.

Jack glanced up the slope, then turned and angrily continued down the trail. "Let's go!" he snapped over his shoulder. "Too late to go back for it now."

They got lost twice coming down, squeezing between boulders, clambering over jagged rocks, and slipping on patches of ice. But just as night had settled on the mountain, and Andy could no longer make out his brother's red hair or his friend's pale face, they all felt the familiar hard-packed earth of the trail beneath their boots.

They were dog-tired and aching by the time they stumbled into camp. They had no flashlights and were too fatigued to try to build a fire. Poor Willie, weariest of all, felt his way to the tent and crawled inside. Andy hung back. In the darkness he heard Jack yawn and slip into the other tent.

He was alone now, with no light but the stars and a sliver of moon, like a great curved mouth. The night was chilly; he knew he couldn't stay out here. With a sigh, he pushed through the tent flaps, trying not to think about what waited for him inside.

The interior of the tent was pitch black and as cold as outdoors. Willie was already asleep. The air, once crisp, seemed heavy with an alien smell; when he lifted the flap of his sleeping bag, the smell grew stronger. Did all new bags smell like this? He recognized the odors of canvas and rubber, but beneath them lurked a hint of something else: fur, maybe, or the breath of an animal.

No, he was imagining things. The only irrefutable fact was the cold. Feeling his way carefully in the darkness, Andy unlaced his boots, barely noticed that his socks were encrusted with snow. Gingerly he inserted one foot into the mouth of the bag, praying he'd feel nothing unusual.

The walls of the bag felt smooth and, moments later, warm. *Too warm.* Surely, though, it was just the warmth of his own body.

He pushed both legs in further, then slipped his feet all the way to the bottom. Lying in the darkness, listening to the sound of Willie's breathing, he could feel the bag press itself against his ankles and legs, clinging to them with a weight that seemed, for goosedown, a shade too heavy. Yet the feeling was not unpleasant. He willed himself to relax.

It occurred to him, as he waited uneasily for sleep, what a clever disguise a bag like this would make for a creature that fed on human flesh. Like a spider feasting upon flies that had blundered into its web, such a creature might gorge contentedly on human beings stupid enough to disregard its warning: *One size eats all. . . .* Imagine, prey that literally pushed itself into the predator's mouth!

Human stomach acid, he'd read, was capable of eating through a razor blade; and surely this creature's would be worse. He pictured the thing dissolving bones, draining the very life-blood from its victim, leaving a corpse sucked dry of fluids, like the withered husk a spider leaves behind. . . .

Suddenly he froze. He felt something damp—no, *wet*—at the bottom of the bag. Wet like saliva. Or worse.

Kicking his feet, he wriggled free of the bag. Maybe what he'd felt was simply the melted snow from his socks, but in the darkness he was taking no

333

chances. Feeling for his boots, he laced them back on and curled up on top of the bag, shivering beneath his coat.

Willie's voice woke him.

"Andy? Are you okay?"

Andy opened his eyes. It was light out. He had survived the night.

"Why were you sleeping like that?" said Willie. "You must be frozen."

"I was afraid to get back in the bag. It felt . . . weird."

Willie smiled. "It was just your imagination, Andy. That's not even your bag."

"Huh?" Andy peered down at the bag. A label near the top said *Arctic Explorer.* "But how—"

"I switched your bag with Jack's when the two of you were starting for the summit," said Willie. "I meant to tell you, but I fell asleep."

"Jack'll be furious," said Andy. "He'll kill me for this!"

Trembling with cold and fear, he crawled stiffly from the tent. It was early morning; a chilly sun hung in the pale blue sky. He dashed to Jack's tent and yanked back the flaps, already composing an apology.

The tent was empty. The sleeping bag, *his* bag, lay dark and swollen on the floor. There seemed to be no one inside.

Or almost no one; for emerging from the top was what appeared to be a deflated basketball—only this one had red hair and a human face.

An Original Revenge

W. C. Morrow

On a certain day I received a letter from a private soldier, named Gratmar, attached to the garrison of San Francisco. I had known him but slightly, the acquaintance having come about through his interest in some stories which I had published, and which he had a way of calling "psychological studies." He was a dreamy, romantic, fine-grained lad, proud as a tigerlily and sensitive as a bluebell. What mad caprice led him to join the army I never knew; but I did know that there he was wretchedly out of place, and I foresaw that his rude and repellant environment would make of him in time a deserter, or a suicide, or a murderer. The letter at first seemed a wild outpouring of despair, for it informed me that before it should reach me its author would be dead by his own hand. But when I had read farther I understood its spirit, and realized how coolly formed a scheme it disclosed and how terrible its purport was intended to be. The worst of the contents was the information that a certain officer (whom he named) had driven him to the deed, and that *he was committing suicide for the sole purpose of gaining thereby the power to revenge himself upon his enemy!* I learned afterward that the officer had received a similar letter.

This was so puzzling that I sat down to reflect upon the young man's peculiarities. He had always seemed somewhat uncanny, and had I proved more sympathetic he doubtless would have gone farther and told me of certain problems which he professed to have solved concerning the life beyond this. One thing that he had said came back vividly: "If I could only overcome that purely gross and animal love of life that makes us all shun death, I would kill myself, for I know how far more powerful I could be in spirit than in flesh."

The manner of the suicide was startling, and that was what might have been expected from this odd character. Evidently scorning the flummery of funerals, he had gone into a little canyon near the military reservation and blown himself into a million fragments with dynamite, so that all of him that was ever found was some minute particles of flesh and bone.

I kept the letter a secret, for I desired to observe the officer without rousing his suspicion of my purpose; it would be an admirable test of a dead man's power and deliberate intention to haunt the living, for so I interpreted the letter. The officer thus to be punished was an oldish man, short, apoplectic, overbearing, and irascible. Generally he was kind to most of the men in a way; but he was gross and mean, and that explained sufficiently his harsh treatment of young Gratmar, whom he could not understand, and his efforts to break that flighty young man's spirit.

Not very long after the suicide certain modifications in the officer's conduct became apparent to my watchful oversight. His choler, though none the less sporadic, developed a quality which had some of the characteristics of senility; and yet he was still in his prime, and passed for a sound man. He was a bachelor, and had lived always alone; but presently he began to shirk solitude at night and court it in daylight. His brother-officers chaffed him, and thereupon he would laugh in rather a forced and silly fashion, quite different from the ordinary way with him, and would sometimes, on these occasions, blush so violently that his face would become almost purple. His soldierly alertness and sternness relaxed surprisingly at some times and at others were exaggerated into unnecessary acerbity, his conduct in this regard suggesting that of a drunken man who knows that he is drunk and who now and then makes a brave effort to appear sober. All these things, and more, indicating some mental strain, or some dreadful apprehension, or perhaps something worse than either, were observed partly by me and partly by an intelligent officer whose watch upon the man had been secured by me.

To be more particular, the afflicted man was observed often to start suddenly and in alarm, look quickly round, and make some unintelligent monosyl-labic answer, seemingly to an inaudible question that no visible person had asked. He acquired the reputation, too, of having taken lately to nightmares, for in the middle of the night he would shriek in the most dreadful fashion, alarm-ing his roommates prodigiously. After these attacks he would sit up in bed, his ruddy face devoid of color, his eyes glassy and shining, his breathing broken with gasps, and his body wet with a cold perspiration.

Knowledge of these developments and transformations spread throughout the garrison; but the few (mostly women) who dared to express sympathy or suggest a tonic encountered so violent rebuffs that they blessed Heaven for escaping alive from his word-volleys. Even the garrison surgeon, who had a kindly manner, and the commanding general, who was constructed on dignified and impressive lines, received little thanks for their solicitude. Clearly the doughty old officer, who had fought like a bulldog in two wars and a hundred battles, was suffering deeply from some undiscoverable malady.

The next extraordinary thing which he did was to visit one evening (not so clandestinely as to escape my watch) a spirit medium—extraordinary, because he always had scoffed at the idea of spirit communications. I saw him as he was leaving the medium's rooms. His face was purple, his eyes were bulging and terrified, and he tottered in his walk. A policeman, seeing his distress, ad-vanced to assist him; whereupon the soldier hoarsely begged,—

"Call a hack."

Into it he fell, and asked to be driven to his quarters. I hastily ascended to the medium's rooms, and found her lying unconscious on the floor. Soon, with my aid, she recalled her wits, but her conscious state was even more alarming than the other. At first she regarded me with terror, and cried,—

"It is horrible for you to hound him so!"

I assured her that I was hounding no one.

"Oh, I thought you were the spir—I mean—I—oh, but it was standing exactly where you are!" she exclaimed.

"I suppose so," I agreed, "but you can see that I am not the young man's spirit. However, I am familiar with this whole case, madam, and if I can be of any service in the matter I should be glad if you would inform me. I am aware that our friend is persecuted by a spirit, which visits him frequently, and I am positive that through you it has informed him that the end is not far away, and that our elderly friend's death will assume some terrible form. Is there anything that I can do to avert the tragedy?"

The woman stared at me in a horrified silence. "How did you know these things?" she gasped.

"That is immaterial. When will the tragedy occur? Can I prevent it?"

"Yes, yes!" she exclaimed. "It will happen this very night! But no earthly power can prevent it!"

She came close to me and looked at me with an expression of the most acute terror.

"Merciful God! what will become of me? He is to be murdered, you understand—murdered in cold blood by a spirit—and he knows it and *I know it!* If he is spared long enough he will tell them at the garrison, and they will all think that I had something to do with it! Oh, this is terrible, terrible, and yet I dare not say a word in advance—nobody there would believe in what the spirits say, and they will think that I had a hand in the murder!" The woman's agony was pitiful.

"Be assured that he will say nothing about it," I said; "and if you keep your tongue from wagging you need fear nothing."

With this and a few other hurried words of comfort, I soothed her and hastened away.

For I had interesting work on hand: it is not often that one may be in at such a murder as that! I ran to a livery stable, secured a swift horse, mounted him, and spurred furiously for the reservation. The hack, with its generous start, had gone far on its way, but my horse was nimble, and his legs felt the pricking of my eagerness. A few miles of this furious pursuit brought me within sight of the hack just as it was crossing a dark ravine near the reservation. As I came nearer I imagined that the hack swayed somewhat, and that a fleeing shadow escaped from it into the tree-banked further wall of the ravine, I certainly was not in error with regard to the swaying, for it had roused the dull notion of the driver. I saw him turn, with an air of alarm in his action, and then pull up with a heavy swing upon the reins. At this moment I dashed up and halted.

"Anything the matter?" I asked.

"I don't know," he answered, getting down. "I felt the carriage sway, and I see that the door's wide open. Guess my load thought he'd sobered up enough to get out and walk, without troubling me or his pocket-book."

Meanwhile I too had alighted; then struck a match, and by its light we discovered, through the open door, the "load" huddled confusedly on the floor of the hack, face upward, his chin compressed upon his breast by his leaning against the further door, and looking altogether vulgar, misshapen, and miserably unlike a soldier. He neither moved nor spoke when we called. We hastily clambered within and lifted him upon the seat, but his head rolled about with an awful looseness and freedom, and another match disclosed a ghastly dead face and wide eyes that stared horribly at nothing.

"You would better drive the body to headquarters," I said.

Instead of following, I cantered back to town, housed my horse, and went straightway to bed; and this will prove to be the first information that I was the "mysterious man on a horse," whom the coroner could never find.

About a year afterwards I received the following letter (which is observed to be in fair English) from Stockholm, Sweden:

"DEAR SIR,—For some years I have been reading your remarkable psychological studies with great interest, and I take the liberty to suggest a theme for your able pen. I have just found in a library here a newspaper, dated about a year ago, in which is an account of the mysterious death of a military officer in a hack."

Then followed the particulars, as I have already detailed them, and the very theme of post-mortem revenge which I have adopted in this setting out of facts. Some persons may regard the coincidence between my correspondent's suggestion and my private and exclusive knowledge as being a very remarkable thing; but there are likely even more wonderful things in the world, and at none of them do I longer marvel. More extraordinary still is his suggestion that in the dynamite explosion a dog or a quarter of beef might as well have been employed as a suicide-minded man; that, in short, the man may not have killed himself at all, but might have employed a presumption of such an occurrence to render more effective a physical persecution ending in murder by the living man who had posed as a spirit. The letter even suggested an arrangement with a spirit medium, and I regard that also as a queer thing.

The declared purpose of this letter was to suggest material for another of my "psychological studies;" but I submit that the whole affair is of too grave a character for treatment in the levity of fiction. And if the facts and coincidences should prove less puzzling to others than to me, a praiseworthy service might be done to humanity by the presentation of whatever solution a better understanding than mine might evolve.

The only remaining disclosure which I am prepared now to make is that my correspondent signed himself "Ramtarg,"—an odd-sounding name, but for all I know it may be respectable in Sweden. And yet there is something about the name that haunts me unceasingly, much as does some strange dream which we know we have dreamt and yet which it is impossible to remember.

The Outsider

H. P. Lovecraft

That night the Baron dreamt of many a wo;
And all his warrior-guests, with shade and form
Of witch, and demon, and large coffin-worm,
Were long be-nightmared.

—*Keats*

Unhappy is he to whom the memories of childhood bring only fear and sadness. Wretched is he who looks back upon lone hours in vast and dismal chambers with brown hangings and maddening rows of antique books, or upon awed watches in twilight groves of grotesque, gigantic, and vine-encumbered trees that silently wave twisted branches far aloft. Such a lot the gods gave to me—to me, the dazed, the disappointed; the barren, the broken. And yet I am strangely content, and cling desperately to those sere memories, when my mind momentarily threatens to reach beyond *to the other*.

I know not where I was born, save that the castle was infinitely old and infinitely horrible; full of dark passages and having high ceilings where the eye could find only cobwebs and shadows. The stones in the crumbling corridors seemed always hideously damp, and there was an accursed smell everywhere, as of the piled-up corpses of dead generations. It was never light, so that I used sometimes to light candles and gaze steadily at them for relief; nor was there any sun outdoors, since the terrible trees grew high above the topmost accessible tower. There was one black tower which reached above the trees into the unknown outer sky, but that was partly ruined and could not be ascended save by a well-nigh impossible climb up the sheer wall, stone by stone.

I must have lived years in this place, but I can not measure the time. Beings must have cared for my needs, yet I can not recall any person except myself; or anything alive but the noiseless rats and bats and spiders. I think that whoever nursed me must have been shockingly aged, since my first conception of a living person was that of something mockingly like myself, yet distorted, shriveled, and decaying like the castle. To me there was nothing grotesque in the bones and skeletons that strewed some of the stone crypts deep down among the foundations. I fantastically associated these things with everyday events,

339

and thought them more natural than the colored pictures of living beings which I found in many of the moldy books. From such books I learned all that I know. No teacher urged or guided me, and I do not recall hearing any human voice in all those years—not even my own; for although I had read of speech, I had never thought to try to speak aloud. My aspect was a matter equally unthought of, for there were no mirrors in the castle, and I merely regarded myself by instinct as akin to the youthful figures I saw drawn and painted in the books. I felt conscious of youth because I remembered so little.

Outside, across the putrid moat and under the dark mute trees, I would often lie and dream for hours about what I read in the books; and would longingly picture myself amidst gay crowds in the sunny world beyond the endless forest. Once I tried to escape from the forest, but as I went farther from the castle the shade grew denser and the air more filled with brooding fear; so that I ran frantically back lest I lose my way in a labyrinth of nighted silence.

So through endless twilights I dreamed and waited, though I knew not what I waited for. Then in the shadowy solitude my longing for light grew so frantic that I could rest no more, and I lifted entreating hands to the single black ruined tower that reached above the forest into the unknown outer sky. And at last I resolved to scale that tower, fall though I might; since it were better to glimpse the sky and perish, than to live without ever beholding day.

In the dank twilight I climbed the worn and aged stone stairs till I reached the level where they ceased, and thereafter clung perilously to small footholds leading upward. Ghastly and terrible was that dead, stairless cylinder of rock; black, ruined, and deserted, and sinister with startled bats whose wings made no noise. But more ghastly and terrible still was the slowness of my progress; for climb as I might, the darkness overhead grew no thinner, and a new chill as of haunted and venerable mold assailed me. I shivered as I wondered why I did not reach the light, and would have looked down had I dared. I fancied that night had come suddenly upon me, and vainly groped with one free hand for a window embrasure, that I might peer out and above, and try to judge the height I had attained.

All at once, after an infinity of awesome, sightless crawling up that concave and desperate precipice, I felt my head touch a solid thing, and knew I must have gained the roof, or at least some kind of floor. In the darkness I raised my free hand and tested the barrier, finding it stone and immovable. Then came a deadly circuit of the tower, clinging to whatever holds the slimy wall could give; till finally my testing hand found the barrier yielding, and I turned upward again, pushing the slab or door with my head as I used both hands in my fearful ascent. There was no light revealed above, and as my hands went higher I knew that my climb was for the nonce ended; since the slab was the trap-door of an aperture leading to a level stone surface of greater circumference than the lower tower, no doubt the floor of some lofty and capacious observation chamber. I crawled through carefully, and tried to prevent the heavy slab from falling back into place; but failed in the latter attempt. As I lay exhausted on the stone floor I heard the eery echoes of its fall, but hoped when necessary to pry it up again.

Believing I was now at a prodigious height, far above the accursed branches of the wood, I dragged myself up from the floor and fumbled about for windows, that I might look for the first time upon the sky, and the moon and stars of which I had read. But on every hand I was disappointed; since all that I found were vast shelves of marble, bearing odious oblong boxes of disturbing size. More and more I reflected, and wondered what hoary secrets might abide in this high apartment so many eons cut off from the castle below. Then unexpectedly my hands came upon a doorway, where hung a portal of stone, rough with strange chiseling. Trying it, I found it locked; but with a supreme burst of strength I overcame all obstacles and dragged it open inward. As I did so there came to me the purest ecstasy I have ever known; for shining tranquilly through an ornate grating of iron, and down a short stone passageway of steps that ascended from the newly found doorway, was the radiant full moon, which I had never before seen save in dreams and in vague visions I dared not call memories.

Fancying now that I had attained the very pinnacle of the castle, I commenced to rush up the few steps beyond the door; but the sudden veiling of the moon by a cloud caused me to stumble, and I felt my way more slowly in the dark. It was still very dark when I reached the grating—which I tried carefully and found unlocked, but which I did not open for fear of falling from the amazing height to which I had climbed. Then the moon came out.

Most demoniacal of all shocks is that of the abysmally unexpected and grotesquely unbelievable. Nothing I had before undergone could compare in terror with what I now saw; with the bizarre marvels that sight implied. The sight itself was as simple as it was stupefying, for it was merely this: instead of a dizzying prospect of treetops seen from a lofty eminence, there stretched around me on a level through the grating nothing less than *the solid ground*, decked and diversified by marble slabs and columns, and overshadowed by an ancient stone church, whose ruined spire gleamed spectrally in the moonlight.

Half unconscious, I opened the grating and staggered out upon the white gravel path that stretched away in two directions. My mind, stunned and chaotic as it was, still held the frantic craving for light; and not even the fantastic wonder which had happened could stay my course. I neither knew nor cared whether my experience was insanity, dreaming, or magic; but was determined to gaze on brilliance and gayety at any cost. I knew not who I was or what I was, or what my surroundings might be; though as I continued to stumble along I became conscious of a kind of fearsome latent memory that made my progress

341

not wholly fortuitous. I passed under an arch out of that region of slabs and columns, and wandered through the open country; sometimes following the visible road, but sometimes leaving it curiously to tread across meadows where only occasional ruins bespoke the ancient presence of a forgotten road. Once I swam across a swift river where crumbling, mossy masonry told of a bridge long vanished.

Over two hours must have passed before I reached what seemed to be my goal, a venerable ivied castle in a thickly wooded park; maddeningly familiar, yet full of perplexing strangeness to me. I saw that the moat was filled in, and that some of the well known towers were demolished; whilst new wings existed to confuse the beholder. But what I observed with chief interest and delight were the open windows—gorgeously ablaze with light and sending forth sound of the gayest revelry. Advancing to one of these I looked in and saw an oddly dressed company, indeed; making merry, and speaking brightly to one another. I had never, seemingly, heard human speech before; and could guess only vaguely what was said. Some of the faces seemed to hold expressions that brought up incredibly remote recollections; others were utterly alien.

I now stepped through the low window into the brilliantly lighted room, stepping as I did so from my single bright moment of hope to my blackest convulsion of despair and realization. The nightmare was quick to come, for as I entered, there occurred immediately one of the most terrifying demonstrations I had ever conceived. Scarcely had I crossed the sill when there descended upon the whole company a sudden and unheralded fear of hideous intensity, distorting every face and evoking the most horrible screams from nearly every throat. Flight was universal, and in the clamor and panic several fell in a swoon and were dragged away by their madly fleeing companions. Many covered their eyes with their hands, and plunged blindly and awkwardly in their race to escape, overturning furniture and stumbling against the walls before they managed to reach one of the many doors.

The cries were shocking; and as I stood in the brilliant apartment alone and dazed, listening to their vanishing echoes, I trembled at the thought of what might be lurking near me unseen. At a casual inspection the room seemed deserted, but when I moved toward one of the alcoves I thought I detected a presence there—a hint of motion beyond the golden-arched doorway leading to another and somewhat similar room. As I approached the arch I began to perceive the presence more clearly; and then, with the first and last sound I ever uttered—a ghastly ululation that revolted me almost as poignantly as its noxious cause—I beheld in full, frightful vividness the inconceivable, indescribable, and unmentionable monstrosity which had by its simple appearance changed a merry company to a herd of delirious fugitives.

I can not even hint what it was like, for it was a compound of all that is unclean, uncanny, unwelcome, abnormal, and detestable. It was the ghoulish shade of decay, antiquity, and desolation; the putrid, dripping eidolon of unwholesome revelation; the awful baring of that which the merciful earth should always hide. God knows it was not of this world—or no longer of this world—yet to my horror I saw in its eaten-away and bone-revealing outlines a leering, abhorrent travesty on the human shape; and in its moldy, disintegrating apparel an unspeakable quality that chilled me even more.

I was almost paralyzed, but not too much so to make a feeble effort toward flight; a backward stumble which failed to break the spell in which the nameless, voiceless monster held me. My eyes, bewitched by the glassy orbs which stared loathsomely into them, refused to close; though they were mercifully blurred, and showed the terrible object but indistinctly after the first shock. I tried to raise my hand to shut out the sight, yet so stunned were my nerves that my arm could not fully obey my will. The attempt, however, was enough to disturb my balance; so that I had to stagger forward several steps to avoid falling. As I did so I became suddenly and agonizingly aware of the *nearness* of the carrion thing, whose hideous hollow breathing I half fancied I could hear. Nearly mad, I found myself yet able to throw out a hand to ward off the fetid apparition which pressed so close; when in one cataclysmic second of cosmic nightmarishness and hellish accident *my fingers touched the rotting outstretched paw of the monster beneath the golden arch.*

I did not shriek, but all the fiendish ghouls that ride the night-wind shrieked for me as in that same second there crashed down upon my mind a single and fleeting avalanche of soul-annihilating memory. I knew in that second all that had been; I remembered beyond the frightful castle and the trees, and recognized the altered edifice in which I now stood; I recognized, most terrible of all, the unholy abomination that stood leering before me as I withdrew my sullied fingers from its own.

But in the cosmos there is balm as well as bitterness, and that balm is nepenthe. In the supreme horror of that second I forgot what had horrified me, and the burst of black memory vanished in a chaos of echoing images. In a dream I fled from that haunted and accursed pile, and ran swiftly and silently in the moonlight. When I returned to the churchyard place of marble and went down the steps I found the stone trap-door immovable; but I was not sorry, for I had hated the antique castle and the trees. Now I ride with the mocking and friendly ghouls on the nightwind, and play by day amongst the catacombs of Nephren-Ka in the sealed and unknown valley of Hadoth by the Nile. I know that light is not for me, save that of the moon over the rock tombs of Neb, nor any gayety save the unnamed feasts of Nitokris beneath the Great Pyramid; yet in my new wildness and freedom I almost welcome the bitterness of alienage.

For although nepenthe has calmed me, I know always that I am an outsider; a stranger in this century and among those who are still men. This I

343

have known ever since I stretched out my fingers to the abomination within that great gilded frame; stretched out my fingers and touched *a cold and unyielding surface of polished glass.*

Over Time's Threshold

Howard Wandrei

A clock ticking in an empty house.

What might that bode? Finch turned to the girl and said, "The agent told me this place has been closed up for four years."

Connie nodded. It was an undeniable ticking, the heavy, clipped chucking sound of a large timepiece. The sound came from the one unexplored room on the ground floor, and Finch walked with the girl toward the door of the room with some curiosity.

The uncovered furnishings of the old house were gray with dust. There had been no caretaker for these four years, and its present condition gave it a cheap place in the market, even among prevailing low prices. The dusty furnishings were of a rather respectable nature, some of them rich enough to give the girl's eyes an incipient sparkle. And those of the room in the left wing which they were approaching were especially interesting. Subconsciously, Finch noted that the door of this room, of the several they had tried on the ground floor, was the only one standing open. The two paused on the threshold of the room and looked in, harking to the ticking of the clock.

A heavy work table in the mathematical center of the room supported a large retort filled with a liquid coloured a pale apple green. The glass arm of the retort appeared to deposit this fluid by slow drops into a fair-sized graduated glass whose capacity must have been about the same as that of the retort. A drop now hung from the extended retort arm, minute accumulation gradually inviting its fall. Finch looked at the litter of test tubes and other apparatus on the table and glanced at the book-lined walls.

"Capal's laboratory," he said. Connie looked at him inquiringly.

"Professor Capal," he said again. "He used to live in this house and it looks as though he worked in this room."

"Oh, he used to teach at the University."

"Yes. He sort of disappeared four years ago, and the house has been vacant since."

Loud ticking filled the room, and now the two watching the clock noted its peculiar character with some astonishment. It was of unusually heavy construc-

344

tion, and had a broad, engraved face set with antique numerals. Around this face the two hands were describing arcs with furious irregularity. The minute hand passed with appreciable movement past the numeral 3, stopped dead and retreated almost to the top of the face. Then both minute and hour hands disappeared in a blurred whirl. The heavy ticking became confused; the sound was full of unaccountable interruptions and double strikings and displayed as many irregularities as the movement of the hands. The weights in the case changed position uncertainly, and the motion of the pendulum could not be followed; it seemed to appear ubiquitously in its arc. The whir of the machinery behind the face suddenly stopped. Finch automatically took out his watch and looked at it. Both pieces gave the same time, 3:10.

At this moment Connie stepped into the room to examine the clock more closely. As she crossed the threshold and Finch was about to step after her, the retort deposited a drop of the green stuff in the fractionally filled beaker on the table. The hesitating hands of the clock leaped and the girl vanished.

Finch looked about blankly.

"Connie . . ." he called questioningly.

The ticking sounded rhythmically, now clear, now confused, as with the sound of another escapement striking somewhat faster. The hands hesitated, whirled, stopped, swung back and forth like the steadying needle of a compass.

"Connie!" Finch ran into the room and looked about him, breathless with fear. And now the clock ticked with precision. But terrifying things were occurring about the house. Finch turned to the room's long windows and looked at the sky. It had blackened in less than a minute. It was night. He looked amazed at the stars, and then turned his shocked eyes from immediately succeeding daylight. The sun had burst like thunder through the belt of Orion. What was happening?

Night again succeeded. The sun became a mere arc of fire across the sky—a yellow golden rainbow, and night was an instant's blur of darkness. The hands of the ticking clock followed precisely the progress of the sun. The alternation of night and day fell swifter and swifter, and for Finch, at the window, it was like looking out of the rapidly shuttering eye of a camera. A time camera. The succession of light and darkness merged into a tone of twilight under a gray sky sliced lower and lower by the arc of the sun, as cold crept in the room, and snow fell abroad over the land. Then the arching sun mounted the sky so rapidly that its many appearances seemed one broad band of fire in the sky.

Now it was midsummer, and the hands of the clock ceased their crazy whirl and hesitated, performing aimless arcs back and forth across the circled numbers of the face. This happening had almost the appearance of malice, as if to allow the man to take account of his disaster.

Finch looked about him. The room seemed the same; there was a thickening of the dust if anything. He wrote "Finch" in the dust on a free end of the apparatus-littered table, and noticed the new accumulation of green stuff at the end of the retort arm.

Capal had been a physicist, and this arrangement of liquid and glass looked like one of his remote experiments in chemistry. Finch thrust his forefinger into the liquid the beaker had collected, and withdrew it hastily. The stuff was so cold it burned, and pain rushed up his arm like a train of exploding needles. In the summer sky the sun marked the month as June, but Finch and the girl had entered the room in early August. He believed nothing, but accepted everything under the name of phenomena.

At the university Capal had propagated a number of scientifically malodorous ideas, and was accounted a trifle mad; Finch pleasantly conjectured that the professor had been tricked by his own queer notions, and wondered what his disappearance had to do with his laboratory.

The retort was mounted upon legs that separated it from the table by almost an inch. To one side was a clockwork mechanism screwed firmly to the table. Projecting from the side was a free metal arm, to the end of which was fastened a small plate of some reddish composition that glinted with metal filings. This plate would swing under the base of the retort, but a test-tube rack had fallen and blocked its progress. Copper wires led from binding-posts on the clockwork to a series of jars of colorless liquid ranged along the side of the apparatus.

The girl had vanished before his eyes and he himself had vanished from his own time. Where was she? Where Capal was. And Capal? Finch had good nerves, and knew the uselessness of dashing about looking for the girl aimlessly. He was caught in a trap, and the spring was set by Capal. The phenomena that played in this room were incident to the professor's clutter of glass and clockwork, and it was by means of these that he would find normality. He was ready to follow any adventure through to its completion, and now ascertained that the clockwork was in order by pushing out the metal arm to the limit of its swing. The composition plate was carried forward by clicking little wheels until it met the test-tube rack again.

As he was about to remove the rack he noticed the arm of the retort, and decided to start evenly by cleaning off the small quantity of liquid that had collected at its mouth. His fingertip wiped the glass, and at the contact his arm jerked convulsively with electric shock as he caught sight of the girl standing opposite him, looking about wildly.

Finch retreated from the table confusedly and called the girl's name. The clock's ticking blurred into one continuous sound of speaking metal, and the hands spun hazily. The room rocked and reeled. Again the world was in twilight, and in the speeding seasons Finch alternatively shook with cold and perspired in summer heat. He was aware of a dim, avalanchian roar that

346

clarified and approached portentively. The old house crashed about his ears, having run into complete decay in a matter of minutes, and he choked in a chaos of dust and falling, rotten timbers.

He found himself prostrated among ruins that dwindled and supported vegetation even before his eyes. As he scrambled to his feet on a pile of crumbled wood and mortar, howling chaos dinned in his ears and then the world was calm and he was looking out over a late autumn wilderness.

There was no house; there was no city about him, and an ancient cotton-wood sank its wrinkled trunk in the ground where the table had stood. A terrific shock tumbled him to the ground and when he arose the world was cold and the sun directly overhead was a great, dim, glowing red ball.

Far off on the horizon was the glow of flame. A creeping blanket of smoke marked some great fire. About a hundred yards off, standing beneath another cottonwood, was the figure of a man anxiously examining the ground about him.

He wore tattered clothes, and spectacles reflected light as he turned his head. A great beast of some odd canine species tightened a leash he gripped in one hand. The animal saw Finch and growled. The man looked up and shouted. Whereupon the beast jumped against the leash, and man and dog beat their way up the knoll toward Finch. All his skin prickled and his throat stiffened in fright.

"Stop!" he screamed.

"I'm Capal!" shouted the other. "Don't move! You *can't* move!"

Finch shuddered and turned white. He heard a confusion of syllables, something about "clockwork," and looked around dazed at the suddenly present room of the old house. A drop was hanging from the arm of the retort. It fell, sparkled globularly on the table of liquid in the glass, and then became a part of it. As he hastily ran through the door and sprawled on the floor outside he thought he heard the girl call his name. At which he raised his abruded cheek from the floor and looked back, but the room was empty. He lay there for long and long, sleeping heavily through the early hours of the morning.

He awakened with the sun pouring through the doorway, shafting the spot his body occupied. His face lay closely against the floor. His cheek hurt with raw soreness.

"God. God. God," he said, and turned stiffly to look into the room, sitting up. A drop of green fell from the retort and Connie's body appeared on the floor, twisted angularly.

"Connie!" He started to his feet and she disappeared. He stopped at the threshold, muttering to himself. The dust in which he had written his name, he noted grimly, was undisturbed. Then, burying his face in his arms, and leaning against the wall, he listened to the aimless, staccato chucking of the clock.

The sportive changes in the room mocked reason and Finch was hungry. After walking around the empty house for a time, absently combing his disordered hair with his fingers, he left the place, slowly, and took his way to a nearby restaurant. The reality of food made Capal's curious laboratory seem exceedingly remote. But the girl was gone. *Where?*

Was that really Capal he had seen running up that confounded knoll? What cursed beast was that with him?

This time Finch circled the house and stood on the ledge that footed the window of the laboratory. He could hear the ticking through the panes, like a mechanical heart. Otherwise, everything was quiet. The windows were curious in themselves. They didn't open, and the panes were of quartz-glass. The place was built solidly and would last a long time. He glued his ear to the glass and listened to Capal's strange clock for a few minutes, and then peered closely at the only other significant object visible—the retort. There was a glimmer of green at the end of the arm.

He dropped from the window and walked across the unkempt lawn to the front steps. Here he looked at his watch and noted that the girl had been absent for nearly sixteen hours. He had awakened at about six o'clock, just as a drop had fallen. Last night one fell at five, when they entered the room, and again at about ten, because of the modicum he removed with his finger. It took about four hours for one drop to accumulate, granting one had fallen while he had been asleep. So. His worried face suddenly straightened. He had seen the girl when he touched the retort, and when the drop fell as he awakened this morning; and heard her voice as he was leaving the room. Coincidences.

Hurriedly jumping the front steps, he snatched open the door, dashed down the hall, and cut through the living room into the left wing. About ten feet from the door he caught sight of Connie lying in the same position in which he had seen her last. He shouted and dived headlong through the yawning door as another green drop fell into the beaker.

His body sprawled into the table and he stood up dazed to find himself once more in the room alone. Thereupon he stumbled toward the door. The capricious clock again forecast the unknown with its spinning hands and syncopated ticking.

The hill on which Capal's house was built flattened, and suffocating, humid masses of foliage crowded the spongy earth. Finch, lying prone, looked on the blanketed peaty leaves and vegetation covering the ground, and saw near his face black beetles and spiders crawling horribly. A train of soft red insects about the size of peas mounted his arm on their clinging, tentacle-like legs, and licked his shuddering flesh with little red tongues like small flames. He shook them off, and rising to his feet, stamped on the lot, and dispatched the beetles and spiders within the area the room would enclose. Then he fearfully returned to the spot his body had occupied when he first recognized this new change. Here he stood waiting patiently, resolved that these things were so. First, two objects cannot occupy the same space at the same time. Second, every four

348

hours the retort introduced a magical green drop into the receptacle under the arm, and time momentarily identified itself with the fall of the drop. It was either Capal's scientific necromancy or coincidence, and Finch didn't care to dispute existence with the table or bookcase; and leaving the room's area might mean never returning.

For four hours he would be lost in time, and therein he was prey to everything about him. He closed his eyes in a savage agony of nostalgia. A curious sensation about his feet attracted his attention. Looking down, he saw the peat-blanketed ground mounting his legs graspingly. All around were palisades of trees, and the surface of the land was jungled with brush and vines. A huge creeper the size of his wrist commenced life at the base of a smooth-boled tree nearby and careened through the air with dizzy life, whipping and cracking as it grew. The peat-level mounted to his knees. He stood stupefied. A shaggy beast hurtled past him, pursued by a barking uproar of wild dogs. He listened to the snarling tragedy dully. The level of earth withdrew suddenly, and whole stands of trees disappeared.

Time in retrograde? Cursing Capal's genius he sat weakly on the ground as he thought of going back and back and back. But there was little time after all to wonder whether the influence of the lost professor's apparatus were limited or not. There was just time to see a stagnant expanse of water, soupy and green and crawling with life. The damp, heavy atmosphere was unbearable. Upward rushes of moisture-laden air choked his lungs and spun his brain. The sun flamed whitely, and the forest reeked and shimmered with wisps of steam. Then the rushing vegetation swept in and buffeted him so that he stood on his feet against the billowing foliage. A lithe, active vine whirled through the air and burst through the fleshy part of his arm. Finch clutched futilely at it, crying out at the pain; the vine had already disappeared in the shuttling years.

Another period was running to its close. Finch looked at his watch, and stooped purposefully in one of time's hesitating moments to pick up from the ground a handy water-rotted root. He heard the ticking of the clock, and the laboratory of Capal's house formed instantly.

He stood anxiously eyeing the clock and retort, gripping the root. The arm gleamed greenly and a drop of liquid hung trembling as the hands of the clock ceased their spasmatic whirling and swung back and forth over the twenty-first hour since the phenomena had begun. Finch gripped the root, poised to throw, while the skipping noise of the clock resolved itself into regular heavy ticking. He looked eagerly for the girl, and now the hands were almost at a dead stop. The ticking became a slow hammering.

Finch trembled; with nervous accuracy he flung the root at the glass works on the table as the body of the girl appeared at his feet.

Quickly he stooped to lift the girl from the floor, although speed was no longer necessary. The root struck the retort squarely and smashed it into a green soup of liquid and shattered glass. The beaker was raked from the table along with the wired jars, and a tinkle of dropping and breaking test tubes and glass rods accompanied him as he left the room.

Where the green stuff touched the table the varnish fumed and blackened.

The clock stopped.

The Palace of the Dead

Robert Peery

The night was cold and quiet. The traffic outside the windows of Gale Parmenter's great brown mansion on Taliaferro Street had moderated until there was heard only now and then the slithering whir of black tires on the frozen pavement. The fire had burned low in the grate and neither of us had thought to replenish it from the black enameled box that stood beside it. The shadows flickered in an eery dance over the walls, the floor and the ceiling of the big room. For four hours we had sat there, slowly exhausting the possibilities of conversation between two old friends who had not seen each other for ten years. The clock in the hall behind us had faithfully ticked the minutes away, and now, after groaning internally, it clanged out the hour from its brass throat.

"The dead," said Gale Parmenter, his cold black pipe still clenched between his teeth, "have devious ways of communicating with the living."

The notes from the clock wavered about us, then died away until only a ghostly echo, small, reverberating, remained.

"And the easiest way is through dreams," he said.

I had been surprised at the change that had come to the face and to the philosophy of my old friend. Where before—when I left him at the ferry at Hoboken on our return from a jaunt with Jack Pershing in France—his face had been ruddy, and alive with the joy of healthy living, it now was the color and seemed of the very texture of old and yellowed parchment. I remembered his eyes as small wells of happiness; I saw them now as burned holes in his cadaverous face. He was thinner by thirty pounds; I had heard that he rarely left his house, but remained cloistered there like a monk, poring over ancient tomes and puzzling his head with various abstruse studies. All night his conversation had been forced. I could tell that much; his manner impressed me strangely. He had appeared all evening to be looking or listening for some horror just beyond the next tick of the hall clock.

I had watched his gaze wander and fasten for minutes at a time upon the painting that hung above the black marble mantel-board. I will admit that the picture held for me also a peculiar sense of fascination. It was Delgari's *The Palace of the Dead,* an excellent copy of original size, in genuine oils. The foreground was a placid lake; tall, exquisite poplars, of a height and beauty not seen even in Lombardy, stood like solitary sentinels on each side of a cavern which lifted its black masses ponderously, majestically, toward a dark and scowling heaven. Upon the lake in a small boat was the figure of a man with outstretched arms, who was pleading with some savage god to renounce the verdict of death to his soul. The colors were somber, dispirited. The very taint of death seemed to exude from that terrible canvas. I shuddered involuntarily when I caught the burning eyes of Gale Parmenter fixed intently upon the painting. And it seemed to me, in that moment as he spoke the words, that it was his own figure in that boat upon the lip of the cavern in which the dead were prisoned for an eternity of darkness and damnation. It was more than merely that there seemed a sort of kinship between that man in the boat of the picture and my friend in the chair before the dying firelight. It was more serious than that; it created strange thoughts in me; I do not know how I might explain this, but it was there, and it was of reality, I think. I have never been called an unduly imaginative man.

"The picture, Frank," said Gale in a flat, almost toneless voice, "is part of a strangely recurring dream that comes to me with the regularity of a booming evening gun—like the guns at Mangapore, you'll remember." At such times, when he recalled a scene, a friend, a time we both had known, there was the slightest wraith of his old self that seemed to flicker past his eyes. But not for long.

"I have dreamed so many times that I have stood in that boat and rowed into that yawning cavern which lips the lake like a grinning god of destruction that I am almost convinced that I am that person who rails so ineffectually against the powers whose shapes one can so dimly discern in the gray and black skies above."

I stood up, the better to examine the picture, and to find what I had at first overlooked. So skilful had been the artist's brush that one had to look closely to see that the very clouds above that darkly mirroring lake were the heads and writhing torsos of enigmatic gods at sportive play and amorous jousts! Their puffed eyes were greedily watching the drama below them. What matter to them that another human being made the dangerous journey to the shades of Death! What cared they! It was a part of their sport, a spectacle for the jaded, eyes of their goddess mistresses! Their limbs were like writhing serpents, their middles bloated and spongy. Their mouths grinned luridly. The figures seemed to shift about in disorderly fashion.

I stepped back. They had gone. The leaden sky was immovable but grim with the power of its implacable, unending surface. A step forward and again I saw the bawdy sport of deism! I could almost hear their voices as they shouted cruel words that would thunder at length upon the ears of the tortured being upon that ebony lake.

"I have heard those voices, too," said Gale. He had not risen from his chair; his eyes searched the last flickering flames within the grate. The room had begun to grow colder. I turned to him with surprize in my face.

"The voices of those terrible gods?" I cried. Was he hypnotizing me? Why should he have twice voiced my thoughts?

"The Voices of the Terrible Gods," he replied. His voice rose as each syllable fell from his lips; unconsciously he had capitalized the letters of his sentence by the inflection, the horror, of his tone. "Shall I tell you about the dream?" he asked.

I sat down once more and he began.

"It has been eight years since first I dreamed of the Palace of the Dead. I bought that picture when the furniture and furnishings of the old Campanis place were sold at auction in New Orleans. It was the only purchase I made. It struck me as soon as I laid eyes upon it. It cost a great deal of money, too, but I wanted it and I bought it.

"I will not try to tell you that the picture has some malign influence over my mind, because we both are sensible men. I have caused myself to dream of these things because of late years my mind has fastened itself tenaciously upon the utter horror of death, upon the imperturbable countenance of death, and upon the necessity for each man 'wrapping the mantle of his couch about him and lying down to'—to what, Frank? What lies just beyond the brightness, the sunlight, the color and the noise of this life? Is it peace? Contentment? Or a vague wandering, an unrest, an eternal search for something which forever eludes? I have imagined ofttimes, have dreamed, that I was lost in an eternity of distance, bodiless, brainless, heartless—searching, groping in a darkness deeper than any Stygian hell, and never finding what I sought! Is it possible that whatever gods there be can be so cruel as to send a soul upon such a fruitless quest? Is it not enough that they should make sport with our destinies while we live and play and dream upon this earth? Can it be true, as Delgari has portrayed in this picture, that their sport has only begun when we leave behind the vestments of reality and take upon our souls the ineffectual garments of death? Will they hound us through all eternity, as they hound us through the black door of death—as they thunderously charge that pitiful figure of a man to enter the Palace of the Dead and its ghastliness? Look at him, Frank! See the horror-stricken countenance, the livid eyes, the grip of death in his clenched hands, the upraised, hopeless arms begging for mercy at the couches of those grinning gods who turn from his plea with mirth to place their hot mouths upon the lecherous lips of their mistresses! See how death hangs in heavy folds about his damp garments! Look how the odor of death beats up from his mouth!"

I arose nervously and placed a stick of wood upon the red coals. I had begun to feel that I could not for a moment longer bear the thought of that room growing darker and colder.

"Always I seem to be waking upon a flat, level ground upon which no living thing grows. The flatlands stretch away to the gray horizon. Always I feel as if the sky above me is pressing down about my body, is strangling me, is imprisoning my heart and lungs with its suffocating embrace. The essence of the sky in that picture, in my dreams, seems to be loosed in my breast and to pluck at the beat of my heart as a skeleton might pluck the strings of a ghostly guitar. And always the rhythm of that serenade is played to the beat of my heart—always I feel it pulsing, quivering, as if trying to escape some indescribable horror.

"My throat becomes slowly more and more constricted—breathing becomes a torture—often I wake at that point, and always I am glad when I do. But more often than not I must go forward on weak limbs until I stumble upon the edge of a lake in which nothing grows, neither green nor brown nor black. And there upon the edge of that dead lake I find my guide with the boat.

"The boat is frail, of a thin, carved black wood, like ebony, and the oarsman is unspeakably dirty and slimy His hair hangs about his face like matted seaweed; his nose is hooked and thin; his lips curl back with disdain for my plight. He speaks no word to me. He is like a madman, now sobbing violently, now laughing as if in merriment; again drawing himself into a shell of reserve as if he knew the answer to the riddles of the world but was afraid to look at any man lest he give something of his knowledge away with a single glance. Silently he paddles the boat along over that lake whose waters are like none in this land of the living. There is great depth to the lake, although one can not see for an inch beneath the surface. There is no slightest ripple upon the surface, because, you see, the wind is dead, too. The paddle makes no ripple as it rises and falls with the slow movement of the guide's arms. That water is thick, like black blood, and a terrible odor arises from it. . . .

"At length we come to the mouth—the yawning, hungry mouth of the cavern that is the Palace of the Dead. Where there was darkness before, there now is complete night. There is no sound; the boat glides on as if upon the air, without motion to the right or to the left, but on, implacably on, toward the horrors of the grave and the musty corridors of that cavern wherein the dead speak without words in a strange idiom of unreality. Beside us, as we go farther into the cave, I see the wraiths walking with solemn, funereal tread, their heads bowed with their great despair. Their clothing hangs from their shoulders in somber folds.

"Here and there along the narrow ledge that borders the channel, pale, yellowish lights throw back the terrible darkness for a few yards, but the water of the canal gives back no answering reflection. Have you ever seen a light that refused the exhilaration of reflection? It is terrible in its finality—it shines for a little way into the blackness, then abruptly throws itself against an eternity of darkness.

"At length we reach land; the stone corridors and the vistas of cathedral spaces filled with strange, bat-like creatures give way at last, and we step out upon the soil, where stretches away a flat, monotonous land without herbage or trees as far as our eyes can reach in the yellowish eternal dusk of that awful place. And as our feet step upon the ground it gives beneath my tread as if it were spongy, unwholesome soil, not built for the tread of living bodies. Always it is only my own feet that sink deep into that strange ground; the feet of my guide, who goes ahead, tread more lightly. Always there is the feeling that I alone of all the creatures in that place am alive, that all my companions are dead things, spinning out the futility of non-existence for the satisfaction of their terrible gods.

"And here comes the strangest part of this dream that recurs. . . ."

During this recitation my eyes had remained upon the face of my friend. The nerves along his temple jerked and fluttered as he unfolded the tale for my ears. Although the fire had mounted to licking amber and red, the room seemed permeated with a strange, unearthly chill.

"I must go back now, Frank, to a day in France when we stormed the canal at St. Quentin," he continued. "During the evening, you will remember, we found a platoon of skulking Germans in the tunnel and routed them out. I can remember still how they came out with their hands in the air, their faces caked with the blue, sticky mud of that uptorn land, their eyes hollows of madness. Do you remember what I did that evening in the dusk near Bellinglis?"

I nodded. How well I remembered! Gale Parmenter, tired, nervous, the rack and tension of the day's battle against the death-rattling pillboxes on the slope, against the clattering cataract of German rifle fire, still tearing with destructive fingers at his brain, had gone mad in an instant. A German boy, wearing the uniform of the Bavarian regiment then in action in that sector, came up out of the tunnel. His face was pasty gray, his eyes pitted sepulchers, his hair matted, and his mouth twisted with horror. And Gale Parmenter, his mind snapping for a moment with frenzy and madness, had lunged once with naked, already reddened bayonet. The German boy fell in a heap before him, a little moan of surprise escaping between his lips. We removed the dripping bayonet. For weeks Gale Parmenter lay on a bed of torment; his mind seemed to us at one time completely upset and beyond all chance of recovery. When he finally regained a degree of sanity he remembered his act, but it required expert nursing and attention to bring him out of the pit of despair into which that mad act had cast his soul.

"The dead, Frank, have devious ways of communicating with the living. In this dream I meet the German boy of Bellinglis. He wears the small skull-cap as he wore it that evening when I spitted him upon my bayonet. His face is just as it appeared to me that day—the matted locks, the horribly staring eyes, the trembling lips. He points his finger at me in that dream, and from his lips, in a voice that is like a woman's, so small and weak and tired it seems, he says to me, 'Der Tag!'—the two German words that one heard so much in those days. 'The Day!' And I know what he means. He is telling me that the day is coming when the gods themselves will take toll upon my life for the wrong I committed upon him at Bellinglis. He was a captured prisoner, Frank. . . ."

Parmenter's voice had weakened considerably at this point. I interrupted.

"You must forget that dream, Gale," I said. "Surely you can not feel that you are responsible for your moment of madness. Surely the gods will not further despise you."

"They must have their sport," he said, casting his glance toward the sportive, greedy gods in the sky above the Palace of the Dead in the picture above the black marble board. "They will visit something more upon me."

The jangling of the door-bell shattered the silence. I sprang half up from the depths of my chair. Gale Parmenter also sprang to his feet, and his face went deathly white.

"Who could be ringing the doorbell at this hour? And Fanning is abed long ago. I shall have to answer it."

I stood up and watched him walk toward the doors of the study. And I knew in that moment that he was going to his doom, but I was powerless to speak. My tongue refused the bidding of my mind. I heard the front door open and I heard a guttural voice repeating the two words that were spoken in the dream: *"Der Tag!"*

I heard the body fall. I ran to the hallway and found Gale Parmenter lying face downward in the door. I looked through the door. A very shabby man with a close-fitting skull-cap was standing there, his eyes distended in horror. His hair was matted beneath the cap; his face wore a yellowish, grayish cast. I tried to order him inside. I could not speak. I lowered my gaze from that apparition, then glanced up again. The figure was still there. The lips were trembling.

He moved through the door and knelt beside me. "I think I am mad," he said weakly.

My hands searched for a spark of life about the stilled heart of Gale Parmenter. He was dead.

"Who are you?" I cried, in horror of the man who knelt beside me.

"My name is Fritz Artmann. I could not sleep tonight. I dressed and walked, not knowing where I was going. I have been out of work. I am a ditch-digger. A German. It is hard to find work because I am not very strong. I do not know why I came to this door and pushed the bell. Something was pushing me along the street."

I knew he was telling the truth.

"Were you in the German army?" I asked.

"I was wounded at Bellinglis during the last days. My comrade, a youth, was killed at Bellinglis with his hands in the air. Sometimes he comes to me in dreams—"

"At Bellinglis? Your comrade killed?" I cried.

I felt the fingers of Gale's unseen ghostly musician plucking at the beat of my own heart. The strange horror closed over me, suffocating, destroying my heart with its deadly embrace. The last thing I remember was a mocking tongue shouting words that must have been my own: "The dead have devious ways of communicating with the living!"

I saw the grins of the gods above the Palace of the Dead; I saw their lecherous sport; I heard the mocking thunder of their gargantuan laughter rolling and resounding along the leaden sky above that implacable lake. Then I fell into unconsciousness.

Past Tense

Brian Hodge

To say that our friendship was based on drinking would be, at best, a grave error. Sober or not, Kristen and I liked each other without reservation. But it seemed, nevertheless, that whenever we got together for a heart-to-heart session, the first crisis was what brand to order. And who shelled out for the lead-off round.

This evening it was stout on tap, and she drew first cash.

We had chosen this fern-infested Rush Street mecca because it was mutually inconvenient to both our workplaces. Comfortably full of furnishings as trendy as its clientele. At its epicenter sat a hollow rectangular bar, all mellow oak and brass; its overhead racks sprouted rows of wineglasses hanging from their stems, like crystal stalactites. Satelliting the bar were tables and booths, abundantly packed with festive groups, quiet pairs, and lone strays trying to hide their hunger to become part of one or the other.

Kristen and I were fringe dwellers, as far removed from the mainstream as we could get. Nestled into a brick corner at a table little bigger than a TV tray. Intimacy was a cardinal mandate.

When our drinks arrived, I held mine up to the light, which was unable to shine through the heavy brew. I ruminated about this, and after disposing of a foam mustache with a flick of her tongue, Kristen accused me of stalling. She was right, of course.

"You probably already know what I'm stalling about," I said.

She nodded, wisdom in her eyes, coupled with bemused patience. "Oh sure. You've lived with Lisa for, what, six months now?"

"Seven and a half."

"Wow, you *are* overdue. I knew it was coming."

"Another live-in love bites the dust," I said softly.

"Poor Lisa. I liked her, I really did." Her voice was light, without reproach. Only a slightly detectable seasoning of concern, as always. I think I might have preferred reproach this time, variety being the spice of life and all. "Have you told her yet?"

I made a muscle with one arm and perched the glass of stout above it. "I was hoping to get psyched up for it first."

Kristen gazed sadly out over the rest of the troops in the bar, as if to set eyes on the next eligible young lovely to set foot through the revolving door of my home and bed. Then she gave me a gray smile, perhaps wondering why her stability couldn't be contagious.

Lisa and I had met in mid-December, an encounter of pure chance when I was reduced by emergency Porsche trouble to relying on the wonders of public transportation. A bus, in this case.

Maybe her tenure in my life was longer than the norm because we met differently. She wasn't another in the parade of models and aspiring starlets I directed in TV commercials on Michigan Avenue.

It had been the peak of the Christmas shopping season, and a three-hundred-pound man bulled into her in his haste not to miss his stop. Sacks and gift-wrapped packages, behind which she had been effectively fortressed, went avalanching to a floor lubed with grimy slush. I helped her pick them up, no ulterior motive. Being on internal slowcook over my car, I hadn't even noticed her looks until after help was offered and underway.

Her looks, her *colors*. Delicately pale porcelain face and rose cheeks, with shoulder-length wisps of hair, shinier and blacker than a raven's wing. Altogether enchanting.

We talked, had coffee. Later that week, lunch, followed by dinners and excursions to the theater. It wasn't until I was already gold-medaling in the head-over-heels Olympics that I learned she was a millionairess-to-be, a department store heiress who kept an extremely low profile because she thought of all that money and its accompanying headaches made her nervous.

And so, by New Year's Eve, she was ready to move in and play at the domestic scene with a frustrated filmmaker who had sold out his dreams of substance and instead cranked out short-shorts in Chicago's megabucks advertising milieu.

While I figured it would probably be wise to first ask her predecessor, Meridy, to move out.

Kristen and I decided to switch to pitchers after the first round. Simpler, more economical. And the unspoken alarm had gone off to signify that, this evening, we were in for a long haul.

"Have you met someone else?" she asked. "Is somebody new going to be moving in?"

I twitched my head no. "Not this time. It just seems better off terminated, that's all. More fair, or something."

"Well, listen. You may be a hopeless satyr," she said, reaching across the table to lightly punch my shoulder, "but I admire your integrity. Most guys'd hang on to Lisa because of the money factor."

"Oh yeah." I polished an imaginary crown. "I'm a real prince."

We veered off course awhile, a normal staple of our serious talks. Cover relevant ground until reaching a good breakaway point for trivia, until one or the other would steer us back on track. In the interim, we'd cover books, music, movies, cabbages and kings.

We paused to watch a guy leave the bar, drink in hand, and maintain a dignified totter to approach a couple of secretarial types near our table. Head in the clouds; drifting smoke, actually. It's a cruel world. They shot him down in fifteen seconds, and he tottered back to the bar to wage war on his liver. Sad.

"I think I've settled on a diagnosis for your condition," she said once the floor show was over. Kristen always looked bright, healthy. With loose, uncomplicated dark blond hair and an outdoorsy complexion, she looked as if she belonged on Colorado ski slopes. And now she was utterly radiant.

"Doctor," I said. "Give it to me straight."

"You, Derek, are subject to what we barroom philosophers refer to as 'serial monogamy.'" She flexed long fingers, then studiously laced them together. "I mean, with a couple of exceptions, you're not a habitual cheater. You're a generally faithful guy . . . just faithful in a never-ending succession. There's always that greener pasture ahead for you, isn't there?"

I pointed down into my lap. "I always figured, to be honest, I'd have to admit I was led around by *that.*"

"Mmmm . . . maybe. But you're still not the average male pull toy." She paused to refill our glasses. Kristen was the one female friend I had found who could keep pace with me all evening. This was important, not to be lost. "And you know why that is? You honestly fall in love. You get shot through the heart every single time."

358

I sent up that peculiar semaphore code for another pitcher. "Yeah, you're right on that. Sometimes I go into each new relationship with all the enthusiasm of a kamikaze pilot gunning for the S.S. *Saratoga*. Feels pretty glorious at the time, but it's ultimately bad for your health."

And I wondered, fleetingly, though not for the first time . . . Would things be different with Kristen? Would duration finally be achieved? I found it paradoxical that a large part of her appeal was precisely the same thing that kept us safe from one another. She was off-limits, in the gonadian sense of things. Her long-term love was a guy named Mark, a good friend of mine from the decade-past Dark Ages of college. But . . . no wedding, no ring, and no such plans so far. There still existed that remote chance of Kristen and me pairing off, slipping beyond the usual bounds of friendship. That one night we might drink just enough to erode the constraints and stoke the libidinal flames, and, so sorry, Mark, but nature has taken its irrevocable course. Hope you understand.

"Don't even think it," she said. But with a smile. One sharp observer, she was. There were times when I thought she could read my face through a ski mask at fifty paces. "I love you too much as a friend to end up hating you as an ex-lover. And we *would* be ex-lovers after a while, you know that. We would."

I looked up from the table, a semiguilty glance, then nodded slowly. We both did, a strange sort of reaffirmation. A residual melancholy rode the crest of the moment, and I think it came from both sides. I'm sure she had entertained the same notions, at least once or twice. Looked at options, risks, probable outcomes. And decided it just wasn't worth it.

"I have this dream, sometimes," I told her. "I'm living alone, for a change. And one morning I wake up and every woman I've loved and messed up with and hurt . . . they're all there waiting for me. It's like there's dozens of them, you know. All there at once. And they form two lines, facing each other, and I have to run the gauntlet. So I run between the rows and I duck and cover my head, but it doesn't do much good, because there's so many of them. They slug me in the face, and kick me in the balls . . . just beat the living hell out of me. Except when I get to the end, see that latest love's face and think it's all over, there are even more of them. Women I don't know, future women, and it just never ever ends."

If anything, that would be poetic justice, but Kristen didn't let on if she felt that way. Her face screwed up, subtly, as if the dream had wormed its way beneath her skin, left a trace of the venom it routinely discharged into me on those mornings after.

The evening wore on, became night. Nothing was resolved, but then, nothing ever was. That was beyond even her capabilities. So we drank up, mutually voted down the idea of another pitcher. Walked out to the street together, where we hugged and swapped the briefest of platonic kisses, then went our opposite ways. As always. As expected. Safe and unentangled for another night.

I headed for my Porsche, mentally gearing up to go home and get into that terribly inevitable task of housecleaning. One more time.

The trip home was rife with memories, mental newsreels of past loves, loves that had withered and died after reaching the same temporal hallmark at which other couples were just hitting their stride. And I remembered one in particular, brought to mind by an otherwise throwaway comment Kristen had made earlier in the evening.

Steffy. Just one of the many whose ties to my life and heart existed solely in the past tense. She was another of the models I seemed to have such a proclivity for. Steffy of the throaty voice, the legs to inspire traffic accidents, and the pathological need to shop that rivaled Tammy Faye Bakker's. I knew from day one it wouldn't last.

But that was okay. Because everything we did was done for laughs. The drinking. The parties. The designer drugs. The sex. The marathon gold card sprees. The weekend morning hangovers and their attempted cures. Everything, one four-month chucklefest. Larry, Moe, and Curly should have had it so good.

Except for the omega day I asked her to move out. Steffy was hurt and furious in equal measures. Somehow I managed to convince her that I'd not met anyone else; I'd had neither time nor energy for that. I just thought it was time for us both to get on with trying to be adults. Or at least as close as *we* could come.

"You know what your problem is?" she said. "You can't handle sticking around after things settle down and get a little more normal. You always need that thrill of something new. You're a junkie for discovery."

In that moment, Steffy displayed more depth than she had during the entire four months. More, in fact, than I had suspected was even there. It was a turn-on; depths unplumbed, uncharted territories. I was ready to change my mind and ask her to please please stay, but knew it was too late. One more bridge was raging in flames.

"And I'm sorry you don't think my waters run deep enough." She heaped on so much sarcasm I wasn't sure if she truly meant that or not. But it didn't matter, not when she was out the door ten minutes later.

I sat down then and wondered. What's worse to do to someone? What's more painful? Leaving them because you've met somebody new . . . or leaving them even though you haven't?

Another of life's great imponderables.

Where are Plato and Socrates now that they're needed most?

* * *

I didn't waste much time after I got home, getting the unpleasantries over with. Repetition breeds efficiency, if not exactly anesthesia. I was just used to the pain. Every time the ax fell, by my own hand, it lopped a chunk out of me, too. Amputations may be quick, but they're never painless, never neat. So much emotional blood had been spilled in my home, the walls must have been sodden. An abattoir of the soul.

Lisa sat in stunned silence until she reached back inside to find her voice. The scene was messy, ugly, with plenty of tears to go around. But I loved her, this was certain. Maybe that was the problem. I loved her—all of them—too much.

At least too much to stand idly by while those initial flames of passion at the beginning of any relationship started to sputter and dwindle into embers of banality. As I often did, I wondered: Why can't every day be like day one?

And damn my overstimulated soul for being dissatisfied with anything less than that.

For the cost, the cost. So high, as the sodden walls could so well attest.

Lisa packed a few things to get her through the night and the next day or two. She made a phone call. And then my department store heiress and her eventual millions went weeping out the door, toward a friend with a vacant couch and an extra-absorbent shoulder. The rest of her belongings could wait until I was elsewhere.

It always takes some getting used to, when they leave. Readjusting to an apartment whose occupancy has just been halved. A loft apartment with seemingly acres of open space, and bohemian brick walls and burnished wood floors, with endearing nooks and crannies and skylights. Doesn't take much of a push for it to feel very big and very empty, and in a hurry.

I settled onto the pit group that made up my sofa, and used the television remote to conjure forth company. Shutting down the higher cranial functions and filling dead time.

Blank, numb. Wretched until the coming dawn, too long away.

But such is the price paid by those who have perfected the artful crime of the sexual hit-and-run.

Lisa was officially past tense. As expected, as was the norm, she still had her key and used it a couple of days later to let herself in while I was away directing my micromasterpieces. She cleansed the loft of her belongings, an orderly exorcism of self.

Occasionally the wounded lady has wanted to enact a little revenge. Symbolic vandalism, sometimes. Twice I had come home to discover large electrical toys missing, a TV or stereo swiped out of anger. One of the especially clever ones rigged my phone to continually redial a recorded message in Zurich, and so it did for the whole of one workday. These I endured without much complaint. If it helps them purge the bile from their systems, it's worth it. No festering *Fatal Attraction* psychopaths waiting in my wings, if I can help it.

Lisa, to my surprise, gravitated toward vengeance.

But for her to have instead left something behind . . . now *there* was a new twist.

At first I wondered where she had gotten them all. Because there were so incredibly many, no two alike. But then I realized that a department store heiress could pull this off with ease. She would have the connections. The resources. The money.

I had just never expected anyone to come up with such a graphic reaction to the situation, such a vivid editorial comment on what I was inside.

And Lisa was, after I'd had a chance to consider it, so damnably on target.

It must have been a week later when Kristen dropped by to check up on me. Wondering how the latest amputation had gone. Wondering about the fresh psychic scar tissue. Wondering, I suppose, why she just hadn't heard from me.

"I've been kind of preoccupied," I said quietly, standing in the doorway and blocking much of any view of the inside of the loft. "You know. Busy."

Her cheeks glowed with the climb up the stairs and general good health. A wide-brimmed thrift shop hat perched jauntily atop her head. "You don't look so hot, Derek. You feeling okay?"

I nodded, shuffled my feet. I wore jeans, a T-shirt, socks. Nothing else. Oh, a five-day beard, if that counts.

"Can I come in?" Her voice was starting to get that edge it honed when she was creeping toward vague unpleasant truths as if they were land mines angled to spray shrapnel into her face.

Should I let her in? I asked myself. Let her in, the first visitor to this brand-new environment and fellowship in which I lived? Would jealousy rear its hideous head? *Oh go on,* I decided. We were, after all, friends.

"Come on in. I'm sorry." I stepped out of the way, let her by.

Two steps in, she stopped frozen in her tracks. I barely had room enough behind her to swing the door shut again.

"Derek?" she said. "Is this . . . from one of your commercials?"

"No," I said. "They're all mine. Or at least, they are now. A special delivery from Lisa. She has a certain sense of style, don't you think?"

Kristen could not answer, but stood gamely trying to take it all in. She was as vacant-eyed and slate-wiped as I'd been upon first walking in a week before and trying to fathom such an extravagant display of angry pain. And while Kristen gave it her best shot, I walked farther in and took a seat on the floor in the midst of my latest soulmates.

She didn't get it, I could tell by her eyes. But then, she hadn't had my

362

week of introspection. And you must admit, the sight of someone's home populated by dozens of mannequins takes some time to grow accustomed to.

But there they were, in perfect frozen poise, staring with their unblinking painted eyes. All different, with long wigs and short wigs, blondes and brunettes and redheads, wearing business clothing and formal wear and swimsuits and lingerie and casual wear of all styles and trends. Standing with motionless grace. Reposing on the pit group. Seated at the kitchen table.

All unique . . . on the outside. And yet identical on the inside, for they were all so very hollow. In her own one-of-a-kind way, I think what Lisa was saying was that I was just as plastic as they.

She wasn't far wrong.

Still, that wasn't the worst of it.

"Oh, Derek," Kristen said, her voice slow and faraway. "Why didn't you get rid of them?"

I smiled and spread my arms wide, bumped into one of the still-life legs. The mannequin wobbled, an eternally slender blonde with blue eyes and thin pink lips that never lost their smile. I had named her Livvy. I steadied her, absently traced a finger down one hard thigh.

"I can't. They're what I always needed. I think Lisa recognized that even before I did."

Kristen still didn't get it. What I think she was starting to get was worried.

"Whatever I'm in the mood for, there's one here who fits the bill. I just have to look. And there aren't any hurt feelings, anywhere. It's a smorgasbord, and I don't have to pretend anymore."

Kristen's look, I knew that look. *He's finally snapped,* that's what it said. With it, I felt a curious liberation in my tongue, in what I could continue to divulge. A little more wouldn't hurt.

"They say that faith can move mountains," I told her, my voice dropping like that of some bewildered prophet. "Love and laughter? Doctors say those release chemicals in your body that add years to your life. Stress eats ulcers into you. Some people get caught up in such religious ecstasy that stigmata open in their hands and feet. But did you ever wonder about hate, and pain, and betrayal, just how much *they* can do? Because you've got to admit, they're the most intense of all."

I then held my hands out to indicate the walls, the ceiling, the floor. The mannequins. Hoping she would *see.*

Kristen wanted to come farther in, I honestly believe she did. But it was as if this plastic battalion held her at bay and turned her back and repelled her out the door, by simple virtue of its presence. This quiet menagerie of variable perfection. They're formidable at first glance, all right.

But perhaps, in time, Kristen would understand. Understand that they

363

were teaching me, and I had no choice but to bend to their imparted lessons, lessons I so desperately needed to learn. And I made a receptive pupil.

I had to be. I was so vastly outnumbered.

I had been an emotional parasite. Taking, and taking, and taking, but giving only what I could easily spare at the moment. I soaked up love and pissed out indifference in return.

I hadn't counted them, didn't want to. But something in me, a new breed of instinct, perhaps, told me that there would be exactly one mannequin for every woman I had ever wronged, ever hurt, for all the wrong reasons. The number would come out a perfect match.

Just as I was a perfect match for *them*.

I live with the mannequins easily enough, now that I'm used to them being around. They're quiet. They make no unreasonable demands. They have no needs. They ask for no commitments. And I've long since dismissed neuroses and psychoses as the cause for when I look at one, and notice the perceptible change in the tilt of a head, the bend of an arm, the stance of a leg, the depth in an eye.

It's ideal.

Except . . .

At night, when I lie awake in the darkness, the skylights admitting just enough of the moon to turn my home into a garden of shadows, I listen. And hear the most minute of shuffling footsteps. And I can hear them conspiring in whispered plastic voices, a message passed along from one to another to the next, like solitary inmates tapping Morse code onto adjoining prison cell walls.

Those sounds . . . They're the stuff of midnight paralysis, of breath uselessly vapor-locked in the throat. Of sweaty palms and stained sheets. And the only thing that frightens me more is the thought of what they might do should I try—one at a time—to remove them from the premises. Or vacate it myself.

They will not be denied their due.

And I know that some morning, come first light, I will awaken to discover that they have formed that inevitable gauntlet I have long since learned to expect.

People Who Love Life

Douglas Clegg

Why did he always have to follow her wherever she went and bring her back? Irene liked to go down to the schoolyard because of the children, the little children. Their faces, *their faces*, their tiny hands, their dresses and shorts and shirts and shoes, so small, so perfect. It bothered her when he volunteered to go, too, because the edge of the schoolyard was her special place, the children were there, and he didn't know anything about children. Children had that edge; they could *smell* things when they were bad, and they weren't afraid to say it. And when things were truly good, children sensed that, too. Children were the thing.

"Oh, but when *we* were children," the girl had said in the kitchen, and Irene had had to stare at her younger sister long and hard before she realized that she wasn't a girl at all, but a woman in her early forties: Gretchen was still pretty and adolescent, even with her slightly etched face and graying hair. Irene could not stand her sometimes, although Gretchen on her own was one thing— sweetness and light even though she *knew*, but Gretchen with this man she'd married was quite another. Irene had never really enjoyed his company, although she couldn't ever tell Gretchen how she felt; and so, she was often stuck with him, this William person, and yes, even when she went to the schoolyard to watch her children play.

"When *we* were children," Irene had replied, "good lord, I can't even remember, barely."

Gretchen was loading the dishwasher, "I remember like yesterday. Days like today, just like today. Look outside the window, it's just like when we were children and mother was in here cleaning, looking out at us." But, of course, there were no children out the window now. Gretchen was the most self-assured person that Irene had ever known, but she lied. Irene knew that about Gretchen: she lied. Gretchen could not possibly remember their childhood accurately, she had no head for memories. She blocked them purposefully, like closing doors on useless rooms. Irene remembered just about everything, but she had lied, also. Irene was not fond of remembering: *days like today, indeed. All days, like today. Unending. I just want to leave. Why won't they just let me leave?* They had been a family of liars, and had never quite grown out of it, although Irene was

365

tired, today, lying to herself about what she felt and what she wanted. Truly wanted. *I just want to go by myself.*

"You were undoubtedly two of the most spoiled girls in creation, all those toys and the way your mother used to dress you up for Sunday school like little dolls," William had said, and Irene had thought: *why do you live here with us when you're so awful to Gretchen? How you did to her what you did, let alone how I must pay for it, is beyond imagining. But you have no imagination, do you? You think it is the way you see it. In front of your face. The way you see it, with no one else allowed to look.* He was an old man who pretended to be young, but she saw right through that, right to that middle-aged heart with its bloodless beating. He pretended things were all right, that there was good to every purpose.

"We were never really spoiled," Gretchen said, "but there's always been someone to watch out for us."

"Amen to that," William said, clasping his hands together.

He had decided to come with her this day, and so there he was at her right arm, helping her every few steps as if she were a complete cripple. "I can handle the steps quite well, thank you, William," she said, and knew she sounded testy. Her right leg twisted as she stepped down to the sidewalk. Again, she had lied; stairs were difficult for her, the way her feet went, one moving almost against the other, but once she was on flat ground she was fine. But she was tired of his help.

"Alright, then," he said, and he was being humorous, *that voice,* so much like he was winking conspiratorially. She could not stand people who spoke like that. People who made fun of everything. People who love life. If only he'd let her *go* sometimes, instead of following after her like a yappy dog.

"I am not so far gone," she told him, "that I can't walk by myself. You know that, don't you?"

"Oh, Irene, I was trying to be helpful."

"Don't think me ungrateful. You and Gretchen have been kind, since the accident. More than kind. But I don't want kindness, not anymore." She had given up on direct sarcasm, and never thought he would get it, anyway. Why couldn't he just let her go?

"You're almost all healed." He reached over and touched around her face. Irene gasped. He was always close to touching her, and *there* of all places, but he had never accomplished more than the slightest graze. She stood still as if he were pulling a stray hair from her forehead. He began reading her scars the way blind people read books in Braille. His fingers were soft along the place where the skin had bubbled and obscured the vision of her left eye. Why did his fingers seem so warm, when she knew him to be so cold, so empty? Was he laughing at her, the way he laughed at the whole of creation?

But his eyes were closed. He was really *feeling* her, and she felt like he was violating her face. But it would be nothing to him. William violated people.

Finally, he removed his hand. "Does it hurt?"

"Not now. Like a headache, sometimes, but the pills take care of that, but please, let's not talk about it, I feel all talked out, and I see it in the mirror every morning, so I don't find it interesting." Would that shut him up? She would like to just have a nice day and watch the children in the schoolyard.

"God loves you, you know, Irene, He really does, and in His infinite wisdom," and he would've gone on with his smug little litany, too.

But she spat at him, "I don't care for your God, William, and I don't care for you. I was going to spend the day alone, in my own way, and you have to come along with your almighty creator and ruin everything once again."

"I know you don't mean that," he whispered, like a hurt child. "I know you're saying it because of great pain."

"You," she said, "you are my great pain. You and your miracles."

He was walking several steps behind her, and she thought of trying to lose him in the village, but she really must go and see the children when they went out to the playground. She must not miss them. Perhaps she'd stop in for a cup of coffee, but only for a minute, because the children would be waiting to see her. Only the children knew how to treat her, how to respect her wishes. They had almost come through for her last time: their tiny hands, so willing, so lovely. It was because children knew things instinctively, they had gut reactions, they were so close to the real pulse of life. Grownups had lost it all, and certainly men like this William person that Gretchen had married were so out of touch, so *clueless*, that everything was like a car: maintenance and repair, tinkering around with things that were best left to the junkyard. And always the male need for possession, possession. *Well, I do not belong to you.*

She limped another quarter mile through the village, and it was empty. It had been mostly empty when she and Gretchen had been girls, and it was empty when they were in their twenties and thirties, and now it was desolate. She had wanted to leave the village for as long as she could remember, but she'd never had the nerve. Now she knew of only one route, and damn him, he was going to shadow her.

The sunlight was flat and nothing escaped it: she saw her reflection in the secondhand bookstore window. The scars weren't healing at all, they were simply drying. Her mouth looked terrible, and she couldn't bring herself to look at her jaw. Her hair was mostly gone, but the scarf hid that. The clerk in the bookstore was pretending not to stare at her from behind his counter, but she saw him stealing glances. *I don't mind,* she thought, nodding to him, *let this be a lesson to you. When it's time, it's time.*

William was behind her. She saw his reflection. "My sister told me once that life was precious," Irene said aloud, knowing he would hear her, "and I believed her. But she meant something different than this."

"Life is the greatest gift," he said. He sometimes had a voice like nails on wood, and in the county they said he had a voice like thunder, but he sounded to her most like teeth grinding. Nothing more than teeth, one bone wearing away at another.

She turned to face him. She counted to ten, silently. Her tongue went dry in her mouth. Sometimes, yes, she was at a loss for words. "I am going to have some coffee, and I want to be alone."

He said nothing, and she walked on down the sidewalk, trying to stay in the shade. She passed Fred Smith, whom she hadn't seen since just after the accident when the town meeting was called, and he actually tipped his baseball cap to her, which seemed a rather pleasant gallantry, considering what he'd said about her in the past. *Way I see it, you belong somewhere between a freak show and a wienie roast,*" Fred had muttered from the safety of his pick-up truck, but she hadn't blamed him because he was right.* "Well, hey, Miz Hart," he said this time, but he didn't look at her, not directly. Her shoes, yes, but not her face. She didn't blame him: she was surprised that the young man in the bookstore had tried. *They're all afraid they're going to turn to stone.*

She went past him, into the Five & Dime, but not before she heard Fred say, more stiffly than when he'd greeted her, "Hello, preacher."

And William's absurdly heartfelt reply, "This is the day the Lord has made, Fred, rejoice."

"Yeah, well . . ." Fred's voice died like the wind had died, too.

The lunch counter was grease-spattered and vacant, as it usually was on Thursdays. Ever since the freeway had been built closer to Blowing Rock, the village didn't even have the trucks coming through. *As if the world knew not to come through here. Like it's a cursed place. Unclean, like in biblical days.* Jeannie Stamp came out from the washroom and leaned over the counter, nodding when Irene sat on the stool.

"It's dying, all my business is gone, just about," Jeannie said as she poured out the coffee, "Black, you like it? I told that old fart Harry to make sure the county money got thrown our way, but he said wait wait, and look what's happened now we been waiting long enough, we ain't even on the map. Used to be, ten, twelve people in here by noon, and now, just you and me, Renie." Jeannie never looked at her directly, either, but Jeannie was always nicer than the rest of the village. She had been to school with Jeannie, and had never thought in all her youth that she would ever depend upon her for friendship, but it was the best that was offered these days.

"I'm going to the school," Irene told her, leaning her elbows on the counter, sipping her coffee. It was lukewarm and smelled like dirty socks, but this was the only place to get coffee in town since the trouble when they'd burned down the ice cream shop. It was the older kids, just going crazy and setting fire to things. Even the teenagers knew when something was wrong, when things needed to be torn down. *Maybe the whole village will go. If I can't leave, maybe it will leave me.*

"You think that's a smart move?"

Irene shrugged. "What's smart?"

"School. All them kids I heard about the other day. What happened."

"*Almost* happened, *almost.*"

"Well, it could."

"Yes, hon, it could," Irene set the half-empty cup down and could not decide if she should go out in the summer heat again and face Gretchen's husband, or if she should wait another fifteen minutes. The children would be in the playground soon, and if she didn't see them today, it would be tomorrow, and if it didn't happen today, they might get used to her presence and never do what she knew they wanted to, never be free to be children, *just be children.* Less than twenty children left in the village at all.

"Preacher's talked about the Lord in our lives," Jeannie said. "He says we should be grateful, that God shines His light on us, even here, to the lowliest."

I am so tired of this fundamentalist town, Irene felt a headache coming on, and all her pills were back at the house, so the headache would just have to hammer away at her. *Gretchen and I should've left long ago, back when we had choices, back when we wanted to get out in the world. I should've learned to drive when I was in my twenties. Not wait until I was forty-six and in a stickshift with a sixteen year old. But they would've laughed at me. Luke was the only one who could teach me, the only one I could trust not to tell William, or even Gretchen. They would've laughed, and then he would've wondered why I wanted to leave so badly, and he would've stopped it. He did stop it. And I should never have been pulled from the car. Not back to this godforsaken place.* "If that's true, Jeannie, about God, what about Luke?"

Jeannie looked like a girl who had been scolded. "That's different. Preacher says God helps those He chooses."

"Who chooses? God, or the preacher?"

"Preacher don't have a choice, way I see it. He just got the gift. Always been miracles, always will be. Ain't you happy, being so special and all?"

Irene put two quarters on the counter. "Look me in the eye and ask me that."

"Oh," Jeannie said, "you know I can't do that. You know what happens. You don't want it to happen, do you?"

Irene waved to William as she came back out, into the sunlight. No one else was on the street, and there he was with his grin, his hopeful grin, like a dog waiting to be kicked. He had that charm, that she found so dull, but in a village like this one, he would be king, he would be adored, and so he had come here and found Gretchen. He was the big fish in the small pond. He was Preacher, and this was his Flock. She had once liked him, a little, but not at all since the accident. She had not even been feeling kindly towards her sister. "I don't understand you," she'd told Gretchen, "why do you even want me here? Isn't it painful?" But Gretchen was so brainwashed by this William person, by his laying on of hands and speaking in tongues, that she was not really the same girl that Irene had grown up with. Gretchen could not see her way out of things, never had been able to; for Gretchen, things were the way they were. Only once had Gretchen asked her about that day, about what happened. And Irene had pretended to have forgotten, as if the accident and the darkness had wiped it away.

"Irene," William called out, his hands tucked almost sheepishly in his pockets; he was rocking back and forth on his heels, "I was afraid I'd lost you." He stepped into the street and crossed over to her. He walked like a boy, all bounce and uncertainty.

"I'm going to see the children."

"I like walking with you."

"Do what you like," she closed her eyes and he touched her elbow with his hand. The bone was broken there, and had not healed where it poked out from her skin. She could move it fine, but she didn't like to be reminded of it. She wondered how he could touch her the way he did; she sensed his discomfort each time he was close, but now, this day, he seemed more relaxed, as if he were no longer fearful of what had happened to her body. She often wondered: *Do you like what you see? Does it please you to be so close to this monster? Do you love life this much, even when it looks this way?* But she had never been beautiful; Gretchen was always the pretty one, which bothered her until the accident, because afterwards, Irene was happy with Gretchen's beauty. She felt her little sister *should* be the lovely one, the one whose flesh was pleasant and fragrant and satisfying. Irene needed no beauty, she needed nothing. What she longed for was death, truly, and in death, an escape from this ravaged flesh.

"You're beautiful in God's eyes," he said, his breath like a warm humid wind along her neck.

"You should have left me."

"I couldn't."

"The children, the ones in the ice cream shop. Told me."

"Liars."

"You let him die."

"Those children are liars."

"Your own son."

"God called me to you. To save you."

370

"But Luke was still *alive*. You could've saved him," she was exasperated. He was so dense, he was so stupid. He only saw what he wanted to see. She moaned in frustration, wanting to hit him as hard as she could. "I was dead. Why can't you just let me go?"

The schoolyard was empty, and she went to sit on a swing. Of course, he followed her, but he hadn't said a word, so she acted as if he were not there. The school was small, and was made up of six rooms; the village had always been a small one, and the population had only diminished over the years. *This would be a place for miracles*, she smelled the dying honeysuckles, the drying grass. She saw their faces in the schoolroom windows, staring and pointing, some calling. She knew their parents. Places like this, you know everyone, you had no secrets.

"It could happen again," he said, and she tried to will him away, but he was standing beside the chain link fence near the Monkey Bars. "You should come home with me now."

When she didn't respond, he said, "You want it to happen, don't you?"

Irene watched the children in the windows: some of them had been at the ice cream shop when the car had smashed into the truck, and the fire had started. She remembered their faces, fascinated, their screaming, excited voices, as they watched the burning wreck. Her last sight had been of them holding their ice cream cones, and she had felt a peace, even in the pain of death, the numbing cold of fire, a peace from those lovely faces, knowing that the world would pass on without her there, that she would leave them, and they would still eat ice cream, and still talk out of turn, and still grow up into the world without some woman they barely knew by sight named Irene Hart who had stayed her whole dull life in the village. Her last thought had been, *children*. It had been a death she enjoyed, and the suffering had only come when she was pulled from the darkness, and opened her eyes to hear him, this man that Gretchen had married, saying, "And as Christ brought Lazarus from the dead, so I call His servant, Irene Hart, come, come to us, live again in the flesh with us."

Irene sat on the swing and began crying. She felt the weight of his hand on her shoulder. She could not help herself, and in spite of her repulsion at his touch, she asked, "Children are closer to God, aren't they? Closer than us? 'Suffer the little children to come unto me', isn't that the quote?"

"God is close to all of us. All who believe, anyway."

"Oh," she stopped crying and laughed. He came and stood in front of her. She hadn't laughed in ages, and he smiled, probably thinking he was finally seeing the light within her, "Oh, that explains it, *that's it*. It's not God who lifted me up from the burning car, it's something else entirely. It was Luke who God took care of, not me. I get it now, oh, William, you should've told me at the time. It was Luke that God loved, not me."

"Irene, you don't know what you're saying."

"Well, if it's not true, why didn't you save your son? Why did you raise me up?"

William looked her in the eye, and she almost fainted because no one had done that since the accident. He whispered something, but she knew it before he whispered it, and she wanted to stop up his mouth before the words had formed, "Because I love you," and she knew he was ashamed and humiliated to have to say it in a schoolyard, in the light of day. *"Ever since I saw you, I loved you. I want to be near you. I never want to let you go."*

So that was it. That was all.

Love.

"You go home now," she said softly, "you go home now." She turned away from him, swinging to the side, her heels scraping the dirt, happy that he had let that awful feeling out, what he called love, out to evaporate in the shimmering heat of August. It had burned all these years within him, and she had been singed by his fire. She had not known what to call it, and she knew that it was not love, not love at all, but desire. Had it been only his desire that had brought her back from the dead? *Well,* she thought, *let desire die, then, and let it have no resurrection.*

"I'll see you at supper," he said, and she heard his footsteps on the soft grass as he headed back to the street.

The swing sagged beneath her weight: *it was made for a child and I am not meant to be here. The children will know, too,* she thought.

The bell rang, and the children poured out onto the playground, and some saw her and some were involved in their games. Children like golden light on the grassy field, coming slowly, curiously towards her. They called her the names she knew children called, their small, delicate hands, and their wondrous faces, their perfect thoughts. She had come before, and they had been close to it, but they had not done what they longed to do. Their hands, their eyes, their instinct so much a part of their flesh.

But today.

Today.

One of the little boys was bold, she thought he must be twelve, and he came up and stared at her fiercely. "You're ugly," he said, "my daddy said you should be dead. You look dead. You even smell dead."

She looked him in the eye, and did not even flinch.

One of the children behind this boy picked up a small stone and threw it at her, hitting her just above her left eye. Irene smiled, *the children know what to do, they are closer to things, to nature.*

She felt another stone, this one larger, hit the back of her head, and then she was surrounded by beautiful, joyful children, and she waited for the darkness as they looked her in the eye and knew what she was.

Sweet darkness blossomed from stones.

It was later, when she thought the Kingdom was opening for her that she regained sight, and she welcomed whatever Kingdom there was, whatever light there was as the place where she belonged, but it was nothing other than the beam of a flashlight, and the lid of a coffin opening, and a madman above her who had scrambled in the earth to dig up a grave, only to say, "Come to us, live again in the flesh with us."

Phantom Brass

Carl Jacobi

Rock River. A water tower, an abandoned freight shed, and a dingy box-like station huddling against the granite wall in the September dusk. Two switch lights gleaming dismally, one at the east, one at the west end of the siding. And telegraph poles diminishing down the long, eastern grade toward Flume, thirty miles beyond.

Inside the little station McFee leaned back in his swivel chair and idly turned the pages of a last week's newspaper. On the instrument desk the train wire sounder rattled incessantly, clicking out an endless chatter into the sultry heat of the room. It was routine stuff. Garnet, the graveyard-trick dispatcher, was talking to some station farther down the line. But abruptly it hesitated, stopped, and then began spelling out call letters:

RR—RR—RR—RR—DS

Quickly McFee reached over, opened the switch, and hammered back:

I—I—RR

Then he poised a pencil over a pad of paper and began copying down a train order. But he did it without interest, scribbling rapidly and finishing long before the sounder had stopped. It was the same old 11.15 order: No. 7, eastbound freight, to wait here in the passing track until the "Coast Limited" roared through. McFee had worked two years in this lonely hole, and he knew in advance what was expected of him.

He set the light against No. 7 and strolled out through the door to the edge of the platform. The glare in the eastern sky was still there, all right. It had grown from a pale yellow to a deep orange in the intervening hour since he had last looked at it. Bad business. If a wind sprang up, there'd be the devil to pay down in the valley.

It had been going on for a week or more, this forest fire. Eating a trail of desolation through some of the finest forest country in the state. Henderson, the young op at Flume, had kept him posted of its steady advance. And messages had come through from the dispatcher, tightening up the schedule because no lumber trains could get through on the inland timber spur.

McFee stepped back into the station, got a package of cigarettes out of the desk drawer and sat down again.

"Wonder how Henderson likes it down there that close to the hot country?" he mused. "He's a funny kid."

The cigarette smoke coiled ceiling-ward, and McFee closed his eyes a moment in retrospection. Yes, Henderson was a funny kid. Came from Montreal. A month ago, before his transfer to Flume, he had worked the day shift here at Rock River. A steady and ambitious operator, scarcely in his twenties, he had an engaging smile and a touch to the key that was clear and precise. McFee liked him, even though he couldn't quite understand the kid's ideas.

Spiritualism. That was Henderson's faith. He became interested in the subject just after the death of his sweetheart—a lovely French-Canadian girl, judging from the snapshot he always carried in his wallet along with his O.R.T. card. The kid must have loved her a lot; he wore on his little finger the engagement ring he'd given her.

Henderson had brought a lot of books along when he came to Rock River—books by Sir Oliver Lodge and other writers—and subscribed to a little paper called *The Doorway* that was tossed off the 2.15 local on the first of each month.

Queer stuff. At first McFee thought it the worst bunk he'd ever set eyes upon. All about communications with our loved ones who were dead and waiting to talk to us from the world beyond. But Henderson seemed to accept it all, and tried to convince McFee. The way he put it did sound logical.

"Everything in this world," Henderson explained with a strange light in his eyes, "leads us to believe that life does not end with the material death of the body, but goes on into some higher and finer existence. You believe that, don't you?" he asked earnestly.

"Sure," McFee agreed. "I been to church."

"The world to which the dead depart is, of course, a spiritual world," the kid went on. "Yet it is close to our own. The boundary wall is thin and can be crossed. Who knows?"

McFee missed the boy when he left. The new day man was a cold and taciturn Scot, a fundamental Presbyterian, not a spiritualist; and the loneliness and monotony of the Rock River station had become a reality once more.

Only one bright spot remained in the recent turn of events. Henderson had been assigned the same trick as McFee's at the Flume Station. Which meant that when things were quiet they could utilize the station-wire to exchange scraps of conversation.

No. 7 arrived on time and waited, puffing impatiently until the "Coast Limited" roared around the curve, screeched a greeting with a blast of its whistle, and disappeared down the grade.

A moment later the freight, too, was only a winking tail-light, and McFee stood alone. Nothing more, he reflected, until 12.26 when that crack "varnish," No. 12, the "Pacific Mail," would shoot by like a flaming rocket.

But the fire down in the valley must be getting worse. Standing there on the platform, McFee looked into a sky that was flushed and sullen. From north to south, high over the horizon, stretched a lurid crimson glare like the advance of a premature dawn. And sweeping to his nostrils came that same pungent smell that had been growing steadily for days. Smoke!

Inside the station once again McFee switched in the station-wire and called Flume. When Henderson replied, he asked:

How's the fire?

The sounder immediately broke into a terse description of the conflagration. And as he listened McFee slowly tightened his lips into a grim frown.

The increasing glow in the sky had told a true story then. The fire was worse. It was sweeping, a raging inferno, on a thirty-mile front, devouring virgin timber and jumping the cut-over open spots as if they had been only a yard wide. The whole western ridge had been wiped out, and the citizens of Flume were making a frantic exodus for safety.

When the sound finally came to a halt McFee queried hurriedly:

U think fire will get far as Flume?

The reply shot back:

No. River too big a gap. Nm. Nw. (no more now)

For a long time after that McFee sat smoking and listening to the flow of conversation over the train-wire. At 11.55 he heard the Rockport man, thirty miles north, report to the dispatcher. The "Pacific Mail" was "by" there. McFee peered absently out of the bay window and made sure the light was green.

And then, without warning, the one kind of hell feared by all railroad men

375

broke loose. The wire suddenly went dead! West, it was all right. But east, where it ran through the fire district, there was no communication. Poles burned down. *Half of the division was running blind!*

McFee swore and called Henderson immediately. If there were any news, Flume was the place to get it.

A moment later the sounder began its chatter, and the Rock River operator was mentally decoding Morse. It came in Henderson's smooth style.

But halfway through the first sentence McFee sat rigid and stared in astonishment. Good Lord, something was wrong with the kid. He must be drunk—or something. Nobody in his right mind would dare to send such stuff over the wire.

All the familiar "box-car abbreviations" were missing. Henderson was spelling out his message word for word, an insane message, an impossible message that seemed to shout its way into the room as it rattled out of the sounder:

Death is a beautiful thing. It is merely a transition from this life to the spirit world beyond. One should not fear it. Those who have lived on this earth are living again. They are waiting for us just beyond the doorway. They try to speak with us but we do not listen. We are foolish not to listen. They could tell us many things and advise us as to the future. Death is not horrible. It is but a natural . . .

McFee slammed open the switch, began pounding his own key:

Stop it! U gone nuts? Don't send that stuff over the wire. Cut it!

A few more meaningless words rattled in; then the sounder stopped abruptly. Henderson put his "sine" on the message without further explanation.

The Rock River operator slumped backward in his chair. His cigarette slipped unnoticed from his lips and dropped to the floor. It was bad business letting an irresponsible person like that handle a key. Damn fool must be off his nut.

A crazy operator at Flume and the wires down beyond, cutting off all messages from the dispatcher's office. This was a night!

Abruptly McFee got to his feet and paced back and forth the length of the room. Everything was quiet now; no sound save the old alarm clock as it pushed its ticks slowly through the heat. Outside, the darkness seemed to gather around the open door and window like a velvet curtain.

All this talk about death and life in the other world—it was enough to give one the creeps. Made a man shudder when he heard it come over the wire like that. Yep, the kid must have taken his girl's death pretty hard, to act that way. In a way you couldn't blame him.

A long drawn-out whistle sounded suddenly from far off. McFee glanced absently out of the open doorway. No. 12, the "Pacific Mail," was entering the hairpin bend five miles northwest on the canyon rim.

It would be roaring by the station any moment now.

Funny about Henderson. He seemed so sober and sincere most of the time. It was only occasionally when he gave in to that bug of his and babbled spiritualism that he seemed to lose his balance. Henderson could believe what he wanted to believe, but he had no business sending such drivel over the line. It would serve him right if some other operator reported it to the dispatcher, and the kid lost his job.

Once again that whistle came, nearer now, shrieking high in the air like the discordant wail of a giant violin.

And then McFee stiffened as though shot. The sounder on the instrument desk had suddenly leaped into life. It was sputtering, hammering like mad, repeating call letters over and over:

RR—RR—RR—RR

McFee flung over the switch and quickly pounded out his reply:

I—I—RR

Then came the question:

No 12 by thr. yet?

There was a strange gleam of bewilderment in the Rock River operator's eyes as he listened to the question. That touch on the brass was familiar. It was evenly-spaced and precise in the Henderson manner he knew well. Yet it didn't seem to be Henderson. It had a curious staccato-like crackle like bottles breaking under heat. McFee raced his answer:

No. 12 due hr 1 min. Wo R U?

The brass chattered back:

Henderson, of course. For God's sake stop No. 12! River trestle burned out by advancing forest fire. Stop her! Stop her! Stop . . .

The last words were still pounding into the room when McFee leaped across to the other wall and pulled the red signal on the outside semaphore.

He was barely in time. Even as the connecting rod groaned under the movement, a shaft of white light wheeled around the canyon and transformed the rails into twin ribbons of silver. Came the bark of the exhaust, the roaring of steel against the rail joints, the thunder of the big 2-8-2.

McFee snatched up a lantern and ran out on the platform. But the engineer of the oncoming Mail had seen the signal against him and answered with two short screams of his whistle.

A moment later the train was stopped at the station, and McFee was shouting the news into the ears of an excited conductor and engineer.

Superintendent Winter looked across his flat-topped desk and toyed with a pencil.

"You are deserving of special citation, Operator McFee," he said. "Had it not been for your excellent foresightedness when the wires on the eastern half of the division were down, the Pacific Mail and everyone aboard would have gone into the river. That means a great deal to the road, and we are proud to thank you."

McFee squirmed uneasily. "But I don't deserve any credit, sir," he said. "I only obeyed orders from the kid down in Flume."

"Flume? I don't understand."

"Why"—McFee cleared his throat—"it's simple enough, sir. Henderson, the operator at Flume, warned me just before the Mail arrived at Rock River that the trestle was down. He ordered Number Twelve stopped, and I simply obeyed orders."

For a moment Winter sat silent in his chair, gazing at the man before him. Then he rose to his feet and moved around to the front of the desk.

"You say you received a call from Flume, informing you of the destruction of the trestle? I didn't know that. When did you receive that message?"

"At twelve twenty-five," McFee replied without hesitation. "Number Twelve was due at Rock River at twelve twenty-six."

The superintendent stood motionless, eyes gradually narrowing to slits. He got a cigar out of his pocket.

"Twelve twenty-five?" he said slowly. "Are you sure?"

"Positive. Why, sir?"

"Listen, McFee," Mr. Winter explained, "the forest fire swept into Flume with the speed of an express train, but because of a cross wind it struck only the tail end of the town. Only two buildings were in its path, and one of those buildings was the station. Henderson was caught in that burning matchbox before he knew what was happening. The fire destroyed the trestle a few minutes later. But when the villagers finally fought their way in to the station, they

378

found a beam from the falling roof had struck the operator on the head and apparently killed him instantly."

McFee nodded soberly. "I know."

"I have the boy's personal effects here, sent to me to forward to his relatives in Canada—a wallet, some letters, a girl's picture, a diamond ring and a watch. The blow from the crashing beam shattered that watch at the same moment it killed Henderson."

The superintendent crossed back to the desk, opened the drawer and drew forth a blackened timepiece with a cracked crystal and broken stem. For a moment he stared down at it.

"Considering what you've told me," he said solemnly, "it's very strange. As you know, an operator's watch should always be correct to the split second. That's a rule this road has always upheld. But according to the hands he was killed at exactly twelve fifteen. At twelve fifteen, do you understand? That would mean the last message you received was sent *ten minutes after the operator was dead!*"

The Ponderer

Eric Frank Russell

The great, tree-topped cliff towered hugely in the sunlight and cast its broad, deep shadow across the flat strip of land which lay between it and the jungle. At the center of the cliff, running its full height from base to crest, jutted an immense outcrop of solid gray rock fantastically molded into semblance of a ruminating giant. Though craggy and rugged, old and worn, so startlingly did it look like a gargantuan statue of someone dreaming of ages long forgotten that ever since the days of the vanished Chiapans it had been named The Ponderer—and mightily feared.

Overhead, the coppery sky of Chiapas poured heat into the rocks, the flat strip and the jungle. To the south lay Palenque with its creeper-covered ruins of a civilization absorbed into the mists of antiquity. There too, in Palenque, was the nearest *finca* where a humble peon could slake his thirst and at the same time rid himself of the eerie feeling induced by this eternally brooding colossus.

Clumsily turning his mule at the end of the strip and edging his primitive stick-plow around behind it, Jose Felipe Eguerola paused to mop his lean, nutbrown face, lick his cracked lips and wave away a horde of mosquitoes. Deep within the jungle to one side of him unseen things yapped and squealed and howled derisively. To his other side soared the cliff and its part-embedded monster of stone. The shadow of The Ponderer's tremendous head slanted far across the lines of new, thin furrows, so high in the sky was it poised.

Jose Felipe Eguerola scrupulously avoided looking directly at the dour shape of The Ponderer. He never gave it eye for eye, never. To do so would be bad. He'd not the remotest notion of why it might be bad, but he was taking no chances. Already he was taking chances enough, in the opinions of some.

Fra Benedictus with his holy water and a few crazy Yanquis with cameras had been the only ones to practice the precept that a cat may look at a king. Nothing terrible had happened to any of them as far as he knew. But he, Jose Felipe Eguerola, had never owned a pair of rawhide sandals, never fascinated a plump señorita, never gained a peso in the State lottery. All that he possessed were a grass hut pleasingly adjacent to the *finca,* seven acres of perilous dirt, the stick-plow, the mule, one pair of torn pants, the sputum of the gods and the will to live despite it. His chief aim in life was to keep what little he'd got.

So for the twentieth time that day he shifted his quid of raw latex from one cheek to the other, turned the end of a furrow, beat off the mosquitoes, glanced hastily and leerily at The Ponderer from out the corners of his black and liquid eyes. In spite of the intense heat the usual shiver raced up his spine. So big, so grandly contemplative, so imperially indifferent to the scrabblings of lesser things around its mountainous feet!

Tilting his hand-woven straw sombrero the better to shield his eyes, Jose Felipe whacked the tough, drab buttocks in front of him and set up an urgent call of, *"Mula, Mula, Mula, Echa, mula!"* Obediently the animal lurched forward. Leaning his weight on the plow he followed bare-footed, splay-toed.

High above, The Ponderer meditated in utter disregard of the tiny, bug-like figures, two and four-footed, as they crawled dustily toward the shadow he was casting. He had posed there so long and eroded so much that none could tell for certain whether he had been carved by oldtime hands of wondrous cunning, or whether he was no more than a freakish product of the elements.

In awful truth, he was neither. The few who had viewed him and theorized about him had erred by rejecting the self-evident in favor of the obscure. He was precisely what he appeared to be, namely, The Ponderer. In that respect if in no other, the wary Jose Felipe's sixth sense was more reliable than the erudition of his betters.

Hesitantly, man and beast toiled through the potent shadow, emerged into the light. Jose Felipe coughed with dust and relief. Invariably he was relieved to escape that darker patch. At any other time, in any other place, he had the true peon's love of the shade; it provided a break from the burning sun, something in which to laze luxuriously, something in which to lie flat on one's back with one's half-naked legs stretched right out. One could then listen idly to the wit of the fat, inactive Señor Don Antonio Miguel Gautisolo-y-Lazares who could both read and write. "Let the Yanquis work—they are more advanced." But not here. Not in that particular shadow. Not in that low-slung silhouette of a countenance which kept away Indians and peons alike, preserving the plot from all but the supremely courageous such as he, Jose Felipe Eguerola. Frequently he regretted that his courage was so supreme. Back in Palenque he was much admired for his hardihood and there had been some talk of it even in far-off Villahermosa. It was gratifying to be admired providing that one was gratified in Palenque, preferably in the *finca*. On this shadow-haunted plot he was called upon to pay the devil for the praise—and the price got upped a bit every day. There were no admirers upon the scene of action; there was only himself and the mule and the monstrous monolith to whose feet even the hungry jungle had dared not push.

Reaching the farther end, he turned mule and plow again, mopped, whooshed the mosquitoes, retilted the sombrero, cautiously eyed the cliff. *"Ho, mula. Mula. Echa, mula!"* The cry wailed and hooted along the rocky ramparts, bounding and rebounding from crevices and corners. *"Mula . . . Echa, mula!"* Parrots screamed in the impenetrable thickness of the green hell, a distant branch snapped and something thrashed heavily amid the growths. *"Echa, mula!"*

The Ponderer awoke.

With slow, titanic deliberation awful to watch, The Ponderer shifted the columnar arm which had propped his head, and removed his massive elbow from his hillock of a knee. His entire tremendous torso edged the merest fraction with this his first movement; the ramparts shuddered along their length and two thousand tons of rock roared down from the cliff's face a mile away. Its sound was like the simultaneous sundering of earth and sky. The jungle yelled its own dumbfoundment with a multitude of hidden voices.

The mule had stopped in its tracks, ears twitching uneasily. Jose Felipe stood paralyzed behind it, not looking up, but down—down to the furrows where the shadow of the elbow had left the shadow of the knee and still was moving. The handles of the plow were wet in his failing grip. Sluggishly, unwillingly, he turned.

His heart at once became a river eel striving to snap at the hawk-moth fluttering within his stomach. Tiny streams of sweat crept down the bridge of his nose, the backs of his ears, the insides of his knees. The muscles of his jaws, thighs and abdomen felt strangely weak. His head was dizzy as if he had stooped too long beneath the merciless sun. He could not move, not one muscle, not one inch. He remained there glued to the earth, as fixed for all time as had seemed the thing he was watching.

Gradually, laboriously, with many harsh sounds as of stone grinding upon stone, The Ponderer came unstuck from the cliff. An avalanche of rock, pebbles and dirt cascaded on either side of him, its dust clouding his feet. Great boulders hopped and hurdled across the flat, some missing the transfixed onlooker by mere yards. With groaning joints The Ponderer straightened, became rigidly erect, at which point his shadow reached the jungle and hushed its agitated crying. The brazen sky glared down while even the birds were silent. The world was awed.

The Ponderer sighed. It was a sibilant sound like that of a venturesome wind lost amid unfamiliar mountains. Then without warning, and with many rasping noises, he bent and grabbed the mule. Its plow-cords broke as he snatched it three hundred feet into the air. Holding it upside-down, its legs kicking furiously, he studied it with mild interest and a touch of contempt. Just as decisively he put it back on the ground, where it lay on its side and panted heavily, tongue out, eyes rolling. Still Jose Felipe remained helplessly rooted to the fateful spot.

As the great hand came for him, Jose called pitifully upon his legs, and called in vain. They refused to respond. The hand closed about him, huge and harsh and hard, a rocky enormity. Opening his mouth, he shrieked on a note so high in pitch that his own ears could not hear it. At terrifying speed he went upward within the hand, his mouth still wide open and emitting the sound which was not a sound.

Nightmarishly he swung close to that immense face, that craggy, lined, corroded travesty of a face. It stared at him, examining him with two granite bulges sculpturally suggestive of eyes and somehow he knew that it could really see—or exercise some queer sense equivalent to sight.

"*Santa Maria!*" Jose Felipe's dangling legs jerked spasmodically.

"Be still!" The Ponderer had no visible mouth, no more than a deeply carved indication of lips, yet he spoke as clearly and surely as the talking Memnon had spoken, and the other could understand his words.

"Be still, little thing who mocks my own shape and form." He turned his captive around, the better to inspect him. His grip was crushing. Jose Felipe screamed again with the sheer agony of it. The fingers loosened slightly.

"So," decided The Ponderer, "this creature has mastery of the other one. This one *thinks*. Well, well!" He chuckled in amused surprise. "You really do think, little one—that is something indeed! I, too, think. What else can one do that is worthwhile? What greater ecstasy can there be than that of sustained and involved thought?"

"*Maria!*" repeated Jose Felipe fervently. His eyes were turned away from that great face and gazing in dread at the drop beneath the hand. From his altitude the mule resembled a mouse. The sight brought on vertigo. He tried to keep well within the cup of the hand, clinging to the fingers. His tattered, sweat-soaked pants had molded themselves to his legs.

"Only in thought may one avoid the torment of endless years," The Ponderer went on. "The long thought, the complicated thought—that is the fundamental pleasure." He crooked a finger which rasped as it bent, used it to nudge his victim. "Isn't it?"

"No!" shouted Jose Felipe hardly knowing what he was hearing or saying. "*Sí! Sí!*" He strove to keep his eyes away from both the fall and the face.

"Alas, I have arrived at the end of a beautiful problem," The Ponderer continued morbidly. "The problem of nine bodies circling a binary, the sixth being retrograde. It has kept me petrified with the pleasure of thought for seventy thousand years." He paused a moment, added, "Or was it seven thousand? I don't know. It is of no consequence and not worth investigating—the solution is too swift and easy." He juggled his huge hand. "But I would guess, little one, that even so simple a puzzle would be too much for your kind, eh?"

The jiggling jerked his tongue free, and Jose Felipe promptly used it to shout, "Put me down! Put me down and I will leave your feet in peace! I swear it by—"

"Be silent!" The hand wobbled again. "Now I am sorely in need of another thought. I yearn to be numbed by a new problem. How unhappy is the silicoid without a problem!" His tremendous thumb caught the victim on the point of sliding helplessly into space, poked him back into the palm. "You, little thing, have a fragmentary life which does not extend from one of my gravitic pulses to the next, and probably any puzzle you could concoct would be equally as short and futile. Yet I need a long one, I need one enjoyable for eons."

"By my father and my mother, I shall never again tread upon your shade or come within sight of here if but—"

"Quiet! Let me consider how I might convert you into a suitable problem." The rocky head came a little closer, staring, staring blindly. "Suppose that I squeeze you? Ah, yes, you will die! Sooner or later others of your kind will come seeking you. I shall squeeze them also. The mystery will grow with the mound of corpses. The tales of it will spread like ripples when a stone has been cast into a pond. Eventually other little things with minds superior to yours will come here to investigate the matter. If I persist, if I go far enough, someone will solve the mystery and employ whatever is available to shatter me to dust."

"I do not wish to die," yelled Jose Felipe. "I do not deserve to die." The jungle came back to life and its parrots screamed in sympathy.

"Now possibly *there* is a problem," mused The Ponderer, completely ignoring his captive's protests. "Somewhat on the short side, but spiced with danger. Can I cast the stone and accurately estimate the speed, distance and amplitude of those ripples? Can I start the chain of circumstance, petrify myself in thought, and awake in good time with the solution of how to avoid my own destruction?" His chuckle sounded again. "This is something decidedly novel; a puzzle loaded with death, my own death. It entices me, yes, it entices me." His fingers began to curl and close in.

383

"Have pity!" gasped the victim, barely finding breath under the awful compression.

The fingers relaxed. "Pity? What a weird concept! Has it an inherent problem?" The Ponderer was silent awhile. "No, I cannot conceive one." More silence, then, "However, I understand what you mean. If I grant you some of this pity it may complicate matters pleasingly. I will therefore grant it by playing a little game with you."

"Put me down. Let me go."

"Not yet. Not just yet—if at all! The game first." The granite eyes were fixed upon him, but blank, blank. "This is the game: I shall release you unhurt if your wits prove the equal of mine. If you can petrify me you will have earned your freedom. So think, little one, *think*. It is you versus a silicoid!"

"Petrify you?" Jose Felipe's mind refused to make sense of the words. His fear was still a potent thing, but anger was outgrowing it.

"With a problem. And not some petty puzzle which can be solved within the space of a gravitic pulse, but one worthy of my time, a long, long time." He tilted the hand slightly. "Come on, petrify me with thought—that you may live!"

Jose Felipe clung desperately to a rocky finger, slid, hung on, slid a bit more. He fought to discipline his scattered wits. He was no intellectual and none knew it better than he. Perhaps of bravery supreme—in given circumstances—but far, far from a genius. Offhand, he could remember nobody who'd ever given him credit for an original thought. Even the mild and inoffensive Fra Benedictus had once pronounced him too stupid to live. Evidently the worthy father had been only too right—for his end was near.

Fra Benedictus!

Had called him stupid!

Why?

Fra—

"Be swift!" The hand slanted alarmingly. "Only the witless are slow!"

Sliding to the verge, Jose Felipe struggled madly to keep his grip while his legs swung in mid-air. Below, the mouse! He could see it in his mind's eye, miles and miles down, a crushed form beside it—the bait, the first link in the hellish chain of circumstance. He tore his nails in frantic effort to stay put.

"Quick!"

More tilt.

A sudden surge of appalling fury filled his being, overwhelming his fear, lending him the strength of desperation. Arcing his body he swung himself onto a great finger, stood upon it erect, at full height, one hand braced against the other's tilted palm. His black, volatile eyes blazing with anger, he shook an absurd little fist at the enormous face, for the first time defying it eye to eye. His voice was shrill, vibrant with emotion as he challenged The Ponderer.

384

"To whom did God say, 'Let there be light!'?"

"Eh?"

Without caring whether it were true or false, the monster accepted the premise for the sake of where it led. His great hand levelled slowly, trembled, began to sink. It went down, gradually down, shivering queerly as it moved. Jose Felipe fell off it when within six feet of earth, landed heavily on his knees, got up and raced twenty paces before he fainted. Dimly and faraway in the instant before his sense left him he heard a grinding, rasping voice high up in the sky.

"To whom?"

The vault of Chiapas was still brazen and hot when his senses returned and he staggered to his feet. Likewise upright and apparently unharmed, the mule was nearby surveying him dolefully. He leaned against the animal, absorbing the comfort of its presence. He tried not to look over its back, but his eyes were drawn as if by a magnet and insisted on seeing. The panorama appeared normal. The mighty ramparts frowned down just as always they had done, and the queer, fantastic outcrop was solidly a part of them as always it had been. The outcrop bore strange resemblance to a brooding giant, a colossus plunged in eternal thought.

Looking longer and with less reluctance, Jose Felipe berated himself. Obviously the supreme courage which was spoken of even in Villahermosa was but the courage of drunken dreams. He sat too often and too long in the *finca*, too stupid to know whether the *tequila* was good or bad—almost too stupid to live. What little there was of his brains had been pickled in a potent jug so that next day he fell even behind the plow and battled the mountains in his stupor.

Moodily he felt for the plow-cords, found them broken. His eyes sought the torn ends. They popped, roamed around, perceived the great fall a mile to the north, the boulders scattered over the flat, the new rubble at either side of the outcrop. His sombrero lay at the outcrop's base. Even as he looked a loosened crag beyond the distant fall gave way and dropped thunderously into a ravine. Its noise echoed and re-echoed, reaching him like a great, booming voice.

"To whom? To *whom?*"

"*Madre de Dios!*" Madly scrambling onto the mule's back and urging its head round to face the Palenque trail, Jose Felipe Eguerola sweated and forgot the mosquitoes while he hammered his mount with his heels until it broke into a steady jog-trot. "*Mula. Mula. Echa, mula!*"

Preparations for the Game

Steve Rasnic Tem

It's the day of the big game. He has a date, oh, a beautiful young date. A member of a leading sorority on campus, auburn hair, perfume behind the ears and down her cleavage, a lure for his young red alcoholic nose. Could there ever be better times?

Certainly not. Not when he has such a beautiful date, his first date in months, and not when they're doubling with the president of his fraternity, who just happens to be seeing his beautiful date's best friend.

Things are looking up for him, oh, certainly.

They pull up in front of his apartment. I'll just be a minute, he says cheerily. Just a change of clothes. His pennant. His flask. Once out of the car, he gazes back in at their fixed smiles. The fraternity president scratches his wool pants. The beautiful date's best friend rubs at her cheekbones distractedly. He reaches into the car and pulls his beautiful date's hand from her fur muff. And grasps rods of bone, well-articulated carpals and metacarpals.

But no. Just the effect of thin winter air against skin. He looks down at her small, narrow hand, with its pale white flesh. So delicate.

It's going to be a great game, he calls, jogging up the apartment building steps.

In his apartment he rummages through piles of clothing. What to wear? He picks up his checkered gray slacks, throws them behind the couch. He picks up the dark-blue monogrammed sweater-shirt, tosses it on top of the refrigerator. He stumbles through piles of books, garbage, unmatted prints with curling edges. What to wear?

He is aware of a skeletal hand curled around the front doorknob. Without looking around he tells her, I haven't the time. I'll be late for the game.

It suddenly occurs to him it's the first time anyone has ever visited his apartment.

But still he tells her, I just haven't the time—I mustn't be late for the game. She slides around the doorframe, her short red shift tight over her emaciated figure, her thin hands twisted into tight fists.

It suddenly occurs to him she may be out to spoil his good time.

He turns around, pretending that she isn't there. He picks up a Nehru jacket, casts it away. He picks up his bright red turtleneck, and drops it on the coffee table. I haven't time, I haven't time, he pleads softly, then silently to himself.

She steps toward him, her eyes two dark stones. He clumsily avoids her, almost tripping over a pile of shoes.

She swings the edge of a cupped hand toward his face. He steps quickly once to his right, his eyes averted, still seeking something to wear to the game. Her blow misses.

What does she want from him? Why doesn't she leave him alone?

Now he is forced to look at her. He's cornered at one end of the small breakfast bar. I'll be late for the game, he repeats, almost crying. Her black hair is filthy, plastered to her skull.

He sidesteps past his television set. Something metallic shines in her moving hand. She smashes the screen. I'll be late, he whimpers. She steps closer. He senses just a hint of corrupted flesh beneath her rough, bluish lips.

The blood is rising into her cheeks and eyes, suffusing them with a light pink color. She swings her hands back and forth, in slow motion.

And still, he attempts to ignore her. He puts on his heavy coat, the dark brown with contrasting tan pattern. He slips his bright orange scarf around his neck, still walking away from her, adjusting the thick folds so that they cut across his neck at the most aesthetically pleasing angle, and still she follows him, swings her hands at him, misses him, and again he stumbles, slightly, before catching himself. His steps become quicker. He attempts to make his movements unpredictable.

He says it rapidly to himself, a magic formula, a prayer: I can't be late for the game. I just can't.

Again, from the corner of his eye he can see she is approaching. He walks briskly, still seeking his spectator's wardrobe, falters briefly, his gaze distracted. She steps around the low couch, directly behind him now, reaching for his coat. Mustn't be late, mustn't be late, he mutters to himself, suddenly deciding to forego the proper dress, to leave now. For wouldn't it be a graver offense to make the president of his fraternity late for the game, not to mention his beautiful young date and her best friend?

He hurriedly, almost running, makes it to the door, jerking it open as she makes a final, determined lunge. He hears the faint knock of her knuckles, or, perhaps, cheekbones, rasping the door panel as he runs down the stairs pulling at his ill-fitting pants, tucking in his shirt, running fidgety hands over his improper clothing.

At the curb he halts in dismay. The car is gone with the president and the two pretty girls inside. The stadium is miles away; he'll never make it in time. What will they all think of him? He sits down on the curb, the sound of footsteps on the staircase growing louder behind him.

* * *

He has been unable to leave his apartment for weeks. He sleeps days at a time, his moments awake so brief they seem like dreams to him. Dinner comes at 2:00 A.M., breakfast twelve hours later. He throws the garbage into a cardboard box under the sink.

One twilight he remembers that he has a date set up for that day. They are all going to the big game. He, his beautiful young date, her best friend and the president of his fraternity who he had never really talked to and probably still wouldn't have gotten to know if their beautiful young dates hadn't been such good friends. What time is it? He's going to be late. The phone is ringing. His parents again? While not quite deciding not to answer it, he fails to answer by default.

He rummages through piles of clothing, attempting to find the one proper outfit for his venture outside, to the game.

He needs to go to the bathroom, but not wanting to walk the ten yards or so down to the restroom in the hall, he walks over to his sink and begins urinating there.

He is aware of a skeletal hand curled around the front doorknob.

Without looking around he tells her, I haven't the time. I'll be late for the game.

It occurs to him it's the first time anyone has ever visited his apartment.

But still he tells her, I just haven't the time. I mustn't be late for the game.

She slides around the doorframe, her short red shift tight over her emaciated figure, her thin hands twisted into tight fists.

It occurs to him that he's seen her before, at one of his fraternity's dances. She danced with Bob, Tom. Perhaps she even danced with the president. It occurs to him that maybe even he danced with her that night.

He can't remember her name.

She approaches him slowly, her arms outstretched. He stumbles backward over the couch. The phone is ringing again. I can't be late for the game, he pleads with her.

The phone stops ringing. Outside a horn is blaring. It must be his fraternity president, his beautiful date, her best friend. He lunges toward the door, forgetting his good clothes. I can't be late for the game, he cries it now. He can hear her quickening steps behind him.

At the curb he halts, looking about in confusion. The car is gone. He'll never make it in time. He suddenly realizes that he is naked: his legs startle him with their chalky whiteness. What will they all think of him? He hears her footsteps behind him. Looking down, he discovers that his feet are bare, bleeding from all the broken glass in the street.

* * *

388

He races down the street. He figures that if he can just find the proper bus, he can make it to the game on time. I mustn't be late, he mutters, then grows self-conscious and worried, thinking some passerby might have heard him talking to himself, and think him strange.

His heavy coattails, dark brown with contrasting tan pattern, flap in the wind. His bright orange scarf hangs loosely around his neck, untying itself with his exertions. His hands grab at the material, trying to maintain his neat appearance.

Occasionally he looks around to see if she is following. Small dogs growl at his feet.

Ahead of him, he thinks he sees the back entrance to the bus station, a tall whitewashed building with a blue roof. But he can't remember which bus it was that traveled the route to the stadium.

He races up the back stairs, seeking information. He pushes open a steel door at the second floor, turns left and jerks open a wooden door.

And he is back in his own apartment once again, the unmade bed, the scattered clothing, the sweet ripe smell of garbage under the sink. She has been waiting for him, his small Boy Scout hatchet clutched tightly in her hand. I can't be late, he starts to whine, then stops. He can't hear his own voice. She walks toward him now, the hatchet slightly raised.

He finds it difficult to move. What is her name?

He sits in the restaurant across from his apartment, sipping his morning coffee. The big game is today, and he waits now for the president to arrive with his late-model Chevy and their two beautiful young dates. He doesn't know the president well, but hopes that will soon change. He is wearing his very best clothing: his brown heavy coat with the tan pattern, his orange scarf, his dark alligator shoes with the small tassels. They'll be here in an hour, he thinks with satisfaction, preparing to eat a leisurely pregame breakfast.

But then he looks up at the clock; hours have passed, the game already started, half over by now, he thinks. He rushes out of the restaurant, looking frantically up and down the street. No sign of cars. He suddenly thinks of all the times he's been forgotten, the times left at the playground, the school parties missed. But they must have come by, waited for hours, he thinks, and somehow he didn't know they were out there. They finally had no choice but to leave; they couldn't be late for the game.

He walks across the street and climbs the narrow stairs to his third-floor apartment. Opening the door he sees her sitting stiffly on his couch, hands clenched in her lap.

Her black hair is filthy, plastered to her skull. He senses just a hint of corrupted flesh beneath her rough, bluish lips.

He thinks he recognizes her. The president had brought her to the house initiation night. After the blindfolded bobbing for peeled bananas in a tub of pudding, after the nose-to-anus farting matches, the hard licks with the paddle and the naphtha poured on the groin, they'd been led one by one into her room. She'd been pale and silent, her high cheekbones flushed in the dim light, and they'd each fucked her, a minute or two apiece.

Her nose had been running the whole time, he remembers.

She rises from the sofa and approaches him. Livid scars crisscross her wrists and forearms.

He gazes about his room, looking for a nice outfit to wear to the game, pretending she isn't there. His eyes rest on a pile of soiled, stained underwear by the couch. He can't smell them, but imagines their corpse-like scent, like a pile of dead white sewer rats. He is suddenly anxious that she might have seen them. He stares at her in intense agitation as she reaches her arms out for him. He is filled with acute embarrassment for himself.

After blocks of strenuous running, he finally makes it to the bus, leaping to the first step just before the driver closes the doors. The driver pays no attention as he drops his coins into the metal box. He momentarily wonders if he could have gotten away without paying, so intent is the driver on some scene ahead.

He strides to the middle of the bus, slightly out of breath, grabbing a seat near the side doors so he can hurry out when they reach the stadium.

The bus contains a half-dozen passengers, all of them old, quiet and somewhat unattractive. One old man has a large purple birthmark covering the side of his face; wartlike growths, also deep purple, spot the area under his right eye. He suddenly realizes he can't hear the sounds of the traffic outside.

When the bus pulls to his stop he leaps out the door, and momentarily the illusion of soundlessness follows him into the street outside. When the traffic noise returns, he is staring up at a whitewashed building with blue tile roof, his apartment house.

He begins climbing the stairs to his apartment on the tenth floor.

Three of his fraternity brothers pick him up at the restaurant across the street from his apartment building. He's just had a leisurely breakfast of coffee, cereal and eggs, the waitress was pretty and smiled a lot, and he is now ready to have a wonderful time at today's big game.

When he gets into the car, the late-model Chevy, his three brothers compliment him on his choice in clothing, the heavy brown coat with tan pattern, the orange scarf. They joke a bit, slap each other's shoulders and pull rapidly out of their parking space.

His brothers ask him if he'd like a little sip from their flask. He replies, No, thank you, I have my own. But as he reaches into his back pocket he discovers it missing, dropped out somewhere in the scramble to be on time, no doubt, so yes, he would care for a small slug.

He raises the flask high over his mouth and pours the warm yellow liquor. Some splashes on his bright orange scarf. He feels panicky, has an urge to wipe it off before it stains the beautiful material, but for some reason seems unable to. He drinks, endlessly it seems. He drinks.

The brothers sing old fraternity and college songs, between various versions swapping stories of fraternity life. Rush. Initiation night and all the fun they had. How all the girls are dazzled by a fraternity jacket. The dumb pledge who almost suffocated when a five-foot mock grave collapsed on him. Chug-a-lugging "Purple Jesuses": vodka, rum, grapes, oranges and lemon juice. The night they caught a pig, beat it, kicked it, dragged it across the parking lot, hung it up by the snout, then finally drowned it in the bathtub.

He remembers his old pledge buddy, a fat kid no one else liked. They had driven him ten miles up into the mountains the day before initiation. He hadn't seen him since.

The brothers are taking a new road to the stadium, one he's sure he's never seen before. It meanders out into the country, through patches of wood and round fields and small farms. He has a moment of uneasiness, worried that perhaps they plan to leave him out there, that he'll never make it to the game on time.

As the car rounds a wide bend in a wooded section, it slows. The brothers stop the car and the driver races the engine. They stare into the clearing a hundred feet ahead and slightly below them.

On a stump beside the road there is a body, lying face up, the back and rump resting on the flat cross-section. Its red shift is tattered and water-spotted.

The driver yells at the top of his lungs, the other two brothers chorusing. They sound like coyotes. The car lurches forward, bearing down on the stump. The brother at the front passenger window pulls a small pistol out of the glove compartment.

As the car suddenly swerves around the stump the brother puts two bullets into the body's torso.

He can see that there are dozens of other bullet holes and torn places in the body's skin. He also notices that it might have been a man, or a woman with short hair. Certainly sexless by now, however.

As the car speeds out of the woods, his brothers laughing and hollering, he looks back at the clearing. He can see another car approaching in the distance. He thinks the body is stirring, about to rise, and his legs tighten up at this thought. He knows that if he were standing by the stump, and if the body did rise, he would not be able to move his legs. He would be unable to run away. But then he realizes this is all just his imagination, that it's the wind rustling the few remaining rags on the corpse, that no, it isn't going to rise.

He sees a gun appear at the window of the distant car, preparing to put more bullets into the body. A road sign, he thinks.

He figures it's no more than fifteen minutes to kickoff.

Outside the stadium he stumbles and falls in the gravel. He's going to miss the kickoff, and he was so close. He'd been lucky to catch the bus; he'd flagged it down, in fact. He is worried about the woman back in his apartment, probably even now looking at all his scattered clothing, his unkempt rooms. He is worried about his torn brown pants, his scuffed alligator shoes. He worries about the fact of the corpse back on the stump, the fact that he will no doubt miss the kickoff.

He runs into his parents as he nears the stadium entrance. They look so old. His old father, his shriveled lips unable to catch the moisture dripping from his mouth as he speaks, pleads with him, wondering why he hasn't answered their phone calls. His aged mother nods, distracted, singing to herself.

His father grabs him by the arm, pulling him closer conspiratorially, whispering hoarsely: Your mother . . . she hasn't been the same, and Don't go in there. First time I had it . . . down by one of the old sorority houses. She pulled me back into the bushes . . . unzipped me, stuck it up there herself . . . was awful, like a big old frying pan in there . . .

He pulls away from the old man and pushes past his mother, seeking the stadium entrance. He sees nothing but a smooth limestone wall. Where is it? He's going to be late.

His beautiful young date is in there waiting for him, her bony fingers encircling a paper cup full of beer.

As he enters the stadium it's a few minutes to halftime. It has been a long walk. The crowd seems strangely silent, as if they were watching an engrossing chess match.

But he's forgotten his tickets, now he knows this, and knows too that he will therefore be unable to watch the game. He searches the crowd for his fraternity president, their beautiful dates, his beautiful date, but it's impossible in this crowd. Everyone looks the same, dressed in grays, blacks, dark blues, their faces pale, hair cropped short. When they try to cheer the players out on the field, no sound comes out.

An usher touches his arm from behind and he begins formulating an excuse for not having a ticket but the usher says nothing, instead leads him to a seat a dozen rows down, on the aisle.

He is sitting next to a family of spectators. They all have light brown hair, the father, the mother, the daughter and son, and perfect smiles, displayed to each other, not to him, in their mutual pride. They clap in unison to approve some play on the field, though strangely, he seems unable to see, to get the field into proper focus. Their clapping makes no sense.

He looks around a bit. Rows of spectators, stacked at an angle, back and upward, as far as he can see. But except for the family sitting next to him, he can discern no movement, not even a nervous tic. He again looks at the family beside him, and is drawn to their smooth, tucked-in lips. And their light blue pallor.

Discomfited, he stands up and starts down the aisle toward the field, still unable to get the players into focus. No one attempts to stop him. He reaches the retaining wall above the sidelines, climbs on top and jumps down, the thud of his feet in the grass the only sound he can hear.

When he reaches the center of the field he turns around. There's no one on the field. The stands seem empty. A slight breeze begins to rustle the grass.

He attempts to reenter the stadium through the tunnel leading to the players' dressing rooms. The light here is dim.

Mummified corpses line the walls, sprawl over dressing tables and tile shower floors. The bodies have lost most of their flesh and only thin strands of hair remain. They still wear their scarlet jerseys, though most of the color has leached away. Bones in white or sporty gold togs peer out of open lockers.

Entering the stadium he discovers to his relief that the game hasn't yet started. All seems well. No corpses, parents or strange women to trouble him. He pulls his ticket out of his unwrinkled pants pocket and makes his way to a seat on the fifty-yard line. His friends are all there and are overjoyed to see him.

The fraternity president slaps him on the back and says, "Great to have you here. Wouldn't be the same without you. And say . . . after the game, I'd like to talk to you about your maybe becoming our new pledgemaster."

His fraternity brothers pass on their congratulations from their seats further down the aisle.

The crowd suddenly leaps to its feet to cheer the upcoming kickoff. He is thrilled by the motion, color and sound. His fraternity brothers are slapping each other on the back, stamping feet, shouting and bussing their pretty dates on the cheeks. Popcorn and empty cups fly through the air. Frisbees are tossed from section to section.

He turns to greet his beautiful young date with an embrace. She opens her mouth widely. He notes the blueness of her throat. She grins and shows her perfect white teeth.

Later he climbs the steps for popcorn and soft drinks for the girls. He wonders if he might not just marry his date someday; she seems so much like him. The day is going so well now, and he wonders if maybe it's time for him to finally settle down, maybe have a family.

He is slowly aware of two arms, clothed in tatters of red, coming around his sides from behind as if to embrace him. The hands are thin, almost bone. Everything is suddenly quiet again.

Purification

Robert Barr

Eugène Caspilier sat at one of the metal tables of the Café Égalité, allowing the water from the carafe to filter slowly through a lump of sugar and a perforated spoon into his glass of absinthe. It was not an expression of discontent that was to be seen on the face of Caspilier, but rather a fleeting shade of unhappiness which showed he was a man to whom the world was being unkind. On the opposite side of the little round table sat his friend and sympathizing companion, Henri Lacour. He sipped his absinthe slowly, as absinthe should be sipped, and it was evident that he was deeply concerned with the problem that confronted his comrade.

'Why, in Heaven's name, did you marry her? That, surely, was not necessary.'

Eugène shrugged his shoulders. The shrug said plainly, 'Why indeed? Ask me an easier one.'

For some moments there was silence between the two. Absinthe is not a liquor to be drunk hastily, or even to be talked over too much in the drinking. Henri did not seem to expect any other reply than the expressive shrug, and each man consumed his beverage dreamily, while the absinthe, in return for this thoughtful consideration, spread over them its benign influence, gradually lifting from their minds all care and worry, dispersing the mental clouds that hover over all men at times, thinning the fog until it disappeared, rather than rolling the vapour away, as the warm sun dissipates into invisibility the opaque morning mists, leaving nothing but clear air all around and a blue sky overhead.

'A man must live,' said Caspilier at last; 'and the profession of decadent poet is not a lucrative one. Of course there is undying fame in the future, but then we must have our absinthe in the present. Why did I marry her, you ask? I was the victim of my environment. I must write poetry; to write poetry, I must live; to live, I must have money; to get money, I was forced to marry. Valdorème is one of the best pastry-cooks in Paris; is it my fault, then, that the Parisians have a greater love for pastry than for poetry? Am I to blame that her wares are more sought for at her shop than are mine at the booksellers'? I would willingly have shared the income of the shop with her without the folly of marriage, but

Valdorème has strange, barbaric notions which were not overturnable by civilized reason. Still my action was not wholly mercenary, nor indeed mainly so. There was a rhythm about her name that pleased me. Then she is a Russian, and my country and hers were at that moment in each other's arms, so I proposed to Valdorème that we follow the national example. But, alas! Henri, my friend, I find that even ten years' residence in Paris will not eliminate the savage from the nature of a Russian. In spite of the name that sounds like the soft flow of a rich mellow wine, my wife is little better than a barbarian. When I told her about Tenise, she acted like a mad woman—drove me into the streets.'

'But why did you tell her about Tenise?'

'*Pourquoi?* How I hate that word! Why! Why!! Why!!! It dogs one's actions like a bloodhound, eternally yelping for a reason. It seems to me that all my life I have had to account to an enquiring why. I don't know why I told her; it did not appear to be a matter requiring any thought or consideration. I spoke merely because Tenise came into my mind at the moment. But after that, the deluge; I shudder when I think of it.'

'Again the why?' said the poet's friend. 'Why not cease to think of conciliating your wife? Russians are unreasoning aborigines. Why not take up life in a simple poetic way with Tenise, and avoid the Rue De Russie altogether?'

Caspilier sighed gently. Here fate struck him hard. 'Alas! my friend, it is impossible. Tenise is an artist's model, and those brutes of painters who get such prices for their daubs, pay her so little each week that her wages would hardly keep me in food and drink. My paper, pens, and ink I can get at the cafés, but how am I going to clothe myself? If Valdorème would but make us a small allowance, we could be so happy. Valdorème is madame, as I have so often told her, and she owes me something for that; but she actually thinks that because a man is married he should come dutifully home like a bourgeois grocer. She has no poetry, no sense of the needs of a literary man, in her nature.'

Lacour sorrowfully admitted that the situation had its embarrassments. The first glass of absinthe did not show clearly how they were to be met, but the second brought bravery with it, and he nobly offered to beard the Russian lioness in her den, explain the view Paris took of her unjustifiable conduct, and, if possible, bring her to reason.

Caspilier's emotion overcame him, and he wept silently, while his friend, in eloquent language, told how famous authors, whose names were France's proudest possession, had been forgiven by their wives for slight lapses from strict domesticity, and these instances, he said, he would recount to Madame Valdorème, and so induce her to follow such illustrious examples.

The two comrades embraced and separated; the friend to use his influence and powers of persuasion with Valdorème; the husband to tell Tenise how blessed they were for having such a friend to intercede for them; for Tenise, bright little Parisienne that she was, bore no malice against the unreasonable wife of her lover.

Henri Lacour paused opposite the pastry-shop on the Rue de Russie that bore the name of 'Valorème' over the temptingly filled windows. Madame Caspilier had not changed the title of her well-known shop when she gave up her own name. Lacour caught sight of her serving her customers, and he thought she looked more like a Russian princess than a shopkeeper. He wondered now at the preference of his friend for the petite black-haired model. Valorème did not seem more than twenty; she was large, and strikingly handsome, with abundant auburn hair that was almost red. Her beautifully moulded chin denoted perhaps too much firmness, and was in striking contrast to the weakness of her husband's lower face. Lacour almost trembled as she seemed to flash one look directly at him, and, for a moment, he feared she had seen him loitering before the window. Her eyes were large, of a limpid amber colour, but deep within them smouldered a fire that Lacour felt he would not care to see blaze up. His task now wore a different aspect from what it had worn in front of the Café Égalité. Hesitating a moment, he passed the shop, and, stopping at a neighbouring café, ordered another glass of absinthe. It is astonishing how rapidly the genial influence of this stimulant departs!

Fortified once again, he resolved to act before his courage had time to evaporate, and so, goading himself on with the thought that no man should be afraid to meet any woman, be she Russian or civilized, he entered the shop, making his most polite bow to Madame Caspilier.

'I have come, madame,' he began, 'as the friend of your husband, to talk with you regarding his affairs.'

'Ah!' said Valorème; and Henri saw with dismay the fires deep down in her eyes rekindle. But she merely gave some instructions to an assistant, and, turning to Lacour, asked him to be so good as to follow her.

She led him through the shop and up the stairs at the back, throwing open a door on the first floor. Lacour entered a neat drawing-room, with windows opening out upon the street. Madame Caspilier seated herself at a table, resting her elbow upon it, shading her eyes with her hand, and yet Lacour felt them searching his very soul.

'Sit down,' she said. 'You are my husband's friend. What have you to say?'

Now, it is a difficult thing for a man to tell a beautiful woman that her husband—for the moment—prefers someone else, so Lacour began on generalities. He said a poet might be likened to a butterfly, or perhaps to the more industrious bee, who sipped nectar from every flower, and so enriched the world. A poet was a law unto himself, and should not be judged harshly from what might be termed a shopkeeping point of view. Then Lacour, warming to his work, gave many instances where the wives of great men had condoned and even encouraged their husband's little idiosyncrasies, to the great augmenting of our most valued literature.

Now and then, as this eloquent man talked, Valorème's eyes seemed to flame dangerously in the shadow, but the woman neither moved nor interrupted him while he spoke When he had finished, her voice sounded cold and unimpassioned, and he felt with relief that the outbreak he had feared was at least postponed.

'You would advise me then,' she began, 'to do as the wife of that great novelist did, and invite my husband and the woman he admires to my table?'

'Oh, I don't say I could ask you to go so far as that,' said Lacour; 'but—'

'I'm no halfway woman. It is all or nothing with me. If I invited my husband to dine with me, I would also invite this creature——What is her name? Tenise, you say. Well, I would invite her too. Does she know he is a married man?'

'Yes,' cried Lacour eagerly; 'but I assure you, madame, she has nothing but the kindliest feelings towards you. There is no jealousy about Tenise.'

'How good of her! How very good of her!' said the Russian woman, with such bitterness that Lacour fancied uneasily that he had somehow made an injudicious remark, whereas all his efforts were concentrated in a desire to conciliate and please.

'Very well,' said Valorème, rising, 'You may tell my husband that you have been successful in your mission. Tell him that I will provide for them both. Ask them to honour me with their presence at breakfast tomorrow morning at twelve o'clock. If he wants money, as you say, here are two hundred francs, which will perhaps be sufficient for his wants until midday tomorrow.'

Lacour thanked her with a profuse graciousness that would have delighted any ordinary giver, but Valorème stood impassive like a tragedy queen, and seemed only anxious that he should speedily take his departure, now that his errand was done.

The heart of the poet was filled with joy when he heard from his friend that at last Valorème had come to regard his union with Tenise in the light of reason. Caspilier, as he embraced Lacour, admitted that perhaps there was something to be said for his wife after all.

The poet dressed himself with more than usual care on the day of the feast, and Tenise, who accompanied him, put on some of the finery that had been bought with Valorème's donation. She confessed that she thought Eugène's wife had acted with consideration towards them, but maintained that she did not wish to meet her, for, judging from Caspilier's account, his wife must be a somewhat formidable and terrifying person; still she went with him, she said, solely through good nature, and a desire to heal family differences. Tenise would do anything in the cause of domestic peace.

The shop assistant told the pair, when they had dismissed the cab, that madame was waiting for them upstairs. In the drawing-room Valdorème was standing with her back to the window like a low-browed goddess, her tawny hair loose over her shoulders, and the pallor of her face made more conspicuous by her costume of unrelieved black. Caspilier, with the grace characteristic of him, swept off his hat, and made a low, deferential bow; but when he straightened himself up, and began to say the complimentary things and poetical phrases he had put together for the occasion at the café the night before, the lurid look of the Russian made his tongue falter; and Tenise, who had never seen a woman of this sort before, laughed a nervous, half-frightened little laugh, and clung closer to her lover than before. The wife was even more forbidding than she had imagined. Valdorème shuddered slightly when she saw this intimate movement on the part of her rival, and her hand clenched and unclenched convulsively.

'Come,' she said, cutting short her husband's halting harangue, and sweeping past them, drawing her skirts aside on nearing Tenise, she led the way up to the dining-room a floor higher.

'I'm afraid of her,' whimpered Tenise, holding back. 'She will poison us.'

'Nonsense,' said Caspilier, in a whisper. 'Come along. She is too fond of me to attempt anything of that kind, and you are safe when I am here.'

Valdorème sat at the head of the table, with her husband at her right hand and Tenise on her left. The breakfast was the best either of them had ever tasted. The hostess sat silent, but no second talker was needed when the poet was present. Tenise laughed merrily now and then at his bright sayings, for the excellence of the meal had banished her fears of poison.

'What penetrating smell is this that fills the room? Better open the window,' said Caspilier.

'It is nothing,' replied Valdorème, speaking for the first time since they had sat down. 'It is only naphtha. I have had this room cleaned with it. The window won't open, and if it would, we could not hear you talk with the noise from the street.'

The poet would suffer anything rather than have his eloquence interfered with, so he said no more about the fumes of the naphtha. When the coffee was brought in, Valdorème dismissed the trim little maid who had waited on them.

'I have some of your favourite cigarettes here. I will get them.'

She arose, and, as she went to the table on which the boxes lay, she quietly and deftly locked the door, and, pulling out the key, slipped it into her pocket.

'Do you smoke, mademoiselle?' she asked, speaking to Tenise. She had not recognized her presence before.

'Sometimes, madame,' answered the girl, with a titter.

'You will find these cigarettes excellent. My husband's taste in cigarettes is better than in many things. He prefers the Russian to the French.'

Caspilier laughed loudly.

'That's a slap at you, Tenise,' he said.

'At me? Not so; she speaks of cigarettes, and I myself prefer the Russian, only they are so expensive.'

A look of strange eagerness came into Valdorème's expressive face, softened by a touch of supplication. Her eyes were on her husband, but she said rapidly to the girl——

'Stop a moment, mademoiselle. Do not light your cigarette until I give the word.'

Then to her husband she spoke beseechingly in Russian, a language she had taught him in the early months of their marriage.

'Yevgenii, Yevgenii! Don't you see the girl's a fool? How can you care for her? She would be as happy with the first man she met in the street. I—I think only of you. Come back to me, Yevgenii!'

She leaned over the table towards him, and in her vehemence clasped his wrist. The girl watched them both with a smile. It reminded her of a scene in an opera she had heard once in a strange language. The prima donna had looked and pleaded like Valdorème.

Caspilier shrugged his shoulders, but did not withdraw his wrist from her firm grasp.

'Why go over the whole weary ground again?' he said. 'If it were not Tenise, it would be somebody else. I was never meant for a constant husband, Val. I understood from Lacour that we were to have no more of this nonsense.'

She slowly relaxed her hold on his unresisting wrist. The old, hard look came into her face as she drew a deep breath. The fire in the depths of her amber eyes rekindled, as the softness went out of them.

'You may light your cigarette now, mademoiselle,' she said almost in a whisper to Tenise.

'I swear I could light mine in your eyes, Val,' cried her husband. 'You would make a name for yourself on the stage. I will write a tragedy for you, and we will——'

Tenise struck the match. A simultaneous flash of lightning and clap of thunder filled the room. The glass in the window fell clattering into the street. Valdorème was standing with her back against the door. Tenise, fluttering her helpless little hands before her, tottered shrieking to the broken window. Caspilier, staggering panting to his feet, gasped—

'You Russian devil! The key, the key!'

He tried to clutch her throat, but she pushed him back.

'Go to your Frenchwoman. She's calling for help.'

Tenise sank by the window, one burning arm hanging over the sill, and was silent. Caspilier, mechanically beating back the fire from his shaking head, whimpering and sobbing, fell against the table, and then went headlong in the floor.

Valdorème, a pillar of fire, swaying gently to and fro, before the door, whispered in a voice of agony—

'Oh, Eugène, Eugène!' and flung herself like a flaming angel—or fiend—on the prostrate form of the man.

A Queer Cicerone

Bernard Capes

I had paid my sixpence at the little informal 'box-office,' and received in exchange my printed permit to visit the Castle. It was one of those lordly 'show places' whose owners take a plain business view of the attractions at their disposal, while ostensibly exploiting them on behalf of this or that charity. How the exclusive spirits of old, represented on their walls in the numerous pictured forms they once inhabited, regard this converting of their pride and panoply to practical ends, is a matter for their descendants to judge; but no doubt the most of them owed, and still owe, a debt to humanity, any liquidation of which in terms of charity would be enough to reconcile them to the indignity of being regarded like a waxworks. For my part, I am free to confess that, did I see any profit in an ancestor, I should apply it unequivocally to the charity that begins at home.

I discovered, when I entered, quite a little party waiting to be personally conducted round the rooms. Obviously trippers of the most commonplace type (and what was I better?), they stood herded together in a sort of gelid ante-chamber, pending the arrival of the housekeeper who was to act as cicerone. A hovering menial, in the nature of a commissionaire, had just disappeared in quest of the errant lady, and for the moment we were left unshepherded.

Assuming the nonchalant air of a chance visitor of distinction to whom palaces were familiar, I casually, while sauntering aloof from it, took the measure of my company. It was not in the least unusual or interesting. It comprised a couple of rather sickly 'gents' of the haberdashery type; two flat ladies in pince-nez, patently in search of culture and instruction; a huge German tourist, all bush and spectacles, with a mighty sandwich-box slung over his shoulder, and a voice of guttural ferocity; an ample but diffident matron, accompanied by a small youth in clumping boots and a new ready-made Norfolk suit a size too large for him, and, finally, a pair of tittering hobble-skirted young ladies, of the class that parades pavements arm-in-arm. All whispered in their separate groups, each suspicious of the other, but with voices universally hushed to the sacred solemnity of the occasion. Only the German showed a disposition to truculent neighbourliness, proffering some advances to the hobble-skirted damsels, which were first haughtily, and then gigglingly, ignored. Whereat the flat ladies, though intellectually addicted to his race, showed their sense of his unflattering preference by turning their back on him.

The room in which we were delayed was the first of a suite, and very chill and melancholy in its few appointments. There were some arms, I remember, on the walls, and a sprinkling of antlers—of all mural decorations the most petrifyingly depressing. They offered no scope to my assumption of critical ease, and—conscious of an inquisition, a little derisive, I thought, in its quality, on the part of the company—I was gravitating towards the general group, when we were all galvanized into animation by hearing the sound of a light, quick footfall approaching us from the direction of the room we were about to traverse. It tripped on, awakening innumerable small echoes in its advance, and suddenly materialized before us in the form of a very elegant gentleman, of young middle-age and distinguished appearance.

'Permit me,' he said, halting, hand on heart, with an inimitable bow. 'I make it my pleasure to represent for the nonce the admirable but unctuous Mrs Somerset, our valued housekeeper, who is unfortunately indisposed for the moment.'

I could flatter myself at least that my manner had so far impressed the party as to cause it to constitute me by mute agreement its spokesman. I accepted, as they all looked towards me, the compliment for what it implied, though with a certain stiffness which was due as much to surprise as to embarrassment. For surely courtesy, in the person of this distinguished stranger, was taking a course as unusual as the clothes he inhabited were strange. They consisted of a dark blue, swallow-tailed coat, with a high velvet collar and brass buttons, a voluminous stock, a buff waistcoat, and mouse-coloured tights, having a bunch of seals pendent from their fob and ending in smart pumps. His hair, ample and dusty golden, was brushed high from his forehead in a sort of ordered mane; the face underneath was an ironically handsome one, but so startingly pale that the blue eyes fixed in it suggested nothing so much as the 'antique jewels set in Parian marble stone' of a once famous poem. He bowed again, and to me, accepting the general verdict.

'It is most good of you,' I said. 'Of course, if we had known, if we had had any idea——'

He interrupted me, I thought, with a little impatience:

'Not at all. It is, as I informed you, a pleasure—a rare opportunity. I fancy I may promise you a fuller approximation to the truth, regarding certain of our family traditions, than you would ever be likely to attain through the lips of the meritorious but diplomatic Somerset.'

He turned, inviting us, with an incomparable gesture, into the next room. He was certainly an anachronism, a marvel; yet I was willing to admit to myself that eccentrics, sartorial and otherwise, were not confined to the inner circle of society. As to the others, I perceived that they were self-defensively prepared to accept this oddity as part of the mysterious ritual appertaining to the sacred obscurities of the life patrician.

'The first two rooms,' said our guide, halting us on the threshold, 'are, as you will perceive, appropriated to family portraits. The little furniture that remains is inconsiderable and baroque. It is what survives from the time of the fourth marquis. We observe his portrait here' (he signified a canvas on the wall, representing a dull, arrogant-looking old gentleman in an embroidered coat and a bob-wig), 'and can readily associate with it the tasteless ostentation which characterized his reign. He was really what we should call now a complete aristocratic bounder.'

His tone suggested a mixture of flippancy and malice, which was none the less emphatic because his voice was a peculiarly soft and secret one. Somehow, hearing it, I thought of slanders sniggered from behind a covering hand. The young ladies tittered, as if a little shamefaced and uneasy, drawing his attention to them. He was obviously attracted at once. Their smart modernity, piquant in its way, proved a charm to him that he made no pretence of discounting. He addressed himself instantly to the two:

'Sacred truth, ladies, upon my honour. He was a "throw-back," as we say of dogs. The mark of the prosperous cheesemonger was all over him.'

'Ach!' said the German, vibratingly asserting himself, 'a dror-back? Vot is dart?'

'A Teutonic reaction,' said the stranger, taking the speaker's measure insolently, with his chin a little lifted, and his eyes narrowed; 'or rather a recrudescence of barbarism in a race or line that has emerged from it. Your countrymen, from what I hear, should afford many illustrations of the process.'

The flat ladies exchanged a little scornful laugh, which they repeated less disguisedly as the German responded: 'I do not ondorrstand.'

The common little boy, holding to his mother's skirts, urged her on to the next picture, a full-length portrait of a grim Elizabethan warrior in armour.

'Look at his long sword, mother!' he whispered.

'*He* didn't wear corsets—not much,' said one of the haberdashery youths facetiously, in an audible voice to the other; and the nearest spinster, with a sidelong stare of indignation at him, edged away.

'A crusader?' said the second flat lady, as if putting it to herself. 'I wonder, now.'

The stranger smiled ironically to the hobble-skirts, one of whom was emboldened to ask him:

'Was he one of the family, sir?'

'By Heraldry out of Wardour Street,' answered our guide. 'Very dark horses, both of them.' And then he added, going a few steps: 'You do us too much honour, sweet charmer—positively you do.' He tapped the portrait of a ponderous patrician: 'The first marquis,' he said, 'created in 1784 out of nothing. The King represented the Almighty in that stupendous achievement. God save the King!'

'Let's go, mother,' whispered the small common boy, pressing suddenly against the ample skirts. 'I don't like it.'

'Hush, 'Enery dear,' she returned, in a whispered panic. 'There ain't nothing to be afraid of.'

'Wasn't there none of you before that, sir?' asked the second haberdashery youth.

The stranger sniggered.

'I'll let you all into a little secret,' he said confidently. 'The antiquity of the family, despite our ingenious Mrs Somerset, is mere hocus-pocus. The first marquis's grandfather was a Huntingdonshire dairy-farmer, who amassed a considerable fortune over cheeses. He came to London, speculated in South Sea stock, and sold out at top prices just before the crash. We don't like it talked about, you know; but it was his grandson who was the real founder of the house. He was in the Newcastle administration of '57, and was ennobled for the owlish part he took in opposing the reconquest of India under Clive. And, after that, the more fatheaded he became, the higher they foisted him to get him out of the way. Fact, I assure you. Our crest should be by rights a Stilton rampant, our arms a cheese-scoop, silver on a trencher powdered mitee, and our motto, in your own admirable vernacular, "Ain't I the cheese!" '

The young ladies tittered, sharing a little protesting wriggle between him. Then one urged the other, who responded *sotto voce:* 'Ask him yourself, stupid.'

'Charmed,' said the stranger. 'Those roguish lips have only to command.'

'We only wanted to know,' said number two blushfully, 'which is the wicked lord—don't push so, Dolly!'

'Ah!' The stranger showed his teeth in a stiffly creased smile, and shook a long forefinger remonstrantly at the speaker. 'You have been studying that outrageous guide-book, I perceive. What is the passage—eh? "Reputed to have been painted by a mysterious travelling artist of sinister appearance, who, being invited in one night to play with his lordship, subsequently liquidated the debt he incurred by painting his host's portrait." '

He turned on his heel and pointed into the next room. Full in our view opposite the door appeared a glazed frame, but black and empty in seeming—an effect I supposed to be due to the refraction of light upon its surface.

'A most calumniated individual,' he protested, wheeling round again. 'There is his place; we shall come to it presently; but only, I regret, to find it vacant. A matter of restoration, you see, and much to be deplored at the moment. I should have liked to challenge your verdict, face to face with him. These libels die hard—and when given the authority of a guide-book! Take my word for it, he was a most estimable creature, morally worth dozens of the sanctimonious humbugs glorified in the Somerset hagiology. Pah! I am weary, I tell you, of hearing their false virtues extolled. But wait a minute, and you shall learn. The "wicked lord," young misses? And so he is the flattered siderite of your regard. Well, it is well to be sought by such eyes on any count; but I think his would win your leniency. Only excess of love proved his undoing; and I am sure you would not consider that a crime.'

We were all struck a little dumb, I think, by this outburst. The two girls had linked together again, both silent and somewhat white; the gaunt spinsters, rigid and upright, exchanged petrified glances; the fat woman was mopping her face, a tremulous sigh fluttering the hem of her handkerchief; the two young shopmen dwelt slack-jawed; even the German tourist, glaring through his spectacles, shook a little in his breathing, as if a sudden asthma had caught him. But our host, as though unconscious of the effect he had produced, motioned us on smilingly; and so, mechanically obeying, we paused at the next canvas—the uncompleted full-length of a beautiful young woman with haunting eyes.

'The Lady Betty,' he said, 'as she sat for "Innocence" to Schleimhitz. The portrait was only finished, as you see, as far as the waist. He was a slow worker, and not good at drapery.'

The German cleared his throat, and pushing his way past the flat ladies (I thought for the moment one was near furiously hooking at him with her umbrella), glanced with an air of amorous appropriation at the hobble-skirts, and spoke:

'Schleimhitz wass fery goot at drapery. There wass a reason berhaps——'

'Ah—tut—tut!' exclaimed the stranger, with a little hurried smile; and led us on.

'Portrait,' he said, 'by Gainsborough, of a boy—unidentified. There was a story of his having been mislaid by his father, the second marquis, on the occasion of that gentleman's first marriage, and never discovered again.'

'Poor little chap,' murmured one of the hobble-skirts. 'I wonder what became of him? Isn't he pretty?'

'An ancestress,' said our cicerone, at the next canvas, 'who married an actor. He played first gentleman on the stage, and first cad off it. I believe he broke her heart—or her spirit; I forget which. She kept them both in one decanter.' He sniggered round at the two girls. 'No, 'pon honour,' he said, 'I vow to the truth of it. You must trust me above Mrs Somerset.

'A collateral branch this,' he said, passing on. 'He buried three wives, who lie and whisper together in the family vault. He himself was buried, by his own direction, at sea. They say the coffin hissed as it touched the water.'

The little common boy suddenly began to cry loudly.

'I'm frightened, mother!' he wailed. 'Take me away.'

The stranger, bending to look for him, made as if to claw through the group. I saw a most diabolical expression on his face.

'Ah!' he said, 'I'll have you yet!'

The child screamed violently, and beat in frantic terror against his mother. I interposed, an odd damp on my forehead.

'Look here,' I said; 'leave the boy alone, will you?'

They were all backing, startled and scared, when there came a hurried, loud step into the room from behind us, and we turned in a panic huddle. It was the commissionaire, very flustered and irate.

'Now, then, you know,' he said, 'you'd no right to take it upon yourselves to go round like this unattended.'

'Pardon me,' I said, resuming my charge of spokesman; 'we did nothing of the sort. This gentleman offered himself to escort us.'

I turned, as did all the others, and my voice died in my throat. There was no gentleman at all—the room was empty. As I stood stupidly staring, I was conscious of the voice of the commissionaire, aggrieved, expostulatory, but with a curious note of distress in it:

'What gentleman? There's nobody has the right but Mrs Somerset, and she's ill—she's had a stroke. We've just found her in her room, with a face like the horrors on her.'

Suddenly one of the women shrieked hysterically: 'O look! He's there! O come away!'

And, as she screamed, I saw. The empty picture frame in the next room was empty no longer. It was filled by the form of him, handsome and smiling, he who had just been conducting us round the walls.

The Rag Thing

Donald A. Wollheim

It would have been all right if spring had never come. During the winter nothing had happened and nothing was likely to happen as long as the weather remained cold and Mrs. Larch kept the radiators going. In a way, though, it is quite possible to hold Mrs. Larch to blame for everything that happened. Not that she had what people would call malicious intentions, but just that she was two things practically every boarding-house landlady is—thrifty and not too clean.

She shouldn't have been in such a hurry to turn the heat off so early in March. March is a tricky month and she should have known that the first warm day is usually an isolated phenomenon. But then you could always claim that she shouldn't have been so sloppy in her cleaning last November. She shouldn't have dropped that rag behind the radiator in the third floor front room.

As a matter of fact, one could well wonder what she was doing using such a rag anyway. Polishing furniture doesn't require a clean rag to start with, certainly not the rag you stick into the furniture polish, that's going to be greasy anyway—but she didn't have to use that particular rag. The one that had so much dried blood on it from the meat that had been lying on it in the kitchen.

On top of that, it is probable that she had spit into the filthy thing, too. Mrs. Larch was no prize package. Gross, dull, unkempt, widowed and careless, she fitted into the house—one of innumerable other brownstone fronts in the lower sixties of New York. Houses that in former days, fifty or sixty years ago, were considered the height of fashion and the residences of the well to-do, now reduced to dingy rooming places for all manner of itinerants, lonely people with no hope in life other than dreary jobs, or an occasional young and confused person from the hinterland seeking fame and fortune in a city which rarely grants it.

So it was not particularly odd that when she accidentally dropped the filthy old rag behind the radiator in the room on the third floor late in November, she had simply left it there and forgotten to pick it up.

It gathered dust all winter, unnoticed. Skelty, who had the room, might have cleaned it out himself save that he was always too tired for that. He worked at some indefinite factory all day and when he came home he was always too tired to do much more than read the sports and comic pages of the newspapers and then maybe stare at the streaky brown walls a bit before dragging himself into bed to sleep the dreamless sleep of the weary.

The radiator, a steam one, oddly enough (for most of these houses used the older hot-air circulation), was in none too good condition. Installed many, many years ago by the house's last Victorian owner, it was given to knocks, leaks, and cantankerous action. Along in December it developed a slow drip, and drops of hot water would fall to seep slowly into the floor and leave the rag lying on a moist, hot surface. Steam was constantly escaping from a bad valve that Mrs. Larch would have repaired if it had blown off completely but, because the radiator always managed to be hot, never did.

Because Mrs. Larch feared draughts, the windows were rarely open in the winter and the room would become oppressively hot at times when Skelty was away.

It is hard to say what is the cause of chemical reactions. Some hold that all things are mechanical in nature, others that life has a psychic side which cannot be duplicated in laboratories. The problem is one for metaphysicians; everyone knows that some chemicals are attracted to heat, others to light, and they may not necessarily be alive at all. *Tropisms* is the scientific term used, and if you want to believe that living matter is stuff with a great number of tropisms, and dead matter is stuff with little or no tropisms, that's one way of looking at it. Heat and moisture and greasy chemical compounds were the sole ingredients of the birth of life in some ancient unremembered swamp.

Which is why it probably would have been all right if spring had never come. Because Mrs. Larch turned the radiators off one day early in March. The warm hours were few. It grew cold with the darkness and by night it was back in the chill of February again. But Mrs. Larch had turned the heat off and, being lazy, decided not to turn it on again 'til the next morning provided, of course, that it stayed cold next day (which it did).

Anyway, Skelty was found dead in bed the next morning. Mrs. Larch knocked on his door when he failed to come down to breakfast and when he hadn't answered, she turned the knob and went in. He was lying in bed, blue and cold, and he had been smothered in his sleep.

There was quite a to-do about the whole business, but nothing came of it. A few stupid detectives blundered around the room, asked silly questions, made a few notes, and then left the matter to the coroner and the morgue. Skelty was a nobody, no one cared whether he lived or died, he had no enemies and no friends, there were no suspicious visitors, and he had probably smothered accidentally in the blankets. Of course the body was unusually cold when Mrs. Larch found it, as if the heat had been sucked out of him, but who notices a thing like that? They also discounted the grease smudge on the top sheet, the grease stains on the floor, and the slime on his face. Probably some grease he might have been using for some imagined skin trouble, though Mrs. Larch had not heard of his doing so. In any case, no one really cared.

Mrs. Larch wore black for a day and then advertised in the papers. She made a perfunctory job of cleaning the room. Skelty's possessions were taken away by a drab sister-in-law from Brooklyn who didn't seem to care much either, and Mrs. Larch was all ready to rent the room to someone else.

The weather remained cold for the next ten days and the heat was kept up in the pipes.

The new occupant of the room was a nervous young man from upstate who was trying to get a job in New York. He was a high-strung young man who entertained any number of illusions about life and society. He thought that people did things for the love of it and he wanted to find a job where he could work for that motivation rather than the sort of things he might have done back home. He thought New York was different, which was a mistake.

He smoked like fury, which was something Mrs. Larch did not like, because it meant ashes on the floor and burned spots on her furniture (not that there weren't plenty already), but there was nothing Mrs. Larch would do about it, because it would have meant exertion.

After four days in New York, this young man, Gorman by name, was more nervous than ever. He would lie in bed nights smoking cigarette after cigarette, thinking and thinking and getting nowhere. Over and over he was facing the problem of resigning himself to a life of grey drab. It was a thought he had tried not to face and now that it was thrusting itself upon him, it was becoming intolerable.

The next time a warm day came, Mrs. Larch left the radiators on because she was not going to be fooled twice. As a result, when the weather stayed warm, the rooms became insufferably hot, because she was still keeping the windows down. So that when she turned the heat off finally, the afternoon of the second day, it was pretty tropic in the rooms.

When the March weather turned about suddenly again and became chilly about nine at night, Mrs. Larch was going to bed and figured that no one would complain and that it would be warm again the next day. Which may or may not be true, it does not matter.

Gorman got home about ten, opened the window, got undressed, moved a pack of cigarettes and ash tray next to his bed on the floor, got into bed, turned out the light and started to smoke.

He stared at the ceiling, blowing smoke upward into the darkened room, trying to see its outlines in the dim light coming in from the street. When he finished one cigarette, he let his hand dangle out the side of the bed and picked up another cigarette from the pack on the floor, lit it from the butt in his mouth, and dropped the butt into the ash tray on the floor.

The rag under the radiator was getting cold, the room was getting cold, there was one source of heat radiation in the room. That was the man in the bed. Skelty had proven a source of heat supply once. Heat attraction was chemical force that could not be denied. Strange forces began to accumulate in the long-transformed fibres of the rag.

Gorman thought he heard something flap in the room, but he paid no attention. Things were always creaking in the house. Gorman heard a swishing noise and ascribed it to the mice.

Gorman reached down for a cigarette, fumbled for it, found the pack, deftly extracted a smoke in the one-handed manner chain smokers become accustomed to, lifted it to his mouth, lit it from the burning butt in his mouth, and reached down with the butt to crush it out against the tray.

He pressed the butt into something wet like a used handkerchief, there was a sudden hiss, something coiled and whipped about his wrist; Gorman gasped and drew his hand back fast. A flaming horror, twisting and writhing, was curled around it. Before Gorman could shriek, it had whipped itself from his hand and fastened over his face, over the warm, heat-radiating skin and the glowing flame of the cigarette.

Mrs. Larch was awakened by the clang of fire engines. When the fire was put out, most of the third floor had been gutted. Gorman was an unrecognizable charred mass.

The fire department put the blaze down to Gorman's habit of smoking in bed. Mrs. Larch collected on the fire insurance and bought a new house, selling the old one to a widow who wanted to start a boarding house.

The Rajah's Gift

E. Hoffman Price

Strange tales are told of the rajah of Lacra-Kai, of the justice he dealt, of the rewards he gave; but the strangest of all these many tales is that of the gift he gave to Zaid, the Persian who had served him long and well. A crafty man was the rajah, who by his devices had retained the sovereignty of his petty state almost unimpaired by British rule. In short, he was an enlightened prince who was left quite to his own devices as regarded the internal administration of his state. But it is of his gift to Zaid whereof we are to deal.

In the privacy of his palace, screened from the view of his people, the rajah was quite European, dispensing with the pomp and formality that is supposed to surround all eastern rulers at all times. Therefore it was that Zaid the Persian, who had served his master long and well, not only sat, but also smoked as he listened.

"Zaid," the prince was saying, "but for your courage and fidelity I would surely have been assassinated. Name whatsoever you desire and it shall be yours, for I mean to reward you richly."

"My lord," replied Zaid, "there is but one request that I make, and that is mad beyond all conception of madness . . ."

"Nevertheless, let me hear it; tell me what is on your mind. Forget that I am rajah, and consider me but as your friend who is indebted to you. Speak freely."

"For ten years I have been favored by your magnificence," began Zaid, speaking slowly. "For ten years I have been the friend of kings; but all that is nothing."

Zaid paused. A far-away look had crept over his features; he seemed to be gazing through and beyond the rajah, and back to some dimly remembered, almost forgotten episode of the past. And then, picking his words as one groping in the dark picks his steps, he told how, twenty years previous, he had stood on the edge of the crowd in the square before the great temple of Kali, awaiting the arrival of the procession at whose head the present rajah would be riding. Zaid, a boy scarcely a dozen years old, ragged, dirty, half-starved, stood that day to watch the rajah ride past in the concentrated, fiery splendor that marked a prince's accession to his throne. And all this the boy saw, yet saw not, for he had eyes for none but the rajah. High above the crowd, on the back of a great elephant he sat, dark, calm, impassive as a god. Not as a man, exultant, but rather as some high, passionless fate solemnly advancing across the wastes of space. The prince was oblivious of the pomp and splendor, oblivious of the tumult and applause; on that day it seemed to Zaid that he saw not a man, but destiny itself in march. And as the rajah drew near, the great temple gong clanged with a reverberation that seemed to shake the very base of the universe; a strange, unearthly vibration that mingled with the resonance of brass, the hiss of serpents and the rustle of silk; a sound that rose and fell, resonant, sonorous, awful. At the sound of that gong, at the sight of that impassive face, a great madness possessed Zaid, so that his blood became as a stream of flame. And he swore that he, too, would some day ride in such a procession, would bear himself with that same godlike hauteur, that same superb arrogance; he, Zaid, hungry beggar-lad dared have such a vision.

Silent were the gongs; vanished the procession; and the new rajah ruled in Lacra-Kai. But with Zaid the vision remained, following him over half the earth, and returning with him to Lacra-Kai, where, ten years later, he entered the service of that same rajah, and, by strange turns of fortune, rose to rank and power in that same court.

Such was the tale Zaid told the rajah.

"You have indeed prospered." Then, suddenly, "And all this is apropos of what?"

Zaid started, as one waking from a dream, then laughed oddly.

"For twenty years that vision has haunted me. Much has happened since then; much have I seen and experienced, but through it all, this desire has persisted. And at last it happened that I entered your service, and that, having served you well, it has pleased you to grant me whatsoever I might desire. Let me ride as I saw you ride twenty years ago."

Whereat the rajah replied in the tone of one who denies some child a dangerous toy: "To grant you that favor would be to sign your death-warrant. Were you to ride thus at noon, poison or dagger would find you before dawn; for no man may enjoy such a mark of favor and live. What? Have you lived in this land all these years and do not realize the penalty you would pay? Consider a moment: my son is dead; the succession to the throne lay among my three nephews. One of them sought to hasten his succession. The plot was discovered, and the plotter I punished by showing him a mark of extraordinary favor. Immediately it was rumored about that I had selected him as my heir; and within ten days he died. But not by my command. That was superfluous. The princes of the blood, and the lords of the court. . . ."

The rajah made a suggestive, sweeping gesture, then continued, "Me you were able to save from assassination; yourself you could not save, nor could I save you. You would ride in state; rumors would drift about. And you know the rest."

"I know the rest. But I will take my chance. It is not good for a man to cherish a vision, however mad, without having made some effort to attain it."

"Think again, Zaid, think again! Choose whatsoever else you will . . . a lakh of rupees . . . ten lakhs if you will . . . jewels the like of which you have never dreamed . . . and I have dancing girls . . . all this, and more is yours, for you have served me well; it is to you that I owe my life. Be reasonable, friend, be reasonable."

"Be reasonable? For me there is no reason. This vision has haunted me entirely too long. So, though it may cost me my life, let me see it to a finish. For there at least would be a roundness, a completeness that in no way else could I attain. In the square before the great temple of Kali I found the inspiration that led me to enter your service, to attain your favor, to serve you well; and in that same square, if need be, I will meet my doom. The cycle will be complete. After that, let come what may, for I shall have cheated destiny of the rare gift of satisfaction, the gift so often denied to kings. And after all, is the assassin so sure of finding me?"

The rajah smiled as one upon whom great understanding has suddenly descended.

"Zaid," he said, "you are more than ever a man after my own heart. Mad, stark mad and raving; I understand, for I, too, have been haunted by visions. But none has understood my thoughts, even as none would understand your mad desire. It would be misconstrued, and . . , you know the result."

Suddenly the rajah arose.

"Come, Zaid, let me tempt you with the things I have but named."

And Zaid was led through treasure-vaults full of gilded arms and armor, trays of flaming jewels, great chests of age-old coins, dinars and mohurs of gold, the secreted plunder of a hundred generations.

"All this leaves you unmoved? Then let me try again."

The Persian accompanied his master to the very heart of the palace, to a hall overshadowed with twilight—a broad, spacious hall whose walls were curiously carved with strange figures in odd postures, engaged in strange diversions. And then his ears were caressed by the soft, sensuously wailing notes of reed and stringed instruments: his senses were stirred by the dull pulsing of atabals, throbbing like a heart racked with passion. And through the purple gloom of incense-fumes he saw the lithe, swaying, gilded bodies of dancing girls, slim and beautiful. One, emerging from the figures of the dance, slowly advanced and made obeisance before the rajah.

"And this is Nilofal. Should she please you. . . ."

The Persian saw that she was perfection, outstripping voluptuous fancy. But when he turned to reply, the rajah had disappeared; and the door through which they had entered was barred.

Nilofal failed in her efforts to separate the Persian from his madness.

Once again Zaid stood before the rajah, who smiled with the air of one whose cleverness has just reaped its reward in the solution of a difficult problem.

"What now, Zaid? Was Nilofal to your taste? Surely she must have been; and certainly she is worth all the dreams that have haunted men since the beginning of time."

"My lord," replied the Persian, "you have tempted me as man has never before been tempted; yet am I to sacrifice the vision of twenty years in favor of a treasure-vault and a lupanar? Although you may refuse it, I nevertheless hold fast to my first desire."

"So be it then; and tomorrow at noon you shall see it satisfied."

And then and there were preparations made for Zaid to ride in royal state through the streets of Lacra-Kai.

Noon, the next day. The rajah, watching from the roof of his palace, saw Zaid in the gilded howdah, mounted on the elephant that carried none but princes of the blood. Calm and serene and godlike sat the Persian: a king he seemed, and the descendant of a hundred kings, for at that moment he was about to fulfil his destiny. Once again understanding came to the rajah.

"It was wrong that I tried to dissuade him," reflected the rajah, "for whatever the end may be, it will be as nothing; Zaid is about to accomplish that which he set out to do when he was a beggar. There is something heroic in this madness . . . but what will happen when he passes the temple of Kali? Can he ever become a man again? . . . for in his madness he is more than a man; he has overturned destiny to fulfil a childish fancy. . . ."

And the prince, watching the procession get under way, was lost in admiration of the man who for half an hour would be rajah.

"And having attained his dream, will not the man Zaid have died, though he live a hundred years thereafter in security? And what would life mean to him?"

The procession, turning, had taken Zaid from the rajah's view. Bestirring himself from his revery, he whispered a few words to Al Tarik, his trusted servant.

". . . And do not fail me in the slightest detail."

The rajah repeated his instructions. Al Tarik departed. And in the meanwhile, Zaid rode to the fulfilment of his dreams.

Through the streets of Lacra-Kai the procession wound. The Persian bore himself not as a man but as the avatar of some god returning to judge the world.

412

On and on he rode, like the slow, sure march of destiny, immutable, irresistible. And but one thought flitted through his brain, the words of some long-forgotten sage: "When indeed they do grant to a man the realization of his dream, they straightway reach forth to snatch from him his prize, lest in his triumph he become god-like and toss them from their thrones."

He smiled. Swift indeed would have to be their envy to defeat him; the temple of Kali was at hand. The great gong in the temple rang, reverberating like the crash of doom, filling the entire universe with its shivering resonance— full-throated, colossal, then hissing with the rustle of silk—a sound that swelled, and died, and rose again.

As slowly as some animated Juggernaut the elephant advanced, pace by pace, deliberately, majestically, as though each step took him from world to world. And again the gong, touched to life by the mallet wielded by a temple slave, rolled forth its sonorous, vibrant crash.

A few more steps, and Zaid, the Persian, whom the rajah loved to honor, was before the temple of Kali. High as Rama going forth to conquer the world; no longer a man, but transfigured beyond recognition. Again the temple gong gave forth its vibrant note, reverberant, awful; diminishing, then rising and swelling again. And the god, who but half an hour before had been Zaid, toppled forward in the gilded howdah. The last roll of the gong had masked the report of a high-powered rifle.

That evening the rajah gazed at the body of the man who had served him well, the man he had esteemed and loved as a friend. Pity and sorrow were on his lean, hard features; but regret was absent.

"A king and more than a king," He regarded the transfigured face of the Persian. "A madman, perhaps—or a god. By his own effort he rounded his destiny. The cycle is complete, the circle has closed upon itself. Yes, it is well that I commanded Al Tarik to fire before Zaid endured the agony of becoming mortal again. . . ."

Such was the gift of the rajah of Lacra-Kai. Yet once, at least, though he did not know it, the rajah had made a futile move: the shot of Al Tarik had missed; and there was no wound on the Persian's body.

Roadside Pickup

Richard Laymon

When the piano stopped, the voice came back. It was soft and friendly, like the music, and kept Colleen's thoughts from dwelling on the empty road. "That was Michel Legrand," it said, almost whispering, "and this is Jerry Bonner bringing you music and talk from midnight till dawn here on easy-listening KS . . ." She rolled the knob of her car radio and the voice clicked off.

It wouldn't be smart to keep listening. Not smart at all, since there was no telling how long she might be sitting here. Maybe all night. You can't play a radio all night without running down the battery. Or can you? She would have to ask that mechanic tomorrow. Jason. He was so good at explaining things.

She sighed with weariness and pressed her fingertips against her eyelids. If only someone would come along, and stop, and offer to help her.

The way Maggie was helped?

She felt her skin tighten.

No! Not like Maggie!

As Colleen rubbed her bare arms, she started to remember it again . . . the telephone that rang in her dream until it woke her to the real ringing, the roughness of the bedroom rug under her feet, the cool slick linoleum in the kitchen. And all the time the sickening lump of fear in her belly because the phone just doesn't ring at 3:00 A.M. unless . . .

"Cut it out," she muttered. "Snap out of it, okay? Think about something pleasant for a change."

Sure, something pleasant.

Otherwise she would start remembering the cop's voice on the phone and the drive to the morgue and the way her sister had looked lying there . . .

"Shine on, shine on, harvest moon," she started to sing. She kept on singing it. Then she began, "Sentimental Journey."

When they were kids, they used to sing those songs on long trips. Mother and Father would be sitting up front, she and Maggie in the back, four shadows holding off the lonely night with sweet, half-remembered lyrics.

Maggie always had lots of trouble remembering the words. Whenever she got stuck, she would listen to the others and sing out the right words a moment later, like a cheery echo.

414

The night her car broke down, nobody was there to sing her the right words.

Colleen caught her breath. A light! A speck of light no bigger than one of the stars high above the cornfields moved in her side mirror. A car was coming.

Would this one stop? Three, so far, had whooshed by without even slowing down. Three in almost as many hours.

Maybe one of them had stopped, somewhere farther on, and phoned the state troopers.

The headlights of the approaching car were set low and close together. Not like a patrol car, more like a sports car.

She flashed her lights on and off, on and off.

"Stop," she whispered. "Please stop."

As the car bore down, Colleen squinted at the glaring slab of her mirror. It hurt to look, but she didn't take her eyes away, not even when the headlights exploded across the mirror in a final brilliant flash.

After the painful brightness, the soft glow of the tail lights felt soothing to her eyes.

When the brake lights flashed, something clutched the inside of Colleen's stomach. She hunched over to ease the pain and saw the cold, white backup lights come on.

Her hand trembled as she rolled up her window. She glanced across her shoulder. The lock button was down. Swinging her eyes to the passenger door, she saw that it too was locked.

The car stopped inches from her bumper.

Colleen filled her lungs with air and let it out slowly.

A sports car, all right . . . small and shiny, with the canvas top of a convertible.

The driver's door swung open.

Colleen's breath made raspy, heartbeat sounds in her throat. Her mouth was parched. Did Maggie feel this way the night she died? She must have. This way, only a lot worse.

A tall, slim man stepped out. He looked to be in his late twenties, close to Colleen's age. His hair was fashionably long, his checkered shirt was open at the throat, his trousers flared at the cuffs.

She couldn't see his lean, dark face until he bent down and smiled in at her. She nervously returned the smile. Then the stranger raised his hand into view and made a circular cranking motion.

Colleen nodded. She lowered her window half an inch.

"What's the trouble?" he asked, speaking directly into the slit. His breath, so close to her, smelled sweet and heavy with liquor.

"It's . . . I'm not sure."

"Something the matter with your car? Your car break down?"

His breath filled her nostrils. She gripped the window crank and told herself to roll it up . . . roll it up *now* because he's been drinking . . . and she saw the dead battered face of her sister.

"You all right?" the man asked.

She rubbed her face. "I'm feeling kind of woozy, I guess."

"You ought to roll down your window, get some fresh air."

"No, thanks."

"The fresh air'll do you good."

"I'm all right."

"If you say so. What's wrong with your car?"

"It overheated."

"What?"

"Overheated," she said into the window's gap. "I was driving along and a red light on the dashboard came on, and then the engine started to make some kind of awful whiny noise, so I pulled over."

"I'd better have a look."

He walked to the front of the car and touched the hood the way a person touches something that might be hot. Then he slipped his hands under the hood's lip. He couldn't get it open. Finally, he crouched, found the latch, and opened it.

He spent only a few moments under the hood before returning to Colleen's window. "You've got a problem," he said.

"What's wrong?"

"What? I can hardly hear you. If you'd just roll down your window a bit more. . . ."

"Roll it down?"

"Sure."

"No, I don't think so."

"Hey, I don't bite," he said, grinning and shaking his head.

Colleen smiled back at him. "Are you sure?"

"I only bite when there's a full moon. It's just a half moon tonight."

"A gibbous," she corrected.

The man laughed and said, "Either way."

Colleen opened the window and breathed deeply. The breeze tasted wet with the freshness of the cornfields. A train, far away, was making a snickity sound. Somewhere a rooster heralded dawn three hours early.

It's a beautiful night, she thought. For a moment, she wondered if the stranger was also thinking about the peaceful sounds and smells. She looked at him. "What's wrong with my car?"

"Fan belt."

"Fan belt? What does that mean?"

He moved his face down closer to hers. "It means, young lady, that it's a good thing you stopped."

"Why's that?" she asked, and turned away from his liquored breath.

"If you go far without a fan belt, you burn up your engine. *Kaput,* kiss your motor good-bye."

"That serious?"

"That serious."

"What could've happened to the belt?"

"It probably just broke. They do that sometimes. Me, I change mine every two years just to be on the safe side."

"I wish *I* had."

"I'm glad you didn't," he said, and grinned a charming, boyish grin that frightened Colleen. "It isn't every night," he continued, "that I'm lucky enough to run into a damsel in distress. Especially one as pretty as you."

She rubbed her perspiring hands on her skirt. "Can you . . . can you fix it?"

"Your car? Not a chance. Not unless you've got a new fan belt in your pocket."

"What'll I do?"

"You'll let me give you a lift to the nearest service station. Or somewhere else, if you'd prefer. Where would you like to go?"

"Well, I don't think I should . . ."

"You can't stay here."

"Well . . ."

"It would be foolish to stay here . . . a woman as pretty as you. I don't want to alarm you, but there've been a number of attacks on this stretch of road."

"I know," she said.

"Not to mention half a dozen murders. Men and women both."

"You've alarmed me." She smiled nervously. "I'll come with you."

"That's what I like to hear." He reached into the car, unlocked the door, and opened it for her. She climbed out. When he shut the door, it made a dull thump that sounded very final.

"Do you live far from here?" he asked, taking Colleen's elbow with cold, firm fingers and leading her toward his car.

"Thirty miles, maybe."

"So close? Why don't you let me take you home?"

"That would be very nice. But I hate to put you to the trouble. If we can find a gas station . . ."

"No trouble. Thirty miles is nothing." He stopped walking. His fingers tightened around her arm. "I guess I'd be willing to drive a woman like you just about anywhere."

She saw the way he smiled and knew it was happening.

"Let go of me," she said, trying to sound calm.

But he didn't let go. He jerked her arm.

"Please!"

He mashed his mouth against hers.

Colleen closed her eyes. She started to remember it again . . . the telephone that rang her awake, the long walk to the kitchen, the rough apologetic voice of the cop.

I'm afraid that somebody assaulted your sister.

Is she . . . ?

She's gone.

Gone. A funny way for a cop to put it.

She bit the stranger's lip. Her forehead snapped against his nose. She jabbed her knuckles into his throat and felt his trachea collapse. Then she ran back to her car.

By the time Colleen returned to the man, he was lying motionless on the road. Kneeling beside him, she lifted his hand and searched for a pulse. There was none.

She dropped the hand, stood up, and took a deep, deep breath. The breeze off the cornfields smelled so fresh and sweet. So peaceful. Yet there was something a little sad about the aroma, as if the cornfields, too, missed Maggie.

Colleen stifled a sob. She glanced at the luminous face of her wrist watch. Then she bent under the hood with her wrench and fan belt, and got to work.

It took her less than six minutes to complete the job.

Not bad.

Faster than ever before.

Schizo Jimmie

Fritz Leiber

Today witch-hunting is an unpopular occupation. Unless the witch happens to be a red, the hunter gets a very bad press. Just the same, today as in the Middle Ages, when a decent man recognizes a real witch—the modern equivalent of a witch by the best scientific standards—then he must instantly strike down the monster for the sake of the community without counting the cost to himself.

That is why I killed my friend Jamie Bingham Walsh, the portrait painter and interior designer. He didn't suicide, nor did he accidentally tumble off that scenic high point of the Latigo Canyon Road in the Santa Monica Mountains. I pushed him off with my little MG.

Oh, the car never touched him, though it very well might have—that was one of the necessary chances I took. But in the end he reacted just as I'd been banking on it that he would—in a senseless panic, avoiding the closest threat to himself, the closest pain.

I stopped the car an exact dozen feet from the verge and he got out and walked around in front to the very edge, to take one of those Godlike looks at things below that he always had to take. He remarked, "The old sculptor poked his finger pretty deep here into the stone, didn't he." Then, as he was staring down at the twisting hazy valley and the lesser hilltops crowned with brown rocks like robed monsters, I silently eased the stick into low gear. Then I softly called his name and as he turned I smiled at him and gunned the car forward an exact dozen feet, thinking of my sister Alice and looking straight at his damned green necktie. I was very precise about it. Two inches more and my front wheels would have been over the edge.

He could have frozen, in which case I'd have knocked him off and he'd have been found with some extra injuries that might have been difficult to explain, or all too easy. Or, if he had reacted instantly, he could have jumped out of the way to either side or even onto the hood of the car—a man as much of a romantic daredevil as Jamie *looked* might have done just that, taking his chance that I didn't intend going over with him.

But he did none of those things. Instead he sprang backward into the great soft sweep of space above the toy valley, away from the nearest hurt. As he did so, as his nerve cracked under that final testing, it seemed to me that he instantly lost all of his black power over me, so that it was a cardboard man, a phantom, who stared wildly at me for an instant from the floorless air across the creamy hood of the MG before gravity snatched him out of sight.

The mind is a funny thing and has curious self-willed blind spots. Mine was so full of the thought that I had destroyed Jamie *utterly* that it never registered at all the thud of his body hitting, though I distinctly heard the distant tinkle of a couple of pebbles as they bounced against the bulges of the rocky wall on their way down.

I sat there calm and cold, thinking of Jamie's two wives and my sister Alice and the five other women I knew about and the half dozen of his close male friends and all his other victims whose names I would never know. I wondered if they'd have given me a round of applause from their various state mental hospitals and private sanitariums if I'd been able to tell them I had just avenged them on the man who sent them there. I couldn't answer that question—some people always love their destroyer—but I knew that now at least there wouldn't be any more unfortunates going to join them and they wouldn't have to endure any more kindly useless visits from Jamie with his vivid neckties and his patter about a person's color. That necktie jazz, you know, was one of the first things that put me on to Jamie—I remembered that he'd told Alice that green was "her color" and then he'd worn a green necktie when he went to visit her at the asylum. Later I noticed the same tie-in (ha!) with others of his victims, except the color would be different in each case. Everybody had a color, according to Jamie—something to do with what he called the atmosphere of your mind. Mine, I now remembered he'd often told me, was blue. Blue, like the cloudless sky over Latigo.

I shivered and smiled and wiped the cold sweat off my forehead and then I backed up my MG and drove off down the canyon. That was the end of it. I never had to exchange a single word with the police. I simply wasn't connected with the affair.

And so Jamie Walsh departed from this life without putting up any resistance whatever. He went away from us like the man who follows the usher without asking any questions when the light tap comes on his shoulder.

But perhaps Jamie didn't expect any attack. Perhaps he never knew how blackly evil he was. Perhaps he never realized he was a witch. This is a possibility I must face.

To me a witch—a modern witch, a *real* witch—is a person who is a *carrier of insanity*, one who infects others with this or that deadly psychosis without showing any of the symptoms himself, one who may be brilliantly sane by all psychiatric tests but who nevertheless carries in his mind-stream the germs of madness.

It's obviously true when you think it over. Medical science recognizes that there are such carriers of physical disease—outwardly untainted persons who spread the germs of TB, say, or typhoid fever. They're immune, they have built up a resistance, but most of those with whom they come in contact are defenceless. Typhoid Mary was a famous instance—a cook who over and over again infected hundreds of people.

By the same reasoning, Jamie Bingham Walsh should have been known as Schizo Jimmie. People with whom he came in really close contact had their minds split and started to live in dream worlds. I secretly thought of him as Schizo Jimmie for years before I gained the courage and complete certainty that let me wipe him out. The immune carrier of insanity is just as real a scientific phenomenon as the immune carrier of tuberculosis.

Most of us are willing to recognize the carrier of insanity when he operates at the national or international level. No one would deny that Hitler was such a carrier, spreading madness among his followers until he grew so powerful that there was no asylum strong enough to hold him. Lenin was a subtler and therefore better example, a seemingly sane man whose madness appeared full-grown only among his successors. And there was surely such a carrier abroad at the time of our own Civil War, there was so much madness then in high places—but I believe I have made my point.

While we generally agree on these top-of-the-heap historic cases, many of us refuse to recognize that there are Schizo Jimmies and Manic Marys and Paranoid Petes operating at all levels of society, including our own. But just think a minute about your friends and relatives and acquaintances. Don't you know at least one person who seems to be a focus for trouble without being an obvious troublemaker? A jinxy sort of guy or gal whose close friends show a remarkable tendency to crack up, to suicide perhaps, to call the headshrinkers a bit too late, to take long vacations in the looney him—or vacations that are longer than long. More likely than not he's brilliant and charming and seems to have the best intentions in the world (Jamie Walsh was all those things and more) but he's just not good for people.

At first you think he's merely unlucky in his choice of friends and maybe you feel sorry for him, and then you begin to wonder if he doesn't have a special talent or compulsion for seeking out and taking up with unstable people, and finally, if circumstances force you as deep into the thing as they did me, you begin to suspect that there's more to it than that. A lot more.

Alice and I got to know Jamie Walsh when Father hired him to do an interior design job on our new home in Malibu and also, it had already been arranged two days later, to paint Mother with the Afghan hounds. Jamie was in his late thirties then, energetic as hell, a real cosmopolite, impudent, flamingly charming, and he hit our soberly intelligent household like a whirlwind. He was a terrific salesman, as you have to be in that sort of job, and every one in the vicinity got an absolutely painless bonus course in general culture—Modigliani, Swedish Modern, the works.

With the price he was getting, we certainly had a bonus coming, but we didn't think about it that way. He'd come in, waving a devil mask, or a sari, or a hunk of period wrought iron or a gaudy old chamberpot, and the day's show would be on. For three months he was a non-resident member of the family. It was exactly like being visited by a pleasantly wicked young uncle you've never seen before because he's been completely occupied having exciting adventures in strange corners of the world and also, quite incidentally, happens to be a genius.

Within two weeks Jamie was painting Alice and myself as a matter of course and in the end he even sculptured a head of Father—cast in aluminum for some abstruse reason—and that was something I'd have given odds against ever happening. But in the end, as I say, even Father was bit by the art bug and for perhaps a month his old airplane factory took second place in his interests—the only time I'm sure, before or since, that ever happened in Father's life.

There was something feverish and distorted and unreal about the interest we all took in art and in Jamie at that time. He was like a hypnotist or some master magician weaving spells, creating wonderful dream worlds.

I dropped my forced interest in Father's business and my vaguer secret ambitions to do something in psychiatry, and determined to devote my life to marine painting, at which I'd earlier shown some talent. I let the others think it was a passing kick, which made things easier, especially with Father, but it was a lot more than that.

As for Alice, she seemed on the surface to be the least affected of all of us—she didn't sprout an artistic talent—but really she was the hardest hit. For she fell in love with Jamie. And he, in his peculiar way, encouraged her.

It wasn't anything obvious, mind you. I'm sure I was the only other person who realized what was happening and at the time I didn't care. In fact it seemed to me to be a fine thing that I should be able to offer up a beautiful sister to Jamie and that he should be interested. Since then I've noticed that many men have the urge, usually unconscious or so they'd claim, to furnish the services of their wives, sisters, and daughters to friends. It seems to be about as common as the opposite urge to clobber any male who so much as looks at their womenfolk, and is probably equally primitive in origin.

Mother may have guessed that Alice had developed a crush on Jamie, but I'm sure that was as far as her guesses went. She was herself too much under Jamie's spell to think unsympathetically of him. You see, by this time we'd learned about Jamie's unhappy marriage—he'd tried or seemed to try, to conceal it, but it had come out all the same—how his wife Jane was a hopeless alcoholic who spent most of her time touring the sanitariums and that one reason Jamie had to work so furiously was to pay the bills. Even I didn't dream at the time that Jane was just another of his victims and that what kept her alcoholism flaring was his ambiguous behavior toward her—his wanting her and not wanting her at the same time, his simultaneous caring for her and getting rid of her via the asylum route. She'd caught the infection he carried and in her case it was alcohol that was nursing the infection along.

But at the time even I knew nothing of this and we were all sympathy for Jamie and his troubles, we were all living in his bright dream worlds. Alice, I'm certain, was existing for the day when Jamie would carry her off—to marriage or a fierce selfish love-affair, I don't imagine she cared which. Just as I didn't care, deep in my old subconscious, whether I became a famous marine painter or merely Jamie's assistant. Alice and I were both of us building up to a big thing happening.

What happened was exactly nothing. Jamie finished the jobs Father had hired him to do and took off for Mexico all by himself. Mother went back to playing bridge. I threw my paint boxes into the ocean I'd been trying to catch on canvas. And Alice flipped, signaling the event by shooting the two Afghan hounds.

Mother and Father were stoned, of course, but they still didn't connect up the tragedy in any way with Jamie. And I must admit that, if you didn't want to dig, there were enough old reasons around for Alice flipping—she'd always been a shy difficult child with a mass of personality problems, she'd a terrific problem fighting overweight, later she'd dropped out of college twice, dithered around with different career dreams, been mixed up with some kids who were on dope, and so on.

No, I was the only one who saw the real part that Jamie played in the business. Mother and Father actually took the attitude that Jamie had been a *good* influence on Alice, that she'd have flipped sooner if it hadn't been for his stimulating presence and the general air of activity and excitement he brought into our otherwise stolid lives. In fact they took this attitude so deeply that when Jamie came bustling back from Venezuela six months later, all shocked sympathy at Alice's tragedy but at the same time yarning of his new adventures—he had a jaguar skin for Mother—they fell in eagerly with his idea of visiting Alice at the mental hospital. They thought it might have a good effect on her, wake her up and all that.

And I was the one who had to drive him there. I, who had begun to shrink from him because I sensed that he was dripping—honestly, that's the way it felt to me—with the invisible germs of madness. I, who remembered how he'd told Alice that green was "her color" and realized now the significance of the green necktie he was wearing.

I don't know, mind you, if *he* realized its significance. All through this, as I've said, I've been uncertain of the degree to which Jamie realized that he was creating the tragedies around him, the extent to which he knew that he was a carrier.

It was a long lonely drive under cloudless skies, prefiguring in a way the final drive I took with Jamie. As we had got in the car he had looked up at the sky and recalled that blue was *my* color. It gave me the shudders, but I didn't let on. I remember thinking, though, of the odd sensitivities painters are supposed to have. Sargent once painted a woman and a doctor who'd never met her diagnosed incipient insanity from the portrait, and the diagnosis was confirmed shortly.

Then after a bit Jamie fell into an odd wistful mood of faintly humorous self-pity and he told me about the dismal end his wife had come to in a New York hospital and about the numbers of his close friends who had flipped or suicided.

I'm sure he didn't realize that he was giving me research materials that were to occupy my real thinking for the next several years.

At the same time I began to see in a shadowy way the mechanism by which Jamie operated as a carrier of insanity—something I understand very well now.

You see, there has to be a mechanism, or else this transmission of insanity I'm talking about would be nothing but witchcraft—just as the transmission of physical disease was once thought by most people to be a matter of witchcraft.

Then the microscope came and *germs* were discovered to be the cause of infectious disease.

What causes insanity, at least the schizoid kind, what transmits it and carries it, is *dreams*—waking dreams, daytime dreams, the most powerful and virulent of all.

Jamie awakened and fostered dreams of romance in every woman he met. They looked at him, they listened to him, they lost themselves in the golden dream of a love affair that would dazzle the ages, they made the big decibands, families, careers, session to abandon their security, position all of that. And then . . . Jamie did nothing at all about it. Nothing brave, nothing reckless, not even anything cruel or merely male-hungry. I'm sure he and Alice never went to bed. Like the others, Jamie just left her hanging there.

In men it was dreams of glory that Jamie roused, dreams of adventures and artistic achievements quite beyond their real capabilities. It was their jobs that the men abandoned—their schooling, their common sense. Just as it happened to me, except that I saw Jamie's trap in time and threw my paints away.

But in one sense I was trapped more completely by Jamie than any of the others, because it was given to me to sense the menace of the man and to realize that I must study this thing and then do something about it, no matter how long it took or how much it hurt me.

Yes, I became aware of all those things in a shadowy way on that first drive from Malibu to the mental hospital—and I also got one piece of very concrete evidence against Jamie, though it was years before I realized its full significance.

After Jamie tired of talking he closed his eyes and went into a sort of uneasy drowse beside me. After a while he twisted on his narrow seat and he began to mutter and murmur in a rythmic way as if, half asleep, he were making up or repeating a jingle to the spin of the wheels and the buzz of the motor. I still don't know what sort of mental process in Jamie was responsible for it—creativity takes strange twists. I listened carefully and after a while I began to catch words and then more words. He kept repeating the same thing. These are the words I caught:

> Beth is sand-brown, Brenda's gray,
> Dottie was mauve and faded away.
> Hans was scarlet, Dave was black,
> Keith was cobalt and off the track.

424

Ridiculous words. And then I thought, "I'm blue."

Jamie woke up and asked what had been happening. "Nothing," I told him and that seemed to satisfy him. We were practically at the asylum.

Jamie's visit to Alice was no help to her that I could see—on her next trip home she was just as out-of-touch and even more disgustingly fat—but that was how I became Jamie's Boswell, interested in every person he'd known, every place he'd been, anything he'd ever done or said. I talked with him a lot and with his friends more. One way or another, I managed to visit most of the places he'd been. Father was alternately furious and depressed at the way I was "wasting my life." He'd have tried to stop me, except that what had happened to Alice had put the fear into him of tampering with his children. We were queer eggs and might crack and smell. Of course he hadn't the faintest idea of what I was doing. I don't think that even Jamie guessed. Jamie responded to my interest with half-amused tolerance, though from time to time I caught an odd look in his eyes.

In the course of five years I accumulated enough evidence to convict James Bingham Walsh a dozen times of being a carrier of insanity. I found out about his younger brother, who had hero-worshipped him, tried to imitate him, done a bad job of it and aberrated before he was twenty . . . about his first wife, who'd only managed to stay a year this side of the asylum walls . . . about Hans Godbold, who ditched his family and an executive job in a big chemical firm to become a poet and who six months later blew out his brains in Panama. About David Willis, Keith Ellander, Elizabeth Hunter, Brenda Silverstein, Dorothy Williamson . . . colored people—scarlet, black, cobalt, sand-brown, gray, mauve—for now I remembered the jingle he'd muttered in my ear . . .

It wasn't just a matter of individuals. Statistics contributed their quota. Wherever Jamie went, if it was a small enough place for it to show up and if I could get the figures, there was a rise, small but undeniable, in the incidence of insanity. Make no mistake, Jamie Bingham Walsh deserved the name of Schizo Jimmie.

And then as I've told you, when my evidence was complete, when it wholly satisfied *me*, I acted. I was prosecutor, judge, jury, and executioner all rolled into one. Sometimes when you're a little ahead of the science of your day, it has to be that way. I marched the prisoner up Latigo Canyon—by chance wearing a green tie, Alice's color, which made me happy—and he made the big drop.

The only thing that really bothers me about it all now is my unshaken conviction that Jamie was a genius. A master manipulator of colors, and, whether he knew it or not, of people. It is too bad that he was too dangerous to let live. I sometimes think that the same is true of all so-called "great men"— they create dreams that infect and rot or crumble the minds of the rest of us.

They are carriers, even the most seemingly noble and compassionate of them. At the time of our own Civil War the chief carrier was that sufferer from involutional melancholia, that tormented man from whom knives once had to be hidden, Abraham Lincoln. Oh, why can't such men leave us little people to our own kinds of safety and happiness, our small plans and small successes, our security firmly based on our mediocrity? Why must they keep spreading the deadly big dreams?

Naturally enough, I haven't escaped from this affair scot-free, though as I've told you I've been in no trouble with the police or the law. But just the same it was too tough a job for one man, too much responsibility for one person to shoulder. It left its mark on me, all right. By the time I'd finished, my nerves were like crackle glass. That's why I'm in this . . . well . . . rest home now, why I may be here for a long time. I concentrated so much on the one big problem that when it was solved I just couldn't seem to attend to life any more.

I'm not asking for pity, understand. I did what I had to, I did what any decent man would do, and I'm glad I was brave enough. I'm not complaining about any of the consequences I'm suffering now, the inevitable consequences of my frazzled nerves. I don't care if I have to spend the rest of my life here—I'm not complaining about the dreams . . . the mental hurting . . . the flow of ideas too fast for thought or comment . . . the voices I hear . . . the hallucinations . . .

Except that I *am* bothered, I admit it, by the hallucinations I have of Jamie coming to visit me here. They are so real that some days they make me wonder whether they aren't the real live Jamie and whether it wasn't just the hallucination of Jamie that I sent hurtling down to his death in Latigo Canyon. After all, he never said a word, he looked like a phantom hanging in the air, and I never heard the sound of his body hitting.

Those are the days when I wish the police *would* come and question me about his death—question me, try me, condemn me, and send me to the gas chamber and out of this life that is no more than a torrent of tortured dreams. The days when Jamie comes to visit me, smiling tenderly and wearing a blue necktie.

Shrapnel

Karl Edward Wagner

It looked like the wreckage of a hundred stained glass windows, strewn across a desolate tangle of wasteland in a schizophrenic kaleidoscope.

The hood of the '78 Marquis buckled in protest as Harmon shifted his not inconsiderable weight. He smeared sweat from his face with a sweatier arm and squinted against the piercing sunlight. Even from his vantage point atop the rusting Mercury, it was impossible to achieve any sense of direction amidst these thousands of wrecked cars.

At some point this had been farmland, although such was difficult to envision now. Whatever crops had once grown here had long ago leeched the red clay of scant nutrients. Fallow acres had lapsed into wild pasture where enough soil remained; elsewhere erosion scourged the slopes with red gashes, and a scrub-growth of pine, sumac, honeysuckle and briar grudgingly reclaimed the dead land. Grey knobs of limestone and outcroppings could almost be mistaken for the shapeless hulls of someone's tragedy.

Harmon wished for a beer—a tall, dripping can of cold, cold beer. Six of them. He promised himself a stop at the first convenience store on the highway, once he finished his business here. But first he needed a fender.

"Left front fender. 1970 or '71 Montego."

"I think it will interchange with a '70-'71 Torino," Harmon had offered—too tired to explain that the fender was actually needed for a 1970 Cyclone Spoiler, but that this was Mercury's muscle car version of the Montego, which shared sheet metal with Ford's Torino, and anyway the woman who ran Pearson's Auto Yard probably knew all that sort of stuff already.

She had just a dusting of freckles, and wheat-colored hair that would have looked striking in almost anything other than the regulation dyke haircut she had chosen. The name embroidered across the pocket of her freshly washed but forever grease-stained workshirt read *Shiloh*. Shiloh had just finished off a pair of redneck truckers in quest of certain axle parts incomprehensible to Harmon, and she was more than capable of dealing with him.

"Most of the older Fords are off along the gully along the woods there," Shiloh had pointed. "If they haven't been hauled to the crusher. There's a row of fenders and quarter panels just beyond that. You wait a minute and Dillon or somebody'll be here to look for you."

The thundering air conditioner in the window of the cramped office might have been able to hold the room temperature at 80 if the door weren't constantly being opened. Harmon felt dizzy, and he further felt that fresh air, however searing, was a better bet than waiting on an office stool for Dillon or somebody.

"You watch out for the dogs," Shiloh had warned him. "If one of them comes after you, you just jump on top of something where they can't get at you until Dillon or somebody comes along."

Hardly comforting, but Harmon knew his way around junkyards. This was an acquaintance that had begun when Harmon had decided to keep the 1965 Mustang of his college days in running order. It had become part hobby, part rebellion against the look-alike econoboxes or the Volvos and BMW's that his fellow young suburban professionals drove each day from their energy-efficient homes in Brookwood or Brookcrest or Crestwood or whatever. Harmon happened to be an up-and-coming lawyer in his own right, thank you, and just now his pet project was restoring a vintage muscle car whose string of former owners had not been overly concerned with trees, ditches, and other obstacles, moving or stationary.

It was a better way to spend Saturday morning than on the tennis court or golf course. Besides, and he wiped his face again, it was good exercise. Harmon, over the past four years and at his wife's insistence, had enrolled in three different exercise programs and had managed to attend a total of two classes altogether. He kept telling himself to get in shape, once his schedule permitted.

Just now he wished he could find Dillon or somebody. The day was too hot, the sun too unrelenting, for a comfortable stroll through this labyrinth of crumbled steel and shattered glass. He rocked back and forth on the hood of the Marquis, squinting against the glare.

"Yoo hoo! Mister Dillion! There's trouble brewin' on Front Street!"

Christ, enough of that! He was getting light-headed. That late-night pizza had been a mistake.

Harmon thought he saw movement farther down along the ravine. He started to call out in earnest, but decided that the general clatter and crash of the junkyard would smother his words. There was the intermittent mutter of the machine shop, and somewhere in the distance a tractor or towtruck, innocent of muffler, was dragging stripped hulks to their doom in the jaws of the yard's crusher. Grunting, Harmon climbed down from the wreck and plodded toward where he thought he'd glimpsed someone.

The heat seemed worse as he trudged along the rutted pathway. The rows of twisted sheet metal effectively stifled whatever breeze there might have been, at the same time acting as grotesque radiators of the sun's absorbed heat. Harmon wished he had worn a hat. He had always heard that a hat was a good thing to wear when out in the sun. He touched the spot on the top of his head where his sandy hair was inclining to thin. Unpleasant images of frying eggs came to him.

It *smelled* hot. The acres of rusted metal smelled like an unclean oven. There was the bitter smell of roasting vinyl, underscored by the musty stench of mildewed upholstery basted in stagnant rainwater. The palpable smell of hot metal vied with the noxious fumes of gasoline and oil and grease—the dried blood of uncounted steel corpses. Underlying it all was a sickly sweet odor that Harmon didn't like to think about, because it reminded him of his smalltown childhood and walking home on summer days through the alley behind the butcher shop. He supposed they hosed these wrecks down or something, before putting them on the yard, but nonetheless . . .

Harmon's gaze caught upon the sagging spiderweb of a windshield above a crumpled steering wheel. He shivered. Strange, to shiver when it was so hot. He seemed to feel his intestines wriggle like a nest of cold eels.

Harmon supposed he had better sit down for a moment.

He did.

"Morris?"

Harmon blinked. He must have dropped off.

"Hey, Morris—you OK?"

Where was he?

"Morris?" The voice was concerned and a hand was gently shaking him.

Harmon blinked again. He was sitting on a ruined front seat in the shade of an eviscerated Falcon van. He jerked upright with a guilty start, like a junior exec caught snoring during a senior staff meeting. Someone was standing over him, someone who knew his name.

"Morris?"

The voice became a face, and the face a person. Arnie Cranshaw. A client. Former client. Harmon decided to stop blinking and stand up. On second try, he made it to his feet.

Cranshaw stared reproachfully. "Jesus! I thought maybe you were dead."

"A little too much sun," he explained. "Thought I'd better sit down in the shade for a minute or two. I'm OK. Just dozed off is all."

"You sure?" Cranshaw wasn't so certain. "Maybe you ought to sit back down."

Harmon shook his head, feeling like a fool. "I'll be fine once I get out of this heat. Christ, I'd kill for a cold beer right now!"

Not a well chosen remark, he suddenly reflected. Cranshaw had been his client not quite a year ago in a nasty sort of thing: head-on collision that had left a teenaged girl dead and her date hopelessly crippled. Cranshaw, the other driver involved, had been quite drunk at the time and escaped injury; he also escaped punishment, thanks to Harmon's legal talents. The other car *had* crossed the yellow line no matter that its driver swore that he had lost control in trying to avoid Cranshaw, who had been swerving all over the road—and a technicality resulted in the DUI charges being thrown out as well. It was a victory that raised Harmon's stock in the estimation of his colleagues, but it was not a victory of which Harmon was overly proud.

"Anyway, Morris, what are you doing here?" Cranshaw asked. He was ten years younger than Harmon, had a jogger's legs, and worked out at his health club twice a week. Nonetheless, the prospect of lugging a semiconscious lawyer out of this metal wasteland was not to Cranshaw's liking.

"Looking for a fender for my car."

"Fender-bender?" Cranshaw was ready to show sympathy.

"Someone else's, and in days gone by. I'm trying to restore an old muscle car I bought back in the spring. Only way to find parts is to dig through junkyards. How about you?"

"Need a fender for the BMW."

Harmon declined to press for details, which spared Cranshaw any need to lie about his recent hit-and-run encounter. He knew a country body shop that would make repairs without asking questions, if he located some of the parts. A chop shop wasn't likely to respond to requests for information about cars with bloodstained fenders and such grisly trivia. They'd done business before.

Cranshaw felt quite remorseful over such incidents, but he certainly wasn't one to permit his life to be ruined over some momentary lapse.

"Do you know where we are?" asked Harmon. He wasn't feeling at all well, and just now he was thinking only of getting back into his little Japanese pick-up and turning the air conditioner up to stun.

"Well. Pearson's Auto Yard, of course." Cranshaw eyed him suspiciously.

"No. I mean, do you know how to get out of here?"

"Why, back the way we came." Cranshaw decided the man was maybe drunk. "Just backtrack is all."

Cranshaw followed Harmon's bewildered gaze, then said less confidently: "I see what you mean. Sort of like one of those maze things, isn't it. They ought to give you a set of directions or something—like, 'Turn left at the '57 Chevy and keep straight on till you pass the burned-out VW bug.' "

"I was looking for one of the workers," Harmon explained.

"So am I," Cranshaw said. "Guy named Milton or something. He'll know where to find our fenders, if they got any. Sort of like a Chinese librarian, these guys got to be."

He walked on ahead, tanned legs pumping assertively beneath jogging shorts. Harmon felt encouraged and fell in behind him. "I thought I saw some-body working on down the ravine a ways," he suggested to Cranshaw's back.

They seemed to be getting closer to the crusher, to judge by the sound. At intervals someone's discarded dream machine gave up its last vestiges of identity in great screams of rending, crumpling steel. Harmon winced each time he heard those deathcries. The last remaining left front fender for a '70 Cyclone might be passing into recycled oblivion even as he marched to its rescue.

"I don't think this is where I want to be going," Cranshaw said, pausing to look around. "These are pretty much stripped and ready for the crusher. And they're mostly Ford makes."

"Yes. Well, that's what I'm trying to find." Harmon brightened. "Do you see a '70 or '71 Montego or Torino in any of these?"

"Christ, Morris! I wouldn't know one of those from a Model T. I need to find where they keep their late-model imports. You going to be all right if I go on and leave you here to poke around?"

"Sure," Harmon told him. The heat was worse, if anything, but he was damned if he'd ask Cranshaw to nursemaid him.

Cranshaw was shading his eyes with his hand. "Hey, you were right. There *is* somebody working down there. I'm going to ask directions."

"Wait up," Harmon protested. *He'd* seen the workman first.

Cranshaw was walking briskly toward an intersection in the rows of twisted hulks. "Hey, you!" Harmon heard him call above the din of the crusher. "Hey, Milton!"

Cranshaw turned the corner and disappeared from view for a moment. Harmon made his legs plod faster, and he almost collided with Cranshaw when he came around the corner of stacked cars.

Cranshaw was standing in the middle of the rutted pathway, staring at the mangled remains of a Pinto station wagon. His face looked unhealthy beneath its tan.

"Shit, Morris! That's the car that I . . ."

"Don't be ridiculous, Arnie. All burned out wrecks look alike."

"No. It's the same one. See that porthole window in back. They didn't make very many of that model. Shit!"

Harmon had studied photos of the wreck in preparing his defense. "Well, so what if it is the car. It had to end up in a junkyard somewhere. Anyway, I don't think this is the same car."

"Shit!" Cranshaw repeated, starting to back away.

"Hey, wait!" Harmon insisted.

A workman had materialized from the rusting labyrinth. His greasy commonplaceness was initially reassuring—faded work clothes, filthy with unguessable stains, and a billed cap too dirty for its insignia patch to be deciphered. He was tall and thin, and his face and hands were so smeared and stained that Harmon wasn't at first certain as to his race. The workman carried a battered tool box in one hand, while in the other he dragged a shapeless bag of filthy canvas. The eyes that stared back at Harmon were curiously intent above an expressionless face.

431

"Are you Dillon?" Harmon hoped they weren't trespassing. He could hear a dog barking furiously not far away.

The workman looked past Harmon and fixed his eyes on Cranshaw. His examination of the other man seemed frankly rude.

"Are you Milton?" Cranshaw demanded. The workman's name across his breast pocket was obscured by grease and dirt. "Where do you keep your late-model imports?"

The workman set down his tool box and dug a limp notebook from a greasy shirt pocket. Licking his fingers, he paged through it in silence. After a moment, he found the desired entry. His eyes flicked from the page to Cranshaw and back again.

"Yep," he concluded, speaking for the first time, and he made a checkmark with a well-chewed pencil stub. Returning notebook and pencil to shirt pocket, the workman knelt down and began to unlatch his tool box.

Harmon wanted to say something, but his mouth was too dry to speak, and he knew he was very much afraid, and he wished with all his heart that his legs were not rooted to the ground.

Ahead of him, Cranshaw appeared to be similarly incapable of movement, although from the expression on his face he clearly seemed to wish he were anyplace else but here.

The tool chest was open now, and the workman expertly made his selection from within. The tool chest appeared to contain mainly an assortment of knives and scalpels, all very dirty and showing evidence of considerable use. If the large knife that the workman had selected was a fair sample, their blades were all very sharp and serviceable.

The canvas bag had fallen open, enough so that Harmon could get a glimpse of its contents. A glimpse was enough. The arm seemed to be a woman's, but there was no way of telling if the heart with its dangling assortment of vessels had come from the same body.

Curiously, once Harmon recognized that many of the stains were blood, it seemed quite evident that much of the dirt was not grease, but soot.

The sound of an approaching motor was only a moment's cause for hope. A decrepit Cadillac hearse wallowed down the rutted trail toward them, as the workman tested the edge of his knife. The hearse, converted into a work truck, was rusted out and so battered that only its vintage tailfins gave it identity. Red dust would have completely masked the chipped black paint, if there hadn't been an overlay of soot as well. The loud exhaust belched blue smoke that smelled less of oil than of sulfur.

Another grimy workman was at the wheel. Except for the greasy straw cowboy hat, he might have been a double for the other workman. The doors were off the hearse, so it was easy to see what was piled inside.

The hearse rolled to a stop, and the driver stuck out his head.

432

"Another pick-up?"

"Yeah. Better get out and give me a hand here. They want both right and left leg assemblies, and then we need to strip the face. You got a three-inch flaying knife in there? I left mine somewhere."

Then they lifted Cranshaw, grunting a little at the effort, and laid him out across the hood.

"Anything we need off the other?" the driver wondered.

"I don't know. I'll check my list."

It was very, very hot, and Harmon heard nothing more.

Someone was tugging at his head, and Harmon started to scream. He choked on a mouthful of cold R.C. and sputtered foam on the chest of the man who was holding the can to his lips. Harmon's eyes popped open, and he started to scream again when he saw the greasy workclothes. But this black face was naturally so, the workman's eyes showed kindly concern, and the name on his pocket plainly read *Dillon*.

"Just sip on this and take it easy, mister," Dillon said reassuringly. "You had a touch of the sun, but you're going to be just fine now."

Harmon stared about him. He was back in the office, and Shiloh was speaking with considerable agitation into the phone. Several other people stood about, offering conflicting suggestions for treating heat stroke or sun stroke or both.

"Found you passed out on the road out there in the yard," Dillon told him. "Carried you back inside here where we got the air conditioner running."

Harmon became aware of the stuttering howl of an approaching siren. "I won't need an ambulance," he protested. "I just had a dizzy spell is all."

"That ambulance ain't coming for you," Dillon explained. "We had a bad accident at the crusher. Some customer got himself caught."

Shiloh slammed down the phone. "There'll be hell to pay!" she snapped.

"There always is," Harmon agreed.

Silent Crickets

John Shirley

The milky moonlight sifted by mercuric clouds, snickers through the dense woods in slippery shafts. The faint light laps at the crotches of trees and catches on tangles of bared branches, giving the moss the silver sheen of mold. The deciduous trees are in bunches infrequently invaded

433

by a lone pine. Roots are choked with fallen leaves. Bared branches are abstracted into atmospheric capillaries. In the inky shadows under a short conical fir tree a man crouches with a rifle in his right hand. He moves slowly forward, trying to make as little noise as he can, and creeps into the crater left by an uprooted pine. The huge dying pine is lying on its side, smaller frustrated trees crushed under its trunk; its roots are thrusting up over the man's head. He hunkers in the shallow pit, his booted feet gripping the mud, rifle barrel catching the light and tinting it blue. The only sound is the *chirr* of a sneaking raccoon and the repetitive song of the crickets.

The crickets go abruptly silent.

The man is on the alert.

Something moves invisibly through the woods. He tenses, raises the .36, props the gunstock against his right shoulder, finger tightening around the trigger. He reaches for the safety catch. *Is it one of them?*

The figure emerges.

It's a man, a man alone. The man with the gun, Buckley, curator of the Deepwood Museum of Modern Art, stands and waves. The stranger, his face only partially visible, nods and comes forward. He stands silently a few feet from Buckley, looking at the long rifle upright at the curator's side. The man wears dungarees and a white longsleeve shirt. The night conceals most of his features.

"Are you Buckley?" He asks in a low, oily tone.

"Yes."

"I'm . . . Cranshaw. I'm from the New York Art Association. I've been looking for you. I believe your story . . . more or less. I want to hear it from your own lips, anyway. I've had a similar . . . experience. I came to talk to you in your study and your servant—she was quite flustered—said that you'd run out here after burning the paintings. A strange business, Buckley, burning eight hundred thousand dollars worth of Miro and Matta and Picasso . . ."

"How many kinds of sexual reproduction are there?" Buckley asks, his voice sounding strange to him in the sucking darkness.

"Well . . . there's mitosis, and cross-pollination and among humanity there's good old—"

"Among humanity there's something *else*," Buckley interrupts, speaking in a rapid clip. "A new kind of mutation. Have you heard it said that an artist doesn't create a 'new' vision, but only siphons it from another dimension of reality where that abstraction is the physical law? Perhaps. Perhaps if the abstract or surrealist artist steals from that world's images, from that other plane long enough, the creatures inherent to that world will take an interest in us and contrive to come here. Perhaps they'll use us as a medium, transferring themselves through a kind of paintbrush insemination. I keep thinking of the words of the dadaist Jean Arp: *Art is like fruit, growing out of man . . . like the child out of its mother. . . .* Someday, Cranshaw, a child will replace its parents."

"Maybe. Come back to your study and we'll talk about it—"

"No. Haven't you been reading about all the artists who've been disappearing? Well, I was visiting Matta when I *saw* something happen to him. I can't describe—"

"All this is interesting but rather xenophobic," the stranger interrupts. "My experiences were not so much like yours as I had thought. It's not easy to be a curator these days, God knows. Those snotty young painters. But come back and have a drink with me, Buckley. We'll work things out from there. Don't be afraid." He reaches out a hand to Buckley's shoulder.

Buckley steps backwards, his hand tightens on the barrel of the gun. If this man is from the Art Association, why is he dressed like a country hick? Cranshaw touches Buckley's shoulder. Suspicions confirmed. Buckley feels it then, the warning tingle, the onrush of activated abstraction. He steps back again, raises the gun. "You lied to me," he murmurs as much to the night as to Cranshaw.

Another movement from the far side of the fallen tree catches his eye. Pure moving anachronism issuing from the areola of upturned roots. It was the abstract figure of Marcel Duchamp's *Nude Descending A Staircase* given its own independent life. A study of strobed motion, the exegesis of a few moments of time into cubism. The creature, viewed literally, glowing against the tenebrous curtain of the woods, resembles a robot strung in Siamese twin extrapolations of itself, leaving behind a hallucinogenic acid trail like a mechanical cape. It might be built of copper-colored tin cans and its torso (futurist extrapolation of pivotal rotation) is built in striations like the gills of a shark. Moving toward Buckley, it is a random tumble of spastic geometry, a carnivorous handy kitchen appliance. The figure is a vector for the bizarre, leaving behind it a wake of abstracted trees, brush distorting into a vision of Siamese triplet belly dancers; treetrunks made Rousseau primitive and perfectly cylindrical-smooth, branches becoming pin-cushion spines. But the voice of the vector is human.

"I couldn't wait any longer. I had to come. Has he been readied?"

"No," the stranger who called himself Cranshaw replies, "not just yet."

"Buckley," came the voice from the golden arachnid whirlpool, "come here."

Buckley pulls a slim penlight from his pocket and shines it on Cranshaw's face. He gasps. A Modigliani simplification, that face, with pits of Munch hollowness around the eyes. The man, while outwardly proportional, is made of rigid planes, unmoving eyes, the same perpetual sardonic smile two inches to the left of his nose. One of his eyes is considerably higher than the other. His arms are blocked into rectangular surfaces with ninety-degree corners.

"It's alright," says the Cranshaw-thing, its voice fuzzy now. "Don't worry." It reaches out a squared-off hand to Buckley's upraised rifle, touches the barrel with a gentle caress at the same moment that the curator touches the trigger.

The gun doesn't go off. There is a conspicuous silence. Instead of an explosion, comes a faint puffing sound. A globular bullet bounces like a soap bubble off Cranshaw's chest and floats up through the clawing trees. Desperately, Buckley feels the barrel of the gun. It sags in his fingers like an exhausted erection, rubbery and pliant. He breaks off a piece of the barrel and puts it to his mouth. Licorice. The gun melts into a snakelike abstraction. He flings it away but already the tingling chill is travelling up his arm. He looks at the two abstract beings standing patiently by, sees them reticulate and waver like an unstable TV picture. He looks down at his body, sees his legs sprout roots which rapidly burrow into the humus under his new hooves.

The Skeptic

Hugh B. Cave

There were only two of them in the silence of the cottage sitting-room: the seventy-eight-year-old woman with her book, and the cat sleeping beside her chair. Suddenly the cat awoke and looked toward the front door.

The woman lowered her book. "Someone's coming, Samantha?"

Samantha, an all-white longhair, voiced a warning meow.

"Are you sure?" the woman said. "I didn't hear a car."

Samantha's expression plainly said, "Of course you didn't. You've been lost in that stupid book all evening." The volume was one Judith Blaine had only just acquired: a new and startling interpretation of the prophecies of that ancient seer, Nostradamus.

Judith Blaine placed the book on the table beside her chair and stood up. With some effort she put her stooped body on a shuffling course toward the door. The doorbell rang when she was only halfway there.

She was not surprised, of course. Samantha always knew when someone was coming. It could be a car in the driveway or the nearest neighbor's little daughter in soundless sneakers. Samantha would hear. If "hear" was the word.

Her caller was a stranger: a young woman in expensive blue slacks and gray silk blouse. Pretty, even beautiful, with short blonde hair and the bluest of eyes.

"Mrs. Blaine?"

"I am Judith Blaine. Yes."

"I'm Delora Moffit. I phoned for an appointment."

"I remember. The lady who is doing a story of some sort."

"About people like you, for our Chamber of Commerce magazine. What you do, exactly. How you operate. I'm one of the magazine's editors."

Judith leaned forward a little to peer into the beautiful young face. "It's more than a story, though," she said gently. "You have a problem, I think." She glanced down at the cat. "Doesn't she, Samantha?"

"If you mean a personal one, I'm afraid you're mistaken." The touch of annoyance in Miss Moffit's voice was so slight, anyone less observant might not have noticed it. "Of course, if you don't like to talk about your work, then I suppose I do have a problem. Coming all the way out here for nothing, I mean."

Judith glanced at the car in the driveway. It had cost a good deal more than the one in her garage. She glanced down at her feet again for Samantha's verdict, knowing that if the cat sensed something she didn't, those orange eyes would tell her so.

There was a message in them. Definitely.

"Of course we'll talk to you," Judith said.

"We?"

Ignoring the remark, Judith stepped aside to let her caller enter, then shut the door and led the younger woman to her conference table. This was about the size of a card table and made of wood obtained by her in India some years before. One of her regular clients, a cabinet maker, had built it for her with loving care, to express his appreciation for her help.

"Sit here, please. What is your name again?"

The young woman sat. "Delora Moffit."

"And what do you want from me, exactly?"

"Well, could you—do you suppose you could give me the sort of reading—if that's what you call it—that you would give any ordinary—ah—customer?" Judith detected a touch of ridicule in both voice and smile. "I mean, could you tell my fortune, if that's what you do?"

"Miss Moffit, we don't tell fortunes. People come to us with problems."

"We?"

Again Judith ignored the remark.

"Well, whatever," Moffit said.

Judith leaned forward and placed both hands on the table, palms up. "Put your hands on mine, please. Palms down."

Moffit obeyed.

It did not always work, of course. Judith was never sure what would happen when her hands and those of a client came together. When nothing did, she simply said she was sorry and charged nothing.

She sensed failure this time and was about to express her regrets when Samantha leaped lightly onto her lap and placed her front paws on the tabletop.

Suddenly the nothing became something. All at once the touching hands, the table, the room itself, were no longer there. Judith Blaine found herself in a strange bedroom, a more expensively furnished one than her own, standing before a dressing table she had never seen before. And the person looking out at her from the dressing-table mirror was not Judith Blaine but Delora Moffit.

The only familiar thing in the room was Samantha, who lay on the bed behind her, head uplifted, orange eyes wide and bright, as though waiting to see what Moffit would do next.

From somewhere came the musical summons of a doorchime.

As Moffit, the old woman turned from the mirror and strode briskly from the room into an upstairs hall. Had she been herself, the flight of stairs confronting her would have intimidated her, without a doubt. Now she trotted down them with ease.

The white cat flowed down behind her like spilled milk.

Briskly, the new Judith proceeded along a downstairs hall to the front door, and opened it.

The person standing there was a woman about Delora Moffit's age, dark-haired, dark-eyed, with an anxious, even fearful, expression on her otherwise attractive face. Her voice was a husky whisper as she asked, "Are you alone, Lorie?"

Judith-Delora felt a twinge of annoyance. "Yes, I'm alone, Marie. Why?"

"He isn't here?"

"If you mean Dane, no. I said I was alone."

"May I come in, then? I have to talk to you!" The "talk to you" was spoken in a higher register and seemed to hang like a wind-sound in the air between them.

Leaving her caller to shut the door, Judith-Delora marched into the living room. Her caller followed. Tight-lipped and stone-faced, Judith-Delora seated herself. With an almost silent sigh, her caller stepped forward to confront her.

Marie spoke first. "Lorie, I know you think I'm interfering. But please, before it's too late, look at this." From the white leather handbag she carried she extracted a long brown envelope. "Ed McNab, at the *Clarion,* found it for me." After handing the envelope to Judith-Delora, who received it in hostile silence, she went to the nearest vacant chair and sat.

The white cat, Samantha, took up a position beside Judith-Delora's chair and watched both women, her head swiveling slowly back and forth.

Judith-Delora opened the envelope. Out of it she took a folded newspaper page. Unfolding the page, she laid it on her knees and looked at it. Underneath a headline that shouted DO YOU KNOW THIS MAN? was a photograph four columns wide of a handsome, clean-shaven male face.

438

Judith-Delora scarcely glanced at the photo. "You must be out of your mind," she said. "There isn't even a resemblance!"

Hands on knees, knuckles white, her caller leaned toward her. "Lorie, please. Look at it again. Lorie, Lorie, I'm your best friend!"

"I tell you they don't look even remotely alike!"

"But they do, Lorie! They do! Can't you see it? If Dane were to shave off his beard . . ."

"Marie, for the last time, you're being totally ridiculous and I wish to God you'd stop it. My Dane is not this man the police are looking for. He hasn't killed anyone, let alone four women—"

"Who looked just like you, Lorie." Her best friend spoke in a whisper now, obviously trying desperately to keep the conversation from being terminated like a telephone talk in which one speaker slams a receiver down in anger. "Lorie, they were all about our age, all pretty, all blondes with blue eyes. And what do you really know about Dane Driscoll except that he appeared in town a month ago and swept you off your feet with his charm? How do you even know Dane Driscoll is his real name?" She thrust out her arms, pleading. Stood up and took a step forward. "Please, please, Lorie. Find out more about him before you get hurt! Please!"

The newspaper page made crackling sounds as Judith-Delora savagely refolded it and jammed it back into the envelope. The envelope flew through the air and thudded to the floor at Marie's feet.

Beside the chair, the white cat arched her back and bared her teeth.

Judith-Delora's voice quavered now with barely-controlled fury. "Marie, please go. Go now, while we're still friends. If we are still friends."

For a few seconds her caller continued to stand there in silence, helplessly gazing at her. Then without speaking she turned and walked toward the hall.

In the hall doorway stood the man in the photograph, waiting.

Waiting with a thin smile on his face and a straight razor—open—in his dangling right hand.

He stepped forward while Marie was still frozen in shock. His empty left hand shot out to grasp her by a shoulder as she faced him. Before she could think of resisting, he had spun her around. Then with her back pressed against him he shifted his grip to her hair and bent her head back.

The blade did its work before she could even scream.

With the smile still on his handsome face, the man who called himself Dane Driscoll flung his victim aside and looked across the room at Judith-Delora. She, out of her chair now, stared back at him in horror. As she turned to run, he hurled himself after her.

But the white cat was in motion, too. With a screech that threatened to shatter the room's windows, she leaped to intercept him.

Her teeth closed on his upflung right wrist.

Blood spurted.

The razor fell from his twitching fingers to the floor.

And Judith Blaine was suddenly back in her own living room, facing Delora Moffit across her conference table.

Between them now on the table, the white cat had already clawed their outstretched hands apart but was still furiously pawing at them, as if to make certain the contact would not be reestablished.

The face of the younger woman wore an expression of annoyance. "Really!" she said, pushing back her chair.

Ceasing her frenzied activity, Samantha seated herself in the center of the table and looked from one woman to the other. The strange light in her orange eyes slowly faded.

Judith Blaine at last stopped trembling and got her breath back. "I'm sorry," she said.

"Well, I should hope so." The young lady from the Chamber of Commerce looked in disgust at Samantha. "Does your cat do that often?"

"She has never done it before. Miss Moffit, may I ask you a question?" Without waiting for permission, Judith plunged ahead. "By any chance, are you seeing a man named Dane Driscoll?"

Moffit gazed at her with obvious suspicion. "So I'm not a stranger to you. What else do you know about me?"

"Nothing, really. But while our hands were touching—"

"Oh, come on." Moffit's laugh was half ridicule, half sneer, and wholly unpleasant. "Don't try to con me, please. I know how you people operate. After I phoned you for an appointment, you made a point of finding out all you could about me."

"You believe that?" Judith shook her head in sadness. "Then there is no point in my trying to warn you against this man, is there?"

"Warn me?" Moffit was more than annoyed now. When she stood up, her pretty face wore a flush of anger. "Warn me about what?"

"That he may try to kill you. That he has killed other women who resemble you. That a photograph of him—without his beard—will even be in the *Clarion* before this happens, and you will be shown it and should not ignore it. Beneath his veneer of charm, Miss Moffit, the man is a monster. You must not—"

"Thank you!" Moffit angrily snatched her handbag from the floor and strode away. "Thank you for so wonderfully revealing yourself to me, Mrs. Blaine!" On reaching the hall she turned, her look of anger now one of triumph. "At least, I now know exactly what to write about you, don't I?"

The front door slammed behind her. A moment later the sound of her car's departure reached Judith Blaine through the silence.

The old woman turned to her beloved cat. "Well, Samantha, what do you think?"

Still seated on the table, the longhair returned her gaze with what appeared to be an expression of sadness.

"Yes, I suppose you're right," Judith Blaine said with a sigh. "Actually, we didn't have a chance, did we? She knew what she believed even before she came here." Turning, she shuffled across the room and sank into her easy chair.

Samantha, following, leaped lightly onto her lap.

"What?" the woman said.

Only silence responded. But the orange eyes were aglow again.

"You won't be there to stop it when it actually happens?" Judith said then. "Is that what you said? Well, I know that, Samantha; of course I do. But if she won't believe us, what can we do about it except call the police and warn them?"

She sighed again. "I'll do that, of course. But they won't believe us either, you know. Not, at least, until it's too late."

The Striding Place

Gertrude Atherton

Weigall, continental and detached, tired early of grouse-shooting. To stand propped against a sod fence while his host's workmen routed up the birds with long poles and drove them towards the waiting guns, made him feel himself a parody on the ancestors who had roamed the moors and forests of this West Riding of Yorkshire in hot pursuit of game worth the killing. But when in England in August he always accepted whatever proffered for the season, and invited his host to shoot pheasants on his estates in the South. The amusements of life, he argued, should be accepted with the same philosophy as its ills.

It had been a bad day. A heavy rain had made the moor so spongy that it fairly sprang beneath the feet. Whether or not the grouse had haunts of their own, wherein they were immune from rheumatism, the bag had been small. The women, too, were an unusually dull lot, with the exception of a new-minded *débutante* who bothered Weigall at dinner by demanding the verbal restoration of the vague paintings on the vaulted roof above them.

But it was no one of these things that sat on Weigall's mind as, when the other men went up to bed, he let himself out of the castle and sauntered down to the river. His intimate friend, the companion of his boyhood, the chum of his college days, his fellow-traveller in many lands, the man for whom he possessed stronger affection than for all men, had mysteriously disappeared two days ago, and his track might have sprung to the upper air for all trace he had left behind him. He had been a guest on the adjoining estate during the past week, shooting with the fervor of the true sportsman, making love in the intervals to Adeline Cavan, and apparently in the best of spirits. As far as was known there was nothing to lower his mental mercury, for his rent-roll was a large one, Miss Cavan blushed whenever he looked at her, and, being one of the best shots in England, he was never happier than in August. The suicide theory was preposterous, all agreed, and there was as little reason to believe him murdered. Nevertheless, he had walked out of March Abbey two nights ago without hat or overcoat, and had not been seen since.

The country was being patrolled night and day. A hundred keepers and workmen were beating the woods and poking the bogs on the moors, but as yet not so much as a handkerchief had been found.

Weigall did not believe for a moment that Wyatt Gifford was dead, and although it was impossible not to be affected by the general uneasiness, he was disposed to be more angry than frightened. At Cambridge Gifford had been an incorrigible practical joker, and by no means had outgrown the habit; it would be like him to cut across the country in his evening clothes, board a cattle-train, and amuse himself touching up the picture of the sensation in West Riding.

However, Weigall's affection for his friend was too deep to companion with tranquillity in the present state of doubt, and, instead of going to bed early with the other men, he determined to walk until ready for sleep. He went down to the river and followed the path through the woods. There was no moon, but the stars sprinkled their cold light upon the pretty belt of water flowing placidly past wood and ruin, between green masses of overhanging rocks or sloping banks tangled with tree and shrub, leaping occasionally over stones with the harsh notes of an angry scold, to recover its equanimity the moment the way was clear again.

It was very dark in the depths where Weigall trod. He smiled as he recalled a remark of Gifford's: "An English wood is like a good many other things in life—very promising at a distance, but a hollow mockery when you get within. You see daylight on both sides, and the sun freckles the very bracken. Our woods need the night to make them seem what they ought to be—what they once were, before our ancestors' descendants demanded so much more money, in these so much more various days."

Weigall strolled along, smoking, and thinking of his friend, his pranks—many of which had done more credit to his imagination than this—and recalling conversations that had lasted the night through. Just before the end of the London season they had walked the streets one hot night after a party, discussing the various theories of the soul's destiny. That afternoon they had met at the coffin of a college friend whose mind had been a blank for the past three years. Some months previously they had called at the asylum to see him. His expression had been senile, his face imprinted with the record of debauchery. In death the face was placid, intelligent, without ignoble lineation—the face of the man they had known at college. Weigall and Gifford had had no time to comment there, and the afternoon and evening were full; but, coming forth from the house of festivity together, they had reverted almost at once to the topic.

"I cherish the theory," Gifford had said, "that the soul sometimes lingers in the body after death. During madness, of course, it is an impotent prisoner, albeit a conscious one. Fancy its agony, and its horror! What more natural than that, when the life-spark goes out, the tortured soul should take possession of the vacant skull and triumph once more for a few hours while old friends look their last? It has had time to repent while compelled to crouch and behold the result of its work, and it has shrived itself into a state of comparative purity. If I had my way, I should stay inside my bones until the coffin had gone into its niche, that I might obviate for my poor old comrade the tragic impersonality of death. And I should like to see justice done to it, as it were—to see it lowered among its ancestors with the ceremony and solemnity that are its due. I am afraid that if I dissevered myself too quickly, I should yield to curiosity and hasten to investigate the mysteries of space."

"You believe in the soul as an independent entity, then—that it and the vital principle are not one and the same?"

"Absolutely. The body and soul are twins, life comrades—sometimes friends, sometimes enemies, but always loyal in the last instance. Some day, when I am tired of the world, I shall go to India and become a mahatma, solely for the pleasure of receiving proof during life of this independent relationship."

"Suppose you were not sealed up properly, and returned after one of your astral flights to find your earthly part unfit for habitation? It is an experiment I don't think I should care to try, unless even juggling with soul and flesh had palled."

"That would not be an uninteresting predicament. I should rather enjoy experimenting with broken machinery."

The high wild roar of water smote suddenly upon Weigall's ear and checked his memories. He left the wood and walked out on the huge slippery stones which nearly close the River Wharfe at this point, and watched the waters boil down into the narrow pass with their furious untiring energy. The black quiet of the woods rose high on either side. The stars seemed colder and whiter just above. On either hand the perspective of the river might have run into a rayless cavern. There was no lonelier spot in England, nor one which had the right to claim so many ghosts, if ghosts there were.

Weigall was not a coward, but he recalled uncomfortably the tales of those that had been done to death in the Strid.[1] Wordsworth's Boy of Egremond had been disposed of by the practical Whitaker; but countless others, more venturesome than wise, had gone down into that narrow boiling course, never to appear in the still pool a few yards beyond. Below the great rocks which form the walls of the Strid was believed to be a natural vault, on to whose shelves the dead were drawn. The spot had an ugly fascination. Weigall stood, visioning skeletons, uncoffined and green, the home of the eyeless things which had devoured all that had covered and filled that rattling symbol of man's mortality; then fell to wondering if any one had attempted to leap the Strid of late. It was covered with slime; he had never seen it look so treacherous.

He shuddered and turned away, impelled, despite his manhood, to flee the spot. As he did so, something tossing in the foam below the fall—something as white, yet independent of it—caught his eye and arrested his step. Then he saw that it was describing a contrary motion to the rushing water—an upward backward motion. Weigall stood rigid, breathless; he fancied he heard the crackling of his hair. Was that a hand? It thrust itself still higher above the boiling foam, turned sidewise, and four frantic fingers were distinctly visible against the black rock beyond.

Weigall's superstitious terror left him. A man was there, struggling to free himself from the suction beneath the Strid, swept down, doubtless, but a moment before his arrival, perhaps as he stood with his back to the current.

He stepped as close to the edge as he dared. The hand doubled as if in imprecation, shaking savagely in the face of that force which leaves its creatures to immutable law; then spread wide again, clutching, expanding, crying for help as audibly as the human voice.

Weigall dashed to the nearest tree, dragged and twisted off a branch with his strong arms, and returned as swiftly to the Strid. The hand was in the same place, still gesticulating as wildly; the body was undoubtedly caught in the rocks below, perhaps already half-way along one of those hideous shelves. Weigall let himself down upon a lower rock, braced his shoulder against the mass beside him, then, leaning out over the water, thrust the branch into the hand. The fingers clutched it convulsively. Weigall tugged powerfully, his own feet dragged perilously near the edge. For a moment he produced no impression, then an arm shot above the waters.

The blood sprang to Weigall's head; he was choked with the impression that the Strid had him in her roaring hold, and he saw nothing. Then the mist cleared. The hand and arm were nearer, although the rest of the body was still

[1] "This striding place is called the 'Strid,'
    A name which it took of yore;
A thousand years hath it borne the name,
    And it shall a thousand more."

444

concealed by the foam. Weigall peered out with distended eyes. The meagre light revealed in the cuffs links of a peculiar device. The fingers clutching the branch were as familiar.

Weigall forgot the slippery stones, the terrible death if he stepped too far. He pulled with passionate will and muscle. Memories flung themselves into the hot light of his brain, trooping rapidly upon each other's heels, as in the thought of the drowning. Most of the pleasures of his life, good and bad, were identified in some way with this friend. Scenes of college days, of travel, where they had deliberately sought adventure and stood between one another and death upon more occasions than one, of hours of delightful companionship among the treasures of art, and others in the pursuit of pleasure, flashed like the changing particles of a kaleidoscope. Weigall had loved several women; but he would have flouted in these moments the thought that he had ever loved any woman as he loved Wyatt Gifford. There were so many charming women in the world, and in the thirty-two years of his life he had never known another man to whom he had cared to give his intimate friendship.

He threw himself on his face. His wrists were cracking, the skin was torn from his hands. The fingers still gripped the stick. There was life in them yet.

Suddenly something gave way. The hand swung about, tearing the branch from Weigall's grasp. The body had been liberated and flung outward, though still submerged by the foam and spray.

Weigall scrambled to his feet and sprang along the rocks, knowing that the danger from suction was over and that Gifford must be carried straight to the quiet pool. Gifford was a fish in the water and could live under it longer than most men. If he survived this, it would not be the first time that his pluck and science had saved him from drowning.

Weigall reached the pool. A man in his evening clothes floated on it, his face turned towards a projecting rock over which his arm had fallen, upholding the body. The hand that had held the branch hung limply over the rock, its white reflection visible in the black water. Weigall plunged into the shallow pool, lifted Gifford in his arms and returned to the bank. He laid the body down and threw off his coat that he might be the freer to practise the methods of resuscitation. He was glad of the moment's respite. The valiant life in the man might have been exhausted in that last struggle. He had not dared to look at his face, to put his ear to the heart. The hesitation lasted but a moment. There was no time to lose.

He turned to his prostrate friend. As he did so, something strange and disagreeable smote his senses. For a half-moment he did not appreciate its nature. Then his teeth clacked together, his feet, his outstretched arms pointed towards the woods. But he sprang to the side of the man and bent down and peered into his face. There was no face.

The Sultan's Jest

E. Hoffman Price

The old sultan sat in his palace at Angor-lana, reflectively stroked his white beard, and smiled as one who recollects an ancient jest. And it was a grim jest that he had in mind, for, though his lips curled in the shadow of a smile, his keen old eyes flamed ominously from beneath brows that, rising to points in the center like Saracenic arches, heightened the sinister expression of his leathery features.

A capricious tyrant was this old despot who pondered on the doom to inflict upon his favorite, Dhivalani, the Kashmiri bayadere, and her lover, Mamoun el Idrisi, the existence of whose illicit amour he had sensed with uncanny intuition. And so sure was he of their guilt that he devised punishment in advance of any confirmation of his suspicions; devised punishment, and awaited the arrival of Ismail, his chief wazir, who had been commissioned to trap the bayadere and her lover, Mamoun of the great house of Idris.

The sultan yawned, as might a tiger consumed with ennui, then settled back among the cushions of his dais. His smile widened; but the sinister light did not fade from his eyes.

"Read!" he commanded, addressing Amru the scribe, who sat at his master's feet.

"The spider spins her web in the palace of Cæsar," began Amru in his rich sonorous voice that time had not cracked, "and the owl stands watch in the tower of . . ."

"Enough!" snapped the sultan. "What news, Ismail?"

"A thousand years," greeted Ismail, bowing himself into the presence; "I have seized el Idrisi and Dhivalani."

"And who was the accomplice that has been smuggling Mamoun into the seraglio?"

"Saoud, the chief eunuch. He has just been sewed up in a bag and dropped into the river."

"Very good," commended the sultan. "Yes, it was just as I suspected. Mamoun has been swaggering about the court too proudly of late; Dhivalani has been entirely too vivacious; and Saoud has displayed more wealth than any honest eunuch could possibly accumulate. And so you trapped them? You did well, Ismail."

446

"My lord is an elephant of wisdom," observed the wazir, who was not blind to the sultan's pride in having so skilfully detected another palace intrigue. "And I, the least of his servants, have but acted upon his infallible judgment."

"Nevertheless, you did well. But tell me, Ismail, how shall we punish this Kashmiri and her lover?"

"Well . . . we might flay them alive and rub them with salt, or we might place them between planks and have them sawn asunder," suggested Ismail.

"Nonsense!" flared the sultan. "Have you no imagination? An amour is carried on in my own harem, under my very nose; and were it not for my intuition, it would still be going on. And here you suggest such commonplace punishments as though they had merely defrauded in the payment of the salt tax, or had stolen a prayer rug from the mosque!"

"My lord is a mountain of sagacity," interposed the wazir, penitently. "What would he suggest?"

The sultan shook his head despairingly.

"Ismail, you are an utter ass! You, my chief advisor, failing me when I am in need of wise counsel! I wish something novel in the way of punishment, and here you suggest the reward of a thieving camel driver!"

Odd and curious punishments were the sultan's forte; and on this occasion he demanded something distinctly different from the sanguinary slaughter and dismemberment that were the portion of petty offenders; he demanded a touch of the unique, something to tickle his sense of humor, of poetic justice. And far into the night the sultan and his chief wazir wrangled and debated, considering the matter from all angles.

All the while, Amru the scribe, whom the sultan had neglected to dismiss, nodded sleepily at the foot of his master's dais, and pondered on the exceeding folly and cruelty of old men who kept young and beautiful girls imprisoned in seraglios. He silently cursed the old man his master, who plotted strange vengeance after the fashion of a scholar resolving an abstruse problem; he cursed that fate which forced him, Amru, to sit impotently among scrolls and reeds, and hear of that which would leave the noble Idrisi a shapeless, mangled horror, a frothing, gibbering madman. And though the Prophet (upon whom be peace and power!) had denied souls to women, he shuddered as he listened to that which might be the portion of the lovely bayadere.

And then a new touch was noted in the sultan's discourse; his imagination was asserting itself in a vein of savage humor that was a distinct departure from even his most novel devices. A decision had been formed. Amru heard, and hearing, gained hope. Reflectively, the old man fingered several gold pieces he had withdrawn from his wallet. To discover where the lovers were imprisoned was by no means impossible. There was still a chance, a chance he would take though it cost him his head; for Mamoun was the friend of Amru, and a noble young man who respected old poets. And as Amru listened to the sultan's perfecting of the device under consideration, his hopes flamed high and fiercely. A word, but a word or two . . .

Yet all this brave hope was vanity: for the sultan, after dismissing his wazir, addressed the scribe.

"Amru, due to my carelessness you have heard more than is good for you. Mamoun is your friend; and to leave you free to work your will tonight would inflict too great a strain upon your loyalty to me, your master."

The scribe's wrinkled features were devoid of expression as he met the sultan's hard, keen gaze; but he sensed that the sultan's intuition had divined his very thoughts.

"And to save you from being torn between loyalty to me and your friendship for Mamoun," continued the sultan, "I shall keep you within arm's reach until sunrise, after which it will be too late for you to be overcome by kindly sentiments."

Again the old despot smiled in anticipation of the doom that was to be inflicted the following morning.

"What is my lord's pleasure?"

"You shall spend the night in shackles at the foot of my couch, guarded by one whose head shall answer for your continuous presence. Follow me."

Sunrise awakened the fierce old sultan to thoughts of the day's wrath.

"Release him," he directed the sentry who had guarded Amru. And then to the scribe, "The few minutes between now and the appearance of the prisoners in the hall of audience can avail you naught. And thus have I saved you from choosing between fidelity to me, or to your friend, el Idrisi. To your duties, Amru!"

The sultan smiled ironically. But he did not observe the curious light in Amru's eye as the scribe bowed himself from the presence; nor did he observe that Amru fingered a golden coin.

It was but a few minutes after the morning prayer that Amru took his post at the right of the sultan's dais in the hall of audience. Disposing about him his inks, reeds, and scrolls, he awaited the appearance of the court, and the pronouncing of doom upon Mamoun and the lovely Kashmiri bayadere. And as he waited, Amru peered anxiously about him, and with nervous impatience.

A moment later Iftikar the executioner, a huge negro, nude save for a scarlet loin-cloth, made his appearance in the hall of audience. Instead of his ponderous, crescent-bladed scimitar with which he usually executed the sultan's judgments, the African bore a tray upon which reposed two small flagons, and two large goblets of ancient, curiously wrought Cairene glass.

"And with you, exceeding peace," returned Amru in response to the negro's salutation. "But where is your scimitar? Is this to be a drinking bout instead of a passing of judgment?"

"Who am I to question the master?" countered the executioner. "Though I doubt that he will make me his cupbearer, for he claims that in the entire world there is no one who can make head and shoulders part company as neatly as I can," concluded the African with a justifiable touch of pride.

The negro turned to pick up the tray he had set on the steps of the dais.

"Just a moment, Iftikar," began the scribe; "since you have traveled so much, perhaps you can tell me what manner of coin this is."

The executioner took the proffered gold piece and examined it closely.

"It is a Feringhi coin, such as I once saw in the *souk* in Cairo," he announced. "And the image on it is that of an infidel sultan, upon whom be the wrath of Allah! But where did you get it?"

Before Amru could explain, a great gong sounded to announce the approach of the sultan and his court. The African tossed the gold piece to Amru, seized the tray, and took his post at the left of the judgment seat.

Eight cadaverous Annamite fan-bearers filed into the hall of audience and disposed themselves about the dais. Following them came a detachment of the guard, resplendent captains of horse, and pompously strutting officers of the sultan's household, officials, and distinguished visitors. Then came Ismail, the chief wazir stalking majestically to his position on the topmost step, and to the left of the dais; and last of all, the sultan himself, lean, hook nosed vulture, who, after taking his seat, signaled to Amru to read, as was the custom of the court, a verse from Al Qurán.

"By the noonday brightness, and by the night when it darkeneth," intoned the scribe, "thy lord hath not forsaken thee, nor hath he been displeased . . ."

"Sufficient! Bring in the prisoners!" commanded the sultan. And again he smiled as one who contemplates a subtle jest.

Mamoun el Idrisi, handsome and arrogant, and calm in the face of certain and unpleasant doom, was escorted to the foot of the dais to face the sultan's wrath; and with him was the Kashmiri bayadere, the wondrously lovely Dhivalani, beautiful, and equally composed in the presence of her sinister lord and master. All hope was gone, if ever hope there had been. No mercy could be expected from that fierce old man who smiled evilly from his commanding position. They had had their hour or two of grace, had tempted fate, had lost; and the utter hopelessness of it all made them unnaturally calm and self-possessed.

"You, Dhivalani, who were my favorite, and you, Mamoun el Idrisi, upon whom I conferred wealth and honor," began the sultan, whose words rolled forth like the cruel, resistless march of destiny, "have merited the sentence I shall pronounce, and more. My father, upon whom be peace, boiled his favorite in a great caldron and fed the broth to her lover until he choked from having had his

449

fill of the lady; and my grandfather, who sits in paradise at the Prophet's right hand, was even more severe."

The bayadere shuddered, more at the sultan's sardonic smile than at the horror he had mentioned. But Mamoun of the great race of Idris met the sultan's gaze unmoved.

"But I shall be merciful," continued the sultan. "No man or woman could live through enough torment to do you justice. In the end, you would die and cheat my vengeance; therefore have I devised so that your punishment shall outlast any that have ever before been inflicted. And to achieve that end, one of you must live."

The sultan paused to observe the effect of his words. In the eyes of each of the lovers he saw hope for the other. And then that fierce old man signaled to the African to advance.

"Here you see two flagons of wine, and two glasses. One is pure, the other charged with a poison laden with all the slow torments and consuming flames of that hell reserved for the infidel. Dhivalani, you shall select a glass for yourself, and leave one for your lover. Each shall drink; and the survivor shall go into exile, free and unharmed. That I swear by the Prophet's beard, and in the presence of the lords of the court. Dhivalani, choose your glass; and if you live, may you live long with the knowledge that you poisoned your lover; Mamoun, drink the glass she leaves you, and if by chance you survive, be happy in the knowledge of the madness and torment that bought your worthless life for you."

The sultan nodded to the African, who poured from each flagon into the glass standing next to it, then, advancing a pace, offered the girl her choice.

With the air of one trapped in the mazes of a hideous dream, the bayadere extended her slim, jeweled arm to indicate the goblet which would doom her to life, or sentence her lover to live at her cost. And then she hesitated.

"May I taste each glass before I make my choice?"

"That you may not do; nor, having made your selection, may you drink together. Each must meet fate alone; therefore, choose, and be happy in your choice," concluded the sultan with a twisted, satiric smile.

"Son of a thousand pigs!" began el Idrisi hoarsely; "inflict whatsoever you will! Do you think that I will buy my life with hers?"

"Indeed? Then perhaps you would rather see her eaten by starving rats, or would you have her as your companion in a bed of quicklime?" And the sultan, in the monotone of a priest chanting a pagan hymn, enumerated that which he could inflict even worse than that which he first mentioned.

"Therefore I fancy that you will accept my merciful sentence. And do not seek to arouse my wrath with rash words, hoping for a swift sword-stroke; for I have set my heart on this jest, and on none other. In half an hour I shall visit you to see whether you have drunk this wine. And if not, you shall both endure

450

that which I but mentioned, and more whereof even I have not dreamed. Dhivalani," he concluded, "make your choice."

And at these words Dhivalani with a gesture indicated the glass from which she would drink, and that which would remain as the portion of her lover. A moment's pause; an exchange of glances; the half parting of lips speaking a speechless farewell; and then members of the guard, followed by slaves who bore the fatal wine, escorted the lovers to separate rooms where each would meet destiny alone, without even the solace of a word of farewell ere the swiftly spreading poison executed the sultan's vengeance.

An attendant approached and presented to Iftikar his great scimitar; and other justice was dispensed, swift, sure, sanguinary. All the while the sultan smiled, as if in anticipation of a rare jest. At last he arose, dismissed the court, and, accompanied by Ismail, entered the room to which Mamoun had been taken to meet his fate.

El Idrisi lay on the tiled floor. A pool of blood testified that a poniard which had eluded the search of the guard had done its work well.

"I have won!" gasped el Idrisi, exultantly. "By your oath, you must set her free, for I did indeed taste the wine, and the bitterness thereof. But rather than drink it and die by her choice, I am dying by my own hand."

To which the sultan smilingly retorted, "But you lose, Mamoun, for the bitterness which you tasted was but that natural to the wine. Neither glass was poisoned; and each of you was to be set free, forever to mourn in exile the life gained at the other's cost. I shall keep my oath and set her free, even as I would have done for you. You two might some day have met on the road of destiny; but now you die, knowing that you have sentenced her to believe that her choice gave her life at your cost."

"Father of many pigs," coughed el Idrisi, "you lie!"

"Then look, Mamoun, see whether or not this wine is poisoned."

And smiling at his own excellent jest, the sultan drank the wine at a draft.

The next day a new sultan ruled in Angor-lana; for Amru, unable to warn the lovers of the sultan's jest, had in the kindness of his heart poisoned both flagons of wine while the African executioner had been examining the Feringhi coin.

Talent

Theodore Sturgeon

Mrs. Brent and Precious were sitting on the farmhouse porch when little Jokey sidled out from behind the barn and came catfooting up to them. Precious, who had ringlets and was seven years old and very clean, stopped swinging on the glider and watched him. Mrs. Brent was reading a magazine. Jokey stopped at the foot of the steps.

"MOM!" he rasped.

Mrs. Brent started violently, rocked too far back, bumped her knobby hairdo against the clapboards, and said, "Good heavens, you little br— darling, you frightened me!"

Jokey smiled.

Precious said, "Snaggletooth."

"If you want your mother," said Mrs. Brent reasonably, "why don't you go inside and speak to her?"

Disgustedly, Jokey vetoed the suggestion with "Ah-h-h . . ." He faced the house. "MOM!" he shrieked, in a tone that spoke of death and disaster.

There was a crash from the kitchen, and light footsteps. Jokey's mother, whose name was Mrs. Purney, came out, pushing back a wisp of hair from frightened eyes.

"Oh, the sweet," she cooed. She flew out and fell on her knees beside Jokey. "Did it hurt its little, then? Aw, did it was . . ."

Jokey said, "Gimme a nickel!"

"Please," suggested Precious.

"Of course, darling," fluttered Mrs. Purney. "My word, yes. Just as soon as ever we go into town, you shall have a nickel. Two, if you're good."

"Gimme a nickel," said Jokey ominously.

"But, darling, what for? What will you do with a nickel out here?"

Jokey thrust out his hand. "I'll hold my breath."

Mrs. Purney rose, panicked. "Oh, dear, don't. Oh, please don't. Where's my reticule?"

"On top of the bookcase, out of my reach," said Precious, without rancor.

"Oh, yes, so it is. Now, Jokey, you wait right here and I'll just . . ." and her twittering faded into the house.

Mrs. Brent cast her eyes upward and said nothing.

"You're a little stinker," said Precious.

Jokey looked at her with dignity. "Mom," he called imperiously.

Mrs. Purney came to heel on the instant, bearing a nickel.

Jokey, pointing with the same movement with which he acquired the coin, reported, "She called me a little stinker."

"Really!" breathed Mrs. Purney, bridling. "I think, Mrs. Brent, that your child could have better manners."

"She has, Mrs. Purney, and uses them when they seem called for."

Mrs. Purney looked at her curiously, decided, apparently, that Mrs. Brent meant nothing by the statement (in which she was wrong) and turned to her son, who was walking briskly back to the barn.

"Don't hurt yourself, Puddles," she called.

She elicited no response whatever, and, smiling vaguely at Mrs. Brent and daughter, went back to her kitchen.

"Puddles," said Precious ruminatively. "I bet I know why she calls him that. Remember Gladys's puppy that—"

"Precious," said Mrs. Brent, "you shouldn't have called Joachim a word like that."

"I s'pose not," Precious agreed thoughtfully. "He's really a—"

Mrs. Brent, watching the carven pink lips, said warningly, "Precious!" She shook her head. "I've asked you not to say that."

"Daddy—"

"Daddy caught his thumb in the hinge of the car-trunk. That was different."

"Oh, no," corrected Precious. "You're thinking of the time he opened on'y the bottom half of the Dutch door in the dark. When he pinched his thumb, he said—"

"Would you like to see my magazine?"

Precious rose and stretched delicately. "No, thank you, Mummy. I'm going out to the barn to see what Jokey's going to do with that nickel."

"Precious . . ."

"Yes, Mummy."

"Oh—nothing. I suppose it's all right. Don't quarrel with Jokey, now."

"Not 'less he quarrels with me," she replied, smiling charmingly.

Precious had new patent-leather shoes with hard heels and broad ankle-straps. They looked neat and very shiny against her yellow socks. She walked carefully in the path, avoiding the moist grasses that nodded over the edges, stepping sedately over a small muddy patch.

Jokey was not in the barn. Precious walked through, smelling with pleasure the mixed, warm smells of chaff-dust, dry hay and manure. Just outside, by the wagon-door, was the pigpen. Jokey was standing by the rail fence. At his feet was a small pile of green apples. He picked one up and hurled it with all his might at the brown sow. It went *putt!* on her withers, and she went *ergh!*

"Hey!" said Precious.

Putt-ergh! Then he looked up at Precious, snarled silently, and picked up another apple. *Putt-ergh!*

"Why are you doing that for?"

Putt-ergh!

"Hear that? My mom done just like that when I hit her in the stummick."

"She did?"

"Now this," said Jokey, holding up an apple, "is a stone. Listen." He hurled it. *Thunk-e-e-e-ergh!*

Precious was impressed. Her eyes widened, and she stepped back a pace.

"Hey, look out where you're goin', stoopid!"

He ran to her and grasped her left biceps roughly, throwing her up against the railings. She yelped and stood rubbing her arm—rubbing off grime, and far deeper in indignation than she was in fright.

Jokey paid her no attention. "You an' your shiny feet," he growled. He was down on one knee, feeling for two twigs stuck in the ground about eight inches apart. "Y'might've squashed 'em!"

Precious, her attention brought to her new shoes, stood turning one of them, glancing light from the toecaps, from the burnished sides, while complacency flowed back into her.

"What?"

With the sticks, Jokey scratched aside the loose earth and, one by one, uncovered the five tiny, naked, blind creatures which lay buried there. They were only about three-quarters of an inch long, with little withered limbs and twitching noses. They writhed. There were ants, too. Very busy ants.

"What are they?"

"Mice, stoopid," said Jokey. "Baby mice. I found 'em in the barn."

"How did they get there?"

"I put 'em there."

"How long have they been there?"

"'Bout four days," said Jokey, covering them up again. "They last a long time."

"Does your mother know those mice are out here?"

"No, and you better not say nothin', ya hear?"

"Would your mother whip you?"

"*Her?*" The syllable came out as an incredulous jeer.

"What about your father?"

"Aw, I guess he'd like to lick me. But he ain't got a chance. Mom'd have a fit."

"You mean she'd get mad at him?"

"No, stoopid. A fit. You know, scrabbles at the air and get suds on her mouth, and all. Falls down and twitches." He chuckled.

"But—why?"

"Well, it's about the on'y way she can handle Pop, I guess. He's always wanting to do something about me. She won't let 'um, so I c'n do anything I want."

"What do you do?"

"I'm talunted. Mom says so."

"Well, what do you do?"

"You're sorta nosy."

"I don't believe you can do anything, stinky."

"Oh, I can't?" Jokey's face was reddening.

"No, you can't! You talk a lot, but you can't really do anything."

Jokey walked up close to her and breathed in her face the way the man with the grizzly beard does to the clean-cut cowboy who is tied up to the dynamite kegs in the movies on Saturday.

"I can't, huh?"

She stood her ground. "All right, if you're so smart, let's see what you were going to do with that nickel!"

Surprisingly, he looked abashed. "You'd laugh," he said.

"No, I wouldn't," she said guilelessly. She stepped forward, opened her eyes very wide, shook her head so that her gold ringlets swayed, and said very gently, "Truly I wouldn't, Jokey . . ."

"Well—" he said, and turned to the pigpen. The brindled sow was rubbing her shoulder against the railing, grunting softly to herself. She vouchsafed them one small red-rimmed glance, and returned to her thoughts.

Jokey and Precious stood up on the lower rail and looked down on the pig's broad back.

"You're not goin' to tell anybody?" he asked.

" 'Course not."

"Well, awright. Now lookit. You ever see a china piggy bank?"

"Sure I have," said Precious.

"How big?"

"Well, I got one about this big."

"Aw, that's nothin'."

"And my girl-friend Gladys has one *this* big."

"Phooey."

"Well," said Precious, "in town, in a big drugstore, I saw one THIS big," and she put out her hands about thirty inches apart.

"That's pretty big," admitted Jokey. "Now I'll show you *something*." To the brindled sow, he said sternly, "You are a piggy bank."

The sow stopped rubbing herself against the rails. She stood quite still. Her bristles merged into her hide. She was hard and shiny—as shiny as the little girl's hard shoes. In the middle of the broad back, a slot appeared—or had been there all along, as far as Precious could tell. Jokey produced a warm sweaty nickel and dropped it into the slot.

There was a distant, vitreous, hollow bouncing click from inside the sow.

Mrs. Purney came out on the porch and creaked into a wicker chair with a tired sigh.

"They are a handful, aren't they?" said Mrs. Brent.

"You just don't know," moaned Mrs. Purney.

Mrs. Brent's eyebrows went up. "Precious is a model. Her teacher says so. That wasn't too easy to do."

"Yes, she's a very good little girl. But my Joachim is—uh, talented, you know. That makes it very hard."

"How is he talented? What can he do?"

"He can do anything," said Mrs. Purney after a slight hesitation.

Mrs. Brent glanced at her, saw that her tired eyes were closed, and shrugged. It made her feel better. Why must mothers always insist that their children are better than all others?

"Now, my Precious," she said, "—and mind you, I'm not saying this because she's my child—my Precious plays the piano very well for a child her age. Why, she's already in her third book and she's not eight yet."

Mrs. Purney said, without opening her eyes, "Jokey doesn't play. I'm sure he could if he wanted to."

Mrs. Brent saw what an inclusive boast this might be, and wisely refrained from further itemization. She took another tack. "Don't you find, Mrs. Purney, that it is easy to make a child obedient and polite by being firm?"

Mrs. Purney opened her eyes at last, and looked troubledly at Mrs. Brent. "A child should love its parents."

"Oh, of course!" smiled Mrs. Brent. "But these modern ideas of surrounding a child with love and freedom to an extent where it becomes a little tyrant—well! I just can't see that! Of course I don't mean Joachim," she added quickly, sweetly. "He's a *dear* child, really . . ."

"He's got to be given everything he wants," murmured Mrs. Purney in a strange tone. It was fierce and it was by rote. "He's *got* to be kept happy."

"You must love him very much," snapped Mrs. Brent viciously, suddenly determined to get some reaction out of this weak, indulgent creature. She got it.

"I hate him," said Mrs. Purney.

Her eyes were closed again, and now she almost smiled, as if the release of those words had been a yearned-for thing. Then she sat abruptly erect, her pale eyes round, and she grasped her lower lip and pulled it absurdly down and to the side.

"I didn't mean that," she gasped. She flung herself down before Mrs. Brent, and gabbled, "I didn't mean it! Don't tell him! He'll do things to us. He'll loosen the housebeams when we're sleeping. He'll turn the breakfast to snakes and frogs, and make that big toothy mouth again out of the oven door. Don't tell him! Don't tell him!"

Mrs. Brent, profoundly shocked, and not comprehending a word of this, instinctively put out her arms and gathered the other woman close.

"I can do lots of things," Jokey said. "I can do anything."

"Gee," breathed Precious, looking at the china pig. "What are you going to do with it now?"

"I dunno. I'll let it be a pig again, I guess."

"Can you change it back into a pig?"

"I don't hafta, stoopid. It'll be a pig by itself. Soon's I forget about it."

"Does that always happen?"

"No. If I busted that ol' china pig, it'd take longer, an' the pig would be all busted up when it changed back. All guts and blood," he added, sniggering. "I done that with a calf once."

"Gee," said Precious, still wide-eyed. "When you grow up, you'll be able to do anything you want."

"Yeah." Jokey looked pleased. "But I can do anything I want now." He frowned. "I just sometimes don't know what to do next."

"You'll know when you grow up," she said confidently.

"Oh, sure. I'll live in a big house in town, and look out of the windows, and bust up people and change 'em to ducks and snakes and things. I'll make flies as big as chickenhawks, or maybe as big as horses, and put 'em in the schools. I'll knock down the big buildings an' squash people."

He picked up a green apple and hurled it accurately at the brown sow.

"Gosh, and you won't have to practice piano, or listen to any old teachers," said Precious, warming to the possibilities. "Why, you won't even have to—*oh!*"

"What'sa matter?"

"That beetle. I hate them."

"Thass just a stag beetle," said Jokey with superiority. "Lookit here. I'll show you something."

He took out a book of matches and struck one. He held the beetle down with a dirty forefinger, and put the flame to its head. Precious watched attentively until the creature stopped scrabbling.

"Those things scare me," she said when he stood up.

"You're a sissy."

"I am not."

"Yes you are. *All* girls are sissies."

"You're dirty and you're a stinker," said Precious.

He promptly went to the pigpen and, from beside the trough, scooped up a heavy handful of filth. From his crouch, Jokey hurled it at her with a wide overhand sweep, so that it splattered her from the shoulder down, across the front of her dress, with a great wet gob for the toe of her left shiny shoe.

"Now who's dirty? Now who stinks?" he sang.

Precious lifted her skirt and looked at it in horror and loathing. Her eyes filled with angry tears. Sobbing, she rushed at him. She slapped him with little-girl clumsiness, hand-over-shoulder fashion. She slapped him again.

"Hey! Who are you hitting?" he cried in amazement. He backed off and suddenly grinned. "I'll fix you," he said, and disappeared without another word.

Whimpering with fury and revulsion, Precious pulled a handful of grass and began wiping her shoe.

Something moved into her field of vision. She glanced at it, squealed, and moved back. It was an enormous stag beetle, three times life-size, and it was scuttling toward her.

Another beetle—or the same one—met her at the corner.

With her hard black shiny shoes, she stepped on this one, so hard that the calf of her leg ached and tingled for the next half-hour.

The men were back when she returned to the house. Mr. Brent had been surveying Mr. Purney's fence-lines. Jokey was not missed before they left. Mrs. Purney looked drawn and frightened, and seemed glad that Mrs. Brent was leaving before Jokey came in for his supper.

Precious said nothing when asked about the dirt on her dress, and, under the circumstances, Mrs. Brent thought better of questioning her too closely.

In the car, Mrs. Brent told her husband that she thought Jokey was driving Mrs. Purney crazy.

It was her turn to be driven very nearly mad, the next morning, when Jokey turned up. Most of him.

Surprising, really, how much beetle had stuck to the hard black shoe, and, when it was time, turned into what they found under their daughter's bed.

The Tapestry Gate

Leigh Brackett

I must have it, Dick. It's exactly what I want for your den."

"But I don't want it, Jane," groaned Dick Stratton. "I want that sporting print of mine."

Jane Stratton's carefully made-up face, under the fashionable monstrosity she termed a hat, was set like a china mask.

"I'm going to have that place decent enough so that I can show it to my friends without apologizing. Will you bid for it, or must I?" Her voice was hard, uncompromising.

"You don't give a damn what I want, do you?" muttered Stratton savagely. "You don't care about anybody but yourself."

Jane shrugged coldly.

"I can't see what possible difference it can make to you," she answered. "You always have your nose poked into some silly book anyway. Are you going to bid?"

Dick Stratton placed his bid. He was filled with cold desperate rage, not so much against the scrap of tapestry itself as what it stood for. To him it was a symbol of Jane's implacable domination, her maddening selfishness and stupidity.

Three times in the last year his house had been torn to pieces and redone in answer to the latest fad. It was no longer a home—it was a showcase for Jane. He was banished to his den, and even there he had nothing to say about the furnishings, though his bank account and salary were drained to the bottom to pay for them.

He got the tapestry for seventy dollars. It was an odd thing, about two feet square, with nothing but a patternless blending of odd colors. Jane took it with a little nod of triumph.

"This finishes the house," she said. "Let's go."

"Until next time," prophesied Stratton, under his breath. Their expensive coupé stood at the curb. Before getting in, Jane unrolled the tapestry in the sunlight.

"Modern as Dali. Pity you can't appreciate these things, Dick. It would make things so much more agreeable for me."

Stratton stifled his mounting fury. The tapestry looked different out in the sunlight, almost as though it would form a picture if one could just find the focus. Black and brown and silver, russet and gold, it shone with a soft lustre unlike any thread he had ever seen. Queer, springy texture, too. He reached out to touch it.

"De Good Lawd have mussy!"

Stratton jerked a quick, startled look upward. The Negro bootblack who kept a stand beside the auctioneer's was staring at the tapestry, wild-eyed with fear. As though drawn by the sheer fascination of terror, he came closer.

"Ah seed one o' dem befo'. Ah look into a conjure-woman's hut way down in de swamps in Loosiana, an' she done had one. She laughin' fit to bus', an' she say Mis' Commeroi's name, and nex' week Mis' Commeroi done gone! De conjure-woman say it's de Devil's joke-rag, whut's used all over de worl' to trap people.

" 'T'aint only in dis worl'!" His gnarled black hand fastened hard on Stratton's arm. "De conjure-people knows conjures in other places. Dey swap souls, jus' fo de laugh. Anywheah dey's hate in de house, it work. It steal yo' soul! Hate's whut make it work. Burn it! Burn it!"

Stratton disengaged his arm in a burst of anger.

"Sorry," he said, "but I just paid seventy dollars for that rag. My wife insists it's modern art, so you must be mistaken. Besides," he added dryly, "there's no hate in our house." And he smiled as he thought of his own growing dark hate.

He turned his back on Jane's sharp look and slid under the wheel. The Negro still stood there, shivering, his gaze on the tapestry, lying now in Jane's lap.

"Look whut it's made of," he whispered. "Den maybe Ah'm not such a fool."

Stratton looked. The sunlight glinted on the haphazard threads, crisp and almost alive looking. It was like—well, like Jane's hair had been when he married her. That was before he had money, before the beauty parlors had created their shellacked perfection.

With a shock of revulsion, he realized what it was.

"Jane! It's human hair!" he exclaimed.

Jane's expensively-gloved hands recoiled from it.

"Ugh!" she shuddered. "How disgusting! Dick, take it back. I won't have it in the house!"

Stratton's mouth twisted in a little smile. After all, what was so disgusting about it? Wigs were made of human hair, and nobody minded.

"Why not? Just think, Jane, there won't be a woman in New York that won't envy you," he sneered. "You'll have something that nobody else can possibly copy. I can just see Mrs. Lydell—"

460

"You needn't make fun of my friends," snapped Jane. Rather reluctantly, she picked it up, turned it in the sunlight. "Still, there's something in what you say. Alice Kelly copied everything in my drawing room and I had to have it completely done over. And after all, it'll be in your den. Yes, I'll keep it."

Jane, thought Stratton as he drove away, was really a horrible woman. His knuckles showed white against the steering wheel as he felt helpless anger welling up in him.

The Negro bootblack watched the car as far as he could see it. Then he shook his head and muttered something as his fingers touched the amulet in his pocket.

That night, when Dick Stratton rose to go to bed, he glanced at the tapestry hanging over the cubistic mantel. The light from the nearby, hideous lamp brought the formless pattern almost into focus. He had a momentary glimpse of people ringed about some central object beneath a darkly branching thing, and just above the center of the little square, he thought he saw a face. An evil, laughing face.

"Nonsense," he grunted. And then the bootblack's half forgotten words came back. He stared at the tapestry, drowsily, thinking of the disappearance of Mis' Commeroi, whoever she was, and thinking—

With a start of horror, he realized what he was thinking. He was thinking how wonderful it would be if the Negro's ravings were true, if Jane might disappear into the picture and leave him free to find happiness. He was thinking of murder.

He turned and fled the room.

Jane didn't sleep well, either, that night. Stratton could hear her tossing in the adjoining room. It kept him awake, and he thought, though he didn't wish to think. Jane was ruining him. She was vain and extravagant and foolish, and cared for nothing except what she could get out of him. But he had no real grounds for divorce. She'd fight to keep him with every bit of strength and every trick at her command. Besides that, he couldn't afford the scandal.

And yet his life was ruined. He was still young. If Jane should die—

"No!" he whispered. "Never that. You can't get away with that!"

After a long time he slept and dreamed of a soul-trap made of human hair and the Devil laughing over Jane's dead body.

Jane was late for breakfast. Stratton, on his way down, was drawn as though by a magnet into his den. Sunlight struck through ultra-violet glass, which, like everything else in the place, he hated. It shone obliquely on the tapestry.

Stratton felt the skin of his back crawl icily.

There *was* a picture!

Twelve people were standing in a ring about a cross-shaped block that was oddly channeled. A most peculiar and unpleasant tree coiled twisting branches above them, and, standing behind the cross-shaped block so that his face was just above the tapestry's center—

He wasn't really a man. Somehow Dick Stratton knew that. He looked like a man, but no normal human ever had such eyes, like mirrors of all the foul, evil thoughts that had been born since time began. Laughing eyes. Horribly laughing. As though sin and wickedness were the most pleasurable, the most amusing, the most soul-satisfying things in the universe.

Involuntarily Stratton closed his own eyes and jerked away; and when he looked again the picture was gone.

"Some trick of the light," he whispered almost fiercely. "Imagination. Those dreams I had."

But he couldn't shake the vision of those laughing eyes. In self-defense, he tried again to find the same spot from which he had seen the picture, but the sun had moved a bit and he could not. For a long time he stood staring at the blurred, mocking little rag, trying to understand the feelings that raged within him. Then, starting almost guiltily at Jane's step in the hall, he shook himself out of the queer mood that held him.

"Just tired," he told himself. "Worried. Mustn't let this—" He'd been going to say "morbid," but the mood was more than morbid. It was horrible. Funny how that Negro's wild ranting had fished up the thoughts he had never admitted even to himself. You didn't think about—murder. You didn't let yourself hate people that way, openly.

Of course, it wasn't really murder. That stuff about the tapestry being a trap was just ignorant superstition. He hadn't really seen that picture. There was nothing to it. But the thought was there just the same, and he couldn't blink it—he wished there were something to it.

"No I don't!" Stratton pressed his fists to his temples. "Jane isn't really bad. Only selfish and stupid. I've got to stop all this right now. After all, I married her. I've got to try to go on."

He didn't look at the tapestry again. But as he left the room, a thought crossed his mind, unbidden:

"If what the Negro said was true, it wouldn't really be murder. Because there wouldn't be any body." He repeated it, half aloud.

Jane faced him across the table like a china doll dressed in peach-colored satin.

"Dick," she said, before he was fairly in his chair, "I've got to have some money."

"But, Jane! Your allowance—"

"It's gone. I spent it on that dress for Mrs. Lydell's reception, but I've got to have another."

Stratton put down his paper.

"Why, Jane?" he asked.

"Alice Kelly has one of the same material. I simply can't wear the thing to the reception."

"Then wear something else."

"Dick! You know perfectly well I haven't—"

"Never mind," he said wearily. "I can't give you any more money this month. You've cleaned me out."

Jane's mouth tightened and her blue eyes went flat with anger.

"I call that gratitude!" she shouted. "I wear myself out trying to keep your home from looking like a hog-wallow. I try to keep up appearances when I go out. And you call me extravagant! Well, if you haven't any pride, I have. I'm not going to let those women laugh at us behind our backs because you're so stingy."

Stratton got up.

"Jane," he said very quietly, "you'd better be careful. I don't want the scandal, nor the trouble. But if you don't learn some sense, by heaven, I'll divorce you!"

Jane smiled.

"You can't," she said smugly. "I won't give you a divorce. And if you try to get one, I'll tell about Doris Rider."

Stratton's heart stopped, jerked, and pounded on. He hadn't known that Jane had ever heard of Doris Rider.

"You can't," he said thickly. "There's never been anything between us. Nothing at all!"

"But you can't prove it." Jane nodded, sure of herself. "Even if you could, I don't think such publicity would do her career any good. She's pretty famous, you know. Child welfare, isn't it? I think you'd best make me out a check, Dick."

He made it out without seeing either pen or figures. Then he left the room. He found himself standing in his den, staring at the tapestry, fists clenched and veins almost bursting with the black rage that shook him.

"I wish it were true!" he whispered savagely. "I wish the damned thing were a trap. I wish Jane were dead and in hell!"

It couldn't be just the light. It was as though the hate in him reached out, touched the little woven square of human hair and brought out the picture like a magic wash. Twelve people ringed around a cross-shaped block, with that high priest of hell laughing down at them. It was clear and unmistakable. So clear that Stratton realized there was an empty place in the ring just at the high priest's right, as though the weaver had intended a thirteenth person.

He went closer. It must be the violet glass that gave the picture the illusion of depth, the sudden dizzy effect of mists parting over an abyss. It was almost as though he could see the trees of that strange forest growing, spreading back and out, shooting upward into an eerie sky.

He found he was trembling violently. He turned away, though it took all his will power. He must get hold of himself—The crazy gibberings of that bootblack, coupled with his own disrupted emotional state, had set everything awry. Suppose he did see a picture. There had been pictures before, done with treated dyes that showed only in certain lights or temperatures. After all, he had no idea how human hair would react as a fabric. The fact that there was a picture in the tapestry didn't in any way mean that what the Negro said was true.

A soul-trap. Conjure-folk of one world bartering souls with the wizards of another. Traffickers in evil, laughing at their secret jokes. Even Satan had to have a laugh now and then.

"Anywheah dey's hate in de house, it work!"

"No," said Dick Stratton. "No. I'm a sensible man. It's impossible. I'll simply get rid of the cursed thing."

But if he did, he'd be admitting fear. And besides, buried deep under his denials, under the revulsion of his civilized, conscious mind, was the fiendish, trembling hope that it was true.

For the second time Dick Stratton fled the room. And it seemed that he took with him a breath of charnel wind from a deep and rotting forest.

Jane slept even worse that night. Dick Stratton shivered in a mad turmoil of thought. In the morning, utterly unable to keep away, he looked at the tapestry.

It must have been the light; but he was almost sure that a nebulous mist was forming in the thirteenth place, the gap in the circle.

In the evening they went to one of Jane's interminable 'musicales.' Stratton, dog-tired, went to his den for some papers he'd want in the morning. And this time there was no doubt. A blurred shape was forming on the weird tapestry.

Jane's voice woke him from troubled sleep, late that night.

"What will you give me?" she was saying, quite clearly.

Stratton smiled grimly, then shivered. There was something unnatural about her voice, about the way she waited, as though she were listening to someone. After a bit she sighed, a little breath of pure ecstasy.

"How wonderful!" she whispered. "Everything I want. Everything! And no one to nag me. But so far away, another world!"

Again the waiting silence.

"What payment?" she whispered. A pause. "It can't be anything very bad, you're so nice. So generous. Everything I want! But my husband?"

There was quite a long wait this time. And then Jane laughed and rolled over into sound, deep sleep.

It was several minutes before Dick Stratton realized what a chillingly horrible sound that little low chuckle had been.

Driven by a feverish wildness, he went quietly downstairs, using a small pocket torch. In the pitch darkness of the den the beam made a brilliant white finger of light and touched unerringly on the thirteenth place in the circle in the tapestry of human hair.

The mist had thickened, grown to the blurred yet recognizable outlines of a woman.

The torch went out as Stratton dropped it. He stood there in the grip of a dense fear that crawled out of some unknown abyss to freeze his heart to ice and his blood to snow-water. Every atom of common sense, of sanity, or normality, rose in him to declare that this was a lie, that it was all a nightmare from which he would awaken.

But he knew. And the Negro had known. Jane, sleeping upstairs with some strange new power, knew.

There was hate in this house. He hated Jane, and his hate had broken the barrier. He had let Jane's selfish little soul be tempted to—to what?

Even in the dark the picture was visible, as though it had light of its own. It was as if some unimagined moon rode an eerie sky, to light a demon's way through that forest. And all the while the high-priest's face was full of laughter.

Shuddering, sick with terror, Dick Stratton pressed his hands to his pounding temples. There was still time. He could burn the tapestry. Jane would be safe. The whole mad business could be forgotten.

But he wouldn't be free. He'd have Jane's selfishness, Jane's extravagance, Jane's smug knowledge of her power over him, until the end of his life, or the end of his money—or both. This way, if he didn't burn the tapestry, he'd be rid of her. He wouldn't really have murdered her. There couldn't possibly be any legal repercussions. They'd never find her body, because it would be in the tapestry. He'd be free.

He could enjoy life, perhaps even marry Doris Rider.

Another thought occurred to him, and he jerked a frightened glance at the picture. If the hated one was trapped into the other world, what happened to the hater?

Then he shook his head. The circle was closed. There was no more room for anyone. Besides, after Jane was gone, he could burn the tapestry. Then the gateway would be closed forever.

For a long, long time Dick Stratton stood in that cold, dark room, looking into the laughing evil eyes of the high priest. Then he turned and went back to bed, leaving the tapestry safe on the wall.

Jane was languid and tired the next day. It was as though some vital force were being drained out of her. Stratton thought of the mist in the tapestry and smiled. He even gave her a check without complaint.

"You dreamed last night. I heard you talking," he said, prompted by a curiosity he couldn't deny.

"Did I? I don't remember." Jane stared vacantly out of the window.

Stratton fought down a shudder and left.

That night Jane, moving almost as though in a dream, put on a white satin gown that had been part of her trousseau. It looked more like an evening dress, with its exquisite white roses at the neck. One of them was loose.

Dick Stratton lay down, but he knew he wouldn't sleep that night. He heard Jane's breathing slow to a deep, steady rhythm. For several hours she slept. Then, without speaking or waking, he heard her get up.

He followed her silently downstairs. Moving slowly at first, Jane went faster and faster, like a child approaching some promised treat. At the doorway of the den she paused, and Stratton saw her shiver, as though some shadow of dread had touched her. Then she went through.

He didn't follow. He knew he couldn't and remain sane. Grabbing a whiskey decanter from the library, he fled back upstairs, where he paced his room all night in a curious and semi-alcoholic state that plunged between light-headed relief and nightmare horror.

Morning brought saner thinking. His first impulse was to burn the tapestry at once, but he decided against it. The act was too abrupt, too senseless. It might even lead to awkward questions. And while there was no danger of a murder charge lodging permanently, there was always the fact that he dared not tell the truth. It would only mean an insane asylum.

Taking a deep breath, he went downstairs to call the police.

He did rather well with his bewildered husband act. He might have managed to get away with it, but there were complications. Jane's maid testified that her lady wasn't the sort of person to leave in the middle of the night without money, or clothes.

The butler hastened to tell of their quarrel over money. Jane's mother, a fat, overdressed, hysterical woman, heaped abuse on Dick Stratton's head. And the Law frowned, having heard before of mysterious vanishings that turned out to have been involuntary.

Stratton was called into the den for private questioning. He stood it for a surprisingly long time, bathed in icy sweat, heart thudding wildly, fists clenched. But his eyes were drawn, slowly, inexorably above the mantel toward the cloth made of human hair.

A shaft of sunlight shone through the violet glass, lighting the tapestry like a spotlight. The ring of people stood there under the monstrous tree, clearer than Stratton had ever seen them. Again he had that dizzy sense of depth, of distance. Their faces were ghoulish, convulsed with a secret mirth that held the shadow of a horror beyond human knowledge. They waited; with a curious, relaxed tensity, they waited. And the eyes of the high priest laughed.

The nebulous mist had thickened to solidity. The thirteenth place was filled.

Dick Stratton's nerves broke. His story lost coherence, became studded with babblings that hung on the brink of madness. He tried to pull himself together. He knew, in some lucid corner of his brain, that it was only the shock of seeing the final, indisputable proof—the mad, the impossible. He achieved silence, but that was all.

The frown of the Law deepened. The half-empty whiskey decanter was found in his room. And then, under the tapestry, almost hidden by the cubistic jut of the hearth, a white satin rose.

Dick Stratton looked at his wife, standing at the high priest's right, at the head of the cross-shaped block. The white satin gown showed bone-white against the dark of the twisting tree, the gown with the satin rose missing at the neck.

"What are you staring at?" demanded the Law, and it was then Stratton realized that the picture was visible only to himself. He laughed, just a shade hysterically.

"You'd better come with us," said the Law, "till we get this business cleared up. Sorry. Suspicion of murder."

Dick Stratton went quietly. He wasn't afraid of a murder charge. But an uneasy question clung in his mind.

"The Devil's joke-rag. What are they laughing at?" he would ask himself, frantically.

After a bit he was glad he was in jail. He hadn't realized what an unhealthy influence the house was beginning to have on him. He stood the grilling of the homicide men well enough, and by nightfall he had so recovered his assurance that he lay down on his cell cot in a mood for healthy sleep. It was all over, and he was rid of Jane. He was safe. All he had to do now was wait until they let him go. Then he would burn the tapestry and forget about it.

He slept—but not well. He woke in the morning, tired and dimly conscious of dreams, dreams he could not quite recall, hideous dreams.

It was then that he began to be afraid.

The next night it was worse. He woke in a cold sweat of fear, his mind breaking with an almost physical struggle from a black web of evil. Then he slept again, dreamed again, and woke, screaming. He fought until they threatened him with a strait-jacket. Then he crouched silently in a corner, trembling because of his knowledge.

He, too, was being drawn into that circle!

Another nebulous mist was growing and thickening on that hellish tapestry of human hair, a mist that would be himself. He knew that, surely as he had ever known anything in his life.

He had to get out. He had to go and burn that tapestry. But he couldn't get out. He had to wait. He fought against sleep, but it trapped him. He dreamed, of a ring of leering faces, of a monstrous, towering tree, of a band of constriction, of heaviness.

Jane's dreams couldn't have been like this. She hadn't been ridden with terror. She hadn't remembered them when she woke. And the circle was filled. There was no place for him to go.

What was happening to him? What inevitable fate was in store for him?

They talked about letting him go the next day. No body, no murder. But the Law was reluctant to give up, just yet. Stratton stayed. And again sleep caught him like an entangling cloak.

He saw the tapestry hanging on his wall, and a little point of light struck full on the high priest's face. His eyes were full of laughter, his face convulsed with some secret, cosmic mirth.

A gateway between two dimensions, a trap woven of human hair to snare souls so that Satan could have his laugh. Stratton felt evil. A black, abnormal sensation brushed his mind with charnel fingers. An evil that attacked the subconscious in sleep and lured the soul away, away into—

He woke shrieking, fighting back a knowledge that struggled to reveal itself. Again they threatened him into silence, and again he crouched—shivering, thinking.

He could feel a vital force draining out of him. First from his soul, then his body. Something was waiting for him in the tapestry, something that made his dreams different from Jane's.

It wouldn't be long now—perhaps tonight. He had to get out, he had to burn the tapestry before it was too late.

Miraculously, his cell door clashed open.

"All right, Stratton," they said. "This still looks fishy, but we can't prosecute without a body. You can go."

His trip home was a nightmare wherein he strove to hurry with his feet buried in quicksand. Everything was against him—traffic lights, all the possible delays of driving. A consuming weakness weighted him, coupled with fear that tottered on the brink of madness. One single thought hammered over and over within his mind:

"Burn the tapestry, burn the tapestry."

The servants were gone, amusing themselves during his absence. He let himself in, ran panting down the hall to his den. The sun was dropping low in the west.

Shaking with frantic haste, Stratton clawed his cigarette lighter from his pocket and reached up to tear the tapestry from its place on the wall.

A level red ray struck through the violet glass full on the waiting, laughing eyes of the high priest. Those eyes drew Stratton's as though an invisible bond had been forged in those minutes when he had stood there in the dark, making his decision.

Stratton screamed once. The lighter dropped from his hand and lay unheeded, burning a hole in the pale rug.

The sunlight dimmed, reddened. Shadows curled across his vision, drew back, showed him depth and thickness. He reeled in icy vertigo as distance opened suddenly into long forest aisles. Tiny trees shot hugely up and up into an eerie sky.

Dick Stratton swayed horribly between two worlds. The little figures swelled dizzily to human size and the shadows thickened around the monstrous tree. A heavy, sepulchral breeze rustled the clothing of the thirteen who stood in the waiting circle, and the laughing face of the high priest was horribly close to his own.

In a wrenching whirl of worlds and dimensions, Dick Stratton looked at the spot where his soul-mist had thickened and shaped. Then he was lying on the grooved and cross-shaped block. Bonds cut his wrists and ankles as he stared up into a face contorted with secret, evil mirth.

A pan-pipe made a reedy, whispering chuckle. A little ripple of laughter ran through the waiting circle. And as though the pipe had been a signal, they closed in.

A ring of faces was over him, blotting out the twisting pattern of the tree above. He saw the stamp of evil on them, the mark of souls condemned mingled with the sins that had brought them there—hate, greed, wickedness. His gaze fled wildly across them, stopped on Jane's haughty, selfish face—a face that had changed. . . .

The high priest laughed, and the deep, gloating sound went round the circle like a litany. The Devil's joke-rag. Why did they laugh, why—

Dick Stratton lay on the cross-shaped block, quite still, and beyond screaming.

In another minute, he would know.

The Terminus

Kim Newman

They had me spend my first month out of training processing statements. It was more like public relations than police work. Nobody the desk sergeant passed on to me was ever going to see any action arising from their complaint. It was my job to give them a polystyrene cup of coffee and politely explain that playing in a public playground was not an offence. The desk sergeant didn't approve of the Metropolitan Police Graduate Entry scheme which had given me the rank of Inspector over him; so I had to deal with all the nutters in Holborn. They felt more comfortable surrounded by blue serge and had vintage stories about Martians in the plumbing. Most were satisfied just to get their loony notions on police notepaper. I filed all the statements, but they might as well have been shredded.

By the time Judyth Staines was sent to my strip-lit cubicle, the novelty had gone. I'd learned all the pigeon holes: she was an Overly Nervous Missing Persons Reporter. She wore her hair in purple tentacles, insisted on the 'y' in her name, and had a cheery *Kill a Pig Today* patch on her jump suit. The disappearee was Robert Webb, the bass guitarist of a band called Slug Death. Ms Staines had last seen Webb in Goodge Street underground station at about quarter past ten the previous night. He had bought (I wrote 'purchased' in the statement) a ticket for Belsize Park and vanished into the lifts. Ms Staines had stayed in town to 'see someone' (cockney rhyming slang for 'buy drugs') and had later taken the tube to Belsize Park herself. She'd arrived at eleven and found the rest of Slug Death, still waiting for Webb. 'And since then he hasn't been back to our place, or rung up, or anything.'

Ms Staines had been up all night. Her charcoal eyeshadow had trickled, giving her that zombie look. She was not happy in a police station. She kept looking around nervously, like the leading lady of a psycho movie exploring an old dark house where, fifteen years before, an entire girls' basketball team had been fed into a giant kitchen blender by a family of demented fast food freaks. I gave her the Telly Savalas speech about calming down, waiting a few days, and not being too worried because although people sometimes disappear they usually turn up with a perfectly logical explanation.

'It's hard to explain without you knowing him. Bobby wasn't just about to

470

disappear. We were going to a party. He had the bottle. He wasn't strung out, or hung up, or anything. He was just normal.'

I asked if she could give a description.

'You can't miss him. He has blue horns.'

I thought of a funny remark, but kept it to myself.

'He had most of his hair off, and the rest shaped like horns. He dyed them blue.'

After another month of statement processing I would have let Webb disappear on his own, but I still had a perverse feeling that being a policeman was all about kicking doors in and getting results. During the next Martian ceasefire I asked around, and ended up at New Scotland Yard. I found Eric Verdon, the liaison between the Metropolitan Police and the London Transport Police, in the smaller of his two offices. The other was filled with eighteen tons of documentation, all the way back to horse-drawn trams.

'Oh yes,' Verdon told me, 'disappearances from the underground are not uncommon. Every once in a while some unfortunate wanders off where he shouldn't and meets with an accident. Sometimes our staff doesn't come across the remains for years. Some people never do turn up. Those are the most interesting, I think. This pile.'

It was an impressive stack of manila folders. On the night of 9 October 1872 (which I like to think of as appropriately foggy) Mr Julian Selwyn-Pitt, a landscape painter, walked into Oxford Street station and was never seen again. Since 1872, fifteen thousand, eight hundred and twenty-four people had followed Mr Selwyn-Pitt into Verdon's files. The figure was exclusive of all those whose disappearance was not reported and those, like Robert Webb, whose folders had not yet drifted down to settle in Verdon's office.

'So there are nearly sixteen thousand people lying around the tube somewhere?'

'Presumably. Over the years whole sections have been closed off, reopened, caved-in or forgotten. Even our maps are nowhere near complete. There are plenty of nooks and crannies that could comfortably accommodate a missing person. I often think of sardines.'

'Pardon?'

'The game. You must have played it as a child. It's like hide-and-seek, only when you find someone you have to hide with them. I always found it unnerving somehow. You'd start with a house full of children, and then one by one they'd vanish. Finally, you'd pull back the curtain and there they all would be, packed in like sardines, waiting for you. I'm sure it's like that down there. Somewhere there's a hidey-hole full of all those people.'

All my deductive prowess could make of that was that Verdon had been filed away for too long and faded out himself. The Singular Case of the Blue-Horned Vanisher remained unsolved. The traditional next step was an inspection of the scene of the crime. After the evening shift I had a couple of shorts to nerve me for my first foray into independent detection.

Goodge Street tube station is one of the deepest in London. It has polite robot lifts whose vocabulary is limited to 'please stand clear of the doors,' and a rude night-watchman whose speech is limited to an incomprehensible Jamaican patois. I used my police identification to borrow a lantern, but the night-watchman's presence was required elsewhere for some important swearing and snoozing. I suspected that he did not want to slip into Verdon's fifteen thousand, eight hundred and twenty-seventh manila folder. The lifts had shut off for the night. I had to go down a spiral staircase, lit by off-white Christmas tree bulbs.

I was conducting my search on the Winnie-the-Pooh principle of looking for a thing lost by losing myself and thus ending up next to the original object. When I passed the third PUBLIC NOT ALLOWED BEYOND THIS POINT notice, I decided to chuck it in. Ms Staines would finally wash her hair and marry an accountant anyway.

I was a couple of levels below the actual railway tunnel and had succeeded in getting lost. Here were the catacombs where broken spades, long-handled brooms, buckets of sand, mops, antiquated ticket machines, lost uniform caps, and stray umbrellas drag themselves to die.

I found a locker full of tin hats and gas masks. A rusted 1930s sandwich box, complete with a green hairy lunch wrapped in pre-cellophane tracing paper. And quiet, no rumbling trains at night. Only the inevitable underground ear-cracking drip. It was a standing tap steadily leaking on to a bale of the *Chronicle*. Prams, bedsteads, army blankets, enamel basins, a rocking horse. After the public lavatory tiling gave way to bare bricks there wasn't even any Persian graffiti or football propaganda. Everything terminated here.

The damp kept the air clean. Verdon's files had been musty, but here the chilly air had a sweet afterscent. I sucked in a lungful, drawing the wind over my tongue, but couldn't catch the taste. I meandered without urgency in search of an exit. The drip was gone. The corridors were smooth and empty. The calm of a sea-bed during a storm. Nothing mattered. Through tunnels, down corkscrew stairs, past uninteresting junctions, at random into empty storerooms. I opened a brassbound door.

The hall was lit blue. The sweetness was stronger, soft yet slowing. There were more of them than I could count. Some pale faces turned without interest. An old man in a frock coat and a wing collar, a stocky type in a khaki sergeant's uniform, a girl in a mini-skirt and stiletto heels. Ulsters, bustles, Norfolk jackets, overalls, flat caps, pinstripes, kaftans, black leather jackets, denims. They weren't dead or alive. Just waiting.

A Terrible Night

Fitz-James O'Brien

By Jove! Dick, I'm nearly done up."

"So am I. Did any one ever see such a confounded forest, Charley?"

"I am not alone weak, but hungry. Oh for a steak of moose, with a bottle of old red wine to wash it down!"

"Charley! beware. Take care how you conjure up such visions in my mind. I am already nearly starving, and if you increase my appetite much more it will go hard with me if I don't dine off of you. You are young, and Bertha says you're tender—"

"Hearted, she meant. Well, so I am, if loving Bertha be any proof of it. Do you know, Dick, I have often wondered that you, who love your sister so passionately, were not jealous of her attachment to me."

"So I was, my dear fellow, at first—furiously jealous. But then I reflected that Bertha must one day or the other marry, and I must lose my sister, so I thought it better that she should marry my old college chum and early friend, Charley Costarre, than any one else. So you see there was a little selfishness in my calculations, Charley."

"Dick, we were friends at school, and friends at college, and I thought at both those places that nothing could shorten the link that bound us together, but I was mistaken. Since my love for, and engagement to your sister, I feel as if you were fifty times the friend that you were before. Dick, we three will never part!"

"So he married the king's daughter, and they all lived together as happy as the days are long," shouted Dick with a laugh, quoting from nursery tale.

The foregoing is a slice out the conversation with which Dick Linton and myself endeavored to beguile the way, as we tramped through one of the forests of northern New York. Dick was an artist, and I was a sportsman, so when one fine autumn day he announced his intention going into the woods for a week to study Nature, it seemed to me an excellent opportunity for me to exercise my legs and my trigger finger at the same time. Dick had some backwoods friend who lived in a log-hut on the shores of Eckford Lake, and there we determined to take up our quarters. Dick, who said he knew the forest thoroughly, was to be the guide, and we accordingly, with our guns on our shoulders, started on foot from Root's, a tavern known to tourists, and situated on the boundaries of Essex and Warren counties. It was a desperate walk; but as we started by daybreak, and had great faith in our pedestrian qualities, we expected to reach the nearest of the Eckford lakes by nightfall. The forest through which we traveled was of the densest description. Overhead the branches of spruce and pine shut out the day, while beneath our feet lay a frightful soil, composed principally of jagged shingle, cunningly concealed by an almost impenetrable brush. As the day wore on, our hopes of reaching our destination grew fainter and fainter, and I could almost fancy, from the anxious glances that Dick cast around him, that in spite of his boasted knowledge of the woods he had lost his way. It was not, however, until night actually fell, and that we were both sinking from hunger and exhaustion, that I could get him to acknowledge it.

"We're in a nice pickle, Master Dick," said I, rather crossly, for an empty stomach does much to destroy a man's natural amiability. "Confound your assurance that led you to set up as a guide. Of all men, painters are the most conceited."

"Come, Charley," answered Dick, good-humoredly, "there's no use in growling so loudly. You'll bring the bears and panthers on us if you do. We must make the best of a bad job, and sleep in a tree."

"It's easy to talk, my good fellow. I'm not a partridge, and don't know how to roost on a bough."

"Well, you'll have to learn then; for if you sleep on the ground, the chances are ten to one but you will have the wolves nibbling at your toes before daylight."

"I'm hanged if I'll do either!" said I, desperately. "I'm going to walk all night, and I'll drop before I'll lie down."

"Come, come, Charley, don't be a fool!"

"I was a fool only when I consented to let you assume the *rôle* of guide."

"Well, Charley, if you are determined to go on, let it be so. We'll go together. After all, it's only an adventure."

"I say, Dick, don't you see a light?"

"By Jove, so there is! Come, you see Providence intervenes between us and wolves and hunger. That must be some squatter's hut."

The light to which I had so suddenly called Dick's attention was very faint, and seemed to be about half a mile distant. It glimmered through the dark branches of the hemlock and spruce trees, and weak as the light was, I hailed it as a mariner without a compass hails the star by which he steers. We instantly set out in the direction of our beacon. In a moment it seemed as if all fatigue had vanished, and we walked as if our muscles were as tense as iron, and our joints oily as a piston-shaft.

We soon arrived at what in the dusk seemed to be a clearing of about five acres, but it may have been larger, for the tall forest rising up around it must have diminished its apparent size, giving it the appearance of a square pit rather than a farm. Toward one corner of the clearing we discerned the dusky

474

outline of a log-hut, through whose single end window a faint light was streaming. With a sigh of relief we hastened to the door and knocked. It was opened immediately, and a man appeared on the threshold. We explained our condition, and were instantly invited to walk in and make ourselves at home. All our host said he could offer us were some cold Indian corn cakes, and a slice of dried deer's-flesh, to all of which we were heartily welcome. These viands in our starving condition were luxuries to us, and we literally reveled in anticipation of a full meal.

The hut into which we had so unceremoniously entered was of the most poverty-stricken order. It consisted of but one room, with a rude brick fireplace at one end. Some deer-skins and old blankets stretched out by way of a bed at the other extremity of the apartment, and the only seats visible were two sections of a large pine trunk that stood close to the fire-place. There was no vestige of a table, and the rest of the furniture was embodied in a long Tennessee rifle that hung close to the rough wall.

If the hut was remarkable, its proprietor was still more so. He was, I think, the most villainous looking man I ever beheld. About six feet two inches in height, proportionately broad across the shoulders, and with a hand large enough to pick up a fifty-six pound shot, he seemed to be a combination of extraordinary strength and agility. His head was narrow, and oblong in shape. His straight Indian-like hair fell smoothly over his low forehead as if it had been plastered with soap. And his black, bead-like eyes were set obliquely, and slanted downward toward his nose, giving him a mingled expression of ferocity and cunning. As I examined his features attentively, in which I thought I could trace almost every bad passion, I confess I experienced a certain feeling of apprehension and distrust that I could not shake off.

While he was getting us the promised food, we tried, by questioning him, to draw him into conversation. He seemed very taciturn and reserved. He said he lived entirely alone, and had cleared the spot he occupied with his own hands. He said his name was Joel; but when we hinted that he must have some other name, he pretended not to hear us, though I saw his brows knit, and his small black eyes flash angrily. My suspicions of this man were further aroused by observing a pair of shoes lying in a corner of the hut. These shoes were at least three sizes smaller than those that our gigantic host wore, and yet he had distinctly replied that he lived entirely alone. If those shoes were not his, whose were they? The more I reflected on this circumstance the more uneasy I felt, and apprehensions were still further aroused, when Joel, as he called himself, took both our fowling-pieces, and, in order to have them out of the way, as he said, hung them on crooks from the wall, at a height that neither Dick nor I could reach without getting on a stool. I smiled inwardly, however, as I felt the smooth barrel of my revolver that was slung in the hollow of my back, by its leathern belt, and thought to myself, if this fellow has any bad designs, the more unprotected he thinks us the more incautious he will be, so I made no effort to retain our guns. Dick also had a revolver, and was one of those men who I knew would use it well when the time came.

My suspicions of our host grew at last to such a pitch that I determined to communicate them to Dick. Nothing would be easier than for this villainous half-breed—for I felt convinced he had Indian blood in him—nothing would be easier than, with the aid of an accomplice, to cut our throats or shoot us while we were asleep, and so get our guns, watches, and whatever money we carried. Who, in those lonely woods, would hear the shot, or hear our cries for help? What emissary of the law, however sharp, could point out our graves in those wild woods, or bring the murder home to those who committed it? Linton at first laughed; then grew serious; and gradually became a convert to my apprehensions. We hurriedly agreed that, while one slept, the other should watch, and so take it in turns through the night.

Joel had surrendered to us his couch of deer-skin and his blanket; he himself said he could sleep quite as well on the floor, near the fire. As Dick and I were both very tired, we were anxious to get our rest as soon as possible. So after a hearty meal of deer-steak and tough cakes, washed down by a good draught from our brandy flask, I, being the youngest, got the first hour's sleep, and flung myself on the couch of skins. As my eyes gradually closed, I saw a dim picture of Dick seated sternly watching by the fire, and the long shape of the half-breed stretching out like a huge shadow upon the floor.

After what I could have sworn to be only a three-minute doze, Dick woke me, and informed me that my hour was out; and turning me out of my warm nest, lay down without any ceremony, and in a few seconds was heavily snoring. I rubbed my eyes, felt for my revolver, and seating myself on one of the pine-stumps, commenced my watch. The half-breed appeared to be buried in a profound slumber, and in the half-weird light cast by the wood embers, his enormous figure seemed almost Titanic in its proportions. I confess I felt that in a struggle for life he was more than a match for Dick and myself. I then looked at the fire, and began a favorite amusement of mine—shaping forms in the embers. All sorts of figures defined themselves before me. Battles, tempests at sea, familiar faces, and above all shone, ever returning, the dear features of Bertha Linton, my affianced bride. She seemed to me to smile at me through a burning haze, and I could almost fancy I heard her say, "While you are watching in the lonely forest I am thinking of you, and praying for your safety."

A slight movement on the part of the slumbering half-breed here recalled me from those sweet dreams. He turned on his side, lifted himself slowly on his elbow, and gazed attentively at me. I did not stir. Still retaining my stooping attitude, I half closed my eyes, and remained motionless. Doubtless he thought I was asleep, for in a moment or two he rose noiselessly, and creeping with a stealthy step across the floor, passed out of the hut. I listened—Oh, how eagerly! It seemed to me that, through the imperfectly-joined crevices of the log-walls, I could plainly hear voices whispering. I would have given worlds to have crept nearer to listen, but I was fearful of disturbing the fancied security of our host, who I now felt certain had sinister designs upon us. So I remained perfectly still. The whispering suddenly ceased. The half-breed re-entered the hut in the same stealthy way in which he had quitted it, and after giving a scrutinizing glance at me, once more stretched himself upon the floor and affected to sleep. In a few moments I pretended to awake—yawned, looked at my watch, and finding that my hour had more than expired, proceeded to wake Dick. As I turned him out of bed I whispered in his ear, "Don't take your eyes off that fellow, Dick. He has accomplices outside; be careful!" Dick gave a meaning glance, carelessly touched his revolver, as much as to say, "Here's something to interfere with his little arrangements," and took his seat on the pine-stump, in such a position as to command a view of the sleeping half-breed and the doorway at the same time.

This time, though horribly tired, I could not sleep. A horrible load seemed pressing on my chest, and every five minutes I would start up to see if Dick was keeping his watch faithfully. My nerves were strung to a frightful pitch of tensity; my heart beat at every sound, and my head seemed to throb until I thought my temples would burst. The more I reflected on the conduct of the half-breed, the more assured I was that he intended murder. Full of this idea, I took my revolver from its sling, and held it in my hand, ready to shoot him down at the first movement that appeared at all dangerous. A haze seemed now to pass across my eyes. Fatigued with long watching and excitement, I passed into that semi-conscious state, in which I seemed perfectly aware of every thing that passed, although objects were dim and dull in outline, and did not appear so sharply defined as in one's waking moments. I was apparently roused from this state by a slight crackling sound. I started, and raised myself on my elbow. My heart almost ceased to beat at what I saw. The half-breed had lit some species of dried herb, which sent out a strong aromatic odor as it burned. This herb he was holding directly under Dick's nostrils, who I now perceived, to my horror, was wrapped in a profound slumber. The smoke of this mysterious herb appeared to deprive him of all consciousness, for he rolled gently off of the pine-log, and lay stretched upon the floor. The half-breed now stole to the door, and opened it gently. Three sinister heads peered in out of the gloom. I saw the long barrels of rifles, and the huge brawny hands that clasped them. The half-breed pointed significantly to where I lay with his long bony finger, then drawing a large, thirsty-looking knife from his breast, moved toward me. The time was come. My blood stopped—my heart ceased to beat. The half-breed was within a foot of my bed; the knife was raised; another instant and it would have been buried in my heart, when, with a hand as cold as ice, I lifted my revolver, took deadly aim, and fired!

A stunning report, a dull groan, a huge cloud of smoke curling around me, and I found myself standing upright, with a dark mass lying at my feet.

"Great God! what have you done, Sir?" cried the half-breed, rushing toward me. "You have killed him! He was just about to wake you."

I staggered against the wall. My senses, until then immersed in sleep, suddenly recovered their activity. The frightful truth burst upon me in a flash. I had shot Dick Linton while under the influence of a night-mare! Then everything seemed to fade away, and I remember no more.

There was a trial, I believe. The lawyers were learned, and proved by physicians that it was a case of what is called *Somnolentia,* or sleep-drunkenness; but of the proceedings I took no heed. One form haunted me, lying black and heavy on the hut floor; and one pale face was ever present—a face I saw once after the terrible catastrophe, and never saw again—the wild, despairing face of Bertha Linton, my promised bride!

The Three

Louise Van de Verg

I never saw such a thick fog," said the man. "Where do you suppose we are by this time?"

"I don't know," returned the woman. "Frank, I'm afraid."

"What nonsense, Margaret! The driver set us in the right path!"

"Did he?"

"Of course he did!" said the man, testily. "Don't let yourself get nervous. Don't you suppose that driver knows his business? He's been meeting the ships from—from—the ships down there at the docks for twenty years. He told me so."

"I heard that." Margaret's little gloved hand moved a trifle frantically. "Frank, you don't remember, either! That's—that's what's unnerved me—not the fog! I can't remember where it is we've come from—nor where we're going!" Tears were near the surface of her voice. "Frank—do *you* remember?"

"Of course I do! We've come from——" There was a long, blank pause, through which the white fog dripped from invisible trees and fell with little pattering sounds to the unseen ground. They could see nothing but a short stretch of beaten path, with a little green at the edges, always the same, receding into the fog at their backs, appearing from the fog in front of them. They continued to walk, but there was panic between them as they paced through the looming and invisible wood.

At last the man spoke. "I don't remember," he said, under his breath. "I—don't—remember." The silence fell again, heavily, oppressive as the fog.

They came to the gate before they knew it was there, and paused before it, doubtfully.

"Shall we go through?" asked the woman.

"The path does; and the driver said——"

"Ah, don't speak to me of the driver!" But she opened the gate, and they went through together. The sound of the dripping trees grew faint behind them, and there were flowers beside the path, now. "I hope Edith has not been worrying about us," said Margaret.

"Edith!" cried the man. "Edith! Then you do——"

"It came to me all at once," she said, wondering. "Until you spoke I didn't realize I hadn't known before."

"Edith what?"

"I—don't remember her married name. She's a widow, and we're—we're——"

As she spoke they came to a house—a small, comfortable cottage, by what they could see of it. "We're what?" asked the man.

"I don't remember that," she answered, the anxious frown on her brow again. "It must be that we have been invited to call—if we were to stay longer we'd have had our own bags. I—almost feel I know this house, Frank! I suppose it's because Edith has sent me pictures, but I don't remember it, if she did—nor Edith, either! It's charming, isn't it?"

"We'll have one like it, Mrs. Dawes," said the man, smiling at her, "after the honeymoon's over."

"I—don't know that I want it," she said, somberly, making no response to his overture. "It's charming, but it—frightens me."

"You're nervous."

"I wish I could remember! If I could remember I'd be all right."

"It'll come back to you," he reassured her. "It's begun already. Isn't there anyone home, d'you think?"

"I don't know." Margaret sighed. "You might ring," she suggested.

A moment later, Edith was at the door. "How do you do?" she said, interrogatively. It was plain she did not know them. Margaret felt a shock of surprise, but was able to answer.

"I am Margaret Chiltern," she said. There! She had made the mistake she had feared to make. Margaret Chiltern, indeed! Margaret Dawes since this morning. She glanced at her husband. There was no expression in his face.

"Come in, Mrs. Chiltern." Edith was opening the door. "And Mr. Chiltern! I'm glad to see you. I was almost afraid you'd be lost in this fog."

Well, well, it was a natural mistake on her part. Why didn't Frank correct her? She was a hospitable soul, thought Margaret, but typical of the women whom matrimony deadens, whose husbands leave them for other women by the time they reach the forties. Perhaps she had been spared a heavier heartache, by her husband's early death. These thoughts were in the top of Margaret's mind as she followed her hostess down the passage. Beneath them surged horror. Horror of what? She would not look at it long enough to find out; she was only able to cast oblique glances, and see the matronly figure of Edith moving kindly in its midst.

"This is your room," said Edith, opening a door.

"Why, our trunks are here!" cried Margaret.

"Yes," said the woman with a surprized look. "What's the matter, Mrs. Chiltern?"

"Nothing—nothing," said Margaret. "You have—unusually quick service here."

"Yes, it's good," assented Edith. "You'll want to freshen up, after your journey, I suppose. I'll see to tea, unless there's something else I can do for you."

"Thank you, we shan't need a thing," said Margaret.

"I don't usually have tea, when I'm alone," Edith said, "and it's such a pleasure to me that you like it. I always had it when Ronny was home." She smiled, and left them.

"Now is Ronny her husband?" wondered Margaret.

"Don't, Meg!" Frank almost moaned the words. "Let's get away from here! I don't like it, Margaret! There's—there's something about that woman!"

"Why, Frank!"

"I didn't dare correct her about the names," he went on. "There's something about that woman," he reiterated. "I'm—yes, I am! I'm afraid of her!"

"You're getting as bad as I am," smiled Margaret, but without mirth. "She's a dear thing."

"Yes, but Margaret, I know her, I tell you! I know her! Only I—can't remember. Did—did you see that scar on her throat?"

"I saw it," she answered steadily. But she was unable to hide a small shudder that possessed her at the moment of speech. "This room's—familiar, somehow, too," she said, after a minute. "I know I've been in this room before."

"How could you have been?"

"I don't know. Maybe it's because it's—it's like the rooms the women's magazines tell you how to furnish. I don't suppose I really have been in it," she added, gazing idly into the fog. "She'd remember me, if I had been. I think the fog's not so thick."

"Let's go back, now, Margaret, before she comes again, while the fog will hide us."

"Back where? Oh, Frank, I *couldn't* go back to those woods again not knowing where we were going, or what would happen!"

"You don't know what's going to happen here. It may be something horrible. I feel it, Margaret, I feel something horrible in the air. Please come away, darling!"

"It's the fog," she assured him.

Edith's knock prevented a repetition of his plea. They went out to sit at a pleasant tea-table and smile politely comfortable smiles at their mysterious hostess, who placidly poured, and served, and chatted in a halo of terror.

"Ronny—my boy, you know—is in South America—with a steamship company. He's a dear boy, and a very capable officer. He's doing awfully well."

"I'm glad of that," said Margaret. "Do you hear from him often?"

A distressed look crossed Edith's face. "I haven't heard from him since the earthquake," she said. "But really, I don't suppose there's any reason to worry. That country, you know! That earthquake was when I lost my husband," she told them.

It was hard for Margaret to sit with a polite face, even a sympathetic face, while icy fear swirled about her. She ventured a glance at Frank. He, too, was tortured.

Edith's voice continued, to an accompaniment of Margaret's murmur of sympathy. "We had been driving, you know, and we were coming home. Frank—my husband's name was Frank, too, like yours, Mrs. Chiltern—Frank had been nervous all day and the traffic had bothered him. You know, I believe there is something in the air, before a quake! At any rate, we both felt it—a kind of tension, you know. We were glad to get home. I went in first, and Frank was right behind me. We had one of those big hat-racks, with mirrors, in the hall, and the first thing I noticed was that it was moving. The next minute I knew nothing."

A hat-rack with a mirror—a dark hall—a woman coming in out of the night. As though in a moving picture, Margaret saw herself in that hall, moving from that shadow with a gleaming—what? Not a knife! Yet in the picture it was a knife, and Margaret seemed quite calm. In a whirl of horror she forced herself to listen.

"The mirror was broken, and a piece of the glass cut me here." Edith touched the scar on her throat. "I had a bad concussion, and was unconscious for several weeks. I never even knew when Mr. Dawes' funeral took place—I have never known the date." She rose. "We need some more jelly," she said placidly, moving to the kitchen.

This horror left her untouched, yet she was part of it. The pictures were whirling now, before Margaret's eyes. She could no longer hide from them the knife, nor its use, nor their flight, nor their capture—nor the plain, bare room from which they had started that morning, with the terrible throne in its center—the throne of death.

"Frank!" she whispered. "Frank! Her husband's name was Frank Dawes!"

"We *had* seen this house before. It was mine—where I lived—with—her." He was breathing heavily. "She doesn't know us," he whispered. "She doesn't know us—and I guess she never will."

"We'll have to get away!"

"We can't. We were brought; we'll have to stay."

"But we're dead, Frank! We're dead! And I thought after we were dead we'd—we'd be together."

"She was dead first; and we *are* together—with her."

"We've *got* to get away, Frank!"

"We can't. I know we can't." There was a dreary and desolate finality in the insistent repetition.

"Even—here—it follows us," she mused, and she did not again think of flight.

Edith was in the room again. "I've been very much alone, since then," she said. "That was why I advertised for a couple, or two ladies to live with me. I do hope," she smiled, "that you won't call me Mrs. Dawes, Mrs. Chiltern. Let's not stand on ceremony. My name is Edith, you know."

Margaret's lips were stiff, but she smiled. "I will call you Edith," she said. "I've felt from the first I knew you well."

"I'm glad. And may I call you Margaret?" She moved to the window. "The fog has lifted," she said. "We can see the woods plainly. I love those trees!"

The Three Marked Pennies

Mary Elizabeth Counselman

Every one agreed, after it was over, that the whole thing was the conception of a twisted brain, a game of chess played by a madman—in which the pieces, instead of carved bits of ivory or ebony, were human beings.

It was odd that no one doubted the authenticity of the "contest." The public seems never for a moment to have considered it the prank of a practical joker, or even a publicity stunt. Jeff Haverty, editor of the *News*, advanced a theory that the affair was meant to be a clever, if rather elaborate, psychological experiment—which would end in the revealing of the originator's identity and a big laugh for every one.

Perhaps it was the glamorous manner of announcement that gave the thing such wide-spread interest. Blankville (as I shall call the Southern town of about 30,000 people in which the affair occurred) awoke one April morning to find all its trees, telephone poles, house-sides and store-fronts plastered with a strange sign. There were scores of them, written on yellow copy-paper on an ordinary typewriter. The sign read:

"During this day of April 15, three pennies will find their way into the pockets of this city. On each penny there will be a well-defined mark. One is a square; one is a circle; and one is a cross. These three pennies will change hands often, as do all coins, and on the seventh day after this announcement (April 21) the possessor of each marked penny will receive a gift.

"To the first: $100,000 in cash.

"To the second: A trip around the world.

"To the third: Death.

"The answer to this riddle lies in the marks on the three coins: circle, square, and cross. Which of these symbolizes wealth? Which, travel? Which, death? The answer is not an obvious one.

"To him who finds it and obtains the first penny, $100,000 will be sent without delay. To him who has the second penny, a first-class ticket for the earliest world-touring steamer to sail will be presented. But to the possessor of the third marked coin will be given—death. If you are afraid your penny is the third, give it away—but it may be the first or the second!

"Show your marked penny to the editor of the 'News' on April 21, giving your name and address. He will know nothing of this contest until he reads one of these signs. He is requested to publish the names of the three possessors of the coins April 21, with the mark on the penny each holds.

"It will do no good to mark a coin of your own, as the dates of the true coins will be sent to Editor Haverty."

By noon every one had read the notice, and the city was buzzing with excitement. Clerks began to examine the contents of cash register drawers. Hands rummaged in pockets and purses. Stores and banks were flooded with customers wanting silver changed to coppers.

Jeff Haverty was the target for a barrage of queries, and his evening edition came out with a lengthy editorial embodying all he knew about the mystery, which was exactly nothing. A note had come that morning with the rest of his mail—a note unsigned, and typewritten on the same yellow paper in a plain stamped envelope with the postmark of that city. It said merely: *"Circle— 1920. Square—1909. Cross—1928. Please do not reveal these dates until after April 21."*

Haverty complied with the request, and played up the story for all it was worth.

The first penny was found in the street by a small boy, who promptly took it to his father. His father, in turn, palmed it off hurriedly on his barber, who gave it in change to a patron before he noted the deep cross cut in the coin's surface.

The patron took it to his wife, who immediately paid it to the grocer. "It's too long a chance, honey!" she silenced her mate's protests. "I don't like the idea of that death-threat in the notice . . . and this certainly must be the third penny. What else could that little cross stand for? Crosses over graves—don't you see the significance?"

And when that explanation was wafted abroad, the cross-marked penny began to change hands with increasing rapidity.

The other two pennies bobbed up before dusk—one marked with a small perfect square, the other with a neat circle.

The square-marked penny was discovered in a slot-machine by the proprietor of the Busy Bee Café. There was no way it could have got there, he reported, mystified and a little frightened. Only four people, all of them old patrons, had been in the café that day. And not one of them had been near the slot-machine—located at the back of the place as it was, and filled with stale chewing-gum which, at a glance, was worth nobody's penny. Furthermore, the proprietor had examined the thing for a chance coin the night before and had left it empty when he locked up; yet there was the square-marked penny nestling alone in the slot-machine at closing time April 15.

He had stared at the coin a long time before passing it in change to an elderly spinster.

"It ain't worth it," he muttered to himself. "I got a restaurant that's makin' me a thin livin', and I ain't in no hurry to get myself bumped off, on the long chance I might get that hundred thousand or that trip instead. No-sirree!"

The spinster took one look at the marked penny, gave a short mouse-like squeak, and flung it into the gutter as though it were a tarantula.

"My land!" she quavered. "I don't want that thing in my pocket-book!"

But she dreamed that night of foreign ports, of coolies jabbering in a brittle tongue, of barracuda fins cutting the surface of deep blue water, and the ruins of ancient cities.

A negro workman picked up the penny next morning and clung to it all day, dreaming of Harlem, before he succumbed at last to gnawing fear. And the square-marked penny changed hands once more.

The circle-marked penny was first noted in a stack of coins by a teller of the Farmer's Trust.

"We get marked coins every now and then," he said. "I didn't notice this one especially—it may have been here for days."

He pocketed it gleefully, but discovered with a twinge of dismay next morning that he had passed it out to some one without noticing it.

"I wanted to keep it!" he signed. "For better or for worse!"

He glowered at the stacks of some one else's money before him, and wondered furtively how many tellers ever really escaped with stolen goods.

A fruit-seller had received the penny. He eyed it dubiously. "Mebbe you bring-a me those mon, heh?" He showed it to his fat, greasy wife, who made the sign of horns against the "evil eye."

"T'row away!" she commanded shrilly. "She iss bad lock!"

Her spouse shrugged and sailed the circle-marked coin across the street. A ragged child pounced on it and scuttered away to buy a twist of licorice. And the circle-marked penny changed hands once more—clutched at by avaricious fingers, stared at by eyes grown sick of familiar scenes, relinquished again by the power of fear.

Those who came into brief possession of the three coins were fretted by the drag and shove of conflicting advice.

"Keep it!" some urged. "Think! It may mean a trip around the world! Paris! China! London! Oh, why couldn't I have got the thing?"

"Give it away!" others admonished. "Maybe it's the third penny—you can't tell. Maybe the symbols don't mean what they seem to, and the square one is the death-penny! I'd throw it away, if I were you."

"No! No!" still others cried. "Hang on to it! It may bring you $100,000. *A hundred thousand dollars!* In these times! Why, fellow, you'd be the same as a millionaire!"

The meaning of the three symbols was on every one's tongue, and no one agreed with his neighbor's solution to the riddle.

"It's as plain as the nose on my face," one man would declare. "The circle represents the globe—the travel-penny, see?"

"No, no. The cross means that. 'Cross' the seas, don't you get it? Sort of a pun effect. The circle means money—shape of a coin, understand?"

"And the square one—?"

"A grave. A square hole for a coffin, see? Death. It's quite simple. I wish I could get hold of that circle one!"

"You're crazy! The cross one is for death—everybody says so. And believe me, everybody's getting rid of it as soon as they get it! It may be a joke of some kind . . . no danger at all . . . but I wouldn't like to be the holder of that cross-marked penny when April 21 rolls around!"

"I'd keep it and wait till the other two had got what was due them. Then, if mine turned out to be the wrong one, I'd throw it away!" one man said importantly.

"But he won't pay up till all three pennies are accounted for, I shouldn't think," another answered him. "And maybe the offer doesn't hold good after April 21—and you'd be losing $100,000 or a world tour just because you're scared to find out!"

"That's a big stake, man," another murmured. "But frankly, I wouldn't like to take the chance. He might give me his third gift!"

"He" was how every one designated the unknown originator of the contest; though, of course, there was no more clue to his sex than to his identity.

"He must be rich," some said, "to offer such expensive prizes."

"And crazy!" others exploded, "threatening to kill the third one. He'll never get away with it!"

"But clever," still others admitted, "to think up the whole business. He knows human nature, whoever he is. I'm inclined to agree with Haverty—it's all a sort of psychological experiment. He's trying to see whether desire for travel or greed for money is stronger than fear of death."

"Does he mean to pay up, do you think?"

"That remains to be seen!"

On the sixth day, Blankville had reached a pitch of excitement amounting almost to hysteria. No one could work for wondering about the outcome of the bizarre test on the morrow.

It was known that a grocer's delivery boy held the square-marked coin, for he had been boasting of his indifference as to whether or not the square did represent a yawning grave. He exhibited the penny freely, making jokes about what he intended to do with his hundred thousand dollars—but on the morning of the last day he lost his nerve. Seeing a blind beggar woman huddled in her favorite corner between two shops, he passed close to her and surreptitiously dropped the cent piece into her box of pencils.

"I had it!" he wailed to a friend after he had reached his grocery. "I had it right here in my pocket last night, and now it's gone! See, I've got a hole in the darn' thing—the penny must have dropped out!"

It was also known who held the circle-marked penny. A young soda clerk, with the sort of ready smile that customers like to see across a marble counter, had discovered the coin and fished it from the cash drawer, exulting over his good fortune.

"Bud Skinner's got the circle penny," people told one another, wavering between anxiety and gladness. "I hope the kid *does* get that world tour—it'd tickle him so! He seems to get such a kick out of life; it's a sin he has to be stuck in this slow burg!"

Finally it was found who held the cross-marked cent piece. "Carlton . . . poor devil!" people murmured in subdued tones. "Death would be a godsend to him. Wonder he hasn't shot himself before this. Guess he just hasn't the nerve."

The man with the cross-marked penny smiled bitterly. "I hope this blasted little symbol means what they all think it means!" he confided to a friend.

At last the eagerly awaited day came. A crowd formed in the street

486

outside the newspaper office to see the three possessors of the three marked coins show Haverty their pennies and give him their names to publish. For their benefit the editor met the trio on the sidewalk outside the building, so that all might see them.

The evening edition ran the three people's photographs, with the name, address, and the mark on each one's penny under each picture. Blankville read . . . and held its breath.

On the morning of April 22, the old blind beggar woman sat in her accustomed place, musing on the excitement of the previous day, when several people had led her—she knew by the odor of fish from the market across the street—to the newspaper office. There some one had asked her name and many other puzzling things which had bewildered her until she had almost burst into tears.

"Let me alone!" she had whimpered. "I ask only enough food to keep from starving, and a place to sleep. Why are you pushing me around like this and yelling at me? Let me go back to my corner! I don't like all this confusion and strangeness that I can't see—it frightens me!"

Then they had told her something about a marked penny they had found in her alms-box, and other things about a large sum of money and some impending danger that threatened her. She was glad when they led her back to her cranny between the shops.

Now as she sat in her accustomed spot, nodding comfortably and humming a little under her breath, a paper fluttered down into her lap. She felt the stiff oblong, knew it was an envelope, and called a bystander to her side.

"Open this for me, will you?" she requested. "Is it a letter? Read it to me."

The bystander tore open the envelope and frowned. "It's a note," he told her. "Typewritten, and it's not signed. It just says—what the devil?—just says: *The four corners of the earth are exactly the same.'* And . . . hey! look at this! . . . oh, I'm sorry; I forgot you're . . . it's a steamship ticket for a world tour! Look, didn't you have one of the marked pennies?"

The blind woman nodded drowsily. "Yes, the one with the square, they said." She sighed faintly. "I had hoped I would get the money, or . . . the other, so I would never have to beg again."

"Well, here's your ticket." The bystander held it out to her uncertainly. "Don't you want it?" as the beggar made no move to take it.

"No," snapped the blind woman. "What good would it be to me?" She seized the ticket in sudden rage, and tore it into bits.

At nearly the same hour, Kenneth Carlton was receiving a fat manila envelope from the postman. He frowned as he squinted at the local postmark over the stamp. His friend Evans stood beside him, paler than Carlton.

"Open it, open it!" he urged. "Read it—no, don't open it, Ken. I'm scared! After all . . . it's a terrible way to go. Not knowing where the blow's coming from, and—"

Carlton emitted a macabre chuckle, ripping open the heavy envelope. "It's the best break I've had in years, Jim. I'm glad! Glad, Jim, do you hear? It will be quick, I hope . . . and painless. What's this, I wonder. A treatise on how to blow off the top of your head?" He shook the contents of the letter onto a table, and then, after a moment, he began to laugh . . . mirthlessly . . . hideously.

His friend stared at the little heap of crisp bills, all of a larger denomination than he had ever seen before. "The money! You get the hundred thousand, Ken! I can't believe . . ." He broke off to snatch up a slip of yellow paper among the bills. *"Wealth is the greatest cross a man can bear,"* he read aloud the typewritten words. "It doesn't make sense . . . wealth? Then . . . the cross-mark stood for wealth? I don't understand."

Carlton's laughter cracked. "He has depth, that bird—whoever he is! Nice irony there, Jim—wealth being a burden instead of the blessing most people consider it. I suppose he's right, at that. But I wonder if he knows the really ironic part of this act of his little play? A hundred thousand dollars to a man with—cancer. Well, Jim, I have a month or less to spend it in . . . one more damnable month to suffer through before it's all over!"

His terrible laughter rose again, until his friend had to clap hands to ears, shutting out the sound.

But the strangest part of the whole affair was Bud Skinner's death. Just after the rush hour at noon, he had found a small package, addressed to him, on a back counter in the drug store. Eagerly he tore off the brown paper wrappings, a dozen or so friends crowding about him.

A curiously wrought silver box was what he found. He pressed the catch with trembling fingers and snapped back the lid. An instant later his face took on a queer expression—and he slid noiselessly to the tile floor of the drug store.

The ensuing police investigation unearthed nothing at all, except that young Skinner had been poisoned with *crotalin*—snake venom—administered through a pin-prick on his thumb when he pressed the trick catch of the little silver box. This, and the typewritten note in the otherwise empty box: *"Life ends where it began—nowhere,"* were all they found as an explanation of the clerk's death. Nor was anything else ever brought to light about the mysterious contest of the three marked pennies—which are probably still in circulation somewhere in the United States.

The Three Sisters

W. W. Jacobs

Thirty years ago on a wet autumn evening the household of Mallett's Lodge was gathered round the death-bed of Ursula Mallow, the eldest of the three sisters who inhabited it. The dingy moth-eaten curtains of the old wooden bedstead were drawn apart, the light of a smoking oil-lamp falling upon the hopeless countenance of the dying woman as she turned her dull eyes upon her sisters. The room was in silence except for an occasional sob from the youngest sister, Eunice. Outside the rain fell steadily over the steaming marshes.

"Nothing is to be changed, Tabitha," gasped Ursula to the other sister, who bore a striking likeness to her although her expression was harder and colder; "this room is to be locked up and never opened."

"Very well," said Tabitha brusquely, "though I don't see how it can matter to you then."

"It does matter," said her sister with startling energy. "How do you know, how do I know that I may not sometimes visit it? I have lived in this house so long I am certain that I shall see it again. I *will* come back. Come back to watch over you both and see that no harm befalls you."

"You are talking wildly," said Tabitha, by no means moved at her sister's solicitude for her welfare. "Your mind is wandering; you know that I have no faith in such things."

Ursula sighed, and beckoning to Eunice, who was weeping silently at the bedside, placed her feeble arms around her neck and kissed her.

"Do not weep, dear," she said feebly. "Perhaps it is best so. A lonely woman's life is scarce worth living. We have no hopes, no aspirations; other women have had happy husbands and children, but we in this forgotten place have grown old together. I go first, but you must soon follow."

Tabitha, comfortably conscious of only forty years and an iron frame, shrugged her shoulders and smiled grimly.

"I go first," repeated Ursula in a new and strange voice as her heavy eyes slowly closed, "but I will come for each of you in turn, when your lease of life runs out. At that moment I will be with you to lead your steps whither I now go."

As she spoke the flickering lamp went out suddenly as though extinguished by a rapid hand, and the room was left in utter darkness. A strange

489

suffocating noise issued from the bed, and when the trembling women had relighted the lamp, all that was left of Ursula Mallow was ready for the grave.

That night the survivors passed together. The dead woman had been a firm believer in the existence of that shadowy borderland which is said to form an unhallowed link between the living and the dead, and even the stolid Tabitha, slightly unnerved by the events of the night, was not free from certain apprehensions that she might have been right.

With the bright morning their fears disappeared. The sun stole in at the window, and seeing the poor earthworn face on the pillow so touched it and glorified it that only its goodness and weakness were seen, and the beholders came to wonder how they could ever have felt any dread of aught so calm and peaceful. A day or two passed, and the body was transferred to a massive coffin long regarded as the finest piece of work of its kind ever turned out of the village carpenter's workshop. Then a slow and melancholy cortège headed by four bearers wound its solemn way across the marshes to the family vault in the grey old church, and all that was left of Ursula was placed by the father and mother who had taken that self-same journey some thirty years before.

To Eunice as they toiled slowly home the day seemed strange and Sabbath-like, the flat prospect of marsh wilder and more forlorn than usual, the roar of the sea more depressing. Tabitha had no such fancies. The bulk of the dead woman's property had been left to Eunice, and her avaricious soul was sorely troubled and her proper sisterly feelings of regret for the deceased sadly interfered with in consequence.

"What are you going to do with all that money, Eunice?" she asked as they sat at their quiet tea.

"I shall leave it as it stands," said Eunice slowly. "We have both got sufficient to live upon, and I shall devote the income from it to supporting some beds in a children's hospital."

"If Ursula had wished it to go to a hospital," said Tabitha in her deep tones, "she would have left the money to it herself. I wonder you do not respect her wishes more."

"What else can I do with it then?" inquired Eunice.

"Save it," said the other with gleaming eyes, "save it."

Eunice shook her head.

"No," said she, "it shall go to the sick children, but the principal I will not touch, and if I die before you it shall become yours and you can do what you like with it."

"Very well," said Tabitha, smothering her anger by a strong effort; "I don't believe that was what Ursula meant you to do with it, and I don't believe she will rest quietly in the grave while you squander the money she stored so carefully."

"What do you mean?" asked Eunice with pale lips. "You are trying to frighten me; I thought that you did not believe in such things."

Tabitha made no answer, and to avoid the anxious inquiring gaze of her sister, drew her chair to the fire, and folding her gaunt arms, composed herself for a nap.

For some time life went on quietly in the old house. The room of the dead woman, in accordance with her last desire, was kept firmly locked, its dirty windows forming a strange contrast to the prim cleanliness of the others. Tabitha, never very talkative, became more taciturn than ever, and stalked about the house and the neglected garden like an unquiet spirit, her brow roughened into the deep wrinkles suggestive of much thought. As the winter came on, bringing with it the long dark evenings, the old house became more lonely than ever, and an air of mystery and dread seemed to hang over it and brood in its empty rooms and dark corridors. The deep silence of night was broken by strange noises for which neither the wind nor the rats could be held accountable. Old Martha, seated in her distant kitchen, heard strange sounds upon the stairs, and once, upon hurrying to them, fancied that she saw a dark figure squatting upon the landing, though a subsequent search with candle and spectacles failed to discover anything. Eunice was disturbed by several vague incidents, and, as she suffered from a complaint of the heart, rendered very ill by them. Even Tabitha admitted a strangeness about the house, but, confident in her piety and virtue, took no heed of it, her mind being fully employed in another direction.

Since the death of her sister all restraint upon her was removed, and she yielded herself up entirely to the stern and hard rules enforced by avarice upon its devotees. Her housekeeping expenses were kept rigidly separate from those of Eunice and her food limited to the coarsest dishes, while in the matter of clothes, the old servant was by far the better dressed. Seated alone in her bedroom this uncouth, hard-featured creature revelled in her possessions, grudging even the expense of the candle-end which enabled her to behold them. So completely did this passion change her that both Eunice and Martha became afraid of her, and lay awake in their beds night after night trembling at the chinking of the coins at her unholy vigils.

One day Eunice ventured to remonstrate. "Why don't you bank your money, Tabitha?" she said; "it is surely not safe to keep such large sums in such a lonely house."

"Large sums!" repeated the exasperated Tabitha, "large sums! What nonsense is this? You know well that I have barely sufficient to keep me."

"It's a great temptation to housebreakers," said her sister, not pressing the point. "I made sure last night that I heard somebody in the house."

"Did you?" said Tabitha, grasping her arm, a horrible look on her face. "So did I. I thought they went to Ursula's room, and I got out of bed and went on the stairs to listen."

"Well?" said Eunice faintly, fascinated by the look on her sister's face.

"There was *something* there," said Tabitha slowly. "I'll swear it, for I stood on the landing by her door and listened; something scuffling on the floor round and round the room. At first I thought it was the cat, but when I went up there this morning the door was still locked, and the cat was in the kitchen."

"Oh, let us leave this dreadful house," moaned Eunice.

"What!" said her sister grimly; "afraid of poor Ursula? Why should you be? Your own sister who nursed you when you were a babe, and who perhaps even now comes and watches over your slumbers."

"Oh!" said Eunice, pressing her hand to her side, "if I saw her I should die. I should think that she had come for me as she said she would. O God! have mercy on me, I am dying."

She reeled as she spoke, and before Tabitha could save her, sank senseless to the floor.

"Get some water," cried Tabitha, as old Martha came hurrying up the stairs, "Eunice has fainted."

The old woman, with a timid glance at her, retired, reappearing shortly afterwards with the water, with which she proceeded to restore her much-loved mistress to her senses. Tabitha, as soon as this was accomplished, stalked off to her room, leaving her sister and Martha sitting drearily enough in the small parlour, watching the fire and conversing in whispers.

It was clear to the old servant that this state of things could not last much longer, and she repeatedly urged her mistress to leave a house so lonely and so mysterious. To her great delight Eunice at length consented, despite the fierce opposition of her sister, and at the mere idea of leaving gained greatly in health and spirits. A small but comfortable house was hired in Morville, and arrangements made for a speedy change.

It was the last night in the old house, and all the wild spirits of the marshes, the wind and the sea seemed to have joined forces for one supreme effort. When the wind dropped, as it did at brief intervals, the sea was heard moaning on the distant beach, strangely mingled with the desolate warning of the bell-buoy as it rocked to the waves. Then the wind rose again, and the noise of the sea was lost in the fierce gusts which, finding no obstacle on the open marshes, swept with their full fury upon the house by the creek. The strange voices of the air shrieked in its chimneys, windows rattled, doors slammed, and even the very curtains seemed to live and move.

Eunice was in bed, awake. A small nightlight in a saucer of oil shed a sickly glare upon the worm-eaten old furniture, distorting the most innocent articles into ghastly shapes. A wilder gust than usual almost deprived her of the protection afforded by that poor light, and she lay listening fearfully to the creakings and other noises on the stairs, bitterly regretting that she had not asked Martha to sleep with her. But it was not too late even now. She slipped hastily to the floor, crossed to the huge wardrobe, and was in the very act of taking her dressing-gown from its peg when an unmistakable footfall was heard on the stairs. The robe dropped from her shaking fingers, and with a quickly beating heart she regained her bed.

The sounds ceased and a deep silence followed, which she herself was unable to break although she strove hard to do so. A wild gust of wind shook the windows and nearly extinguished the light, and when its flame had regained its accustomed steadiness she saw that the door was slowly opening, while the huge shadow of a hand blotted the papered wall. Still her tongue refused its office. The door flew open with a crash, a cloaked figure entered and, throwing aside its coverings, she saw with a horror past all expression the napkin-bound face of the dead Ursula smiling terribly at her. In her last extremity she raised her faded eyes above for succour, and then as the figure noiselessly advanced and laid its cold hand upon her brow, the soul of Eunice Mallow left its body with a wild shriek and made its way to the Eternal.

Martha, roused by the cry, and shivering with dread, rushed to the door and gazed in terror at the figure which stood leaning over the bedside. As she watched, it slowly removed the cowl and the napkin and exposed the fell face of Tabitha, so strangely contorted between fear and triumph that she hardly recognized it.

"Who's there?" cried Tabitha in a terrible voice as she saw the old woman's shadow on the wall.

"I thought I heard a cry," said Martha, entering. "Did anybody call?"

"Yes, Eunice," said the other, regarding her closely. "I, too, heard the cry, and hurried to her. What makes her so strange? Is she in a trance?"

"Ay," said the old woman, falling on her knees by the bed and sobbing bitterly, "the trance of death. Ah, my dear, my poor lonely girl, that this should be the end of it! She has died of fright," said the old woman, pointing to the eyes, which even yet retained their horror. "She has seen something *devilish.*"

Tabitha's gaze fell. "She has always suffered with her heart," she muttered; "the night has frightened her; it frightened me."

She stood upright by the foot of the bed as Martha drew the sheet over the face of the dead woman.

"First Ursula, then Eunice," said Tabitha, drawing a deep breath. "I can't stay here. I'll dress and wait for the morning."

She left the room as she spoke, and with bent head proceeded to her own. Martha remained by the bedside, and gently closing the staring eyes, fell on her knees, and prayed long and earnestly for the departed soul. Overcome with grief and fear she remained with bowed head until a sudden sharp cry from Tabitha brought her to her feet.

"Well," said the old woman, going to the door.

"Where are you?" cried Tabitha, somewhat reassured by her voice.

"In Miss Eunice's bedroom. Do you want anything?"

"Come down at once. Quick! I am unwell."

Her voice rose suddenly to a scream. "Quick! For God's sake! Quick, or I shall go mad. *There is some strange woman in the house.*"

The old woman stumbled hastily down the dark stairs. "What is the matter?" she cried, entering the room. "Who is it? What do you mean?"

"I saw it," said Tabitha, grasping her convulsively by the shoulder. "I was coming to you when I saw the figure of a woman in front of me going up the stairs. Is it—can it be Ursula come for the soul of Eunice, as she said she would?"

"Or for yours?" said Martha, the words coming from her in some odd fashion, despite herself.

Tabitha, with a ghastly look, fell cowering by her side, clutching tremulously at her clothes. "Light the lamps," she cried hysterically. "Light a fire, make a noise; oh, this dreadful darkness! Will it never be day!"

"Soon, soon," said Martha, overcoming her repugnance and trying to pacify her. "When the day comes you will laugh at these fears."

"I murdered her," screamed the miserable woman, "I killed her with fright. Why did she not give me the money? 'Twas no use to her. Ah! *Look there!*"

Martha, with a horrible fear, followed her glance to the door, but saw nothing.

"It's Ursula," said Tabitha from between her teeth. "Keep her off! Keep her off!"

The old woman, who by some unknown sense seemed to feel the presence of a third person in the room, moved a step forward and stood before her. As she did so Tabitha waved her arms as though to free herself from the touch of a detaining hand, half rose to her feet, and without a word fell dead before her.

At this the old woman's courage forsook her, and with a great cry she rushed from the room, eager to escape from this house of death and mystery. The bolts of the great door were stiff with age, and strange voices seemed to ring in her ears as she strove wildly to unfasten them. Her brain whirled. She thought that the dead in their distant rooms called to her, and that a devil stood on the step outside laughing and holding the door against her. Then with a supreme effort she flung it open, and heedless of her night-clothes passed into the bitter night. The path across the marshes was lost in the darkness, but she found it; the planks over the ditches slippery and narrow, but she crossed them in safety, until at last, her feet bleeding and her breath coming in great gasps, she entered the village and sank down more dead than alive on a cottage doorstep.

Tom Toothacre's Ghost Story

Harriet Beecher Stowe

What is it about that old house in Sherbourne?" said Aunt Nabby to Sam Lawson, as he sat drooping over the coals of a great fire one October evening.

Aunt Lois was gone to Boston on a visit; and, the smart spice of her scepticism being absent, we felt the more freedom to start our story-teller on one of his legends.

Aunt Nabby sat trotting her knitting-needles on a blue-mixed yarn stocking. Grandmamma was knitting in unison at the other side of the fire Grandfather sat studying "The Boston Courier." The wind outside was sighing in fitful wails, creaking the pantry-doors, occasionally puffing in a vicious gust down the broad throat of the chimney. It was a drizzly, sleety evening; and the wet lilac-bushes now and then rattled and splashed against the window as the wind moaned and whispered through them.

We boys had made preparation for a comfortable evening. We had enticed Sam to the chimney corner, and drawn him a mug of cider. We had set down a row of apples to roast on the hearth, which even now were giving faint sighs and sputters as their plump sides burst in the genial heat. The big oak back-log simmered and bubbled, and distilled large drops down amid the ashes; and the great hickory forestick had just burned out into solid bright coals, faintly skimmed over with white ashes. The whole area of the big chimney was full of a sleepy warmth and brightness just calculated to call forth fancies and visions. It only wanted somebody now to set Sam off; and Aunt Nabby broached the ever-interesting subject of haunted houses.

"Wal, now, Miss Badger," said Sam, "I ben over there, and walked round that are house consid'able; and I talked with Granny Hokum and Aunt Polly, and they've putty much come to the conclusion that they'll hev to move out on't. Ye see those 'ere noises, they keep 'em awake nights; and Aunt Polly, she gets 'stericky; and Hannah Jane, she says, ef they stay in the house, *she* can't live with 'em no longer. And what can them lone women do without Hannah Jane? Why, Hannah Jane, she says these two months past she's seen a woman, regular, walking up and down the front hall between twelve and one o'clock at night; and it's jist the image and body of old Ma'am Tillotson, Parson Hokum's mother, that everybody know'd was a thunderin' kind o' woman, that kep' every thing in a muss while she was alive. What the old crittur's up to now there ain't no knowin'. Some folks seems to think it's a sign Granny Hokum's time's comin'. But Lordy massy! says she to me, says she, 'Why, Sam, I don't know nothin' what I've done, that Ma'am Tillotson should be set loose on me.' Anyway they've all got so narvy, that Jed Hokum has ben up from Needham, and is goin' to cart 'em all over to live with him. Jed, he's for hushin' on't up, 'cause he says it brings a bad name on the property.

"Wal, I talked with Jed about it; and says I to Jed, says I, 'Now, ef you'll take my advice, jist you give that are old house a regular overhaulin', and paint it over with tew coats o' paint, and that are'll clear 'em out, if any thing will. Ghosts is like bedbugs,—they can't stan' fresh paint,' says I. 'They allers clear out. I've seen it tried on a ship that got haunted.' "

"Why, Sam, do ships get haunted?"

"To be sure they do!—haunted the wust kind. Why, I could tell ye a story'd make your har rise on e'end, only I'm 'fraid of frightening boys when they're jist going to bed."

"Oh! you can't frighten Horace," said my grandmother. "He will go and sit out there in the graveyard till nine o'clock nights, spite of all I tell him."

"Do tell, Sam!" we urged. "What was it about the ship?"

Sam lifted his mug of cider, deliberately turned it round and round in his hands, eyed it affectionately, took a long drink, and set it down in front of him on the hearth, and began:—

"Ye 'member I telled you how I went to sea down East, when I was a boy, 'long with Tom Toothacre. Wal, Tom, he reeled off a yarn one night that was 'bout the toughest I ever hed the pullin' on. And it come all straight, too, from Tom. 'Twa'n't none o' yer hearsay: 'twas what he seen with his own eyes. Now, there wa'n't no nonsense 'bout Tom, not a bit on't; and he wa'n't afeard o' the divil himse'f; and he ginally saw through things about as straight as things could be seen through. This 'ere happened when Tom was mate o' 'The Albatross,' and they was a-runnin' up to the Banks for a fare o' fish. 'The Albatross' was as handsome a craft as ever ye see; and Cap'n Sim Witherspoon, he was skipper— a rail nice likely man he was. I heard Tom tell this 'ere one night to the boys on 'The Brilliant,' when they was all a-settin' round the stove in the cabin one foggy night that we was to anchor in Frenchman's Bay, and all kind o' layin' off loose.

"Tom, he said they was having a famous run up to the Banks. There was a spankin' southerly, that blew 'em along like all natur'; and they was hevin' the best kind of a time, when this 'ere southerly brought a pesky fog down on 'em, and it grew thicker than hasty-puddin'. Ye see, that are's the pester o' these 'ere southerlies: they's the biggest fog-breeders there is goin'. And so, putty soon, you couldn't see half ship's length afore you.

"Wal, they all was down to supper, except Dan Sawyer at the wheel, when there come sich a crash as if heaven and earth was a-splittin', and then a scrapin' and thump bumpin' under the ship, and gin 'em sich a h'ist that the pot o' beans went rollin', and brought up jam ag'in the bulk-head; and the fellers was keeled over,—men and pork and beans kinder permiscus.

" 'The divil!' says Tom Toothacre, 'we've run down somebody. Look out, up there!'

"Dan, he shoved the helm hard down, and put her up to the wind, and sung out, 'Lordy massy! we've struck her right amidships!'

" 'Struck what?' they all yelled, and tumbled up on deck.

" 'Why, a little schooner,' says Dan. 'Didn't see her till we was right on her. She's gone down tack and sheet. Look! there's part o' the wreck a-floating off: don't ye see?'

"Wal, they didn't see, 'cause it was so thick you couldn't hardly see your hand afore your face. But they put about, and sent out a boat, and kind o' sarched round; but, Lordy massy! ye might as well looked for a drop of water in the Atlantic Ocean. Whoever they was, it was all done gone and over with 'em for this life, poor critturs!

"Tom says they felt confoundedly about it; but what could they do? Lordy massy! what can any on us do? There's places where folks jest lets go 'cause they hes to. Things ain't as they want 'em, and they can't alter 'em. Sailors ain't so rough as they look: they'z feelin' critturs, come to put things right to 'em. And there wasn't one on 'em who wouldn't 'a' worked all night for a chance o' saving some o' them poor fellows. But there 'twas, and twa'n't no use trying.

"Wal, so they sailed on; and by 'm by the wind kind o' chopped round no'theast, and then come round east, and sot in for one of them regular east blows and drizzles that takes the starch out o' fellers more'n a regular storm. So they concluded they might as well put into a little bay there, and come to anchor.

"So they sot an anchor-watch, and all turned in.

"Wal, now comes the particular curus part o' Tom's story; and it was more curus 'cause Tom was one that wouldn't 'a' believed no other man that had told it. Tom was one o' your sort of philosophers. He was fer lookin' into things, and wa'n't in no hurry 'bout believin'; so that this 'un was more 'markable on account of it's bein' Tom that seen it than ef it had ben others.

"Tom says that night he hed a pesky toothache that sort o' kep' grumblin' and jumpin' so he couldn't go to sleep; and he lay in his bunk, a-turnin' this way and that, till long past twelve o clock.

"Tom had a 'thwart-ship bunk where he could see into every bunk on board, except Bob Coffin's, and Bob was on the anchor-watch. Wal, he lay there, tryin' to go to sleep, hearin' the men snor'n' like bull-frogs in a swamp, and watchin' the lantern a-swingin' back and forward; and the sou'westers and pea-jackets were kinder throwin' their long shadders up and down as the vessel sort o' rolled and pitched,—for there was a heavy swell on,—and then he'd hear Bob Coffin tramp, tramp, trampin' overhead,—for Bob had a pretty heavy foot of his own,—and all sort o' mixed up together with Tom's toothache, so he couldn't get to sleep. Finally, Tom, he bit off a great chaw o' 'baccy, and got it well sot in his cheek, and kind o' turned over to lie on't, and ease the pain. Wal, he says he laid a spell, and dropped off in a sort o' doze, when he woke in sich a chill his teeth chattered, and the pain come on like a knife, and he bounced over, thinking the fire had gone out in the stove.

"Wal, sure enough, he see a man a-crouchin' over the stove, with his back to him, a-stretchin' out his hands to warm 'em. He had on a sou'wester and a pea-jacket, with a red tippet round his neck; and his clothes was drippin' as if he'd just come in from a rain.

" 'What the divil!' says Tom. And he riz right up, and rubbed his eyes. 'Bill Bridges,' says he, what shine be you up to now?' For Bill was a master oneasy crittur, and allers a-gettin' up and walkin' nights; and Tom, he thought it was Bill. But in a minute he looked over, and there, sure enough, was Bill, fast asleep in his bunk, mouth wide open, snoring like a Jericho ram's-horn. Tom looked round, and counted every man in his bunk, and then says he, 'Who the devil is this? for there's Bob Coffin on deck, and the rest is all here.'

"Wal, Tom wa'n't a man to be put under too easy. He hed his thoughts about him allers; and the fust he thought in every pinch was what to do. So he sot considerin' a minute, sort o' winkin' his eyes to be sure he saw straight, when, sure enough, there come another man backin' down the companion-way.

" 'Wal, there's Bob Coffin, anyhow,' says Tom to himself. But no, the other man, he turned: Tom see his face; and, sure as you live, it was the face of a dead corpse. Its eyes was sot, and it jest came as still across the cabin, and sot down by the stove, and kind o' shivered, and put out its hands as if it was gettin' warm.

"Tom said that there was a cold air round in the cabin, as if an iceberg was comin' near, and he felt cold chills running down his back; but he jumped out of his bunk, and took a step forward. 'Speak!' says he. 'Who be you? and what do you want?'

"They never spoke, nor looked up, but kept kind o' shivering and crouching over the stove.

" 'Wal,' says Tom, 'I'll see who you be, anyhow.' And he walked right up to the last man that come in, and reached out to catch hold of his coat-collar; but his hand jest went through him like moonshine, and in a minute he all faded away; and when he turned round the other one was gone too. Tom stood there, looking this way and that; but there warn't nothing but the old stove, and the lantern swingin', and the men all snorin' round in their bunks. Tom, he sung out to Bob Coffin. 'Hullo, up there!' says he. But Bob never answered, and Tom, he went up, and found Bob down on his knees, his teeth a-chatterin' like a bag o' nails, trying to say his prayers; and all he could think of was, 'Now I lay me,' and he kep' going that over and over. Ye see, boys, Bob was a drefful wicked, searin' crittur, and hadn't said no prayers since he was tew years old, and it didn't come natural to him. Tom give a grip on his collar, and shook him. 'Hold yer yawp,' said he. 'What you howlin' about? What's up?'

" 'Oh, Lordy massy!' says Bob, 'we're sent for,—all on us,—there's been two on 'em: both on 'em went right by me!'

"Wal, Tom, he hed his own thoughts; but he was bound to get to the bottom of things, anyway. Ef 'twas the devil, well and good—he wanted to know it. Tom jest wanted to hev the matter settled one way or t'other: so he got Bob sort o' stroked down, and made him tell what he saw.

"Bob, he stood to it that he was a-standin' right for'ard, a-leanin' on the windlass, and kind o' hummin' a tune, wher he looked down, and see a sort o' queer light in the fog; and he went and took a look over the bows, when up came a man's head in a sort of sou'wester, and then a pair of hands, and catched at the bob-stay; and then the hull figger of a man riz right out o' the water, and clim up on the martingale till he could reach the jib-stay with his hands, and then he swung himself right up onto the bowsprit, and stepped aboard, and went past Bob, right aft, and down into the cabin. And he hadn't more'n got down, afore he turned round, and there was another comin' in over the bowsprit, and he went by him, and down below: so there was two on 'em, jest as Tom had seen in the cabin.

"Tom he studied on it a spell, and finally says he, 'Bob, let you and me keep this 'ere to ourselves, and see ef it'll come again. Ef it don't, well and good: ef it does—why, we'll see about it.'

"But Tom he told Cap'n Witherspoon, and the Cap'n he agreed to keep an eye out the next night. But there warn't nothing said to the rest o' the men.

"Wal, the next night they put Bill Bridges on the watch. The fog had lifted, and they had a fair wind, and was going on steady. The men all turned in, and went fast asleep, except Cap'n Witherspoon, Tom, and Bob Coffin. Wal, sure enough, 'twixt twelve and one o'clock, the same thing came over, only there war four men 'stead o' two. They come in jes' so over the bowsprit, and they looked neither to right nor left, but clim down stairs, and sot down, and crouched and shivered over the stove jist like the others. Wal, Bill Bridges, he came tearin' down like a wild-cat, frightened half out o' his wits, screechin' 'Lord, have mercy! we're all goin' to the devil!' And then they all vanished.

" 'Now, Cap'n, what's to be done?' says Tom. 'Ef these 'ere fellows is to take passage, we can't do nothin' with the boys: that's clear.'

"Wal, so it turned out; for, come next night, there was six on 'em come in, and the story got round, and the boys was all on eend. There wa'n't no doin' nothin' with 'em. Ye see, it's allers jest so. Not but what dead folks is jest as 'spectable as they was afore they's dead. These might 'a' been as good fellers as any aboard; but it's human natur'. The minute a feller's dead, why, you sort o' don't know 'bout him; and it's kind o' skeery hevin' on him round; and so 'twan't no wonder the boys didn't feel as if they could go on with the vy'ge, ef these 'ere fellers was all to take passage. Come to look, too, there war consid'able of a leak stove in the vessel; and the boys, they all stood to it, ef they went farther, that they'd all go to the bottom. For, ye see, once the story got a-goin', every one on 'em saw a new thing every night. One on 'em saw the bait-mill a-grindin', without no hands to grind it; and another saw fellers up aloft, workin' in the sails. Wal, the fact war, they jest had to put about,—run back to Castine.

"Wal, the owners, they hushed up things the best they could; and they put the vessel on the stocks, and worked her over, and put a new coat o' paint on her, and called her 'The Betsey Ann;' and she went a good vy'ge to the Banks, and brought home the biggest fare o' fish that had been for a long time; and she's made good vy'ges ever since; and that jest proves what I've been a-saying,—that there's nothin' to drive out ghosts like fresh paint."

Tombstone Moon

Norman Partridge

Black entered the cemetery shack and tossed the severed ear onto the desk, between a can of Brown Derby beer and a salami sandwich that was missing a bite.

The desert wind whipped through the open doorway, salting the warped floorboards with gritty sand. Black was already sick of the desert—sick of the earthy smell, sick of the unyielding heat, sick of the sand in his boots.

He closed the door, but that didn't help much. The shack's only window was open a fraction of an inch, and the steady wind whistled through its corroded metal lips. The sound was unsettling. Black leaned on the latch, but the window was rusted in place and wouldn't budge.

Black sighed. Only open a fraction of an inch, but that fraction was enough to mess with his senses.

Well, there was nothing to be done about it. Black rubbed a clean circle on the grimy glass. His '73 Toyota Corolla sat about twenty feet from the shack. The engine ticked and pinged, trying to cool without much success. Rust spots on the hood and trunk shone like pools of dark rum in the light of the setting sun.

A week's parking at McCarran International Airport in Las Vegas had cost twenty-five bucks, and that little fact irritated Black. He doubted he could sell the damned car for twenty-five bucks. But the Toy was inconspicuous, and that was the important thing.

Black scanned the desert. There wasn't much to see besides his car. Whistler's limo was nowhere in sight. Neither was the prospector's Ford pickup—Black had hidden it in an arroyo on the other side of the old state road. Only the cemetery lay before him, a borderless expanse dotted with tombstones that had been sandblasted blank over a period of forty years.

Anonymous graves, forgotten by a town that had folded when the interstate opened. Black thought about that. If your grave went untended, if your sacred piece of ground was forgotten—or worse, desecrated—was there a chance that something evil might get its hands on your soul even though you'd been laid to rest in a proper Christian cemetery?

Black wondered if it made a difference. He supposed that every grave was forgotten sooner or later. He toyed with the severed ear, flipping it between the beer and the sandwich. He'd never thought about graveyards, or tombstones, or Christian burial before in his life. He'd never thought about heaven or hell, either. He knew that such worries could get in the way of a man in his business, and he'd always felt fortunate to consider them a waste of his time.

Before today.

Even now, he wasn't sure that he wanted to start thinking about those things. He'd never felt comfortable tackling life's little intangibles.

He looked at the sandwich and his stomach growled.

The prospector wasn't coming back for it.

The salami was greasy and good. Black ate the meat and threw away the bread because the latter was salted with sand. He chased the salami with warm Brown Derby beer and tossed the empty can over his shoulder. It bounced off a filthy duffel-bag and rolled to a stop against the rusty blade of the prospector's shovel.

Black wanted to sort through the old-timer's duffel, but he didn't want Whistler to come barging in while he was at it. Instead, he pulled up a chair and rested his feet on top of the desk.

Soon it was dark. Black lit a few candles and watched faint shadows dance over a map of the cemetery that was mounted next to the door. The map was dotted with black pins, except for one spot in the right-hand corner where a white pin stood out, as stark and unexpected as a corpse at a family reunion.

Black grinned, thinking *I Bury the Living*. He'd seen that movie late one night in a cheap hotel room in Denver. It starred Richard Boone, and that was the only reason that Black stayed awake for it, because more than a few clients had told him that he resembled the young Richard Boone. He did, kind of— they were both all ruined around the eyes, and they both had noses that were of equal thickness from skull to tip, like carelessly fitted hunks of pipe.

Anyway, the movie was about a guy who thought that he was murdering people by sticking black pins in a map that marked pre-sold cemetery plots. Boone was pretty good in it, worrying that he was some kind of psychic monster or something. It wasn't *Have Gun, Will Travel*, but it was okay, until the ending.

Because the ending was a cheat—it turned out that Boone wasn't a monster after all. He hadn't killed anyone. The deaths were only a cheap coincidence, nothing to do with God or the Devil. And while Black had certainly never believed in anything supernatural—or much of anything at all, for that matter—he thought that in the movies there should always be something spooky, something unknown, or unknowable.

The wind whistled through the window's corroded lips.

A dirty yellow halo bloomed on the glass.

Bright light seeped beneath the bottom rail of the door.

The glow of headlights.

Whistler's limo.

Black reached behind him and straightened the knife that was tucked under his belt, then covered the weapon with his shirttail.

The cold steel felt good against the small of his back.

Black stepped to the window and watched a tall man ease out of a black Cadillac limousine. Even in the flat, uncritical light of the full moon, Black didn't like the look of Diabolos Whistler, Junior. He didn't like the man's accountant eyes, and he didn't like his spotless snakeskin boots, and he didn't like the silver-and-turquoise studs that sheathed his collar like a couple of gigantic arrowheads.

Whistler came through the doorway, his distressed-leather duster wind-wrapped around his ankles, and stood poised in the center of the room like a shootist ready to slap leather.

"You've come to the wrong place," Black said.

"Huh?"

"You want to go west on the interstate. Stop when you hit the water."

"What are you talking about?"

"Beverly Hills. Rodeo Drive, to be precise. Looks like where you belong, in that getup."

"Okay, you've had your little joke."

Black grinned. "Close the door, Tex."

Whistler did, his nose wrinkling. "God, it stinks in here. . . . We could have done this in Vegas, you know."

"Too many tourists," Black said. "Besides, I didn't much notice the stink. Maybe because I stink too. Last shower I had was at the hotel, before I climbed aboard a taxi with four sweaty tourists. Then I had a two-hour wait at the Baja airport. If you've ever been there this time of year you know it's like a sauna. I flew out on Aero Mexico, which is like flying in a school bus. They fed me a

502

lousy lunch and didn't even have any coffee. I got mad and tossed the plastic cup on the floor, and the smart-assed stewardess got all huffy—told me that I was breaking up a matched set. Then came Vegas where I had to pay twenty-five damn bucks to get my Toy—"

"Okay. Okay." Whistler dabbed his sweaty brow with a silk handkerchief that was supposed to look like a cowboy's bandana but didn't.

Black said, "I just wanted you to know that things haven't been going according to expectations today."

"Like I said: okay. Let's drop it."

Black shrugged.

"Well, did you do it?"

"Of course I did." Black pointed at the ear. "Let's do business, Junior."

"Don't call me that."

"No need to get testy." Black looked away, at the map. God, he hated this guy. He didn't care if Whistler had made the cover of *Newsweek*. That wasn't anything to him. After all, hadn't *Newsweek* put Max Headroom on the cover once? Hadn't they run that silly story, IS GOD DEAD?

Maybe *Time* had done that one. Black thought about it but couldn't remember, and he decided it didn't much matter.

Junior took a ziplock bag and a pair of tweezers out of his coat pocket and made a big production of bagging the ear. "We'll run tests on this, you know. My lab people have Father's complete medical records, and we'll know if you're trying to pull anything."

"I fulfilled our contract," Black said simply. "I brought the ear to prove that, per your instructions. It was a fairly easy job, except that it took me a week to find your father. He was staying in a beachfront condo at the tip of Baja, all alone, unless you want to count those mummies that were stacked in the bedroom closet. Anyway, I did him and buried his body at the end of a road that no cop will ever bother with. If you want to know the details, he went pretty easy. I came up from behind and stabbed him just above the first vertebra. He gasped a little bit. Then he started mewling . . . sounded more like a newborn babe than an eighty-five-year-old master of occult sciences. It didn't last more than a second or two, but—"

"That's enough."

"No, it's not. It might be for you, but it's not for me. If you want me to shut up about it, pay me." Black grinned. "That'll shut me up."

"Come out to the limo."

"No. That thing looks like a hearse." Black pretended to scratch his back; his fingers closed on the hilt of the knife. "You put the money in my Toy. I trust you, Junior."

"Have it your way, Mr. Black." Whistler left the shack.

Black closed his eyes and used his ears, listening through the wind. He believed you could learn a lot by listening, especially if you knew what to listen for. He heard a car door opening. He was sure that it was a door, not the trunk, and that made him happy; Whistler was the kind of guy who would hide a gun in the trunk if he had one.

The door closed easily, smoothly. Junior was nice and relaxed. Then Black heard a long creak as Whistler opened the door of the Toy.

An instant later he heard a rusty slam.

Black chuckled. "Temper, temper."

Black was surprised when Whistler returned to the shack.

"I've been thinking," Whistler began. "I could use a man like you on a permanent basis. I'm sure you can appreciate that mine is an organization on the move. With my father out of the way and me at the helm, we'll be more than just another cult. We'll be an accepted religion." He slapped a magazine down on the desk. "Just take a look."

Newsweek. Black glanced at Junior's picture above the blurb that read, THE NEW HEDONISM.

Black slid the magazine toward Whistler. "Look, I'm not much of a joiner. You bought me once. You can buy me again, should the need arise. But I only work when I need money." He smiled. "Besides, I want to see how things develop. I wouldn't want to make too many commitments with the end of the world so close at hand."

Whistler laughed.

Black said, "You don't believe any of it, do you?"

"What?"

"All that stuff your old man preached. All that stuff about a new satanic age coming on the heels of his death. Satan rising from the ruin of Diabolos Whistler's corpse like Jesus born of Mary. The end of the Christian era and the beginning of—"

"You've been doing your homework, Mr. Black."

"Hanging around airports, you have plenty of time to read. You run into all sorts of interesting folks selling all sorts of interesting pamphlets."

"Very funny." Whistler snatched up the magazine and shoved it into his coat pocket. "Look, this is a job to me. Some people put on suits and ties and run corporations. They tell their stockholders what the chumps want to hear. I put on a black leather jacket and run a religion."

"But *you* don't pay taxes."

"Come, come, Mr. Black. Neither do the corporations."

"But your father—"

Whistler cut him off with a sigh. "My father didn't have much business sense. He was wasting our money, frittering it away on archaeological expeditions and medieval manuscripts without the slightest concern for the bottom line. Our operation was poised on the brink of a sinkhole called debt, and my father was determined to shove us over the edge."

"And now he won't have the chance."

"Now he'll be my ace in the hole. People love a good mystery. They still talk about Ambrose Bierce disappearing into the Mexican desert, don't they? They even speculate about Jim Morrison . . ."

Black yawned. "Morrison died choking on his own vomit in a bathtub in Paris. Your old man died with six inches of steel jammed through his neck."

Whistler's breaths came short and hard through flared nostrils. Finally, he said, "You think about my offer. If you change your mind, you know where to find me."

"Right. Rodeo Drive."

"Wrong, Mr. Black. You watch for me on the financial page."

Whistler left the shack. Black let him go wondering how long the kid would last. He thought about how nice it would be to milk Junior for some extra green, but he doubted either of them would be around long enough for that. As it was, he felt lucky to be paid for this job.

Black closed his eyes. "You go find a lab and play with your ear," he said. "You see if you still think it's important in a day or two."

A car door slammed. A sound you could recognize if you knew what to listen for: an angry man hurrying on a treadmill to nowhere.

Headlight beams washed over the grimy window.

Black opened the desk drawer and stared down at the lump of leathery red flesh that came to a twisted point.

When Black severed Whistler Senior's ear out on that Baja backroad, it looked like any other human ear. But when he arrived at the cemetery shack and removed the ear from the false bottom of his suitcase, he realized what it had become.

The prospector returned to the shack at almost the same moment, thirsty for Brown Derby beer and surprised as hell to see a rusty rice-rocket parked in front of his current digs. Black slipped the ear into the drawer just as the old-timer stepped through the doorway with a big, "Howdy, stranger." Then he listened to the prospector's story, the old one about milking silver from an abandoned mine up in the mountains.

Mine, hell. One look at the prospector's flimsy shovel told Black what kind of mining this guy was doing. He'd heard about scavengers who hit abandoned cemeteries, but he'd never run into one. He'd never been eager to mix with that kind of man.

Funny, doing what he did for a living and feeling like that.

So Black let the prospector gab and drink Brown Derby beer. After a while, Black told the old guy that he had an ice chest full of Anchor Steam out in the Toy's trunk. Said that he was bringing it in from San Francisco for a buddy, but what the hell. The prospector went for it with a nod and a wrinkled grin—Black imagined that it was the same grin the old guy wore when he hit pay dirt.

In the heat, in the blowing sand, Black stabbed the prospector just above the first vertebra and watched him crumple like a puppet shorn of strings.

When the old guy stopped bleeding, Black severed his left ear.

Black rolled the prospector's body out of the Toy's trunk. He returned to the shack to get the duffel and the shovel. Old man Whistler's ear lay in the drawer. It had sprouted a hedge of tiny white spikes that were as thin as cactus thorns but as hard as teeth.

Black pulled the last white pin out of the cemetery map. Found a black pin in the desk. Stabbed it through Whistler's ear and pinned it to the spot where the white pin had been.

Outside, the moon crested the ash-colored mountains like an enormous tombstone. Black took off his shirt and let the evening breeze caress his sweaty back. His sweat smelled like beer. He dragged the prospector's skinny corpse through the graveyard. The dead man's heels dug little ditches in the sand.

Black found the empty plot and was kind of surprised that it wasn't marked with a big white pin. He started to dig. He felt a little better. The wind had dried his sweat, and the desert air smelled good. Dry and clean, like the sky. The baked-earth smell that had bothered him in the heat of the day was long gone.

He went down about two feet before the sand started to sift back into the hole. He rolled the prospector's body into the grave, upended the duffel and poured diamond rings and gold teeth and silver crosses over the corpse, and covered it up.

The cool wind smoothed the mounded sand. Black tossed the empty duffel to the wind and watched it tumble past a row of blank tombstones. He thought about the ear pinned to the map in the cemetery shack, and he thought about the body that he had buried on that Baja backroad, remembered burying that body without a second thought. He wondered what it looked like right now, that body.

Black stared at the moon. Maybe he should make a marker for the prospector's grave. Maybe he ought to dig the registration slip out of the old-timer's truck and pin it to a cross so the skinny old guy wouldn't go unknown. Maybe . . . He shook his head. That was the flip side of all right, but he didn't have any proof that it really existed.

What he had was the ear.

What he figured he didn't have was a whole lot of time.

Black hesitated, then planted the shovel at the head of the grave.

506

The wind picked up, howling like something evil, something young and strong. Blasts of sand worried the anonymous tombstones. Black imagined the sound of hoofbeats—cloven hoofs racing sharp and fast over a stretch of blacktop somewhere south of the border.

He hurried to his car, wondering if he'd hear that sound.

Wondering if he knew what to listen for.

The Torture by Hope

Villiers de l'Isle Adam

Many years ago, as evening was closing in, the venerable Pedro Arbuez d'Espila, sixth prior of the Dominicans of Segovia, and third Grand Inquisitor of Spain, followed by a *fra redemptor*, and preceded by two familiars of the Holy Office, the latter carrying lanterns, made their way to a subterranean dungeon. The bolt of a massive door creaked, and they entered a mephitic *in-pace*, where the dim light revealed between rings fastened to the wall a blood-stained rack, a brazier, and a jug. On a pile of straw, loaded with fetters and his neck encircled by an iron carcan, sat a haggard man, of uncertain age, clothed in rags.

This prisoner was no other than Rabbi Aser Abarbanel, a Jew of Arragon, who—accused of usury and pitiless scorn for the poor— had been daily subjected to torture for more than a year. Yet "his blindness was as dense as his hide," and he had refused to abjure his faith.

Proud of a filiation dating back thousands of years, proud of his ancestors—for all Jews worthy of the name are vain of their blood—he descended Talmudically from Othoniel and consequently from Ipsiboa, the wife of the last judge of Israel, a circumstance which had sustained his courage amid incessant torture. With tears in his eyes at the thought of this resolute soul rejecting salvation, the venerable Pedro Arbuez d'Espila, approaching the shuddering rabbi, addressed him as follows:

"My son, rejoice: your trials here below are about to end. If in the presence of such obstinacy I was forced to permit, with deep regret, the use of great severity, my task of fraternal correction has its limits. You are the fig tree which having failed so many times to bear fruit, at last withered, but God alone can judge your soul. Perhaps Infinite Mercy will shine upon you at the last moment! We must hope so. There are examples. So sleep in peace to-night. To-morrow you will be included in the *auto da fé:* that is, you will be exposed to the *quémadero*, the symbolical flames of the Everlasting Fire: it burns, as you know,

507

only at a distance, my son; and Death is at least two hours (often three) in coming, on account of the wet, iced bandages, with which we protect the heads and hearts of the condemned. There will be forty-three of you. Placed in the last row, you will have time to invoke God and offer to Him this baptism of fire, which is of the Holy Spirit. Hope in the Light, and rest."

With these words, having signed to his companions to unchain the prisoner, the prior tenderly embraced him. Then came the turn of the *fra redemptor*, who, in a low tone, entreated the Jew's forgiveness for what he had made him suffer for the purpose of redeeming him; then the two familiars silently kissed him. This ceremony over, the captive was left, solitary and bewildered, in the darkness.

Rabbi Aser Abarbanel, with parched lips and visage worn by suffering, at first gazed at the closed door with vacant eyes. Closed? The word unconsciously roused a vague fancy in his mind, the fancy that he had seen for an instant the light of the lanterns through a chink between the door and the wall. A morbid idea of hope, due to the weakness of his brain, stirred his whole being. He dragged himself toward the strange *appearance*. Then, very gently and cautiously, slipping one finger into the crevice, he drew the door toward him. Marvelous! By an extraordinary accident the familiar who closed it had turned the huge key an instant before it struck the stone casing, so that the rusty bolt not having entered the hole, the door again rolled on its hinges.

The rabbi ventured to glance outside. By the aid of a sort of luminous dusk he distinguished at first a semicircle of walls indented by winding stairs; and opposite to him, at the top of five or six stone steps, a sort of black portal, opening into an immense corridor, whose first arches only were visible from below.

Stretching himself flat he crept to the threshold. Yes, it was really a corridor, but endless in length. A wan light illumined it: lamps suspended from the vaulted ceiling lightened at intervals the dull hue of the atmosphere—the distance was veiled in shadow. Not a single door appeared in the whole extent! Only on one side, the left, heavily grated loopholes, sunk in the walls, admitted a light which must be that of evening, for crimson bars at intervals rested on the flags of the pavement. What a terrible silence! Yet, yonder, at the far end of that passage there might be a doorway of escape! The Jew's vacillating hope was tenacious, for it was *the last*.

Without hesitating, he ventured on the flags, keeping close under the loopholes, trying to make himself part of the blackness of the long walls. He advanced slowly, dragging himself along on his breast, forcing back the cry of pain when some raw wound sent a keen pang through his whole body.

Suddenly the sound of a sandaled foot approaching reached his ears. He trembled violently, fear stifled him, his sight grew dim. Well, it was over, no doubt. He pressed himself into a niche and, half lifeless with terror, waited.

It was a familiar hurrying along. He passed swiftly by, holding in his clenched hand an instrument of torture—a frightful figure—and vanished. The suspense which the rabbi had endured seemed to have suspended the functions of life, and he lay nearly an hour unable to move. Fearing an increase of tortures if he were captured, he thought of returning to his dungeon. But the old hope whispered in his soul that divine *perhaps,* which comforts us in our sorest trials. A miracle had happened. He could doubt no longer. He began to crawl toward the chance of escape. Exhausted by suffering and hunger, trembling with pain, he pressed onward. The sepulchral corridor seemed to lengthen mysteriously, while he, still advancing, gazed into the gloom where there *must* be some avenue of escape.

Oh! oh! He again heard footsteps, but this time they were slower, more heavy. The white and black forms of two inquisitors appeared, emerging from the obscurity beyond. They were conversing in low tones, and seemed to be discussing some important subject, for they were gesticulating vehemently.

At this spectacle Rabbi Aser Abarbanel closed his eyes: his heart beat so violently that it almost suffocated him; his rags were damp with the cold sweat of agony; he lay motionless by the wall, his mouth wide open, under the rays of a lamp, praying to the God of David.

Just opposite to him the two inquisitors paused under the light of the lamp—doubtless owing to some accident due to the course of their argument. One, while listening to his companion, gazed at the rabbi! And, beneath the look—whose absence of expression the hapless man did not at first notice—he fancied he again felt the burning pincers scorch his flesh, he was to be once more a living wound. Fainting, breathless, with fluttering eyelids, he shivered at the touch of the monk's floating robe. But—strange yet natural fact—the inquisitor's gaze was evidently that of a man deeply absorbed in his intended reply, engrossed by what he was hearing; his eyes were fixed—and seemed to look at the Jew *without seeing him.*

In fact, after the lapse of a few minutes, the two gloomy figures slowly pursued their way, still conversing in low tones, toward the place whence the prisoner had come; HE HAD NOT BEEN SEEN! Amid the horrible confusion of the rabbi's thoughts, the idea darted through his brain: "Can I be already dead that they did not see me?" A hideous impression roused him from his lethargy: in looking at the wall against which his face was pressed, he imagined he beheld two fierce eyes watching him! He flung his head back in a sudden frenzy of fright, his hair fairly bristling! Yet, no! No. His hand groped over the stones: it was the *reflection* of the inquisitor's eyes, still retained in his own, which had been refracted from two spots on the wall.

Forward! He must hasten toward that goal which he fancied (absurdly, no doubt) to be deliverance, toward the darkness from which he was now barely thirty paces distant. He pressed forward faster on his knees, his hands, at full length, dragging himself painfully along, and soon entered the dark portion of this terrible corridor.

Suddenly the poor wretch felt a gust of cold air on the hands resting upon the flags; it came from under the little door to which the two walls led.

Oh, Heaven, if that door should open outward. Every nerve in the miserable fugitive's body thrilled with hope. He examined it from top to bottom, though scarcely able to distinguish its outlines in the surrounding darkness. He passed his hand over it: no bolt, no lock! A latch! He started up, the latch yielded to the pressure of his thumb: the door silently swung open before him.

"HALLELUIA!" murmured the rabbi in a transport of gratitude as, standing on the threshold, he beheld the scene before him.

The door had opened into the gardens, above which arched a starlit sky, into spring, liberty, life! It revealed the neighboring fields, stretching toward the sierras, whose sinuous blue lines were relieved against the horizon. Yonder lay freedom! Oh, to escape! He would journey all night through the lemon groves, whose fragrance reached him. Once in the mountains and he was safe! He inhaled the delicious air; the breeze revived him, his lungs expanded! He felt in his swelling heart the *Veni foràs* of Lazarus! And to thank once more the God who had bestowed this mercy upon him, he extended his arms, raising his eyes toward Heaven. It was an ecstasy of joy!

Then he fancied he saw the shadow of his arms approach him—fancied that he felt these shadowy arms inclose, embrace him—and that he was pressed tenderly to some one's breast. A tall figure actually did stand directly before him. He lowered his eyes—and remained motionless, gasping for breath, dazed, with fixed eyes, fairly driveling with terror.

Horror! He was in the clasp of the Grand Inquisitor himself, the venerable Pedro Arbuez d'Espila, who gazed at him with tearful eyes, like a good shepherd who had found his stray lamb.

The dark-robed priest pressed the hapless Jew to his heart with so fervent an outburst of love, that the edges of the monochal haircloth rubbed the Dominican's breast. And while Aser Abarbanel with protruding eyes gasped in agony in the ascetic's embrace, vaguely comprehending that *all the phases of this fatal evening were only a prearranged torture, that of* HOPE, the Grand Inquisitor, with an accent of touching reproach and a look of consternation, murmured in his ear, his breath parched and burning from long fasting:

"What, my son! On the eve, perchance, of salvation—you wished to leave us?"

510

Two Doctors

M. R. James

I t is a very common thing, in my experience, to find papers shut up in old books; but one of the rarest things to come across any such that are at all interesting. Still it does happen, and one should never destroy them unlooked at. Now it was a practice of mine before the war occasionally to buy old ledgers of which the paper was good, and which possessed a good many blank leaves, and to extract these and use them for my own notes and writings. One such I purchased for a small sum in 1911. It was tightly clasped, and its boards were warped by having for years been obliged to embrace a number of extraneous sheets. Three-quarters of this inserted matter had lost all vestige of importance for any living human being: one bundle had not. That it belonged to a lawyer is certain, for it is endorsed: *The strangest case I have yet met*, and bears initials, and an address in Gray's Inn. It is only materials for a case, and consists of statements by possible witnesses. The man who would have been the defendant or prisoner seems never to have appeared. The *dossier* is not complete, but, such as it is, it furnishes a riddle in which the supernatural appears to play a part. You must see what you can make of it.

The following is the setting and the tale as I elicit it.

The scene is Islington in 1718, and the time the month of June: a countrified place, therefore, and a pleasant season. Dr Abell was walking in his garden one afternoon waiting for his horse to be brought round that he might set out on his visits for the day. To him entered his confidential servant, Luke Jennett, who had been with him twenty years.

'I said I wished to speak to him, and what I had to say might take some quarter of an hour. He accordingly bade me go into his study, which was a room opening on the terrace path where he was walking, and came in himself and sat down. I told him that, much against my will, I must look out for another place. He inquired what was my reason, in consideration I had been so long with him. I said if he would excuse me he would do me a great kindness, because (this appears to have been common form even in 1718) I was one that always liked to have everything pleasant about me. As well as I can remember, he said that was his case likewise, but he would wish to know why I should change my mind after so many years, and, says he, "You know there can be no talk of a remem-

511

brance of you in my will if you leave my service now." I said I had made my reckoning of that.

' "Then," says he, "you must have some complaint to make, and if I could I would willingly set it right." And at that I told him, not seeing how I could keep it back, the matter of my former affidavit and of the bedstaff in the dispensing-room, and said that a house where such things happened was no place for me. At which he, looking very black upon me, said no more, but called me fool, and said he would pay what was owing me in the morning; and so, his horse being waiting, went out. So for that night I lodged with my sister's husband near Battle Bridge and came early next morning to my late master, who then made a great matter that I had not lain in his house and stopped a crown out of my wages owing.

'After that I took service here and there, not for long at a time, and saw no more of him till I came to be Dr Quinn's man at Dodds Hall in Islington.'

There is one very obscure part in this statement—namely, the reference to the former affidavit and the matter of the bedstaff. The former affidavit is not in the bundle of papers. It is to be feared that it was taken out to be read because of its special oddity, and not put back. Of what nature the story was may be guessed later, but as yet no clue has been put into our hands.

The Rector of Islington, Jonathan Pratt, is the next to step forward. He furnishes particulars of the standing and reputation of Dr Abell and Dr Quinn, both of whom lived and practised in his parish.

'It is not to be supposed,' he says, 'that a physician should be a regular attendant at morning and evening prayers, or at the Wednesday lectures, but within the measure of their ability I would say that both these persons fulfilled their obligations as loyal members of the Church of England. At the same time (as you desire my private mind) I must say, in the language of the schools, *distinguo*. Dr A. was to me a source of perplexity, Dr Q. to my eye a plain, honest believer, not inquiring over closely into points of belief, but squaring his practice to what lights he had. The other interested himself in questions to which Providence, as I hold, designs no answer to be given us in this state: he would ask me, for example, what place I believed those beings now to hold in the scheme of creation which by some are thought neither to have stood fast when the rebel angels fell, nor to have joined with them to the full pitch of their transgression.

'As was suitable, my first answer to him was a question, What warrant he had for supposing any such beings to exist? for that there was none in Scripture I took it he was aware. It appeared—for as I am on the subject, the whole tale may be given—that he grounded himself on such passages as that of the satyr which Jerome tells us conversed with Antony; but thought too that some parts of Scripture might be cited in support. "And besides," said he, "you know 'tis the universal belief among those that spend their days and nights abroad, and I would add that if your calling took you so continuously as it does me about the country lanes by night, you might not be so surprised as I see you to be by my suggestion." "You are then of John Milton's mind," I said, "and hold that 'Millions of spiritual creatures walk the earth/Unseen, both when we wake and when we sleep.' "

' "I do not know," he said, "why Milton should take upon himself to say 'unseen'; though to be sure he was blind when he wrote that. But for the rest, why, yes, I think he was in the right." "Well," I said, "though not so often as you, I am not seldom called abroad pretty late; but I have no mind of meeting a satyr in our Islington lanes in all the years I have been here; and if you have had the better luck, I am sure the Royal Society would be glad to know of it."

'I am reminded of these trifling expressions because Dr A. took them so ill, stamping out of the room in a huff with some such word as that these high and dry parsons had no eyes but for a prayer-book or a pint of wine.

'But this was not the only time that our conversation took a remarkable turn. There was an evening when he came in, at first seeming gay and in good spirits, but afterwards as he sat and smoked by the fire falling into a musing way; out of which to rouse him I said pleasantly that I supposed he had had no meetings of late with his odd friends. A question which did effectually arouse him, for he looked most wildly, and as if scared, upon me, and said, "*You* were never there? I did not see you. Who brought you?" And then in a more collected tone, "What was this about a meeting? I believe I must have been in a doze." To which I answered that I was thinking of fauns and centaurs in the dark lane, and not of a witches' Sabbath; but it seemed he took it differently.

' "Well," said he, "I can plead guilty to neither; but I find you very much more of a sceptic than becomes your cloth. If you care to know about the dark lane you might do worse than ask my housekeeper that lived at the other end of it when she was a child." "Yes," said I, "and the old women in the almshouse and the children in the kennel. If I were you, I would send to your brother Quinn for a bolus to clear your brain." "Damn Quinn," says he; "talk no more of him: he has embezzled four of my best patients this month; I believe it is that cursed man of his, Jennett, that used to be with me, his tongue is never still; it should be nailed to the pillory if he had his deserts." This, I may say, was the only time of his showing me that he had any grudge against either Dr Quinn or Jennett, and as was my business, I did my best to persuade him he was mistaken in them. Yet it could not be denied that some respectable families in the parish had given him the cold shoulder, and for no reason that they were willing to allege. The end was that he said he had not done so ill at Islington but that he could afford to live at ease elsewhere when he chose, and anyhow he bore Dr Quinn no malice. I think I now remember what observation of mine drew him into the train of thought which he next pursued. It was, I believe, my mentioning some juggling tricks which my brother in the East Indies had seen at the court of the Rajah of Mysore. "A convenient thing enough," said Dr Abell to me, "if by some arrangement a man could get the power of communicating motion and energy to inanimate objects." "As if the axe should move itself against him that lifts it; something of that kind?" "Well, I don't know that that was in my mind so much; but if you could summon such a volume from your shelf or even order it to open at the right page."

'He was sitting by the fire—it was a cold evening—and stretched out his hand that way, and just then the fire-irons, or at least the poker, fell over towards him with a great clatter, and I did not hear what else he said. But I told him that I could not easily conceive of an arrangement, as he called it, of such a kind that would not include as one of its conditions a heavier payment than any Christian would care to make; to which he assented. "But," he said, "I have no doubt these bargains can be made very tempting, very persuasive. Still, you would not favour them, eh, Doctor? No, I suppose not."

'This is as much as I know of Dr Abell's mind, and the feeling between these men. Dr Quinn, as I said, was a plain, honest creature, and a man to whom I would have gone—indeed I have before now gone to him—for advice on matters of business. He was, however, every now and again, and particularly of late, not exempt from troublesome fancies. There was certainly a time when he was so much harassed by his dreams that he could not keep them to himself, but would tell them to his acquaintances and among them to me. I was at supper at his house, and he was not inclined to let me leave him at my usual time. "If you go," he said, "there will be nothing for it but I must go to bed and dream of the chrysalis." "You might be worse off," said I. "I do not think it," he said, and he shook himself like a man who is displeased with the complexion of his thoughts. "I only meant," said I, "that a chrysalis is an innocent thing." "This one is not," he said, "and I do not care to think of it."

'However, sooner than lose my company he was fain to tell me (for I pressed him) that this was a dream which had come to him several times of late, and even more than once in a night. It was to this effect, that he seemed to himself to wake under an extreme compulsion to rise and go out of doors. So he would dress himself and go down to his garden door. By the door there stood a spade which he must take, and go out into the garden, and at a particular place in the shrubbery, somewhat clear, and upon which the moon shone (for there was always in his dream a full moon), he would feel himself forced to dig. And after some time the spade would uncover something light-coloured, which he would perceive to be a stuff, linen or woollen, and this he must clear with his hands. It was always the same: of the size of a man and shaped like the chrysalis of a moth, with the folds showing a promise of an opening at one end.

'He could not describe how gladly he would have left all at this stage and run to the house, but he must not escape so easily. So with many groans, and knowing only too well what to expect, he parted these folds of stuff, or, as it sometimes seemed to be, membrane, and disclosed a head covered with a smooth pink skin, which breaking as the creature stirred, showed him his own face in a state of death. The telling of this so much disturbed him that I was forced out of mere compassion to sit with him the greater part of the night and talk with him upon indifferent subjects. He said that upon every recurrence of this dream he woke and found himself, as it were, fighting for his breath.'

Another extract from Luke Jennett's long continuous statement comes in at this point.

'I never told tales of my master, Dr Abell, to anybody in the neighbourhood. When I was in another service I remember to have spoken to my fellow-servants about the matter of the bedstaff, but I am sure I never said either I or he were the persons concerned, and it met with so little credit that I was affronted and thought best to keep it to myself. And when I came back to Islington and found Dr Abell still there, who I was told had left the parish, I was clear that it behoved me to use great discretion, for indeed I was afraid of the man, and it is certain I was no party to spreading any ill report of him. My master, Dr Quinn, was a very just, honest man, and no maker of mischief. I am sure he never stirred a finger nor said a word by way of inducement to a soul to make them leave going to Dr Abell and come to him; nay, he would hardly be persuaded to attend them that came, until he was convinced that if he did not they would send into the town for a physician rather than do as they had hitherto done.

'I believe it may be proved that Dr Abell came into my master's house more than once. We had a new chambermaid out of Hertfordshire, and she asked me who was the gentleman that was looking after the master, that is Dr Quinn, when he was out, and seemed so disappointed that he was out. She said whoever he was he knew the way of the house well, running at once into the study and then into the dispensing-room, and last into the bed-chamber. I made her tell me what he was like, and what she said was suitable enough to Dr Abell; but besides she told me she saw the same man at church, and someone told her that was the Doctor.

'It was just after this that my master began to have his bad nights, and complained to me and other persons, and in particular what discomfort he suffered from his pillow and bedclothes. He said he must buy some to suit him, and should do his own marketing. And accordingly brought home a parcel which he said was of the right quality, but where he bought it we had then no knowledge, only they were marked in thread with a coronet and a bird. The women said they were of a sort not commonly met with and very fine, and my master said they were the comfortablest he ever used, and he slept now both soft and deep. Also the feather pillows were the best sort and his head would sink into them as if they were a cloud: which I have myself remarked several times when I came to wake him of a morning, his face being almost hid by the pillow closing over it.

'I had never any communication with Dr Abell after I came back to Islington, but one day when he passed me in the street and asked me whether I was not looking for another service, to which I answered I was very well suited where I was, but he said I was a fickleminded fellow and he doubted not he should soon hear I was on the world again, which indeed proved true.'

Dr Pratt is next taken up where he left off.

'On the 16th I was called up out of my bed soon after it was light—that is about five—with a message that Dr Quinn was dead or dying. Making my way to his house I found there was no doubt which was the truth. All the persons in the house except the one that let me in were already in his chamber and standing about his bed, but none touching him. He was stretched in the midst of the bed, on his back, without any disorder, and indeed had the appearance of one ready laid out for burial. His hands, I think, were even crossed on his breast. The only thing not usual was that nothing was to be seen of his face, the two ends of the pillow or bolster appearing to be closed quite over it. These I immediately pulled apart, at the same time rebuking those present, and especially the man, for not at once coming to the assistance of his master. He, however, only looked at me and shook his head, having evidently no more hope than myself that there was anything but a corpse before us.

'Indeed it was plain to anyone possessed of the least experience that he was not only dead, but had died of suffocation. Nor could it be conceived that his death was accidentally caused by the mere folding of the pillow over his face. How should he not, feeling the oppression, have lifted his hands to put it away? whereas not a fold of the sheet which was closely gathered about him, as I now observed, was disordered. The next thing was to procure a physician. I had bethought me of this on leaving my house, and sent on the messenger who had come to me to Dr Abell; but I now heard that he was away from home, and the nearest surgeon was got, who, however, could tell no more, at least without opening the body, than we already knew.

'As to any person entering the room with evil purpose (which was the next point to be cleared), it was visible that the bolts of the door were burst from their stanchions, and the stanchions broken away from the door-post by main force; and there was a sufficient body of witnesses, the smith among them, to testify that this had been done but a few minutes before I came. The chamber being, moreover, at the top of the house, the window was neither easy of access nor did it show any sign of an exit made that way, either by marks upon the sill or footprints below upon soft mould.'

The surgeon's evidence forms of course part of the report of the inquest, but since it has nothing but remarks upon the healthy state of the larger organs and the coagulation of blood in various parts of the body, it need not be reproduced. The verdict was 'Death by the visitation of God.'

Annexed to the other papers is one which I was at first inclined to suppose had made its way among them by mistake. Upon further consideration I think I can divine a reason for its presence.

It relates to the rifling of a mausoleum in Middlesex which stood in a park (now broken up), the property of a noble family which I will not name. The outrage was not that of an ordinary resurrection man. The object, it seemed likely, was theft. The account is blunt and terrible. I shall not quote it. A dealer in the North of London suffered heavy penalties as a receiver of stolen goods in connexion with the affair.

The Visitor

John Bender

After a hard day which had included two rows with Mr. Greck—the middle-aged, second-floor Lothario—concerning some peculiarly objectionable behavior of his cat, Mrs. Mulvaney was in no mood for midnight callers that stormy Saturday night. When the jangle of the front bell roused her from her sleep, she was of a mind to turn over and ignore the ringing. But finally, disheveled and annoyed, she padded out into the hall and put on the lights.

With a sigh of impatience she opened the door, and admitted a tall young woman, wet to the bone, whose thin face was fairly shrunken with the cold.

"Do you have a room?" the young woman asked, and her dark brown eyes in that dead white face wrenched at Mrs. Mulvaney's very heart.

Mrs. Mulvaney told her to come inside, carefully inspecting her the while. The girl seemed a good deal better than some who had come to her door in the thirty years she'd been letting the upstairs rooms, since her husband—may the Lord have mercy on his soul!—had up and died one night of the cough. Mrs. Mulvaney thought it something of a coincidence that the girl had come this very night: but she liked the fact that the young lady had luggage—and a ready twenty-dollar bill in her hand.

In fact, the shivering girl who said her name was Jula de Mise didn't ask the price of the room. She held out the twenty and said, "Of course, I'll pay the first week in advance," and from that point on—since the room had been bringing only fifteen a week—Mrs. Mulvaney was inclined to think very well of her.

So she showed her to the newly unoccupied room, second floor, back—the one next to Mr. Greck—and that was all there was to it. Mrs. Mulvaney slipped the twenty into her ample bosom, brushed at the faded bedspread and explained about the bathroom, which was in the hall.

She noticed that Miss de Mise seemed extremely pale and drawn, nervous like, but then the girl said she'd been looking for a room all day and it had only been by chance that she'd come to this rooming house. Mrs. Mulvaney said that was the way, now, wasn't it? Why, it had only been the day before that Mrs. Hutchins, who'd had the room for seven years, had up and— Here, Mrs. Mulvaney checked herself in time and added that the aged Mrs. Hutchins had *left* them for another place.

On leaving, Mrs. Mulvaney congratulated herself that she had not mentioned that Mrs. Hutchins had had the misfortune to die in that particular room.

As Mrs. Mulvaney went down the hall to the stairs she noticed that Mr. Greck—oh, he was a one for knowing everybody's business!—had his door open. Wrapped in his eyesore of a robe—which he no doubt fancied as a romantic touch—he came out into the corridor, smiling as he always did when he was after something.

"A new tenant, eh?" he observed. "A young lady?"

She said yes, but no more. Despite the goodness of her heart, she could not find it in herself to like this man. He looked too much like what he was—an undertaker's assistant—and Mrs. Mulvaney had uneasy convictions about him and his profession. The work of preparing bodies for the grave was, in her opinion, hardly an honorable one. In this, her ancestry shaped her thoughts: as a little girl in Ireland she had had an aunt whose mode of occupation had called for whispers when it was discussed—something to do with the making of "lay-away" clothes.

"Quite young," said Mr. Greck, in that slick-lipped way of his, whenever discussing pretty young women. "And—ah—very attractive, wasn't she?"

"Scrawny," said Mrs. Mulvaney, meaning no disrespect for the new young woman. Indeed, had Miss Jula de Mise known of this little slug of a man, she'd have been grateful for the statement, Mrs. Mulvaney thought. Mr. Greck looked upon anything in skirts as fair prey, and he could be a bother. "No flesh on her at all. Pale, too. 'Tis anemic, that young lady is. I'll tell her of a tonic—"

"Oh," said Mr. Greck, his thin lips frowning. "Oh. . . ."

So she left him there, and satisfied she was with herself for having cooled him some. The lecherous old body snatcher!

Mrs. Mulvaney smiled within her vastness, and considered it good payment for the troubles he caused her. Him and that bloody cat of his! If she'd had the full say of it, she'd have had done with him and that terrible, razor-clawed animal which kept tearing at her hall runners. But being a landlord was not as simple as it had been in the old days. Once, she'd have turned him out—for no other reason than that she didn't like the cut of him, or the fact that his tawny, striped cat was destructive and a smell about the place. But with all the present regulations, a landlady had a time of it, for fair.

So she went and put the twenty dollars in the coffee can behind the stove, said a simple prayer for her late lamented good man and settled her hulk in bed. It was not until the following morning that Mr. Greck brought up the subject of the new lodger.

He came early, pounding on the door less than half an hour after Mrs. Mulvaney had had her breakfast tea and toast.

"I want my cat," he demanded in his shrill voice. "I want you to get my cat."

"Do you, now?" Mrs. Mulvaney frowned. "Where would I be keeping the animal?"

"*She's* got him, damn her! That new girl!"

"And what would she be wanting with it?"

His thin face blanched. "That's what I want you to find out. This morning I let Tommy out, and that new girl got him into her room. I saw him going into her room, I tell you! I saw it myself!"

"Perhaps she likes cats," Mrs. Mulvaney said.

"But she wouldn't answer when I went to get him. I knocked and knocked, and she wouldn't let me in. She's up to no good."

Mrs. Mulvaney thought otherwise, but to keep him quiet she went upstairs and knocked on Miss de Mise's door. The girl was quick to answer, and Mrs. Mulvaney apologized for the early disturbance and informed her of the purpose of the call.

"A cat?" said Miss de Mise. "I have a cat?"

"Mr. Greck thinks his cat may have come in here."

The new girl frowned. "You're mistaken, I'm sure. I don't like cats, really."

Then she smiled, and Mrs. Mulvaney was surprised, for the new girl seemed so much the better for the night of sleep she'd got. Her cheeks, indeed, were a new and healthy pink glow; she seemed much fresher and attractive.

Mrs. Mulvaney apologized again and went downstairs and brewed another cup of tea. She was a bit on edge, though for the life of her she could not tell just why, and she decided to forget about it. She gave her small place a brushing up, just a lick and a promise; then she put on her hat and went to an early Mass. She returned, much fortified, and was content until, once again, Mr. Greck came knocking on her door.

His face was a study in anxiety. "She's killed him!" he exclaimed abruptly. "I know it. I know it. Do you hear?"

"Now, now," said Mrs. Mulvaney, still full of Christian tolerance. "What's all this about?"

"My cat, Tommy! I tell you she's killed him. I know it!" He wrung his waxy hands, and the sound was like the rattling of dead flowers. "Come on, I'll prove it!"

His annoyance, or fear, brought beads of sweat right out on his forehead. He was clutching her arm. "Out in back," he said. "In the garbage can."

Almost tugging, he led the way through the narrow corridor of the downstairs floor, to the small courtyard in the rear. Then he rushed to a waste receptacle and threw back the cover. He pointed.

Mrs. Mulvaney looked. She saw the usual debris discarded by her tenants, but certainly nothing more.

"It's gone!" Mr. Greck was deflated. "But I saw her. I *saw* her! She brought a towel down here and put it in the can just a little while ago. There was blood on it, I tell you—"

"Now," she said. She was sure the man was going off his head. His work, no doubt. Why, it was enough to give anyone the shakes. "Now, why don't you let me make you a cup of nice hot tea . . . ?"

His imperiously cocked eyebrows were disdainful. "You think I'm just making this up?"

Mrs. Mulvaney wondered just what to say. She ran her tongue across her lips, ill at ease, then decided on the obvious. "Well, there's nothing here that looks like a towel—or blood," she said as crossly as she could.

"But she's killed my cat, she has!"

"Killed, my foot! 'Tis probably in someone's backyard you'll be finding the blasted animal," Mrs. Mulvaney declared.

Upon that she closed the subject. She started for her room, hoping that Mr. Greck would go for his.

"She's killed him," he muttered, ignoring what she'd said. "No matter what you think. I know it, I tell you. I'll get the truth out of her. You just wait and see."

"You leave the poor girl alone," Mrs. Mulvaney said sharply.

Mr. Greck laughed his nasty laugh. "You'll see," he said. "You'll see."

And she did see. Later on, toward the end of the afternoon, she observed a remarkably subdued Mr. Greck standing in the corridor outside Miss de Mise's room; and from what she saw, Mrs. Mulvaney could tell that he was being very friendly. Slick and polished in his Sunday suit, he was, with his slippery laugh running softly through the hall. He was saying, "I'm sure that we've met somewhere before. . . ."

The girl's seductive murmur came back, "Why, yes. Of course. I was wondering if you would remember me. . . ."

Then the door opened just a shade more, to admit him to the room.

Mrs. Mulvaney could hardly contain her surprise. Why, the little devil, working an old dodge like that! But, really, it was the new girl's responsiveness that bothered her the more. Mrs. Mulvaney hadn't thought that she was that kind; frankly, the suddenly realized ramifications of the action upstairs filled her with a certain dread. She'd never had any trouble of *that* sort in her place!

She fidgeted for long minutes in her room, trying to decide upon her action, while keeping her ears open for any sounds upstairs. Once she thought she heard a foot on the stairs, and someone going to the back door, but she could not be sure it was Mr. Greck, and the suspense grew within her. Finally, she determined on the phone-call ruse. Carefully and silently she went into the hall and dialed the three numbers which would ring her right back. That done, she called loudly upstairs:

"Mr. Greck! Oh, Mr. Greck! Telephone!"

When several minutes went by without answer, she tried again. Then, when that produced no response, she was fully justified in climbing the stairs and knocking at his door.

There was no answer. At length, decided, she went to the girl's door and rapped sharply.

To her surprise it opened almost immediately, and a remarkably bright and spirited Miss de Mise looked down at her.

"Yes?"

"I—I thought I saw Mr. Greck come in here," Mrs. Mulvaney said, "and now there's a phone call waiting for him down—"

"But he's not here," the girl said quickly. "He—he's gone."

"Gone, is he?"

"He won't be back." She smiled with those startling blood-red lips of her. "At least, not for some time."

As Mrs. Mulvaney stood there, absorbing this bit of information, the girl disappeared for a moment, then returned with some money in her hand. "His rent. He—he asked me to give you this." She held out the money.

Mrs. Mulvaney took the two ten-dollar bills, thoroughly amazed. Surely Mr. Greck was a strange one, for fair: at least he could have had the decency to wish her good-bye.

As she placed the money in her pocket, she realized that Mr. Greck's week's rent had been the same as Mrs. Hutchins'—fifteen dollars. And she found herself heading for the staircase with a peculiar pattern of thoughts chasing around in her head. The queer behavior of this new young lady, with her cadaverous look that had a way of changing to almost radiant, flush-faced beauty; the remarkable actions of Mr. Greck: his fears about the missing cat, and his insistence on a bloody towel; and above all, this sudden disappearance. . . . Could that have been himself she'd heard, the while back, when she thought there'd been footsteps and a closing back door?

She would have thought more of it, then, if she had not been still the landlady that she was, and had not noticed the sound of running water in the bathroom as she went past.

With a further sigh over the mysteriousness abruptly visited upon her house, Mrs. Mulvaney turned to the partially opened bathroom door, intent upon shutting off the tap. She had her hand almost on the doorknob when she felt the fingers on her shoulder, stopping her.

"Please—if you don't mind," Miss de Mise said apologetically, getting between her and the door.

Mrs. Mulvaney frowned. "But the water's running." Through the opened door she could see it was the cold-water faucet, splashing into the sink on what seemed to be a towel. The water, sloshing about the upper edges of the basin, looked faintly pink. . . .

"I'll take care of it," said Miss de Mise, and hurried into the small room, turning the key in the lock behind her.

Mrs. Mulvaney waited for some time outside, but presently it grew very dark in the hall because it was getting late in the afternoon and the daylight was fading rapidly.

Finally, she had to go downstairs to turn on the house lights, but she went back upstairs immediately.

The bathroom door was ajar, and she found nothing in the empty room but the still-damp towel, hanging folded on its rack. She thought she could detect very faint discolorations on it. The sink, of course, was clean.

In Miss de Mise's room, where she looked next, there was a chilling emptiness.

The curtains fluttered against the open window, and the wash of cold air made her shiver. She had no idea where the girl could have gone until she saw the note, propped on the table. Just a short note, written in a quick, somehow unreal hand:

> Dear Mrs. Mulvaney—Thank you for everything. You were very kind, but you must forget me. And Mr. Greck, as well. He may never be back. But in case he or his cat do return, it would be best to have your crucifix with you.
>
> J. de Mise.

Wave Scars

Joel Lane

Some people never really leave home; they just carry on where their parents left off. For other people, leaving home is what makes them who they are. Steven was the latter type. When he took me back to his home, it was to show me the things he'd had to leave behind in order for his life to start. It was very different from taking me back to the house where he was living in Birmingham. Obviously, there was the physical distance involved. And there were some factors which I still don't understand.

I'd known Steven for a year or so. He was one of a group of friends I used to see quite often, at the pub or at various people's parties. At twenty-three he was a few years younger than most of us, and had a disconcerting tendency to look younger still. Steven was so thin you wondered where the rest of him was. He always wore plain T-shirts or shapeless pullovers, which served to accentuate his fairly stunning looks. He had nervous blue eyes and a semi-quiff of dense black hair. One or two of our group had slept with him, but most of his relationships were with men of an older generation. Talking to Steven could be hard work. He spoke in a rapid, stumbling kind of way, with a strong Welsh accent. It was impossible to lip-read him, which you always try to do in a crowded pub. He amazed everybody when he got a job as a citizens' advisor.

But then, Steven had a way of surprising people. It surprised me how he and I drew closer together after Craig left me. I knew he was fond of Craig, and expected him to be quite distant with me. But instead, he used his knowledge of the breakup to help me talk through what had happened. It was partly that he wanted to understand. Craig and I had lived together happily for as long as he'd known us, until a newcomer had suddenly taken Craig away from me. The speed of it had shocked our friends. And Steven was nothing if not curious about people and their emotions. But also, he really did care; and some part of his diverse character felt sharply what it had been like for me. Maybe he too felt rejected by Craig; I don't know.

At this time, I'd moved into a studio flat not far from the house which Steven shared with two other men. The first time he came round to see me, I discovered that we liked a lot of the same books and the same music. I taped a k.d. lang album for him, and he introduced me to Dory Previn. That was the first time I'd heard that scary, desolate voice, cracking jokes on the edge of suicide.

Steven also began to tell me about his life. A lot of it sounded pretty dreadful: a small town full of bullies and bigots; a claustrophobic family; a mother so transformed by mental illness that he hardly knew her. He'd come to Birmingham to study, and to live. Recently, his parents had moved inland from Fishguard, breaking his most important link with the place. At one level, he was fiercely independent; at another, he seemed to be in need of a surrogate family—and in particular, a father. But he was already learning that familial instincts didn't sit well alongside other instincts and other needs.

The first time I saw Steven's room, I found it quite disconcerting. The walls were covered with photographs of semi-naked men, taken from calendars and magazines. Many of them were framed, some behind glass. I suspected that their role had changed: originally chosen to be looked at, they had become witnesses. But if Steven's love life was fuelled by adolescent fantasies, it was focused in an adult way. Anyone who tried to manipulate him very soon regretted it. He saw more and understood more than the people he dealt with. Many times, I heard him dissect another man's beliefs and perceptions with a sudden clarity that scared me. But he wasn't cruel, at least not often. He was simply judging people by his own standards. For him, being Steven wasn't a natural given: it was a craft, a vocation.

Don't get me wrong. There was nothing cold or scheming about him. But you knew everything he said and did reflected the way he had chosen to be. Part of him took pride in this. Another part ached with the lack of authority. Steven's personality was a labyrinth; but there was no beast at the centre, only a whorl like a smudged fingerprint where the tunnels had collapsed into each other. You could see that sometimes when he just fell into himself, sat in complete silence with his arms folded over his chest; when you asked him if he was OK, he'd either reply 'I'll be all right in a bit' or simply not answer.

We only slept together once. It took me weeks to find the courage to make a pass at Steven; and I didn't want him to think I was just on the rebound from Craig. Eventually I asked him in a night-club, where he could walk away if he wanted to. I was as nervous as hell, though I could have chatted up complete strangers without fear. He paused before answering. Wavy lines of shadow flickered in the air around him. I must have been drunk to see that. 'I don't know, David,' he said at last. 'I'm sorry, I just don't know what to say . . . Best to leave it for now.' He gripped my arm, very gently. 'Are you all right? I'll stay here if you want.'

I shook my head. 'I'm fine, don't worry.' I could see in his face that the answer was not an unequivocal *no*. And although the way I felt was painful, there was a great sense of relief in having been able to try. All I wanted to do now was go home and sleep. Steven came round the next day to lend me a tape; he borrowed a Ramsey Campbell novel in exchange. We didn't talk about what had been said the night before, but he invited me round for dinner in midweek.

Steven lived on an industrial estate somewhere between Kings Heath and Yardley Wood. That part of the city is at a higher altitude than the rest; so there's no skyline, which makes you feel exposed. The complete absence of trees didn't help. Outside his house, some children were kicking a football against the side of a van; the crashes echoed in the narrow street. I felt as though the concrete garages at the top of the road were on a cliff-edge, poised to fall into nothingness.

We covered a lot of ground that evening, spurred on by a bottle of wine and the kind of still August atmosphere that makes you want to listen and talk. In a group, Steven would often become tense and take refuge in a kind of adolescent vivacity; but on his own, he was thoughtful and alert. I asked him what he felt for Craig, and he admitted that Craig meant a lot to him. No doubt the strength of Craig's personality had a lot to do with that. But it was also the fact that when he'd arrived on the scene, all bright-eyed and bushy-tailed, Craig was the only person who'd taken him seriously. Now it looked as though Craig and Michael, his new lover, would be going away to live together. Which of course was hard for me; but I hadn't realised until that moment how hard it would be for Steven too. In any case, Steven said, he didn't want to get too involved with anyone just now. And it always threw him when someone he was friendly with asked him out: 'I always think of . . . like, a beautiful summer night, and some perfect stranger who just comes up to me out of nowhere.' He laughed; it was a naive way of putting it, but I knew what he meant. It can be very hard to change the way you look at someone. I tried to reassure him that what he'd said in the night-club hadn't offended me at all, and that he could trust me not to push my luck. I always think of seduction as a false concept; you shouldn't take what's not given.

He also told me about his mother's breakdown. It happened when he was twelve. He came home from school and half the family were there. His mother had been taken away in an ambulance; she'd tried to cut her wrists. Steven's aunt was still in the bathroom, scrubbing the blood from the floor. Steven went into his room, closed the curtains and wouldn't come out. 'I hoped she was dead. That's terrible, isn't it? But I couldn't understand how she could do such a thing. And I was closer to her than any of my sisters. She was in hospital for a year and when she came out, she wasn't the same person. The drugs made her either dopey or violent. She's more stable now.'

I asked him if he knew what had caused it. 'I don't know,' he said. 'I think it was having too many children. Four of us, for God's sake. And she had to look after us, when she didn't even *like* children. To be honest, I don't think she liked being married either. But what choice did she have? That's why I had to get away.'

By now, it was nearing eleven. I said I'd catch the last bus in half an hour. Steven made some coffee, and we sat down together on the couch. I'm still not sure whether it was kindness or need that made him reach out for me. When we kissed, his head was almost perfectly still; I had to shape his mouth with my own. When I paused, not sure if he wanted to go on, Steven embraced me tightly and touched me in ways I couldn't mistake. He led me up to the bedroom in silence, and we made love more slowly and tenderly than I could have dreamed. There were points when he smiled for no immediate reason, and other points when he seemed about to cry. Every touch and movement and sound of that night seemed to echo in the back of my head. I remember one moment just before Steven came; he was lying on his back, and seemed to become entirely still, as if he were reduced to a single image. I glanced up at the wall and saw a pattern of blurred ridges in the air, like a crumpled piece of gauze. Then Steven cried out, and the illusion of stillness was gone. He slept very deeply in the night, only once turning over and twitching as though trying to shake something off. I never sleep well in a strange bed.

The next morning he told me, gently but decisively, that it wouldn't happen again. That didn't kill the friendship; if anything, we became closer. But at the time, I couldn't help wondering if I had disappointed him. Later I realised that his reasons went deeper than that. Perhaps I wasn't old enough; more probably, I wasn't a strong enough person for him. I rather suspect that, without ever letting me know, he decided I wasn't worth it. Even so, I didn't feel hurt. I could have told Steven that I loved him; but that would have made him feel threatened, and perhaps even insulted. He didn't want to be told that, unless by someone who had been with him for a long time and who intended to make the relationship permanent. Love wasn't a word that Steven used lightly.

At the end of August that year, a burning summer turned into a strange, chilly autumn. Rain darkened the air for days on end. A number of my friends lost their jobs due to the recession. Nobody seemed to know quite how or why the Government had been re-elected, but their economic promises were already as stale as yesterday's car exhaust. It seemed ironic that the people being made redundant now were the accountants, the salesmen, the designers. I remembered how 1989 had ended in a wave of global optimism, and wondered where it had all gone. There was a current of unease that affected everything. I saw couples splitting up, old friends losing touch, people hiding behind grudges. I began to cry a lot without really knowing why.

Steven went to earth, as he was inclined to do at difficult times. I saw him occasionally in the pub, and we met for lunch once or twice in town. He was more withdrawn than usual. Another love affair had ended badly for him, and he was beginning to doubt that two men could ever be happy together. I didn't realise what else was bothering him until later. In mid-October, he asked me if I'd like to go to Wales with him. He wanted to go back to Fishguard for the day. 'I don't want to travel alone,' he said. 'It's just that going home is such a ride.'

526

It was certainly a long and tiring journey by train—from Birmingham to Aberystwyth, then out along the coast via a succession of branch lines and small, iron-sheltered platforms. As the landscape took on depth and age, Steven seemed to come alive. He sat by the window, reaching out with his eyes. There were long stretches of hillside or quarry without any roads or buildings. When we reached the coastline, the sky had cleared; so that our first glimpse of the sea was of innumerable points of light, like a duvet covered in ground glass.

As its name suggests, Fishguard is a small town clustered around a harbour. We arrived late in the afternoon; the tide was out. Chained down in the muddy sand, the boats were ill-defined shapes under canvas hoods. Steven and I walked along the seafront until we found a bed-and-breakfast place. Steven hesitated before going in. 'Better ask for two rooms,' he said. I nodded. Even if we'd been lovers, it wouldn't have done to arouse suspicions in a place like that. As it turned out, the landlady offered us a room with two single beds. Steven spoke to her in Welsh, while I tried not to look as foreign as I felt. I still wasn't sure why he'd come here, since he'd said nothing about meeting any friends or relatives.

After a quick meal in a café where the only vegetarian item was some overcooked lasagne, Steven led me up onto the cliff path towards Dinas. A thin arm of land ended in broken fingernails. On the far side, a crescent of lights marked the coastline. Under the gathering clouds the sea was like a sheet of iron, hammered flat by the wind; the waves appeared not to be moving. On whitish areas of sand, I could just make out the pattern of thin scars left by the tide.

Steven was quiet; he'd been quiet all day. I didn't want to intrude on his memories. Every so often, as we walked back into the town, he'd point to some building or seafront construction and say 'That's new' or 'That's always been here.' We stopped at a pub, where a man with a guitar was encouraging the drinkers to sing 'Yesterday' and 'Let It Be.' Steven smiled at me over his glass. 'Weird isn't it,' he said. 'Places change and people change, but music . . . I don't know, are they being faithful or have they just got no imagination?' He sat in silence for a while, looking around the pub. Then he stood up, muttered 'Come on' to me and walked out. I followed him; he was standing in the street, looking frightened and angry. 'I don't belong here any more,' he said quietly. Instead of going straight back to the guest-house, he led me up a narrow side-street to a viewpoint overlooking the sea. The harbour boats were tugging at invisible chains; further out, the sea looked and sounded like a gradually shifting mass of gravel. Steven frowned and looked out towards Dinas, where the promontory was faintly sleeved in mist.

'What are you looking for?' I asked.

He shook his head and stepped back. 'It's not here yet.' Although it was a Saturday night, the town was all but dead. Occasional car headlights photographed the mist coming in from the seafront. Steven wrapped his arms across his quilted jacket, pulling at the sleeves. I didn't feel the cold as much; but even so, I felt as though I were standing on a block of stone with the sea all around.

Back in our room at the guest-house, we sat up for a while talking. Steven described things from his childhood: learning to swim by diving off the harbour wall; the crowded house he grew up in; how the adults of his family discouraged him from making friends, so that he'd always be there for them. Several of his relatives were still here, he said, but he hadn't kept in touch with them. 'I see most of them at Christmas anyway. And I see my parents every few months, that's enough I suppose.' He went to the window and looked out. I asked him what he'd tried to see earlier. 'Nothing really,' he said. 'Tell you tomorrow.' Whatever it was, he seemed relieved that it wasn't there. We went to bed before midnight, too tired to go on talking. Darkness surged over me: a tide finding ridges and hollows in the sand.

It was still dark when I woke up. Steven was gripping my shoulder. 'David. David.' He was dressed; I wondered if that was because the room was so cold. 'It's out there,' he said. I got dressed without asking any questions. It was just after three o'clock. We felt our way down the stairs and out the front door in the dark. Mist was a series of blurred fingerprints behind the streetlamps. The sea was invisible, a whisper of movement. Steven walked one pace ahead of me. He was shivering. There was nobody else on the streets, so it felt like being outside the town. He led me up a stone staircase to the point where the roads disappeared, and there was only a narrow footpath along the cliff edge. It was difficult to keep walking, knowing that the impression of emptiness on one side was a sheer and unguarded drop. Steven took my hand. He seemed to know every step of the way.

After a while, he stopped and pointed down towards the sea. 'Look,' he said quietly. The mist was rising to expose patches of grey shimmering water. Sharp fragments of rock broke the surface, distorting it into a network of tiny ripples. The wind's teeth combed through the dark waves, bringing up highlights of spray. Then I could see what Steven was pointing at: a boat coming rapidly inland, between us and the promontory. It was like an elongated yacht, or a barge with a sail; the jib swung erratically as the boat tried to slow down. There were several people on board, and for an insane moment I could make out their terrified shiny faces.

A few yards ahead of us, a very steep flight of stone steps led down to the beach. Steven ran down ahead of me, gripping the rail for support. The boat was lurching closer, coming in to land. They had some kind of lamp on board, but they didn't appear to be navigating with its help. At the head of the beach, Steven lost his footing and fell over a rock. I helped him up; he was shaking, and seemed about to pass out. In spite of the cold, his face was drenched in sweat. We were still standing there when the boat hit something, rode up out of the water and then capsized. At first, I thought nobody had survived.

By the time Steven and I reached the water, a few dark figures were struggling towards us over the rocks. They appeared to be badly hurt. The nearest of them was covering his face with one arm. I pulled him up onto the sand before realising that his head was in some way joined to his forearm, so that there was no face to cover. Both his arms ended in smoothly healed stumps.

I turned back to the water, where Steven had caught hold of somebody and was trying to lift him. More of the survivors were emerging from the wreck. Some were holding on to each other. One of them collapsed as a wave struck him from behind; I caught his arms and helped him to stand up. A rock had gashed his shoulder, but there was no blood. His eyes and mouth appeared to be incapable of opening, so that his sealed face gave an impression of peace. He stepped past me onto the sand, and fell again. From behind him, a woman reached up with a child in her arms. I caught hold of the child; but her arms were joined to its body, her fingers spread across the child's shoulders like embryonic wings. A few yards away, Steven was carrying someone whose back was crusted with broken ribs. He looked at me, and I could see in his face the same question I was asking myself. *How could there be so many of them?*

But there was no question of what to do about the survivors when they were on the beach. They simply came apart. Their faces, if any, misted over with a pain so great it left them no identity. They became glass, snow, driftwood. They wrapped their damaged limbs around themselves, and bled their own substance into the sand. In less than an hour, the beach was empty. The only marks on the sand were the long curved ridges left by the outgoing tide. I looked out towards the rocks; but there was no sign of the boat. Then I turned and followed Steven up the stone steps to the clifftop. It was getting light; I could just see the outlines of trees and distant buildings inland.

We walked back along the cliff path in silence. When we reached the edge of the town, Steven paused. 'It's always like this,' he said. 'Every year. I need to come back. But it's always just the same.' His hair was matted with sweat, and he looked even thinner than before. I wanted to say *It's not your fault,* but I couldn't find the words. Back at the guest-house, Steven lay down and went to sleep, still fully dressed. We had to be out of the room by ten o'clock, but I let him sleep for a couple of hours while I sat and tried to understand. Perhaps it was remarkable, I thought, that a grown man should be so imprisoned by his childhood. But it was just as remarkable that someone carrying such a weight of guilt and terror could still have so much to give. I knew he'd come with me, if I had a similar trip to make.

And it happens all the time. Boats go down, cars crash, houses burn; and damaged people spill out into the road. The only way to go on is to realise that it *is* always the same. You have to hold on to the few who mean enough to you to bring out the healer. And sometimes the healer is very difficult to find.

We left the guest-house a few minutes after ten. Outside, it was still cold but the sun was shining. The tide had come in, and some children in cutoff jeans were diving off the breakwater. Steven looked at me. 'A Sunday morning and they're not in church! Maybe there's hope for them yet.' We walked slowly up through the still town to the train station. The platform was like a metal and glass shell; I imagined I could hear the sea echoing in it.

A Wedding Chest

Vernon Lee

No. 428. A panel (five feet by two feet three inches) formerly the front of a *cassone* or coffer, intended to contain the garments and jewels of a bride. *Subject:* "The Triumph of Love. Umbrian School of the Fifteenth Century." In the right-hand corner is a half-effaced inscription: *Desider . . . de Civitate Lac . . . me . . . ecit.* This valuable painting is unfortunately much damaged by damp and mineral corrosives, owing probably to its having contained at one time buried treasure. Bequeathed in 1878 by the widow of the Rev. Lawson Stone, late Fellow of Trinity College, Cambridge.[1]

By Ascension Day, Desiderio of Castiglione del Lago had finished the front panel of the wedding chest which Messer Troilo Baglioni had ordered of Ser Piero Bontempi, whose shop was situated at the bottom of the steps of St. Maxentius, in that portion of the ancient city of Perugia (called by the Romans Augusta in recognition of its great glory) which takes its name from the Ivory Gate built by Theodoric, King of the Goths. The said Desiderio had represented upon his panel the Triumph of Love as described in his poem by Messer Francesco Petrarca of Arezzo, certainly with the exception of that Dante, who saw the Vision of Hell, Purgatory, and Paradise, the only poet of recent times who can be compared to those doctissimi viri P. Virgilius, Ovidius of Sulmona, and Statius. And the said Desiderio had betaken himself in this manner. He had divided the panel into four portions or regions, intended to represent the four phases of the amorous passion: the first was a pleasant country, abundantly watered with twisting streams, of great plenty and joyousness, in which were planted many hedges of fragrant roses, both red and blue, together with elms, poplars, and other pleasant and profitable trees. The second region was some-

[1] Catalogue of the Smith Museum, Leeds.

what mountainous, but showing large store of lordly castles and thickets of pine and oak, fit for hunting, which region, as being that of glorious love, was girt all round with groves of laurels. The third region—*aspera ac dura regio*—was barren of all vegetation save huge thorns and ungrateful thistles; and in it, on rocks, was shown the pelican, who tears his own entrails to feed his young, symbolical of the cruelty of love to true lovers. Finally, the fourth region was a melancholy cypress wood, among which roosted owls and ravens and other birds, of evil omen, in order to display the fact that all earthly love leads but to death. Each of these regions was surrounded by a wreath of myrtles, marvellously drawn, and with great subtlety of invention divided so as to meet the carved and gilded cornice, likewise composed of myrtles, which Ser Piero executed with singular skill with his own hand. In the middle of the panel Desiderio had represented Love, even as the poet has described; a naked youth, with wings of wondrous changing colours, enthroned upon a chariot, the axle and wheels of which were red gold, and covered with a cloth of gold of such subtle device that the whole chariot seemed really to be on fire; on his back hung a bow and a quiver full of dreadful arrows, and in his hands he held the reins of four snow-white coursers, trapped with gold, and breathing fire from their nostrils. Round his eyes was bound a kerchief fringed with gold, to show that Love strikes blindly; and from his shoulders floated a scroll inscribed with the words—"Sævus Amor hominum deorumque deliciæ." Round his car, some before, some behind, some on horseback, some on foot, crowded those who have been famous for their love. Here you might see, on a bay horse, with an eagle on his helmet, Julius Cæsar, who loved Cleopatra, the Queen of Egypt; Sophonisba and Massinissa, in rich and strange Arabian garments; Orpheus, seeking for Eurydice, with his lute; Phædra, who died for love of Hippolytus, her stepson; Mark Antony; Rinaldo of Montalbano, who loved the beautiful Angelica; Socrates, Tibullus, Virgilius and other poets, with Messer Francesco Petrarca and Messer Giovanni Boccaccio; Tristram, who drank the love-potion, riding on a sorrel horse; and near him, Isotta, wearing a turban of cloth of gold, and these lovers of Rimini, and many more besides, the naming of whom would be too long, even as the poet has described. And in the region of happy love, among the laurels, he had painted his own likeness, red-haired, with a green hood falling on his shoulders, and this because he was to wed, next St. John's Eve, Maddalena, the only daughter of his employer, Ser Piero. And among the unhappy lovers, he painted, at his request, Messer Troilo himself, for whom he was making this coffer. And Messer Troilo was depicted in the character of Troilus, the son of Priam, Emperor of Troy; he was habited in armour, covered with a surcoat of white cloth of silver embroidered with roses; by his side was his lance, and on his head a scarlet cap; behind him were those who carried his falcon and led his hack, and men-at-arms with his banner, dressed in green and yellow parti-coloured, with a scorpion embroidered on their doublet; and from his lance floated a pennon inscribed: "Troilus sum servus Amoris."

But Desiderio refused to paint among the procession Monna Maddalena, Piero's daughter, who was to be his wife; because he declared it was not fit that modest damsels should lend their face to other folk; and this he said because Ser Piero had begged him not to incense Messer Troilo; for in reality he had often portrayed Monna Maddalena (the which was marvellously lovely), though only, it is true, in the figure of Our Lady, the Mother of God.

And the panel was ready by Ascension Day, and Ser Piero had prepared the box, and the carvings and gildings, griffins and chimeras, and acanthus leaves and myrtles, with the arms of Messer Troilo Baglioni, a most beautiful work. And Mastro Cavanna of the gate of St. Peter had made a lock and a key, of marvellous workmanship, for the same coffer. And Messer Troilo would come frequently, riding over from his castle of Fratta, and see the work while it was progressing, and entertain himself lengthily at the shop, speaking with benignity and wisdom wonderful in one so young, for he was only nineteen, which pleased the heart of Ser Piero; but Desiderio did not relish, for which reason he was often gruff to Messer Troilo, and had many disputes with his future father-in-law.

For Messer Troilo Baglioni, called Barbacane, to distinguish him from another Troilo, his uncle, who was bishop of Spello, although a bastard, had cast his eyes on Maddalena di Ser Piero Bontempi. He had seen the damsel for the first time on the occasion of the wedding festivities of his cousin Grifone Baglioni, son of Ridolfo the elder, with Deianira degli Orsini; on which occasion marvellous things were done in the city of Perugia, both by the magnificent House of Baglioni and the citizens, such as banquets, jousts, horse races, balls in the square near the cathedral, bull fights, allegories, both Latin and vulgar, presented with great learning and sweetness (among which was the fable of Perseus, how he freed Andromeda, written by Master Giannozzo, Belli Rector venerabilis istæ universitatis), and triumphal arches and other similar devices, in which Ser Piero Bontempi made many beautiful inventions, in company with Benedetto Bonfigli, Messer Fiorenzo di Lorenzo and Piero de Castro Plebis, whom the Holiness of our Lord Pope Sixtus IV afterwards summoned to work in his chapel in Rome. On this occasion, I repeat, Messer Troilo Baglioni of Fratta, who was *unanimiter* declared to be a most beautiful and courteous youth, of singular learning and prowess, and well worthy of this magnificent Baglioni family, cast his eyes on Maddalena di Ser Piero, and sent her, through his squire, the knot of ribbons off the head of a ferocious bull, whom he had killed *singulari vi ac virtute.* Nor did Messer Troilo neglect other opportunities of seeing the damsel, such as at church and at her father's shop, riding over from his castle at Fratta on purpose, but always *honestis valde modibus,* as the damsel showed herself very coy, and refused all presents which he sent her.

Neither did Ser Piero prevent his honestly conversing with the damsel, fearing the anger of the magnificent family of Baglioni. But Desiderio di Città del Lago, the which was affianced to Monna Maddalena, often had words with Ser Piero on the subject, and one day well-nigh broke the ribs of Messer Troilo's squire, whom he charged with carrying dishonest messages.

Now it so happened that Messer Troilo, as he was the most beautiful, benign, and magnanimous of his magnificent family, was also the most cruel thereof, and incapable of brooking delay or obstacles. And being, as a most beautiful youth—he was only turned nineteen, and the first down had not come to his cheeks, and his skin was astonishingly white and fair like a woman's—of a very amorous nature (of which many tales went, concerning the violence he had done to damsels and citizens' wives of Gubbio and Spello, and evil deeds in the castle of Fratta in the Apennines, some of which it is more beautiful to pass in silence than to relate), being, as I say, of an amorous nature, and greatly magnanimous and ferocious of spirit, Messer Troilo was determined to possess himself of this Maddalena di Ser Piero. So, a week after, having fetched away the wedding chest from Ser Piero's workshop (paying for it duly in Florentine lilies), he seized the opportunity of the festivities of St. John's Nativity, when it is the habit of the citizens to go to their gardens and vineyards to see how the country is prospering, and eat and drink in honest converse with their friends, in order to satisfy his cruel wishes. For it so happened that the said Ser Piero, who was rich and prosperous, possessing an orchard in the valley of the Tiber near San Giovanni, was entertaining his friends there, it being the eve of his daughter's wedding, peaceful and unarmed. And a serving wench, a Moor and a slave, who had been bribed by Messer Troilo, proposed to Monna Maddalena and the damsels of her company, to refresh themselves, after picking flowers, playing with hoops, asking riddles and similar girlish games, by bathing in the Tiber, which flowed at the bottom of the orchard. To this the innocent virgin, full of joyousness, consented. Hardly had the damsels descended into the river bed, the river being low and easy to ford on account of the summer, when behold, there swept from the opposite bank a troop of horsemen, armed and masked, who seized the astonished Maddalena, and hurried off with her, vainly screaming, like another Proserpina, to her companions, who, surprised, and ashamed at being seen with no garments, screamed in return, but in vain. The horsemen galloped off through Bastia, and disappeared long before Ser Piero and his friends could come to the rescue. Thus was Monna Maddalena cruelly taken from her father and bridegroom, through the amorous passion of Messer Troilo.

Ser Piero fell upon the ground fainting for grief, and remained for several days like one dead; and when he came to he wept, and cursed wickedly, and refused to take food and sleep, and to shave his beard. But being old and prudent, and the father of other children, he conquered his grief, well knowing that it was useless to oppose providence or fight, being but a handicraftsman,

533

with the magnificent family of Baglioni, lords of Perugia since many years, and as rich and powerful as they were magnanimous and implacable. So that when people began to say that, after all, Monna Maddalena might have fled willingly with a lover, and that there was no proof that the masked horseman came from Messer Troilo (although those of Basita affirmed that they had seen the green and yellow colours of Fratta, and the said Troilo came not near the town for many months after), he never contradicted such words out of prudence and fear. But Desiderio of Castiglione del Lago, hearing these words, struck the old man on the mouth till he bled.

And it came to pass, about a year after the disappearance of Monna Maddalena, and when (particularly as there had been a plague in the city, and many miracles had been performed by a holy nun of the convent of Sant' Anna, the which fasted seventy days, and Messer Ascanio Baglioni had raised a company of horse for the Florentine Signiory in their war against those of Siena) people had ceased to talk of the matter, that certain armed men, masked, but wearing the colours of Messer Troilo, and the scorpion on their doublets, rode over from Fratta, bringing with them a coffer, wrapped in black baize, which they deposited overnight on Ser Piero Bontempi's doorstep. And Ser Piero, going at daybreak to his workshop, found that coffer; and recognising it as the same which had been made, with a panel representing the Triumph of Love and many ingenious devices of sculpture and gilding, for Messer Troilo, called Barbacane, he trembled in all his limbs, and went and called Desiderio, and with him privily carried the chest into a secret chamber in his house, saying not a word to any creature. The key, a subtle piece of work of the smith Cavanna, was hanging to the lock by a green silk string, on to which was tied a piece of parchment containing these words: "To Master Desiderio: a wedding gift from Troilo Baglioni of Fratta"—an allusion, doubtless, *ferox atque cruenta facetia,* to the Triumph of Love, according to Messer Francesco Petrarca, painted upon the front of the coffer. The lid being raised, they came to a piece of red cloth, such as is used for mules; *etiam,* a fold of common linen; and below it, a coverlet of green silk, which, being raised, their eyes were met *(heu! infandum patri sceleratumque donus)* by the body of Monna Maddalena, naked as God had made it, dead with two stabs in the neck, the long golden hair tied with pearls but dabbed in blood; the which Maddalena was cruelly squeezed into that coffer, having on her breast the body of an infant recently born, dead like herself.

When he beheld this sight Ser Piero threw himself on the floor and wept, and uttered dreadful blasphemies. But Desiderio of Castiglione del Lago said nothing, but called a brother of Ser Piero, a priest and prior of Saint Severus, and with his assistance carried the coffer into the garden. This garden, within the walls of the city on the side of Porta Eburnea, was pleasantly situated, and abounding in flowers and trees, useful both for their fruit and their shade, and

534

rich likewise in all such herbs as thyme, marjoram, fennel, and many others, that prudent housewives desire for their kitchen; all watered by stone canals, ingeniously constructed by Ser Piero, which were fed from a fountain where you might see a mermaid squeezing the water from her breasts, a subtle device of the same Piero, and executed in a way such as would have done honour to Phidias or Praxiteles, on hard stone from Monte Catria. In this place Desiderio of Castiglione del Lago dug a deep grave under an almond tree, the which grave he carefully lined with stones and slabs of marble which he tore up from the pavement, in order to diminish the damp, and then requested the priest, Ser Piero's brother, who had helped him in the work, to fetch his sacred vestments, and books, and all necessary for consecrating that ground. This the priest immediately did, being a holy man and sore grieved for the case of his niece. Meanwhile, with the help of Ser Piero, Desiderio tenderly lifted the body of Monna Maddalena out of the wedding chest, washed it in odorous waters, and dressed it in fine linen and bridal garments, not without much weeping over the poor damsel's sad plight, and curses upon the cruelty of her ravisher; and having embraced her tenderly, they laid her once more in the box painted with the Triumph of Love, upon folds of fine damask and brocade, her hands folded, and her head decently placed upon a pillow of silver cloth, a wreath of roses, which Desiderio himself plaited, on her hair, so that she looked like a holy saint or the damsel Julia, daughter of the Emperor Augustus Cæsar, who was discovered buried on the Appian Way, and incontinently fell into dust—a marvellous thing. They filled the chest with as many flowers as they could find, also sweet-scented herbs, bay leaves, orris powder, frankincense, ambergris, and a certain gum called in Syrian fizelis, and by the Jews barach, in which they say that the body of King David was kept intact from earthly corruption, and which the priest, the brother of Ser Piero, who was learned in all alchemy and astrology, had bought of certain Moors. Then, with many alases! and tears, they covered the damsel's face with an embroidered veil and a fold of brocade, and closing the chest, buried it in the hole, among great store of hay and straw and sand; and closed it up, and smoothed the earth; and to mark the place Desiderio planted a tuft of fennel under the almond tree. But not before having embraced the damsel many times, and taken a handful of earth from her grave, and eaten it, with many imprecations upon Messer Troilo, which it were terrible to relate. Then the priest, the brother of Ser Piero, said the service for the dead, Desiderio serving him as acolyte; and they all went their way, grieving sorely. But the body of the child, the which had been found in the wedding chest, they threw down a place near Saint Herculanus, where the refuse and offal and dead animals are thrown, called the *Sardegna;* because it was the bastard of Ser Troilo, *et infamiæ scelerisque partum.*

Then, as this matter got abroad, and also Desiderio's imprecations against Ser Troilo, Ser Piero, who was an old man and prudent, caused him to depart privily from Perugia, for fear of the wrath of the magnificent Orazio Baglioni, uncle of Messer Troilo and lord of the town.

Desiderio of Castiglione del Lago went to Rome, where he did wonderful things and beautiful, among others certain frescoes in Saints Cosmas and Damian, for the Cardinal of Ostia; and to Naples, where he entered the service of the Duke of Calabria, and followed his armies long, building fortresses and making machines and models for cannon, and other ingenious and useful things. And thus for seven years, until he heard that Ser Piero was dead at Perugia of a surfeit of eels; and that Messer Troilo was in the city, raising a company of horse with his cousin Astorre Baglioni for the Duke of Urbino; and this was before the plague, and the terrible coming to Umbria of the Spaniards and renegade Moors, under Cæsar Borgia, *Vicarius Sanctæ Ecclesiæ, seu Flagellum Dei et novus Attila.* So Desiderio came back privily to Perugia, and put up his mule at a small inn, having dyed his hair black and grown his beard, after the manner of Easterns, saying he was a Greek coming from Ancona. And he went to the priest, prior of Saint Severus, and brother of Ser Piero, and discovered himself to him, who, although old, had great joy in seeing him and hearing of his intent. And Desiderio confessed all his sins to the priest and obtained absolution, and received the Body of Christ with great fervour and compunction; and the priest placed his sword on the altar, beside the gospel, as he said mass, and blessed it. And Desiderio knelt and made a vow never to touch food save the Body of Christ till he could taste the blood of Messer Troilo.

And for three days and three nights he watched him and dogged him, but Messer Troilo rarely went unaccompanied by his men, because he had offended so many honourable citizens by his amorous fury, and he knew that his kinsmen dreaded him and would gladly be rid of him, on account of his ferocity and ambition, and their desire to unite the Fief of Fratta to the other lands of the main line of the magnificent House of Baglioni, famous in arms.

But one day, towards dusk, Desiderio saw Messer Troilo coming down a steep lane near Saint Herculanus, alone, for he was going to a woman of light fame, called Flavia Bella, the which was very lovely. So Desiderio threw some ladders, from a neighbouring house which was being built, and sacks across the road, and hid under an arch that spanned the lane, which was greatly steep and narrow. And Messer Troilo came down, on foot, whistling and paring his nails with a small pair of scissors. And he was dressed in grey silk hose, and a doublet of red cloth and gold brocade, pleated about the skirts, and embroidered with seed pearl and laced with gold laces; and on his head he had a hat of scarlet cloth with many feathers; and his cloak and sword he carried under his left arm. And Messer Troilo was twenty-six years old, but seemed much younger, having no beard, and a face like Hyacinthus or Ganymede, whom Jove stole to be his cup-bearer on account of his beauty. And he was tall and very ferocious and magnanimous of spirit. And as he went, going to Flavia the courtesan, he whistled.

And when he came near the heaped-up ladders and the sacks, Desiderio sprang upon him and tried to run his sword through him. But although wounded, Messer Troilo grappled with him long, but he could not get at his sword, which was entangled in his cloak; and before he could free his hand and get at his dagger, Desiderio had him down, and ran his sword three times through his chest, exclaiming, "This is from Maddalena, in return for her wedding chest!"

And Messer Troilo, seeing the blood flowing out of his chest, knew he must die, and merely said—

"Which Maddalena? Ah, I remember, old Piero's daughter. She was always a cursed difficult slut," and died.

And Desiderio stooped over his chest, and lapped up the blood as it flowed; and it was the first food he tasted since taking the Body of Christ, even as he had sworn.

Then Desiderio went stealthily to the fountain under the arch of Saint Proxedia, where the women wash linen in the daytime, and cleansed himself a little from that blood. Then he fetched his mule and hid it in some trees near Messer Piero's garden. And at night he opened the door, the priest having given him the key, and went in, and with a spade and mattock he had brought dug up the wedding chest with the body of Monna Maddalena in it; the which, owing to those herbs and virtuous gums, had dried up and become much lighter. And he found the spot by looking for the fennel tuft under the almond tree, which was then in flower, it being spring. He loaded the chest, which was mouldy and decayed, on the mule, and drove the mule before him till he got to Castiglione del Lago, where he hid. And meeting certain horsemen, who asked him what he carried in that box (for they took him for a thief), he answered his sweetheart; so they laughed and let him pass. Thus he got safely on to the territory of Arezzo, an ancient city of Tuscany, where he stopped.

Now when they found the body of Messer Troilo, there was much astonishment and wonder. And his kinsmen were greatly wroth; but Messer Orazio and Messer Ridolfo, his uncles, said: " 'Tis as well; for indeed his courage and ferocity were too great, and he would have done some evil to us all had he lived." But they ordered him a magnificent burial. And when he lay on the street dead, many folk, particularly painters, came to look at him for his great beauty; and the women pitied him on account of his youth, and certain scholars compared him to Mars, God of War, so great was his strength and ferocity even in death. And he was carried to the grave by eight men-at-arms, and twelve damsels and youths dressed in white walked behind, strewing flowers, and there was much splendour and lamentation, on account of the great power of the magnificent House of Baglioni.

As regards Desiderio of Castiglione del Lago, he remained at Arezzo till his death, preserving with him always the body of Monna Maddalena in the wedding chest painted with the Triumph of Love, because he considered she had died *odore magnæ sanctitatis.*

What Can a Child Do?

Chet Williamson

She saw the boy the first day she moved in. It was close to eight o'clock, and she had just stepped from the shower, when she saw him standing naked by the bathroom closet. For a split second the thought that the boy was real was strong in her exhausted mind, but almost immediately she realized that he was a ghost.

His pale pink body was translucent, and she could just make out the brass hinges of the closet door through the child's shallow chest. She noticed dark blotches on the arms and legs, grayish-blue marks, like bruises. And she knew it was the Bradley boy.

What was his name? The real estate agent had said. Tom? No, Timothy. Yes, that was it. "Timothy," she called softly, her own nakedness forgotten, "Timmy?"

The boy slowly disappeared, like a Polaroid print in reverse, she thought. He hadn't moved. He had just stood there, as if waiting for someone (his mother? *Not* his father, surely) to lift him into the tub.

Linda hadn't been frightened while it was happening, but now she trembled uncontrollably, whipped the towel from the rack she had put up that afternoon, and wrapped it around her shivering body. She sat on the toilet bowl and ran her hand through the salt-wet tendrils of hair that stuck to her forehead. The bathroom was warm from the electric heater, but she felt chilled.

It seemed so real that not for a moment did she think it was her imagination. She had seen him, she was certain. Timothy Bradley. She had read the stories in the papers last year when it had happened. The boy was four years old. His father had been abusing him, and evidently the mother did nothing to stop it. The child was finally taken to a hospital with a concussion. He went into a coma and died a few days later. The father was sentenced to eight years in prison, the mother to three years for complicity. A small enough payment, Linda had thought at the time, for stealing seventy years of a person's life.

He'd been so thin, so brittle looking. The bruises had stood out so clearly. His father must have been brutal.

She stepped back into the shower for a minute to wash the sweat away. The water swept into her face and hair, cold at first, then growing hotter. She closed her eyes and let the steam wrap around her like a shroud. She thought about the boy.

Paul above her, towering like the giant in Jack and the Beanstalk, his big red-knuckled hand coming down again, and the red before her eyes—not blood but rage, stop, stop won't you stop, and crying harder until the wet tears ran

The pipes started banging, and she wiggled the faucet handles until they stopped. She slid back the shower door, half expecting to see him again, but there was nothing more than the light of the fluorescents and the mist that hung in the air and settled like dew on the mirror and tiles. The rough towel felt good on her skin. When she was dry, she put on her bathrobe and went into the kitchen.

All the papers were there. She'd have to take them to the bank and rent a lockbox tomorrow. As she picked up the mortgage she smiled. Even at the high interest rate the house had been a great buy. It must have been small for the Bradleys, she thought, but for a single woman who wanted a little equity, it was perfect. After the boy's death and the arrest of the mother and father, the house had been vacant for over a year while the price went lower and lower. It was due, the real estate woman had told her, simply to the fact that most people were leery of a house in which (technically at least) a murder had taken place. Linda had scarcely thought about that. She liked the house, it was the right size for her, and the price was low enough for her to handle on her new salary. The fact that it had once had sorrow and pain within its brick walls was irrelevant to Linda, who had had those things within her heart. She didn't fear the ghosts of past acts, didn't believe in them until tonight, when she accepted the existence of ghosts—or *a* ghost—as easily as she accepted and believed in the neighbors' laundry hanging on the line next door. She had seen the boy. That was a fact.

And now as she looked up from the papers on the kitchen table she saw him again. He was standing by the refrigerator, his face and hands smeared with something purple, or maybe red—it was hard to be sure because of the light coming through his body. She read fear in the wide eyes, and as she watched tears started to roll down his cheeks and his tiny mouth opened in a wail she could barely hear, as if he were calling from outside, and the doors and windows of the house were shut tight against him.

Again she felt no terror, no sudden thrill of fright, but a pity so deep it gripped her bowels, and something like love that urged her to reach out to that frail insubstantial thing across the kitchen.

As if in a dream she rose and walked toward the boy, and as she drew nearer his fear seemed to increase, and he raised his shadowy arms in a defensive gesture and drew back from her.

"No," she whispered, "no, it's all right." And at her words his face changed into a mask of outrage and hate whose force stunned her. She stopped and watched as he faded away once more, and the warm hand of pity became a cold claw of fear around her spine.

But *what* frightened her, she asked herself. Was she scared of the little boy, a weak four year old? No, even less, a *shadow* of a four year old with no substance, no solidity with which to harm her. A *wraith* (her mind tingled at the word) bound here by past hurts, a sad little thing caught between death and life—was she scared of *this?*

Or was she scared of the look in the child's face, the look that her own face still remembered how to wear, the futile gesture of defense she too had made a hundred times?

The belt snaking through the trouser loops, like a python uncurling from around a tree branch in the Tarzan movies, and the sound of it, that soft shhhhh as it whispered around his waist, always so slow, so slow, and she could feel the pressure of her bladder, feel the wispy hairs on the back of her neck nearly pull away from the skin as he came closer, finally flinging her over his bony knees, his rough hands pushing her skirt above her waist, pulling down her cotton panties so she felt the autumn chill on her buttocks, and then the pain that murdered the cold, the redness that seeped up her belly, over her chest, and onto her cheeks, her forehead, her ears and her eyes until everything was red and she could only think kill me, kill me, I'll kill you, I will, just kill me and be done, and it would stop and Paul would push her onto the floor and leave her there, saying that'll teach you, little bitch, and she would lie there alone in the red darkness and the stale smell of beer, and the sound of her mother crying downstairs only made the red hurt more

The refrigerator motor kicked on, and she lost the memory in a mechanical whir of hidden fans. Dear God, she thought, is this what it's going to be like to live here, that boy showing up every few minutes? What would she do, what *could* she? The thought occurred to her to call someone, but she was new in the town and had made no friends in whom she could confide a crazy ghost story. She thought of calling her mother, but the difference in time zones made it certain that she'd be asleep by now. Besides, since Linda's stepfather had left her mother a few years before, she'd been withdrawn and strange in Linda's presence.

She gave up the phone idea and suddenly realized that she felt hungry. She'd had no dinner, and a sandwich would taste good, maybe some Tab too. The breadbox door squeaked as she opened it, and she made a mental note to get some 3-in-1 tomorrow when she bought paint. She pulled open the refrigerator and saw Timothy Bradley inside, staring up at her.

She shrieked and leaped back. The door swung slowly shut with a muffled thud and she screamed again. The sight was etched with steel on her mind's crystal surface. He'd been huddled, shivering, on the flat enamel of the bottom, his body occupying the same space as the groceries Linda had bought earlier that day. The boy's form passed through the wire rack next to the bottom, but seemed pressed against the second one up, as if he'd been jammed in there for . . . for what? Punishment? *Yes.* She'd seen the marks again, this time on his face, and some blood on his lips, which were turning blue with the cold.

Christ, she thought, *monsters, monsters!* and her heart beat fast and her stomach churned until she was afraid she would throw up. She sat down heavily in the kitchen chair and moaned softly. Then it struck her. *He's in there. He or his ghost or whatever I'm seeing is still in there,* and she leaped up and swung the door open again. This time she didn't step back or scream, but held the door open for the whimpering child to crawl out. He was still there, and the sounds of his sobbing seemed far away as before. As if underwater, he fumbled his way out of the refrigerator, his hands touching and then going through the floor, until his whole body disappeared beneath the house. She had noticed his eyes again before they passed from sight. There was something primal in them, a fear and an urge she could not quite read, and then he was gone.

She would not stay. She would not be a noble idiot and stay in that house. She would go to a motel and think about this and maybe call the real estate agent in the morning. There were still three days to get this straightened out before she started her new job, and if there was a problem she would leave and live somewhere else. But she would not stay here tonight.

She got dressed, threw some underwear and some toilet things in her flight bag, and grabbed her purse. She locked the door, thinking as she did that if a burglar *did* go in, the boy would probably scare the living bejesus out of him. Then she shuddered, took out her car keys, and wished for the first time in her life that she had a dog.

She found a motel three miles down the road, one of those places that manage to stay open with only three cars at the most in front of the U of brick compartments. But it was cheap, it was warm, and it was private. There was no little boy to pose for her nightmares, no boy bound to the bed, no boy locked in the closet, no boy forced to kneel in the shower as cold water beat down upon him, or whatever else they had done to him.

The bed was too soft, but she sank into its embrace thankfully, and fell asleep fully clothed. She awoke the next morning around seven, amazed that she hadn't dreamed, or, if she had, hadn't remembered it. In retrospect, she thought her night should have been filled with lurking terrors, but in reality she could not recall when she had slept more soundly.

She made some instant coffee on the wall-mounted machine, sat at the desk, and thought about the previous evening. In the hatchwork of bright sunlight coming through the opened venetian blind, her experience softened, became almost romantic—not the boy's maltreatment, not that, but the idea of his remaining in the house. She thought she knew why.

All the ghost stories—true or false—that she had ever heard had given the ghost a reason for remaining on the earthly plane. Perhaps it was to show where buried treasure was hidden, perhaps for revenge to right a wrong, perhaps to find something the ghost didn't have in life.

Could that be it? Could the little boy, who had lived with fear and madness and torment all his young life, could he be looking for that which he had never had? A kind word, a touch, a gesture of loving concern?

It could be just that simple, she thought. If she ran away from him, if no one would live in the house because of the haunting, then he would remain chained there forever.

But if she tried to comfort him, perhaps she could free him.

She shook her head to clear it of doubts and sentimental illusions. First of all, she would go back to the house—now, in the clean unshadowed light of the sun. It was her home, and today she would do what she had planned to do— clean it, fix it, rearrange it until it was hers even more. And when . . . if the boy came . . . well, she would do what she thought was right, that's all.

He was waiting for her as she came up the driveway. He had on a powder blue snowsuit that was too small for him, and she could see his bare ankles above the rubber boottops. The air was cold, and the brisk wind seemed to ruffle his hair and make him shiver. She stopped the car, opened the door, and got out slowly. When she held out her hand and started to walk toward him, he turned and ran through the back yard to the hedge, into which he merged and disappeared.

The look had been there again; she had seen it just before he had bolted. Panic, fright . . . outrage.

She went inside. He didn't reappear that morning at all, and she did what she had planned. The house was terribly dusty, and she made cleaning her first priority, reaching high up on door sills and cupboard tops with the vacuum cleaner extension until no more thick streamers of dust clung to her exploring fingertips. The loud roar of the Hoover pounded her ears all morning, and at last she gratefully turned it off and made a light lunch of soup and plain yogurt. When she opened the refrigerator door, she felt a chill that was not due to the escaping cold air, but she saw nothing, and reached into the back for a Tab with only a slight shiver.

After lunch she mixed some powdered cleanser in water and started on the woodwork. On the back of the door of the smaller bedroom, which she planned to turn into a study/sewing room, she found some penciled marks that she could not bring herself to wipe off. The first was a short horizontal line with the notation, "Mar 84," beside it. The next was a few inches up, marked "Aug 84." There were six in all, the last and highest marked "Dec 85," about three feet off the floor.

Linda half expected to see Timothy suddenly appear before her, looking up in fear and expectation as he must have looked at *them* to see whether they would use the ruler to mark his height or to strike him again. She made a bitter face, closed her eyes in pain, and suddenly felt very tired.

No one was coming to see her today—the telephone man was due next week, and the washer and dryer were being delivered tomorrow. There was no reason for her not to lie down for a few minutes, and the floor with its deep carpeting seemed so comfortable that she lowered herself down onto her side and rested her head on her arm, the rich muskiness of her sweat bearing her on an onyx cloud down into sleep.

And in her sleep and in her dream the smell of sweat grew stronger until Paul stood over her, and the belt came off, and he took her over his knees, but now she was bigger and stronger and so he would not whip her again, and she bit his leg hard until she heard him gasp in pain and surprise. Then the hand with the belt curled around her head and wrenched it away from his leg, and she heard his heavy breathing turn ragged, and felt something beneath her stir and press into the softness of her stomach. There was no transition. One second she was over his lap and the next he was on top of her, pinning both her arms with one of his own while his other hand roughly guided himself into her.

But she was no longer there. Instead she hovered over the bed like a ghost, watching herself struggle beneath Paul's massive body, feeling the pain dully through the anesthesia of disembodied memory.

The eyes of the girl on the bed grew wide, and as they stared into hers as she hung suspended in the air the terror in them faded and was replaced by a hot flame of lust, not for the grunting that aped passion on that bed, but lust for the blood of the defiler, the blood of those who rob the innocent of innocence, who turn childhood into nightmare.

Then the face beneath her changed again; the brown eyes turned a pale blue, the dark hair lightened, the thin nose flattened, until the face of the twelve-year-old girl was that of a four-year-old boy, and the look of savage vengeance on that face was the one she had seen him wear before. The raw power of it frightened her, and she rose higher and higher until the face was only a dot and the bed a red smear in a black void.

She awoke with the slanting rays of the late afternoon sun in her eyes, her blouse soaked with perspiration, her heart tripping over its beats. When she staggered to her feet, the boy was standing in the doorway. She could not see through him now.

There was something else. He had changed subtly in some other way. He still seemed small, frail, but there was a power around him that she could feel, that drove her slowly backward into the corner of the room. And now the reddish rays of the falling sun shone full on his young face as he stood there glaring at her, every bruise and mark on his body a living thing that screamed out its agony in a voice she heard only in her soul.

She could not think of extending her hand to the thing that wielded that power. She could not feel compassion, or pity, or sympathy. She could only feel terror and the need to escape from the force that surged out from that demonic face.

She knew now that he had not come back for love.

And as the boy drifted across to her with the speed of a thought, her head flew back in astonishment, and his right hand sheared across her exposed throat, showering petals of blood that sparkled in the sun, and ran from her throat like a penitent's tears.

What Say the Frogs Now, Jenny?

Hugh B. Cave

Striding briskly along the road shoulder, the girl raised her left hand and turned her slender wrist to let the moonlight shine on her watch. Its hands stood at 2:19 A.M. and the road was empty of headlights as far as she could see in either direction. At any second now, though, she would be hearing the eighteen-wheeler, empty road or no. Heaven help her.

The road was a divided four-lane highway in central Florida, and since the accident to her car she had been forced to walk a mile of it every night after work. Her evening job was at the Lake Serena Café, a truck stop on the southern edge of town. Afternoons she worked as cashier in the prescription department of the Lake Serena Drugstore.

She was nineteen years old, pretty enough in face and figure to be justified in believing she might have been named Miss Florida had she been sponsored in the state's recent beauty contest. Her name was Jennifer Forrest and she was frightened. Not even the familiar croaking of frogs in the roadside ditches could diminish her terror as she waited for the tractor-trailer to come snarling up behind her. The rig she never saw, even when darting from the road to avoid becoming its victim.

Three weeks ago, when she had first heard it behind her, it had not been invisible as it was now. And she had not been on foot but proudly and happily driving her own car—the very first car she had ever owned.

It was not a new car, of course. It was a five-year-old Datsun that had already been driven more than fifty thousand miles when she bought it. But it was hers, and the good-looking young examiner who tested her for her driver's license had told her she was a first-class driver. (She hadn't told him how many guys had helped to teach her.) What she hadn't expected, on seeing the tractor-trailer come barreling up behind her at 2:15 in the morning, was that its driver would be stupid enough to play games.

She had known Willard Allison ever since getting the job as waitress at the café. He owned his own rig and thought he owned any girl he took a shine to, though he could still laugh his crazy, booming laugh on finding out he was mistaken. He was as big as a wrestler and had an enormous beard the color of the sandy soil in the citrus groves.

Half an hour before, while eating at the restaurant, he had grabbed her by a wrist and told her, with a grin, that she ought to quit slinging hash and marry him.

"Oh, sure, I'll do that."

"Hey, I'm serious, Jenny," he said, his grin making a liar out of him. And he pulled her down onto his knee and tried to kiss her.

Others had tried that, and she had learned how to handle them. You grabbed where it hurt. Not hard enough to make them really sore at you, of course, but enough to make them let go. Willard Allison had let go and laughed like a clap of thunder, then reached for her again so fast she fell down when leaping away from him. Then he jumped from his chair and lifted her to her feet, saying, "Jeez, Jenny, I'm sorry."

"Look at my knee!" It was scraped and bleeding, and she was furious. "It's a lucky thing for you I'm not wearing stockings, Willy Allison!"

He pulled a handful of paper napkins from the holder on his table and wiped the knee with them, all the time saying how sorry he was. "Jeez, girl, I was only horsing around. You know that. You know me."

"Well, you can horse around with Evelyn or Nadeen," she said, "because I'm not waitin' on you!"

"Aw, come on, Jenny. I never meant nothin'."

"Well"—it was hard to stay mad at the big ape sometimes—"I'm off now, anyway."

"I'll drive you home," he said. He had done that a few times when he was heading south and didn't have a buddy along. The house she lived in with her folks was right on the highway. In return, of course, he expected the right to do a little pawing . . . but didn't every man, these days?

Tonight was different, though. "I have a car now, Mr. Allison, thank you very much," she told him with a toss of her auburn hair.

"You have? Since when?"

"Since this morning."

"Well, whatta ya know! Where is it? Let's have a look at it."

She would have shown Jack the Ripper her car that night, she was so proud to be the owner of it. (So proud, too, of what the handsome young examiner had said about her driving.) Leading him out the back door, she unlocked the car and stood there with her arms folded over her breasts while he appraised it inside and out.

"Looks good if the price was right," was his verdict. "How much you pay for it?"

"None of your business." Just about every cent she'd had in the bank was what she had paid for it.

"Okay, kiddo," he said, grinning. "You leaving now?"

"When I've changed." She never wore her uniform home as some of the other girls did. How could you know who you might meet?

"This is for luck," he said, and kissed her.

She stepped back and slapped him, and his crazy laugh boomed through the almost empty parking lot. Again angry with him, she stormed back inside. When she drove out of the lot some ten minutes later, in a white pantsuit that showed off her figure, Allison was just stepping up into his cab. She had to pass within fifteen feet of him to reach the exit, and he waved to her. With what she hoped was obvious indifference she lifted an arm languidly in reply.

It was just under a mile from the café to her house. She had covered about half the distance, doing only thirty to thirty-five miles an hour in her brand-new (that morning) secondhand car, when she heard Allison's rig behind her. Just ahead the road sharply curved to the right in a blind bend hidden by a thick stand of pine trees. Allison sounded his horn as he swung out to pass her.

She pulled well over because she knew the size of the Goliath he was driving. As a new driver—even though pronounced first class by her good-looking young examiner—she was leery of anything that big, with that many wheels. He had plenty of room to zoom on by. Plenty. But did he? No.

He veered in at her, playing a game. Slowing to her speed, he swung the monster at her, then out again, like a cowboy making a skittish horse do tricks. Into the curve they went side by side, she clutching her wheel for dear life, he trying to frighten her while filling the night with his booming laughter.

Even before he gunned his rig and left her behind on the turn, she had lost control of her car and was headed for the deep, boggy ditch just off the pavement.

By the time she crawled out of her car, miraculously unhurt, he and his Goliath were long gone. Even the whine of the many tires had faded away to silence. Frogs croaked again in the ditch where her precious car lay on its side. Tears streamed down her face as she trudged homeward.

Bitter hatred for Willard Allison and his booming laugh filled her heart.

Again Jennifer raised her arm to catch the moonlight on her watch. The rig was a few minutes late tonight, or else her watch was slow. Most likely it was the watch—getting old now and only a cheapie to begin with. On leaving the café she hadn't stopped to set it by the electric wall clock as she usually did.

The highway was still empty. The only sound other than her own hurrying footsteps was the croaking of the frogs. What a fantastic mix of sounds frogs made, when you stopped to think about it. Anyone who thought they all croaked alike was plain crazy.

When, oh God, *when* would she get her car back? It was three weeks now, and she had been hearing the rig for two. Every night for two weeks! She should have spent the higher towing fee and had the work done by someone reliable, not given the job to Jarrett's just because they were closer. Jarrett's was probably the poorest garage in thirty miles.

But she hadn't known then that Willard Allison would be paying the bill, had she? How could she when the car had been in the garage for a week before he even showed up at the café again?

But, anyway, let them finish repairing it. Let them give it back to her before she got so scared of walking this road that she would have to give up her waitress job. She couldn't get by on the little she made by working part-time at the drugstore. Let them stop making excuses about waiting for parts, for God's sake. There were plenty of Datsuns on the road here. Parts must be available somewhere.

Maybe tonight—just this one night— the rig would not come. Or if it did come, maybe she would reach home ahead of it. Please God . . .

Evidently God was not tuned in to scared waitresses just then. The truck noise was in her ears already.

She stopped. Trembling all over, she turned swiftly to look down the road. She wouldn't see it, of course. She never saw it. But she always looked.

It made the same noise it had made when it came up behind her car and caused her to drive into the ditch. It always did, and because it did she knew it was always the same rig. His. Allison's. People thought all the big rigs made the same kind of noise, but they didn't. Not to her, anyway, and she'd been living within two hundred feet of this highway since she was born. They were as different as the frogs were different.

The noise that rushed toward her along the empty road now was a blend of many sounds, all terrifying. There was the high whine of all that rubber on the concrete. There was the snarl of a huge diesel engine being pushed to its limit. Even the invisible body of the trailer made a noise as it flung the sleeping air aside.

Now it set up a vibration in a stretch of metal guardrail that she had not yet put behind her. That told her how close it was and how little time she had.

Too scared to cry out, she leaped the rail like a hurdler and landed in a heap on the far side of it, in grass a foot high. As she struggled to her feet and continued running, she heard the unseen rig veer in her direction. Would it shatter the guardrail to pursue her? It could if it wanted to, she was certain. But it straightened—the sound of it did—and went on down the highway.

She had a feeling that if she could see it, it would be roaring along just an inch or so from the rail. With him at the wheel, of course, looking back to let her know there would be another time.

"Dear God," she sobbed as the silence returned, "let my car be finished tomorrow. I can't take this anymore!"

God didn't answer. The frogs began their serenade again.

The café had been crowded when Willard Allison parked his tractor-trailer and walked in, a week after causing her to wreck her car. "Leave him to me," Jennifer had told the other girls. "I've been waiting for this."

When she went to his table he had tried to talk to her, but she had silenced him with a curt, "We're busy, buster," and taken his order. He wasn't clowning as he usually did. He looked downright unhappy, in fact—probably afraid she would start yelling at him for what he had done, in front of all those customers.

She would have, too, if she hadn't already figured out a better way to get even.

He wanted coffee, of course. At every meal he drank three or four cups of coffee laced with so much sugar it must have tasted more like honey. Also he ordered the day's special, corned beef and cabbage, which was unlike him. He was usually in too big a hurry for that much food.

When he got it, he just picked at it until the place was almost empty. Then when she went to his table to fill his coffee cup for the umpteenth time, his hand closed over her wrist and he said with a sheepish kind of grin, "Sit down a minute, Jenny."

"With you?" she snapped. "Am I crazy?"

"Please. Sit down," he said, and there was no wild laugh to put a curse on it. "We were on a sharp curve there, remember? I never knew what I did to you till yesterday when Nick told me in Orlando." Nick DiAngelo was a regular at the café and a buddy of his. "I hadn't figured on coming down this way today," Allison went on, shaking his bushy face at her. "But here I am. How much is the car costing you?"

"What do you care?" she said.

"I care. It's why I'm here. How much?"

"Three-hundred sixty, Jarrett said. That's just the estimate. It'll be more, you can bet."

He reached into his hip pocket for his billfold and took a handful of hundred-dollar bills out of it. He counted out ten of them and pressed them into her hand. She was surprised not only by the amount but by his not having clapped the money down on the table with one of his crazy loud laughs.

He stood up, still holding on to her hand with the money in it. Reaching for her other hand he held both and stood there on wide apart legs solemnly looking down at her—a bearded bull moose gazing at a frightened fawn.

"I'm sorry," he said. "It was a stupid thing I did. I clean forgot you only just got your license to drive. Try not to be too sore, huh?"

For a second she thought he was going to try kissing her again, and she wasn't sure she could handle it. Not after what she had just done to him. But he didn't. He just grinned again—or almost did—and dropped her hands and walked out.

From the front window she watched him step up into his cab and wondered if she ought to tell him. But she was afraid to.

Her left hand, pressed hard against her stomach but shaking all the same, still clutched the thousand dollars he had given her.

She had been wrong about Jarrett. When he delivered her car to the café the evening after her crazy leap over the guardrail, he stuck to his estimate. Prepared for the worst, she had kept the whole thousand dollars in her handbag ever since Allison had given it to her two weeks before, and now most of it was pure profit. She could have kissed him. Not Allison. It was too late for that. She could have kissed old man Jarrett.

"Sorry it took so long, Miss Forrest," he said. "I really had a tough time finding some of the parts." He was a little dried-up man and his gaze roved happily over her bosom while he talked to her. Evidently he thought more of her looks than of her mind, though, for he didn't bother going into detail about what he had done to the car. Most of his customers had to hear it down to the last cotter pin, whether they wanted to or not.

Jenny was pleased with him, though. "Boy, will I be glad to be driving home tonight instead of walking!" she exclaimed as she paid him.

At her 2 A.M. quitting time she was so glad to have her brand-new once-wrecked secondhand car waiting for her in the parking lot, she sang all the time she was changing from her uniform into her white pantsuit. Then she sang some more as she slid in behind the wheel and started home.

She had almost forgotten Willard Allison when she heard the sound of his rig behind her. With her car windows wide open she was even enjoying the chorus of frog calls from the roadside ditch. It was like an accompaniment to her own happy warbling, she had been thinking with a grin.

The roar of the rig destroyed her mood, of course. But completely. She sent a terrified glance into the rearview mirror and saw nothing but empty highway, but the sound became louder so rapidly that she knew she had to outrace it. Her sandaled right foot shoved the gas pedal flat onto the floor.

The little car leaped forward like a frightened deer, its speedometer streaking from thirty-five to over seventy before she knew what was happening. She had no idea how fast the car would go. After all, she hadn't owned it for even a day when the same rig that was now pursuing her had caused her to wreck it. Oh my God, she mentally wailed, I don't know how to drive this fast!

And even at seventy-five she was not outdistancing her pursuer. The tractor-trailer was roaring up beside her.

She saw it then for the first time since her nightly ordeal had begun. There was no moon tonight, and the God-awful thing was only a faint, misty outline—but it was his rig, all right. It was the same one that had carried him to his death when he fell asleep at the wheel after she laced his coffee with stuff from the drugstore. And he was at the wheel now, glaring accusingly across at her as the cab of his Goliath came abreast of her.

She saw him shaking his head as if to say, "You shouldn't have done that, Jenny. No, baby, you shouldn't have done that. After all, I more than paid for the repairs to your car."

"I know you did!" she shrieked at him as the monster veered over toward her. "Oh my God, Willy, I know you did. But I doped your first cup of coffee and you'd already drunk it. I wanted you to know what it was like to have an accident."

His roaring Goliath and her little car were tearing along the highway together, only inches apart, and he still shook his head at her. "You should have listened when I asked you to marry me, Jenny," he was saying. "A cute trick like you and a big lug like me—we'd have had fun. Killing me was the dumbest thing you ever did, baby."

Then he said "So long" and began laughing. And as the little car went off the road into the ditch, and through the ditch end over end into a bog full of frogs, she heard the bellow of his laughter long after the frogs were shocked into silence.

It was the last sound she ever heard.

Wild Grapes

August Derleth

The echo of his neighbors' mocking voices lingered in Luke Adam's mind—"Wild grapes!" scornfully said, pityingly whispered from mouth to ear, from farm to farm and on into Sac Prairie. Standing there on his rickety porch, he smiled, his grim lips curving only slightly, his eyes hard and cold. His gaze went from the farmyard across the fields to the clump of cedars fringing his land to the southwest. Dividing the trees from the fields were the wild grapes he had planted.

He had planted them at night. Did those fools think of that? Not they, and the better for him. Darkness was a welcome cloak for his work, since the body could not have been handled in the daytime.

Twilight did not obscure the strong green of the wild grapes. He considered them in the growing darkness, the long line of them curving along the slope, and finally drove his eyes to the thick clump growing where the body of his Uncle Ralsa lay. He complimented himself again on the sagacity he had shown in setting wild grapes to grow on the spot where the body was buried. No expense had been incurred, and the broken earth on the edge of the field had excited no comment but the scornful voices of his farming neighbors, who thought him crazy to go to any trouble about wild grapes when there were so many of them in the bottoms not far from his land.

He was glad, too, that the old man had the reputation for taking long and mysterious journeys and staying away for months at a time without communicating with anyone. All the old man's friends nodded solemnly and said, "Ralsa's gone on another tear." No one had suspected anything. Luke could appreciate the irony of their laughter over his wild grapes.

The stars brightened, and the afterglow faded to a fan of emerald light flung upward against the western sky. Luke lit his pipe and watched the slow smoke trail upward from his lips. A whippoorwill began to call from the bottoms. Abruptly a small dark shape dropped noiselessly to the roof of the corncrib and shrilled its flute-like call into the growing night.

Luke thought of the legend about whippoorwills calling for a dying man's soul. He caught up a clod of earth and flung it at the bird on the corn-crib.

"Get out," he muttered harshly. "You got Uncle Ralsa—you don't get me." He laughed at his words, grimly.

One by one the whippoorwills assaulted the silence, and from the sky came the harsh calls of nighthawks and woodcocks. An owl hooted mournfully from the grove of cedars. Presently the moon pushed itself into the sky above the low range of hills to the east, and long shadows haunted the ground.

Thinking of his uncle, Luke experienced a shudder of irritation at himself that he had not killed the old man with one blow. "They'll get you for this, Luke, and if they don't, I will," he had had time to say before the second blow. And he had cursed him, too. Luke smiled, took his pipe from his mouth, and spat at a stone not far from the porch steps.

"C'mon, Ralsa," he murmured. "I'm still waitin'."

He felt warmth creeping over him at the satisfactory knowledge of his ownership of his uncle's farm. He had always wanted it; now it was his, even if the fools thereabouts considered him only a caretaker. When it would be plain to them that the old man was never coming back, even they would have to acknowledge him as owner.

He knocked out his pipe presently and stood up, stretching himself. Then he turned to go into the house. From the threshold he looked once more toward the line of wild grapes, fixing his eyes on the large clump in the center, now lost against the dark background of the cedars.

As he looked, he reflected that he had never before been aware of that patch of sky showing through between the trees above the grapevines.

Even as he thought it, the sky moved gently to one side. For a breathless moment Luke felt a shock of terror; then he took a deep breath, pressed his lips firmly together, and stared long and hard at the patch of sky.

The sky wavered a little, moved casually to the north, and drifted southward again.

It was not sky! It was a whiteness above the secret grave, standing out against the cedars—not sky showing through from beyond!

Luke flung himself into the house, banging the door behind him, and stood with his back against it. Sweat flecked his forehead, and his hands shook despite his determination to control himself. He strove to convince himself that he had seen nothing, that his eyes and the night had combined to play a ghastly trick on him.

Presently he moved away from the door. He halted just before he reached the west window, hesitation looped about his legs, stopping their advance. If he went forward, he would look out of the window. He would look at the grave. And his eyes might trick him again.

He stood there, feeling that the house was pressing its walls toward him. A sense of ominous closeness enveloped him. Presently he groped for the table, found the lamp, and the box of matches. He struck one and held the flame to the wick, his shadow grotesque against the wall and the ceiling. The small, poorly furnished room sprang into dubious life.

A feeling of security returned to him with the light, and he sat down at the table, resting his head on his clenched fists. The noise of the whippoorwills dinned into the room, insistence in the wealth of flute-like notes that welled across the fields from the lowlands and the marsh beyond. As he sat listening to them, unreasonable anger grew at their calls, and he determined to go whippoorwill-hunting in the morning, intent upon paying them back for the fright he had got.

The fear having gone completely out of him, he rose abruptly and strode boldly to the window. He looked out. The white mass had grown. It lowered threateningly above the row of wild grapes, uncanny movement breaking its outlines. As he looked, the moonlight faded suddenly, clouds blanketing it away from the earth, and the white shape against the cedars seemed to glow as if from some inner light.

He fell back from the window, his heart pounding with maddening insistence. There *was* something at the grave. Terror possessed him suddenly, terror driven into fierce life at the fear that somehow Ralsa Adam was coming back to get him, as the dead man had promised.

He made a frantic calculation. It was almost a month now since he had killed the old man. No one had suspected. No one had come for him. No solid flesh could rise from that grave. Yet the old man had said that he would return, if Luke—

The door swung suddenly wide, forced by a gust of wind, and the night gaped blackly beyond. Lamplight lit the porch floor tentatively, fingers of flickering light turned back by the darkness.

Luke looked out through the doorway toward the southwest, where the grave was. The white thing was still there, moving with the wind, now this way, now that, and occasionally there were flaffing white arms seeming to beckon him, or grotesque heads lolling horribly against the night.

He dragged himself from the room to the porch, where he leaned against a post, looking with fear-maddened eyes toward the line of wild grapes. There was something about that whiteness—something that brought sudden hope to him. He stared, cold sweat smarting in his eyes.

Then he remembered. Phosphorus from decaying bodies. He had read of that somewhere. It sometimes happened. So-called ghosts in graveyards were nothing but phosphorus— he remembered reading about it. He almost sobbed his relief, and for a moment laughed weakly at himself.

He tempered his relief with the thought that he had better make sure about the phosphorescence. Immediately another thought occurred to him and brought apprehension. If it were phosphorescence, someone might possibly notice it and investigate, though the spot was out of sight of all farmhouses and all roads save the poorly marked trail to his own house, and in sight of strange fields only during the day.

He stepped from the porch, leaving the lamplit doorway open behind him, and strode away into the darkness, frightening up whippoorwills as he went. As he came into the southwest forty, uneasiness took possession of him at recognition of the fact that the phosphorescence did not fade, that it seemed to have descended more closely about the clump of grapevines growing from the spot where the body lay concealed.

He halted uncertainly ten feet from the vines and looked. The whiteness was phosphorescence, he was sure of that. He felt vaguely that it ought by rights to be closer to the ground, but he could not be sure. And it moved oddly, sometimes with the wind, but sometimes not. There was a very odd shape to it, too. He felt misgivings, and cast a glance backward for the reassuring sight of the rectangle of light from the house.

Despite a sudden feeling that he should go no farther, he stepped forward. He came up to the mass of vines and looked carefully down at the unmarked spot where he had nocturnally buried Ralsa Adam almost a month ago.

The ground seemed oddly broken.

He pushed away the grapevines and peered closer.

Suddenly he felt something close about his ankle, felt something whip toward his uncovered head. He jerked upward—and felt his arms, too, caught. Then he looked up.

His hoarse, terror-fraught screams were muffled by the writhing mass of grapevines which descended upon him, their rustling like an echo of Ralsa Adam's dying voice, their sentient movement vengefully alive.

He was found two mornings after. He had been strangled; there were still vines wound oddly about his throat. It was said in Sac Prairie that he had probably entangled himself somehow and had caused his death. Everybody said it served him right. In his struggles he had kicked up the ground so that the body of Ralsa Adam was discovered.

The farmers who dug the old man out said he was not a pleasant sight. The big grapevine which Luke had planted above his victim had rooted itself firmly in the decaying flesh and clung fiercely to the body when they moved it.

Will

Vincent O'Sullivan

I

Have the dead still power after they are laid in the earth? Do they rule us, by the power of the dead, from their awful thrones? Do their closed eyes become menacing beacons, and their paralyzed hands reach out to scourge our feet into the paths which they have marked out? Ah, surely when the dead are given to the dust, their power crumbles into the dust!

Often during the long summer afternoons, as they sat together in a deep window looking out at the Park of the Sombre Fountains, he thought of these things. For it was at the hour of sundown, when the gloomy house was splashed with crimson, that he most hated his wife. They had been together for some months now; and their days were always spent in the same manner—seated in the window of a great room with dark oak furniture, heavy tapestry, and rich purple hangings, in which a curious decaying scent of lavender ever lingered. For an hour at a time he would stare at her intensely as she sat before him— tall, and pale, and fragile, with her raven hair sweeping about her neck, and her languid hands turning over the leaves of an illuminated missal—and then he would look once more at the Park of the Sombre Fountains, where the river lay, like a silver dream, at the end. At sunset the river became for him turbulent and boding—a pool of blood; and the trees, clad in scarlet, brandished flaming swords. For long days they sat in that room, always silent, watching the shadows turn from steel to crimson, from crimson to grey, from grey to black. If by rare chance they wandered abroad, and moved beyond the gates of the Park of the Sombre Fountains, he might hear one passenger say to another, "How beautiful she is!" And then his hatred of his wife increased a hundredfold.

So he was poisoning her surely and lingeringly—with a poison more wily and subtile than that of Cesare Borgia's ring—with a poison distilled in his eyes. He was drawing out her life as he gazed at her; draining her veins, grudging the beats of her heart. He felt no need of the slow poisons which wither the flesh, of the dread poisons which set fire to the brain; for his hate was a poison which he poured over her white body, till it would no longer have the strength to hold back the escaping soul. With exultation he watched her growing weaker and weaker as the summer glided by: not a day, not an hour passed that she did not pay toll to his eyes: and when in the autumn there came upon her two long faints which resembled catalepsy, he fortified his will to hate for he felt that the end was at hand.

At length one evening, when the sky was grey in a winter sunset, she lay on a couch in the dark room and he knew she was dying. The doctors had gone away with death on their lips, and they were left, for the moment, alone. Then she called him to her side from the deep window where he was seated looking out over the Park of the Sombre Fountains.

"You have your will," she said. "I am dying."

"My will?" he murmured, waving his hands.

"Hush!" she moaned. "Do you think I do not know? For days and months I have felt you drawing the life of my body into your life, that you might spill my soul on the ground. For days and months as I have sat with you, as I have walked by your side, you have seen me imploring pity. But you relented not, and you have your will; for I am going down to death. You have your will, and my body is dead; but my soul cannot die. No!" she cried, raising herself a little on the pillows: "my soul shall not die, but live, and sway an all-touching sceptre lighted at the stars."

"My wife!"

"You have thought to live without me, but you will never be without me. Through long nights when the moon is hid, through dreary days when the sun is dulled, I shall be at your side. In the deepest chaos illumined by lightning, on the loftiest mountain-top, do not seek to escape me. You are my bond-man: for this is the compact I have made with the Cardinals of Death."

At the noon of night she died; and two days later they carried her to a burying-place set about a ruined abbey, and there they laid her in the grave.

When he had seen her buried, he left the Park of the Sombre Fountains and travelled to distant lands. He penetrated the most unknown and difficult countries; he lived for months amid Arctic seas; he took part in tragic and barbarous scenes. He used himself to sights of cruelty and terror: to the anguish of women and children, to the agony and fear of men. And when he returned after years of adventure, he went to live in a house the windows of which overlooked the ruined abbey and the grave of his wife, even as the window where they had erewhile sat together overlooked the Park of the Sombre Fountains.

And here he spent dreaming days and sleepless nights—nights painted with monstrous and tumultuous pictures, and moved by waking dreams. Phantoms haggard and ghastly swept before him; ruined cities covered with a cold light edified themselves in his room; while in his ears resounded the trample of retreating and advancing armies, the clangour of squadrons, and noise of breaking war. He was haunted by women who prayed him to have mercy, stretching out beseeching hands—always women—and sometimes they were dead. And when the day came at last, and his tired eyes reverted to the lonely grave, he would soothe himself with some eastern drug, and let the hours slumber by as he fell into long reveries, murmuring at times to himself the rich, sonorous, lulling cadences of the poems in prose of Baudelaire, or dim meditative phrases, laden with the mysteries of the inner rooms of life and death, from the pages of Sir Thomas Browne.

On a night, which was the last of the moon, he heard a singular scraping noise at his window, and upon throwing open the casement he smelt the heavy odour which clings to vaults and catacombs where the dead are entombed. Then he saw that a beetle—a beetle, enormous and unreal—had crept up the wall of his house from the graveyard, and was now crawling across the floor of his room. With marvellous swiftness it climbed on a table placed near a couch on which he was used to lie, and as he approached, shuddering with loathing and disgust, he perceived to his horror that it had two red eyes like spots of blood. Sick with hatred of the thing as he was, those eyes fascinated him—held him like teeth. That night his other visions left him, but the beetle never let him go—nay! compelled him, as he sat weeping and helpless, to study its hideous conformation, to dwell upon its fangs, to ponder on its food. All through the night that was like a century—all through the pulsing hours did he sit oppressed with horror gazing at that unutterable, slimy vermin. At the first streak of dawn it glided away, leaving in its trail the same smell of the charnel-house; but to him the day brought no rest, for his dreams were haunted by the abominable thing. All day in his ears a music sounded—a music thronged with passion and wailing of defeat, funereal and full of great alarums; all day he felt that he was engaged in a conflict with one in armour, while he himself was unharnessed and defenceless—all day, till the dark night came, when he observed the abhorred monster crawling slowly from the ruined abbey, and the calm, neglected Golgotha which lay there in his sight. Calm outwardly; but beneath perhaps—how disturbed, how swept by tempest! With trepidation, with a feeling of inexpiable guilt, he awaited the worm—the messenger of the dead. And this night and day were the type of nights and days to come. From the night of the new moon, indeed, till the night when it began to wane, the beetle remained in the grave; but so awful was the relief of those hours, the transition so poignant, that he could do nothing but shudder in a depression as of madness. And his circumstances were not merely those of physical horror and disgust: clouds of spiritual fear enveloped him: he felt that this abortion, this unspeakable visitor, was really an agent that claimed his life, and the flesh fell from his bones. So did he pass each day looking forward with anguish to the night; and then, at length, came the distorted night full of overwhelming anxiety and pain.

II

At dawn, when the dew was still heavy on the grass, he would go forth into the graveyard and stand before the iron gates of the vault in which his wife was laid. And as he stood there, repeating wild litanies of supplication, he would cast into the vault things of priceless value: skins of man-eating tigers and of leopards; skins of beasts that drank from the Ganges, and of beasts that wallowed in the mud of the Nile; gems that were the ornament of the Pharuohs; tusks of elephants, and corals that men had given their lives to obtain. Then holding up his arms, in a voice that raged against heaven he would cry: "Take these, O avenging soul, and leave me in quiet! Are not these enough?"

And after some weeks he came to the vault again bringing with him a consecrated chalice studded with jewels which had been used by a priest at Mass, and a ciborium of the purest gold. These he filled with the rare wine of a lost vintage, and placing them within the vault he called in a voice of storm: "Take these, O implacable soul, and spare thy bond-man! Are not these enough?"

And last he brought with him the bracelets of the woman he loved, whose heart he had broken by parting with her to propitiate the dead. He brought a long strand of her hair, and a handkerchief damp with her tears. And the vault was filled with the misery of his heart-quaking whisper: "O my wife, are not *these* enough?"

But it became plain to those who were about him that he had come to the end of his life. His hatred of death, his fear of its unyielding caress, gave him strength; and he seemed to be resisting with his thin hands some palpable assailant. Plainer and more deeply coloured than the visions of delirium, he saw the company which advanced to combat him: in the strongest light he contemplated the scenery which surrounds the portals of dissolution. And at the supreme moment, it was with a struggle far greater than that of the miser who is forcibly parted from his gold, with an anguish far more intense than that of the lover who is torn from his mistress, that he gave up his soul.

On a shrewd, grey evening in the autumn they carried him down to bury him in the vault by the side of his wife. This he had desired; for he thought that in no other vault however dark, would the darkness be quite still; in no other resting-place would he be allowed to repose. As they carried him they intoned a majestic threnody—a chant which had the deep tramp and surge of a triumphant march, which rode on the winds, and sobbed through the boughs of ancient trees. And having come to the vault they gave him to the grave, and knelt on the ground to pray for the ease of his spirit.

Requiem æternam dona ei, Domine!

But as they prepared to leave the precincts of the ruined abbey, a dialogue began within the vault—a dialogue so wonderful, so terrible, in its nature, its cause, that as they hearkened they gazed at one another in the twilight with wry and pallid faces.

And first a woman's voice.

"You are come."

"Yes, I am come," said the voice of a man. "I yield myself to you—the conqueror."

"Long have I awaited you," said the woman's voice. "For years I have lain here while the rain soaked through the stones, and snow was heavy on my breast. For years while the sun danced over the earth, and the moon smiled her mellow smile upon gardens and pleasant things. I have lain here in the company of the worm, and I have leagued with the worm. You did nothing but what I willed; you were the toy of my dead hands. Ah, you stole my body from me, but I have stolen your soul from you!"

"And is there peace for me—now—at the last?"

The woman's voice became louder, and rang through the vault like a proclaiming trumpet. "Peace is not mine! You and I are at last together in the city of one who queens it over a mighty empire. Now shall we tremble before the queen of Death."

The watchers flung aside the gates of the vault and struck open two coffins. In a mouldy coffin they found the body of a woman having the countenance and warmth of one who has just died. But the body of the man was corrupt and most horrid, like a corpse that has lain for years in a place of graves.

Acknowledgments

Grateful acknowledgment is made to the following for permission to publish their copyrighted material:

"Ashes of Circumstance" by J. U. Giesy, copyright © 1925 by Popular Fiction Publishing Company. Reprinted by permission of Weird Tales, Ltd.

"At the Bend in the Trail" by Manly Wade Wellman, copyright © 1934 by Popular Fiction Publishing Company. Reprinted by permission of Frances Wellman.

"Beside the Seaside" by Ramsey Campbell, copyright © 1976 by Ramsey Campbell. First published in *The Height of the Scream*. Reprinted by permission of the author.

"Best of Luck" by David Drake, copyright © 1978 by David Drake. Reprinted by permission of the author.

"Boo, Yourself!" by Joe R. Lansdale, copyright © 1987 by Joe R. Lansdale. First published in *Whispers*, Vol. 6, No. 34, October 1987. Reprinted by permission of the author.

"The Broken Thread" by Kirk Mashburn, copyright © 1932 by Popular Fiction Publishing Company. Reprinted by permission of Weird Tales, Ltd.

"The Chill" by Dennis Etchison, copyright © 1981 by Dennis Etchison. Reprinted by permission of the author.

562